The author taught pre-school children for twenty years, and now lives in rural Perthshire with her husband Richard, enjoying the quiet life amidst red squirrels, roe deer and partridges; an ideal environment for thinking and writing. She is currently working on the last chapters of her next novel.

WHERE CROWS GATHER

To my husband, Richard, whose patience and good humour have greatly
contributed to this work.

To Gail

with best wishes

Lisa

Liz Todd

WHERE CROWS GATHER

AUSTIN MACAULEY

A CIP catalogue record for this title is
available from the British Library.

ISBN 978 1 84963 155 6

www.austinmacauley.com

First Published (2012)
Austin & Macauley Publishers Ltd.
25 Canada Square
Canary Wharf
London
E14 5LB

Printed & Bound in Great Britain

There was no doubt about it: he could still turn the ladies' heads. As he walked briskly from the taxi to the Rutland Hotel he was aware of the attention bestowed upon him by dozens of interested pairs of eyes, young and old, pretty and plain, yet all of them alight with curiosity.

His clothes, of course, were not of this country, nor was the tan: it was the kind of tan which 'evolved' over years spent in a hot climate, rather than the tan people were seeking - for one or two weeks - on the Costa Brava and such places. He sighed at the very idea: package holidays indeed! Who would have predicted such a thing in the '20s, when only the chosen few could spread their wings and visit foreign places? Nowadays he had even seen the hoi-polloi on a Spanish beach. How much further could things degenerate?

As he approached the Rutland, he decided to linger outdoors on such a lovely day and to take a wander through Princes Street gardens. His suitcase was light enough - he would simply buy what he needed here - and so he crossed the street and entered the gardens. As he strolled, he was aware of his heart beating faster: he was here at last!

He sat down on one of the park benches and lifted his face to the spring sunshine. Was she sitting somewhere, doing the very same? His eyes flew open: did he have the courage for what lay ahead of him, or would it have been wiser to leave things as they were?

He took a deep breath. Behind him, in Princes Street, a taxi hooted, as if prompting him to forget this mad quest and go home; but that was the damnedest part about it.

He *was* home.

Part One: 1969

Chapter One

Harry Gillespie stretched and stood up, scowling at the mess of papers on his desk and moving off before the sight depressed him further. It was five o'clock already and he had had nothing to eat since breakfast, a predictable consequence of Beth's absence. Despite the 'women's lib' atmosphere of the times, he was ashamed to admit that he had fallen into the habit of leaving the household tasks to his wife, and – more to her shame than his – she had never uttered a word of complaint.

'I don't have to study now,' she told him cheerfully, the first time he sat around reading the newspaper while she cooked and cleaned. 'You just take it easy, have some time off.'

'You used to condemn your father for this. Didn't you always say that he had Grace tethered to a chain in the back garden?'

'It's true, he does.'

'Well then, I don't want to do it to you.'

'You can pay me back in bed,' she had smiled, glancing at him in a way that made his heart lurch. 'If I'm not too tired, of course, with all this housework.'

Harry looked down to the street, choc-a-bloc with rush-hour traffic, throbbing engines at the lights, exhaust fumes spiralling past his closed windows and the occasional blast of a horn when someone lost their cool.

He wandered back into the room and through to the small kitchen, shocked to discover half a dozen unwashed coffee mugs in the sink, along with several breakfast dishes caked with congealed muesli.

Pausing for a long moment, he thought about hiring someone to clean the place while Beth was away, but the 'someone' would inevitably be a girl and if Beth should find out, his life would not be worth living. She was rarely guilty of throwing jealous tantrums, but after her suspicions over the cocktail waitress at the Athenaeum Hotel, he had trodden warily, given her no cause.

The contents of the fridge, stocked by Beth the week before, were sufficient for his needs; the only trouble was that he had to prepare meals, another task he tended to avoid. At the back of his mind he had a niggling sense of guilt that he was not taking good enough care of Grace Melville's daughter and that his father's generation would never have been so neglectful.

'Oh, come on,' he said irritably, grabbing his jacket from the kitchen chair. 'Go to the fish and chip shop and be done with it!'

*

Frank had prepared the tea for the two of them, having caught the early bus from school to rush around the kitchen for half an hour; thereby ingratiating himself with his father. Since his sister's marriage, Frank was sole beneficiary of James Melville's wrath but had devised several methods of toning it down, the most effective one being his willingness to become head chef of the household in his mother's temporary absence.

'This is very tasty,' his father had said with some degree of surprise, the first night he arrived home to a hot meal on the table. 'I'd no idea you could cook, son.'

'I sometimes watch Mum,' Frank had said, which he did, but not to pick up culinary skills, rather to spend time with her and get to know her better. His selfish, arrogant big sister had been the centre of attention for almost twenty years and Frank was only now beginning to carve out his own little niche in the affections of his parents. Despite

15

frequent censure from his father he felt he was on the winning stretch.

'What's this?' his father had asked him at the end of the first week. 'It looks like skirlie.'

'It is,' Frank said, hoping his father's appreciative smile would not be premature. 'I know that Granny used to make it, and Mum told me it was your favourite.'

'It was,' his father nodded. 'And it's ages since your mother made it. Good for you.'

When it tasted as good as it looked Frank breathed a sigh of relief and notched up another victory in his mind.

'D'you think Mum's enjoying herself?'

James glanced across at his son and shrugged. 'I expect so.'

'It seemed an odd choice of holiday, didn't it?'

'Did it?' his father asked, but the hand holding the fork paused in mid-air.

'Yes,' Frank went on, pushing his luck. 'I never thought she liked her aunt.'

For a moment he thought a reply was imminent, but then his father pointed to his plate and laughed.

'This is really tasty. I'll expect nothing less tomorrow.'

*

Aunt Helen's idea of a holiday was to be up at the crack of dawn, aboard a tour bus by eight o'clock, off to savour the delights of Dutch culture. After three days they had been to Maduradam, Gouda and Vollendam and by nightfall they had collapsed into bed, feet aching, heads spinning, dreading the next day.

'Why don't we just tell her that we've seen enough?' Beth asked on the Thursday morning as they lay listening to the sound of the banister brush beating the rugs to death over the balcony. 'We could maybe spend the day here for a change, couldn't we?'

'I suppose we're seeing Holland,' Grace sighed, eyes still closed. 'No one could accuse her of short-changing us tourists.'

'But I want to go shopping, buy something for Harry. What d'you say I ask her if we can do that today?'

'It's worth a try, I suppose,' Grace said, marvelling at the way her aunt had bullied them in the past few days and wondering why they had allowed her to do so. 'The good thing is, it passes the time quickly, don't you find? I mean, we hardly seem to have arrived and it's Thursday already, half way there.'

In the single bed alongside, Beth laughed and reached for her mother's hand.

'It's hilarious, isn't it? You'd think it was a concentration camp, not a holiday.'

Suddenly, there was a thud on the door and Helen's voice boomed out.

'Wakey-wakey! Time to get up, breakfast's on the table!'

'Not another plate of stewed rhubarb,' Beth groaned, clutching her stomach. 'Has the woman never heard of cornflakes or weetabix?'

Over the breakfast table, Beth broached the subject of a day's shopping and, faced with Grace's agreement, Helen gave in and ordered a taxi.

'We can take the bus, surely?' Grace said, unwilling to give her aunt the slightest cause for complaint. 'There's a tram passes outside too, I saw it this morning.'

'Too crowded,' Helen said with a sniff. 'We'd never get a seat and we'd have to stand all the way into town. No, if you must go shopping, there's no option, and I'm paying for it.'

Beth donned jeans and a t-shirt, glad to relax in casual clothes after spending so many days dolled up for the coach tours. As she passed through the hall on her way to the living room, she heard her great-aunt's gasp of horror.

'You're not going out dressed like that, are you?'

Surprised, Beth turned. 'Why not?'

'Those jeans,' Helen said. 'They're not even clean.'

'Yes they are, Mum washed them the day before we left.'

'But they're covered in stains.'

'It's paint,' Beth shrugged. 'Harry and I were re-decorating the flat. It'll never come off.'

'People don't walk about like that here,' Helen said in hushed tones. 'Heaven knows what they'd think.'

Over-hearing from the bedroom, Grace joined her daughter in the hall and prepared herself for an argument.

*

The day was warm and sunny and as she and Beth wandered in and out of shops Grace was reminded of the holiday she and her mother had spent in the West of Scotland one summer; only a month before her mother's death.

She endured the wave of nostalgia, mentally braced herself against the pain of loss. Even after twenty years, she could not forget the sense of desolation that had lingered in the wake of that fateful day.

'You're looking sad,' she heard Beth remark.

Grace dragged her thoughts from the past. 'Sorry, dear.'

'What were you thinking about?'

'How lucky we are to be able to spend time together.'

Beth linked arms with Grace. 'You still miss her, don't you?'

'Yes, I do.' Grace made an effort to brighten up. 'But I'll always be grateful that I had a girl.'

'You must have felt like an orphan when she died,' Beth said unexpectedly.

When Grace turned to look at the girl, however, she was peering idly in a shop window.

'That one's nice,' Grace said, to change the topic. 'It would suit you.'

'Too expensive. Until Harry passes his finals, we'll have to be careful.'

'I could buy it for you.'

Beth laughed. 'What? And have him think he couldn't afford to keep me?'

'Is that what he'd think?'

'Oh, yes.' Beth pulled a comical face. 'I'd be in heap big trouble.'

As Beth examined various cufflinks in the jeweller's window, Grace wondered if the girl were truly happy. She was certainly jolly enough, laughed and teased at the appropriate moments; but Grace had spent many a sleepless night worrying about the girl, especially since she had completed her degree and seemed in no hurry to find a job. In fact, contrary to the ethos of the 'swinging sixties', Beth seemed content to fall into the role of housewife.

'Have you decided what you want to do yet?' she had asked Beth one day as they sat in the garden.

'No, not yet.'

'But you want to do something with your languages degree, don't you?'

'I suppose so. Eventually.'

'How about teaching?'

Beth had screwed up her nose at the idea. 'Oh no! Can you imagine me in front of a class of spotty twelve-year-olds, trying to dodge the missiles? A fate worse than death.'

'What does Harry think?' Grace had ventured to ask.

'He says he's not bothered. Besides, fingers crossed, he'll be working next August and earning enough for both of us.'

'But you'll soon be bored, won't you?'

'Not for ages.'

Grace had dropped the subject but she resolved to speak to Harry once his Law Degree course was over. She had sabotaged her own career for stupid reasons that she now regretted, and she would do what she could to save her daughter from the same mistake.

'Hey, look at this,' Beth was saying, holding up a pair of silver cufflinks. 'I think he'd love them.'

'I thought you said you'd to be careful with money?'

'But it's a present. That's different.'

'You're so lucky he wears suits and shirts,' Grace said, eyeing the price on the cufflinks and trying to convert guilders into pounds. 'Most young men are so sloppy these days. It makes a nice change to see Harry dress so smartly.'

'He has a thing about it,' Beth grimaced. 'In fact, he and Helen should get together, they're two of a kind.'

'Heavens above,' Grace smiled. 'He has absolutely nothing in common with Helen. I'll never know how her husband survived so long.'

'These are fabulous,' Beth said happily. 'I'll buy them. Oh, and maybe this tie pin as well.'

Grace's eyes widened at the cost, recalling that, when she was twenty, the same amount could have bought a bedroom suite.

'You're sure it's not too expensive?' she felt obliged to ask.

'He'll love them,' Beth grinned cheekily. 'Oh, by the way, do we have time for a coffee before we have to meet her?'

'Half an hour, but if we're late there's no supper for us tonight, so we'd better behave.'

They sat in the café of a large department store, sipping coffees frothed high with cream, and Grace wondered why it should feel so decadent.

'Since I got married we don't spend so much time together,' Beth was saying now, and Grace was sure the girl was upset.

'Beth, what is it?'

'Nothing,' she smiled, blinking rapidly. 'Just being nostalgic, that's all.'

'Nostalgic? At twenty two years of age?'

'Yes, for old times.'

'Winning a prize for being a daffodil at primary school, you mean?'

Beth grinned. 'That as well.'

'You'd tell me if something was bothering you, wouldn't you?'

'Of course,' Beth replied, spooning a dollop of cream into her mouth. 'But I'm fine really. I expect when I settle down to a job I'll feel better.'

Grace seized the opportunity, for the topic had not been mentioned for months. 'Have you looked for one?'

'Vaguely.'

'How vague would that be?'

'You're funny, Mum. I envy you. You always know exactly the right thing to say.'

'Do I?'

'Yes, you're very shrewd,' Beth smiled. 'You may fool some people, but not me. And not Harry either,' she added unexpectedly.

'The two of you have time to discuss your old mother?'

'Of course, and you're not old.'

'Oh look at the time! ' Grace exclaimed, glancing at her watch. 'Drink up, for Heavens' sake, or we'll break the curfew and never hear the end of it.'

*

Grace persuaded Beth to borrow Helen's bicycle for a couple of hours in the afternoon whilst she and Helen had a quiet afternoon.

Beth shook her head. 'I can't leave you on your own with her.'

'Beth, dear, she is my aunt. You'd think she was a monster. And don't say another word. You're going cycling, and that's that. Let's go and get her old bike out.'

As Beth checked the tyres and adjusted the height of the saddle, Grace reminded her to ride on the opposite side of the road.

'No problem, it's easy.'

'You'll have to take care at the roundabouts, remember. Go right, not left.'

Beth gave her mother a grateful glance. 'I hadn't thought of that. You've probably saved my life, not to mention dozens of pedestrians as well.'

Grace watched as Beth negotiated the crossroads at the end of the avenue and then she went inside; to have a talk with her aunt.

Helen was on edge, as if half expecting her niece to be confrontational. As Grace entered the living room her aunt jumped up and began smoothing out the velvet cover on the dining table.

'I can never get this to sit properly,' she said nervously. 'If it's not one thing, it's another.'

'It's hardly a matter of life or death though. Is it?' Grace asked, settling down in one of the armchairs by the hearth.

'Perhaps not,' Helen replied, eyes narrowing. 'What's ailing you today?'

'Me? Nothing that a little talk won't put right.'

'A talk? What kind of talk?'

'Come and sit down, Helen, there's something I want to discuss.'

Being the elder, Helen did not take kindly to her niece's tone; nor was she inclined to accede to the request, sensing as she did the element of aggression in the girl's attitude. She moved over and sat opposite Grace, however, and folded her hands in her lap, as if to intimate her disapproval.

'I'll come straight to the point,' Grace said, and there was no going back.

'I've the tea to prepare,' Helen said firmly. 'So I hope this won't take long.'

'I want to ask you about my father.'

Helen's jaw dropped. 'What?'

'You heard. I want to know everything about him.'

'But you know everything.'

'All I know is that he abandoned my mother when she was pregnant with me.'

Helen shifted in her chair, hands working together. 'That's all there was.'

'Why do you think he married her?'

'Because it was the decent thing to do.'

'Did my mother want to go with him when he left?'

'No,' Helen said firmly. 'She was glad to see the back of him.'

'That's not what she told me.'

'She didn't want you to grow up hating him.'

Grace smiled. 'Well, she failed then, because I do.'

'Why are you asking now?' Helen frowned. 'You've never bothered about it before.'

Grace pondered the question, for, in truth, she had no idea. With a shrug, she let the

19

question drift.

'Did she ever hear from him again?'

'He…' Helen paused, but the look in her niece's eye prompted her to continue. 'He sent money for you until you were seven. She still wrote to him after that.'

'But, no money?'

Helen shook her head. 'Not that I know of.'

'And did he and Mum ever divorce?'

'No.'

'So, he might have been a bigamist?'

Helen was shocked. 'What makes you say that?'

'Mum didn't die until '44. Years after he left her. Do you think he stayed single all these years?'

Helen's tone was surly. 'I have no idea.'

'You're hiding something, I know you are.'

Helen flinched in her seat, but remained silent; and Grace knew she would have to resort to more robust tactics.

*

Grace sat in the park, her eyes on the path that Beth would have to take on her way back to the flat. Luckily, anticipating a long, draughty vigil, she had donned coat and scarf, superfluous at the start of the holiday but essential today to ward off the cold wind that swept across the recreation park.

An hour after the conversation with her aunt, Grace was still suffering the effects of the acrimonious discovery. Even armed with the knowledge that she would be opening old wounds, resurrecting old grievances, she had not been prepared for the information.

As the light began to fade and the first anxious thoughts of her daughter's late homecoming began to take precedence, Grace was suddenly delighted to see Beth's red hat bobbing towards her.

'Hi! Is this the sum total of the search party?'

'I needed some fresh air,' Grace lied, taking Beth's arm and setting off across the park. 'How was the cycle trip?'

'Oh, it was fine,' Beth said cheerfully. 'But I'd hate to live in this place.'

'Really? You mean, apart from the fact that Helen's here?'

'Naughty! No, it's got nothing to do with her, more to do with everything being perfect.'

'No one wearing jeans covered in paint, you mean?'

'Exactly. Far too smart and posh for me.' Beth stopped walking suddenly and turned to her mother. 'How did you get on with old torn face?'

'Beth, dear, I –'

'Did she bully you all afternoon?'

'No. We talked about my mother, and I think I upset her a bit.'

'No supper for us then, I presume?'

Despite the rigours of the day, Grace had to laugh. 'Maybe not.'

'We could go out busking,' Beth suggested. 'I saw lots of them in the town.'

'Well, that's hardly conducive to the smart and posh theory.'

'Did you really upset the old dear?' Beth asked as they stepped onto the pedestrian crossing outside the block of flats.

'Yes, I think I did.'

'You don't sound too worried about it.'

'I'm not, but I'd rather you didn't mention anything.'

Beth laughed and pressed the intercom button on the front door.

'Mention what? I've forgotten it already.'

'Just don't speak and you'll be fine.'

'When we were kids, Dad used to say we should be seen and not heard.'

'That's good advice for tonight,' Grace said pointedly. 'She'll probably be in a bad mood, but at least we have each other.'

'I know,' said Beth mischievously as the buzzer sounded and the door swung open. 'Let's talk about sex, get her really annoyed.'

'Beth, please!'

*

Helen was polite but distant all evening and, despite Beth being in the dark about the reasons for it, Grace sensed that the girl was doing her best to keep things cheerful.

After supper, when Grace imagined she and Beth could just sit quietly and read their books, Helen announced that the downstairs' neighbours were to visit for the evening.

'They won't stay long,' she added, in direct contradiction to the spirit of an invitation. 'I'll make a cup of tea at nine and they'll be gone by half past.'

Beth and her mother exchanged a brief glance, at which Helen bristled:

'I take it you're not keen on the idea?'

'What's it got to do with us?' Grace heard herself say unkindly. 'It's your house, Helen, you can do as you please.'

She saw Beth hold her breath at the dispassionate tone of voice and resolved to have a heart-to-heart with the girl, once they were alone.

'It is, as you say, my house,' Helen repeated frostily. 'But I would hope that you make the effort.'

Grace toyed with the idea of scuppering the entire evening, but her daughter's unhappy expression pulled her up sharply.

She forced a smile. 'Of course we'll make the effort. We'll behave ourselves perfectly, won't we, Beth?'

After an uncomfortable hour of constrained conversation, the neighbours took their leave, happily, Grace imagined. When she and Beth offered to help with the clearing up, Helen, who had her own fastidious system and regarded help as a criticism, declined, thereby allowing them to have an early night.

'Hey, did you know I can get radio Hilversum on this transistor?' Beth asked, as they prepared for bed.

'What on earth is that?'

'A pop music station. It's quite good, even better than Radio Luxembourg.'

'If you say so, dear.'

'Come on, Mum, tell me what went on this afternoon.'

Grace was taken aback: her daughter had switched off the transistor radio and was lying back on her pillow with a determined look on her face. Despite her earlier decision to have the heart-to-heart with Beth, Grace was having second thoughts.

'I told you, we talked about my mother, and things like that.'

'You must have said something terrible. Her face was tripping her all night.'

'If you must know, she and my mother never got on. I suppose it brought it all back.'

'Never got on? Why not?'

'I have no idea,' Grace said, turning from the scrutiny of her daughter's gaze and combing her hair at the dressing table. 'To be honest, it was so long ago that I wonder why I'm still thinking about it.'

'They say that every family has skeletons in its cupboard,' Beth yawned. 'I'd be really interested to know what ours were.'

'Skeletons?' Grace repeated warily. 'What's that got to do with my chat with Helen?'

'Do we have any?' Beth persisted.

'As far as I know, we only had the one,' Grace said, knowing that she had the power to end Beth's speculation. 'And that was me.'

'Oh Mum,' her daughter said contritely. 'I didn't mean to –'

'Least said, soonest mended,' Grace said with a smile; and the subject was dropped.

Later, as she lay listening to her daughter's peaceful breathing, Grace longed to be home, settled into the familiar routine of her own house, her own family. She had done what she had come to do, although she was hard-pressed to ignore the fact that her mother would have been horrified at such impudence; and particularly at Grace's disrespectful attitude towards her aunt.

The mystery of her mother's marriage and subsequent abandonment had been Grace's constant companion all her life. She was convinced that anything she had ever been told about the situation had been untrue. Her grandfather was primarily to blame, but also her two aunts, and even her own mother: all perpetrators of lies so unwavering, that Grace had come to accept them unquestioningly; until now.

But, why now?

She could think of no reason for her sudden interest in her father's treachery. The only possible excuse was that she had too little to do; or was it the sudden realisation that she had reached middle age without discovering the whole truth?

Now, as she lay remembering every sentence, every word of the afternoon's conversation, she was wondering how it had been possible to remain inwardly calm as she had bullied an elderly woman in such an uncharitable manner.

'What does it matter now anyway?' Helen had asked irritably. *'These things happened, people made the best of it.*

'I suppose you said the very same thing to my mother?'

Helen appeared aggrieved. 'I gave her all the help she needed.'

Grace had scoffed at that, but Helen had continued angrily:

'You can think what you like, but I know the truth of it.'

'The truth?' Grace had repeated sarcastically. 'You wouldn't recognise it, Helen, not if it flew into this room and slapped you in the face.'

'Which is what you've done,' her aunt had retorted, her voice breaking. 'I don't deserve this... this inquisition, Grace, and I have to tell you that I can never feel the same about you again.'

'Well, that's fine by me,' Grace retorted, surprising them both. 'I doubt if we'll have much to do with each other in future anyway.'

After a moment's silence wherein both women suffered from varying degrees of shame, Helen was the first to speak.

'I wanted to tell you when you were younger, but your mother wouldn't hear of it.'

'How convenient.'

Helen flinched once more, but went on: 'Father forbade it and his word was Law, you know that.'

'I would never have said anything to him. You should have told me.'

'If your mother had found out, she'd have told him and Lord knows what he would have done.'

The hall clock struck midnight. Grace sighed and closed her eyes. She found sparse consolation in finally having the courage to broach the subject, for her aunt's revelations had been disappointing: Thomas Blake had married his sweetheart as soon as she told him she was pregnant; a man of honour, one might have judged him – but for his speedy abandonment of his wife and unborn child.

To her surprise, Grace had bullied Helen into divulging Thomas Blake's destination – South America – and even into admitting that her mother had paid for his ticket; a fact that deepened Grace's hatred of the man.

'You mean she gave him money to leave her?'

'It's what Charlotte wanted.'

'You mean, it's what you all wanted to believe. Anyway, at least I know where he went.'

'What does it matter now?'

'I just wanted to know for certain that he left and never gave us a second thought.'

'How can that help you?'

'Because now I can hate him and feel justified.'

Helen had refused further information, but it was enough for Grace, although she suspected there was much more. As the clock in the hallway struck two, she was still alert, racking her brains for another likely source of information.

There was one other person in the area who had known her father, and that was his old school friend, Ralph Fergusson. Friends stuck together, however, and so Grace had never considered going to see the man. Besides, he had the reputation of being a spinner of yarns. Could she believe anything he told her?

Outside in the street the sound of a motorcycle ruffled the air, disturbing the peace and quiet of the room. Wearily, Grace closed her eyes and thought of home.

Chapter Two

Thomas Blake strode down Perth High Street, occasionally glancing at his reflection in a shop window, adjusting his expression if he thought it too un-complimentary. He had a habit of frowning, the creases formed and confirmed by years under the Buenos Aires sun and, despite the Scottish light being more subdued, he frequently caught himself scowling, a most unattractive feature in an otherwise handsome face. At least, he considered it to be a handsome face for a man of sixty-seven; which was as many years as he admitted to, and no-one had raised an eyebrow at him yet.

The changes in the city were astonishing. His absence might have been for a hundred years, not fifty, the way everything had altered. The biggest difference was in the inhabitants, the young particularly, strutting around looking like scarecrows, with filthy, tight-fitting jeans, sloppy vests, and hair so long that, had it not been for the advent of the mini-skirt, he would have had difficulty distinguishing male from female.

He averted his eyes from the girl walking ahead of him, for the sight of so much bare flesh, even at his age, was unsettling. All at once, a young woman pushed past him, bruising his shoulder; and an image of Charlotte Shepherd flashed into his mind, catching him off-guard, taking his breath away, causing his heart to thud in his chest.

*

They bumped into each other, quite literally, on the station platform. Whose fault it was at the time they could not decide, but much later, when they were regular companions, they laughingly blamed the other.

'Ouch!'

'Oh, steady on!'

Thomas had composed himself first, and so he had time to take in the flushed cheeks, the merry blue eyes, the sweet curve of her mouth; but, just as he was about to introduce himself, she flew up the steps of the train and into the carriage.

'Hey, wait a minute, please wait!' he called after her, and she turned and looked at him.

'I beg your pardon, but, are you speaking to me?'

'I'm Thomas. I work across the street from your office.'

'Oh, yes,' she said, glancing up the platform at the guard who was closing the carriage doors and preparing to whistle the train from the station.

'Can I see you sometime, for luncheon maybe?' Thomas asked, not caring how desperate he sounded.

'No, I hardly think so.'

'Why not?'

'Because I'm only just sixteen if you must know,' the girl told him pleasantly, and he stared at her.

'You're....you're only....?'

'I am indeed,' she said with a mischievous smile, and he knew immediately that she was the one.

*

He stood for a moment in the doorway of a shop, bringing himself back to the here and now, utterly astonished at the depth of emotion induced by the memory; and if he were honest with himself, terrified at the idea that she might never want to see him again.

It was quite feasible, of course, after the way he had treated her and their daughter, and for years he had convinced himself that any kind of reconciliation was out of the question.

Recently, however, in the past six months, in the wake of Maria's death, he had fantasised about seeing Charlotte again, and the speculation had developed into a full-blown obsession; until he was compelled to give up everything and come home to find her; and their daughter.

Once he had recovered his composure, Thomas glanced around for a café that might serve lunches, but he knew that he would end up at the George Hotel for he was more at ease with the clientele of a salubrious establishment than with the riff-raff currently thronging the streets.

The receptionist, a young, blowsy girl called Sarah, eyed him with the usual interest as he entered the foyer, leaning over to give him the benefit of her cleavage as he stood at the desk.

'May I have my key?' he smiled, eyes deliberately, albeit with difficulty, avoiding the cleavage. 'Room num –'

'As if I would forget your room number, Mr Hudson,' she twittered, using his assumed name. 'We don't get many guests from America, you know.'

He was about to correct her, to remind her it was South America, but he decided that her mistake might be fortuitous: this place was barely ten miles from the Shepherd's village, and he would rather that Charlotte heard of his arrival from him, not from some snip of a girl unconnected to the story.

'Thank you, Sarah,' was all he said before turning towards the stairs.

'Will you be having lunch today, Mr Hudson?' she called after him and he turned back.

'I rather think I will. Can you remind me of the times again?'

'Twelve until two,' she said, and, was it his imagination or had she loosened another button of her blouse? 'Shall I reserve a table for you, Sir?'

'I'd be most grateful,' Thomas smiled, recalling how fortunate he had been with Charlotte Shepherd, a girl whose modesty and decorum were indisputable; until she met him.

*

Harry fretted on the station platform, glancing at the clock every few minutes, becoming increasingly impatient. To pass the time, he had allowed his mind to drift back to the day he had first met Beth Melville, on a platform similar to this one, and had summoned up the nerve to chat her up. How fortuitous that they had both chosen Aberdeen University for their degrees. If his Uncle George had had his way, Harry would have been married to a Southerner by now.

'Since your father's dead, I'm responsible for you and I suggest you apply to the best universities,' the man had said pompously.

'My mother is Scottish and she –'

'Your mother is not interested,' Uncle George had said without altering his austere tone. 'She's too wrapped up in her new family to bother about you.'

Perhaps the nature of his thoughts was adding to the chill of the day, but Harry considered Perth station to be one of the coldest and draughtiest spots on the planet; only marginally kinder than his digs in the Granite city, where it had not been uncommon for him to wear old-fashioned long-johns under his linen trousers and a thick vest as buffer between his chest and the freezing North.

Years before, as he had studied the latitude of Aberdeen from the warmer climes of the Borders, he had thought himself prepared for life in the far North, but the reality of it had continually shocked him, literally, with its unforgiving, relentlessly bitter temperatures. Even in summer, he had been glad to escape to Perth to take advantage of its more sympathetic temperatures, and had often wondered if Beth's initial attraction for him was the latitude of her village…

'You'll come out with an inferior degree,' his uncle had predicted sullenly. 'No-one this side of the border will want to employ you.'

The fact suited Harry: his mother was Scottish and, despite her running off with the family doctor years before she was made a widow, she still wrote occasionally to her son and assured him he was always in her thoughts.

It was impossible for Harry to condemn her: his father had been the most over-bearing, intolerant man. How she had endured his tantrums for fifteen years was a mystery. At last, the sound of the train reached Harry's ears, and his mind flew at once to Grace. He had to chastise himself for feeling more elated about seeing his mother-in-law than his wife.

Beth alighted first, however, her blonde hair flying around her face, untamed by clasps or bands, and when she caught sight of him her face lit up, causing him a fleeting moment of guilt.

'Harry!' she cried, hurrying towards him, arms outstretched. 'Oh, I've missed you so much!'

He hugged her tightly and the touch of her fingers on his neck was enough to remind him why she drove him crazy.

'Hey, watch the new jacket,' he laughed and she stepped back.

'Been spending more dosh, Gillespie?' she asked, 'Just as well I'm frugal with money.'

'That, my love, will be the day, now help Grace with her case.'

As usual, he had to tread the fine line between concern for Grace and keeping Beth's resentment at bay. Despite her love for her mother, there had been occasions when Beth had glanced at him with suspicion, jealousy almost, and he had quickly diverted his attention back to his wife.

'Grace,' he smiled now, with what he hoped was the right balance of affection and politeness. 'Please, allow me.'

'Thank you, Harry. This thing has weighed a ton since Abbotsinch.'

'I could have met you at the airport, you know. It's hardly any distance at all.'

'What, in the middle of rush-hour?' Grace smiled. 'No, it was easier for us to catch the train.'

'Mum's a brick,' Beth said, taking her mother's arm. 'She's the toughest cookie on Earth, never moaning or complaining.' She grinned suddenly. 'Not like me, who never stops.'

'Remember it was you who said it,' Harry said humorously. 'Now tell me, how was the trip, and how was Helen?'

*

Had it not been for James expecting her home in the afternoon, Grace would have been tempted to spend some time in Perth. There was nothing more harassing than arriving home in a state of fatigue and being obliged to relate every detail of the holiday. She would much rather have taken advantage of Beth's offer of an hour's rest at the flat before going home to face James's inquisition, for that was what it would be.

She accepted their offer of a lift to the village, however, despite the fact that James had suggested she telephone him from Perth.

26

'I can pick you up,' he had offered when she called him from Abbotsinch that morning. 'It's no trouble, my dear, no trouble at all. I've missed you so much I can hardly wait to see you again.'

She had a fleeting wave of guilt when she lied about not being sure of the time of the Perth train, nor did she understand why she should want to deceive him like this, although the lingering effect of her argument with Helen was the probable cause of her unrest. Now, in her daughter's flat, Grace sat down for a few minutes, to get her breath back.

'Is it all right if I phone your father, let him know I'm on my way?'

'Mum, you don't have to ask! For Pete's sake, there's the phone, pick it up!'

From his first words, Grace heard the disappointment in her husband's voice, but she insisted.

'We're leaving shortly,' she told him, and a fresh wave of fatigue washed over her. 'See you in an hour then.' She replaced the receiver slowly, a hundred thoughts and ideas cascading around her mind. Had it really been a good idea to confront Helen, to resurrect such a disturbing past when life was relatively tranquil?

'It's a pity you can't stay, Mum, put your feet up, have a bit of a snooze.'

'I can do that when I get home,' Grace smiled but they both knew it would not be possible. 'Besides, we've spent over a week together, maybe you're fed up of the sight of me.'

'Never,' Beth said, grabbing her mother in a crushing hug. 'In fact, I'll spend the next week missing you like anything.'

'Me too, darling, but you can phone me if you want to come out.'

'It depends on Harry,' Beth said, turning to look at him.

'How could it depend on me?' he asked in astonishment. 'May I remind you, Madam, it would be the first time you'd asked my permission to do anything.'

Beth laughed. 'I'd never do anything you didn't want me to, you know that.'

'That's not quite the same thing as asking my permission. Are we all ready then for the last lap? Let's get you home, Grace.'

He picked up the suitcase and headed for the door and Grace had the greatest difficulty in mustering a smile.

*

It was light until nine o'clock. Grace and James sat in the garden and she relayed to him the least significant details of her holiday, omitting any reference to her talk with Helen, although she wondered if he heard the frequent hesitations in the catalogue of events.

'Next year we might go to France,' James announced as Grace came to the end of her list. 'Maybe Beth will want to come.'

'Not without Harry,' Grace said, forestalling any idea he might have of leaving the boy out. 'In fact, he might enjoy it too.'

She did not look at him as she spoke, but she had known him long enough to pick up his dissent. She waited for his response, her eyes on the yellow bush flowering at the side of the bench. It was Meadowsweet, she remembered suddenly, the herb her mother had used in the kitchen.

'He'll be working by then,' James said eventually and Grace understood the implication.

'Surely, you can't think it a good idea for Beth to go without him?'

'She went to Holland without him,' James reminded her quickly.

'True, but that was only for ten days. If you mean to drive there and back, it would mean she'd be away for at least three weeks.'

'You don't think their marriage would stand up to it?' he asked. Grace sensed the effort it had taken him to inject humour into his voice.

'That's not the point, and of course it would, but I think Harry would be keen to go. We should at least give him the chance.'

She wanted to tell him that this autocratic manner of dealing with his daughter should have ceased when she became Mrs Gillespie, but she was tired; longed to fall into bed and sleep for hours, and wake up with her disrespectful behaviour towards Helen a distant memory.

'Better to discuss it some other time,' James said, preparing to stand up. 'I think you should rest now.'

'Yes, I'm exhausted,'

'I'll be up later, once you've had a good sleep.'

'Did Frank say when he'd be home?'

'He's at football training, and with the new lights at the pitch, they can play until late.'

'He was telling me he did some of the cooking,' Grace remarked as they walked down the path towards the house. 'I could hardly believe it.'

'He's a good son.'

After the long years of animosity between father and son, the words should have filled her with delight; but Grace found it irksome that something as nondescript as a plate of food could turn the boy from sinner to saint.

*

Beth yawned and stretched, her long legs extending beyond the bed.

Beside her, although it was only seven in the evening, Harry lay asleep, features relaxed, mouth curved into a smile, She studied him for several minutes, taking in the long eyelashes – sadly, the prerogative of men – the strong jaw-line, the tanned skin.

It was always a relief to her that she still retained the ability to excite him, although she had no idea why it should be so. After two years of marriage she had envisaged a decrease in their passion, but then, what had she known about men before Harry? A couple of frenzied, hurried kisses to find out if He was The One hardly qualified her as a femme fatale. When she had asked Harry what he found appealing about her, he had looked at her with some amusement.

'Why should it matter? You do appeal to me. That's the main thing.'

'I like to analyse things.'

'What, even sex?'

'Especially sex.'

'I should have asked about your birth sign before I married you.'

'Yes, well, you know what they say. Love me, love my birth sign'

'I love you in spite of it.'

Beth had been caught unawares, for he rarely uttered the words.

'Do you really love me?' Harry had sighed then, a long-suffering sigh that a five-year old might expect.

'Beth, honestly, I wonder how seriously you take this marriage.'

'How can you ask that?'

'Because,' Harry had said patiently. 'If you don't even know that I love you, maybe you have doubts that *you* love *me*.'

She had been horrified, had thrown herself at him in a conciliatory gesture, after which they went to bed and made love, their only way of confirming their love for one another, a fact that frequently perturbed her.

Now, gazing at him in such a vulnerable state, she wondered how she could ever doubt him. Was it her own feeling of insecurity that was to blame, and would she have to take more care not to drive him away with her constant need for reassurance?

He stirred and opened his eyes. 'What's up with you, Lady Godiva?'

'Sometimes I think I'm a prat.'

Harry yawned and sat up, arranging the pillows behind his head.

'Go on, tell me every single detail, and I'll write a best-seller.'

'I know I can be irritating, and I wouldn't blame you for losing your patience with me.'

Harry laughed. 'You think too much, Beth, that's your only trouble.'

'I didn't think it could be possible to think too much.'

'Well,' he said, his eyes closing. 'You do, and it's not necessary either.'

'You always seem so laid back.'

'That's because I'm old and you're still a kid.'

'Maybe I'll grow up when I get a job.'

'And maybe I don't want you to grow up.'

'I thought you were going to say you didn't want me to get a job.'

'Wishful thinking, sweetheart,' Harry smiled wryly. 'And you'll have to start looking for one pretty soon. That's the reason you're fed up, you know, stuck in this flat all day. You're an intelligent girl, Beth, you need something to do.'

'Maybe,' Beth replied, chastened. 'What d'you think I should do?'

'Whatever you want. Just don't leave it too long.'

'What is there to do, apart from teaching?'

Harry shrugged. 'There are dozens of businesses in Perth. Maybe someone needs a language expert.'

'Like who?'

'Find out. Go and sell yourself.'

Catching sight of Beth's wicked expression as he uttered the words, he knew it was a provocative thing to say and that it would be another hour before he could get out of bed.

*

After an unsuccessful foray among the back copies in the public library, Thomas Blake sat in the guests' lounge of the hotel and skimmed through the Perthshire edition of the *Courier and Advertiser*. He was scouring the local news items in the hope of coming across any up-to-date snippet of relating to Charlotte or her family; but so far he had found nothing.

He had been tempted, but only briefly, to strike up a conversation with the couple opposite him in the dining room, for they seemed to be local, chattering on about events and people from the area. He had changed his mind, however, just in case they knew her, or any of the Shepherd clan and might mention him to his daughter before he could speak to her himself.

His heart thudded again: *speak to her himself!*

*

'Please let me see you again,' he pleaded, without the slightest shame. 'Just for a cup of tea or something, it doesn't have to be in private.'

The guardsman, who had been witness to this situation every night for the past week, approached sympathetically but purposefully, withdrawing his whistle and closing the final door.

'I'll write you a note, send it across,' Thomas said desperately. 'Please say you'll write something back!'

His pitiful expression had caused the dimple to reappear in her cheek. She hesitated, and then the guard blew his whistle and the train began to slide away from Thomas, furtively, as if it had taken the girl's side. He was obliged to walk with ever-increasing speed alongside, in a last bid to secure some sort of answer from her.

'Promise me you'll write back?' he urged and he saw that she was relenting.

'Oh, all right,' she whispered, glancing back into the carriage for fear that others had over-heard the conversation.

'Great! Thanks!' he called after her, and, within seconds, she was out of sight.

When the train pulled out of the station and vanished amid clouds of smoke, Thomas stared after it, trying to retain an image of the girl... Charlotte. He had not been at all disappointed when they had met at close quarters: her skin was delicate, not ruddy, as you might expect in a country girl, and her eyes were so incredibly blue that he had found it impossible to look away.

It was only when he found himself walking home in the wrong direction, when he glanced around and discovered that the street names were unfamiliar to him, that he fully appreciated the influence the girl had on him, with her soft skin and sparkling blue eyes.

He laughed aloud, startling a blackbird from its perch on a nearby cherry tree. The bird flew up, chattering a reprimand in Thomas's direction and took up a new position, from where it regarded him suspiciously, as if anticipating another burst of laughter.

Thomas retraced his steps to the nearest bus stop, where he would catch a bus back into the centre of Perth and start all over again. The lateness of his return would normally have caused him some concern, but tonight he was too preoccupied with thoughts of a pair of lovely blue eyes to be apprehensive about the fuss his mother would create at his late home-coming.

*

The hand that held the newspaper trembled slightly and brought Thomas's attention back to the present. Surreptitiously, he glanced around the fellow guests, but none was paying him any heed. He sighed, laid the newspaper aside, and wondered if he would have the courage to go and find her tomorrow.

Chapter Three

As she had done for the past few days, Grace was perusing the employment section of the *Courier* in case there should be a suitable job for her daughter. She was undecided as to whether Beth actually wanted a job or not, but it did no harm to look on her behalf.

The trouble was that the girl had no inclination to teach and Grace could see no other option with languages, at least not in this backwater. Had the girl been motivated to work in Edinburgh or Glasgow, there would be numerous openings for the holder of an English and foreign languages degree, but there was not the faintest possibility that Beth would agree to move, especially since Harry would be a junior partner in a solicitors' practice in Perth.

After two cups of the new, powdered variety of coffee – so much more enjoyable than Bev – and a fruitless search for employment for her daughter, Grace rose and cleared away the breakfast dishes. Frank, taking advantage of his last day of the Easter break, had switched on his record player – Beth's old one – and the sound of the Rolling Stones hurtled down the stairs and into the living room.

Grace climbed the stairs and knocked loudly on his bedroom door.

'Sorry, Mum,' the boy said as soon as he opened the door. 'I'll turn it down.'

'I wasn't coming for that,' Grace said magnanimously. 'I was just wondering if you wanted anything. I'm going to pop up to Molly's for half an hour.'

'Thanks, but I'm fine,' he said, and she marvelled anew at the scarcity of his demands; unlike Beth, whose list had been endless. 'Will I just get my own lunch if you're not back?'

'I'll be back in plenty time, dear, don't worry. Your Dad will expect a sandwich at half past twelve.'

'I could make it if you like.'

Grace looked closely at her son, who fidgeted under the scrutiny.

'That's kind of you, Frank, but you'll have years of work ahead of you, so I forbid you to do any housework.'

'Making a sandwich is hardly housework,' he laughed.

'That's as may be, but I forbid you anyway,' she said, adding cheerfully. 'Except when I'm away, of course. Then you can do all the cooking.'

'I hated when you were away,' Frank blurted out, his cheeks turning pink.

'Did you?' Grace asked with some surprise. 'Your father said you managed fine.'

'Yes,' the boy agreed. 'I managed, but that was all. The house isn't the same when you're not here.'

Grace smiled, more at her son's embarrassment than the compliment.

'That's the nicest think anyone's said to me in years, but I won't be going away again,' she told him. 'Only if we all go together.'

'Does Dad want us to go to France next year?'

'Probably.'

'That's good, I could arrange to meet my pen pal, Claude, then, and we can swap records and go down to the beach.'

Grace descended the stairs in a daze: just when she had foreseen a struggle to persuade the boy into going abroad, Frank had appeared delighted at the prospect. Grace had to smile: she had never been any good at summing people up, regardless of their age.

*

Molly was in the middle of baking a tray of scones for the Church Daffodil Tea. She bustled around the kitchen like a hospital matron whilst Grace poured out her third cup of tea and pondered over her own contribution to the sale. She had not even begun the baking and it was due to be handed in the following morning. In her mind she was organised but the reality was quite the opposite. She would have to slave over a hot stove until after midnight; as usual.

'I've done three already,' Molly said smugly, dusting yet another tray with flour. 'And I've also made a couple of fruit loaves and two gingerbreads. Will I have time for potato scones?'

'I doubt it,' Grace told her friend truthfully, but she suspected it would only serve as incentive. 'Anyway, you've done enough, surely? I mean, if we all did what you do, the Church hall would be filled to the ceiling.'

'But so many of them do nothing,' Molly said, lips pursed. 'And the worst one is Mary Campbell. Have you ever seen her hand in one single thing for one single coffee morning? No,' she answered her own question. 'Yet she's on the Committee and expects to be re-elected every blooming year. Honestly!'

Grace had heard it all before and, over the years, had developed immunity to her best friend's criticisms, not to the extent of contradicting her naturally, but tempering the most brutal. The Women's Guild was, after all, an organisation affiliated to the Church.

'I'll have to be up all hours baking mine,' she said now, looking round for the milk jug so that she could add milk to cool the tea. Molly preferred lemon tea, perhaps for snob value, Grace always thought uncharitably. Her friend was delighted to regale Grace with the benefits of keeping company with the Websters in the big house.

'Oh, of course, I forgot you don't take it with lemon,' Molly said, her tone signifying disapproval. 'The milk's over there, in the blue jug.'

As Grace sipped the tea and watched Molly bound back and forward across the room, she tried not to think she was wasting her time. Her house was in need of a good clean, the washing from her holiday was lying in the twin tub, and she had umpteen trays of scones and cakes to bake before the day was out. Why on earth was she sitting in Molly's kitchen, putting everything off?

'You haven't told me about the holiday,' she heard her friend say.

'Oh well, Helen's Helen, isn't she?'

Molly paused in her trek from sink to cooker and looked closely at Grace.

'Why did you go then, if you're not keen on the woman?'

Grace shrugged. 'Beth wanted to go,' she lied. 'I didn't want to disappoint her.'

'Oh, I see. How is she, by the way? Still married?'

Grace ignored the implication and nodded. 'Yes, still happy.'

'Jonathan's thinking of getting married soon. At least, that's what he told his brother.'

'Funny, isn't it, that your younger one got a serious girlfriend first?'

'I suppose it depends when you meet the right one.'

'How old were you when you met yours?'

'Nineteen, but it took him a while to persuade me.'

'Really? I thought you were smitten right away.'

'What on earth gave you that idea?'

'Any time I saw you, you seemed to have eyes only for him.'

'Aye, that's what he thought too.'

Molly, never one to keep a secret, gave Grace a knowing glance, as if to encourage further questions. When her friend only shrugged and smiled, however, she was obliged to complete the puzzle herself:

'Remember Ronnie?'

'Yes, your boyfriend before Derek.'

'My boyfriend the same time as Derek,' Molly corrected archly, as if it were something to be proud of.

'Goodness me, I'd no idea you were two-timing him.'

Molly threw Grace an aggrieved look. 'That's not a very nice word, dear, between friends.'

'What would you call it then?'

'As my mother would say: two men, two different loves.'

Grace was shocked at the very idea.

'Did you hear me?' she heard Molly ask. 'Two men –'

'Yes, I heard you.'

'She'd have been wasting her time saying it to you,' Molly said disparagingly. 'I can't imagine you ever two-timing James.'

'Well I didn't, of course.'

'No, you wouldn't.'

'Well, I really must get on,' Grace said, standing up and moving over to deposit her cup at the sink. 'I'll be up until the small hours.'

'You'll manage. And I bet your scones turn out better than mine again.'

'It was my mother's recipe,' Grace told her friend and it sounded as if she were unwilling to take the credit. Why was she always doing that?

'Anyway, see you tomorrow morning. Oh, and don't forget to bring half a dozen cups and saucers, just in case it's a lovely day and we're inundated with customers.'

'James is giving me a lift up to the hall, shall I ask him to call in for you?'

'You'll have to sit in the front then,' Molly smiled impudently. 'Or I won't be responsible for my actions.'

As with all her friend's innuendos, Grace returned the smile and passed no comment.

*

Thomas Blake picked up the telephone directory and flicked through to the 'S' section, being of the opinion that she would have reverted to her maiden name soon after he stopped writing and sending money. It was only the first step, of course, for he knew that her old friend Lily Morris still lived there, the name that had come to him the night before and which he had found immediately in the directory.

Lily Morris! Thomas let out a slow sigh at the memory of Charlotte's friend, provider of frequent alibis for them in the beginning; how she had been the only one to understand their commitment to each other, even under such deplorable circumstances. Had it not been for Lily, he would never have won Charlotte. He frowned. The words were not strictly true, since they had spent their lives on opposite sides of the globe.

After a fruitless search through the 'S' section, he turned, even less optimistically, to the 'B's. If she was not listed here either, then it might mean she had remarried.

Remarried!

His mind refused to dwell on the word, despite the fact that he himself had remarried – bigamously too – with nary a second thought. Still, Charlotte was not like him and he would have placed money on it, that she had never given her heart to any other man.

Twenty minutes later, having exhausted all possible leads in the directory, Thomas opened his wallet and looked at the number he had jotted down the night before. Taking a deep breath and, his confidence diminishing with every passing moment, he lifted the receiver and dialled quickly before he changed his mind.

*

33

Lily Morris sat down heavily on the kitchen chair and mopped her brow. She was getting too old for this caper, baking a dozen chocolate cakes and banana loaves that would be virtually given away, so low was the price label. Five shillings for two chocolate cakes? She had never seen anything so ridiculous. It hardly seemed a just reward for three days' labour, not to mention the cost of the ingredients; and her well on her way to celebrating her seventy-third birthday too.

She studied the result of her latest morning's work and wondered if it would only be her baking that people missed once she had passed away; or whether there were any other of her attributes that people noticed.

The telephone rang in the hall and she sat waiting for it to stop, since her days of running to answer it were long gone. If they wanted to speak to her, they would call again, when she was closer to the contraption.

When it rang the second time she frowned and waited, satisfied moments later when whoever it was hung up. She knew it was no-one important. Only Grace and the next-door neighbours were of any significance to her and, because they knew her dislike of going out these days, they would arrive unannounced, fully expecting to find her at home.

Half an hour later, as she passed through the hall to the parlour, the telephone rang again and she paused to stare at it. Why in Heaven's name had she allowed her brother to have the damned thing installed? Was it not the most unwelcome, intrusive contraption in the whole world, even more so than the television set? At least you could switch that off, get some peace; whereas this thing could jangle at any time of the day or night and, when she did answer it, the voice at the other end was always asking her to do something.

Angrily, Lily grabbed the receiver off the hook and waited.

'Is that Lily Morris?' a man's voice asked, a voice she did not recognise, one with an unusual accent.

'Aye, it is,' she replied and was greeted by a silence. 'I said, aye, it is.'

'You might remember me,' said the voice, but still she thought him a stranger.

'I used to live in the village…years ago…in the '20's.'

The first faint signs of recognition were flickering in Lily's mind but she dismissed them as preposterous: even if he were still alive, he would never have the audacity to show his face in this place again.

'Who is this?' she demanded abruptly, suppressing her worst fears.

'Lily, I apologise for this, but I couldn't think of anyone else to ask.'

With a crash, Lily dropped the receiver into its cradle and sought the nearest chair. She could hardly think for the pounding of her heart. It was him! It was Thomas Blake!

How wrong could she be? He did have the audacity to come back here and show his face. Lily took out her handkerchief and mopped her brow. It was the worst moment of her life since it had all gone horribly wrong.

What could possibly go wrong?

Lily gasped: she could see Lottie standing there as clear as day.

*

Charlotte looked at Lily imploringly, the blue eyes unwavering, and they both knew that she would get her own way.

'Oh, all right,' Lily agreed irritably. 'But please remember you're only sixteen and if anything goes wrong, you're on your own, Madam!'

'Wrong?' laughed Charlotte. 'We're only going for a walk, for Heaven's sake. What could possibly go wrong?'

'I'm just saying be careful, Lottie. Your mother's no fool.'

Over the years, Betsy Shepherd's boundless energy and cheerful disposition had been sorely tried by her husband's intransigent adherence to the rigid doctrine of the United Free Church. Alexander's word was law and neither his wife nor his daughter would have dared to question him. However, Lily, having no surviving parent, was spared the trouble of treading warily at home. There were only her brothers to worry about, and they were rarely interested in what she did.

As she and Charlotte sat in the tiny scullery of Lilac Cottage that evening, Lily watched Betsy for any sign that she had caught on to what the girls had been concocting together.

'You're lookin' wabbit tonight, pet,' Betsy told her daughter. 'Did you not have a good day at work?'

Neither Lily nor Charlotte were fooled by the lightness of the older woman's tone, nor by the relaxed smile which seemed to indicate she was simply passing the time of day: Betsy Shepherd – Chapman that was – had an easy, amiable manner that belied the shrewdness of her observations about people and events and often lulled her neighbours into divulging their innermost thoughts. They were unaware that Betsy's casual, almost absent-minded glances and smiles concealed an excellent comprehensive filing system.

Lily had come to appreciate that no piece of information, however isolated or insignificant, was ever disregarded; rather it was absorbed and categorised, stored indefinitely until it might be used to her advantage.

'No, work was fine,' Charlotte said, avoiding Lily's eye. 'What's for tea?'

'Mutton stew and boiled tatties, as if you didn't know. It's Monday, pet, and what does your father always have on Mondays? How's your office training coming along anyway?' Betsy asked her daughter pleasantly 'Are you any nearer to earning fifteen shillings a week?'

'Oh, I can type three words a minute now,' Charlotte laughed, but Lily was sure that the older woman must have heard the nervousness in the laugh.

'Och, you'll be the manageress there within the year,' Betsy smiled. 'Thank the Lord your father had connections in Perth. Now, you two go and set the table through there and we can eat whenever Sandy comes home.'

As they laid out cutlery and crockery, the two girls exchanged wary glances, each of them wondering if they would have the courage to carry out their plan.

'Remember,' whispered Charlotte in her best friend's ear. 'We're going to spend the whole afternoon in Perth, home with the later bus.'

'I swear, Lottie Shepherd,' Lily whispered back. 'If I ever survive this, I'll never speak to you again!'

*

The clock struck mid-day and Lily woke with a start. The effect of the tablets would take at least another hour to wear off and she cursed herself for being so stupid; but the sound of his voice and the terrible memories it evoked had driven her to desperate measures. Groggily, she tried to stand up but the effort was too much and so she sank back onto the bed, too sleepy even to wipe the tears from her eyes.

*

Grace had just begun to mix the first batch of scones when the telephone rang. Hands covered with flour, she hurried to the hall and picked up the receiver, still unaccustomed to the luxury of having one in the house after decades of telegrams and the dank, smelly public box down the road.

'It's me,' Molly said 'Lily's not well. I went round to borrow some eggs and she's in bed.'

'Maybe she's just tired,' Grace replied, and it was feasible, for the old lady was well over seventy.

'No, I think it's more than that. I knocked on the bedroom window and couldn't waken her up.'

Grace's heart sank: it was the moment she feared; the moment when her mother's old friend took seriously ill, and Grace would have to face it all again.

'I'll pop up and see what's wrong,' she told Molly. 'I have a key, so it's no bother.'

'Good, I just thought I'd let you know, and you'll be in the middle of your baking too, you poor thing,' Molly added, but there was little sympathy in her tone.

'It's all right, I'll be up 'til all hours anyway. Oh, and thanks for telling me, I'll call you later if anything's the matter.'

*

Grace walked slowly up to Lily's front door, key at the ready. It had taken her twenty minutes to pop the tray of scones in the oven and wash up all the bowls – James was due home any minute and he would take a dim view of an untidy kitchen, regardless of the reason.

As she pushed open the door, Grace paused and listened. The prospect of finding the old lady lying dead in her bed was the most horrible thing she could imagine. Grace shuddered. It was almost thirty years since she had come downstairs to find her mother lying on the kitchen floor; and she still suffered the same distress at the memory.

She walked around the house, peering into each room as she passed by. Hesitating, but only for a moment, she went upstairs to the bedrooms and found, to her relief, that they were all empty. Her heart soared, for it meant that Lily was probably sitting in the back garden having her tea and would soon be chastising her young friend for all the fuss.

She glanced from the kitchen window and saw Lily sitting in the sunshine.

Her spirits rising, Grace opened the door and went out.

'Oh, it's you, Grace?' Lily called cheerfully.

'Yes, it's me,' Grace said, her whole world re-assembling in a heartbeat. 'Are you busy?'

'When am I not busy?' Lily asked. 'Are you short of something, pet?'

'Yes, I could do with some eggs,' Grace lied, for she could pop into Molly's on the way back and hand them in. 'Have you enough?'

'Aye, the hens were very obliging yesterday, must be the mild weather. Help yourself. They're in the larder; take as many as you need.'

Grace picked half a dozen of the smallest eggs, before rejoining Lily in the garden. She looked at the old lady carefully, trying to assuage the nature of her 'turn', but she appeared perfectly normal.

'I'm exhausted,' Grace said, a ploy to find out Lily's state of health. 'I had to lie down an hour ago, put my feet up, have a snooze. Heaven knows how you manage at your age.'

Lily smiled wryly. 'As if I needed reminding.'

'Have you had a rest this morning?' Grace persisted, although her companion was regarding her with some suspicion.

'Aye, I did lie down for a wee while. Why d'you ask?'

'I came up earlier,' Grace lied. 'For the eggs. But there was no reply.'

36

Lily seemed satisfied with the explanation and Grace thought how easy it had been to tell so many lies in one day. Years ago, when she was a girl, she would never have contemplated telling lies, far less have had the guile to express them.

'I did have forty winks,' Lily admitted, turning her face to the sun. 'But I feel fine now.'

'You're sure you're fine then.'

'Aye,' Lily frowned. 'As fine as I can be, At my age,' she added.

'I'd best be getting down the road, back to a mountain of baking for this damned coffee morning. And James is due home any minute, expecting his tea, and I haven't even looked anything out.'

'Look,' Lily said, pointing to the trays of banana loaves. 'You take them and hand them in, I've plenty stuff. I hate to think of you up half the night, especially when nobody else bothers their backsides about it.'

Grace laughed, but more in relief that Lily was in good health.

'No, honestly, I'll manage fine.'

'If you don't take them,' Lily stated firmly, hands on hips. 'I'll not be happy.'

'Oh well,' Grace acquiesced reluctantly. 'I'd not want to make you unhappy. Suit yourself, I'll take the loaves.'

'And you promise me you'll not stay up all night baking now?'

'I promise. Just a couple more trays of scones and they're easy enough.'

*

A few minutes later, Lily watched the girl as she carried her bundles carefully to the gate and tried to wave goodbye with her hands full. When Grace had disappeared from sight, the old lady sighed and went inside. How she had survived the past twenty minutes was down to a miracle.

She had done her best to keep her thoughts away from the phone call, but the effort had taken its toll. She was furious that, for the second time in her life, she had been left with bearing the worst kind of news you could think of. It was almost impossible for her not to blame Charlotte.

Her heart went out to Grace Melville when she considered how the girl might react to the information Lily was concealing; and *would* conceal, for as long as she could. There was no fear of her telling Grace about Thomas Blake's call, no fear that she would pass on such dreadful – catastrophic – tidings that could only turn the world on its head. No, they had all suffered enough; and it had to stop.

*

Oblivious to the passage of time, Thomas Blake sat with his head in his hands. As soon as he heard the crash of the receiver in his ear he knew that his quest would fail. Lily Morris was the only link he had to Charlotte and their daughter, and now that she knew he was home she would be warning them; turning them against him, even as he was sitting there considering his next move.

His only other alternative was to walk up the path to the cottage and knock on the front door. With a sigh, he shook his head and glanced at the clock: five to four and no further forward.

He picked up the *Perthshire Advertiser* and leafed through; simply to pass the time, for he did not expect to find her name in its pages, although once upon a time, or so he had discovered in a back copy from the '40's, his daughter had been featured for her singing abilities.

37

Thomas opened his wallet and looked again at the photograph they had copied for him, of the lovely young girl holding her Festival certificate, joyous eyes lifted to the camera, appearing as happy as a girl could possibly be; never giving her absent father a single thought since his hasty and undignified departure.

She was his spitting image, of course, as was his son; notwithstanding that Maria Caro had been raven-haired. Thomas still found it hard to believe that Joseph spoke Portuguese better than he spoke English. It seemed to alienate the boy from his father's side of the family; although Thomas had never felt sufficient affection for either his second wife or child for the idea to preoccupy him.

Down in the street, a heavy vehicle rumbled to the traffic lights and ground to a throbbing halt, vibrating the glass in Thomas's hotel room window, disturbing his thoughts. Quickly, he replaced the photograph in his wallet and stood up. If he had to abandon this quest, then he may as well eat lunch before he checked out. At the back of his mind, however, he felt a wave of guilt at the idea of abandoning his daughter a second time.

Chapter Four

With Frank back at school and Harry off to Aberdeen for his final few months, Grace and Beth were enjoying each other's company; lunching in Perth or having afternoon tea in the garden of Lilac cottage.

It was a warm, hazy afternoon in May, the kind of day that stirs up the scents of spring blossoms and fills the air with sweetness; and it was so bright that Grace had to don sunglasses.

'You look like Marilyn Monroe,' Beth told her as they drank tea and consumed several pieces of homemade shortbread. 'In that film with Joseph Cotton.'

'Darling, you know I don't go to the cinema.'

'I thought you said you'd seen all the Fred Astaire films?'

'Mum and I went to see them when I was a girl, but I haven't been for ages.'

'That's because he never takes you.'

'Who's 'he', Beth'? The cat's father?'

'Dad never takes you anywhere.'

'You've certainly changed your tune about your father, my lady. Once upon a time you'd have defended him with your life.'

Beth gave her mother a resentful glance. 'No, I didn't.'

'You know perfectly well you did, dear, and there was nothing wrong with that. You and he were – are – two of a kind.'

'Not so much now,' Beth said quietly, helping herself to a third piece of shortbread. 'Not since I got married.'

'Are you still happy?'

'Yes, deliriously.'

Grace lowered her sunglasses and studied her daughter's face.

'You're sure you did the right thing then, that you weren't too young to get married?'

'Yes, Mrs Fusspot, I did the right thing, and don't change the subject, I said you look like Marilyn Monroe in that film about Niagara.'

'And I said I never go to the cinema, so I guess we're back where we started.'

Beth grinned as her mother readjusted the sunglasses and leaned back into the deckchair.

'I was just thinking,' she giggled, and Grace opened one eye.

'What?'

'You never let me tell you about my sex life.'

'I should think not either,' Grace said, outwardly unruffled; her sang-froid evoking a glance of admiration.

Beth laughed. 'That's the great thing about having you for a Mum, the fact I can tell you anything and you're never shocked.'

'Mine was the same,' Grace smiled, recalling Charlotte Blake's unshockable personality. 'We were more like sisters.'

Something I can't tell you.

'I wish I'd known her.'

'She'd have worshipped the ground you walk on,' Grace said, her heart aching at the idea.

'Did she ever mention…? I mean, did you ever…?' Beth hesitated and her mother removed the sunglasses for the second time in as many minutes.

'My father, you mean?'

'You don't have to talk about it if you don't want to.'

'That's true, and I don't.'

'But remember, he was my grandfather.'

'I'm aware of that, Beth.' Grace said, flashing her daughter a reprimand.

'I'm just saying,' Beth went on unashamedly. 'Sometimes I'm dying to know the whole story.'

'The whole story is that he abandoned Mum and me before I was born and that he never wanted either of us.'

Grace sat up in the deckchair, the memory of her conversation with Helen springing into her mind. Such was the strength of it that she had to take a deep breath.

Beth frowned and leaned towards her mother. 'What is it?'

'Nothing. Too much shortbread gives me heartburn.'

'Is that all you're going to tell me?'

'Well, I think it must be the sugar content in the mix.'

Beth burst out laughing and slapped her mother playfully on the wrist.

'You are the funniest, wittiest person I know, and I hate you!'

'Oh, good Heavens, is that the time?' Grace asked, jumping up and preparing to clear away the tea tray. 'I'll have to get you back to Perth, young lady.'

'I could always stay the night,' Beth suggested hopefully.

'Not a good idea. I'd get used to it and keep asking.'

'Well, what's wrong with that?'

'Nothing, except it would be better to ask Harry first.'

'What?' Beth shrieked. 'Why should I do that?'

'Because he's an interested party.'

'Well, *I* have no intentions of being tethered to the back green,' Beth said, and it seemed to Grace that the girl flinched.

'What an odd thing to say,' Grace smiled. 'Of course Harry wouldn't tether you to the back green, but I do feel you should consult him.'

'Fair enough,' Beth agreed. 'But I'm only saying it to keep the peace. Now, let me take these down and help with the washing up.'

'Two cups and plates?' her mother queried. 'Oh, I think I'll manage. You go and gather your belongings together, be ready in ten minutes.'

'I wish I could afford my own car, then you wouldn't have to give me a lift back.'

'Maybe if you found a job?'

Beth frowned. 'I suppose so.'

'Do go and get ready, dear. We'll hit the rush hour if we don't go now.'

'Will Dad come with me when it's time to choose a car?' Beth asked later, as Grace reversed onto the main road.

'You'd fall out, as sure as rain falls downwards.'

'No, we wouldn't.'

'Yes, you would. It would be better to ask Harry.'

'You must be joking! He's not too keen on my having a car.'

'Isn't he?'

'But, if I did get a job, I could buy one with my own money and he'd have no say in it.'

'Still, you should take him with you if you buy one. It makes them feel they're in charge.'

Beth paused in her examination of her red fingernails and looked across at her mother.

'Ah, ha, so you *do* know that we have to pander to their egos?'

'And then you and I could go here, there and everywhere,' Grace said, ignoring her daughter's remark. 'Only not to Holland. I can only take Helen in very small doses.'

40

Grace walked to the car and raked for her key. As she opened the door, she glanced up to the window of the flat and waved to her daughter, before throwing her handbag onto the passenger seat and preparing to drive off. She much preferred the location of Beth and Harry's new flat; closer to the centre of the city, closer to shops and civilisation, although she thought the place too big, especially for Beth, who was alone during the week.

Grace eased into the flow of traffic and crawled towards the Queen's Bridge. How she would have loved the girl to stay the night, to hear the sound of her laughter around the house, to enjoy the banter between her and Frank, for recently brother and sister had settled into a more amicable sibling relationship; and, of course, to take advantage of the girl's influence on her father...

Occasionally, alone in the house with no fear of interruption, Grace would take out the old photograph album and pore over the snapshots of Beth as a baby, and, at the first sight of the spiky blonde hair, the cheeky face, she would reach for her handkerchief and cry her eyes out. It was unreasonable, she knew, and perhaps it was her age, but, at times, she seemed unable, unwilling, to move on, to accept things as they were. She was over forty; perhaps this weepy, nostalgic phase was simply a consequence of the mid-life crisis.

The traffic was light and so she arrived in the village just before half past three. On the spur of the moment, she decided to pop in and see if Lily Morris had fully recovered from her 'turn'.

*

Beth ran across the street, dodging cars and pedestrians, cursing herself for running out of milk. Such a stupid oversight obliged her to walk several blocks for just one item and, although she could have used the powdered rubbish that Harry often chucked in his cup, she would have had to be pretty desperate first: the stuff tasted like wallpaper paste.

As she jay-walked between crawling cars, she caught sight of a chauffeur's cap in the big car she almost collided with: the wearer was young, smartly turned out, and he was giving her the kind of smile she was accustomed to. Her bad mood, however, ensured that her glance at him was not of a similar nature and, obviously taking umbrage, he glowered back.

Within seconds, she had manoeuvred her way to the other side of the road and, with an involuntary backward glance at the big car, was jogging the last few yards to the grocer's shop.

*

Thomas Blake had been staring into space, trying not to dwell too much on his failed mission; but the thought of flying back to Edinburgh and an uncertain future was turning this into the most depressing day of his life; even worse than the day in Reform Street when he had made the biggest mistake a man could make.

'Look at that,' he heard his driver mutter, and Thomas raised his eyes.

'What is it?' he asked disinterestedly.

'That girl looks like she wants to commit suicide,' the youth said, eyes meeting Thomas's in the rear-view mirror. 'Mind you, she's a looker and no mistake,' he added, and it aroused his passenger's curiosity.

What he saw caused Thomas Blake's heart to stop.

*

The nights were lengthening. Beth waited until the last moment before switching on the standard lamp. She had been reading *Girl with the Green Eyes*, laughing uproariously one moment, shedding a tear the next, and she knew that when she finished the book the characters would stay with her for days, maybe even weeks; the sign of a good book, she maintained.

She stood at the window but there was little sign of activity now, particularly in this street, which, despite being only yards from the city centre, was a virtual backwater at night. A solitary car drew up at the lights and she suddenly missed the old flat in Rose Crescent, dispensed with, Harry had told her, because it was too small for them.

Beth glanced back into the huge room and, involuntarily, she shivered. The place was so big that a burglar could be ransacking the bedrooms and she would never hear a sound.

'Stop that, you twit!' she cried aloud, swishing closed the heavy curtains and stepping towards the television set. It was Thursday and she had missed *Top of the Pops*, a chance to see The Stones maybe, or Manfred Mann, whose lead singer could drag her off to his cave any day.

Before she switched on the set to watch the late news, she wandered through the long hallway to their bedroom, quickly turning lights on and resisting the temptation to glance behind her as she went. If Harry knew what a wimp she was on her own, he would laugh himself silly.

'This flat is huge,' she had frowned, the day he brought her for the first time. 'We'll rattle around the bloody place.'

'The other one was a bachelor pad,' Harry had replied patiently, checking the white goods in the spacious kitchen. 'This is for a married couple.'

'Yes, with six kids,' she had said before thinking, and he had turned to look at her, a faint smile at his mouth, a smile so tantalising that she could hardly shift her gaze.

'Presumably we'll have kids?' he asked, and Beth's heart sank: not that she did not want them, just that she figured she still had lots of time before she was tethered to the back green…

'Yes, of course we will, but not for ages.'

'That goes without saying,' he said, his attention returning to the faulty fridge door. 'I'll have to get this seen to before we move in. One swing and the thing will be off its hinges.'

'This bedroom could sleep six people,' Beth had pointed out, standing on the threshold and staring into the room. 'We can always take in lodgers.'

'Only if they're female, Swedish, and seventeen,' Harry had smiled, and she had the greatest difficulty trying not to imagine his mouth on hers.

Now, the clock began striking and Beth jumped. She really would have to buy a cat or a budgie. This ridiculous nonsense was pathetic. All of a sudden the doorbell rang and she leaped three feet into the air. She stood for a moment, trying to get her breath back, imagining what kind of person would be at her door at ten o'clock. Worse still, she was perplexed that she had missed the footsteps on the stone staircase.

The bell rang again and she tiptoed along the hallway, her heart pounding.

'Who is it?' she had the bravado to inquire, ear pressed against the door.

'Please don't worry, I'm a friend of your mother's,' a man's voice told her and she was stunned into silence.

'I knew the family years ago,' he asserted, and the accent escaped her; she who was

42

a whiz at languages. She could opt to speak or to remain silent, but she decided that speaking might get rid of him quicker.

'Are you still there?' he asked before she had thought of something to say.

'Yes, but anyone could say they were a friend of mother's and she might be dead, for all you know.'

'She's not,' the man replied, but she heard the uncertainty in his voice. 'She's not nearly fifty yet and the Shepherds were all fairly healthy.'

'So much for...' Beth started to say, and then she realised what she would be giving away if she told him about Charlotte. If he was a know-it-all, let him prove it.

There was a short silence, during which she held her breath and listened closer, but heard nothing. After a full minute, believing him to be gone, she sighed and straightened up.

'I know your grandmother, Charlotte,' the voice started up again, taking Beth by surprise. 'Her maiden name was Shepherd. She's Sandy's daughter.'

'A likely story,' Beth responded rudely, disturbed by the strange pseudo-American accent. 'I'm going now, I'm busy.' She could have bitten off her tongue for using the word 'I' instead of 'we'; a trap for beginners.

'They lived at Lilac cottage' he persisted. 'And Grace was born in 1926.'

'You're wasting your time,' Beth said, but less forcefully, for she was still transfixed by the accent and how he could have known the year of her mother's birth. 'I have no idea who you're talking about.' She was pleased with that bit: it made up for the blunder about 'I'.

'I know you're her daughter,' the man said, and, even through the thickness of the door she heard the nervousness in his tone. 'You're as like her as two peas in a pod.'

'I also look like Brigitte Bardot,' Beth said belligerently. 'And she's no relation of mine.'

She heard the man laugh then, and there was something in his laugh that allayed her fears. She remained alert, however, for if he knew what she looked like, he had already been watching her and that was a situation fraught with peril.

'When Grace was thirteen, she won two second prizes at Perth Music Festival. I have the photograph in my wallet.'

Beth was taken aback: surely, only relatives kept photos in their wallets. She sighed with exasperation: was she doomed to spend the whole night crouched behind this damned door conversing with a complete stranger; or could he be genuine? Her decision was not weighed in the balance, but that was nothing new.

'Look, I'm going in now. Goodnight, whoever you are.' She turned to walk back towards the sitting room and had taken several steps when he called out again:

'I won't give up, I'll be back.'

Beth halted in her tracks; frowned at the implication. Although his words had not been uttered in sinister tones, her imagination broke free of the constraints of common sense and ran amok: she might never feel safe in this place if she refused to confront it head-on, now, tonight, before he stalked her and made her too scared to leave the flat; and what about her mother and her safety? No, she would have to get rid of him, albeit gradually.

She retraced her steps to the door.

'Come back tomorrow morning then,' she said rashly, biting her lower lip and foreseeing the torrid newspaper headlines on her demise. 'I'll meet you down on the South Inch at ten,' she concluded without thinking it through.

'That would be great!' the man exclaimed so loudly, that she jumped back. 'Thank you, I'm really grateful! South Inch, ten o'clock, I'll be there.' There was a short pause. 'But, how will you know me?' he asked now.

43

'You say you know me, isn't that enough?'

'Ten o'clock,' the man repeated with such delight that Beth began to worry again. 'I'll see you tomorrow then. Goodbye, and thank you!'

She listened to his footsteps receding down the staircase, along the tiled hallway and then the street door swung shut with a thud. Too late, the idea came to her that she could have rushed to the window to try and get a look at the man but, in retrospect, she had had enough excitement for one night. When she finally switched on the T.V. she was trembling. For the first time in her life, she went to the drinks cabinet and poured herself a whisky.

*

Despite James's disapproving glances, Grace sat up in bed reading until after midnight. Not only was she wide awake, she was also mulling over Lily Morris' sudden suggestion that the three of them – she, Grace and Beth – should travel up to Inverness to visit an old friend of hers. It was so contrary to Lily's nature, coming up with such an idea on the spur of the moment, that Grace had stared at her in disbelief.

'What's brought this on?'

'I haven't had a holiday in years, and you're the only person I could think of to take me.'

'But I've only just come back from Holland.'

'Weeks ago that was,' Lily had said, and her fingers had shaken as she held the teacup. 'You could do with another break, surely?'

'I don't know,' Grace said, adding tactfully, 'I'll think about it, see what Beth says.'

'I'm going somewhere anyway,' Lily had announced, and her whole demeanour rang so false that Grace had wondered if the old dear was having some sort of breakdown.

'Where would you go, if not to Inverness?'

'Anywhere, it doesn't matter, as long as it's a change.'

'If you're really serious,' Grace said, mostly to humour her companion. 'I suppose we could arrange something.'

Lily's eyes lit up. 'Oh, I'd like that, pet, I really would. I've not been well lately and it would do me the world of good.'

Grace was engulfed by shame; leading the old lady on with no real intention of carrying it through.

'Let me think about it,' she had said on her way out.

'Oh it has to be soon,' Lily had said with a degree of desperation and Grace had paused on the threshold.

'Lily, what's the matter?'

'I need a holiday,' Lily reiterated, but avoiding Grace's gaze. 'I haven't been well and I just need a change of scenery.'

'We'll get something organised,' had been Grace's parting shot, although she held out little hope.

Eventually, James having fallen asleep an hour previously, Grace turned out the lamp and settled down; but, for some reason, her conversation with Lily had unnerved her and she knew that sleep would not be possible unless she could come up with some rational explanation for her old friend's behaviour.

*

In his room at the George – hurriedly re-booked a couple of hours before – Thomas

Blake lay on the bed and contemplated his joy at the unexpected turn of events. Had his driver, Jack the Lad, neither noticed the girl, nor drawn Thomas's attention to her, then they would have continued on to Edinburgh and Thomas would be looking up flights for London this very minute, bound for who-knew-where.

He shook his head at the complete randomness of the discovery. Even if he *had* glanced at the girl, even if he *had* admired her mini-skirted legs – which, thankfully, considering he was her grandfather, he had had no time to do – it was a view of her back, nothing to distinguish her from any other young girl in the city.

What quirk of fate had made her turn round to glance at the car, to meet his gaze for that split second? Whatever it was he might never know, but, hopefully, after tomorrow it would be irrelevant, for he had made contact and that was all that mattered. He lay awake until well after midnight, his mind agile, his heart pounding out of control.

He was going to see Charlotte again.

Chapter Five

Harry yawned and peered at the clock: seven thirty; time he was up.

He switched on the radio before going into the bathroom to wash and shave and was regaled with a report of some drunken lad throwing himself off the Bridge of Don.

As he passed through the living room he reached for the 'Off' button, deciding that the looming interview with David Routledge would be quite sufficient drama for one day. It was ridiculous to be anxious for he was confident of achieving his degree and a permanent position in Perth; but the best laid plans of mice and all that; he was taking no chances. He would sacrifice arrogance for humility; just this once.

He chose his best suit – a dark blue pin stripe – a crisp white shirt laundered lovingly for him by old Elma at the Union Street laundromat, and a conservative tie that reflected both discretion and sense of purpose. Once dressed, he surveyed himself in the hall mirror and decided he would want to employ this chap himself.

David Routledge had become more of a staunch friend than a tutor in the years Harry had been a student, even inviting him for a drink in his office after hours when neither had anywhere else to go, but today, Harry knew, was not an informal chit-chat about sports cars and yachts and he would play the role of professional legal eagle as best he could.

Idly, he wondered what Beth was doing this early; decided that she was still in bed. As soon as he had secured his Degree, he would set about finding his wife a job. Already, having languished at home for a year, she had lost some of her glimmer and, though he might have to tread warily for fear of igniting the temper, he had a fairly good idea of how to go about it.

With a final check of his reflection and a fleeting regret that his father was not here to see him, Harry picked up the car keys and left the flat.

*

For the best part of a week, David had been wondering how he could change tack from friend to tutor. The boy had become an enjoyable part of his week, delighting the older man with humorous tales and countless witty anecdotes, not to mention his skill at chess, a game that few people played nowadays.

In retrospect, he sorely regretted now suggesting the Perth practice to the boy at the end of his first year, because now he was tempted to persuade young Gillespie to remain in Aberdeen, to take up the junior partnership of Routledge and Barclay and allow David to retire happily; the rudder in safe hands, so to speak.

Looking down at the car park, he spotted Harry's red sports model driving through the gates, too fast as usual, and into his normal space – David's space. He had not been surprised at the alacrity with which the boy had accepted the vacant parking place, for it only served to underline David's opinion that young Harry Gillespie would soon make a name for himself in legal circles. There was nothing of the shrinking violet about this boy.

In the few minutes before the interview was due to start, David Routledge flicked through the papers in front of him, thrilled to be the bearer of good news but saddened by the inevitability of its being the last time he could relish the prospect of the boy's company.

*

Beth sat in the kitchen making no attempt to eat breakfast. The cornflake packet stood uninvitingly on the table, bowl and spoon to keep it company, but she had no appetite whatsoever. In fact, she had been up during the night with a pain in her stomach, a pain she knew was related to this morning's imminent tryst.

Despite her occasionally outrageous traits, Beth Gillespie was no Mata Hari; nor had she any desire for rocking the boat, and that was what she would be doing if she met this weirdo on the Inch. Why had it all sounded so reasonable the night before?

Man comes to door, knows mother, seems nice enough, only wants to meet and chat, so why not?

'Because I don't want to, that's why not,' Beth scowled at the Kellogg's cockerel. 'He's probably a bloody psycho, bolt through the neck, huge hands, black-ringed eyes.'

She rose and wandered to the window, her legs hardly strong enough to carry her. It was stress that made you so lethargic, or so she had read in a popular glossy magazine; and they should know since there were more psychos contained in its pages than you would expect to find in an institution.

For the hundredth time since she entered the kitchen, she glanced at the clock: half past nine. How she wished for a crystal ball that could see into her future! At half past nine tonight, would she be laughing merrily about this moment, wondering what all the fuss was about; or, more likely, would she be in the Intensive Care Unit of PRI, detectives at her bedside, eager to jot down notes on her lucky escape from the new serial killer in Perth?

Beth shook herself and jogged on the spot for a few minutes, trying to bring some energy back into her fatigued body. Elspeth, her pal at Aberdeen, had sworn by this jogging lark, although it seemed to Beth to be a complete waste of time. Out of breath, she stood and weighed up her options. The trouble was, she had none.

*

Thomas sat on the bench closest to her apartment, feet restless, hands fidgeting. He resisted the temptation to keep looking round, for he had no doubt that she would find him easily enough: apart from the dustman picking up litter on the grass and the elderly man out walking his dog, Thomas was the only male on the Inch.

So anxious had he become in the past half hour that he repeatedly had to ask himself if it was the North or South Inch she had mentioned, perhaps choosing the one furthest from her flat not the nearest; and was he now sitting like an idiot at the wrong end of the city? Had she said nine o'clock or ten?

He had hardly slept a wink the previous night, as his mind had refused to shut down, darting back to the past, then catapulting forward to the present with as much control as a kite in a force 10. Eventually, he had dropped off some time after three, only to awaken at seven, feeling – and looking – like a man who had slept in his car for a week.

Nothing disgusted him more than not looking his best; especially for the girl. He had spent his life impressing the opposite sex with his numerous God-given attributes and he knew his script off by heart; but his granddaughter! That was an entirely different story: to convince her of his sincerity could be his only route to Charlotte and if he mucked it up, he would want to throw himself off the bridge that was visible from his seat.

The elderly man with the dog wandered past, nodding in a friendly manner, but it was not what Thomas had in mind, a casual chat with a lonely old man, not when he was waiting for someone important. In an attempt to get rid of the man, Thomas barely glanced at him and, inexplicably, was beset by a wave of guilt when the fellow, still smiling, wished him 'good morning'. Thomas felt so mean-spirited that he murmured a greeting.

*

As she made her way across the road, Beth could see him sitting alone on the bench nearest the flat, in conversation with the old guy who walked his dog every morning at ten. She slackened her pace, waiting until the old man had moved on, and then she took a deep breath. Nothing ventured, nothing gained, she was reciting as she covered the final few yards. In for a penny, in for a pound and all that drivel.

'You must be the psycho,' she said unkindly to the back of his head, having rehearsed it for the past ten minutes; and, caught unawares, the man leaped to his feet.

'I'm sorry if I gave you cause to think that,' he said with an injured expression that almost made her regret her remark. 'I didn't mean to frighten you.'

Beth was speechless: as he turned to look at her, she could have sworn she recognised him. But it was impossible: she had never met the man in her life. She was not thinking straight. Suddenly, she knew what made him familiar: the deep green eyes and blonde hair had passed down through the generations.

'You didn't actually frighten me,' she admitted now, in light of the family resemblance. 'But it's a bit unnerving having some strange man knocking at the door late at night.'

'I know, and I do apologise,' he said in that undecipherable accent she was having trouble with. 'Perhaps we can start again?'

'I'm not keen,' Beth said, sticking to her plan, and his face fell. 'In fact, even if you do know my mother and my grandmother, to be honest, I couldn't care less.'

She had rehearsed both sentences, and ones yet to come, until she was word perfect, and she had the satisfaction of witnessing the stranger's discomfort.

'Oh dear,' he smiled sadly. 'I'm so sorry to hear that. I've come such a long way to see them both.'

'Do you think they'll want to see you?' Beth asked; hedging her bets, for she could be wrong about the green eyes and blonde hair. The effect upon him was severe.

'I...I'm not sure,' he said despairingly.

'You're not sure?' Beth repeated suspiciously. 'Why wouldn't they?'

'It's been such a long time,' he told her, rather lamely she thought, and in that instant she knew she had the upper hand. 'People change. I've changed,' he added, and he seemed surprised by the admission.

'I can't speak for my mother and ...' Beth hesitated. 'My grandmother. You realise it would be up to them.' She had no idea why she kept implying her grandmother was still alive: she just knew it was the right thing to do.

'I understand, of course it would be up to them.'

'Who are you anyway?'

Despite the flimsy evidence regarding eye and hair colouring, she had to find out for certain. The question appeared to make the man uneasy, and it flashed through Beth's mind that he knew perfectly well her mother would not want to see him.

'Who are you?' she asked again and he averted his gaze from her face.

'I don't want to...It might be a bit of a shock for you.'

Beth frowned. 'A shock? What, you mean you're the black sheep of the family or something?' Her suspicions about his being her grandfather were being slowly confirmed; but she would not make it easy for him. It would have to come from his own lips.

'Perhaps we could go somewhere more...?'

'Here will do,' Beth heard herself say abruptly. 'Say what you have to and be done with it.'

The man dropped his gaze to the ground, as if this were proving more arduous than he had imagined. Had he thought her an easy pushover then, whatever his intention?

'I was married,' he said slowly and the effort caused perspiration to seep into his brow. 'Married to your grandmother, Charlotte Shepherd.'

Her fears confirmed, Beth nodded and shrugged; thumping heart and reckless thoughts fighting with outward calm.

'You're Thomas Blake,' she said as dispassionately as she could, at which he remained silent, his eyes on her face.

'Yes.'

Beth shook her head, for there had been no necessity to rehearse what she was about to say. It fell effortlessly from her lips and filled the space between them.

'There's not a snowball's chance in Hell that they'll ever want to see you.'

His face crumpled, like a little boy's, and she knew that with one sentence she had wreaked havoc in this man's life. Without another word or glance in his direction, Beth turned on her heel and quickly walked away. Thomas Blake made no attempt to stop her.

*

Grace trudged up the path and laid down the laundry basket. Lifting the forked pole and raising the clothesline, she bent to pick up the first pegs. The wind was from the West, a common occurrence, and the sheets and towels would be dry before early afternoon, when she could peg out a second washing. She would burden herself with a huge pile of ironing as a consequence, but she was accustomed to that.

She sighed and lifted the first towel, her mind continuing to seek out the reason for Lily's sudden desire for a holiday. The old lady had not been further afield than Blairgowrie for the past ten years. Even that outing had taken a considerable amount of persuasion on Grace's part, culminating in half an hour's shopping with a reluctant Lily in tow and Grace condemning her plans as futile.

The postman's van drew up at the front gate and she listened for his steps on the path, expecting any day now to receive the latest, welcome letter from Alice, the next instalment of her affair with Brad, a man whose habits and personality were so familiar to Grace that she would recognise the man if he appeared at her door.

She smiled to herself at the unlikelihood of such an event, although she had been encouraged by Alice's last letter, in which she expressed a desire to visit Scotland again.

'*Oh, Grace,*' she had written; and Grace could visualise her friend as she wrote, the long dark hair plaited and twisted at the nape of her neck, the immaculate make-up, the long painted fingernails.

'I'm so desperate to come home again, and I know you'll think me daft, because this is supposed to be my home, but you know what I mean!

I think I may have persuaded hubby Martin to let me go on the rampage again, as I have been a very dutiful wife for a very long time, if you get my meaning!'

As the wind caught the double sheet and almost whipped it from her fingers, Grace could only hope and pray that she would see Alice soon.

1953!

She could hardly believe that over fifteen years had passed since the two of them had shed tears on a station platform; fifteen years of monthly letters to-ing and fro-ing across the Atlantic with so many confidences and intimate disclosures that, had James ever intercepted one, he would have been utterly outraged.

Grace was reminded of her own letters to James and how easy it had been to divulge her innermost thoughts to him on paper; and yet, when they were married, when she might have expected their love-making to unlock her most profound feelings, she had always been dismayed by the constraint between them.

'Mrs M,' called the postman from the corner of the house. 'Letter for you, from your pal in New Jersey!'

Grace dropped the bath towel she had been about to pin on the line and went to meet him.

'Just the thing I've been waiting for,' she told him. 'A letter from Alice always cheers me up.'

'You needing cheered up?' Bob asked with a frown. 'That's not like you.'

'Wash day,' Grace smiled, a feasible excuse. 'I hate it.'

'Sadie's the same,' Bob grinned. 'I often think men take the easy way out, but if you repeat that to anyone, I'll deny it.'

'How is everyone?' Grace asked, taking the proffered letter and secreting it in her apron pocket. 'Are the children all at school now?'

'Thank the Lord for that,' Bob said, pretending to mop his brow. 'When the last one walked up the school steps we breathed a sigh of relief. My goodness, but the house is quiet!'

'If you think that's quiet,' Grace said, surprising herself. 'Wait until they're up and married.'

'You still miss her then?'

'Yes, I do, but she's only as far away as Perth, so it could be worse.'

'Yes,' Bob winked as he headed down the path. 'But you'll be wishing it was further away once the grandkids come along. Baby-sitting every night, eh?'

'I won't mind,' Grace said, recalling, with a sharp stab, that her mother never had the opportunity.

'Well, must rush, don't work too hard now. See you tomorrow!'

Rather than go back to the washing, Grace sat down on the wrought-iron bench and opened Alice's letter, cheered up immediately by the familiar handwriting.

*

An hour later, despite the darkening sky and cool wind, Thomas Blake was still sitting on the bench where she had left him. From her window, Beth could see him now, his desolate figure shrinking a little more each time she looked out.

The few minutes after she had let herself back into the flat had been the most traumatic she had ever endured. She contemplated the various reactions of her mother, but always came back to the same one: there was absolutely no chance of Grace Melville seeking a reconciliation with a father who had abandoned her twice; before she was born and then in the middle of a Dundee street when she was old enough to understand. That was the story Beth had wheedled out of Helen the month before.

'You mean, he just left her there?' Beth had asked, not comprehending the circumstances.

'No, I mean she was with Charlotte and me, so he knew damn fine who she was. As like him as anything. He fairly ran up that street, he was so desperate to get away from them both. Quite disgusting it was.'

'And did Mum see him?'

'No,' Helen had said, but her cheeks had gone pink. 'At least she was spared that. Anyway, you can ask her yourself, if you're brave enough. And there's more,' Helen had finished hotly. 'But I've told you quite enough already.'

50

Since the disturbing revelation, Beth had made an extra effort to be considerate to her mother, often casting surreptitious glances at her to figure out if she were truly happy or not. The trouble with Grace Melville, of course, was that her acting skills were second to none. Beth was still a raw beginner when it came to playing a part; but she was learning; as today's meeting with her grandfather had confirmed.

Her grandfather!

She gasped at the very idea. How could she ever lay claim to such a selfish and cruel man, someone who would run away from his own daughter, a creep of the first order? As she paced the floor in the hall, the phone rang and she rushed to the window to see if he still sat there or if it was him at the other end of the line.

It was Harry, and she suffered from a huge bout of guilt for forgetting that his final interview had taken place an hour ago.

'Sweetheart, I passed,' he said casually, no obvious trace of pleasure in his voice. 'So that's settled. Have you missed me?'

'What do you think?'

'There's something being delivered to the flat this afternoon,' Harry told her, and this time she was sure she heard a greater degree of enthusiasm. 'Make sure you're at home between two and five, otherwise you'll be sorry.'

'What is it anyway? Is it a new table for the dining room?'

'Something like that,' he said, and she gave up.

'Don't worry, I'll be here all afternoon. But, aren't you going to tell me what Mr Routledge said?'

'The usual. Nothing exciting. Oh, but the good news is I'll be home Thursday, don't have to come back here now. You'll have me all to yourself.'

Beth could not decide whether to laugh or cry: she was desperate for the two of them to settle down into a real marriage, not just a week-end relationship; yet, on the other hand, Thomas Blake had just turned up and, whether she liked it or not, she would have to protect her mother from the heartache this man continued to drag in his wake.

'I can hardly wait to see you, Harry, you know that, and the first thing we'll do is go to –'

'Don't be too sure,' he laughed and she was annoyed at the implication.

'What do you mean, 'don't be too sure'?'

'Enough said. See you Thursday, and don't go out this afternoon.'

He hung up before she could think of a suitable retort.

This time when she wandered to the window and looked down at the South Inch, Thomas Blake had gone.

*

Grace heard the telephone ring and rushed through the living room. James could let it ring, but Grace had to know immediately who it was. To miss a call from Beth would be a disaster.

'Hi, Mum!' the voice said, and Grace was happy she had made the effort.

'Darling, it's lovely to hear from you, is everything all right?'

'It's better than all right,' Beth laughed and her mother suddenly recalled Harry's final interview.

'You mean he passed?'

'What? Oh, yeah, he did, but that's not why I'm phoning.'

'For Heaven's sake tell me, what is it?'

'You'll never guess what he bought me, what's just been delivered to the flat?'

'A new dining room table? You said you needed one.'

51

'A piano!' Beth shrieked. 'Can you believe it? He bought me a brand new piano!'

Grace was so delighted that she suppressed the fact that her own piano would now be obsolete; that Beth would have fewer reasons to visit.

'Oh, Beth, that's wonderful. You'll be able to play whenever you like now.'

Only then did it strike Grace that the old piano in the parlour might sit idle for weeks on end; unless she herself resumed playing.

'Don't worry, Mum, I'll still want to come and play yours and I'll visit you all the time.'

'Beth, you're a sweetie.'

'So when can you come in to see it?'

'When do you want me to come?'

'This is Tuesday. How about Thursday, give me enough time to practise?'

'I can hardly wait. What make is it?'

'A Knight, one of the best modern things, and the sound is heavenly! See you Thursday.'

Grace hung up, marvelling at the ease with which young people could throw money around these days. The new flat had cost six thousand pounds, give or take a hundred or so; then the furniture had added up to another thousand, and now they had bought a piano that had probably cost the earth!

How different from Grace's youth, with its hand-me-downs from relatives and its homemade summer sandals, not to mention the walks to the picture house because taxicabs were a luxury.

Happy to receive two pieces of good news in one day, however, Grace sighed and retraced her steps to the garden, looking forward to reading more of Alice's Adventures in America.

**

Thomas Blake had been walking around the city for hours, neither stopping for something to eat, nor even caring where he was. When, eventually, he glanced at one of the street signs, his heart lurched, for it had been in this very street, on this very pavement, that he had stood, distressed, almost fifty years ago, trying to prevent her marching off, out of his life forever; trying to sort it out.

*

His mind was racing: he had said the wrong thing, done the wrong thing, and what happened in the next few moments would determine their future.

'Right,' he said, more firmly than he intended. 'We're going to sort this out right now.'

Charlotte appeared surprised but said nothing, simply stood silently, looking up at him.

'When I said we should go somewhere more private, it wasn't because I was ashamed to be seen with you. It was because I wanted to...' He hesitated, gulped for air. 'I wanted to ask you something.' He paused again and watched her face, but she was staring at her shoes, contributing nothing. 'Is it you who doesn't want to be seen with me?'

She seemed horrified at this idea, raising her blue eyes to his and frowning.

'Of course I don't mind being seen with you, I thought it was the other way round, that you didn't want to be seen with me.'

'You ninny,' Thomas said, squeezing her arm affectionately. 'You look like a film

star. Why wouldn't I want to be seen with you?'

'That's all right then,' she said, blushing, half turning away. 'I'm sorry I got the wrong idea.'

'Where do you get such lovely clothes anyway?' he asked as they made their way back to the restaurant.

'London,' came the astonishing reply.

'Goodness me,' he said, drawing her arm through his, and musing that his mother could only afford five-shilling frocks from Marks and Spencers.

'They'll think we're mad,' Charlotte smiled. 'Going back into the restaurant just minutes after marching out.'

'Let them think what they like,' he had grinned, the happiest young man on earth at that particular moment.

*

A bus hooted to warn him that he was about to step into its path and Thomas jumped back with a gasp. He looked around for the nearest taxi rank and checked the money in his pocket; he would go back to the George for another week and if he had not succeeded in winning her over by then, he would leave this damned place, never to return.

Chapter Six

Beth finished the Chopin Mazurka with a flourish and turned to her mother.

'Well? Are you impressed?'

'Oh Beth, that's the best I've ever heard you play, it was uplifting.'

'You would say that,' Beth grimaced, easing herself from the piano stool and crossing the room. 'You'd have been absolutely hopeless as a music teacher. You would, always tell them they were great even when they were bloody useless.'

'Probably,' Grace agreed with a smile. 'It's a wonder I won any prizes myself.'

As she came to the end of the sentence, she must have noticed the sudden rush of colour to Beth's cheeks.

'Are you all right, Beth?'

'Er... yes, I'm fine, just thinking. Fancy a cuppa now?'

'Yes, but why don't I make it for a change?'

'That's a nice way of saying my tea's like dish-water?'

'Would I say that?'

'No, but everyone else does.'

Beth followed her mother into the kitchen and sat watching her prepare the tea tray, wondering if it would ever be possible for her to broach the subject of Thomas Blake without seeming to make a point of it; simply drop his name into the conversation. It was impossible!

*

Grace glanced several times at her daughter, trying to work out if there was something she wanted to talk about, for she certainly appeared on edge.

'Beth...'

'Mum...'

They both laughed and waited, but it was Grace who spoke first.

'Is there something worrying you, darling? You seem a bit... well... not your usual self.'

Beth bit her lower lip, a sign to her mother that there was something wrong.

'I'm not sure, Mum, honestly. I have to think it over for a while.'

'It's not...' Grace hesitated. 'It's not something to do with your health, is it?'

'God, no!' Beth said irreverently, and Grace thought immediately of how Sandy Shepherd might have viewed such a blasphemous exclamation.

'That's a relief, I'd be worried sick about you if you were ill.'

'Well I'm not.' Beth hesitated and grimaced. 'The thing is, Mum...'

'What, for Heaven's sake?'

'There is something keeping me awake at night, and you could probably help.'

'Darling, of course I'd want to help. What is it?'

'It's my grandfather,' Beth said bluntly.

Grace caught her breath, torn between helping her daughter and opening old wounds. Sometimes there was a limit; even for her.

'Mum, did you hear me?'

'I heard you.'

'I've been lying awake worrying about you.'

Grace frowned and poured out two cups of tea before responding.

'Why would you worry about me?'

'I may as well tell you,' Beth blurted out, avoiding her mother's gaze. 'Helen told

54

me about that day in Dundee, the day your father ran away, the day he had another woman with him and you said you'd never forgive him.'

She came to a halt, perhaps deterred by the look in Grace's eyes. 'I just had to ask her, I'm sorry.'

Slowly, Grace raised the cup to her lips and drank. She had the power to erase the anguished expression on her daughter's face and, under normal circumstances, she would have done so; but this was Thomas Blake, and there were some things best left alone.

'It was a long time ago, Beth, and I don't want to talk about it.'

'Even if it hurts me to think about it?'

Grace fought back the temptation to air her own sense of hurt. After all, it was hardly Beth's fault.

'I'm sorry darling, but it would hurt me more to talk about it. I'm sorry, I just can't.'

Beth's shoulders sagged. 'I suppose I can't force you.'

'Why did you ask Helen about him?'

'You never speak about him and I was curious.' She gave her mother an apologetic glance before adding: 'And I've seen the photos of him and Charlotte.'

'Where did you see them?' Grace asked, envisaging her daughter snooping around the bedroom.

'You'd left them in Gran's old room, at the back of a drawer.'

'But you moved into that room when you were ten, Beth,' Grace reminded the girl. 'You must have found them years ago. Why did you never give them to me?'

'It was the only evidence I had of my grandparents.'

With something of a shock, Grace was starkly reminded that she had been so wrapped up in her own resentment that she had over-looked the possibility of Beth's interest in her family history.

'There are lots of photographs of my mother,' she said lamely.

'But none of *him*,' Beth said accusingly, as if it were her mother's fault. 'These few are the only ones of him.'

'Why should you be interested in the man now?'

'Because I am,' Beth replied stubbornly.

'And you asked Helen?'

'Yes.'

'She's hardly the one to tell you the truth.'

'Well, how am I supposed to know the bloody truth if everyone avoids telling me?' Beth expostulated, slamming the teaspoon down on her saucer and making her mother jump.

'Beth, please!'

'You've got to tell me the truth,' demanded Beth angrily.

Grace recalled vividly how she herself had been duped by her entire family. Could she do the same to her own daughter?

'Let me think about it,' she conceded and was rewarded by an immediate softening of her daughter's attitude.

'That's all I ask, that you think about it. Even if he was the most horrible man on the planet, he was still my grandfather and I have the right to know.'

Grace regarded the girl closely, wondering how she could possibly benefit from the truth; convinced it would only cause the two of them further grief.

'We could go and see Lily Morris,' she heard herself say. 'Maybe the three of us could even take a short break somewhere, up to Inverness perhaps; discuss things far away from here.'

'I'd like that,' Beth said happily, and her mother marvelled at the speed of the girl's mood swings. 'Lily's great fun.'

'And she knows everything there is to know about the past,' Grace said, perhaps unwisely; although Lily would never divulge anything important.

'Does she? Even about …?'

'Yes, even about him.'

'Well then,' Beth said, sitting on the arm of her mother's chair and putting an arm round her. 'Let's do it, go up to Inverness for a few days, have a change of scenery, talk about things.'

'I'm not promising anything,' Grace warned her daughter. 'I can't promise.'

'It's enough that you're thinking about it,' Beth told her happily. 'Do your best.'

As she drove home later, Grace's spirits were sinking by the minute. What had possessed her to make such a rash suggestion? There was nothing more repugnant to her than giving Thomas Blake the opportunity to ruin her life a second time; but now she was faced with her daughter's obsession with the truth of the matter. Did the girl have a right to know? If she, Grace, had known the truth at the beginning…

Something I can't tell you.

The traffic lights at the Queens Bridge turned to green and she prodded the gear stick into first, her fingers trembling. How ironic that, in the space of a few hours, her joyful mood could have been superseded by such misery.

Just when she was congratulating herself on having had several pleasant surprises in one week, here she was plunged into despondency again, fearful of the next day. She knew it was an uncharitable thought, but why was it that people found it so easy to trample over her feelings in order to satisfy their own?

*

Harry frowned as the phone started to ring. In the tiny garden of his studio flat in Roslyn Place, he had just thrown himself into the white plastic chair and picked up the book he had been ploughing through – a legal tome detailing the numerous differences between Scottish and English law; and he was tempted to let the damned phone ring.

With a sigh, thinking that it might be Beth, he stood up and stepped into the room.

'Harry, it's Grace.'

His spirits rose when he heard her voice; and then he imagined the worst.

'Is anything wrong?'

'Nothing at all. Everything's fine down here. Look, Harry, I'm sorry for springing this on you, but I wonder if we could meet?'

'Well, of course, but there is something wrong, isn't there?'

'It's not what you think, I mean nothing to do with any of us.' She paused and he heard her sigh. 'It's complicated, Harry, too complicated to talk about over the telephone. Beth said you were coming home tomorrow?'

'Yes, it should have been today, but David wanted to treat me to a celebratory dinner this evening. I'll be on my way first thing tomorrow. Do you want me to call in and see you on my way home?'

'Oh, could you?' she asked, and the gratitude in her voice made him feel good.

'I could and I will,' he told her, quickly re-scheduling his itinerary for the following day. 'How about half past eleven?'

'I'd rather James didn't come in for lunch and interrupt us,' she said bluntly, and a minuscule blip of hope flashed into his mind at the idea of her keeping a secret from the man. 'Could you make it half past ten?'

'Half past ten it is, and don't worry,' he said recklessly. 'Whatever it is, we can sort it out together.'

'I'm relying on you,' she said unexpectedly, causing him to doubt his own abilities.

'Oh, and I'd rather you didn't tell Beth,' she added tentatively. 'At least, not yet.'

'That's fine,' Harry said truthfully, grateful for a spark of excitement in his life. 'See you tomorrow, and don't worry.'

He stood in the room long after he had replaced the receiver, mulling over possible crises that might have arisen; but, apart from her wanting to leave her odious husband, Harry was hard-pressed to come up with one. It was odd, he was thinking now, that he had taken an instant dislike to Beth's father and nothing had happened in the intervening years to alter the fact. The man was a boar. Not for the first time did Harry consider Grace to have settled for second best.

Turning back into the garden a few minutes later, he found he was smiling: what were the chances of her divorcing the man and finding a whole new life out there?

He shook his head at the improbability of such an idea, but when he picked up the legal tome once more the first section he turned to was divorce Scottish-style and his hand trembled.

*

Thomas Blake stood at the corner of the girl's street and waited for her to reach the main entrance to the block. Rather than scare her by suddenly appearing, he called out as she fiddled with the key in the lock.

'Hello there!'

She turned and hardly seemed surprised to see him, which he took as a good sign: had she spoken to Charlotte and his daughter then, and had she managed to broker some sort of a deal?

'Oh, it's you,' she said sullenly, and the prospect of a brokered deal fell away.

'Look, I know how much of a pain in the arse I've been,' Thomas said briskly, not taking the trouble to maintain the veneer. 'But would you at least read this?' he asked her, holding out an envelope and grateful that his hand had stopped shaking.

'What is it?'

'An explanation. Something you should know.'

Despite the girl's reluctance to take the envelope, he saw the interest in her eyes and knew that she would find the offer irresistible. What she had learnt from Charlotte and his daughter he could only guess, but there was every chance it had been derogatory, Now, if she wanted, she could learn his side of things.

'Even if I read whatever it is, and even if it changes my mind, it won't make one iota of difference to....' The girl paused and then added: '...to them.'

'All I ask is that you read it,' Thomas said, although her summing up of his wife and daughter's reaction had detracted somewhat from her acceptance of the envelope. 'My phone numbers in there. If you want, we can meet.'

'We're meeting now, aren't we?' she asked impudently, and he had to restrain himself from a comment on her upbringing.

'True, but I meant to talk over what's in the letter.'

'I have to go now,' she told him, turning her back on him and inserting the key in the lock.

'Thanks for agreeing to read it,' Thomas said, and he could have kicked himself, for she had only agreed to take the envelope from him and he had deduced from the start that this girl was no pushover. Her retort echoed his opinion.

'I didn't say I'd read it,' she threw over her shoulder as she entered the lobby and closed the door on him. Thomas walked back to his hotel, perversely delighted that, not only had he assessed his granddaughter's character accurately, but also, he and Charlotte, between them, had produced a pretty sharp girl; and that was immensely satisfying. More

57

than anything, he admired a woman with spirit.

*

Lily Morris had walked down the village for the first time in years, pausing several times to get her breath back and to readjust the walking-stick in her hand. She had been pleasantly surprised at the number of toots and waves she received on her short journey, as she had not taken an active part in village life for some time now; other than the inevitable baking requests. Six days had elapsed since his telephone call, and with the dawning of each new day her sense of hope and optimism increased, so that today, Friday, she was beginning to think that he must have gone back to wherever it was he lived, and that Grace would be spared further agony.

She stopped to admire the flowerbeds in the front garden of the lodge leading to big house, and, suddenly, an image of previous incumbents flashed into her mind. Could it really be over thirty years since the Flower Festival, and since the War had broken out? Assailed by mild chest pains, Lily let her breath out slowly. Her heart condition was a consequence of her weight presumably; although the new doctor lacked the courage to say so; unlike old Malloy, who would tell you the truth in words that were never carefully chosen.

'You're fat,' he had once told Charlotte. 'And are you still smoking?'

'No, the fire brigade put me out,' she had responded sweetly, much to his disgust and the two friend's amusement.

She still missed Charlotte Blake, regretted that they had not experienced the luxury of growing old together, of reminiscing over people and times that only they had known. She could blether away to Grace and her generation but there was no substitute for friends of your own age who had stuck with you through thick and thin, who knew what you were thinking before you spoke and who you never had to tiptoe round for fear of upsetting.

As she reached the front door of Lilac cottage, Lily saw a red car slow down and draw into the kerb. She knew who it was, of course, as she had heard all about the flashy car from Beth. As the young man stepped from the car, Lily thought how handsome the boy was. 'Handsome is as handsome does' her mother had often quoted.

'Lily!' he called and gave her a friendly wave, waiting for her to reach the gate. 'You're looking fine.'

'Do you think so?'

'Yes I do, now tell me what you've been up to.'

'Well,' she said, declining his arm. 'I've been sleeping, eating, sleeping and eating. Such a busy life I lead, you've no idea.'

'Not unlike my own for the last few years,' he laughed and even his laugh was beguiling. 'But that's me fully qualified, a lawyer.' He slapped the side of his head. 'No, sorry,' he smiled, recalling where he was. '*A solicitor*. If ever you need one.'

'Aye, Grace was telling me,' Lily said as they walked up the path to the front door. 'A job in Perth too.'

Despite the faint whiff of resentment in her tone, Harry reminded himself that she was Grace's confidante.

'Oh, here's the lady herself,' he said breezily as Grace appeared to welcome them. 'Grace, you look great.'

'He said the same to me,' Lily told Grace wryly. 'I wouldn't put any store by it.'

'That's not a very nice thing to say,' Grace said unexpectedly, taking both her guests by surprise. 'I've never doubted Harry's sincerity,' she added, not looking at either. 'Come on in, I've everything ready.'

Harry noticed the pallor of her skin, despite the recent sunny spell, and the faint dark rings beneath her eyes that only highlighted her lack of colour. If there were anything in his power to help this woman he would move Heaven and Earth to use it. He frequently judged himself to be her only true ally.

They sat in the garden, under the branches of the ancient apple tree. Each time he sat here, Harry could see Grace in this very spot, laughing, chatting, with a boyfriend perhaps. She had never mentioned anyone apart from James Melville, but, with her looks and personality, Harry suspected she had broken numerous hearts.

'I hope you don't mind,' Grace was addressing him now, bringing his attention back. 'I asked Lily to come down, She knows all about him.'

It was obvious by Lily Morris' desperate glance that she been oblivious to the reason for her invitation that afternoon, and Harry was intrigued by the glance, for it signalled apprehension; yet how could Lily know what was coming?

'Now you mention it,' Lily said slowly, her gaze on Grace. 'You never gave a reason. You just asked me to come down. I thought it was to get me out of the house for a wee while.'

Grace appeared slightly embarrassed. 'That too. Help yourself to a piece of cake, Harry. Don't stand on ceremony.'

'So, who is this '*him*' that Lily knows about?' Harry asked as she handed him a plate.

Before she had time to reply, Lily, in an agitated manner, had begun to speak, her eyes darting around the garden, not settling on anything for longer than a heartbeat.

'If it's about Thomas Blake, I've nothing to say. I don't want to get involved.'

Astounded, Grace looked at her friend, then, apologetically, at Harry, who almost shook his head at the rapidity with which she assumed the burden of guilt for all and sundry.

'But you don't know what it's about,' Grace frowned. 'It's more to do with Beth actually.'

Lily's agitation lessened, but only slightly, and she turned her attention to Harry.

'Do you know what it's about?'

'No idea. I'm only here as a *friend.'*

The barb did not go unnoticed by either woman, but he was determined to remind the old biddy that their main concern should be Grace.

'Beth asked me about him yesterday,' Grace said quickly, hoping to avoid further aggravation. 'She got quite heated up when I said I didn't want to discuss him.'

'Why would she suddenly be interested now?' Harry wondered aloud.

'That's what was worrying me,' Grace shrugged. 'She's never shown the slightest interest in him before. Why now?'

Lily gasped and they both turned to look at her. Harry was convinced that the old woman knew something about it.

'Lily, what is it?' Grace asked, leaning forward to touch her friend's arm.

'I can't tell you,' Lily said sharply. 'I won't.'

By the expression on Grace's face, Harry could deduce that she had a fairly shrewd idea of what Lily was keeping to herself, for there was a look of such fear in her eyes that it could only have been evoked by something the two women shared; information relating to Thomas Blake.

'Lily, you have to tell me, no matter how bad it is.'

Grace's eyes were no longer filled with fear, Harry saw, but rather resignation. She was sitting quite still, poised even, preparing herself for what she thought she knew was coming. His heart went out to her, even before Lily spoke.

'I didn't want to tell you, Grace,' the elderly woman said tonelessly. 'But it seems as if he's...'

Harry watched Grace's face, saw the momentary closing of her eyes, the holding of her breath. It was as if she knew what Lily would say.

'You may as well say it, Lily. It won't change anything, but you may as well come out with it.'

With a brief glance towards Harry, Lily shook her head, shoulders slumping.

'He telephoned me last week. He's here, in Perth.'

*

The lambs' bleating kept her awake; such a soulful sound meandering through the dark night, matching her mood, confining her thoughts within the bleakness of its boundaries. Occasionally, the screech of an owl would stab the air, wrenching her mind back to the present, and she would lie for a moment, wondering where she was.

She had been perplexed at not shedding a tear, wondered if it signified that she was failing to appreciate how catastrophic the situation was; or was she stronger than she had imagined and could confront it with impunity?

When all was said and done, of course, she would never speak to him, never agree to even a single written word passing between them; and so the knowledge that he was here looking for her meant nothing at all; not to her. Her life would remain unaffected by the man and, sooner or later, he would tire of her constant refusal to make contact and go back to wherever it was he lived now; back to his family, the one he had chosen over her.

As the clock in the hall struck another half hour and the bleating from the hillside faded with the lightening sky, Grace was more optimistic: she had done it once and she would do it again; she would assume control of her own life, and any intentions her father might have with regard to a family he so readily discarded would be thwarted right at the beginning.

*

Harry's finger traced the outline of Beth's shoulder, smiling as she stirred in her sleep and reached for him. She was the most contrary of females, Beth Melville – for so he still thought of her – with her puritanical adherence to the habits and rituals of daily routine, and the wantonness of her lovemaking, displaying no shame at some of the demands she made on him.

Sometimes, he thought himself the luckiest man on the planet, and at times the most unfortunate, for with the acquisition of something so valuable came the inevitable anxiety over its possible loss. He sighed and touched the blonde hair resting on the pillow beside him.

'Harry,' she murmured, and her arm stretched out to find him.

'I love you, sweetheart,' he told her, believing her to be too drowsy to respond.

'This is my very favourite place,' Beth said distinctly, and her eyes flew open. 'You hardly ever tell me you love me,' she accused him, but gently.

'It's not a manly thing to say, is it?'

'I can't think of anyone more manly than you, Harry bloody Gillespie, so that's a fallacy. You're the very model of a chauvinist caveman.'

'I thought you were asleep, you minx.'

He heard her chuckle and then she rolled over and eased her body across his.

60

'You thought wrong then, didn't you?'

'Fancy another drink, Miss whatever your name is?'

Beth laughed and refused to allow him to leave the bed.

'I'm not going to tell you my name either,' she said archly, her fingers playing a silent Chopin waltz on his chest. 'Nor will I give you my phone number.'

'But I must see you again,' Harry told her, grasping her fingers and spoiling the Chopin piece. 'Give me a clue then, if you won't give me your name.'

'Well, I enjoy music, and sex, and music and sex.'

'Ah, in that case, you must be Beth Melville.'

'Right first time,' Beth smiled, endeavouring to free her fingers from his grip. 'And you are?'

'Can't remember.'

'Mmm. Maybe I can give you a clue.'

'Fire away.'

'You like Beth Melville and sex, and sex and Beth Mel –'

'I've remembered!' Harry laughed, sitting up and rolling out of bed. 'I must be Harry Gillespie.'

'Why do you still call me by my maiden name?'

'Because it's who you were when we met.'

Beth frowned and covered herself with the sheet. 'But that's the old me.'

'And the one I love. Red or white?'

'White sparkly, and don't use the small glass, use the plastic bucket.'

They lay, entwined, Harry thinking that this was the best part about sex, the aftermath, with its lazy, fulfilled contentment; far more intimate than the act itself. Beth sipped from the glass and looked up at him.

'Were you annoyed with me earlier, about Thomas Blake?'

'Not at all, why should I be?'

'Honestly?'

'Honestly, now drink up and be quiet.'

As she sipped the wine and showed no inclination to talk, Harry's mind drifted back to the restaurant, where they had sat only an hour ago, mulling over what Beth had told him. Thomas Blake, until recently a dim and distant figure in someone else's history, had now pushed himself to the forefront of the lives of two young people who should have been celebrating Harry's degree, but who, instead, were struggling to keep the conversation going.

'You're very quiet, my love,' Harry had ventured to say after the main course had been served. 'Is the piano what you'd expect?'

'Harry, it's magnificent,' Beth said truthfully. 'I played it all day yesterday.'

'If you're not too tired, you can play it for me when we get home.'

'Were you sorry to leave Aberdeen?' Beth had asked, an innocuous question, he might have though once, but there was no such word with Beth.

'No, the only thing I'll miss is David Routledge, a lovely old guy.'

'You won't miss any of your class mates, then?'

'Not in the slightest,' Harry frowned, and the first inkling as to her discontent had wheedled its way into his mind. 'You can't think I'd miss any of that lot, surely? I mean, you met them all, didn't you? Was there even one that you'd miss yourself?'

She laughed and shook her head, for his whole demeanour was honest.

'I suppose not.' She glanced across at him, fleetingly, and added: 'But that girl with the very short haircut and the even shorter skirt seemed to fancy you.'

His surprise had pacified her. No one, not even her mother, could play the part of innocence quite so competently; and yet, behind the façade she would ferret for

61

information like a dog nosing for scraps.

'Did she? I never looked at her twice,' Harry said truthfully. 'She was more like a man, such short hair and the moustache too.'

'She didn't!' Beth laughed. 'You're making it up.'

'No, it tickled whenever I snogged her.'

She shook her head and relaxed. So, whatever it had been that had kept him late was not little Miss Mister...

'You're wondering why I came home late, aren't you?' Harry asked, the best approach with Beth being the direct one. Although he had been only nine years old at the time, he had seen his father doing it and it always yielded results; mostly beneficial.

'Yes, I suppose I am,' she had replied. 'At least I know you weren't seeing the stick insect with the moustache.'

'It was your mother actually,' Harry said, catching her unawares.

'My mother? What, in Aberdeen?'

'No, dopey, at the cottage.'

'You mean you dropped in to see her on the way past?'

'I did.'

'So why didn't you say?'

'It's complicated. Let's just say it's a surprise.'

Beth's face lit up and Harry had suffered a momentary twinge of guilt. He hated deceiving her, but Grace took precedence every time.

'That's all right then,' she told him happily, believing it to be a surprise related to their anniversary the following month. 'I won't ask again.'

'Remember, if anyone says they saw me outside the house, don't worry.'

'You're so good to me, you know,' Beth said suddenly, biting her lower lip. 'I hate...'

'Hate what?'

She had looked at him with a gloomy expression. 'Hate deceiving you.'

His heart lurched at the thought of her being spirited away by some hunk who looked like Bob Dylan and owned a multi-million pound business.

'You're not trying to tell me you've —' He stopped, for it was too painful to voice, even when he knew it could not be true.

'What?' Beth had shrieked, attracting several disapproving glances from the more salubrious diners. 'You thought I meant that? You must be bonkers.'

'How else would you deceive someone?' he asked, whilst reserving the right to do just that to Beth.

'I know I should tell you.'

'Tell me then.'

'I want to.'

Harry caught his breath at the confusion in her eyes. She was always at her loveliest when she was vulnerable.

'Beth, sweetheart, how can you not tell me now?'

She had hesitated, moving the piece of fish around her plate with the elaborately carved fork.

'You must promise not to tell Mum.'

'I promise,' Harry lied, for he would not conceal something that could ever hurt Grace.

'It's her father, my grandfather.'

It was his turn to be surprised. 'Thomas Blake, you mean?'

'Yes, he... he turned up at the flat last week.'

'Tell me you didn't let him in,' Harry said quietly and it sent a shiver of fear through

Beth.

'No, of course I didn't.'

'How did you know who he was if you didn't let him in?'

'He was waiting for me on the...' She readjusted her sentence. *'...In the street outside.'*

'He just came up and spoke to you?'

'Yes, he just came up and spoke to me,' Beth repeated, the first sign of her temper fizzing to the surface. *'You sound as if it were my fault.'*

'I'm sorry, I didn't mean to. How did he know you?'

Beth shrugged, genuinely flummoxed. *'I have no idea. I've been trying to figure it out.'*

'He might have seen you in the street before, noticed your resemblance to Grace.'

'I suppose so. If he'd been in Perth for a few days, it's a possibility.'

'What did he say to you?'

'He handed me a letter, told me to read it.'

'And did you?' Harry asked pleasantly, but his amiable tone did not fool Beth.

'Yes, I did, but it was predictable, his side of the story.'

'Did you write back?'

'No!' Beth said firmly. *'I read it, then I stuffed it in the kitchen drawer and forgot all about him.'*

'Yet we're discussing him now.'

'Have you always been such a smarty-pants, Gillespie?'

'Oh yes, from way back.'

Beth smiled, despite herself. *'Me too.'*

'Can we sleep on this problem?' Harry had asked and had not been surprised by her reaction.

'Sleep is not what I had in mind. Not on your first night home.'

He raised his wine glass and chinked it against Beth's.

'Here's to not sleeping,' he smiled, and she blushed faintly.

'Yes, here's to that,' Beth had said, her features suffused with equal measures of primness and lasciviousness; and Harry's pulse rate ran crazy.

The clock in the hallway struck midnight and brought Harry back to the present. He glanced down at Beth: she had fallen asleep, the empty glass in her hand. As if attuned to the moment, she opened her eyes.

He removed the glass from her hand. 'I do love you,' he said.

'That's the second time you've told me tonight, so it must be true.'

'I'm the luckiest man on the planet.'

'That's quite a coincidence then, for I'm the luckiest female.'

'Come here,' Harry smiled. 'I haven't finished with you yet.'

'Don't I have a say in it?'

'No, you don't.'

'In that case, I'm never going to tell you my name, whoever you are.'

*

In his room at the George Hotel, Thomas Blake sat in the uncomfortable chair with a glass of whisky in his hand, the sixth since dinner; served in his room by the bimbo, Sarah, who, in another life, he might have thrown on the bed and ravished. Now, however, he was approaching seventy and hardly eligible for casual one-night stands. No, what he wanted now was Charlotte Shepherd, a mature and sophisticated woman who could give him the companionship he so desperately wanted; a woman to sit opposite him at the fireside and talk to him about her ordinary day; a woman who had known him fifty years ago, who still knew all there was to know about him and loved him for what he was.

He knew she would accept him again. She had done it once and there was no possibility that she would spurn him now, such an idea being totally alien to her amenable nature. He drank swiftly, draining the glass and reaching for the phone beside him. One more would be his limit for the night, and then he would have a good sleep and...

Thomas paused in his ramblings, trying to work out what he would do the next day. Had the girl even read the letter? Moreover, would she put in a good word for him with her grandmother?' Everything depended on Charlotte.

Chapter Seven

For the following few days Grace carried out her daily tasks automatically. It was easy to wander around the place like a zombie, for she spent most of the day alone, never seeing anyone except James and then only for half an hour at lunchtime.

Lately, he had forsaken the bus and taken the car to work and was able to take a longer lunch break, but the change in his routine resulted in a change to her own. Household tasks had to be reorganised; visits curtailed. Also – a notion that she tried to suppress – she wondered if he were checking up on her; but when she applied rationality to the idea, it seemed quite ridiculous. Besides, she was capable of playing the part of a dutiful wife for three quarters of an hour.

Beth, occupied as she was now with finding employment, telephoned every night, but now that Harry was at home permanently, Grace hardly expected her daughter to pop in every afternoon. It had been for this reason that she had never encouraged the girl to stay the night: once the habit had been formed, breaking it would have been a wrench, and Grace was doing her best to fashion a new life without her children.

Frank, almost eighteen and working in the local bank, was akin to a boarder, flying into the house at five o'clock for his meal and then dashing out again, either to football practice with his father, fishing with his pals or, more frequently nowadays, to woo his many girlfriends.

'Who was that you were talking to out there?' Grace had asked him the week before. 'She was a lovely girl, long black hair, very pretty.'

'Just a friend,' he had told her, too old now to blush. 'No one special.'

'But that's half a dozen you've had in the past month,' Grace had said, trying to sound interested rather than disapproving.

Frank had looked at her, a wry smile on his face. 'Yeah, I know.'

'And none of them special?'

'Nope, just friends.'

'Hasn't Mike got engaged recently?' Grace asked, referring to her son's best friend.

'Stupid git,' had been the gruff response, and he moved off before his mother had time to reprove him.

Now, as she packed his laundered shirts into his chest of drawers, she glanced around his bedroom, Beth's old room, and Charlotte Blake's before that. Her son's first posters – of The Rolling Stones and The Kinks – had been supplanted by girly shots, and Grace usually averted her eyes when she was in the room; today, however, she glanced, embarrassed, at several of the wide-eyed, provocative full-bosomed members of his gallery and wondered how on earth her son could have turned from the shy, timid boy into someone who enjoyed looking at such pictures.

Shrugging and thinking that, strictly speaking, it was none of her business, she went downstairs to prepare her husband's lunch. As she passed through the hall, the front doorbell rang and, for a moment, Grace stood motionless behind the door, reluctant to open it. The man could turn up at any minute of the day or night and the last thing she wanted to do was even to let him look at her.

'Who is it?' she called, not caring how foolish it sounded.

'It's me, Lucy Webster.'

'I'm sorry,' Grace said as she opened the door to her visitor. 'I've been trying to avoid the onion Johnny. I thought it was him.'

'Oh yes, he's been at me twice this week,' Lucy laughed. 'I've no idea why I buy the dashed things, There's enough in my own vegetable plot to sell to half of Perthshire.'

'Come in, there's only me here but if you have time to stay, James will be home in half an hour or so.'

'Such a gentleman,' Lucy said unexpectedly; to Grace's knowledge she had not even met James. 'But I won't come in, thanks. I only popped down to ask you if you'd like to come with me to Perth this afternoon, perhaps have a coffee in town?'

Ever conscious of the presence of Thomas Blake in the city, Grace politely declined on grounds of limited time. Lucy was not in the least offended.

'In that case, why don't you come to the Birches and we can sit in the garden if it stays nice?'

'That would be better,' Grace agreed, although she was at a loss as to why Lucy would ask her in the first place. They were acquaintances, it was true, but hardly friends; certainly not accustomed to visiting each other's houses.

As she watched Lucy walk down the path and turn into the street, Grace's mind was roaming through her wardrobe, trying to select something suitable for a guest invited to the big house.

*

Over lunch, James expressed his approval of social contact with Lucy Webster; in fact, when he appeared delighted, Grace was irritated.

'You're at home most of the time,' he said, and Grace was tempted to remind him it had been his idea. 'You need to get out and about, and she's the best kind of friend for you. Like Molly,' he added, cutting his sandwich into small pieces and arranging them neatly on the plate, akin, Grace always thought, to an inspection of his former gun crew.

'You hardly know her,' she reminded him, barely touching her own sandwich, her appetite adversely affected by the situation with her father. 'Neither do I really,' she mused. 'But she's not typical of the gentry at all, and I have a feeling we'll get on fine.'

Immune to the various accents of the locals, and unconcerned as to their class or the state of their finances, James was largely unaffected by their prejudices. Having forsaken his Oxford roots to join up in '41, he had lost contact with any surviving family, and was more than content with his lot. It was an attitude that Grace envied, her own upbringing having been inextricably entangled in the class system of the village. Even now, her opinions and actions were moulded around it.

James changed the subject. 'Has Beth been looking seriously for a job?'

'Oh, yes, every day.'

'Nothing yet?'

'No. Nothing yet.'

'She needs to work,' James frowned, draining the last of his tea. 'All that studying going to waste.'

'Something will turn up,' Grace said. 'You'll see.'

*

Lucy was in a flap: there was something wrong with the kettle and her guest was due any minute. Kathleen, excellent maid though she was, had no head for technical problems, her only solution being to run across to the manse and borrow one from the minister's wife.

'Do you think we could?' Lucy asked doubtfully.

'Oh yes, Madam, she's a very nice lady, she'd want to help.'

'Well, if you're sure...'

Kathleen rushed off, almost bumping into Grace on her way down the path.

'Sorry, Mrs Melville,' she said, already out of breath. 'Have to hurry, sorry again!'

When she learned of the reason for Kathleen's frenzied exit, Grace offered to go back for her own kettle, but Lucy would not hear of it.

'Just you sit down there,' she said, taking her visitor by the elbow and leading her into the sunroom. 'I think it's too chilly now to sit outside, don't you? Here, this is the most comfortable chair. Make yourself at home.'

No sooner had Grace sat down, but Lucy began urgently: 'I'll get straight to the point,' she said briskly. 'Someone told me that Beth's looking for a job. True or false?' she added humorously.

'True, but she only just started looking last week.'

'The thing is, my son, Charlie, would be grateful for the services of a language graduate. If Beth were interested....?' Lucy's voice tailed away, giving her companion time to digest the idea.

'Yes, she might be.'

'Charlie's in import-export, the antique trade, you know. Beth's languages would come in handy.'

'She prefers French,' Grace pointed out. 'I'll never know how she succeeded in passing her German, for she tells me she hates it.'

'Weren't you good at languages?'

'My mother wanted me to go to University, but, thankfully, War broke out.' Grace gasped at the insensitivity. 'I only meant...'

'I know exactly what you meant,' Lucy smiled. 'Sometimes parents are the least qualified to steer their children through life. So, do you think you could mention it to Beth? It's mostly French, with the odd German customer. But they tend to speak perfect English.' Lucy's mouth turned down in disapproval. 'The French, on the other hand, don't seem at all keen to speak anything other than their own language, and it makes it a bit of a problem for my son's patchy school-boy French.' She gave Grace an inquiring glance. 'Do you think she'd be at all interested?'

'I can't be sure,' Grace said truthfully. 'Sometimes I look at both my children and wonder who they are.'

Lucy Webster appeared to enjoy such frankness. 'Same with me,' she said sadly, and Grace's mind flashed to Charlie. 'Oh, Charlie's a fine boy,' she went on hastily. 'It's the other one.'

Grace had never heard of the 'other one' and perhaps the manner in which the words had been delivered helped to explain.

'The other one?'

'The black sheep,' Lucy grimaced, hands spread out in a gesture of despair. 'Matthew, almost thirty now, and Lord knows where he is.'

'You mean you don't keep in touch?'

'Matthew's choice,' Lucy said wistfully. 'Anyhow, enough of this whining. We can have coffee as soon as Kathleen comes back with the kettle. What a pity it's too cool to sit outside. I do love the flowers at this time of year.'

Grace smiled, her gaze drawn to the flowerbeds. 'The flowers are lovely. I was admiring them on the way up the drive.'

'I adore the old-fashioned roses, don't you? These modern things never seem to have the scents. All colour and perfect petals,' Lucy went on in disgust. 'And absolutely useless at raising one's spirits.'

Grace had known the woman for only a short time; not long enough to ask the reason for flagging spirits. She glanced from the window and made no reply.

'You must be missing your daughter,' Lucy said, taking a seat opposite. 'But at least she's in Perth, not London.'

'Yes, and if she takes the job with your son...'

'Do you think she will?'

'I hope so.'

'Me too,' Lucy said with an uninhibited display of joy that Grace envied. 'She'll be so good for Charlie.' Lucy's hand flew to her mouth. 'Oh, Grace, I didn't mean in that way, I...'

Grace laughed and waved away the explanation.

'I know what you mean and I agree, except I think Charlie will be good for Beth.'

'It's such a relief to have your company,' Lucy sighed, sinking back into the leather settee. 'So often I feel I have to tiptoe round people, minding my 'p's and 'q's. Ghastly! Sometimes I think I've been dropped from outer space.'

At that moment Kathleen arrived with the tray and the conversation was halted briefly. Whilst the girl was pouring and serving, Grace gazed from the window and fended off discordant thoughts of Thomas Blake, but she was dismayed by the possible consequences of the man's sudden presence in Perth.

'A penny for them?' she heard her hostess say quietly.

'I was just thinking of Beth's new job,' Grace lied.

The colour was rising in Lucy's cheeks. 'I don't mean to pry,' she began hesitantly. 'But I'd like to be honest with you, Grace. I may as well tell you. I bumped into Lily Morris the other day.'

'You did?'

'And I'm afraid she told me all about it.'

Grace's heartbeat picked up. 'All about what?'

'Lily took a bad turn just outside the back gate,' Lucy explained, brave enough to look Grace in the eye. 'So I brought her in here, just to give her time to recover.' She paused; gave Grace an anxious smile.

'And she told you about my father running out on us?'

'Yes, she did, but I accept full responsibility, I think I rather bullied it out of her, demanded to know the reason for her dizzy spell.'

Despite the circumstances, Grace had to smile at her companion's woeful expression. There was a naiveté in Lucy Webster that refuted condemnation, even for such a blatant invasion of privacy.

'What did Lily tell you?' Grace asked, fully prepared for a reply relating to the '20's.

'That he's here, in Perth, staying at the George Hotel.'

*

The city was thronging with tourists and, despite the fact that he should have remembered he was one of them, the crowds irritated him. Fifty years ago there had been ample space on pavements for everyone, enough distance between people so that you were happy to meet and greet.

Thomas weaved in and out, dodging mothers with twin buggies, small children on wobbling tricycles, and layabouts who looked as if they had never done a hand's turn in their lives, busking on every corner, even outside Marks and Spencers, would you believe?

He paused to look in a jeweller's window, his eye alighting upon an engagement ring not dissimilar to the one he had bought for Charlotte: a cluster of sapphires and diamonds set in a gold filigree band. His heart skipped a beat as he thought of her wearing it now, today, as he stood here, so close to her, yet as far away as the moon.

*

She preferred the cheaper one, of course, as he had anticipated, but he was hell-bent on buying the sapphire and diamond ring at eight pounds.

'What?' she had gasped as he pointed it out to her. 'I couldn't wear something like that to do the dishes, for Heaven's sake!'

'I thought you'd use a dish mop,' he joked, tweaking her hair.

'Very funny, but you know what I mean.'

'Quite frankly, Charlotte, whether you agree to marry me or not, that's the ring I'm buying for you and that's the ring you'll wear.'

'Oooh!' she had breathed, gazing into his eyes with an expression fairly akin to coquetry. 'Haven't we gone all masterful and demanding?'

As always, her blue eyes and their explicit message gave him goose pimples.

'So, let's go in,' Thomas said firmly. ' And you can try it on, just to see.'

'Eight pounds is more than seven times my weekly wage,' she complained as they entered the shop, but it was her last attempt to dissuade him and they both knew it.

'It's lovely, Madam,' the girl had enthused, but her expression implied to Thomas that he could have done better in his choice of sweetheart; which angered him into contemplating going elsewhere to buy the ring. By this time, however, Charlotte had worn the ring for a few minutes and now it was her *heart that was set on it.*

'And the wedding ring,' Thomas told the assistant, despite Charlotte's scowl of disapproval. 'Let me see a tray of wedding rings.'

In the end, he had paid twelve pounds for both rings, a sum he considered satisfactory, but Charlotte had kept voicing the cost of various basic necessities until he was forced to reprimand her. He was not despondent, though, for he took heart that she had not yet refused his offer of marriage; and, in his mind, the buying of the rings had sealed their union.

'Charlotte, dearest, is there the slightest possibility that you'll stop this harangue about the cost before we're old and grey?'

She giggled then, squeezing his arm affectionately and looking up into his face with an expression of such love that it rendered him quite breathless.

*

Thomas straightened up, having become aware that he was slouching in despair. He walked on quickly, away from the jeweller's window and so many painful memories. As he fought his way through a crowd of school children barging down the High Street, the thought occurred to him that, if he had not heard from his granddaughter by tomorrow, he might take a bus that went past Lilac Cottage and then, from his anonymous position in the rear seat, he could ascertain if she still lived there or not.

By the time he was running up the steps to his hotel, Thomas had regained some of his joie de vivre and was rehearsing his lines for the moment he came face to face with Charlotte Blake; and the first thing he would ask her was why she had stood by and watch him buy the two rings when, all the time, she had made up her mind never to marry him.

Chapter Eight

Charlie Webster picked up his wallet and pushed it into his inside pocket.

He never took the time to do things properly and so both wallet and pocket ended up the worse for wear, but he had always relied on his charming manner and upper crust accent to carry him through, so a little scruffiness hardly mattered.

His receptionist in the front office called him on the intercom, intimating that the girl with the language degree was waiting and could she send her through?

'Yes, go on,' Charlie told her, and he heard the sigh of frustration from Mrs Wilson, an old-fashioned stickler for detail who disapproved of her employer's lack of business skills; namely, *'go on'* instead of *'certainly, Mrs Wilson, you may.'* Idly, he pushed papers around his desk to make it seem that he was busy.

*

Outside in the draughty corridor, Beth Gillespie was unnerved by the receptionist's critical stare and was beginning to wish she had worn a business suit rather than her tartan mini-kilt. Still, if you had the legs to show off…

'You may go in now, Mrs Gillespie. First door on the left.'

'Thanks,' Beth smiled, but the woman was already typing.

Beth knocked politely and waited.

'Yes?' asked a male voice and Beth opened the door and went in.

He stared at her for a full twenty seconds – Beth counted in her head – and then Charlie Webster's features broke out into the broadest smile.

'You're Beth?'

'Yes.'

He was still staring when Beth looked down at the chair.

'Shall I sit down?'

'Please do. I'm so sorry, I should have suggested it. Yes, sit down, do.'

Beth manoeuvred her legs and feet into a decorous arrangement and placed her hands in her lap.

'You're here about the language job?' Charlie asked unnecessarily.

'Yes, I qualified a few years ago, haven't worked yet.'

'You haven't worked? You mean, you've been at home wasting your talents?'

'No, I've been keeping house for my husband.'

'Ah yes, of course,' Charlie said, thinking that the way she had reminded him she was a married woman had been quite brutal. 'But now you'd like a job of some sort?'

'Yes.'

'It's yours if you want it,' he said simply and, under the desk, he kept his fingers crossed.

'Well of course I want it,' Beth frowned. 'What would be the point of this interview if I intended to turn it down?'

'Look,' Charlie said, hands in a gesture of surrender. 'I'm nervous. I've never interviewed anyone before. I've made a bad impression and there's nothing I can do to change that.' He ploughed on, giving her no time to contradict him. 'But I really need someone to translate for me and to talk to potential clients. If you want the job, you can start tomorrow and, as for thinking that I'm a ninny, well, I'll do my best to convince you I'm not.'

He had hoped for a placating response, but she appeared to enjoy his discomfort. Besides, he suspected that she was the type of girl who had the knack of putting men at a

70

disadvantage. His heart skipped a beat.

'So, I can start tomorrow?'

'Yes, or today if you're free.'

'What, now?'

'Yes, now.' Charlie leaned across the desk and handed her several leaflets. 'These have to be translated into French pretty soon. Potential clients, coming over next week. They'd appreciate information about the pieces.'

Beth gave the leaflets a cursory glance, decided she could do it standing on her head.

'Yes, well, I suppose I could do it today.'

'You could?'

'Shall I work here?' Beth asked glancing around. 'Or would you mind if I worked at home this afternoon, considering I'd no idea I'd have to start right away?'

'Home would be fine,' Charlie smiled, wondering if his smile looked as gormless as it felt. 'If you can hand them in by the end of the week, that's great.'

'Would I have an office here?'

'Ah, that's a slight problem at the moment. The storeroom at the end of the corridor is being renovated. That's where you'd be, an office to yourself.'

'And when's that likely to happen?'

'Not until the end of next month, maybe even the beginning of August.'

'So, I might be able to work from home until then?' Beth asked sweetly.

'I don't see why not. Where do you live anyway?'

'Here's my address,' Beth said, handing him a card that Harry often used.

'It's my husband's number, of course, but mine too obviously.'

'Fine,' Charlie said, and his spirits plummeted at the tangible proof of the husband. 'I'm here most days, and Mrs Wilson's here all the time. Any problems, just call.'

Beth stood up, pushing the chair in neatly.

'I guess that's settled then,' she said, offering her hand.

'Yes, I guess it is,' Charlie agreed, taking it.

He stood at his office door as she walked past Mrs Wilson, saw the girl give his secretary a broad smile; braced himself for the icy glare that would follow.

'Thank you, Mrs Wilson,' the girl said meekly and, to Charlie's astonishment, his secretary actually smiled.

'That's all right, Mrs Gillespie,' she said condescendingly. 'Nice to have met you,' she added, perhaps never imagining that someone in such a short skirt could be considered for the position. Charlie opted to wait for a few days before telling her. It would give him time to sweeten the old girl up.

*

Lily Morris let Grace run around the kitchen seeing to the morning tray. She was too old and weary now to bother and, besides, Grace had a flair for this sort of thing, laying out matching napkins, the best crockery, the finest silver teaspoons. Such an adherence to old-fashioned etiquette was a joy to behold. In that respect, the girl was exactly like her mother.

'There, I think that's the lot. Tea or coffee?'

'Not that instant rubbish,' Lily frowned. 'Have you time to make the proper stuff? The percolator's brand new.'

'It's done,' Grace said happily. 'I prefer it myself. And there's brown sugar too.'

Lily peered at the bowl. 'I didn't think I had any.'

'You didn't, but I did, so I brought some just in case.'

They sat at the kitchen window looking out at the effects of a wet summer's day.

The lupines and monkshood were drooping morosely in the middle of the flowerbeds, their long stems unable to support the weight of a whole night's rain. Grace was always tempted to go around the garden after a storm and prop them all up again, shake the water from their petals and cheer them up. There was nothing quite so miserable as a stiff, proud stem being brow-beaten by the elements. She considered it a gross injustice.

'So, tell me about Beth's new job then,' Lily said as they took their first sip of the coffee. 'In Perth you said?'

'Yes, only yards from her flat. Most convenient. She has the interview today, but I know she'll get it.'

'It's a relief that she won't have to travel,' Lily said. 'All that traffic nowadays, makes my head spin just seeing it rush past.'

'She'll be able to pop home at lunchtimes, do some housework, wash up the breakfast dishes.'

Lily shook her head. 'Does your mind never take a holiday from household chores?'

'Speaking of a holiday,' Grace said slyly. 'I suppose you won't want to be going to Inverness now?'

Lily had the grace to appear sheepish. 'I suppose not.'

'You should have told me, you know. I hate to think of you worrying about him for a whole week. It's not fair.'

Lily smiled at the girl. If there was a kinder, more considerate person in the district she had yet to meet her. It reminded her of the reason for the girl's visit.

'I hope you're not worried either,' she said, watching her young friend's face. 'Tell me you're not lying awake every night.'

'I'm not. He won't affect me one little bit, for I have no intention of seeing him, or speaking to him, or even writing to him. He had his chance and he's not getting another one.'

'Aye well, he might not take 'no' for an answer.'

'He'll have no choice,' Grace said quickly. 'He can do what he likes, but he'll not have the satisfaction of telling me a load of lies.'

'Is Beth still asking about him?'

'No, she'll be too busy with her new job. Did you know her boss will be Charlie Webster, from the big house?'

Lily's eyes met Grace's. 'No, I didn't. He can be a bit of a lad, you know?'

'Gossip,' Grace tutted. 'Nothing but gossip.'

'A little bird told me something interesting,' Lily smiled. 'Well all right then, Kathleen's mother told me. She saw him entertain a married woman.'

'Probably his aunt,' Grace said dismissively. 'I'm not listening.'

'So, what will Harry think about the job?'

'He'll be delighted.'

'Jealous, more like,' Lily smiled mischievously. 'Beth's a lovely girl. He must have a heart attack every time another fellow even looks at her.'

'You're wrong about Harry,' Grace insisted pleasantly. 'Besides, Beth won't let anything get in the way of a good job, believe me.'

'If you say so. By the way, I meant to ask, how are you and James doing these days?'

'So-so.'

'I expect that's all you can expect if you've been married for almost twenty-five years.'

'Gosh, you are a cynical old thing,' Grace laughed. 'And what would you know about the state of a marriage after twenty-five years?'

'Precious little, thank the Lord.' Lily glanced away and fiddled with her napkin.

72

'About your father,' she said suddenly, still not catching Grace's eye.

'What about him?'

'D'you think he'll come to the village to look for you?'

If she had been horrified at the very thought, Grace gave no sign. Her composure was unruffled.

'No, I can't see the point of him coming to find me,' she remarked calmly. 'He must know that you've told me he's in the area, and if I'd wanted to see him I'd have telephoned all the hotels to find him. No, he'll not come here and risk being rejected.'

'That's fine then.'

'As for James, he and I are fine as well.'

Lily leaned forward in her chair. 'I thought you described it as 'so-so'?'

'As you said, after twenty five years that's as good as it gets.'

Lily smiled and sat back. Grace Melville knew what she was doing. Everything would work out fine.

*

Grace dusted the bookcase and went to the back door to flick the duster clean. She had wandered around the house for an hour, filling her hands and mind with menial tasks, to ward off other, more weighty matters. She knew she had succeeded in putting Lily's mind at rest, but the truth was that, until her father was well away from this place, she herself would find no peace.

Every time the doorbell rang, or the telephone clanged in the hall, or some driver tooted his horn in the passing, Grace's heart almost stopped for fear it was him; and the other, unforeseen, consequence of the man's sudden appearance was the emergence of painful memories involving her mother's staunch defence of an errant husband; memories that had lain dormant for years.

The alternative – of meeting the man, telling him how she hated him and never wanted to see him again – had insinuated itself into her thoughts over the past few days but, surely, he would have won then, and she could never allow that to happen. No, she would just have to endure it as best she could, play the waiting game until he had gone.

Grace heard the four o'clock bus pass the cottage: it was time to think about making James's tea.

*

Harry sighed, cleared the few papers from his desk and surveyed his new office, freshly-painted and refitted for him, complete with his own nameplate on the door. His eyes rested on the oak desk, a good choice, for the wood was light and matched his own preference. He had viewed David's office in Aberdeen with some scepticism, laden down as it was with heavy, dark furniture and gloomy décor; more conducive to an undertaker's parlour than a lawyer's office.

A junior partner now in Gilmour and Barclay, Harry had enjoyed his first week immensely. As a joke, he had envisaged the day when his own name would be added to the company nameplate; had abbreviated the name to GGB, an acronym for Gorgeous Great Bastard, which had greatly amused Beth.

'Just don't blurt it out on the phone to a client,' she had giggled the previous night as they sat in front of the television set not caring what programme they were watching: the luxury of being together during the week was taking precedence over everything.

'I won't,' he smiled, fondling her hair and contemplating taking her to bed early. 'You don't seem very nervous about the interview.'

73

'I'm not,' she had shrugged, her fingers ruffling his blond hair. 'Why should I be?'

'Your first interview since you left university? I think I'd be nervous.'

'Rubbish! You, Harry Gillespie, are the coolest thing on two legs.'

'Except when I'm sitting next to you.'

Beth never tired of compliments, which often amazed him since she must have received so many.

'Flattery gets you anything you want.'

'In that case, I want a glass of whisky.'

'What? Sitting next to the hottest thing on the planet and all you can think of is a whisky?' Beth feigned outrage, but released him. 'Make mine a sparkly.'

'Have you seen or heard from Grace's father again?'

He was in the kitchen by the time he called through to her and he had imagined at first that his voice had not carried. The second time he asked, however, she had appeared at the kitchen door, glum-faced, and he knew the man had contacted her again.

'I take it you have seen or heard from him.'

'No, but I...' She bit her lower lip, the same habit as Grace's, he noted. 'I suppose I did a foolish thing.'

'Which was?' Harry asked pleasantly, but her glance conveyed that she had picked up the warning tone.

'I followed him yesterday, to the George Hotel.'

'And?' he had asked, handing her the glass of wine

'And that's all,' Beth said grumpily, turning away. 'Isn't it bad enough?'

'Only if he saw you.'

'He didn't,' she told him proudly, and he was reminded of how young she was. 'I was the perfect spy.'

'So he's staying at the George, is he?' Harry asked, wondering if the man had sampled the delights of a cocktail waitress. The very idea filled him with horror as he recalled his own foray into unfaithfulness in Aberdeen.

'You're not thinking of confronting him, are you?' Beth had asked anxiously.

'Why would I? The man's got nothing to do with me.'

Now, as his office clock struck four, Harry leaned back in the massive leather chair and placed his hands behind his head. The thought of going to warn off Grace's father had never entered his mind; until Beth had broached the subject; after which he had thought of nothing else.

There was a knock on the door and he jumped, so wrapped up had he been in family problems.

'Come in,' he called, experiencing a rush of excitement as he realised that he was now a boss.

'Just a few letters to sign, Mr Gillespie,' the woman told him, laying them on the desk and waiting politely. Sandra, his secretary, was elderly, a fact which suited Harry very well, considering his wife's unpredictable temper

'Oh, I almost forgot,' Sandra said, as she opened the door to leave. 'Mr Gilmour said there's nothing to keep you today if you want to pop home.'

'Thank you, Sandra, I might do that.'

The door closed quietly and Harry sat for a few minutes, counting his blessings.

*

It had been James's suggestion that they treat Beth and Harry to dinner for their second wedding anniversary. Grace had been astonished, as James had shown no enthusiasm for even visiting the new flat and had stepped over the threshold of the old flat on only one occasion.

'That's a good idea,' she said, as eagerly as she could, but her mind was racing ahead, seeking out potential pitfalls. 'I'll tell Beth when she phones later.'

'Didn't she let you know how the interview went?'

'No, she always phones after six, so I expect she'll be full of it then.'

'You'd think it would be the first thing she'd want to do,' James frowned. 'She must know you'd be worried sick.'

'Oh, yes,' Grace said slowly, remembering that she should not be quite so relaxed about her daughter's future. 'I am worried, of course, but I think she'll sail through.'

'You think so?'

'Yes, definitely,' Grace confirmed and James appeared mollified.

'I've to go up to see Stuart about the general meeting,' he said as they cleared away the tea things. 'Tell Beth I was thinking about her all day.'

'What a nice thing to say.'

James paused at the door and gave her a puzzled look.

'Why wouldn't I be thinking of her when it's her first interview?'

He had gone before Grace had the opportunity to reply and she was left with the familiar sense of inadequacy.

*

Beth could hardly contain her excitement. Her mother had to beg her to slow down in the telling of the tale, so exuberant was her rhetoric.

'Sorry, Mum, it was just such a great day. Anyway, you'll never – and I mean never – guess how much he's offering me?'

'Is it enough?' Grace asked, but Beth was so thrilled with the day's events that she was barely listening.

'I'm to be paid twenty pounds a week!'

'Goodness, that's certainly enough.'

'Oh, and I think he and I will get on really well. As boss and employee, I mean,' Beth added hastily.

'I know what you mean, dear, and I'm so happy for you. It's exactly the kind of job you were looking for.'

'And there's another thing you'll never guess. I've been working at home today, started already.'

'Gosh, that was quick. He must be desperate.'

Beth's raucous laughter drew her mother's attention to the ambiguity of her remark.

'Honestly, Beth! Does this generation think of nothing else?'

''Course not! By the way, is there any chance of you coming into Perth this week for a visit?'

'This week?' Grace repeated uneasily. 'I'm not sure, darling. Can I let you know?'

'Sounds more depressing than 'we'll see',' Beth said bluntly and her mother was remorseful.

'Perhaps on Thursday then.'

'Great! Oh, and was it really Dad's idea, about the anniversary treat?'

'Yes it was. He even suggested that we go into Dundee for a change,' Grace lied, in an effort to avoid the city of Perth.

'Dundee?' her daughter asked dubiously. 'That's surprising. I thought he hated Dundee.'

'No, I don't think he does. Anyway, it's a few weeks off yet, plenty time to organise things.'

She hung up, ashamed of herself, ashamed that her fervent resolve not to allow her father's presence to affect her life had come to this: that she was not only allowing him to affect hers, but was also affording him the right to spoil the relationship she had with her loved ones.

*

Thomas Blake picked up his glass and caught the waitress' eye. Ordering another, he ignored her disapproving glance and gave her a dazzling, if false, smile.

'Another of the same, Deirdre,' he smiled, and her flash of anger delighted him.

'It's Laura,' she snapped, almost forgetting that he was a guest, but then, in an effort to soften her tone, she forced a smile and added: 'But Deirdre's one of my favourite names.'

He watched her wriggle across the room towards the small bar in the corner and wondered how any man could ever find such a lump attractive; and yet, one had, for she wore a wedding ring. As he pondered his options for the evening, the receptionist came into view, hurrying towards him with an apologetic grimace.

'Mr Hudson, I'm so sorry, and I have no idea how it happened, but this letter was left in your box yesterday and someone seems to have overlooked it.'

Breathless by the end of the sentence, the girl – Sarah something or other, he recalled – was regarding him with what she probably considered her most alluring eye contact; and he had to admit she was not unattractive. The large bust helped, of course, and he had been offered a share in its delights each time he stood at the reception desk.

'Oh, I daresay no harm's been done,' he smiled tolerantly, taking the letter from her fingers and allowing his own to touch hers briefly. To his immense satisfaction, he saw the slight shock his action produced, not to mention the sudden, implicit, acceptance in her eyes.

'I'm still sorry, Mr Hudson,' she said, seemingly unwilling to take her leave. 'If there's anything I can do to make up for the oversight...'

'Thank you, Sarah. If there is, you'll be the first to know.'

With a weary sigh, Thomas followed her progress to the door, congratulating himself on such self-restraint. It was all in a good cause; otherwise he might have sampled the girl's wares on the first night. Even at his age, a man had appetites.

He brought his attention to the envelope in his hand and when he caught a glimpse of handwriting instead of a typed label his pulse quickened: it was from his granddaughter.

*

Beth lay in the bubble bath sipping her wine, her face flushed with the alcohol and the heat in the bathroom, her hair pinned up, the tendrils damp at the nape of her neck,

She had never imagined that she could deceive so many people in so short a time, had never believed that it was in her nature to do so, having always tended towards honesty; not because it came so naturally, though it did, but because it was the coward's way out of embarrassing situations. Before it got too messy, before one tiny fib layered itself onto another tiny fib and made it impossible to recall exactly what she had said in the first place, Beth Melville chose the truth; right at the beginning.

Now, here she was, lying pondering her recent spate of fibs – lies then! – and projecting her mind forward to the moment she would be found out.

She had lied to Harry about only following the man to the hotel; then she had lied to her mother – by omission, but a lie nevertheless – and she had lied to her grandfather by

76

not telling him Charlotte Blake was dead. Furthermore – and was this the worst? – she had avoided talking to her father that evening, phoning the house when she knew he would be at the meeting.

Lying to everyone else, reprehensible though it might be, was not on a par with lying to her dad, and it was ruining her night.

'Have you melted in there?' she heard Harry ask at the door.

'Come in, it's open.'

'Are you decent?' he laughed and it cheered her up; until she remembered how she was deceiving him.

'Not likely, so get in here.'

He opened the door and gasped at the heat and steam.

'My God, Beth, it's like a bloody sauna in here.'

'Never been in one, wouldn't know.'

'I'll leave the door open, let the steam out. Here, I brought the bottle with me.'

'Why don't you come in? The water's lovely.'

He sat on the edge of the bath, and regarded her with what she thought was an odd expression; or was her life of duplicity making her imagine things?

'Are you all right today, Beth?'

'Yes, of course I am, What d'you mean?'

'You've just landed a great job, the kind you've been dreaming about, and yet you seem... well... a bit introverted. I thought you'd be jumping for joy.'

'Not easy in a sea of bubbles.'

'Are you sure you want the job?'

'Yes,' she told him, injecting as much enthusiasm into her voice as was possible. 'I'm going to love it, honestly.' Inwardly, she cringed at the word. 'Do you know Charlie Webster by any chance?' she asked, by way of mitigation of the more significant lie.

'No, I don't think so.'

'He's my boss, very handsome, most charming.'

'I hate him already,' Harry said, throwing the yellow plastic duck at her and sending a spray of bubbles around the bathroom.

'Silly man,' Beth smiled, reaching for his hand. 'There's no one could steal my heart like you have.' She thought it was a bit theatrical, that he might suspect she was trying to butter him up, but it was said and there was no going back.

'That's one of the nicest thing you've ever said to me.'

Beth looked at him, trying to gauge his mood, but with Harry Gillespie it was well-nigh impossible. He and her mother were two of a kind...

'It's true, Harry,' she said and he gave her one of his enigmatic smiles.

'It won't stop me going to see this Charlie Webster for myself.'

'He lives up the road from Mum actually.'

'Really? And you've never met him before?'

She was used to his innocent demeanour hiding a shrewd mind, but she had honed her skill of counterattack by indulging in the truth, confronting it head-on; when it suited her, of course.

'I think I've seen him once or twice,' she smiled, flicking frothy bubbles at him. 'He drives a BMW.'

'Very swanky. Is he good-looking as well, by any chance?'

'Not in your league,' Beth said with a shrug, and she heard the ring of truth to it.

'So, he's your new boss?'

'Yes, and I'll be able to wind him round my little finger,' she smiled wickedly.

'That, my love, goes without saying.' Harry began loosening his tie and unbuttoning his shirt. 'As long as it's only your finger he winds himself around.'

'Your bits and pieces are the only ones that interest me.'

'Well that's lucky,' Harry smiled, stepping out of his trousers and folding them neatly onto the toilet seat. 'I happen to have them with me, at this very moment.'

Beth sighed as his mouth touched hers, but she knew that the thought of her grandfather would intrude on the intimacy of the next hour and that the fault was hers alone. What had she done?

Chapter Nine

In the first week of June, Grace received a letter from Alice and, to her shame, she was dismayed at what she read.

'Lucky me! I'm to be let loose again - for the second time in twenty years too, ain't that grand?'

The prospect of her friend coming over for a holiday should have been the best news Grace had had for months; yet, with her father snooping around the area, presumably hoping to contact her, Grace could only dread Alice's visit. Inevitably, her guest would want to go shopping in Perth and Dundee, even to Edinburgh. Now that Beth and Frank were adults, there was no excuse for Grace to linger close to home.

When James noticed the postmark on Alice's letter, he asked if she and the family were well, the first time he had enquired after them in all the years of trans-Atlantic correspondence.

'They're fine,' Grace told him, still pondering the implications of Alice's news. As her resolve not to worry James with the information on Thomas Blake was unwavering, she relayed only the briefest details of the letter, completely omitting any reference to a holiday at Lilac Cottage.

'It's a long time since she was here,' James said unexpectedly over breakfast, glancing several times at the letter that was lying on the table beside Grace. 'Does she ever mention coming back again?'

Grace could hardly believe what she was hearing: why was it, when she was fully committed to deceiving everyone, that they seemed to sense the change in her manner? Despite her reliance on her acting skills, was she, in fact, an open book, exhibiting the symptoms of disloyalty to people who knew her better than she knew herself?

'No,' she said now, meeting James's eyes. 'She never mentions it. But,' she added, hoping to put an end to this line of conversation. 'She often asks me to go out there.'

As she had anticipated, James shook his head, the corners of his mouth turning down.

'I don't think we could afford it.'

'No, money's the problem,' she agreed, but the fact she had cited money as the reason and not an unwillingness to travel alone, would sit heavily on James's shoulders.

'Maybe one day,' he said, rising from his chair and avoiding her eyes.

'Yes, maybe.'

Once alone in the house, Grace set about writing a delaying letter to her friend, not a happy pursuit but, in the light of Thomas Blake's appearance, a very necessary one.

By mid-morning she had succeeded in composing a reply, although duplicity was taking its toll. Here was yet another example of her father's destructive influence in this family and, once again, she had allowed herself to be manipulated. With each fresh incident confirming the man's power to ruin her life, Grace felt that she was being manoeuvred into a corner.

*

Thomas Blake was waiting for Beth when she left for work at the start of her first week at Charlie Webster's office. In the aftermath of her letter he anticipated a friendlier attitude.

'What the hell are you doing here?' she asked him sharply, moving quickly into the street and glancing around. 'You've no right to snoop.'

Though surprised at the girl's tone, Thomas smiled and shook his head.

'I'm not snooping. More like lurking,' he joked, hoping the girl would soften. She frowned, however, and emitted a sigh.

'What do you want anyway?' she asked unkindly.

'Your letter,' he said slowly, trying to fathom the expression in her eyes. 'You said you might…'

'I know what I said,' Beth cut him off shortly. 'That was only a few days ago. I have a life to live, you know, I'm not just here to suit you.'

Thomas made a conciliatory gesture. This would be harder than he had imagined. 'Yes, and I apologise. The thing is, I'm pretty keen to see them again, as you'd imagine, and I…'

Again, Beth interrupted him. 'If you'd stuck by them in the first place, we wouldn't be having this conversation.'

For an instant, he was taken aback: the tone of her letter was in such sharp contrast to her present attitude that he could hardly believe it had been written by the same person.

'You seemed willing to help me,' Thomas told her, unable to conceal his disappointment. 'Have you changed your mind?'

'I don't know,' Beth said, and she was fidgeting from one foot to the other. 'My Mum isn't an easy person to convince.'

'Look,' Thomas smiled, attempting to ease the tension. 'I'll be staying here for at least a month, maybe longer.' In truth, he had nowhere else to go but he was not about to divulge such a thing to the girl. 'You have all the time you want. I promise not to rush you, or 'lurk' about,' he laughed, his fingers adding apostrophes to the word. 'You won't even see me unless you call me.'

He fished in his pocket for something. 'Here, it's my room number at the George. Please call me if you want to talk. Please,' he added, hoping to appeal to the girl's sympathetic instincts which he knew she must have, being Charlotte's granddaughter too.

'I can't promise anything,' Beth said bluntly, but she took the card.

'I'm just grateful that I've spoken to you,' Thomas said, although she must have guessed it was lip service.

'I have to go now,' she said briskly. 'Or I'll be late for work.'

He was tempted to ask where that was exactly, but he only smiled and allowed her to pass. It would be fairly easy to follow her.

*

Charlie Webster was playing hard to get. He had decided that, against all odds, he was intent on winning Beth Gillespie – he almost choked on the surname, for it reminded him of her status – on stealing her from the suave, sophisticated, legal eagle that was her husband; and he had just the ally: Frank Gilmour, his best mate, a chap game for anything. More significantly, he was in the right place at the right time, only yards away from Gillespie's office.

On Beth's first day at the office, Charlie had opted to disappear, to take the opportunity to court the new clients he had been too busy to see these past few months. Now he would be spared long hours with his old French dictionary stuck in front of him; now he had the girl to do all the translating,

Charlie savoured the lovely whiff of freedom in the air, the freedom to be out of the office when he pleased; but not simply to waste his time, for he had numerous clients to visit, valuations to make and sale rooms to wander around looking for potential money-spinners.

Mrs Wilson gave him a critical glance when he told her he might be out for most of the day.

'Out?' she repeated and, like a schoolboy, he fidgeted. 'You mean, the new girl will be in her office for the first time, and you won't be here?'

Charlie was used to the old dear's manner but, because she was an old friend of his mother's, he was also used to biting back the odd, snide remark, added to which Marjory Wilson was an excellent secretary and the business would suffer for her absence.

'She'll be fine,' he smiled. 'Mrs Gillespie is an honours graduate in French and German,' he went on. 'And I've left instructions for her. She can't go wrong.'

'But you'll be back later in the afternoon?' Mrs Wilson asked, more of a statement than a question.

'Should be,' Charlie said, risking further reprimand. 'I promised to meet mother in town,' he lied, and the result was predictable.

'Oh well, give her my regards and have a lovely time.'

He bounced down the steps and almost knocked Beth Gillespie into Kingdom come.

'Ow!' she cried, grabbing the handrail and staggering to a halt.

'Ouch!' Charlie exclaimed, clutching the knee he had bashed on the rail.

'For Heaven's sake!' Beth said irritably. 'Can't you watch where you're going?'

Confused by her icy tone, and considering he had set plans in motion to woo the girl, he backtracked rapidly.

'I'm so sorry,' he said desperately. 'I've an appointment with a new client and I'm late already. Any bones broken?'

'No. No thanks to you,' Beth said, as surly as he ever imagined she could be. The situation called for desperate measures.

'Look, I'll come back in, phone the client, put him off, see you're all right.'

'I'll be fine, Nothing that a week in intensive care won't cure.'

He burst out laughing and was relieved to see her expression soften.

'Beth, I really am so sorry, honestly. If you don't forgive me and let me take you out for a coffee, I'll hurl myself off the Queen's Bridge.'

'Whatever suits you,' she smiled and his plans were going haywire. 'I'll be fine. Don't let me prevent you from seeing clients.'

She had turned to climb the remaining steps and Charlie's resolve crumbled like dry leaves underfoot.

'Wait, I really must see you're fine,' he said, following her into the building.

As he approached Mrs Wilson's desk, he threw her a radiant smile and wondered if he should pretend to have taken note of her disapproval and changed his mind about being out of the office.

'Mr Webster was flying down the steps and crashed into me,' he heard Beth say, scotching his rehearsed speech. 'He's just making sure I'm in one piece, but I told him I was fine and that he should carry on.'

The look of admiration that passed from Marjory Wilson to the new employee was not lost on Charlie. It annoyed him, if the truth be told, for in all the years he had known the old bag she had never endowed him with anything other than mild tolerance at best, frigid disapproval at worst.

'I think the two of us can manage without him,' Mrs Wilson smiled sweetly, and Charlie felt the conspiratorial air of dismissal.

'Well, if you're sure you're fine?' he asked of Beth.

'Perfectly. As Mrs Wilson said, she and I will manage without you.'

Charlie smiled and took his leave but, before the door closed behind him, he heard Mrs Wilson's voice.

'You can call me Marjory, my dear.'

With a last, disgruntled sigh, Charlie let himself out of the building.

*

Beth smiled and held out her hand in a most old-fashioned gesture that she suspected would appeal to the old dear.

'And I'd like you to call me Beth.'

'I have a feeling we'll get on just fine, Beth.'

Once in her small office that still smelt of emulsion paint and damp woodchip wallpaper, Beth settled down with her list of instructions. She withdrew the new French dictionary she had used at Aberdeen University and laid it neatly on the desk, her first action as a businesswoman.

She was satisfied with Charlie Webster's departure, not to mention the abruptness of her attitude to him, for it meant she could start as she meant to go on: a happily married woman who intended to keep it that way.

Perturbed, Beth paused in her work. Was she envisaging a struggle to keep it that way? Otherwise, why would she have to consider it at all? She tried to concentrate on the list in front of her; but her thoughts kept drifting to Charlie Webster.

*

Harry Gillespie stepped out into the warm sultry afternoon and looked up the street. He had forgotten which direction he should take into town, particularly if he wanted a late lunch, as not all eateries served it after two thirty. As he stood weighing up his chances of choosing correctly, he became aware of an elderly man on the pavement opposite. At the last moment, as Harry's gaze had come to rest on the man, the collar had gone up, rather swiftly it occurred to Harry, and the man had walked away, dashing round the corner and out of sight.

Harry shrugged. He supposed they had them even in this far neck of the woods.

As the day was lovely, he decided to walk to the end of North Inch and from there along Tay Street and into High Street where, surely, he would find a café that sold sandwiches and coffee. After the incident with the elderly psycho, he turned sharply when he heard footsteps behind him. It was Frank Gilmour, a senior partner.

'You'd rushed off before I knew you'd gone,' he said, out of breath, as he caught up with Harry. 'If you're heading off for something to eat, mind if I join you?'

'Not at all. In fact, you'll know better than I do where there's a café.'

'Haven't you lived in Perth for a few years?' Frank asked, falling into step.

'Yes, but only at week-ends.'

'Ah, of course, you were up in the windy city during the week. But your wife was here, wasn't she?'

Harry was no fool, especially where Beth was concerned. If he had a pound for every time a man passed an innocent remark about her, he could have saved enough to fly to the island of Ibiza.

'Yes, she was quite happy to stay at home for a while. In fact, she's only just started work today.'

'Has she?' Frank asked, steering them towards McEwens. 'Is she a solicitor too?'

'No, a language buff.'

'Wow, she sounds the brainy type.'

Harry stopped in his tracks and afforded Frank Gilmour the kind of smile he had seen his father employ so often.

'Oh she is, as you say, the brainy type, but, fortunately, she's a pretty shrewd judge

82

of character too.'

The expression on Frank Gilmour's face was vindication to Harry, although he could have no idea of the man's interest in Beth. The only thing he knew was that he would stamp it out while it was still small enough to be within the scope of his heel.

'I... I imagine she is,' Frank swallowed hard, gaze flickering away from Harry's. 'I just meant...'

'Yes, I'm sure you did,' Harry said pleasantly, patting the man's arm in a condescending manner. 'And I just meant she's a pretty shrewd judge of character.'

Because of David Routledge's recommendation for the position at Gilmour and Barclay, Harry had no fear of losing it, and if his relationship with one of the partners were not to be of the hail-fellow-well-met variety, it would not cause him a single sleepless night.

'They serve a good lunch in here,' he heard Frank Gilmour say nervously as they drew level with the front door of the first hotel they came to. 'I often come here.'

They sat in the hotel restaurant, at the window, and Harry was the more relaxed, talking easily about any subject his companion initiated, smiling at the right places, even joking when the occasion demanded; but his eyes missed nothing. When he saw how well known Gilmour was in the restaurant and that it must be his usual lunch venue, Harry resolved never to give the place the benefit of his custom again.

*

An hour later, Charlie Webster picked up the phone and listened to his friend's tirade, shocked by the first angry sentence.

'If you want that girl, you'll have to do it without me.'

'What the hell do you mean?' Charlie asked, mystified.

'I'm not getting involved in your little scheme to lure that girl away from her husband, that's what I mean.'

'You've met him?'

'I've met him.'

'And you won't help?'

'The man's got a razor sharp mind, and I think he even suspected what was going on.'

'But we haven't done anything yet. Unless you said something, put your bloody foot in it.'

'That's charming, thank you very much, and no, I did not put my foot in it. I told you, the guy's smart, not the type you should upset.'

'What did he say?'

'Nothing. He said absolutely nothing, and that was worse than saying something.'

'Oh, drop dead!' Charlie told his friend unwisely before slamming down the receiver.

*

Grace had been sitting in the garden, on the bench that was furthest from the house, for the best part of two hours. So animated had been her thoughts that she was drained of energy; but she had come to a decision and she felt there was something to show for her efforts.

Rising to her feet, she smoothed down the apron she had been wearing to do the washing and then loosened the ties, removing it slowly and folding it neatly over her arm. As she stood there, she had a sudden vision of her mother sitting there, smoking the inevitable cigarette, relating some outrageous anecdote, rendering the world a happier place.

Grace walked down the path, touching the occasional flower head and stooping to breathe in the faint scent of the meadowsweet. She felt surprisingly calm after her hours of deliberation, calm enough to decide to telephone Harry and tell him of her predicament.

In the kitchen, she hung her apron on the back of the cupboard door, checked the cakes through the glass door of the oven and then glanced at the clock: half past three. She raked in the drawer for his number and went through to the hall.

*

The lunch had taken as little time as Frank Gilmour could engineer, with the result that Harry had been back in his office by half past two, his mind mulling over the various reasons for Gilmore's mentioning Beth. It had not been the utterance of her name that had been disturbing, more the expression on the man's face as he had spoken. It was not the casual interest a colleague might show in a new employee's family, but a determined attempt to ferret out information.

Harry had seen it before in Aberdeen, when fellow students – fortunately too young and self-centred to be endowed with powers of observation – had asked seemingly innocent questions about Beth's relationship with him and had aroused his curiosity.

'So, she likes music, does she?' had been the most frequent, and Harry had deliberately misled them by naming the Rolling Stones as her favourite pop group, thereby having the satisfaction of seeing her reaction to the gift of their latest album.

'You can have it if you want,' she would say irritably, casting the record aside. 'Whatever gave him the idea I would like it anyway?'

He considered his most successful ploy to have been the one involving bunches of flowers: there had been nothing quite so appalling to Beth Melville than the sight of cut flowers: even the tiny posies that frequently graced the tables of restaurants brought out the worst in her. Harry smiled now at the memory of so many lovesick students being struck off her list of friends; although the flowers had soaked for days in the sink, since it was hardly their fault; innocent victims of a human foible.

Sitting at his brand new desk in his brand new job, he was beginning to wonder if he were paranoid about his wife. Just as he prepared to grapple with the idea, the telephone rang and it was Grace.

'Is this a bad time for you?' she asked predictably.

'You could never call at a bad time,' he told her truthfully, leaning back in the sumptuous chair and putting Beth from his mind.

'I'd like to see you,' she said firmly.

'Right,' he said, reaching for his blank diary of appointments. 'I can meet you for lunch tomorrow if you like?'

'I don't want to come into Perth,' Grace said, and, for a moment, Harry was stumped. 'It's difficult to explain,' she added apologetically.

'Well, in that case, how about if I pop in to see you after work some night? I'm sure Beth will manage to cook the tea herself.'

'Oh don't tell her I asked to see you.' The voice at the other end of the line was urgent, and he was confused for the second time in as many minutes. 'She mustn't know.'

'Is it about your father?' he asked, for it was only thing he could think of.

'Yes,' was the dull response, and so he resolved to go that evening.

84

*

It was Marjory Wilson who interrupted her with the message from Harry. The woman had been so kind to Beth the whole day that Beth had revised her first impression. Where, originally, Marjory had appeared abrupt and over-critical, she was actually efficient and attentive to detail; the old-fashioned kind of secretary who was more of a P.A. than a typist, capable of running the business with or without Charlie Webster.

In fact, by the end of the first day, there was no doubt in Beth's mind that Marjory did run the business and that C. Webster esquire was nothing more than a name on the ornate front door.

'You know what men are like,' Marjory had confided to Beth during the lunch-hour, sitting in the main office sharing Marjory's sandwiches because Beth had forgotten to bring any. 'They're handy for mending the washing machine and moving heavy furniture, things like that, but, as for having a head for business, well, to be honest, I'm amazed that the world survives in spite of them.'

Beth had almost choked on her coffee, for it reflected her own view of the male population, apart from the sex, of course, which would have to be excluded from the list of topics in this office.

'It's dreadful,' Beth grinned. 'But I feel the same way. I often wonder why we allow them to think they're so wonderful.'

Marjory had laughed at that and Beth was astonished to see the difference it made to the woman's demeanour. Suddenly, she looked more like forty than fifty-five.

'Oh stop it, you're worse than me,' she had said, wagging a finger at Beth.

It was such a relief to get on with the old dear, although had it turned out differently, Beth would have coped: she was quite happy working away by herself, content with her own company, secure in the knowledge that the work itself was well within her scope. However, getting along with the only other person in the office was fairly satisfying.

'Your husband called, my dear,' Marjory was saying now, her head round the door of Beth's office. 'Left a message, won't be home until later.'

'Oh, all right,' Beth said, disappointed that he would not be there to hear the exciting exploits of her first day. 'Thank you, Marjory. In that case, I'll just finish this leaflet, start another one tomorrow.'

'You really should be going now, it's long past four thirty.'

'You mean I don't work until five?'

Marjory tutted. 'Dear me no. After all, Charlie's been out and about all day, and we've no proof that he's been working.'

Beth grinned and shrugged. 'Fair enough, but I'd still like to finish this.'

'I have some letters that have to catch the post. Would you mind locking up?'

'No, just point me in the direction of the key and I'll be fine.'

Alone in the office, Beth completed the translation of the glories of a George the Third writing desk for a potential French client and laid the document out for Marjory to type the next day; and then she locked her desk – despite its being empty – and picked up the key to the main door.

As she walked down the stone steps, hand on the rail as her leg was still painful after her earlier clash with Charlie Webster, Beth decided that, if she could not regale her husband with the thrilling account of her first working day, she would seek her mother's receptive ear.

It took her only minutes to reach the flat, the best aspect of the job, and within seconds she had swapped her office attire for jeans and one of Harry's old shirts. Deciding against having a lonely glass of wine to celebrate her day, she plumped for tea instead, carrying the mug through to the sitting room and setting it beside the phone.

*

As soon as she opened Lily Morris' door to welcome him. Harry was concerned over Grace's demeanour. Her desire to change the venue had not surprised him, for he knew that James would be home by five thirty and he was certain that the man had been kept in the dark regarding the recent appearance of Thomas Blake.

'I'm sorry for the cloak and dagger stuff,' she smiled wanly, leading the way to Lily's best room. 'But I haven't told James about it, yet.' He heard the hesitancy over the word 'yet'. 'Has Beth been plaguing you with more questions?'

'Oddly enough, no.'

'Perhaps she's lost interest,' Grace said hopefully, sitting down, but unable to keep still. She waited for him to sit opposite her before continuing: 'Do you think she has?'

'Without a doubt,' Harry lied. 'She'll be onto the next thing now, whatever that might be. Are you all right? You look rather tired.'

'I was up half the night, trying to decide what to do for the best.'

'And have you decided?'

'Yes, but I wanted to ask your opinion first,' she said, and, not for the first time, Harry wondered if he were worthy of such trust.

'Fire away,' he smiled. 'Although you've made me nervous now.'

She revealed to him her innermost thoughts about the situation, including her fear that, whatever action she took, the man would wield enough power over her and her family to ruin their lives. She could ignore him or confront him and, after long and hard consideration, she had settled on the latter, her eyes now searching Harry's for his immediate reaction.

'I think you should meet him,' he told her, albeit reluctantly. 'It's not ideal, but, if you don't, you'd have no idea where he was, what he was intending to do. You didn't fancy going into Perth today,' he reminded her gently. 'Obviously because you might bump into him.'

'Exactly,' Grace concurred unhappily. 'I couldn't bear the thought.'

'On the other hand, if you agree to meet him, I'd advise you to tell him to get lost once and for all.'

'You think he would leave us alone then?'

'Yes, I do.'

She relaxed then, her hands stilling on her lap, her eyes coming to alight on his face.

Harry had no idea what prompted him to ask it, but he had uttered the words before he could stop himself.

'Was James Melville the first man you ever loved?'

She stared at him, her mouth tightening, a tiny frown appearing on her brow, and he knew he had upset her.

'What has this got to do with Thomas Blake?' she asked, eyes opening wider, and displaying more hostility than he suspected her capable of.

'Any man would have been crazy about you. Why did you accept him?'

Harry's mind was seizing up: what the Hell was he thinking about?

Abruptly, Grace stood up to take her leave, hurrying past his chair towards the door. Instinctively, he stretched out his hand and held her fast.

'Grace, wait, please. I'm sorry, it was a stupid thing to say.'

'Quite the wrong thing to say,' she amended. She looked at him and then at his hand, still locked around her wrist.

'Please, Grace, don't go. I promise I won't mention it again.'

86

She sighed heavily, shifted her gaze from his, withdrew her arm as soon as he released it. For a moment she seemed undecided about staying or leaving and, wisely, Harry made no further demand on her. She spoke at last.

'What on earth got into you, asking such a stupid question?'

'I haven't a clue. But I promise it won't happen again.'

Grace sat down and twisted her wedding ring around her finger.

'Anyway,' Harry went on, 'do you want me to come with you when you meet your father?'

She stared at him as if the thought had never occurred to her.

'Oh, no,' she replied quite vehemently and he was hurt. 'That wouldn't be a good idea at all.' Perhaps seeing the disappointment in his eyes, she continued more gently. 'Harry, I'm sorry, I didn't mean to—'

He admonished her with a finger to his lips. 'There's no need to apologise. It's me who should be sorry, butting in when it's none of my business.'

The fact that Harry was part of the family made them both aware that the matter could easily be regarded as his business, and he had crafted the sentence so that it would leave doubts in her mind. At the moment, however, he was here to lend support; that was all.

'But there is a small thing you can do for me,' Grace ventured.

'Consider it done,' Harry said, grasping for the proverbial olive branch.

*

Beth was irritable by the time Harry returned home. He could tell at once, even before she spoke, that he was in for a frosty reception and, quite frankly, he was too tired for a confrontation. With the onset of her first frown, and before the accusing words had left her lips, he made the decision to tell her where he had been; and why.

Half an hour later, after she had sobbed her heart out with relief that her spell of lying was over, Beth was hanging on Harry's every word. She was only too willing to admit her failings as Head of Subterfuge, the greatest of these being that she found it almost impossible to deceive people. The odd white lie may be acceptable – and sometimes even that was debateable –but lies were trickier; and holding back the truth was even worse.

'I'm so glad Mum knows about him,' she sighed happily as they ate a late evening meal. 'I was a nervous wreck, dreading how I was going to tell her.'

Harry glanced across at his wife, cheeks still flushed from crying, eyes still shiny with tears, and he marvelled that she could look so lovely at a time when most other women were at their worst.

'Dread no more, sweetheart,' he smiled, raising his glass of wine. 'Cheers, and here's to us sticking together, you me and Grace.'

'And Dad,' Beth added stubbornly, clearly annoyed at the omission. 'Do you think she's told him yet?'

'No, she hasn't. Nor,' Harry continued, meeting her eyes. 'Nor is she likely to.'

Beth was horrified. 'But it's as much his business as it is yours,' she blurted out before her brain had time to catch up. 'Ooops,' she added with a grimace. 'The famous Beth Melville footwork again, in the mouth before it knows where it is.'

'No offence taken,' Harry said, but it rankled.

'So what now?'

'Now she's agreed to meet him it's up to her really.'

'And you're sure she's not letting you go with her?'

'Sure,' he said, and again it rankled.

'Why ever not?'

'Haven't a clue,' Harry said abruptly, and she fought hard to ignore his tone.

'Will she let me go, d'you think?'

'She doesn't know you've met him yet, or that I've told you about her going to confront him.'

'I have to do something,' Beth frowned, and the first seeds of anger were scattering themselves across her fertile mind. 'Or things could go on without me, although no one seems to have thought to include me up to now.'

Harry smiled at her predictability. It gave him more control over the volcanic temper tantrums. for he had already formed an answer. 'You have a lot to learn about being loved, my sweet.'

'Like what, for instance?'

'If someone really loves you, he'll do anything in his power to protect you from nasty things. That's true love. Very rare.'

Beth lowered her gaze and played with the food on her plate. Harry sensed she was reminded of her youth, her inexperience. She would often complain that, with one sentence, he was able to placate her.

'You mean that I don't really love you then, since I wouldn't dream of protecting you from nasty things,' she said moodily, not looking at him.

'What kind of a wimp needs a woman to protect him?'

She glanced across at him, saw that he was grinning, and the beginnings of her foul mood dissipated within seconds.

'Well, you're certainly not a wimp,' she said grudgingly, trying to hold back a smile. 'And let's face it, I doubt if I'd be any good at the protecting lark either.'

Harry congratulated himself on his increasing ability to defuse the temper.

'So... truce?'

'Truce,' Beth said, and their glasses chinked together. 'Did you know, by the way, that Annie thinks you look like Steve McQueen?' Harry choked on the mouthful of wine as Beth continued: 'You know when he was in '*Nevada Smith*'? She fancies you something rotten as a matter of fact.'

'I've only met her a couple of times, for Heaven's sake. I can't even remember what she looks like.'

He was treading carefully: Annie Kerr was vivacious and interesting; the kind of girl he would not crawl over to get to Beth. 'She's very sexy.'

Harry shook his head and feigned disinterest; took a long sip of wine before responding.

'Does she play Chopin like an angel?' he asked.

'No.'

'Or like moonlight walks?'

'Don't think so.'

'Well,' Harry shrugged amiably. 'I prefer that kind of female. Oh, and she must hate cut flowers in restaurants and abhor housework.'

At the sight of Beth's irrepressible laughter, Harry congratulated himself: he had deflected yet another jealous tantrum.

'Speaking of housework, will you manage the washing up, sweetheart?' he asked as they rose from the table. 'I've to pop out to post something.'

'At this late hour?'

'In case I miss the morning post,' Harry lied and she appeared satisfied.

He picked up his lightweight jacket, checked that the note was in the pocket and left the flat. As he ran down the staircase, his mind was not on Grace and her father. He was pondering the possible delights of Annie Kerr's voluptuous breasts.

Chapter Ten

Thomas Blake crossed the street with jaunty steps. His morning was going splendidly, thanks to the note that had been left for him at the front desk the night before, a note that had been delivered after half past ten he had been informed by the departing night porter.

'Was it a young girl who delivered it?' Thomas had asked the man, expecting to hear it confirmed.

'Oh, no, Sir, it was a very handsome young man.'

'It must have been my granddaughter's husband,' he had returned jovially. The expression made him feel he was already part of Grace's family.

'If you say so, Sir,' the man had smiled obsequiously.

Thomas had a day to kill before meeting his daughter and he had written a healthy cheque at the hotel in exchange for cash, with which he now intended to buy her an expensive gift.

The thought came to him that he had no idea what she would like: in fact, did she wear any jewellery at all? Was he wasting his time buying her a pearl brooch, for instance, the kind that Charlotte had always admired? He stood in the middle of the pavement, hardly aware of people having to dodge around him. What would his daughter consider to be lovely?

*

'This is just the loveliest thing I've ever owned.'

'The first of many,' he told her, not caring how lovesick she might think his expression. 'I'll shower you with so many gifts that your house won't be big enough to hold them.'

'Och, for Heaven's sake!' Charlotte tutted, walking away from him. 'I don't need showers of gifts, I just need you.'

It had been the first time she had uttered the words, and, suddenly, his feet hardly seemed to touch the ground.

'What did you say?' he called after her, striding out to catch her up.

She halted in her tracks, causing him to collide with her.

'Hey!' she cautioned. 'Watch where you're going!'

'Sorry, Charlotte, but what did you say back there, about needing me?'

She laughed mischievously, the dimple showing on her cheek, and he thought her the most beautiful creature he had ever set eyes on.

'I said I didn't need gifts, I just needed you, as if you don't know.'

'Will you marry me, Charlotte?' he heard himself blurting out. it was impossible to gauge which of them was the most astonished.

'What did you say?'

'Will you marry me, Charlotte Shepherd?' he asked, not so cockily this time, for he was now dreading a refusal.

She said nothing, simply stood looking at him, scrutinising him, with the deep blue eyes. He had absolutely no idea what she was thinking.

'Charlotte, say something,' he whispered, suddenly becoming aware that they were standing in the middle of a crowed pavement. 'Please say you will.'

'Needing you doesn't mean... I'm not... maybe we can just...'

Taking advantage of her confusion, Thomas seized her arm and drew her into the shop doorway, where she seemed to regain her composure.

'Marry me,' he managed to say before she had time to speak. 'Or, I swear, I'll die.'

He would never forget the look on her face as he had come to the end of his plea: she was shaking her head at him, albeit in a kindly fashion, and his heart sank. She had no intention of accepting his proposal and he had never felt so thoroughly wretched in his life.

*

Thomas felt himself buffeted by a group of school children, sauntering along behind their teachers in search of the meaning of life, presumably. He glanced round, to confirm where he was and, as he made his way up High Street, despite his new-found optimism that he would soon be given the chance to woo her a second time, the pain of her initial rejection of him was taunting him.

*

For the umpteenth time in a few minutes, Beth pushed up her sleeve and looked at her watch, a fresh wave of resentment for Harry engulfing her at the thought of being left out of things, of having to wait on the sidelines until someone deigned to give her a snippet of information, a tiny scrap to keep her happy. His cosy relationship with her mother irked her, albeit irrationally, she had to acknowledge.

It was proving such a contentious issue with her, that she had even suspected them of frequent meetings behind her back. Only the previous evening, she had telephoned her mother to chat about the new job; perhaps to divulge the contact with her grandfather.

'Your mother's out,' her father had said. 'She might be at Molly's.'

Angrily, Beth flicked over to the next page of the catalogue and began to translate, not into French this time but into German, which had never come as easily to her; a most rigid and austere language with none of the quirky, romanticisms of the Gauls.

A knock on the door disturbed her and she presumed it was Marjory.

'Come in, Marjory,' she called, not looking up. 'You know you don't have to knock.'

'Old habits and all that,' she heard Charlie Webster say.

'Oh, it's you.'

He feigned disappointment and clowned his way into the office, although his antics were not sufficiently amusing to make her laugh, not in her present frame of mind.

'I wish I could be Marjory,' he smiled, closing the door behind him and taking the chair at the other side of her desk. 'Maybe then you'd smile at me.'

Beth put down her pencil and looked at him, heartened to witness his discomfort. When she had the upper hand, she was pretty good at keeping it.

'I'm in a bad mood,' she said bluntly. 'Not much chance of a smile today, I'm afraid.'

He nodded, but lowered his gaze to the desk.

'You're not happy here then?'

Beth frowned. 'Yes, of course I'm happy here.'

'But you said you were in a bad mood.'

'That has nothing to do with here.'

'Ah,' he said brightly, and she could have kicked herself for insinuating that her bad mood was a result of her private life. 'That's good, that you're happy here. Mrs Wilson tells me you're wonderful.'

'She's pretty wonderful herself,' Beth responded, her hand hovering over the pencil.

'Am I keeping you from your work?' Charlie asked, following the progress of the hovering hand.

'Obviously.'

'Have I said something to upset you?'

'No, I told you I'm just in a bad mood. Some guy almost knocked me over this morning as I was crossing the road,' she lied, drawing attention away from her private life.

'Oh, I see,' he said, and, to her satisfaction, the corners of his mouth turned down. 'Hope you got his number.'

'Sadly, no.'

'Were you hurt at all?'

'Not as much as when you crashed into me on the stairs.'

Charlie laughed, although he must have known it was the daftest thing he could have done. Beth studied him for the moments he was laughing and was hard-pressed to keep her face straight.

'I'm sorry, Beth, but you're honestly the most delightful girl I've ever met, you really are.'

Graciously, she awarded him a smile. 'You're easily satisfied.'

His eyes met hers and she realised she had said the wrong thing. She stood up and moved to the window to hide the blush that was creeping across her cheeks.

'I like this office,' she said with her back to him. 'The view is lovely.'

'Sure is,' he said pointedly and she felt the blush deepen.

'Were you successful in finding new clients?'

'Yes, three as a matter of fact,' he told her, sounding surprised. 'It was great.'

Having banished the pink from her cheeks, Beth turned to look at him.

'Was there something specific you wanted me to translate?'

'No,' he replied, appearing confused. 'Why?'

'I was just wondering why you'd come in here.'

Taken aback at her abruptness, he stared at her momentarily and then stood up, saying brusquely, 'Methinks the lady hath tired of my scintillating presence. Forsooth, I shall not tarry longer.'

Beth tried to keep her face straight. Much to her disgust, however, she failed and burst out laughing.

'At last,' Charlie grinned, pausing at the door. 'I consider that's one up to me.'

With that, he opened the door and disappeared, leaving Beth in a worse mood than ever.

*

Grace was more than grateful for Harry's sympathetic support. Now, as she recalled how composed and relaxed he had been as she burdened him with her problems, she thought how much he had come to depend on him, especially when her spirits were low. With a twinge of guilt, she acknowledged it should be her husband to whom she turned at such times.

She listened to James upstairs, clomping around in his shoes, never wearing the slippers she bought for him. For the past hour, she had been dwelling on past memories – vivid and heartbreaking – brought to the forefront of her mind by her father's presence.

One of the most vivid memories was a rainy day in Dundee; standing on a shiny wet pavement, clutching her mother's hand, listening to Aunt Helen shouting for a policeman. It was a bewildering experience for a seven-year-old child.

'Stop that man! Get the police! Stop him, someone!'

'Grace?'

She turned quickly to see James in the doorway.

'Are you all right?'

'I've just been remembering old times,' she smiled. 'It's stupid, I suppose.'

'If it makes you unhappy, then it is stupid. It's odd that you should be gloomy about the past,' James said slowly. 'I thought that our past was happy.' Despite his concern, he made no attempt to advance into the room. 'Wasn't it happy?'

'Yes, it was,' Grace said quickly. 'I was over the moon when you came home from France, for good.'

'It's a strange phrase,' James smiled, but still not responding to her touch. 'Home for good. But it wasn't always good, Grace, I know it wasn't.'

'It was my fault mostly,' Grace admitted. 'And don't say it wasn't,' she cautioned before shifting her gaze back to her hands.

'All right, I won't then, but come and sit down, I'll make you something to drink.'

Grace laughed and shook her head.

'James, dearest, you wouldn't know your way round the kitchen without a map. I'll make us something to drink.'

They sat opposite each other at the oak table, and it seemed to Grace that it had been years since they had sat here together, spontaneously, out with meal times, free from the tedium of routine.

'I love you as much as I did then,' she heard him say, but his eyes were on the cup in front of him.

It was such a deviation from James's normal line of conversation, that Grace was unsettled: she had no idea how to respond. When she hesitated, James spoke again.

'We can't stay young forever, Grace.'

She forced a light-hearted laugh. 'We're an old married couple,' she told him, injecting an element of fun into the atmosphere.

'Is there something bothering you?' James asked, out of the blue.

'No, nothing.'

'You've been distracted lately.'

'Have I?'

'You would tell me, wouldn't you?'

Grace nodded. 'Of course I would. But there's nothing.'

James rose and picked up his cup. 'I'll just go and do some gardening, if you don't need me in here?'

'No, I'm fine.'

'Oh, by the way, Beth called last night.'

Grace began gathering up cups and saucers to give herself time to reply. 'When I was up at Lily's, you mean?'

'Is that where you were?'

Grace nodded. 'Poor Beth. She'll have wanted to tell me all about her first day in the office.'

'No doubt she'll phone again.'

'Of course.'

A few minutes later Grace stood at the kitchen window, watching James work; wondering at the ease with which she could lie to a man whom she had known for over twenty years, and yet baulk at the idea of withholding the truth from her son-in-law.

As for Beth, she would have to telephone the girl and make her peace.

*

Harry rattled the key in the lock and then checked that he had the right one. Just as he confirmed it was, the door opened and Beth was grinning at him.

'Don't tell me you've been sacked already,' he said as she stepped aside to let him in.

'Nope, the painter's back to finish off the varnishing, so Mr Webster said I could work at home.'

'Mr Webster? Sounds a bit formal.'

'Just the way I like it,' Beth said; and then grimaced.

Harry did not respond but she would be in no doubt that he had picked up the inference.

Keep it formal in case I dive into bed with the guy.

'How's your job?' she asked casually, following him into the kitchen.

'Oh, fine,' he smiled absent-mindedly, throwing his briefcase on the nearest chair and loosening his tie. 'God, I hate these things.'

'I love you in a suit.'

'Fancy a drink yet, or are you still on duty?'

'I hate people who are wittier than me.'

Harry glanced at her. 'I doubt if you'll find that many, sweetheart.'

'You, Gillespie,' she said, putting her arms around him and impeding the bottle opening, 'are the nicest man I know.'

'I'm not sure about the word '*nice*',' Harry smiled, disentangling her arms from his neck. 'Especially since it's not a true description of me.'

Beth stepped back and frowned at him. 'What? Of course you're nice.'

'Frank Gilmour wouldn't agree with you.'

'Who's he?'

'One of the partners.' Harry looked at Beth closely. 'Do you know him at all?'

'Never heard of him,' she shrugged and he knew it was the truth. 'Why?'

'He was asking about you a couple of days ago.'

'Was he? How odd. Oh, make mine a whisky for a change.'

They sat in the kitchen with the late afternoon sunshine seeping through the glass, casting small square boxes of light across the table. Beth sighed as the first sip of whisky touched her lips.

'This Gilmour chap might have designs on you, for all I know.'

'How many times do I have to tell you I'm crazy about you?'

'I can never hear you say it often enough.'

'Why is it I can't stay mad at you for longer than ten seconds?' Beth frowned.

'That's a bad thing?'

'Extremely.'

'Do me a favour.'

'Depends.'

Harry laughed at her expression and touched his glass to hers.

'Don't then.'

'You're annoying, did you know that?' she asked, the words belied by her smile.

'Of course, but you're not far behind me.'

'Flattery gets you anything. Tell me then, what's this favour you want?'

'Charlie Webster.'

'What about him?'

'Ask him, in a roundabout way naturally, if he knows Frank Gilmour.'

'Yes O.K., if it's important to you.'

'Oh, it is,' Harry smiled, and the element of unpleasantness in his tone reminded Beth how lucky she was to have this man on her side.

'Incidentally, I phoned Mum this morning, but the line was engaged for ages.'

'You intend to tell her about Thomas Blake?'

Beth must have heard the note of disapproval. 'Shouldn't I?'

93

Harry shrugged. 'Maybe you should wait.'

To his astonishment, she nodded agreement. 'She has a lot on her plate at the moment. You're right. I should wait.'

Harry's mind searched for a reasonable explanation for her change of heart. She might be apprehensive of falling out with Grace; or, could it be cowardice on her part; leaving it to him to broach the subject with her mother?

Either way, he suspected he would be the one to smooth things over.

*

Grace was perturbed when her husband demanded to know what was upsetting her. They were sitting outside, after their meal, with cups of tea on their laps, when he broached the subject, not casually as before, but purposefully, catching her unawares.

'Upsetting me?' she flustered, cheeks fiery red. 'There's nothing upsetting me.'

'I think there is,' he told her, looking right into her eyes. 'And the sooner you tell me the better.'

Grace struggled with the idea of bluffing her way out, telling him she was simply feeling unwell; something – anything – but not Thomas Blake. She had never intended to tell James.

'Come on, Grace,' he was saying impatiently. 'If you don't tell me, I'll ask Beth. She'll know.'

'She doesn't know anything,' Grace said firmly, and then realised her mistake.

'So, there is something.'

'It's not important.'

'I'll decide what's important,' James said, taking her cup and saucer and setting it aside. 'Now, please, tell me.' His fingers covered her hand and, despite the warmth of the evening, she felt her flesh cold.

'I didn't want you to know,' she began, and the hopelessness of her situation engulfed her. 'Oh, James, it's…' She burst into tears and he held her tightly.

Fully clothed, she lay on top of the bed listening to the sounds of children playing in the next garden; new people, not the friendliest neighbours since the Stewarts had moved on; but pleasant enough in the passing.

Grace was astonished at her stupidity: how could she have imagined that she could handle this situation herself? Now that she had confided in James she felt such a surge of relief that she wished she had done it sooner, rather than carry the burden alone. The only negative aspect now was that she had taken the boy into her confidence before her husband and so the relief was tinged with guilt.

Unfortunately, even after her confiding in James, her options remained unchanged: she had to meet her father and make it clear she wanted nothing to do with him; to get rid of him once and for all. Moreover, she would do it alone.

She had witnessed the hurt in the boy's eyes as she spurned his offer to accompany her, but her guilt had been assuaged by the need to keep Beth out of it. Harry's involvement would lead, inevitably, to Beth's. Whatever she did, Grace was determined to confine Thomas Blake's existence to as few people as possible.

*

Thomas Blake lay on the top of the bed listening to the muffled sound of traffic in the street. He had exchanged his earlier room at the front for this one at the back, although the furnishings and décor were hardly in the same class, with its Chinese restaurant wallpaper, discordant pine bedside tables; not to mention the flimsy lampshades available at any jumble sale for five bob.

He was pleased with the five bob idea, for he had been in this country for only a few weeks and yet already he had cottoned on to the modern slang words for various things; 'bob' for shilling; 'fuzz' for the police; 'groovy' as the new word for 'grand'; and ''pop' to describe the disgusting racked that was modern music.

He was endeavouring to retain his accent, however, believing it to be the most distinguishing aspect between him and the locals. Each time he met someone for the first time, the accent was quite a talking point.

'You must be from America,' they would say, looking at him as if he had dropped in from a distant planet.

'The States,' he would correct, for it was how Americans described their country. 'I'm from the mid-west.'

In truth, he had very little notion where the mid-west was, but he suspected that, unless they were geography teachers, neither would they.

From his relaxed position on the bed, his gaze wandered to the dressing table, to the neatly wrapped little box sitting primly beside his wallet, waiting for Charlotte Shepherd to open it and show her gratitude. Thomas gave a grunt of dissatisfaction: why did he always think of her as Charlotte Shepherd? She had been his wife. Had she not taken his name; borne his child? His mind dismissed the idea that she might have married again, borne more children. It was a step too painful.

After the first flush of courtship, he recalled her reluctance to get married, and how, at one stage, he had almost given up hope. Had it not been for his determination to… Thomas caught his breath at the implications.

*

'Thomas, you must stop this,' she was saying, her face upturned to his. 'It's no use. The sooner you realise it, the better for all of us. We can stay good friends, can't we?'

'Is that what you want?' he had asked her, utterly aghast at the idea.

'Yes,' she replied, but her eyes moved to her gloved hands.

'I don't believe you.'

'I don't care.'

'Yes, you do,' he persisted, grabbing her hands and forcing her to look at him. 'I know you love me, so don't deny it.'

Charlotte had shrugged, presumably because they both knew it would be pointless to deny it.

'It's not that easy,' was all she said, trying to wrestle her hands from his.

'It's easy for me,' he told her roughly, losing his patience. 'I love you and want to marry you, and what does it matter if my mother has other ideas? It's my life, my choice. Why can't you see that, Charlotte?'

'Because she'll just make our lives miserable, that's why.'

'And what can she do once we're married, tell me that? How can she possibly affect us one way or the other?'

'Please don't pretend you're naive, Thomas Charles Blake,' she had smiled, using his full name, the only person to do so. 'Your mother won't stand by and see you ruin your life on someone like me.'

'For Heaven's sake!' he had cried loudly, jumping up and frightening her. 'I refuse to listen to this nonsense about the bloody gentry and Jock Tamson's bloody bairns!'

She had sat still then, making no attempt to calm him, which she usually did; saying nothing. From time to time, in his meandering around the park bench, Thomas cast *furtive glances at her, to gauge her mood; but she was giving nothing away and, eventually, he had to strike up the conversation again.*

'Where you live and what your father does for a living is of no interest to me whatsoever, Charlotte, and you know that perfectly well.' He knelt down on one knee and took her hands once more. 'Please think about it, that's all I ask, just to think it over for a little while.'

'All right,' she smiled, raising her eyes to his. 'I promise I'll think about it.'

He resumed his seat beside her but they both knew that her answer would remain the same, no matter how long she took to think it over. As they sat in silence, however, Thomas had already come up with a plan that was foolproof.

*

He groaned at the memory of that hopeless day when she had promised to think it over, his eyes alighting again on the little box with her gift inside. Maybe she would even prefer this one to the original. It had certainly cost him the earth.

As the steeple clocks began to chime, Thomas felt the first tingle of excitement: he was about to meet his daughter for the first time; a sure sign that it would not be long before he and Charlotte were reaffirming their love for each other.

Thomas laughed aloud: he could hardly wait to court her again; but this time he had every hope of success.

Chapter Eleven

Grace rose early and had bathed and dressed by half past seven. She had been astonished at her deep sleep the previous night, and this morning she was feeling unexpectedly refreshed and calm. After a heated exchange of views, James had been persuaded not to go with her to Perth, but it had been a hard-fought victory and the doubt still lingered in Grace's mind that he might change his mind at the last moment.

'You're looking fine,' he told her over breakfast. 'You realise I won't be happy until you telephone me later.'

'As soon as I've got rid of him,' Grace assured her husband. 'I'll call your office and ask to speak to you.'

'Mr Dickson won't mind. I never get any calls. Unlike the office girls,' he added, censure clearly discernible.

'I'm seeing him at ten, so I should call you about quarter past.'

'As short a time as that?' James asked in surprise.

'Long enough, I should think,' Grace said lightly, standing up to clear away the dishes. 'I only have one thing to say to him.'

'But he may have more to say to you.'

Grace glanced at her husband briefly before placing the dishes in the sink.

'I doubt if he'll want to say anything after I've spoken.'

'Remember, you can always change your mind; let me go with you.'

'I have to do this on my own, James.'

He shrugged and left it at that, but Grace sensed his disapproval.

At half past nine, after a successful search through her wardrobe for suitable attire, she was preparing to lock up the house when she heard the telephone ring. Unwilling to let it go unanswered, she sighed and retraced her steps to the hall.

It was Harry.

*

Harry put down the receiver and settled back in his leather chair, ecstatic that he had something significant to add to her armoury, smiling to himself at the thought of the information he had just shared with her; thankful that he had remembered it, albeit at the last minute.

Had it not been for Beth's impromptu call to ask him to buy more wine on the way home, he would never have reminded her of Grace's meeting with Thomas Blake, he and Beth having exhausted the topic the previous night.

I wonder if she'll tell him about Charlotte?' Beth had asked casually after he agreed to pick up a bottle of fizz.

'What about Charlotte?'

'Did I forget to tell you? He doesn't know she's dead.'

'What?' Harry asked, astonished, his thoughts forging ahead.

'I decided not to tell him,' Beth had said with a triumphant little smile. *'I didn't think he deserved to know right away, thought I'd let him sweat a bit, you know?'*

Harry did know; and once she had hung up, he had immediately called Grace, hoping against hope that she was still in the house.

Now, as he turned to the first legal problem of his day, he hummed a little tune to himself and wished he could be a fly on the hotel reception wall.

*

Thomas had to change his shirt half an hour before the meeting. He had been so nervous, that the sweat was pouring off him by half past nine and though he had no time to shower, he had selected another crisp white shirt from his wardrobe, hurling the previous one into the laundry bag.

Fastening the buttons and tying his tie, his fingers were jittery. He swore several times, projecting his thoughts to how pathetic he would appear in his daughter's presence if he acted like a schoolboy in front of the Headmaster; which was what he was doing now.

'Shit!' he cursed, as the button pinged off and vanished from sight. 'That's all I need now,' he growled, pulling the collar together and wondering if the tie would hide the gap. With a glance at his watch, he reckoned it would have to.

At ten minutes to ten he closed the room door, locked it with the key – separated on the first day from its grotesque, plastic attachment – popped the key into his pocket, and walked to the top of the stairs.

*

Grace sat, calm and relaxed, hands in her lap, feet neatly together, emitting an impression of composure, a role she had played so many times before. Her lines were perfect, her mannerisms rehearsed at length and, apart from her ignorance of her father's script, she was ready.

It was the jacket she spotted first – a garish ochre colour – that only an arrogant man could wear; a man who wished to draw attention to himself.

Out of the corner of her eye she saw him descend the stairs and it took a gargantuan effort for her to sit still and breathe normally. Emboldened by the fact that it would be a full thirty seconds before he had his first sight of her, Grace used the time wisely, reciting in her head the only reason for meeting him.

Just as she sensed he would be seeing her for the first time, she looked away, out of the window, waiting for him to walk over.

'Excuse me,' she heard the voice say, and, slowly, she turned her head.

'It is… Grace, isn't it?'

'Yes,' she said, as if she had ordered a coffee.

'May I…?' he asked, glancing at the settee opposite her.

She shrugged politely and he sat down. Because it was obvious that he was more nervous than she was, Grace looked straight at him, satisfied to witness the apprehension in his eyes; having no intention of speaking first.

'I'm so grateful that you came,' he said, swallowing hard. 'I can understand how you feel…' He paused, as if expecting her to pass some comment and, when she remained silent, he continued, his eyes darting to and fro, sometimes on her face but more often on his hands. 'I can't expect you to be glad to see me, Grace, and I think I know how you feel about me, but, I never stopped loving Charlotte. She must know that, she knows me better than anyone.' He paused and glanced at her unresponsive form. 'Has she said anything about you meeting me?"

Grace shook her head, but still said nothing.

'She hasn't?' her father asked, perplexed. 'I thought she might…' The sentence was left hanging and, suddenly confronted by his daughter's intransigence, he appeared to lose his composure. 'This hasn't been easy for me either, you know,' he told her testily, meeting her impersonal gaze. 'You've no idea how much pain I've endured over the years, worrying about you and your mother, never having a moment's peace of mind. Aren't you going to say anything?'

'No,' Grace said flatly and her father seemed to shrink before her eyes.

'I have to see her, to explain...' He looked at Grace with such a plea in his eyes that she was glad her mother was dead: Charlotte Shepherd would not have been able to resist such a look.

'And she'll want to see me,' he said confidently. 'Now she knows I'm back. She does want to see me, doesn't she?' he added, less sure of himself now. Grace had to force herself to speak slowly.

'No, it's out of the question.'

Her father was stunned. Distraught, he looked away and fidgeted with his tie, and then he looked back at Grace, this time smiling, shaking his head with newly found optimism.

'I don't believe you. Charlotte would want to see me, I know she would. You haven't told her about me, have you?'

'No, I haven't,' Grace smiled. Despite the acrimonious situation, the image had an element of humour.

'I knew it!' her father declared, slapping the arm of the settee. 'You didn't tell her because you knew she'd want to see me. Isn't that the truth?'

Grace waited, forming the words in her head until she was certain she could do them justice. As she watched his reaction, saw it turning from despair into hope, from apprehension to arrogance, she felt a twinge of pity for the man; but in a disinterested way, as she might feel sorry for any stranger down on his luck.

'I didn't tell her,' Grace said tonelessly, but with an inner joy that was hard to conceal. 'Because she's dead.'

She refused to avert her eyes at the crucial moment and it afforded her the most immense pleasure to see the contortions of the man's face. For him to endure this agony was bad enough, but to endure it in front of a daughter who hated him and was happy to witness his agony must have added an extra twist to the knife. Grace waited but only for a moment. Without a further word, she rose from the settee and picked up her handbag.

'I never want to see you again,' she said, without rancour. 'I never want to hear from you again, or have you pestering any member of my family. In fact,' she concluded, lowering her voice. 'As far as I'm concerned, you don't exist.'

Making a huge effort not to hurry, Grace brushed past him and walked towards the exit.

Once in the street she paused and tried to remember where she had parked the car. As she glanced despairingly up the street, she caught sight of a familiar figure: it was James.

*

He drove in silence, allowing her time for her own, private thoughts, but she had been so heartened by the sight of him that her only thought was how much he loved her. To have stood outside the hotel, waiting for her, knowing the toll that such a meeting would take on her, fearing that she might be angry with him for not heeding her wishes.

Grace looked across at her husband and wondered how she could have been so insensitive as to exclude him from such an important issue.

'Thank you, James,' she said, touching his arm gently. 'I was so glad to see you.'

'So, I won't be made to stand in the corner with a cap on my head then?'

Grace laughed, the first time she had felt jolly all week.

'No, but you can make the lunch instead.'

'Oh, we're not going home for lunch.'

'We're not?'

'No, we're going to Beth's.'

Grace stared at him. 'But, you've never been to her new flat before.'

'Better late than never.'

'When did you arrange this?'

'Yesterday, when you were having a rest.'

'I'm speechless,' Grace said, glancing again at James. 'You're not joking, are you?'

'Here we are, and we're in luck, there's a parking space.'

'But it's too early for lunch, and how did you get away from work anyway, now that I come to think of it? And how did you get here?'

'Beth's at home, waiting for us, so we can have a chat before lunch, and as for your second question, Mr Dickson gave me time off when I said I had to fix a problem.' He turned to smile at her. 'I took the bus, which was a most interesting experience.'

'Now I know you must love me,' Grace said humorously.

'Oh, and Frank's sorry he can't come, but he sends his love and will see you tonight.'

Grace frowned. 'Does he know?'

'About your father turning up? Of course, he does. He's part of the family too.'

'Well, you seem to have had everything organised,' Grace said wryly and James turned to look at her.

'You may think you're on your own, Grace, and you may even want to be on your own, but I won't stand by and see you hurt. Not by anyone.'

*

Beth was hovering at the door when they reached the top of the stairs, her anxious frown being the first thing her mother spotted.

'Oh, Mum!' she cried, hurling herself at Grace and ignoring her father's cautionary glance. 'I was so worried about you. Are you all right? What did he say? What happened?'

'Beth,' James said sternly. 'Perhaps we can go in first?'

'Sorry.'

She led her mother into the kitchen and sat her down on the nearest chair before remembering that her father had never visited the flat before.

'You sit here, Mum, get your breath back, and I'll just whiz Dad round the place, let him see the grandeur of it all!'

'Will she be O.K.?' she whispered to her father once they were in the dining room.

'She'll be fine now, now that she's with us.' He stood in the middle of the room, casting admiring glances at the furnishings. 'Very nice, Beth, very nice. The two of you have done very well.'

'Thanks,' Beth grinned, noting the oblique reference to Harry. 'But you ain't seen nothin' yet.' She took her father's arm and led him into the sitting room.

'Ah, this is grand,' her father said, eyes widening. 'But it's cosy too. Large but cosy. You have the same good taste as your mother.'

'You're right.'

'I'm always right,' her father laughed. 'Goodness me, this room is huge.'

'I thought so too, until the piano arrived. Come and see it. It's fabulous!'

*

Alone in the kitchen, Grace smiled to hear the opening notes of the 'Moonlight Sonata' float through. It brought her back to the present, for she had been sitting in a trance for the past few minutes, hearing and seeing nothing.

She stood up and wandered to the window but, instinctively, drew back in case he should be down there somewhere, spying, snooping, trying to find her. She sighed with exasperation: surely, she had told him he did not exist to her, and was that not enough to send him away forever? Now, only twenty minutes after walking out on him and being so certain she had done the right thing, the first doubts were clamouring in her head. Would he be the kind of man who gave up so readily? In her heart of hearts, Grace thought she knew the answer.

*

Harry was out of the office by twelve, having cleared it with Andrew Barclay. He had made the decision not to defer to Frank Gilmour until Beth had discovered if there were a connection between him and Webster; which he suspected there would be.

'Of course you can have an early lunch,' Andrew had told him, obviously mystified that Harry felt he had to ask. 'You're free to come and go at any time, as long as you get the work finished by the end of the day.'

'Thanks, I'll be back by one thirty at the latest,' Harry smiled. 'And I'll work on until my desk's cleared.'

'Special occasion?' Andrew asked cautiously.

'Sorry?'

'Just being nosey about the early lunch. Apologies, old chap, didn't mean to pry.'

'It's a special day for Grace, my wife's mother.'

'We all call them the mother-in-law,' Andrew laughed. 'The dreaded mother-in-law.' If he had expected Harry to join in, he was disappointed; in fact, in the face of polite indifference, he appeared silly. 'Just a poor joke,' he added. 'See you later.'

'Thanks, goodbye,' Harry smiled, wondering why people so often made fools of themselves without any assistance from him.

He glanced at his watch and walked briskly along the street, resisting the temptation to listen for footsteps behind him. For the past few days he had imagined – probably erroneously – that he was being followed, but he was beginning to think he had been watching too many Hammer horror movies.

As he passed Grace's car at the kerb, he noticed James Melville's jacket on the back seat. Harry paused and took a deep breath. Any hope of having Grace to himself was dashed immediately. Also, he had the added problem of socialising with a father-in-law whose antagonism towards him was well documented.

He ran up the stairs two at a time and steeled himself.

'Oh, here's Harry now,' he heard Beth call out, and she flew to meet him in the hallway. 'So glad you're here,' she whispered in his ear as he hugged her. 'I'm hopeless at things like this.'

His eyes asked the question: things like what? But she had moved off and was already back in the kitchen. Harry hung up his jacket and went to see how Grace was.

*

Whenever she saw him, Grace nodded and gave him a reassuring smile. Later, she would thank him for the invaluable snippet of information he had passed to her, the 'addition to her armoury', as he had termed it, but which had turned out to be the only weapon she wanted to wield.

'Grace, are you all right?' Harry asked, after a brief smile to James Melville. 'Did he cause you any trouble?'

101

She shook her head. 'None at all. In fact, after I told him about my mother he just seemed to give up.'

'We're grateful for your support,' James said suddenly, stepping forward and offering his hand to Harry, who, surprised though he was, took it.

'Family's important to me,' he said, wondering if it sounded contrived.

'And to me,' James smiled. 'Thank you, Harry. I know that you've been a great help to Grace, and I...'

'Oh, come on,' Beth butted in, and Harry was astonished at her courage in interrupting her father. 'Let's go and get a comfy seat next door and have some wine to celebrate.'

'I don't think it...' Grace began and then changed her mind.

'You don't think it what?' Beth frowned. 'Is there something you're not telling us about him, and what he said to you?'

'No, honestly, we hardly exchanged two sentences. It's just that he may....I mean, once he's had time to mull it over, perhaps he might persist.'

Harry glanced at James, who shook his head imperceptibly, as if to caution against prolonging this line of conversation.

'Beth's right,' James said, taking his wife's hands and pulling her to her feet. 'Let's all go and have that drink, and maybe our daughter can play the new piano for us?'

Beth, who never needed a second invitation to fling her fingers around a keyboard, jumped to her feet.

'I only take requests that I'm able to play,' she laughed. 'No melody that has more than one sharp, please!'

As they settled down with their drinks and prepared to be entertained to the full version of the 'Moonlight Sonata', Grace did her best to relax. Despite the fact that the whole problem of her father might not have been resolved, she had, at least, met him, made it quite clear that he was not welcome in her life. To be hell-bent on pursuing his original course of action after such a blatant rejection by his daughter would surely be the most foolhardy decision Thomas Blake could make. The trouble was that she had no idea what the man was like, no idea of his character or even if he were capable of malice.

Malice! She could hardly believe she was using such a word in relation to her own father; a man who had inspired such a profound an unwavering love in Charlotte Shepherd that she had defended him to her dying day. Irrationally, Grace had a growing sense of having betrayed her mother's memory. Was there something she was refusing to see, something that...?

'Grace?' she heard Harry whisper beside her. 'Feeling better?'

'I love when Beth plays,' she smiled back at him, aware it was not a response to the question. 'I could listen to her all day.'

'It's not the playing I mind,' Harry said, repressing a smile. 'It's the bloody practising.'

'You know, I knew there was a reason I was happy to see her married and out of the house.'

'I heard that!' Beth called, in the middle of an intricate passage of the Sonata. 'Practice makes perfect you always told me.'

After the last notes had faded away, James, who had been standing at the piano during his daughter's performance, patted her on the shoulder as he moved off.

'That's the best you've ever played it,' he told her, and Grace saw the look of sheer joy on Beth's face.

'Thanks, Dad, you can take the hat round for me while I slave over a hot stove.'

'You're doing the cooking?' Harry asked. 'That'll be the day.'

An hour later, as they prepared to leave the flat and go their separate ways, Grace had yet to commit herself one way or the other as to the success or failure of her meeting with her father; but the pleasure she had derived from her family's company this past few hours was a heartening aspect. James was right: she was not alone in this; she had her family around her.

*

From his position at the far end of the street, Thomas watched the group leave the block of flats and congregate at the silver car. Suddenly, and to his horror, he was filled with an overpowering urge to ruin the happy state of their family.

'Steady on, old boy,' he told himself quietly, revising his current train of thought. 'Just calm down, think rationally.'

He might never forgive the brutal manner his daughter had employed to break the news about Charlotte's death, nor for her displaying such delight as she told him; but she was Charlotte's daughter too and he had loved the woman every single moment of every single day and he would not resort to malice.

There was another aspect to it as well: maybe the Shepherds had concealed the truth of the matter; perhaps Grace was ignorant of Charlotte's absolute refusal to join him; perhaps her opinion had been disfigured by a lie.

Thomas's heart mellowed a little at the thought of his daughter's being lied to, for there was nothing in the world he himself hated. No, he would not employ underhand means against the girl; but he was determined to have his say, to at least make her listen to his side of the story.

He waited until the silver car had disappeared round the corner, waited until the two youngsters had gone their separate ways, back to work presumably, and then he began the trek back to the hotel. The first thing he would do the next day was to check out of the George and find rented accommodation. He was here for the long haul.

Part Two: 1970

Chapter One

The September sun was beating down relentlessly and turning the interior of the car into a furnace, or what Beth imagined a furnace to be. She lowered the window and hung her head out, endeavouring to cool herself with the rush of passing air. The trouble was, the air itself was hot.

'Are we nearly there?' she asked Harry, who still appeared as cool as the proverbial cucumber.

'You sound just like our kids will sound one day.'

Beth flinched to hear the word again, for he had mentioned 'kids' or 'children' several times on the journey down. It may be true that she was not getting any younger, but – what the heck – she was only twenty-five, or was it four? She had plenty time yet before she had to endure the rigours of childbirth, the end to her freedom and the ignominy of being tethered to the back green.

'Was that Brignolles we just passed?'

'Oh we left that ages ago,' Harry said, eyes on the twisting road ahead. 'We should hit Le Lavandou in about an hour, maybe less.'

'And the first thing I'm going to do is throw myself into the sea and not come out for a week.'

'Just imagine the state of your skin.'

'Do you ever notice my skin?'

Harry braked sharply to avoid a cyclist, an old man wobbling like a jelly across the road, a French breadstick under his arm.

'What kind of daft question is that? Of course I notice your skin. I crawl all over it once a week, sometimes more.'

Beth giggled. 'That's the second thing I'm going to do when we get there.'

'Think again, sweetheart, if you're skin's to be like a prune.'

She laughed and turned to look at his profile, stretching her arm across the back of his seat and allowing her fingers to touch his neck.

'It sounds funny, when you say things like 'daft'.'

'Funny?'

'Yeah, with your uppercrust, plummy accent, all hoighty-toighty.'

'Is that how I sound?' Harry asked, knowing that he did.

'Absolutely. In fact, I often have to look twice, in case it's Prince Philip.'

'You should be so lucky.'

'I think I am,' Beth said and there was no teasing in her tone.

'Well, I could have told you that,' Harry smiled, denying her the right to be serious.

Beth yawned. 'Golly, I'm knackered,' she said without thinking and immediately braced herself for a bawling out.

'Don't say things like that,' she was told brusquely. 'It's vulgar.'

'Sorry.'

'Oh look, here's the turn off at last. Not long now.'

They arrived in the town just after five o'clock, in time to book in to the hotel and have a snooze, before finding a good restaurant. From the outside, the building appeared ancient, but inside it had been modernised to a high degree, the only modern part that interested Beth being the new toilet. On the way down, regardless of the grandeur of the establishment, the toilet had consisted of two raised footprints, a hole and a flushing mechanism that swamped your feet before you could dive from the cubicle.

'Oh, heavenly!' she cried as she opened the door to the bathroom. 'A real loo at last!'

Harry shook his head. If he had charged her a pound for every time she had moaned about the state of French toilets, he would be a couple of hundred francs up. Beth could be mind-numbingly dogmatic if she had the slightest grievance, although he himself had not been particularly enamoured of the Paris pissoirs.

'I'm sure it will smell all the sweeter, my love,' he retorted sarcastically, as he examined what the room had to offer.

'I thought you said I was vulgar?' she asked, her head round the bathroom door. 'That's even worse.'

'May I remind you that no one does it perfumed.'

'Disgusting man,' she muttered, disappearing into the bathroom and closing the door.

Having satisfied himself as to the facilities in the room, Harry wandered to the balcony and looked down at the street. The hotel was perfectly placed in the centre of Le Lavandou and their room was equally suitable; on the second floor, overlooking the beach, with the entertainment of the street vendors setting up on the esplanade and the hubbub of café life beneath them. He sighed and stretched his arms above his head, refraining from sitting down, for he had been sitting in the car for days.

He leaned on the balcony railing and wondered how Grace was coping without him.

'The South of France?' she had asked, an anxious tremor in her voice. 'As far away as that?'

'Grace, it's only a few hours' flight home if you need us.'

'But by car,' she said. 'Such a long journey.'

'You have the hotel address and phone number. Just call, even just to say you're fine.' He had looked at her, hoping she did not see how reluctant he was to leave her. 'Remember, pick up the phone and keep in touch. And don't worry, I'll take good care of her,' he added.

She had nodded and smiled, but her eyes had conveyed to him that her anxiety over his absence was not related to Beth.

'Look, we've heard nothing from him since the day you met at the hotel, well over a year ago,' Harry had reminded her soothingly. 'He's long gone, Grace, out of your life forever. I promise you,' he vowed with less confidence than he was feeling, 'that he'll never give you any more trouble.'

'Have a good holiday,' she had told him, and it was almost a dismissal of his promise. She was right, of course: how could he possibly promise something that was completely out with his control?

His last sight of her had been at the door of the cottage, standing quite forlornly, such an expression of distress in her eyes that he had almost cancelled the holiday there and then; which would have been financial idiocy, not to mention grounds for divorce...

Now, in the soft light of the Mediterranean afternoon, he breathed in the scent of pine and sea and resolved to have the time of his life. Well, it would be the best time he could have without Grace anyway.

*

Lucy Webster rang the doorbell and waited. The cool breeze that had sprung up in the morning was whistling along Lily Morris' garden path like a steam train, slicing through Lucy's thin jacket and leaving her breathless.

Within seconds, the door opened and Lily ushered her in quickly, closing the heavy door immediately against the cold.

'Gosh,' said Lucy, rubbing her hands together. 'It's like winter out there, and only the middle of September too.'

'I've got the fires on,' Lily said, leading the way into her best room. 'You'll soon get warmed up. Oh, and I've a nice sherry too, the best way of heating yourself up I always find.'

As they entered the parlour, Lucy was pleased to see that Grace was there, already ensconced in the most comfortable chair, face flushed from the heat of the room.

'Trust you to beat me to it,' she laughed, taking the chair opposite. 'You've certainly got the best spot.'

She was surprised when Grace did not give up her seat, for it was typical of the woman to do so; ever willing to sacrifice her own comfort for her friends.

'I was freezing,' Grace told her, wiggling her toes at the fire. 'Can you believe that it's still summer?'

'And here's just the thing we need,' Lily said behind them. 'Sherries all round and then the others will have arrived and we can get started.'

The three of them drank in relative silence, lulled by the crackle of the fire and the ticking of Lily's mantle clock.

'Is Molly coming?' Lucy asked eventually, the first to drain her glass.

'Yes, she is,' Grace confirmed. 'I spoke to her this morning and she mentioned she'd be here.'

'She's always late,' Lily said, a stickler for punctuality. 'And Joanna too, but we're not in a hurry. I daresay we can wait.'

'We need some men,' Lucy said without thinking, and Lily laughed.

'Speak for yourself, I manage fine on my own.'

'You know what I mean,' Lucy smiled with some embarrassment, and Grace was touched by the woman's old-fashioned values; similar to her own.

'Bobby Findlay said he might join,' Lily remarked, face flushed with the sherry. 'Oh, and whatsisname, the reporter for the *P.A.* the one that fancied Grace all these years ago.'

Lucy gave Grace a wide-eyed stare. 'Oh, sounds interesting.'

'She's having you on,' Grace said, although her heart lurched. 'Graham was only being polite.'

'Liar,' Lily laughed. 'He was completely smitten with you, still is probably. We'll have to be careful not to cast the two of you as the lovers in Romeo and Juliet.'

'Now you're being silly,' Grace smiled tolerantly. 'He's one of the nicest men in the village.'

'Doesn't stop him having a roving eye,' said Lily, determined to have the last word. 'Anyway, he's keen to join, for obvious reasons,' she added quickly with a sly glance at Grace. 'Then there's Ronnie. I might be able to twist his arm.'

'That would defeat the purpose,' Lucy grinned. 'Unless you wanted him to play a one-armed pirate.'

'There's been too much sherry in this conversation and not enough sense.' Lily said, to the amusement of her guests. Further comment was delayed by the sound of the doorbell.

'I'll go,' Lucy offered, jumping up. 'You sit here, Lily, rest your legs.'

Lily, however, rose almost as soon as Lucy had left the room and gathered up the sherry glasses.

'If they see these, they'll all want some,' she frowned. 'I'll just pop them in the sink and be right back.'

Left alone, Grace's eye focussed on the calendar above the fireplace: only five days to go until they started home again and she could hardly wait. She missed Harry more than she had anticipated, for, in the past few months, he had been a constant source of reassurance to her; telephoning her every day to ensure she was fine, dropping in to see her on his way to see a client in the area. She knew it was foolish, but she had come to rely on the boy far too much recently, and his absence was unsettling.

Lucy re-entered the room with Graham Smeaton in her wake, the *P.A.* reporter who had favoured Grace Melville in his articles about the Dramatic Society in the '50s.

'Grace,' he beamed, and it was clear to everyone that the man was thrilled. 'You're something of a stranger, aren't you?'

'Well, I could say the same about you,' Grace smiled, taking his hand in an old-fashioned greeting, her mind flying back to the heady days of their romance.

'I keep meaning to pop in,' Graham said, taking the chair nearest to hers. 'But I'm always worried in case you're busy and I'd be taking up your valuable time.'

'Oh, I'm never busy,' she smiled. 'In fact, I'm getting so lazy these days that I keep expecting James to sack me.'

'You'd not be short of a job if he did.'

Grace glanced at Lily, who shrugged and pulled a face behind Graham's back. As if suspecting he had taken friendship a step too far, the poor man blushed and added:

'I didn't mean... I only meant...'

'Graham, for Heaven's sake,' Grace smiled, patting his arm. 'You're among friends. Don't worry.'

'Still, it was a stupid thing to say,' he said apologetically.

'So,' chipped in Lucy hastily. 'Are there any other men in the village you can persuade to join us?'

'I think so, but you know how it is nowadays, with folks stuck in front of their televisions every night. Years ago,' he smiled with a glance towards Grace. 'It was all home entertainment, isn't that so, Grace?'

'And much more fun too.'

'Do you still play the piano and sing?'

'Oh, I sometimes give the keys a rattle, now that Beth's away and the piano's not used so much.'

A silence ensued and Lucy took advantage of it to change the subject.

'How many years is it since the Society has met?'

'Not since the late '50's,' Lily replied. 'Grace here was our star.'

'I thought Joanna was pretty good,' Grace said, evoking a sigh from Lily.

'Aye, you would. If she'd spent as much time learning her lines as she did making eyes at all the men, she'd have been the darling of Hollywood.'

'Lily,' Grace said reprovingly. 'She tried her best, you know, we all did.'

'Do you remember Alice Cameron?' Graham suddenly asked.

'Yes, of course,' Grace said. 'She and I write regularly.'

'Mum heard that she's divorced now,' Graham said, and the effect on Grace was profound.

'Divorced?' she asked, aghast, sitting on the edge of her seat. 'But, that can't be right. Surely, she'd have told me.'

Graham shrugged. 'Oh well, maybe Mum got it wrong,' he smiled, but it was clear to them all that the man was only trying to placate Grace.

The doorbell rang once more and, this time, Lily stood up and waved Lucy back into her chair.

'That'll be Molly, and maybe Joanna. We are definitely going to need more men!'

'It can't be right about Alice,' Grace frowned to Lucy. 'I'm sure she'd have told me if she'd been having any problems at home. I'm sure she would.'

'Of course she would,' Lucy said calmly, although she could know nothing of the nature of the two women's friendship. 'No need to worry over nothing, my dear.'

Grace smiled and nodded but, settling back in her chair once more, she was suddenly aware that her casual response to Alice's desire to visit had not been the most considerate thing to do, particularly if her friend were going through a bad patch in her marriage. Trust Grace Melville to have been only thinking of herself; as usual.

*

Beth's idea of a swim was to wallow in shallow water for twenty minutes and then clamber back to her beach towel for another hour's sunbathing. She had lost sight of Harry, far off shore now and hardly visible, and as usual she was beginning to fret.

Being the middle of the day, the beach was almost deserted, with only the 'mad dogs and Englishmen out in the mid-day sun.' She examined her arms and legs, satisfied that they had assumed their normal golden hue; unlike the girl up the beach from her, whose red shoulders looked painful, even from a distance.

Not for the first time in her life, Beth Melville put up a silent prayer of gratitude for having inherited her father's skin. Poor Frank, with his fair, sun-resistant skin, had always had to cover up in the heat of the day, even in Scotland, where Beth and her father could lie outdoors from morning 'til night without adverse effects.

She glanced at her watch and suddenly wondered where her brother would be at this very moment: sitting behind his teller's desk in a claustrophobic, stuffy bank... He had been so thrilled at gaining two Higher grades – Maths and English – and she had poured scorn on him at the time, but at least he had a well-paid job with reasonable hours and good 'perks', the cheap mortgage 'perk' being the one she envied herself. Almost a third of Harry's salary went towards their own mortgage, whilst her contribution, modest though it was, helped with household bills and groceries.

She sighed at the banality of her thoughts: lying on an exclusive beach on the Riviera, surrounded by azure sky and sparkling sea and here she was dredging up thoughts of mortgages and the price of sausages.

'Honestly!' she said aloud, attracting the attention of the peanut seller.

'You buy?' he asked, and Beth wondered why these men were always the handsomest men on the planet.

'No, thank you,' she replied, never in French, much to Harry's disgust, and the youth passed on.

'What's the point of having a language degree and expecting me to do all the talking?' he had asked angrily the first time they bought something in the north of France.

'Because you're the boss,' Beth had quipped brightly, hoping it might pacify him.

'And you're the linguist,' he retorted, turning on his heel and leaving her to pay for the bread and cheese.

Once they had entered the land of *supermarches*, of course, the problem had disappeared, for they simply took stuff off the shelves, placed it in the trolley and steered it to the check-out, where Beth handed over a huge amount of cash and the girl gave her back two centimes.

'Do we really need tins of anchovies?' Harry had frowned at her as they had unloaded their first trolley-load of at the hotel. 'We're half board here, remember? Dinner's included.'

'Yes, but we've a packed lunch to take to the beach,' Beth had smiled back. 'And you're always telling me I'm lazy, so I'm on the lunches to prove you wrong.'

Now, as her eyes scanned the sea for the top of his blond head, she was not so sure that tins of anchovies had been such a great idea: too fishy to use on a sandwich, too salty to eat on their own, she was wondering how she could use them up. The welcome sight of Harry's head stopped her rambling thoughts. She lay on her stomach and picked up the book she was reading:

'*Madame Bovary*,' by Flaubert; in French for the first time, to impress the natives.

A few minutes later Harry appeared, shaking cold water on her searing back and making her jump.

'Ow! You rotter!'

He laughed and towelled himself dry, flopping down beside her and laying a cool hand across her *derriere.*

'Watch it, stranger, we haven't been introduced.'

'In that case,' Harry whispered in her ear. 'I'm the man who's intent on ravishing you later.'

Beth turned on to her back and closed her eyes. 'Oh, really? Any chance of a preview then, to let me know if you're any good at it?'

She heard the soft laugh, sensed his mouth closing on hers, felt his hand on her neck.

'Mm, I think you'll do,' she told him as he lay on the mat beside her. 'Where did you say you learnt your love-making?'

'From a harlot in Perth,' Harry replied, much to the delight of his wife.

'Flattery gets you everywhere.'

'Are you happy, Beth?' he asked, out of the blue.

'Yes, of course I'm happy,' she replied, turning to look at him. 'Are you?'

'Utterly.'

'And I should think so too. Glamorous companion, gorgeous hotel, sun, sea and sand – the three 's's.'

'You've forgotten one.'

'What?'

Harry rolled over and played with the string of her bikini top.

'Sex. You forgot that 's',' he said with a look in his eyes that made Beth's heart skip a beat.

'Wish it was later,' she sighed.

'It won't do you any harm to be patient.'

*

They lay in the hot sun, each with their own thoughts. The only thing on Harry's mind, however, was not sex, but how Grace was managing without him and how desperate he was to see her again.

*

Beth was too impatient to wait: as soon as they had showered off the sand and sun cream from their bodies, she dragged Harry to the bed, refusing to take 'no' for an answer. He had never been able to resist her advances, not in over three years of marriage and he presumed that it would always be so. As her fingers began their journey around the small of his back, however, and as he smiled down at her soft mouth, anticipating an hour of self-indulgent pleasure, he was suddenly presented with an image, not of Beth but of Grace, lying beneath him, waiting for his kiss.

'Shit!'

'What is it?' Beth asked in alarm as he leaped from the bed.

'Shit, shit!' he repeated and because he cursed so rarely she was scared.

'Harry, tell me, for Heaven's sake, what's wrong?'

He took several deep breaths in an attempt to steady himself, began wandering around the room aimlessly, naked, not caring if anyone saw him as he passed the window.

'Harry,' he heard Beth whimper behind him and, suddenly aware of how it must seem to her, he turned and picked up his robe, wrapping it around him-self and tying it loosely; and then he looked at her, wondering how the hell he was going to get out of this.

'Beth, I'm so sorry, honestly, I'm really so sorry.'

'But, what is it?' she persisted, when all he wanted her to do was go away and leave him alone. 'You can tell me, surely?'

He sat on the edge of the bed and she moved beside him, tentatively reaching for his hand. For a few moments his mind ran through several possible explanations, but it was hopeless; he could think of nothing that would sound at all reasonable to her. She spoke first, however, and saved his life.

'Look, I know you weren't keen to...well, you know...have sex just now. It's my fault, Harry, I'm just too pushy, I know that.' She gazed at him with tears in her eyes and, despite his situation, he thought her the loveliest creature on earth. 'Forgive me?'

He smiled and shook his head. 'Beth, sweetheart, it's my fault, not yours, and there's nothing to forgive. Come on, get back to bed, let's...'

'No!' she said loudly, and he had to admit to some relief. 'I promise not to be so bossy, to push you around. I don't mean to.'

'Beth, you're not bossy, or pushy. Come on, cheer up. Let's get dressed and go and paint the town.'

'Great!' she said happily and his heart lurched at the speed with which she had given in to him. 'I'll wear my sexiest outfit.'

As she raked in the wardrobe for her red, wrap-over dress, Harry sat on the bed, slowly recovering from the events of the past five minutes; but even when he had dressed and was satisfied that his mood was back to normal, he had a tiny doubt in the recesses of his mind that the problem had been postponed; not resolved.

*

Arm-in-arm, they wandered along the esplanade, glancing briefly at the wares of the vendors, laid out in stalls by the sea wall, but buying nothing. Beth had eyed some of the African carvings with the intention of buying one for her mother but Harry had talked her out of it.

'She won't like that sort of thing,' he said dismissively, walking on.

'How do you know she won't?' Beth had asked him, irritated that he was presuming to know what her mother liked. 'I've known her longer than you and I can assure you, that's exactly the sort of thing she likes.'

'Well, buy it then,' Harry had called over his shoulder, but by then she had begun to doubt the wisdom of her choice and had followed on reluctantly.

Now, as they lingered by the jewellery stall, Harry picked up a necklace, a replica of a tiny seahorse encased in coloured silicon.

'Now, that's the kind of thing Grace would like,' he told Beth, turning it over in his hand and examining the detail. 'If I were you, I'd buy it for her.'

With that, he walked on, leaving her in a quandary.

She caught up with him, the necklace in her handbag and her wallet depleted by several francs.

'You'll be pleased to know I bought it,' she said moodily, linking her arm in his.

He smiled down at her with such affection that she melted.

'She'll love it, Beth, just wait and see.'

'How about a glass of wine?' she asked, pointing to their favourite café.

'Only if you're paying. I've left my wallet at the hotel.'

111

'Typical! Don't you feel any shame at being a kept man?'

'No, and mine's a dry Martini,' Harry smiled, sitting down on one of the chairs on the pavement.

'What? You never drink Martini.'

'I do now,' he said, pulling out the chair beside him. 'Sit down and I'll snap my fingers at the waiter.'

'He'll bop you one if you do,' Beth reminded him, recalling the previous night's incident when the boy in question had slapped one of the customers.

'What was all that about?' Harry had asked, eyebrows raised at the fracas.

'Sounds like his ex-girlfriend,' Beth had whispered, somewhat disappointed. 'He told her never to go back to the house again. Wouldn't it have been much more fun if she'd been a complete stranger?'

'Sometimes I worry about you, Beth Melville.'

'So,' Beth was saying now. 'One dry Martini and a glass of Chablis coming up.'

As she made her way to the bar, Harry felt his mood changing for the worse: after a couple of drinks and a cosy chat, he would be expected to go back to the hotel room and make love to his wife. Under normal circumstances it was a prospect to relish. Tonight, however, if there were anything he could do to avoid it, he would be the happiest man in the world.

*

Grace sighed and laid down her book, a pictorial record of Scottish tartans she was researching for a word competition. She glanced at the clock and could hardly believe it was only half past eight. Surely, she had been poring over this book for hours; not just twenty minutes?

Hearing her sigh, James looked across, probably thinking that her headache was returning; the headache that had plagued her for days; despite her constant swallowing of Askit powders, sometimes up to half a dozen a day.

'You should have an early night,' he suggested tentatively, for in her present mood he knew she was likely to be uncooperative. After her initial gratitude for supporting her over Thomas Blake's sudden appearance in the area, Grace acknowledged she had become withdrawn and taciturn.

'Good idea,' she replied, interrupting his thoughts and surprising him with her eagerness to retire so early. 'I think I will.'

'You go up,' James said, laying his newspaper aside. 'I'll bring you up a hot chocolate if you like?'

She rose wearily from her chair and endowed him with a fleeting smile.

'Thanks, that would be nice.'

'I'll be up in five minutes, Cherie.'

She paused at the door and looked back at him, her hand on the doorknob.

'You haven't called me that for years.'

'Haven't I?'

'It's very nice,' Grace smiled. 'Reminds me of the old days.'

He nodded but said nothing, for she had fallen into the habit recently of re-marking on 'the old days' a dozen times in any given week; not that there was anything untoward about an occasional nostalgic perusal of the old photos that had lain gathering dust in the attic; but she had brought the box down a few weeks ago and every time James had walked in on her unexpectedly she had been engrossed it one or other of them, hardly glancing at him as he entered the room.

Grace suspected he was disappointed at her recent moods, especially after her affectionate response in the wake of her woeful tale about her father. She had felt like her old self; but the feeling had been short-lived.

Ten minutes later, she heard James downstairs, opening and closing cupboards to find what he needed. Rather than be amused that he knew where nothing was, she felt a surge of anger. If anything ever happened to her, how would he manage on his own? Or, more likely, would he marry again; find someone else to chain to the kitchen sink?

Immediately, she was ashamed of such uncharitable notions. Besides, it was Thursday today, and her spirits rose at the prospect of Beth and Harry arriving home the day after next. She wondered if they had missed her at all.

'I know what's wrong with you,' Molly had told her several days previously, as they sat learning their lines for the new play.

'There's nothing wrong with me,' Grace had smiled, hoping to fend off a lecture.

'Yes, there is,' Molly said firmly, finger on her next line in her copy of the play. 'You're missing Beth, that's what.'

'Well of course I'm missing Beth. I hate when she's away, even in Perth. You can imagine how I feel when she's hundreds of miles away, and in a strange country.'

'It's not strange to Beth,' Molly corrected. 'She speaks French like a native, so you told me. She'll be quite at home there, I should think.'

It had not been the kindest thing to say to Grace, for she had dwelt upon the remark for days, dreading that her daughter would find she preferred France and decide to move there on a permanent basis.

And Harry too!

She had shuddered suddenly, although Molly's kitchen was warm. Eyes on the page in front of her, Grace continued to read her lines, but Molly butted in quickly.

'Are they still as happy as ever, the two of them?'

Grace raised her gaze to meet Molly's. 'Of course they are.'

Molly shrugged. 'Young people nowadays, honestly.'

'Which ones do you have in mind?' Grace heard herself ask, perhaps rudely, although Molly did not appear to notice.

'We took our marriage vows seriously, didn't we, Grace? Yet some of them aren't even bothering to get married now, far less take it seriously. Johnnie, for instance.'

'Jonathon? I thought he was engaged.'

'He is, but that's just the point,' Molly had said, lowering her voice despite the two of them being alone in the house. 'He's been engaged for months, and no mention of marriage. And,' she leaned forward confidentially. 'They're even sleeping together.'

'Lots of them do now.'

'Anyway, I've no say in the matter, so I'm wasting my breath.'

The finality of Molly's tone put an end to her foray into the social ills of the modern day and, with a sigh, Grace had turned her attention to the play.

Now, in the darkness of her bedroom, Grace stared out at the gloomy shapes of the flowerbeds beneath her window, viewing the scene with melancholy eyes. She wondered if she should take James's advice and go to the doctor's, to find out exactly what might be ailing her and if he could recommend a remedy.

It was the inconsistency of her moods that alarmed Grace most: one day she loved James with as much ferocity as at the beginning, but the next, she kept recalling the many disagreements along the way; most involving his determination to brow-beat her into accepting his decisions. It was proving a perplexing time for her; a time of so many conflicting thoughts that sometimes she convinced herself she was going mad; and it was all because of her father.

The door opened slowly and James came in with her mug of hot chocolate, and it was odd to see how hesitant he appeared to be to enter the room at all.

'Here you are, dearest, just the way you like it.'

'Thanks, it smells delicious. Did you make it with hot milk?'

'Yes, I remembered the way you do it.'

She looked at him closely and saw the anxiety in his face, anxiety for her state of well-being, anxiety because he loved her; and, as always, when she witnessed the extent of his love for her, Grace was besieged by her failings as a wife.

'James…'

He turned on his way to the door and glanced back at her.

'Yes?'

'I do love you, James.'

She almost winced to see the joy on his face.

'I know you do,' he said, remaining at the door. 'And I love you.'

'I think I'll go and see the doctor tomorrow, find out if he can improve my mood swings.'

James's joy increased and she thought how easy it had been to make him happy. This time he did move away from the door but came back to hold her hands and give her an affectionate kiss on the cheek.

'That's a good idea,' he told her. 'I've been so worried about you. He'll maybe be able to help you.'

Grace nodded. 'I'm sure he will. I'll go tomorrow morning, first thing.'

Alone again, she sat looking at the hot chocolate, recalling the numerous nights she and her mother had rushed home in adverse weather to sit by the fire with hot drinks, feet wriggling in front of the flames, happy voices, chattering about their day; not a care in the world.

Her nostalgia for the 'old days' and for times she considered to be the happiest of all, were symptoms, Grace knew, of her father's sudden intrusion into her life. Even from a spot on the map as distant from this village as the moon, Thomas Blake had caused his daughter unimaginable grief; but, with the passing of decades and the fulfilment that came with having own family, Grace had succeeded in coming to terms with the situation; in confining her hatred for him to a place known only to her.

Now, however, her father's arrogant assumption that she would welcome him back into her life had unleashed emotions and thoughts that were impossible to hide. Apart from her family, even her closest friends had noticed the change in her attitude. She recalled Harry's words regarding the time that had elapsed since her father had made his presence known. Despite his assurances, Grace had never felt so vulnerable in her life.

She moved away from the window, her mood one of unutterable gloom. It hardly mattered what she decided to do, for the result would be the same. Thomas Blake was hell-bent on ruining her life a second time, and she felt powerless to stop it.

Downstairs in the hall, the clock struck the half hour and roused Grace from her reverie; but then the image came rushing back: her father deserting her on a rain-soaked pavement; her mother seizing hold of Grace's hand, as if fearing that the child would run after him.

'Who was that, Mummy?'

'No-one.'

No-one.

Grace picked up the mug of hot chocolate and sat on the edge of the bed.

She had never felt so wretched in her life; yet, she was determined that Thomas Blake should receive just punishment. She had to pull herself together. She had to make the man suffer.

Chapter Two

Lily Morris read and re-read the note in her hand, surprising herself at remaining so calm. She had recognised the handwriting immediately, as she still had a few letters belonging to Charlotte, letters that her friend had pleaded with her to keep, letters that Charlotte had sat reading again and again long after Thomas Blake had gone.

She folded the piece of expensive notepaper in half and placed it in her apron pocket before stepping outside to hang out the washing. As she pegged up each item, her mind refused to move on from the note, and she wondered how long it would be before her nerves got the better of her.

*

'Nerves?' Charlotte repeated disparagingly. 'I doubt if you even know the meaning of the word, Lily Morris.'

'How can you say that?' Lily had laughed in return, as the two friends wandered arm-in-arm across the fields by the church. 'Why, only this morning they flew up and walloped me right on the chin, made me jump, they did.'

'Hey,' said Charlotte, as if suddenly tiring of the conversation and keen to change the subject. 'Is there any chance you'll keep this for me?'

'Keep what?'

'This,' Charlotte sighed, pulling an envelope with the familiar handwriting from her pocket. 'He wrote it yesterday and it made me cry.'

'Aye, well,' Lily had said wryly. 'That wouldn't be difficult, the way you've been lately.'

Charlotte had looked at her, cheeks paling, eyes troubled. 'What d'you mean?'

'The way you've been lately,' Lily repeated patiently, perturbed at the pallor of her friend's face. 'You know, up and down like a see-saw, never the same mood two minutes in a row?'

'Is that the way I am?'

'Aye, it is. Are you sickening for something, by any chance?'

She had meant it as a joke but the sight of her friend's fearful expression made Lily's heart turn over: it could mean only one thing.

'Oh, my God, you're pregnant,' she said numbly, at which Charlotte had burst into tears.

'I want to die,' she sobbed, leaning on Lily's shoulder and clutching her friend's arms. 'What can I do? Oh, tell me, what can I do?'

'Wheesht now, it's not the end of the world,' Lily had said, forcing lightness into her tone. 'Let's face it, it won't be the first or last time such a thing's happened in this village, will it?'

After a moment, Charlotte drew apart from her friend and gave her a red-eyed, watery smile.

'But my sister! What will she say?'

Lily had sighed. 'Helen? Och, she'll not be bothered.'

'Of course she'll be bothered!' Charlotte had cried, in near hysterics. 'And then my mother will go mad and throw me out, I know she will.'

'Don't be daft, Lottie,' Lily said angrily. 'She's many things, your mother, but she's not completely heartless. She'll not throw you out, so stop thinking like that.'

'But, what will I do?' Charlotte wailed.

'What does he want to do?' Lily asked and her friend's face calmed at once.

'Oh, he wants us to get married.'

'Well then? Isn't that the kindest man on earth?'

'I don't want to marry him,' Charlotte said matter-of-factly. 'I'd never any intention of marrying Thomas Charles Blake and fine he knows it.'

'So,' Lily had said slyly. 'He tricked you, did he? Made you pregnant without you even being there?'

'That's a horrible thing to say!'

'Well, listen to yourself, Charlotte, telling me you've never wanted to marry him and yet letting him...' Her voice tailed off and she turned to walk on.

'You don't understand,' Charlotte said stubbornly, remaining where she was at the field gate. 'I never thought I would love him this much, otherwise I'd not have started it.'

'But if you love him,' Lily frowned in exasperation. 'If you love him, Charlotte, why the hell can't you get married?'

'His mother would make our lives a misery.'

Lily looked at her companion from her ten yards' distance and scowled.

'I don't think you're being honest with me, Lottie Shepherd.'

'What d'you mean?' Charlotte asked, but her mouth was slack.

'It's not Isabella Blake that's bothering you.'

'Who is it then, Miss Know-it-all?'

'It's the Jock Tamson's bairns thing again, isn't it, that nonsense you hear from your father about the difference between the classes.'

'Don't you dare insult my father,' Charlotte returned angrily, cheeks aflame. 'It's not nonsense at all, it's fact.'

'No, it's his fact, no one else's. You're just scared.'

'Scared? You've got a cheek!'

'Yes, scared to take on responsibility for your own life, Madam.' Despite her friend's indignant stare, Lily carried on. 'You'd be quite happy to stay at home, wouldn't you, have your father make all your decisions, run your life for you? That's no life, Charlotte, that's washing your hands of it, that is.'

They had gone back to the village their separate ways after that, without a single word being uttered, Charlotte along the top of the field, Lily down the railway path. Lily had not been sorry for losing her temper: it was time that Charlotte was put right about Sandy Shepherd's influence on his daughters, Charlotte in particular. Why, the girl couldn't even breathe in and out without the old man's say-so.

Lily walked home, despondent; not because she feared that she and Charlotte would fall out permanently over this, but because she knew that her outburst would have no effect whatsoever on the goings-on at Lilac cottage. So what now?

*

So what now? Lily shivered in the cold September air. Pegging up the last item on the clothesline, she picked up the laundry basket and hurried inside. After she had cleared everything away and prepared her tea for that night, she went to the telephone and looked up Grace's number. She had worked out the best thing to do about Thomas Blake's letter to her: first light Monday morning, she would contact Harry Gillespie. If he were half the man she suspected him to be, he would know exactly what to do.

*

Thomas wandered from room to room, examining cupboards and wardrobes to find adequate space for his belongings. He had spent the past month buying almost

116

everything he could think of for both the house and himself, and he was surprised to find he had any money left. Not that he could not easily access more, of course, but that entailed transfers half way round the world and back again and took nail-biting days until he had proof it had not been lost somewhere across the Atlantic. It had happened once, years ago, to the monthly money he sent for his daughter.

His daughter! He paused in his critical study of the electrical cupboard and stood in the middle of the hall. His daughter, Grace, the loveliest little girl he had ever seen. Well, strictly speaking, he had not actually seen his little girl in the flesh, but her photographs had relayed her beauty to him, photographs he still had in his suitcase, a record of her early years, the sight of which reduced him to the occasional tear.

Thomas sighed. It was no longer her early years that interested him now, but this one, the year he had earmarked for his return; the time when he would pick up where he and Charlotte had left off. Charlotte... Despite the cold treatment he had received at the hands of his daughter, and despite his initial reaction of anger against the entire Shepherd clan, Thomas's heart ached at the idea of never seeing Charlotte again.

How many times had he imagined their reunion? How many times had he rehearsed his opening words to her, envisaged her joy at seeing him again? And she would have been joyful, he knew that, for she had loved him more than any man could hope to be loved; and she in return had known the depths of his love for her. In spite of the unfortunate turn their life together had taken all these years ago, Thomas was convinced that, had she not passed away...

Passed away!

He endured the pain that coursed through him at the silent words and moved into the living room, a spacious and bright room overlooking the garden at the rear of the property and which had the bonus of two windows, one facing south, the other west to take advantage of afternoon sunshine. Sunshine?

He grimaced, for the day was as dreich as you could get in this country, a relentless drizzle falling from a bad-tempered sky and a wind as chilly as you might find at the North Pole.

Granted, it was the first week in October, but he seemed to recall, as a boy, enjoying autumn days by the river, guddling trout, wading bare-foot through the peaty water from one field to another before the icy temperature caused him to spring out and rub his toes with his hands until the feeling came back.

Thomas decided now that the house would suit him fine, for, if it pleased him on a day like today, then it would be most welcoming on a good day. He glanced down at the solicitor's number and made his mind up: he would sign the rental agreement first thing tomorrow.

*

Harry was back to the trauma and excitement of subterfuge. He parked the car in the lane behind the Church and walked the hundred yards or so to Lily Morris' house, knowing full well that he was probably fooling no one, not in this small village.

As the gate clicked behind him, the front door opened and Lily appeared on the step, giving him a wave before going in again, out of the wind presumably, for it was fairly flying down the path, bowling him along.

'I'm sorry for all the secrecy,' she said as soon as he set foot in the hall. 'And I appreciate you coming out here.'

'You sounded worried,' Harry said, handing her his coat. 'I hope you're not putting your trust in me for nothing.'

She smiled wryly at that and he wondered what meaning she had taken from the words.

'I doubt if it'll be for nothing,' Lily said, her back to him as she led the way into the kitchen. Idly, he pondered the number of people in this place who sat in their kitchens and not their living rooms, a habit Beth had never copied, thankfully. Kitchens were all very well; but only for meals.

'You don't mind if we sit in here?' she asked and he suffered a momentary twinge of guilt. 'Only it's cosier than the parlour, and a lot brighter.' She shrugged philosophically. 'Not that you'd notice on a day like this, but most days it's fine. Tea or coffee?'

'Coffee, please.'

'Sit there,' Lily told him, indicating the chair nearest the window. 'If there's a wee bit of sun, you'll be the first to feel it.'

He watched her bustle around the kitchen, an old lady set in her ways, her actions and movements probably the same since Adam was a boy. He was startled to remember that she must have known Grace's father.

'You knew Thomas Blake, didn't you?' he asked, taking advantage of the moment in case she assailed him with her 'problem' before he could find out about Blake.

'Aye,' she replied warily.

'Did you like him?' Harry dared to ask, for there was something in her tone that warned him.

'No, I can't say I did.'

'I see.'

'It was a shame really, because it wasn't his fault alone.'

'Sorry?'

He witnessed the flush on her cheeks, the biting of the lower lip and he knew that she might not be persuaded to say more.

'It's all in the past,' she said briskly, pouring hot water into his cup. 'Now, I've forgotten if you take sugar or not.'

'No thanks. You know,' Harry said, deliberately manoeuvring his way to a conclusion. 'No one ever tells me anything about him. It's as if it's a huge secret.'

'Chocolate biscuit?'

'Yes. Thanks,' Harry smiled, although it was only to encourage the old dear to talk.

'Now,' Lily said firmly. 'About my little problem.'

'Fire away.'

'It's this,' Lily said, handing him a letter. 'I got it on Friday, but, of course, you didn't come back from holiday until yesterday.'

He noticed that she bypassed the niceties of asking about the holiday; presumed it was to do with the generation gap. Even in a few months of dealing with legal issues, Harry had found that older people got right to the point.

'It's from Grace's father,' she added, just as he spotted the signature at the bottom of the page. 'I'd be grateful if you read it aloud to me.'

'Dear Lily,

You're the only person I can turn to, and I know that despite our past differences, you, more than anyone, understood how much I loved her. You were there when it all happened and she told me you were the best friend a girl could have, always there if she wanted a shoulder to cry on, and never turning her away, not like some others did.

I met Grace last year and she was very cruel to me, not telling me until the last moment that Charlotte had died. I never imagined that my daughter could be quite so heartless, and I can only think that no one

118

has told her the truth about Charlotte and me. If they had, she'd not have treated me the way she did.

Do you have it in you, Lily, to tell her? She'll not listen to me, I saw that in her eyes when we met. Isn't one Shepherd secret bad enough? You have it in your power to tell her exactly what happened between Charlotte and me, and Helen's part in it all. I'm putting my faith in you, Lily, because I know that you loved her as much as I did and this present hatred is not what she'd want. I'm not a vindictive man. The only thing I really want is to be part of my daughter's family, to end my days not being hated when it wasn't my fault.

Please help me, Lily, if not for me, for your best friend. Wherever Grace learned her hatred of me, it was never from Charlotte. She would not have said an unkind word about me because there was none to say.

I am renting a house in Perth with the idea of staying here permanently, so once I know my fixed address I will send it to you and you can do what you like with it.

Yours sincerely,

Thomas. '

Harry looked up when he came to the end of the letter. Lily was staring at the cup in front of her but when his voice stopped she glanced up.

'Thank you. I have a bit of bother with my eyes now, even with the glasses.'

'What did he mean about it not being his fault?' Lily shrugged and was silent. 'So, what do you want me to do about him?' Harry went on, flapping the letter in her direction.

'It's up to you,' she said tonelessly. 'You can tell her or not, I'm past caring.'

'Was Charlotte the one to blame then?'

'As I said,' Lily repeated, standing up. 'I'm past caring. Maybe you should talk to him yourself.' Harry frowned and she added: 'He can tell you what you want to know.'

'You have no idea what I want to know.'

Lily smiled at that. 'Don't be too sure.'

Harry was immediately apprehensive: she could not possibly know of his interest in Grace; yet she was looking at him with eyes that were suddenly shrewd. He kept calm, however, while she moved around the kitchen, clearing up the coffee cups and rattling them in the sink.

'So you think I should meet him?'

'I do.'

'What about Grace? What will she say if I do?'

'She'll be fine,' Lily said, facing the window, her expression concealed.

'I go and talk to her father behind her back and she'll be fine? I doubt it.'

Lily turned to meet his gaze. 'She'll not want to fall out with *you*.'

Again, Harry could hardly meet the old woman's gaze.

'How can you be so sure?' he asked coolly.

'Oh, take my word for it,' she advised him cynically. 'She won't want that.'

He stood up then, realising that he would not glean more from her.

'Thank you for the coffee,' he smiled. 'I can see myself out.'

She made no attempt to dissuade him and, as he collected his coat and left the house, Harry wondered what he had let slip to arouse the old bat's suspicions about his feelings for Grace Melville.

119

Whenever she heard the front door close, Lily stopped the pretence of washing dishes and stood, motionless, at the window, her hands still in the soapy suds but not moving. It was so quiet that she even heard the metallic click of the garden gate as it closed behind him. Only then did she remove her hands from the sink and dry them on the nearest towel, automatically hanging it over the cooker rail before resuming her seat at the table.

She pressed her fingers to her temples in an attempt to ease the nagging pain, but she knew she would eventually have to take a pill. Contacting the boy had been the most difficult thing she had done for a while. There was no knowing how Grace would react to his involvement. Lily was not one to dwell on fairy stories, but the way Grace Melville looked at the boy did not sit lightly with Lily's Christian conscience.

However, despite everything, she had still made the right decision, She sat back in her chair and allowed a slow smile to touch her lips: it was out of her hands now; let the boy deal with it.

*

Beth rushed to the window for the tenth time in as many minutes. The sound of cars drawing up had her on tenterhooks, for she had still the potatoes to roast, and the oven – brand new and horrendously expensive – was playing up, added to which Harry was nowhere in sight and she had expected him an hour ago.

She thought she heard his key in the lock, but the door was furthest from her position in the kitchen that she could not be sure; until his voice called out.

'It's me, home from the hills.'

She smiled, as it was what he said most nights, and rushed through to greet him. At the sight of his weary expression, she frowned.

'You look done in.'

Harry sighed, beckoned for her to come forward. 'I am. Come here and work your magic on me.'

'Can't. Visitors in twenty minutes,' she recited, but went to hug him anyway. He groaned and she bristled. 'May I remind you, it was you who invited them.'

'No, you invited them, I said it was O.K.' He smiled, refusing to let her go. 'No-one will notice that we're not here. Just set the table, put arrows on the floor and they'll manage fine by themselves.'

Beth had to laugh, although she reserved the right to ask where he had been until seven in the evening.

'You're wondering where I've been until this time of night,' Harry said and she glared at him for being a mind reader.

'Honestly, Gillespie, you're the limit! Have you planted a bug in my hair or something?'

He grinned, pulled her closer. 'No, I just study the script before I leave for work in the morning.'

'You're a pain,' she said, her face against his coat. 'And I hate you.'

He prised her from him, lowered his head and kissed her, taking her mind off the cooking and everything else for that matter; other than the bedroom.

'I liked that,' she sighed, eyes still closed, face upturned. 'Do it again.'

'Can't,' Harry teased. 'Visitors in seventeen minutes.'

She flew back into the kitchen, her carefully pinned hair falling around her

120

shoulders, just the way he liked it, he thought, hanging his coat in the hall cupboard and following her through.

'What did you say Annie's boyfriend's name was?' he asked.

'Alan.'

'Two 'l's or one?'

Beth gave him a withering glance. 'Three, and open the wine.'

'And Catriona's boyfriend?'

'It's her fiancé, and his name is Kevin, or is it Keith? Damn!'

'You look gorgeous.'

'Red wine's in the rack, sparkly's in the fridge.'

'You really suit that colour.'

Beth halted in her trek around the kitchen and looked at him. 'What?'

'That colour you're wearing. You really suit it.'

'Are you going bonkers?'

Harry laughed and began loosening his tie. 'Probably.'

Had she not been so busy, so flustered with the arrangements for her first dinner party in the new flat, Beth might have reminded her husband that he had avoided her question as to his reason for being so late home; but she was busy – and flustered – and they were due in five minutes now.

Their guests arrived together on the stroke of seven thirty, dragging the cold air in their wake and hugging coat collars tightly. Annie, small and slim, reminded Harry of Beth, except for the large breasts, which he struggled to ignore. The dress she was wearing made his endeavours more arduous.

He was on his best behaviour, he knew, especially since he had come home late; with no explanation.

Before Beth's agile imagination blew it out of perspective, he mentioned it whenever they had congregated around the fireplace.

'I thought I'd be too late for the pre-dinner cocktails,' he remarked casually and they all looked at him.

'I didn't think solicitor's worked after two o'clock,' Annie said mischievously.

'Oh cruelty, thy name is Annie' Harry quipped, and she blushed. 'I was working late in a way. Had to go and see an old friend of Grace's.'

Beth's eyes widened. 'Who?'

'Lily Morris.'

'You didn't say.'

'If you remember, sweetheart, you were too busy accosting me in the hall to care.'

It was Beth's turn to blush and Harry smiled, glancing briefly at Annie, who was gazing at him with willing eyes. To reciprocate, however, would be utter folly with a wife like Beth, despite the fact he could successfully manoeuvre the constant tightrope walks.

'Is she in any trouble?' Beth was asking now.

'A bit,' he replied and she visibly relaxed.

'Poor thing. Nothing too bad, I hope?'

'Not for her, no, but it's...' He paused, reluctant to say the word 'confidential' in case she took umbrage, thought he was trying to conceal something.

'It's O.K.,' she said happily and he wondered if he would ever be able to predict her moods. 'Client confidentiality, I know. Another slurp, Alan?'

'Please.'

Harry could never figure out what Annie Kerr saw in the boy: dark features, glum faced, hardly ever spoke, sat like a zombie half the time; yet she was an attractive girl, not beautiful but pretty, contributing merrily to the group chat, compatible with everyone.

'Beth was telling me that you think I look like Steve McQueen,' Harry told her suddenly, feeling only a tiny twinge of guilt at her discomfort.

'Harry!' Beth said sharply. 'For Heaven's sake, do you have to blab everything I tell you?'

'Not the things you say in bed, no.'

He had no idea why he said it. Perhaps it was the aftermath of Lily Morris' letter, or perhaps he was annoyed that he had not had time to pop down to see Grace after such a prolonged absence; whatever it was, he seemed to have no control over his mouth, not even when Beth fixed him with a look that would have stopped a horse in its tracks.

'What's wrong with you this evening?' she asked him tersely.

'Nothing. Well, nothing that a good stiff…'

'Stop it!' she cried angrily, when all he intended to say was a stiff drink.

'I was just going to say…'

'No one wants to hear what you were going to say,' she snapped.

Harry looked at her for a long moment. There was a very thick line between being tethered to the back green and being a nag; and at the moment she was nagging.

'One thing I can't stand,' he said quietly and they all turned their heads towards him. 'Is a woman with a petty mind backed up by a loud mouth.'

Beth's face crumpled but he had no intention of backing down. She was not the only one who had a temper; simply the only one who let it show.

'I'll go and see to the food,' she said, springing up and leaving the room.

Silence reigned for a full minute, and Harry could sense the tension in the group. Idly, and feeling no guilt whatsoever at spoiling the party, he wondered who would speak first.

'I'm sorry, Harry,' Annie said, and he glanced across at her. 'I'll talk to her.'

'No, don't,' he told her quickly, motioning her to sit down again. 'She has a lot to learn about being a woman.'

Annie and Catriona exchanged glances and he knew he had given them the impression he was an expert in women; but it hardly mattered, for neither would ever find out; nor would they tell tales to Beth.

'Actually,' he heard Catriona remark lightly. 'I think you look more like Michael Caine. When he played '*Alfie*'.'

'So does Beth,' Harry laughed. 'She's always going on about him playing Laertes in '*Hamlet*' when she was studying for her English exam.'

'Golly, you mean she saw him in the theatre?' Annie asked.

'No, on telly apparently,' Harry smiled. 'Me, I tend to think I'm more like Boris Karloff when he was staggering around as the monster.'

Although the others joined in the laughter, it suddenly hit him that he had ruined the evening; her first dinner party in the new flat. Inwardly he sighed. Why was he doing so much of this now? Was it his growing obsession with Grace that was affecting his moods?

'I'll go and grovel to Beth,' he smiled, rising to his feet and laying his glass down on the mantelshelf. 'Back In a moment.'

Beth had been crying and, as soon as he saw her, his heart ached and he was filled with remorse.

'Sweetheart,' he said.

'It was my fault again,' she mumbled, trying to take the roasting tray from the oven without chipping her nail polish. 'I'm too bossy and pushy, and I don't want to be.'

Harry walked towards her but she met him halfway, throwing her arms around him and sighing into his shirt. In light of her taking the blame, he felt more of a heel than if she had flown into a rage.

'Oh, Beth, I don't know what's got into me lately, I'm so sorry.'

She raised her face to his and gave him a smile. 'Maybe it's the male-o-pause.'

He laughed and shook his head, and then kissed her, not caring about the four people left in limbo next door; his only concern being to make it up to his wife.

'You did say it wouldn't happen again until the next time,' he heard her murmur into his cheek.

'I tell you what,' he said, drawing back and meeting her gaze. 'Every time I'm horrible to you, I give you my permission to look for someone else.'

It was hardly as risky as it sounded for he knew she was crazy about him, and his love for her was less insecure now; to the extent that he could even utter such words, albeit in jest.

'I don't want anyone else,' Beth said with a pout. 'Just stop being horrible.'

'Come on, I'll help you put the meal out before the guests rush out to the chip shop.'

He watched her as she slept, her arms across his chest, fingers lightly intertwined with his, her breath on his skin. She was the loveliest girl he had ever seen and he had treated her like dog shit on the heel of his shoe. Harry raised his eyes to the ceiling and emitted a long sigh of despair.

Beth stirred in her sleep, moaning faintly, the way she did when they were making love, a sound that aroused him more than the feel of her body against his.

'Harry?'

'Sweetheart.'

'I'm sorry.'

'No, I'm sorry.'

'I shouldn't have told you what Annie said about Steve McQueen. She told me in confidence.'

'But I shouldn't have…'

'Sshh,' Beth whispered, her mouth close to his. 'Don't speak.'

'I love you, Beth.'

'There you go again, disobeying a direct order.'

He laughed and kissed her, taking her into his arms and thinking everything would be fine now, that he had nothing to worry about; but it had been a close thing, and he would be obliged to watch his step for a while.

Something bright flickered and woke him up, but it was only the curtain flapping at the open window, playing with the glow from the street light. He lay for a moment, wondering if she were asleep, and then he heard the slow, rhythmical breathing and knew that she was.

Drowsily, he glanced across at the luminous dial of the alarm clock: two in the morning. As he drifted back to sleep, his last thought was of Grace and that he should call her the next day.

*

Grace tossed and turned and eventually crawled out of bed and tiptoed downstairs. Yawning, she sat in the glow of the dying fire embers and peered at the clock: only two o'clock, not even halfway to the morning. As she allowed herself to doze in the chair, her last thought was of seeing Beth very soon and how much she had missed the girl; and Harry too.

Chapter Three

Beth was guilty at having missed her mother's birthday. When she ought to have been taking her out to lunch and handing her a big bunch of flowers, she had been sunning herself on the beach at Le Lavandou and fluttering her eyelashes at the peanut vendor. Today, however, she was making up for it, a week late, but with the lunch and flowers well in hand.

They were in Dundee, at the Café Val D'or, in the heart of the city. The restaurant was so impressive, the cutlery and crockery evoking memories of a bygone, glamorous era, that Beth was slightly peeved at never having been before. It was her mother who preferred Perth but now, with Thomas Blake hovering around the fair city, Grace rarely set foot there, not even to the flat.

'You look tired, Mum,' she felt obliged to say, for had she plied her mother with platitudes, she was certain she would have been told off. Where once Grace Melville had been considerate and sensitive, she was now capable of presenting her daughter with long silences and brusque words.

'I am tired,' her mother said. 'I think it's old age.'

'Not at forty three.'

She received a brief smile and then it was gone. 'Forty-four dearest.'

Beth's hand flew to her mouth in a gesture of shock and distress: how could she have made such a miscalculation?

'Mum, you can't be! I was sure I'd got the year right. That means the card's rubbish now, since I put forty three kisses on the damned thing.'

'Hush, Beth,' her mother smiled again and this time it reached her eyes. 'I'll take that as a compliment, don't worry.'

'Oh, Mum,' Beth muttered, head down, utterly dejected. 'I'm the most awful daughter a mother could have.'

'Don't be so dramatic, Beth,' her mother frowned and it was the intolerant frown that hurt Beth the most. 'What difference does it make anyway?'

'None to you maybe, but a lot to me.'

'Come on, choose the macaroni cheese. Doesn't that always cheer you up?'

'You were always having to make that for me, weren't you?'

'You could eat the whole dish yourself, if I remember rightly. I'm amazed you never put on weight.'

'Listen to who's talking. What do you weigh, as a matter of fact?'

'I've no idea. Why?'

'Because you don't look an ounce over eight stones, that's why. Too thin, especially for your age.'

She grimaced, for it was a reminder of her gross negligence about the number forty-four.

'Oh my goodness!' Grace suddenly said, her face lighting up at something over Beth's shoulder. 'It's Harry!'

Beth turned in her chair and saw him making his way across the restaurant, oblivious to the admiring glances he was attracting from the female diners. She could hardly believe that he had taken the trouble to come all this way to gate-crash her lunch date; supposedly a cosy tête-à-tête with her mother. Irrationally, she was annoyed at him.

'Harry, what a lovely surprise,' Grace said as he took her hand and raised it to his lips.

'Surely, you didn't think I'd let your birthday pass unheralded?'

Beth glowered at her husband. 'Presumably you know she's forty-four today and you watched me write forty-three on the card?'

'I didn't see the card,' Harry said patiently.

'You can't convince me you didn't know her age,' Beth said sullenly.

'Who's 'she'?' Grace asked, critical eyes on her daughter. 'The cat's mother?'

'What's wrong with everyone today?' Beth whispered irritably as Harry pulled up a chair and sat down. 'Is there some bug going about?'

Harry and Grace shook their heads, both of them speaking at once.

'Beth, dear...'

'Please Beth...'

'Sorry, sorry, sorry,' Beth recited curtly, seizing the menu and fixing her gaze on the list of starters. 'Don't mind me. This treat was only my idea.'

'And I appreciate it,' Grace said, more kindly. 'What makes you think that I don't?'

'I think I'll have the soup to start with,' Beth said briskly, aware of the glance that passed between her companions. 'Let's hope it's tomato and I can walk down the street with a red moustache.'

'Perhaps you can tell me about your holiday,' her mother said pleasantly.

'It was the four 's' kind of holiday,' Beth replied, giving her husband a defiant stare.

'Beth, really,' Harry said wearily. 'I don't imagine Grace wants to know about that.'

'Well I want to tell her, so there.'

As soon as the words were out, Beth pulled a face and shook her head.

'For Heaven's sake, what the hell is wrong with me these days?' She looked at each of them in turn, abject apology in her expression. 'Mum, I'm really sorry for being such an idiot, and Harry, please forgive me for still being a spoilt brat.'

The atmosphere lightened then and Beth's mood altered immediately. She chattered on about their holiday in the South of France and how much they had enjoyed it, but she could still sense her husband's resentment at her childish antics and her mother's sense of guilt at having produced such a wayward child.

*

Grace sat in the passenger seat of the red sports car and waited for Harry and her daughter to stop arguing. She could see Beth's animated arm movements, see the angry set of her mouth, and was just on the brink of stepping from the car and allowing the girl to have her own way, when, suddenly, the discussion stopped, Harry walked away and Beth stood where she was, looking as wretched as Grace felt.

'Sorry about that,' Harry said as he opened the driver's door and swung himself into the seat. 'But it's settled now. I'm taking you home, Beth's going back to work.'

He had laughed as he said it and Grace was sharply reminded that she had no idea of the boy's true nature.

'I hate to see her like that,' Grace said, although there was no censure in her tone, simply a mother's remorse. 'I should have gone with her. After all, it was her idea to treat me to lunch. I feel bad now, honestly, I do.'

Harry drove past the Angus hotel and up towards the Repertory Theatre, switching on the windscreen wipers as the first spots of rain splattered on the glass.

'Beth and I are having a dip just now,' he said. 'Not the swimming pool kind, the marriage kind. But it's not serious, so don't worry. It happens to us all,' he added and, because of his choice of personal pronoun, Grace suspected he was fishing.

'Does it?' she asked lightly and he turned to look at her.

'Of course it does,' he smiled, refusing to even glance at the road ahead.

'Watch the lorry,' she warned him and he braked sharply.

'Oops, another near miss.'

'She'll be upset all day now,' Grace bemoaned. 'I should have…'

'Sshh,' Harry said swiftly. 'Least said, soonest mended.'

'How on earth do you know that old phrase?'

'My mother used to say it all the time, especially to my father, poor sod.'

Grace remained silent and it was not until they were in the countryside, driving sedately up the hill towards Tullybaccart that she thought of something to say. Her eyes followed the line of the bedraggled hedgerows and she pitied the doleful cattle in the fields.

'You know that she loves you desperately.'

'I know,' Harry replied so quickly that Grace guessed that his own thoughts had been running parallel to hers. 'Whoever said marriage was easy had absolutely nothing at all to do with women.'

'Do you mind?' she laughed. 'I'm one.'

'Oh yes,' Harry said, and, although she was not looking at him, she heard the smile in his voice. For a moment she was embarrassed: how could two simple words that were spoken thousands of times a day sound so implicit?

'How did your holiday go anyway?' she chose to ask. 'I mean, was Beth difficult at all?'

'Heavens no,' he laughed, turning to glance in her direction. 'She's not like a spoilt brat all the time, Grace. In fact, she's an absolute delight.'

A tiny, illogical pang of jealousy flitted through Grace, leaving her shocked and disgusted at herself, but the resentment of her daughter for being a delight was not easily cast aside. What on earth was wrong with her? During her days, she pretended to content herself with the doctor's diagnosis of her ills – the impending menopause – but, in her heart of hearts, in the minutes before she fell asleep, she knew it was more to do with her father and the re-emergence of past deceits.

'I'm glad,' she said to Harry eventually, but she knew that the reply had been too long delayed and the boy might have deduced her true feelings from the length of the delay.

'How about a coffee in the next place?' Harry asked, as they descended the steep hill where, on a fine day, you could see the Strathmore valley stretch out for miles.

Instinctively, she consulted her watch. 'I'm not sure if I have time.'

'You have five minutes to make your decision,' Harry laughed; imbued with satisfaction. She knew then that he had sensed her pang of jealousy for her daughter.

'Perhaps the next time,' she managed to say firmly, her eyes on the road ahead. 'I really should get James's tea ready.'

'Of course,' he said politely, pressing his foot down on the accelerator and speeding up.

As he dropped her at the door of the cottage, she refrained from asking him in.

'Thank you, Harry,' she smiled, the smile of a grateful mother-in-law. 'Do tell Beth that I thoroughly enjoyed the lunch and that I'll phone her soon.'

'Will do,' he said, giving her an amusing salute. 'Take care.'

She stood in the doorway, waiting until the car had disappeared round the corner, recalling the day, some five years previously, when she had first set eyes on Harry Gillespie as he helped her daughter from the car.

Grace closed the door behind her and made her way upstairs, where she sat on the bed staring into space. The pills prescribed by the doctor a few weeks before lay on her dressing table, the packet unopened. She had been quite sceptical about the need for anti-depressants and had resisted taking them, despite the doctor's advice.

'At your age,' he had smiled. 'I suspect it's the menopause, and that you're depressed.'

When Grace had informed him that she did not feel depressed, he had regarded her with the sort of patience that he might employ on a five-year old.

'Perhaps not,' he said slowly, pen poised over the prescription pad. 'But I've known you for a long time, Grace, and I can see – professionally, not just as a friend – that you're not your usual self. At your age,' he had glanced at her apologetically for repeating the phrase, 'there's no reason to take risks with your health. These tablets I want to prescribe are very mild and I won't give you so many that will make you dependent on them.' He had raised his eyebrows at that point, as if asking for her permission.

'Well, all right,' she had agreed reluctantly. 'As long as it's just a few.'

Now, reading the leaflet from the box, Grace sighed and decided that she would take some, only a couple, to see what difference it made. One thing was perfectly clear to her: it was nothing that a pill could cure: it was Thomas Blake's fault, turning up after all those years, upsetting everyone, making demands on them, caring for no one but himself; and although he had left her alone for over a year now, she was not convinced that she had seen the last of him.

*

Beth was pouring her heart out to Marjory Wilson, who, in the past hour, had acted more like a mother than Grace Melville. Putting a brave face on it was all very well, Beth had decided as she entered the office after the public row with her husband, but Marjory had taken one look at her and started it all.

'Beth, dear girl, whatever's the matter?'

Now, after an hour's dry-eyed heart-to-heart, both women's mood was much improved; Beth's because she had been able to tell someone, and Marjory's because she had never married, never had a daughter, and it was still high on her Might-Have-Been list. She was thrilled to be able to listen to Beth's out-pouring of anger and disappointment and had not been shy about giving her opinion.

'But men are all the same,' she had assured Beth, within minutes of the first grievance. 'My mother told me that, and her mother before her, so it's nothing new.'

'Honestly, he treats me like the housekeeper,' Beth had groaned, but, even through her anxiety, she saw the funny side of it. 'To be honest, I'm a useless one at that,' she added, hunching her shoulders with glee.

'Well, it must be the only thing you're not good at,' Marjory had said, defending her charge. 'I'd be over the moon if you were married to my son.'

She did not have one, of course, another item high on her MHB list, but Beth took it as a compliment.

'Thank you, Marjory, and I'd be pleased to have you as a mother-in-law.'

She had stopped short of saying 'Mum', out of a lingering respect for her own mother, but also because this kind of cosy, confidential situation could never be allowed to get out of hand: Marjory, nice and sympathetic though she may be, was still her immediate boss.

'I've had an idea,' Marjory was saying now, just as Beth had stood up to go into her own office.

'What?'

'Why don't you spend the afternoon with Mr Charlie? He's to see some clients, French, I think he said, and he'd be sure to need your language skills. What do you say?'

Beth pondered the idea, but only for ten seconds. Spending time with Charlie Webster in the wake of a heated argument with her husband was not on her agenda, no matter how appealing it might seem.

'I think I'd be too fed up,' she smiled, and she knew as she spoke that the words had sealed her fate.

'You see?' Marjory said triumphantly. 'You've just admitted you're fed up. An hour in the town with exciting people is just what you need.'

It was the most unpropitious moment for Charlie to walk in, for, without any preamble, Marjory launched in.

'Beth's fed up today and I suggested she go with you this afternoon, to meet the French people?'

'Brilliant!' Charlie exclaimed, and his expression of sheer joy did nothing to cheer Beth up. 'And don't argue, I'm not listening.'

'She wasn't going to argue,' smiled Marjory, no doubt thinking she was doing this for the best. 'Were you, dear?'

Beth shrugged. If she made a fuss, he would know.

The French people turned out to be English speakers who wanted to practice their English, a rare occurrence in Beth's experience of the Gauls. The couple, Colette and Christophe, were young and lively and, after an embarrassing moment when Beth and her boss were taken for man and wife, the group set off for the nearest auction rooms, where Charlie had reserved a porcelain figurine for Colette.

'Were you named after Colette?' Beth asked the young woman, and Charlie gave her a confused glance.

'Who's Colette?' he asked, before his client had time to reply.

'"Cheri", and the 'Last of Cheri',' Beth told him, much to Colette's amazement.

'You have read this?' she asked Beth.

'Oh yes, lovely books. I so enjoyed them.'

'But they are very…' Colette paused and winked. 'Very naughty, yes?'

Beth's heart sank: the word 'naughty' in Charlie Webster's presence was not her most favourable circumstance.

'Are they?' she asked innocently. 'I never thought so.'

'It must depend then,' Charlie said, perhaps seizing upon the opportunity, 'On our individual notions of what 'naughty' means.'

'Listen,' Beth said pleasantly, giving him the benefit of her most virginal look. 'The books are about an older lady and her young friend. I'm sure it happens all the time in France.'

'Ah, oui,' Colette sighed, her hand on her heart. 'C'est l'amour, n'est-ce-pas?'

Beth smiled, shrugged and turned to examine the figurine. Despite the risk attached to the afternoon, perhaps she was acting like a stuffed shirt. All he was asking her to do was to be nice to a couple of clients for an hour and here she was resorting to the Wee Free attitude that her mother had endured from Alexander Shepherd. She advised herself to loosen up and stop being such a killjoy. Besides, had Harry not treated her badly that morning? What harm would a little competition do?

*

Harry parked the car in his designated space and ran up the steps two at a time. For some reason, just as he reached the door, he turned to glance down the street, for he had spotted a blonde head in a crowd of people.

He watched his wife laughing and joking with a tall dark handsome youth in the group, her hand sometimes touching his arm, her face raised to his. As they walked slowly up the street towards him, Harry opened the office door and quickly went inside, resuming his observation of her from the tiny side window in the vestibule.

As she drew level with his office, although on the opposite side of the street, he saw her take the youth's arm as they prepared to cross the road. He had no idea who the man was, nor why Beth should be so enamoured of him, but one thing he did know: he would find out. He had tolerated one disaster today, when he reneged on telling Grace about the letter Lily Morris had received. There was no chance that he would indulge in cowardice twice in one day.

*

After the French couple had returned, exhausted, to their hotel, Beth and Charlie spent an enjoyable half hour in the café in the centre of the city. The rain clouds had dispersed and a weak October sun was struggling to assert itself. After her initial resistance to enjoyment had worn off, Beth did appear to be enjoying herself; or at least so Charlie Webster was thinking as he handed her a milky coffee and a slice of chocolate cake.

'There you are, now eat up, for Pete's sake and get some meat on these bones.'

'If you think I'm skinny, you should see my mother.'

'You have a mother? You mean, an angel didn't drop you from Heaven?'

Her hand paused as she was guiding coffee cup to lips and Charlie thought he had never seen such a voluptuous mouth in his entire life. So engrossed was he in its examination, that she frowned and said sharply:

'You'd like to know my shade of lipstick, maybe?'

'Sorry, just thinking how lovely you are.'

He saw the amusement in her eyes, noticed the slight twitch of her mouth before she sipped the coffee.

'Yes, I'm sure.'

He stared at her. 'You don't think you're lovely?'

'Well of course I'm lovely,' she smiled, but he wondered if she were serious.

'In fact, I must be the loveliest girl in the whole of Perthshire.' She hesitated and then added, 'Apart from my mother, that is.'

Tactfully, Charlie let it go. Sensing that she had had some sort of contretemps before he had stepped into the outer office two hours before, he had been so delighted at her agreeing to spend the afternoon with him that he was content to let her keep it to herself, whatever it had been. Now, with the second remark about her mother, plus the accompanying tone of derision, he was beginning to believe that she had simply rowed with Mum. But, so did everyone; and did it not wash off like water from a duck's back?

'Are you still enjoying the work you're doing?' he opted for instead.

'Yes,' she said, brightening up. 'It's just ideal for me, the relaxed atmosphere in the office, Marjory being such a nice person.'

'And the boss?' Charlie asked, his face straight. 'What's he like?'

Briefly, her eyes met his and he was struggling to read the message.

'He's fine,' she said, glancing from the window at passers-by. 'Except he makes me nervous.' Taken aback, Charlie could think of nothing to say, and so Beth added, 'He tries too hard.'

'Do I?'

'Yes.'

'Only because I want to impress you.'

'Why would you want to do that?'

'Because I really like you, but you know that already.'

'I suppose.'

'If I asked you out to dinner... with clients, I mean... would you say 'yes'?'

She had been swishing the dregs of her coffee round the cup but now she paused and studied his face for a long moment. He almost held his breath.

'I don't know,' she said slowly, eyes still fixed on his face. 'It depends.'

'On what?' he asked, throat dry, dreading that he might blow his chances at any second.

'On whether my husband agreed or not.'

Charlie fought to maintain his polite smile but the mention of the husband had his spirits spiralling to earth. Why did he keep forgetting she was married?

'Of course, that goes without saying,' he smiled. 'But if he didn't object?'

'Then it would be fine,' she said, focussing her attention once more on the coffee cup.

'Good. If the occasion arises, then we'll see how you feel.'

'Agreed,' Beth said and Charlie's heart skipped a beat.

*

Harry put his key in the lock and braced himself for the virago that would greet him. After his chauvinistic behaviour that morning, he could not expect anything less that the frosty treatment, closely followed by the temper tantrum. Her dalliance with the dark-haired handsome youth apart, he would have a fair bit of grovelling to do in the next fifteen minutes.

As he hung up his coat and threw the car keys into the bowl on the hall table, he could hardly believe his eyes when she sauntered from the kitchen to welcome him, a broad smile on her face.

'Gosh,' he said, sounding like a '30's movie star. 'You look happy.'

'I am,' she smiled sweetly and his stomach lurched at the image of the dark-haired youth.

'Beth, I was a shit to you this morning and I don't have an excuse. Can we start the day again?

She shrugged, but happily. 'If you like.'

'I didn't mean to spoil your lunch with Grace, I just wanted to pop by and surprise you both.'

'Which you certainly did,' Beth said, waggling her fingers at him as though he were a naughty child and, whereas he should have been relieved that she was in a good mood, he was not consoled by the dark-haired youth's being the reason.

'Did you have a good day afterwards?' Harry dared to ask her, hardly anticipating an honest answer.

'Yes, it was very nice, My boss... remember, Charlie Webster? Well, he had some French clients to see, so I tagged along, but they spoke English as it happened, so I wasn't required really.'

'So you left them to it?' he asked, testing her.

'No, I tagged along some more,' she said and, not for the first time, did he thank his lucky stars for her brutal honesty. 'And we wandered round a couple of salerooms, then they went back to their hotel and Charlie and I had coffee and a chat.'

His heart froze at the word 'chat', for, in his experience, if women strayed at the beginning, it was not so much for sex as for a sympathetic ear.

'I hope you told him about your abusive husband then,' he smiled, crossing the kitchen and searching for the gin bottle.

'No, I didn't,' Beth frowned. 'Why would I even mention you?'

Harry stopped what he was doing and went to take her in his arms.

'I don't know what I did to deserve you, Beth Melville, but whatever it was I intend to bottle it and sell it for a thousand guineas an ounce.'

130

She laughed then and he should have been happy that she had put this morning's row behind her; but, at the back of his mind, he had the niggling idea that Charlie Webster had been charming enough company to wipe the whole incident from her mind.

'Dinner's in the oven,' Beth was saying. 'and the drinks are waiting by the fireside, and I'm just going to phone Mum and apologise. Back in two secs.'

Harry wandered into the sitting room and marvelled at his wife's constant ability to astound him; although the quality had been part of her appeal at the start, her incredible capacity to switch from spoilt brat to angel within the blink of an eye. Idly, as he poured their drinks and made himself comfortable in his favourite chair, he wondered if grouchy Uncle George would have liked her.

When she came into the room a few minutes later, a frown was etched across her brow.

'That didn't take long,' Harry said lightly, although he feared that mother and daughter had not had enough time to make up. 'Must be some sort of a record, two minutes on the phone to Grace.'

'Dad answered, said she'd taken a sleeping pill and was still in bed.'

'Really?' Harry asked and it was his turn to frown. 'That's not like her.'

'No, it isn't, and I'm so worried I might just pop out there after dinner.'

'We'll both go.'

'No,' Beth contradicted him, the first sign of dissent rising to the surface. 'I'm perfectly capable of dealing with my mother.'

'Beth, I didn't mean that you weren't,' he told her firmly. 'I'm only concerned for you both.'

'We can take care of ourselves,' she said quietly, stretching out on the rug in front of the fire, bare feet touching the hearth.

'When I married you,' he reminded her gently. 'I promised to protect you, take care of you, whether you like it or not.'

At first he thought she was annoyed at the remark; but, all at once, she laughed and shook her head at him.

'You men are all the same, with your primeval instincts. You'll be hauling me into the cave by the hair next.'

'Into the bedroom more like.'

She pressed her lips together and threw him a look, which he could not decipher.

'So, we'll have dinner,' she reiterated, staring into the fire glow. 'Then I'll drive out and see Mum.'

Despite her swift change of mood, and despite the odds being against it, he decided that this was as good a time as any to drop the bombshell. Quickly, before he took cold feet, he cleared his throat and prepared to speak.

'You know I went to see Lily Morris a week or so ago?'

Beth glanced up. 'Yes.'

'It was concerning Grace.'

'Go on,' Beth said slowly, eyes on his face.

'Lily had received a letter from Thomas Blake.'

'Lily?' she frowned. 'Why Lily?'

'Because she was your grandmother's best friend.'

'I'd forgotten that. So, pray continue,' she smiled wryly, but he suspected it was to conceal her anxiety.

Harry took his time over the next sip of gin and tonic, rehearsing the words in his mind before setting them free.

'He asked Lily to speak to Grace, to tell her the truth about what happened, when he and Charlotte were courting.'

'That's a real old-fashioned word. Courting.'

'That's why I like it,' Harry smiled.

'And is Lily going to tell my mother the truth, whatever it is?'

'No, she wants me to do it.'

Beth was aghast. 'But you've nothing to do with it.'

He was shocked at how the remark cut through him, but could see no sign of malice in her eyes, for it had been a reasonable thing to say.

'That's true, but she asked me to do it.'

'What exactly do you intend to do?' Beth asked warily.

'I'm not sure,' he lied, avoiding her gaze. 'I'll have to give it some thought.'

'Do you think he's still hanging around here?'

'Possibly.'

'Is there any way we can find out?'

Harry brought his attention back to his wife's face, saw the interest in her eyes, suspected that she wanted to contact her grandfather.

'Can't think of one,' he lied again, knowing he would have Thomas Blake's address within days. 'Let me mull it over.'

'I wouldn't mind meeting him myself,' Beth said casually and he was hardly surprised; although, for some reason, she averted her eyes from his. 'After all, he is my grandfather and everyone seems to forget that.'

Harry had great difficulty in keeping his voice level, for to have his wife in direct conflict with Grace was not only undesirable, but also divisive.

'We'll work something out,' he smiled, standing up to replenish his drink. 'In the meantime, I'm starving, what's for dinner?'

'Something I spent hours slaving over,' Beth replied humorously, but, for the life of him, he could not deduce her mood now. Only time would tell.

During the meal Harry surreptitiously plied his wife with half a bottle of wine, topping her glass up regularly so that she had no accurate idea of how much she had consumed; until she stood up to clear the dishes away.

'Wow!' she frowned, clutching the edge of the table. 'How many have I had?'

'Not that many,' Harry lied, eyebrows raised innocently. 'Why?'

'I'm squiffy,' Beth said and sat down again. 'Maybe it's not such a good idea to drive to Mum's tonight.'

'Well, I've certainly had too much anyway,' Harry laughed, happy that his plan had worked. 'No chance that I'll be straying far from the telly between now and bedtime.'

'Sounds good to me,' Beth said, and her words slurred together. 'But I doubt if I'll be able to keep my eyes open long enough to watch anything.'

'You go and sit next door,' Harry suggested, reaching for her hand across the table. 'And I'll clear up here.'

He was rewarded with such a smile of gratitude that he was assailed by a wave of guilt. Fortunately, being his mother's son, it lasted only a few seconds: if you were looking for the essence of remorse, Rachel Gillespie was not a name that sprang to mind.

Later, as he placed the final piece of cutlery in its drawer, Harry pondered the situation regarding Thomas Blake: he had no intention of allowing Beth to become personally involved with him; rather, he had every intention of meeting the man himself and getting rid of him; for Grace's sake.

If he were forced to choose between Beth's interests and those of Grace Melville's, there was not a snowball's chance in Hell that he would choose his wife's.

Chapter Four

November brought with it the first freezing weather to the Shire, short-lived normally, but inconvenient for a few days, coating roads, pavements and cars with their daily doses of ice and salt. The countryside fared worse, as usual, for there were so many side roads and tracks, vital to the lives of villagers and delivery drivers, but not so uppermost in the minds of the local Council, whose devotion to the city was far more evident in winter than at other times of the year. Whilst city streets and pavements were treated regularly and the main roads passing through villages were kept clear, there was the usual disregard for rural dwellers, the state of their pavements and side streets being left to individual householders

One morning, the second Saturday of the month, Grace woke to find the attic bedroom window laced with ice. She could hear James sweeping the path round the house, the harsh sound of the bass broom having awakened her.

She yawned and stretched and sat up in bed, but made no attempt to rise. It had become her husband's habit to bring her breakfast in bed every Saturday and she was finding the ritual welcoming, even though she had long dispensed with the pills; his reason for indulging her in the first place. Grace enjoyed the lazy start to her Saturdays, not to mention the fact she would be spoiling James's pleasure in preparing the tray.

She arranged the pillows behind her back and looked around the room. Very little had changed in the thirty odd years since she had moved into this room as a ten year old girl, having shared her mother's room until then. After her grandmother's death, the bedrooms had been reallocated, giving Grace a new degree of privacy.

Now, as her gaze wandered over familiar things, particularly the old oak suite, she was horrified to acknowledge the passing of the years – decades, in fact – in the blink of an eye. So wretched had she felt at the end of the summer, that she had hidden the photograph albums in the back of the hall cupboard, out of sight behind the old frocks and coats and boxes of sewing cottons.

Refraining from leafing through the old photographs had been the doctor's suggestion to allay some of her more emotional symptoms, and she had not been certain enough of her own diagnosis to contradict him; although the suspicion lingered on, that the hostile meeting with her father had been the real cause of it.

With the passing of each month and the absence of further demands being made on her, however, Grace's hope was increasing that she would never see the man again.

The sad old photographs apart, however, she might still be swallowing the pills to this day had it not been for Harry. He had been stalwart in his support, telephoning each day to ascertain her mood, encouraging her out of the doom and gloom of which her mother had so often accused her, and reassuring her in a way that neither James nor Beth could do, being, as they were, too close to the problem; unable to view things objectively.

She must have dozed, for a knock on the bedroom door startled her.

'Good morning,' James said, and she waited for his usual joke to follow. 'Or maybe I should say 'good afternoon'.'

Grace smiled as she always did and raised herself further up the pillows, so that he could lay the tray flat on her lap. He was out of breath, strangely enough, and she wondered if there had been much snow to shovel.

'Is it still snowing?'

'No, just icy,' he replied, sitting on the stool at her dressing table and watching her eat. 'And absolutely freezing, so don't rush to get up.'

'What time is it anyway?'

'Half past nine, but there's nothing for you to do,' James told her. 'I've tidied up downstairs, even made the sandwiches for lunch.'

'Oh, James, you should leave that to me,' she protested, ever mindful of the rigours of his working week. She should be doing her best to see that his weekend was light. 'I'm not ill, you know.' She glanced at him, wondering if she should mention it. 'In fact, as much as I enjoy breakfast in bed on a...'

'Stop right there,' James said, but his eyes were twinkling.' Don't you dare deny me the right to make toast and tea for you. You never give me the chance to show you that I've appreciated you over the years.'

Grace was so surprised that such a sentiment could stem from tea and toast that she stared at him for a moment.

'I know you appreciate me, James,' she said eventually. 'And you show it all the time.'

'Do I?'

'Yes, you do,' Grace affirmed, drinking the tea – too strong and sweet. 'I see it every day.'

They looked at each other, but it was James who broke the silence.

'I never see a letter from Alice now,' he said, glancing at the dressing table where such letters usually lay. 'Has she stopped writing?'

It was a dreadful reminder to Grace that she had let her friend down: the postponement of Alice's visit in early summer the previous year had led to an uncanny silence from Pennsylvania. Despite Grace's two apologetic letters, discreetly enquiring as to the state of her marriage, Alice had never replied, and it was the first time in over thirty years that there had been a cessation of criss-crossing letters between the two friends. Now, as James waited patiently for an answer, Grace could only blame herself.

'I've written a few times, 'she said, looking down at her plate. 'But she hasn't replied. I don't know what can be wrong.'

'Didn't she want to come and visit you last year?'

Grace was caught unawares: she had never mentioned Alice's intention to visit, preferring to keep it to herself so that she could handle the situation in the way most suited to her.

'Did she want to visit?' she asked James, her heart pounding.

'Yes,' James said, but it was his turn to appear shame-faced. 'She wrote to me.'

'Alice wrote to you?' Grace asked in utter astonishment. 'Why on earth would she do that?'

He shrugged but it was obvious, despite his discomfort at the topic, that he was relieved she had mentioned it.

'Because you told her you were ill and that it would be best if she came over later in the year, or even this year.'

Grace could hardly absorb the implications: one of her dearest friends had written behind her back and James had been party to the deceit for the best part of six months. The most puzzling aspect, however, was how the letter had escaped Grace's notice, for James was never at home to receive the mail. Aware that her next question would have the tone of interrogation attached to it, she asked it nevertheless.

'She wrote to you here?'

'No, to the depot in Perth,' James said, having the grace to drop his gaze.

'I don't understand why you didn't tell me.'

'You had told her yourself that you were ill, Grace, and I didn't want to worry you.'

Grace pushed the tray aside and flicked back the blankets. This time James made no attempt to persuade her to stay in bed, and so she brushed past him and opened the wardrobe door.

'Grace, please, I didn't say anything because she asked me not to, and I didn't tell you a lie, did I?'

Grace turned and looked at him, wondering why it was, that only her son-in-law had displayed any loyalty towards her in recent days.

'As I have often discovered, not telling the truth is the same as a lie,' she said bluntly, turning back to select her dress for the day. When she continued to push the coat hangers back and forth for several minutes, she heard James leave the bedroom and close the door quietly behind him.

*

Thomas Blake paced the luxuriously carpeted floor of his lounge and tried to calm down. For one thing, he was too old for this kind of aggravation and, for another, he had not envisaged Lily Morris' washing her hands of Charlotte with such haste; hardly an exponent of the old adage: *a friend in need is a friend indeed.*

For the umpteenth time that morning, he glanced at the clock and was annoyed to see it was only ten past nine; still an hour and fifty minutes before he was to meet the boy.

The boy! If he were older than Beth – and, even from a distance Thomas had surmised he was – he must be almost thirty by now, yet he was still referring to him as a boy. Thomas moved into the kitchen, switched on the kettle and assembled cup, saucer and spoon, setting them neatly on the small table. He opened the cupboard door and looked at the jar of instant coffee left by the previous tenant, and lamented that anyone could drink such foul-tasting liquid in preference to freshly-ground beans.

Ten minutes later, waiting for the percolator to work its magic, he stared from the kitchen window at the ice on the path, still glistening well into the morning, and on a south-facing roof. It had been years since he had last seen ice or snow, for there had been nary a sign of it in Buenos Aires; and, in a strange way, he had missed the sights and smells of a Scottish winter; despite the upheaval it delighted in causing to mere mortals.

He smiled as he recalled her resistance to the ice-skating he had suggested that freezing winter. He had not known about the baby, of course, had not been sympathetic to her pleas to stay on the sidelines when all his friends had been donning skates at the pond.

*

'You go on your own,' Charlotte had repeated so often that it was irritating him. 'I'll watch from the side.'

'But I bought these skates especially for you,' he told her, hardly able to conceal his frustration. 'You haven't even tried them on, don't know if they fit or not.'

'I will try them on,' she smiled patiently. 'But not today, some other time.'

'But the ice won't last much longer. They're saying it'll be over by the end of the week.'

She had remained silent then, not even looking in his direction; and, for the first time that day, he was suddenly beginning to notice how pale and tired she was. Remorse set in and he put his arm around her.

'Charlotte, what is it? Are you not well, ma chere?'

She shook her head at his dreadful French accent and smiled briefly.

'I'm fine, Thomas, really. I just don't feel in the mood of ice-skating, that's all.'

'No,' he disagreed, aware now of the furtiveness of her glances. 'There is something that you're not telling me, I'm not leaving, Charlotte, until you tell me.'

He had stood, intransigently, still with his arm around her shoulder, gazing down into the wary blue eyes. Normally, he could read her like a book but today he was struggling.

'I can't.'

'Can't what?'

'Can we go somewhere more private?' she had asked, and a finger as icy as the surrounding air draped itself across his heart. She was meaning to leave him!

Numbly, he accompanied her up the main street to the Park, a distance of at least half a mile, during which neither had spoken, she striding out beside him, Thomas not even feeling his legs beneath him.

When, at last, they sat on their favourite bench in the Park, she turned at once and told him:

'I'm going to have a baby.'

To tell the truth, he was overjoyed and would have seized her in his arms and danced around the bench with her; but there was a look in her eyes that stopped him. He was afraid of what she would say next.

'I don't want to marry you, Thomas,' she said bluntly. 'So you needn't worry.'

His fury must have shown in his face, for she visibly shrank from him.

'What? I needn't worry? What the hell does that mean?'

She was more hesitant then, giving him frequent sidelong glances, as if weighing up his reaction, perhaps testing his sincerity.

'I'm sorry,' she said, finally able to look at him. 'We can't be married, and there's nothing you can say that will change my mind. I'm sorry,' she repeated and he lost his temper completely.

He never regretted a thing he told her that afternoon, sitting on a cold bench in a freezing Park; and, to his credit, he had meant every word of it. Even she could see that.

He told her he had loved her the moment he set eyes on her, when she was sixteen, precocious, and the most exciting girl he had ever been with. He told her that he would rather die than spend his life without her; and then, just when she believed there was nothing more to be said, he warned her that, if she refused to marry him, he would tell their offspring that Charlotte Shepherd had deliberately chosen to pronounce their child a bastard.

She had wept then, but whether from love or shock at his vindictiveness he could not guess. The only thing he cared about was if she would marry him, and he had ensured that she would.

'On one condition,' was her tearful entreaty; and Thomas prepared to abide by anything she asked.

*

Thomas put the cup to his lips and found that the coffee was cold. With a sigh, he poured it down the sink and wondered if he could be bothered going through the rigmarole again. It was a quarter past ten now and he must stop this clock watching, for it was getting him no nearer to his meeting with the young man,

On impulse, he decided to rake through his photographs and choose the best ones to be framed. He had a house now, walls to hang photographs, flat surfaces where he could arrange his daughter's life in sequence, look into her eyes whenever he wanted to; and there was nothing she could do to prevent him.

*

Harry was not nervous: other than the man being Grace's father, Thomas Blake had nothing to do with him; he was only meeting him to issue an ultimatum, after which, hopefully, Grace would be rid of him and would never have to worry about driving into Perth again.

He had not asked Barclay for the hour off, since the man had already made it clear that Harry was free to come and go as he pleased so long as the work was done, Being the junior partner, the bulk of his work was paper-pushing anyway and, as a last resort, he could always take it home. He often found Beth in their little office, translating the details of a particular piece for a foreign client. If he ever asked her about her workload, she would smile at him absentmindedly, tell him that, by and large, she pleased herself as to what she did. Apparently, Charlie Webster was as easy-going a boss as you could hope to meet.

Harry had been correct in his assumption of a link between Webster and Frank Gilmour, for Sandra – the legal secretary – had confirmed that the two had attended Perth Academy together and were as thick as thieves.

There was no doubt in Harry's mind that Gilmour was in cahoots with Webster, the dark-haired youth he had spied in the street; or that one of them was interested in Beth. Thanks to his brusque treatment of Gilmour the day of their one and only lunch date, Harry had not crossed paths with the man since, hearing his voice on the telephone occasionally through the office wall; nothing more.

As the clock struck eleven, Harry stood up and pushed his chair in. He would be five minutes late but that was exactly how he had planned it. There was no one in the outer office and so he removed his coat from the rack and left quietly.

*

Thomas was on tenterhooks. It was five past eleven and he had been sitting in his seat since half past ten, having been unable to stay longer in the house. From his position at the window he had views both up and down the street, and, regardless of which direction the fellow took from the office, Thomas would spot him first, have time to prepare his opening speech.

When someone brushed past him and he glanced up, he almost fell off his seat: it was the boy, appearing out of thin air.

'Mr Blake' he smiled politely, extending his hand in an old-fashioned gesture. 'I'm Harry Gillespie, Grace's son-in-law. We spoke briefly on the telephone.'

'Yes, that's right,' Thomas mumbled, half standing, feeling and looking like a bumpkin, his opening speech forgotten. 'Thomas Blake, pleased to meet you.'

The boy sat down opposite, his eyes sweeping around the hotel reception area before alighting on Thomas's face.

'You have an odd way of showing your love for your daughter,' the boy began, taking Thomas completely by surprise.

'I beg your pardon?'

'This vendetta you seem to have put in place to frighten her,' the boy smiled. 'I said it's an odd way to show that you love her.'

For a moment there was silence, during which Thomas fidgeted but the boy sat calmly, studying his companion's face.

'You don't know anything about how I love my daughter,' Thomas said at last, a modicum of control returning. 'What would you – a stranger – know of it?'

The boy – Harry – shrugged and smiled. 'I think you know perfectly well that I'm not a stranger to this family.'

'What is it you want?' Thomas asked rudely, his patience depleting.

137

'Your daughter is afraid of you,' the boy said pleasantly. 'All she wants is to be left alone, for you to go back to wherever it was you came from. She's made her decision and she asked me to relay it to you.'

'She told me that herself, months ago.'

'True, but she wanted to be fair about it, give herself time to mull it over. Now she's certain that she doesn't want you in her family.'

'I'm her father,' Thomas said harshly. 'I'm in her bloody family whether she likes it or not.'

The boy smiled and Thomas's patience dissipated: that she should dispatch this boy to do her work, knowing he was a complete stranger, rankled with him.

'I've rented a house in Perth,' he said, finally having the courage to meet the boy's gaze. 'So I'll be staying here for the foreseeable future, and there's no law against it.'

The boy was still smiling and it worried Thomas. Casually, he brushed an imaginary speck of dust from his trouser leg and waited. At last, the boy spoke

'No, that's quite true, and I should know, being a solicitor. But I believe there is a law against bigamy,' the boy added, and the look in his eyes caused a shiver to surge through Thomas.

'Bigamy?' Thomas repeated numbly.

'Yes, you know, the state of marrying someone while you're still married to someone else? That kind of bigamy.'

Thomas had never expected to encounter the word, for Charlotte had promised not to make a fuss, and also to record in a letter to their daughter that it was not her wish to have the subject raised; not her wish to punish him in any way.

'Prove it,' he heard himself say, unwisely, perhaps; especially to a lawyer.

'Oh, I don't need to,' the boy smiled, preparing to leave. 'But I suggest that you do.'

'It was years ago, no one will be interested.'

'I wouldn't be too sure,' the boy said and this time there was not the trace of a smile on his face. 'If I were you, Mr Blake, I'd give it some serious thought.'

With that, he stood up and walked away; was out of sight before Thomas had time to rise to his feet.

*

Back in the office, Harry found he was trembling. The effort of maintaining a cool and collected exterior had taken its toll, particularly as it was a bluff, for it could blow up in his face were Grace to hear of it and be forced to suffer the consequences of Harry's interference.

He reached for the sheaf of papers on his desk and cast his eye over the top one. A few minutes later, having re-read the first sentence countless times and still making no sense of it, he abandoned any attempt to work and sat back in his chair, thinking through the possible recriminations of his action.

'A bit late now,' he muttered to himself, hands behind his head, eyes closed. 'You should have thought of that before today.'

His main worry was that Thomas Blake would be so incensed by the reference to 'bigamy' that he would contact Grace directly and make something of it; or, he might write to Lily Morris again, a frail old woman unable to cope with such turmoil in her life, who, in utter desperation, could decide to spill the beans to Grace.

Harry took only a few minutes to make up his mind: he had to see her; and soon.

*

Beth was engrossed in the description of a nineteenth-century snuff box when Marjory knocked and popped her head around the door.

'Oh, Mrs Gillespie,' she began, eyes widening to indicate she had donned her official hat. 'There's a gentleman to see you. Is it convenient to show him in?'

Beth gave Marjory an enquiring look and mouthed, 'Who is it?'

'Very good, Mrs Gillespie,' came the reply and Marjory disappeared with a parting apologetic grimace.

Although astonished when she saw him in the doorway, Beth was neither pleased nor annoyed. In deference to her mother, however, and their recent cooling relationship, she waited for him to speak first.

'Would it be permissible for me to come in?' her grandfather asked.

'If it won't take long,' Beth said, in as neutral a tone as she could.

He smiled and closed the door but stood at the other side of her desk, not even glancing at the chair.

'Thank you for seeing me,' he said. 'I didn't know if you would.'

Beth shrugged and covered the paper she was translating, and then she waved her hand at the chair behind which he was hovering.

'Sit down if you like.'

Despite the hardness of her tone and the lack of welcome in her eyes, he sat down and shifted the position of the chair before he spoke again.

'Thank you. I've just met with your husband,' he told her and it took all her acting skills to meet his gaze dispassionately.

'And?'

'You don't appear surprised,' he said and Beth noticed a slight flicker of disappointment on his face.

She shrugged. 'Why would I be?'

'So you knew he was meeting me?'

'Of course.'

'And you agree with what he proposed?'

Beth smiled grimly, for she could have no idea what the proposal had been; nor even that Harry had gone behind her back like this. Had her mother put him up to it? Her only option was to play it calmly.

'We tend to make family decisions.'

'I find that hard to believe,' her grandfather said unexpectedly. 'Grace would never have agreed.'

Beth was in the dark, flailing blindly for clues that he was withholding, either deliberately or by sheer luck.

'Why did you come here?' she asked bluntly.

'To reason with you.'

'If you knew me at all,' she said unkindly, 'You would know that I am not at all reasonable.'

He appeared uncomfortable at that, lowering his eyes for the first time, albeit briefly.

'I'll be honest with you... Beth, isn't it?' When she said nothing, he continued, but with less conviction. 'I think I wrote in my letter to you that the Shepherd family had told their side of things... what passed between Charlotte and me, I mean. But it wasn't the truth, and I don't know you, as you've quite rightly reminded me, but I hate being lied to, and maybe you're the same.'

Predictably, although he could not have guessed it, the words struck a chord with Beth. Momentarily, she hesitated and, perhaps taking hope from the slight delay, his eyes brightened.

'What was the particular lie you think they told?' she asked, too interested now to

139

allow attitudes and mannerisms to block her path. His letter had only whetted her appetite for the Shepherd Lie and she was beginning to care less and less about her mother's or her husband's agenda.

'They let everyone think that I had deserted Charlotte and our daughter,' her grandfather said, but she heard the effort it took for him to utter the words.

'But the truth was that she sent me away.' He met Beth's eyes then and she knew he was being honest with her. For a split second she felt sorry for him, until she remembered she was supposed to be playing it cool.

'She sent you away? She didn't want to see you again?'

'Exactly so,' he nodded. 'And, if the truth be known, I thought I would die without her.'

It was the flatness of his tone, a tone she, herself, often employed to ward off extremes of emotion, that led Beth to believe him; moreover, along with her abhorrence of people lying to her ran the parallel interest in justice being served. It was her husband's profession that had attracted her to him at the very beginning; not his looks, nor his personality. Sometimes, in the darkness of the night, she wondered if she would have noticed him had he been studying chemistry.

'Tell me what happened,' she invited him, sitting back in her chair, arms folded, a sign that she might hear him out but that it would have to be pretty convincing.

'I loved your grandmother,' he said first and, whether it was a calculated remark or not, the term was a point in his favour, for Beth's mind had already accepted that she was Charlotte Shepherd's own flesh and blood, not simply a spectator of a 1920s drama.

The man sitting in front of her was directly responsible for Beth's existence and she could not – would not – relegate him to a small scene in historical events. What was the famous phrase her English teacher had often used?

'Even the fool has his story.'

Well, Beth thought, let him speak. She took a deep breath and waited.

He talked for at least half an hour, stating facts without embellishment, describing his feelings without sentimentality; and as he told his tale, Beth could appreciate his humiliation at having to bare his soul to a slip of a girl. By the end of his monologue she had been won over: she was completely on his side.

'So,' he concluded sadly. 'She even told me to stop sending money, and, worse, to stop writing, said she wouldn't be opening any more of my letters.'

He pressed his lips together in what seemed to be the highpoint of his emotional journey. 'She wasn't bluffing either, sent them back. I still have them.'

'Do you?' Beth asked, and it was the first time she had spoken for half an hour.

He must have picked up her interest, for he smiled and nodded.

'You're welcome to read them any time you want.'

'Really?'

'Of course,' he replied, appearing surprised. 'You're perfectly entitled to read them, being our granddaughter.'

Again, he had drawn her in, made it personal. Beth sighed and looked at him for a long time; but she knew she was only delaying the moment, knew full well that she would read them; deal with the consequences when they arose.

Chapter Five

The amateur dramatic society was in its second month of rehearsal. With a great deal of persuasion and their fair share of luck, the few existing members had roped in enough volunteers to stage most productions, this one being Noel Coward's '*Blithe Spirit*'. Grace was playing Elvira and she was enjoying every moment of it. After a month or so in the depths of despair, she had clambered out of the misery that had influenced so many of her thoughts and decisions and she was now as happy as she could expect to be.

She had long since made her peace with James regarding Alice's secret correspondence, having slowly come to the conclusion that the two of them had been worried on her behalf and how could they be condemned for such a sentiment?

Just occasionally, however, when she had nothing more taxing to occupy her, she would feel the old sense of grievance bubble up inside her, that the people who were supposed to love her most had conspired behind her back, but largely she dwelled upon the positive aspects.

On the last day of November, she had received at last a letter from her old friend, profusely apologising for her negligence in writing and making up for it with a five-page epistle. Now, in the ten minutes left before she had to leave for the rehearsal, Grace re-read Alice's welcome letter.

'Oh, Grace, I'm so happy that I could dance a jig in the main street! Brad is the most wonderful husband you can imagine, and, with the heartache and animosity of my divorce behind me, I can look forward to a peaceful and loving future. AND I won't have to be careful what I say or how I say it either. You know what it's like, this constant tightrope walking, but at least James loves you more than anything. Martin never truly loved me, and that's the most humiliating bit about it. I keep thinking that I wasted half my life on him, and that if he'd only told me he didn't love me I could have made a new life for myself long ago.

The awful part is the children, but they're grown-up really and can understand what's happening. The laugh is, they blame their father for some reason and I feel rather guilty at times! My affair with Brad was so discreet that no one seems to be blaming me. I should be glad, but I'm not as hard-necked as all that!

If you're agreeable, my dearest friend, I'd love to visit in the Spring - April perhaps. Is it still your favourite month? If it's possible to stay with you, then I'd be delighted, but if I'm too much to handle, you have my permission to book me into a local hotel!! Whatever you decide, we can go out and about every day and spend the money I've saved for the trip. You remember how it burns a hole in my pocket?!

I'm so glad that you're feeling better, although you never

said what the problem was. Women's troubles, perhaps? I've had my share too and when I come back into this world, I'll come back as a man!!'

Grace smiled and tucked the pages back into the envelope. This time, however, she did not leave it lying on the dressing table for James to read, but slid it into the top drawer beneath her handkerchiefs. James's disapproval of divorce was well known, and the news of Alice's marriage to the man who had been her secret lover for years was best confined to Grace; at least, for the moment.

She checked her purse, in case someone was selling raffle tickets at the meeting, and then combed her hair, cut shorter recently but still showing no signs of greying.

Suddenly, poignantly, she missed her daughter's influence in the house, her readiness to tame Grace's hair or to wield the lipstick brush to cheer her up. Grace paused at the top of the stairs; tried to recall the last time Beth had visited. Her mind searched swiftly: it was at least six weeks; and even the regular telephone calls had lapsed.

Slowly, Grace placed her foot on the first step. Had she been so distracted by her father; so wrapped up in her own selfish needs, that she was oblivious to the effect the whole affair was exerting on Beth? Had she even given the girl more than a few minutes' thought in past weeks? Doubtlessly, her reliance on Harry had caused resentment between them; in which case Beth would hold her mother responsible.

Mindful of the time, Grace wrenched her thoughts free and descended the stairs. She would have to contact Beth first thing; sort things out.

When she went downstairs, James gave her a look of appreciation, a far cry from the old days when she had not had enough courage to argue when he derived most satisfaction at her staying at home; garbed in drab grey.

'You suit that dress,' he said, glancing at her above the spectacles he now wore. 'It's lovely. Is it new?'

'Goodness, no. It's one of the hand-me-downs from years ago.'

His eyebrows rose. 'You've done well to keep your figure.'

'I hide it beneath this cardigan.'

'You look the same as the day I met you,' James said, giving her a wink. 'As soon as I saw you I told my best friend that I would marry you.'

It was the first time Grace had heard of it. 'Did you? I'd no idea you decided to marry me at first sight.'

'Oh, yes,' he smiled, laying aside his book and removing his spectacles. 'You were so lovely, I couldn't take my eyes off you.'

'I remember thinking I wouldn't mind dancing with you either.'

'You didn't show it.'

'Didn't I? I thought it was pretty obvious.'

James shook his head. 'I often wondered.'

'Wondered what?' Grace asked in astonishment.

'Whether you were only being polite.'

'Polite? Goodness me, no. I was willing you to come over and ask me.'

For a moment they sat in silence, mulling over their own thoughts, but Grace was late already and time was short.

'I should go now,' she said, standing up reluctantly. 'I'll be back before ten tonight because Lily won't be there and I won't be walking her home.'

'She had the doctor in this morning, so I heard at the Post Office.'

'Yes, I'll pop in for five minutes, just to check on her.'

Grace picked up her purse and went to find her stout walking shoes, for the pavements were already icing up. As she made her way up the village street, her mind

142

was not focussed on the Noel Coward play, but on her daughter, and the best way to make things up to the girl.

*

Beth heard Harry's key in the lock and swiftly stuffed the letters into her underwear drawer. She took several deep breaths to compose herself and then walked casually into the hall to meet him.

'Hi,' he said, giving her an appreciative look. 'You're a sight for sore eyes.'

'What, in an old t-shirt and baggy trousers? You're desperate.'

He grabbed her and planted a kiss on the top of her head, but she snuggled into him and held on tightly. She hated deceiving him; and her mother. There was only so much of it she could endure.

'I have to talk to you about something,' she heard herself say; but was she ready for it yet?

'I hope you're pregnant,' he said and she jumped back in astonishment. 'Ah, you're not then,' Harry smiled, releasing her and hanging up his coat.

'Why would you want to have kids yet?'

'I'm thirty, you know, and time's clanking on.'

'You look twenty and you know it.'

'And you look twelve, so are you old enough to have any?'

'Seriously, there's something bothering me.'

Harry looked at her closely, and she wondered if he had seen the flicker of apprehension in her eyes

'Let me get changed,' he said. 'I'll be through in five minutes.'

Beth nodded, but five minutes was a long time to think about it, long enough to take cold feet.

'O.K. I'll pour us some drinks. What's yours?"

'Red wine if there's any left. I slugged it back something rotten last night.'

'I didn't notice,' Beth called from the kitchen. 'I was too busy slugging back the white. Anyway, make it quick. I've something to tell you.'

Harry retraced his steps to the living room door.

'Tell me now.'

Beth's attention wavered from the oven, but her eyes refused to meet his directly.

'A few minutes won't make that much difference. Go and change.'

Harry shrugged and swung on his heel.

*

In the bedroom, Harry changed into cords and a loose sweater, one that Beth had knitted him years before – two sizes too big and in a sombre shade of maroon. Still, it pleased her when he wore it and tonight, after she had told him whatever was bothering her, he would have to tell her what was bothering him.

The smell of shepherd's pie wafted through the flat: he knew it would be shepherd's pie because it was Thursday. If anything, Beth Melville was a creature of habit when it came to mundane things, whilst in others, she was utterly unpredictable.

'Smells good,' he told her as he joined her in the sitting room.

'You'll never guess what's bothering me,' she began hesitantly.

'Nope, you'll have to tell me.'

'Harry...'

Hearing the tremor in her voice, he turned sharply; just before she burst into tears.

143

Grace's ability to get the most out of the character was appreciated by most members. Only Molly, her best friend no less, was grudging in her praise; not that Grace cared a jot, but Graham Seaton was quite vociferous in his opinion, perhaps to counter Molly's lukewarm response.

'You're a great actress,' he often told her, well within earshot of her friend. 'If you were the only one on stage, the audience would get their money's worth.'

'Graham, honestly,' Grace would counter jovially. 'I enjoy what I do, but I'd be pretty miserable up there on my own.'

She hoped it was the line between false modesty and blowing her own trumpet, for she knew that she could act and that she had an instinctive flair for character; but, at the same time, it was a small community and she had to live alongside the rest of the cast. There was no reason to cause resentment, especially for something so trivial.

'Did you ever see '*Zulu*'?' he suddenly asked her.

'No, I didn't.'

'Oh, it was fabulous,' he enthused, shaking his head in what Grace presumed was admiration. 'That new actor, Michael Caine, was just perfect in the part, absolutely perfect. Actually,' he said, as if it had only occurred to him. 'He looks a bit like your son-in-law.'

'Does he?'

'You must have noticed, surely?'

'No, I can't say I have. Of course,' Grace smiled apologetically. 'I really have no idea what Michael Caine looks like.'

'Like Harry,' Molly chipped in, moving to stand beside them. 'If I were ten years younger...'

Grace caught sight of Graham Seaton's disapproval.

'Perhaps we should get started again?' she asked him, completely ignoring Molly. 'I've to pop away early to see Lily.'

'Oh, she's fine,' Molly said airily. 'I saw her an hour ago and she's up and about already.'

'I'll go in on my way home anyway,' Grace insisted, wondering for the umpteenth time why she and Molly were best friends. 'Just to check if she needs anything tomorrow when I'm in Dundee.'

'That's the third time you've been in Dundee this month,' Molly told her accusingly, as if it were a crime. 'Why do you never go to Perth now?'

Grace shrugged. 'I don't know really. It was Beth's idea the first time,' she lied. 'She wanted to have lunch in the Café Val D'Or.'

'Oooh, very swish,' Molly laughed. 'Have you won the pools?'

'Maybe we should get started,' Graham suggested diplomatically. 'I'll go and get them prised away from the sandwiches.'

Whenever Graham had moved off. Molly turned and whispered confidentially to Grace.

'I think I know why you don't go into Perth now.'

'Do you?'

'I heard from Lily Morris that your father's still there, rented a house on Kinnoull Hill apparently, a big one with lots of rooms.'

It was news to Grace, but she was so accustomed to fending off the adverse effects of Thomas Blake's influence that she smiled and shook her head.

'Is that so? Well, I never.'

'Apparently he's got money,' Molly said, with the reverence of someone who aspired to it. 'Sarah – you know, the girl who works at the George? She said he used to chuck it around like it was going out of fashion.'

'I daresay he'll have made lots of friends then,' Grace said pointedly. 'Now, I think they're ready to begin again.'

She moved to the stage and picked up her script but she was relieved that her first lines were easy, for the pounding of her heart and the sense of anger at the mention of her father would not dissipate so quickly.

*

Harry sat opposite her, waiting for her to speak again, although he could hardly trust himself to answer her. The idea that she had colluded with the very man he and Grace wanted removed from their lives was so appalling that he felt physically sick.

He stared into the fire, unwilling to raise his eyes to hers lest she read his mind. As the minutes ticked by, however, and she remained silent, he had to glance up eventually, surprised to find she was looking at him.

'You're angry,' she said, the handkerchief at her nose. 'I know you are, so don't pretend.'

'Of course I'm angry,' he said, but without raising his voice. 'But more than that, I'm disappointed.'

'He's my grandfather,' she said for the fourth or fifth time, as if it explained everything. 'Besides, I want to be fair, to find out the truth.'

'You're interfering in Grace's past, going against her wishes. You know that, don't you?'

'The only thing I know is that it's important to ferret out the truth.'

'*His* truth,' Harry said bluntly, to be rewarded by a scowl.

'No, not his, the actual, plain truth of it,' Beth responded impatiently.

'I can't see how it will help, even if you do 'ferret' out the truth, as you put it. Sometimes truth isn't the best remedy.'

Her eyes widened in horror, reminding him of the one-way street that was Beth Melville's mind in the realm of high moral values, and affirming how much of James Melville was in his daughter.

'How can you say that?' she asked now, throwing him a disdainful glance. 'And you being a solicitor makes it even worse.'

Harry sighed, which was quite the wrong thing to do to his wife when she was in full indignant flow. She leaped to her feet and stormed from the room.

He sat patiently, waiting for her to come back, but to his surprise she had still not returned after half an hour and he was left with no option but to go and find her; this time, however, he would not be begging her forgiveness.

*

Beth hurled herself on top of the bed and discarded the damp hanky in favour of a box of tissues. She found to her delight, however, that her eyes were dry and that the spell of weepiness had subsided, leaving her with a quiet determination not to be swept aside. She had seen it happen to her mother and she had learnt from the experience: ten tips on how to avoid being stamped on, then having the stuffing ripped out of you, and then, the ultimate indignity of being tethered on a short chain to the back green; in the drabbest grey frock imaginable.

Why was it that so many strong-willed women – and she counted her mother in their

145

ranks – allowed themselves to be turned into serfs who spoke only when they were spoken to and then only to say 'yes'? If it were not for the need to have sex, would things be remarkably different? She sighed into the tissue – lavender-scented; supposed to be calming – and considered her options.

She had blundered by telling him anything, should have kept it to herself; but it was well-nigh impossible to deceive him about something so important for such a long time, and she had struggled with it for weeks now. If Harry would only agree to read the letters, he might see her point, but would he relent and read them? Beth thought not.

Sitting up in bed, listening for his tread in the hall, she held her breath and waited. If he were to prove intransigent, she could always withhold her favours as a last resort, as a Barbara Cartland heroine might say. She had suspected her mother of doing it on the odd occasion, and she was of a generation that was naive about sex, so, if Grace Melville could do it, so could her daughter, a child of the swinging sixties, a bra-burning women's libber.

At last, Beth heard the sitting room door open and close and she lay down with her eyes firmly closed.

*

Grace let herself into Lily's vestibule with the spare key she had in her purse and called out to put the old lady's mind at rest.

'It's only me. Are you in bed yet?'

'No, I'm making scones,' came the reply from the kitchen. 'Come through.'

Shaking her head at a woman who was stubborn enough to be baking at ten o'clock after the doctor had confined her to bed, Grace followed the aroma of fresh baking and pushed open the kitchen door.

'Tea's in the pot,' Lily said, her floury hand waving in the direction of the tray, already set with two cups, two plates and some butter in a dish. 'And there's jam in the larder if you'd like.'

'Butter's fine, and what the heck are you doing up at ten o'clock at night, when you should be resting in bed, you thrawn cratur?'

Lily gave a wry smile. 'I haven't heard that one for a while.'

'Don't change the subject. Why aren't you resting?'

'The honest truth?' Lily asked, turning and giving Grace her full attention.

'Aye, the honest truth.'

'If I'm going to drop dead, I'd rather it was in here than in my bed. All that blood and gutters on the sheets. I'd never hear the end of it.'

'What blood and gutters, for Heaven's sake?'

'When you kick the bucket,' Lily told her companion irreverently. 'There's an awful mess behind, you know. Everything falls out, and I mean *everything*. Better it's on this tiled floor and can be swilled away, than on the mattress. It's new, that mattress, and somebody can have it when I'm gone.'

Grace sat down, watching her old friend remove the last tray of scones from the oven.

Humour apart, Grace took no pleasure in the conversation, for it reminded her too much of a morning in March '44 when she had heard her grandfather's anguished cry at the sight of his youngest daughter lying on the living room floor. Even twenty years later, it was a sound that still haunted Grace.

'I'm not listening to all this talk of death and swilling kitchen floors,' she said firmly. 'You look well enough to me, Lily Morris.'

'And you seem much better too,' Lily said, giving Grace a sidelong glance as she wiped the griddle clean. 'Have you stopped these daft pills you were taking?'

Grace had to smile. 'Yes, Professor, I've stopped them.'

'What you need is a grandchild,' Lily remarked with a cheeky smile. 'Once Beth and Harry get going, you'll not have time to wonder if you're feeling fine or not. Any sign that Beth's broody yet?'

'Not a chance. She's enjoying her life too much.'

'Bairns soon put a stop to that, sure enough.'

'And she says she's far too young, and I agree with her.' Grace chose the smallest scone and placed it on the plate. 'They don't seem to be in any hurry to be mothers these days.'

'You mean they're not in any hurry to give up their good salaries,' Lily corrected with a sniff. 'They've more money in a year than we saw in a life-time and yet they want more. I always say –'

'Yes, we know what you always say,' interrupted Grace. 'If you want to know what God thinks of money, just look at the people he gives it to.'

'Aye, it's one of my favourite sayings.' Lily said happily, helping herself to a pancake and giving it a critical examination. 'That's too doughy,' she added, turning it over in her hand. 'I must be getting old.' Suddenly, she fixed Grace with a disconcerting stare and asked: 'Did your son-in-law tell you about the letter?'

Grace's hand froze on the way to her mouth. 'Letter? What letter?'

'The one your father sent to me a few months back.' Lily appeared confused. 'You mean, he hasn't told you yet?'

'No, he hasn't,' Grace answered, trying to sound casual. 'Was it important?'

'I'll say it was. He wanted me to tell you the truth about him and your mother.'

'I know the truth about him and my mother.'

'Maybe not.'

Grace laid the untouched scone back on her plate and met her companion's eyes. 'What?'

Lily shrugged and pulled a face. 'Sometimes the truth's not the best thing to hear, pet, at least not when you're young.'

A familiar sense of trepidation rippled through Grace. It was always the same: whenever she thought she had survived the latest crisis, another rose up and slapped her in the face. Would there ever be a day when they were all behind her? Bitterly she decided that the day would dawn only after her coffin lid had been nailed down.

'Do *you* know the truth?' she frowned at Lily.

'Oh, aye, I do indeed.'

'And you never thought to tell me?'

'Charlotte wanted to…'

'She's been dead for bloody years!' Grace heard herself exclaim. 'Why are you still harping on about what she wants? Do you not think it's about time you asked what I wanted?'

Lily's face fell but Grace was not for turning back. She had been duped by all and sundry and she was losing her patience. Lily remained silent.

'Oh, for Heaven's sake!' Grace cried out, frightening the old lady. 'Say something!'

Lily sighed and shook her head. 'I'm sorry, Grace, I should have told you about the letter, but I didn't feel up to it. I telephoned your son-in-law, asked him to deal with it.' She gave Grace an apologetic smile. 'It never occurred to me that he wouldn't tell you, pet, honest to God.'

'Well, I'm sorry you were left with it all,' Grace said more calmly. 'What a mess.'

'If you want to read his letter, the one Thomas Blake sent me, I should imagine that Harry still has it.'

'You know, Lily,' Grace said wearily. 'I'm so fed up with all of it that I'm not even sure if I want to read it.'

'That's your choice, of course,' Lily said, but there was disapproval in her tone. 'Anyway, if you feel you want to, you can ask young Gillespie about it.'

'I'll have to think about it.' Grace stood up to take her leave. 'But, why didn't Harry tell me about the letter?'

Lily opened her mouth to say something, but changed her mind.

'I'll see myself out,' Grace said a few minutes later, after an uncomfortable silence.

'Ask your son-in-law,' was Lily's parting shot.

*

Grace walked slowly along the slippery pavement, hanging on to railings and fences on her way home. Her slow progress suited her fine, for she had a lot of thinking to do.

Her legs aching from keeping her balance on the icy pavement, Grace stood for a moment at the front gate, unable to recall a time when she had felt so uncertain about the future.

*

Lying awake in the spare room, Beth raked in the tissue box and found it empty. With a sigh of exasperation, she climbed from the uncomfortable single bed and padded her way to the kitchen, where she grabbed a roll of paper towels and marched back to bed. Despite not being lavender-scented and calming, they would have to do.

She was unsettled in this room, being as it was at the back of the flat and furthest from the master bedroom. She jumped at every little sound, for it was three in the morning and she hated being here alone; her own choice, of course, but it was still pretty scary, even with the curtains half open and a faint glow from the street light seeping in.

He had issued her with an ultimatum; that had been the problem. No-one –not even her father – gave Beth Melville an ultimatum. If they did, only trouble and chaos could follow.

'I forbid you to have anything more to do with him, Beth,' Harry had said at last, presumably having reached the limits of his patience.

'Who are you to forbid me?' she had asked coldly, and after that it all went downhill, culminating in talk of separation, divorce even, and her marching from the bedroom clutching her nightdress. She had forgotten to pick up her makeup bag, with all her cleansers and toners and night creams, and she was beginning to feel like a vagrant in a shop doorway.

Reluctantly, she settled into the bed as best she could and closed her eyes.

Maybe it would all seem better in daylight. Yes, and pigs could fly.

*

Harry awoke with a start, lay listening to the strange sounds in the flat. It was only Beth, scrambling in the kitchen for something, crashing around like the proverbial bull in the china shop; to wake him up probably just because she had insomnia.

It had been the ultimatum that had pushed her over the edge. No one, not even James Melville, issued that girl with an ultimatum. He smiled at the thought, but knew he would not back down, He had said it to himself before and he would say it again: if he had to choose between his wife and Grace, it was no choice at all.

He sighed and settled down as best he could in the huge, empty bed. Per-haps things would seem better in the morning; and then he marvelled that he could entertain such an idiotic idea.

*

Lily Morris sat by the fire long after Grace had left. She even stoked it at midnight in case she could not sleep and had to come back down. Why on earth had the boy not mentioned the damned letter? With one simple phrase, the whole thing could have been resolved and the girl would finally have some peace. Lily knew it had been foolhardy to blab about truth not being the best thing to hear. Had she ever heard such nonsense in her life? She shivered; drew her chair closer to the fire. The words clamoured inside her head until she could contain them no longer.

*

'Charlotte Shepherd, I have never heard such nonsense in my life.'

'It's not nonsense to me.'

'Have you lost your mind? Have you thought what you're doing to the bairn, if not to yourself?'

'The two of us will be fine,' her friend had said, walking away from Lily, making her way up the garden. 'Now, if you don't mind, I've the Angoras to see to.'

'You'll be the laughing stock of this village... you and the bairn, until the day you die. Don't be so stupid, Lottie Shepherd.'

'And I wish you'd stop calling me that,' Charlotte had said irritably. 'My name's Blake now. I'm married, remember?'

'I thought marriage meant you were man and wife,' Lily had snapped, at the end of her tether. 'You're still living here and he's to be living God knows where. Call that a marriage?'

'If you must know,' Charlotte said, more quietly, picking up one of the Angora rabbits from the cage and stroking the silky coat, 'I'm not going to travel half way round the world in this state.' She patted her stomach. 'Anything might happen and I'll not risk it.'

'But your father told me you were never going to join Thomas, not even when the bairn comes.'

Charlotte had turned and looked at her friend then, an expression of sadness in her eyes that she was not quick enough to hide. For a moment she was silent, and then, her face brightening up, she laughed and lowered the rabbit back into the cage.

'We'll see,' she said, avoiding Lily's gaze. 'Only time will tell.'

Lily took her courage in both hands and decided to say it.

'Your father was telling me that you were so anxious to get rid of...' she hesitated long enough for Charlotte to turn and look at her. '...your husband,' she pronounced with heavy sarcasm. '...that you even paid for his fare out there.'

The anger on Charlotte's face was unprecedented: Lily had never seen such a look in her friend's eyes in the twenty years they had been friends.

'Maybe you'd like to post a bulletin in the shop, Lily Morris, and that way the whole village would know my business.'

The venom in the tone shocked Lily momentarily, but she recovered quickly and prepared to reply. Charlotte, however, spoke first, still as angry, her cheeks aflame.

'I'm not brave enough, if you must know, to go with him.'

'Yet you were brave enough to lift your skirts for him.'

Lily flinched at the memory of her words, for, even after forty years, she could hardly believe what she had said. The two of them had not spoken after that, not for months, each of them waiting until the heat of the moment had cooled, looking for the opportunity to heal the rift; but it had only been after Grace was born that, with no real enthusiasm at the start, they met one day for a brief chat and even shook hands.

The fire crackled and spat, rousing Lily from her reminiscing. The words rang in her head, like a tune she wanted to stop singing, but could not.

Brave enough to lift your skirts for him

With a groan, she lay back in the armchair and closed her eyes; but neither the words nor her friend's heart-broken expression were so easily shed. The worst thing, however, was that she had never been able to make up for it in her devotion to Charlotte's daughter, and now Lily had allowed the child's life to be as blighted as the mother's. She could blame Alexander Shepherd, she supposed, or Helen, his spiteful daughter, or she could even blame Thomas Blake himself for being such a spineless twerp that he allowed his wife to dictate their future; in an age when men ruled the roost.

The clock struck one and Lily rose from her chair, set the fireguard on the hearth and switched off the lamp.

Chapter Six

Harry drew up at the house and saw her at the window. Despite the fact he had let her down, and despite the fact that she was at liberty to harbour a grievance against him, she waved and smiled, making him feel worse than before. As she opened the front door and met him on the path, an overwhelming sense of disloyalty blocked his mind to what he had meant to say to her.

'Harry, how nice of you to come all this way,' Grace said, taking his arm in an unexpected gesture of affection and walking slowly by his side towards the door. 'I feel like a silly old woman, not being able to face going to Perth. You must think you've married into a family of lunatics.'

He could have told her that the marriage she had in mind was at breaking point at the moment and, had he been a betting man, he would have laid no odds on its survival. Instead, he smiled and tried to sound as if everything were normal at home.

'Don't be daft. Although,' he paused and rolled his eyes humorously. 'I have known the odd occasion when Beth gets up in the middle of the night to see if she can still hit middle 'c' without hearing it on the keys.'

Grace glanced at him in surprise. 'Does she still do that?'

'Frequently,' he smiled, standing back to let her through the doorway first. 'But I have my own little foibles too.'

'Like what?' she asked, but warily.

'Like thinking I'm doing things for the best and then falling flat on my face.'

She turned and looked at him with no trace of accusation, and then she smiled, a slow, encouraging smile that banished his blues completely.

'Oh, Harry,' she said quietly. 'Don't ever think you've let me down.'

Although he had not used these words to her, they had been romping around his mind for the better part of two days, and he thought it strange that she should have echoed them.

'I can't help it,' he shrugged, aware that they were still standing in the hall, front door open to the cold wind. 'Shall I close this?'

'Oh, yes, what I am thinking of? Another sign of a silly old woman. James is at a meeting, won't be back until late. Did you have to lie to Beth?'

'No, she wasn't home, so I left her a note,' Harry said tactfully. It was partly true: she had not been at home; but he had not bothered to leave a note. At the moment, neither of them cared where the other was.

'Come through to the kitchen, I've made pancakes, or at least tried to. Lily's so much better than I at things like that.'

At the mention of Lily's name he was sharply reminded of the reason for his visit. In his mind, jumbled words and phrases vied for his attention, lining up in order of priority.

'Please sit down,' Grace was saying now. 'Is it tea or coffee?'

'Tea, please, if that's what you're having.'

'No sugar, a little milk,' she said, turning to hand him the cup. 'Have I got it right?'

'Perfect.' Harry took the cup and saucer. 'These are lovely,' he indicated the china crockery.

'They were a wedding present.'

They sat opposite each other and there was a short silence. Harry knew he should be the first to speak, but his courage was deserting him. If there were one thing that upset him most of all, it was failing to live up to Grace Melville's expectations of him.

*

Grace sat opposite the boy and stirred sugar into her cup. After her anxiety as to how she could broach the subject, it seemed her fears were being confirmed: that her courage would seep away at the last moment. At last, she took a deep breath.

'What did he say in the letter?'

When Harry spoke, his words rushed out in a constant stream, confirming her suspicions that the boy was equally anxious.

'He said he wanted her to go with him, but she refused, said she couldn't travel when she was pregnant, and not even after that, and he did try.'

She flinched at the starkness of words when they were separated from the frailties of the people who had once lived them. To hear it in such a blunt setting was more disturbing than the events themselves.

'What else?'

'He said she was under her father's thumb and could never go against the old man's wishes.'

Suddenly feeling the stuffiness of the air in the room, Grace straightened up in her chair and took several deep breaths. Harry leaned forward.

'Are you all right? We can stop this if you'd rather?'

'No, I think it's best if we get it over with'

'Only if it's best for you,' he insisted, and she was reminded of his loyalty to her. 'I couldn't care less about anyone else, but if it's distressing you, we'll stop.'

Even in the midst of such turmoil, Grace had to smile. The boy had no qualms about showing his feelings; displayed no embarrassment in front of her

'Did you believe him?' she asked quietly.

Immediately, Harry shook his head. 'Not for a moment.'

Because of his compassion for her, Grace suspected that the words had been chosen to placate her.

'Why not?'

'Because if you love someone, you'll do anything to be with them.'

It was said with such passion that Grace suffered a fierce stab of resentment over her daughter's relationship with Harry Gillespie. Her swift intake of breath aroused the boy's interest.

'You know what I mean, don't you?' he asked now.

'Yes, of course,' Grace responded automatically.

'So Thomas Blake couldn't have loved your mother enough.' Harry lowered his eyes to his cup. 'Otherwise he would have moved Heaven and Earth to be with her.'

Grace nodded. 'That's always been my opinion. But now, with Beth being taken in by the man...' There was no need to complete the sentence, for they both knew the implications.

'I'm doing my utmost to talk her out of it.'

'Don't jeopardise your marriage,' Grace felt obliged to advise him.

'Some things are more important than our own selfish needs.'

He looked at her with such affection that Grace could think of nothing to say.

*

Beth trudged up the street, forgetting exactly where she had parked the car. The wind was howling down the High Street, almost knocking her over, and now the snow was falling, thick flakes that were piling up on the pavement, sticking to the heels of her boots, making her teeter off-balance and lose her temper. The parcels she was carrying were too bulky, not heavy, just bulky, and every so often in her Captain Scott trek to wherever she had left the car, she had to stop and rest them on a shop window, so that she could reposition them before she could go any further.

There was no getting away from it: she was as wretched as she had ever been in her life and, had she been blessed with company at this very moment and obliged to speak, she would have burst into tears at the drop of a hat.

'Beth! Wait!'

Even muffled up to the eyeballs in thick scarf, woollen tammie and high collar, she recognised the voice, swithered about dashing into the ladies' loo in McEwens and sitting there until the coast was clear. She halted – mostly because the bulky parcels were sliding from her grasp – and made a valiant attempt to recover them; too late, however, for they cascaded to the pavement where they slithered around on the cover of snow like a gangly Bambi.

'Here, I'll help you,' Charlie Webster said, upon which Beth nodded dumbly, not trusting herself to speak. 'Give me your bag, it's awkward on your shoulder, slipping off like that. There, now we can save you from doing a Sonja Henje impression.'

Beth looked at him, his face lit by the bright Christmas lights in McEwens' windows. 'Sonja who?'

'A famous ice skater long before your time.'

'And before yours, I think.'

'My grandmother,' he explained humorously. 'She's in her eighties and was an ardent admirer apparently. Come on, I'll buy you a coffee. You look utterly miserable, you poor soul.'

It was not so much the word itself, but the sad way he said it, and, at the last moment, Beth did make a huge effort not to give in; but the chill in her toes matched the chill in her heart and she knew she was about to make a fool of herself.

The café was as cheerful and happy as Beth was gloomy. She sat waiting for Charlie to come back to the table with her coffee and a chocolate éclair and dabbed her eyes with a tissue that had seen better days. The laugh was that she was past caring who saw her or if she looked like a scarecrow in a field. Harry was the only one she dressed up for, pampered her skin for, fluttered her eyelashes at; and if he were out of the equation she had no incentive to do any of it. She looked at her watch and wondered where he was.

*

As he moved towards her, balancing the tray with over-filled coffee cups, Charlie's heart skipped a beat: she was the most beautiful creature, especially with moist eyes, dishevelled hair and a bloom on her skin from such a cold night. What the hell was her dolt of a husband thinking, not keeping her in sight twenty-four hours a day? The man needed his head examined.

'Here we are, just what the lady ordered. It's on me, no arguing.'

'I wasn't going to,' she said, and the first hint of a smile touched her lips.

Having focussed on the said lips, Charlie had a heck of a job to tear his eyes away.

'So, what's a nice girl like you doing in a cold, snowy street in the middle of the night?'

'It's only half past seven.'

'You should be at home being waited on hand and foot.'

He had no idea what had possessed him to blurt it out. In fact, had he not recognised his own voice, he might have imagined it was someone else speaking.

'Gosh, I'd hate that,' she frowned. 'Heaven help your future wife.'

Inwardly, he cursed himself. Now he had blown it, surely?

'I only meant tonight,' he amended with a smile and a prayer. 'Because you look so

153

miserable and cold.'

'Don't get me bubbling again,' she pleaded, glancing across at him and stabbing him with the piercing green eyes. 'I've only just got control.'

'I'm just glad I was passing,' Charlie lied, having followed her from work. 'Where did you park your car anyway?'

'At the kerbside,' she said, deadpan.

'You're very witty, but I think I told you that a long time ago,' he said, giving some substance to their non-relationship.

'I remember.' She was looking at his sandwich, at his attempts to remove the wrapper. 'Don't you have your scout knife handy?'

He laughed. 'Funnily enough, I was in the Scouts.'

'Were you? Let's see your knife then.'

He laughed again and was delighted to see that she almost did the same; almost, but not quite.

'I could ask you to come back and see it, but that's as corny as etchings, isn't it?'

'No,' she said unexpectedly. 'It's perfectly acceptable.'

For a moment Charlie floundered, aware of her studious gaze and knowing that, at any time between now and opening his mouth, he would ruin everything.

'So,' she smiled, eyes on him. 'Are you, or aren't you going to ask me back to see your Scout knife?'

*

Harry let himself into the flat and knew at once that she was out. The place was in total darkness, which meant that, not only was she out, but she had never been in; a slightly disconcerting thought despite their recent impasse.

He wandered to the central heating cupboard and turned the dial up, and then, retaining his overcoat until he felt warmer, he went into the kitchen and took the gin bottle out of the fridge, adding it to the tray of clean glasses that always awaited his arrival home. There was no tonic, for she had been so contrary that morning that he had hardly spoken to her, far less ask her nicely if she could pop into the corner shop for him.

There was a half a bottle of flat lemonade in the cupboard and he decided it would do. Switching only one or two lights on, Harry meandered through to the bedroom, glass in hand, swilling the ghastly combination down before the taste put him off. After the first few, he would not even notice.

He sat down on the bed and, for the first time in his life, he could not be bothered to smooth his coat under him, even foreseeing the garment's crushed state, his resemblance to every other man walking the streets of Perth. It was one of those things that he had never understood: why any man would be content to be seen in public wearing a coat he had obviously slept in. Perhaps tonight he had the answer: they were all unhappily married suckers, sitting on their coats in a darkened room, guzzling back the booze for all they were worth; waiting for their wife to come home.

After the glass was empty, he stood up and set off to replenish it, chucking his coat at the bottom of the hall cupboard with a flourish; slamming the door shut before he suffered remorse at the crumpled result.

He blinked at the sudden spread of light when he switched on the kitchen spotlights. They had been Beth's idea, but he thought them too bright, too invasive, and, at 100 watts each, too expensive to run. He glanced at the clock and saw that it was half past eight. Where the heck could she be?

Unhappy marriages apart, he was beginning to worry, for she was a creature of habit and her habit was to come home after work, no matter what; besides which, the snow was so heavy now that it obliterated his view of the Inch, and she hated getting cold and wet. In fact, when she became victim to the rigours of inclement weather, Beth Melville was the most contrary girl he could think of.

Harry sighed and decided he had no option but to run out for fish and chips; or – a more salubrious idea – he could nip up the road to the Station Hotel and dine like a gentleman. He looked at himself in the hall mirror as he passed it for the third time in his quest for oblivion. He looked like something the cat had dragged in. If he wanted to secure the best service in a hotel, he would have to sober up, smarten up, and get the hell out of here before she came back and spoiled his plans.

When he sauntered back into the kitchen, however, and opened the fridge, he discovered cheese slices and a jar of pickle and decided it would do. He spread a very untidy sandwich and took it into the sitting room with his fourth gin and flat lemonade. Had Beth been around, of course, he would have sat in the kitchen with his meagre supper, for one of her edicts was 'no food to be consumed out with kitchen and dining room'.

As he sat eating and dropping crumbs on the carpet, he pondered what he and Grace had discussed; their joint course of action. Rather than spurn his idea of opposing Beth, Grace had been only too willing to support him. His one reservation had been setting mother against daughter: Harry would have preferred to keep Grace out of the conflict, but she was quite resolved to stick by her principles, regardless of the consequences; especially after the shock of discovery.

'You mean, she's been meeting him behind my back?'

'I shouldn't have told you.'

'I'd have been extremely hurt if you hadn't.'

She hád hardly uttered another word on the subject of her daughter. They had stuck to strategy thereafter. Only when he had risen to take his leave did she revert to the topic of Beth's duplicity.

'And to think I was going to phone her and apologise.'

'Look, Grace,' Harry had pleaded, trying to forestall the inevitable animosity between mother and daughter. 'I think it's best if you pretended not to know.'

'I doubt if I could.'

Harry had stifled a smile. 'Oh, I think you're fairly skilled at treading the boards.'

'This is my daughter we're talking about,' she had mused unhappily. 'I don't want to fall out with her, but, at the same time, she's completely ignored my feelings.'

Despite his protestations, and despite the freezing night, she had insisted on walking to the gate with him. He had hurried to the car to shorten her vigil.

'I'll call you soon,' he had told her, doing his best not to see the distress that lingered in her expression. He knew it had been a mistake to tell her; and chose not to dwell on his reasons for doing so.

Now, Harry closed his eyes. He suspected that Grace had no real understanding of her daughter's personality and that he should have warned her of the perils of thwarting the girl.

Regardless of Beth's reaction to the new situation, however, Harry took heart at the empathy he and Grace shared. They were united in the desire to get rid of Thomas Blake and he had persuaded her that they would succeed; words uttered only to gain her complete trust and affection.

Grace Melville was the one person Harry would die for; and his wife could go to Hell.

*

The sight of the house took her breath away. Beth had believed that The Birches was his only main residence and that he might keep a modest flat in Perth for the few days he had business in the city. When she caught sight of the house from the bottom of the driveway, she almost gasped. Talk about Manderley!

'This belongs to mother,' Charlie said as he drove slowly towards the house. 'I can lay no claim to it, other than I'm a paying guest during week.'

'You pay rent for it?' Beth asked, amazed.

'Oh, yes, I wouldn't rob the old girl. She could easily rent it out, so she's doing me a favour really. Here we are. Wait there and I'll just open the garage door.'

She watched him dash through the blizzard and wrench the door open, and then he ran back to the car, covered in snowflakes in the few short minutes, and dived into the driver's seat.

'Wow, that isn't very nice out there. Hope the place is warm enough for you.'

'Don't you have a servant to switch it on for you?' she asked facetiously.

He drew into the garage and stopped the car, turning the key and dousing the headlights. With an apologetic smile, he glanced in her direction.

'Yes, I do have someone who comes in from five until nine.'

'Oh, my sainted Aunt!' Beth exclaimed, but she was too happy not to be stuck in the middle of the freezing High Street to vent any anger on him. 'Will she be there now, to wait on you hand and foot?'

'Come on,' Charlie said, stepping from the car and heading for the inner door. 'We can have a warm drink and forget our troubles.'

'A warm drink? Think again, pal. Mine's a white wine, bubbly if you've got it.'

She meant sparkly, of course, not champagne, and she almost gawped at him when he told her he would bring up a magnum from the cellar.

'Real bubbly?' she asked, not caring how impressed she sounded.

'Yes,' he frowned, pausing at the kitchen door. 'Isn't that what you meant?'

'Absolutely, but I didn't reckon you'd have any.'

'The kitchen's in there. In you go, get warmed up. I'll be back in a jiffy.'

'Will I bump into the hired help?'

'Er... possibly. Her name is Vera and she's not young.' With that he disappeared down a set of stone steps and Beth was left to wander into the kitchen on her own.

When she crossed the threshold, she wondered how many gasps you could emit in five minutes; if there were a finite number of them. It was a dream, the only word to describe it: huge free-standing oak furniture, massive Aga with gold trim, and the most luxurious parquet floor she had ever seen; except in French chateaux. She cast her wet shoes off at the thresh-hold – surprised to feel the floor warm under her feet – and ambled around the room, discovering gems at every turn.

A door opened and an elderly lady came in; white apron, little starched cap, and, most disconcertingly, no expression of surprise on her face to see a strange young girl standing in Charlie Webster's kitchen.

'Good evening, Madam,' she said in a country brogue. 'Is Mr Charlie with you?'

'Yes, he is, just popped down the cellar to get some plonk.'

The hired help smiled, but grimly, and inwardly Beth sighed. She was as cultured as a pig's snout.

'My boy uses that word 'plonk',' the white-aproned figure said, and Beth turned back to look at her. 'He's an engineer, in the Royal Navy.'

'Oh, that's ...good,' Beth smiled, wishing desperately for Mr Charlie's return.

'Will you be having dinner this evening, Madam?'

'Er, no, I don't...'

'Yes, Vera,' came a voice from the door. 'We'll be eating in half an hour, if it's not

156

too late for you?'

'Oh, no, Mr Charlie, that's fine. It's all ready, just to be heated up'

With that, the old dear left the room. At ease in the spacious village that was his kitchen, Charlie popped the champagne cork with a flourish that let Beth know he did it every day; and then he poured it slowly, expertly, into a flute and handed it to her. She was doing her best not be over-awed.

'Come on,' he smiled. 'Let's go and sit next door.'

He led the way through the hallway, its size and splendour akin to what Beth imagined Buckingham Palace to have, and she resolved, whatever the room was like, not to gasp at the next room.

The only reason she did not gasp was because she had just taken a sip of bubbly and her mouth was full. The first thing she noticed was the size of the fireplace, large enough to have seating inside the nook; and the next thing she noticed were the curtains: heavy brocade dripping with gold threads and fancy tassels and sufficient material to start a small draper's business.

'The sofa's comfortable,' she heard him say and her eyes followed his pointing finger to the cosy arrangement by the fire. 'I promise not to molest you,' he said, seriously.

'Well, I should hope not,' Beth countered, but she wondered if she truly meant it.

'Come and sit beside me, tell me what's wrong.'

Taken aback, she paused in her bare-footed progress towards him.

'What do you mean 'what's wrong'?'

Charlie gave her the benefit of his most dazzling smile and beckoned her over.

'Listen, Beth, you and I are good friends, or, at least, I like to think we are.' He hesitated just long enough to allow her time to sit beside him and then he added: 'You're a married woman and I want you to know that you're perfectly safe with me. I would never make a pass at you, now that you have a husband. So, come on, as a friend, tell Uncle Charlie what's wrong.'

He sipped from the champagne flute and glanced at her over the rim of the glass.

*

Harry awoke with a start and, no sooner had his eyes opened, than a fresh wave of despair washed over him: his wife was still not home...

He glanced at his glass and realised that, because of the gymnastics of his mind before he nodded off, he had not touched the gin. Now, he made up for the omission by swigging it back in one gulp after which his thoughts were temporarily numbed.

He sat up and manipulated his body into a comfortable position, kicking off his shoes and knocking over the bottle of lemonade. Even when the sticky liquid seeped into the carpet, Harry made no attempt to mop it up.

His mind cleared slowly and he looked at the clock. It was almost ten o'clock and Beth had not appeared. Harry was beginning to think that their 'disagreement' was proving more significant than he had anticipated; or perhaps he had never fully understood his wife.

As he stood up, his feet landed on the damp carpet; fuelled his temper. If Beth had walked in at that moment, he knew he would say all the wrong things. With a sigh, he went into the kitchen and picked up a cloth; then he carefully mopped up the remnants of the lemonade and moved the armchair's position to cover the stain. He was trying to work out what phrase had incensed his wife during their recent argument.

'I'm perfectly aware he's your grandfather,' Harry had said the previous day, at the height of their blazing row. 'But Grace is your mother and she's done a bloody good job of raising you, caring for you, watching out for you. In fact,' he had even added, unwisely as it turned out, 'If it hadn't been for her, you'd be serving in a village shop at this very minute, shackled to a country yokel and picking summer fruit to make ends meet.'

'And what makes you think this is any better for me?' she had asked, with the most scathing glance she had bestowed on him. 'Maybe I'd prefer the country yokel.'

'Be my guest,' Harry had smiled, his heart sinking. He could have stopped it there and then, by giving in to her whim about the letters, but it was the old story in a different guise: he would never choose Beth over Grace, not even if it meant the end of his marriage.

He had told her then that she could stuff the man's letters, that he had no intention of reading them or even hearing a single word from their pages. To make it worse – much worse – he also told her not to leave them lying around for him to see, otherwise they would end up in the bin. All in all, it had not been his finest hour.

Harry waited as the hall clock struck the hour. He counted ten and wondered again where the hell she could be at this time of night, in the middle of winter, in a snowstorm.

*

Beth's cheeks were rosy from the dual effects of the roaring fire and three glasses of champagne; but she was still sober, although she could not make up her mind as to whether that was exactly what she wanted. Every time she cast her mind forward to the moment she would enter her flat, she reached for another sip.

Charlie, the perfect gentleman, had been great fun and a sympathetic listener. She had not divulged her innermost secrets, of course, nor any snippet that would point the finger at Harry's being a stinker; no, she had stuck to the story of her grandfather appearing again after fifty years' absence and how much distress it was causing her mother, Half a truth was better than none.

'And you, poor thing,' Charlie said at the end of the sad tale. 'You must be caught in the middle, not knowing who's in the right.'

'Exactly so,' Beth had nodded, sipping slowly, trying to eke out her third glass of bubbly. 'I don't want to hurt my Mum, but I feel I should give the old boy a fair hearing.' She looked at Charlie, doing her best to ignore the tenderness in his eyes in case she forgot that it was too late in the evening and that she had consumed far too much bubbly. The fact she was a married woman came low down on the list. She sighed and wriggled her feet free from under her.

'Sorry to be such a wet blanket, but I must get going. Harry will be sending out a search party.'

'I'll get the coats,' Charlie said immediately and she wondered if her charms were fading already, at the age of twenty-four, or was it five? 'I think I should drive you home, actually,' he frowned. 'Would you be outraged at the suggestion?'

Beth laughed. 'No, not at all. I can't even remember where I left the car anyway.'

'Outside the library,' Charlie told her and, at once, she witnessed his grimace.

'How could you know where my car was?'

'I think I passed it on my way into the city centre,' he said, but Beth was not convinced. 'Hang on,' he added quickly, turning away and almost sprinting across the room. 'I'll be back in a second.'

As the door closed behind him, Beth allowed a slow smile to creep over her face. She was thinking of an abandoned husband, and how it served him right.

*

Grace sat by the fire waiting for James to come back from his meeting. In the silence of the room, especially when she closed her eyes, she could almost imagine that her mother was sitting opposite, in her favourite chair, with the crochet needle clicking back and forth.

Since Harry had left, Grace's mood had swung from euphoria to despair: euphoria because she had found a loyal ally in the boy; despair because Thomas Blake had settled in the area and was still determined to use any means at his disposal to force her to accept him as part of her family. She had mulled over every possibility of ridding herself of the man, but even she had to admit that there was no law against his living here.

The fire was low and she stoked it up, although she had been so deep in thought for the past hour she had neglected it completely; allowed the chill to creep back into the room. She shivered at the inert layer of coal that would take its time to burst into life, and decided to change her clothes, to swap the tailored dress she had donned for Harry for a warmer skirt and cardigan.

As she raked through her wardrobe to find something suitable, she wondered if Harry had been secretly shocked at the hatred she displayed for her father; although the boy assured her he understood her emotion.

'You must feel he betrayed you,' he had said, and the word had caught her breath.

'Yes, that's exactly how I felt…betrayed.'

'About Beth?' he had asked and Grace was puzzled.

'What about her?'

'I'll try to dissuade her if she mentions him to me again,' the boy had smiled and it had put her mind at rest.

'It would be the worst thing that could happen to me, Beth taking his side.'

'Don't worry,' he had assured her. 'I won't let it happen.'

Now, as she selected a tartan skirt that James had bought for her, Grace was becoming more philosophical about Beth's decision to meet the man. She decided that, as with most things, her daughter would blow hot and cold about the matter, and that the interest she was showing in Thomas Blake this month would soon become yesterday's pursuit. Slowly but surely this family would come together and keep him out. Grace smiled to herself. She was optimistic again.

*

Harry heard the car draw away from the kerb and then, a few moments later, her key in the lock. He took courage from her noisy entrance; for it signified she was not skulking.

'Beth?' he called out from his position in the unlit sitting room. 'Is that you?'

Her footsteps clicked along the hall and he found his pulse picking up at the prospect of another row.

'Yes, it's me,' she said from the doorway, making no comment on the darkness. 'Are you disappointed?'

'No, I was worried about you, thought I might charter a rescue helicopter to scour the streets.'

'I wasn't in the streets,' she told him. 'I was with Charlie Webster.'

'Good, at least you were safe.'

He had guessed right, said the right thing, for she gave him an impromptu smile before moving off.

He could have followed her into the kitchen; made some attempt at conversation; but his instinct told him that she was glad to be home and that he should bide his time. If she had something to tell him, he would hear it soon enough.

*

In the kitchen, Beth raked around the cupboards until she found oatcakes and peanut butter, an unlikely culinary combination after champagne, but the old familiar habits were comforting at such times, and peanut butter was her best friend in this kitchen.

She listened for the sound of Harry's feet in the hall, but was disappointed when he did not join her. His remark about her being 'safe' with Charlie Webster was precisely what he should have said: Harry Gillespie knew her better than anyone; and she missed him. As she spread a thick layer of the peanut butter onto the last oatcake, Beth had begun to wonder if there might be room for manoeuvre in the week-long impasse.

When, eventually, she took her tray into the sitting room, the first thing he commented on was that she was breaking her own rule about eating only in the rooms designed for such a purpose.

'Trust you to remind me,' she said, but not irritably, for it was the truth.

The truth!

'I've a confession to make,' Harry said, switching on a lamp beside him.

Beth had a fleeting image of him with Annie but, of course, it was impossible.

'Oh?' she asked, settling herself on the settee and crunching through the peanut butter. 'What confession would that be?'

'I had a sandwich in here.'

Try as she might, she failed to conceal her amusement.

'How terrible.'

'As long as my sentence isn't to be hung by the neck until dead, I reckon I can take anything you dish out.'

For a moment they looked at each other. Beth stopped chewing. Harry was awarding her a look that usually preceded throwing her on the bed.

'So,' she said at last. 'How was your day?'

'Fine, how was yours?'

'My day was fine,' she shrugged. 'But my evening was a disaster.'

'Tell me,' he smiled so lovingly that she almost dropped her plate.

'I went shopping and it was so cold, freezing, in fact, and I had so many parcels and they were so bulky, and then I...' She hesitated.

'Then you what?' Harry asked patiently.

'Then I was miserable and Charlie Webster appeared out of nowhere and took me for a coffee.'

'Well, I'm grateful to him for that,' he lied. 'And to you, for telling me the truth.'

'I haven't finished yet,' Beth said, lowering her eyes and fiddling with the last oatcake. So, perhaps she was leading him on a bit, but, so what? He did deserve it.

*

Harry waited, although he knew there would be nothing more to tell. On the spur of the moment he decided to put his cards on the table.

'If I may interrupt,' he said, and she made no objection. 'I think I know the rest.'

'You think so?' Beth asked, as mysteriously as she could. 'Go on then.'

'Well, let's see. You didn't fancy coming home so early, and so when he suggested you went back to his place, you agreed, and he drove you there, left your own car in the city.' Spurred on by the mild astonishment on her face, Harry continued. 'Then you had a few drinks, got warmed up, by a roaring fire presumably, and then you said you had to

160

go and you went.'

'How do you know we didn't roll around on the bearskin rug together?'

'Because,' Harry said slowly. 'You are the most honest person I know, Beth, and there isn't a snowball's chance in Hell that you would be unfaithful to me until you'd told me first.' He smiled ruefully. 'You'd tell me you fancied someone and would I mind terribly?'

He sat back in his chair, enjoying the astonishment on her face. Even before she spoke, Harry guessed that there might be room for manoeuvre in this week-long impasse.

*

Later, as they lay in the huge double bed, Beth's spirits were low: despite the intimacy of the past hour, despite the joy at making up with a husband who completely understood her, she knew that the problem still lurked in a dark corner, like a bird of prey waiting to pounce.

She would still re-read her grandfather's letters and feel so sorry for him that she would want to meet him and have a chat – grandfather to granddaughter – and then what? Did she have the guts to do it on the sly, no harm done, the rest of the family never knowing? After all, in the grand scheme of things it would be a fairly tiny white lie and if it kept the family together, surely that was acceptable?

She snuggled closer and laid her cold feet against Harry's warm legs.

'Ouch! You're bloody freezing.'

'I'd have thought that heating up your wife's legs is a small price to pay for a night of passion.'

'A night of passion? It's only half past eleven, the night's only just begun.

'What? I'm exhausted.'

'Weakling.'

'Give me ten minutes and I'll think about it.'

*

As she nuzzled his neck and he looked forward to the familiar spontaneity of Beth's lovemaking, Harry knew that the problem still hovered in the shadows. He would still refuse to read the letters, still refuse to have any sympathy for Thomas Blake, and then what? Did he have the courage to pretend he had no idea she was still involved with the man, let her do it on the sly, no harm done, keeping the truth from the rest of the family? If it kept the family together, he would have to give it some thought.

He shuddered as her fingers worked their magic, and all thoughts, other than his own pleasure, vanished from his mind.

Chapter Seven

Thomas Blake strolled down the main street of Bridgend towards the paper shop – as they called it here. It was a fair distance from his house on the outskirts of Perth to the shop but, at his age, he could do with the exercise; furthermore, he was making friends with Daphne. They had passed each other several times just outside the Isle of Skye hotel, she walking her dog – a spaniel – and Thomas striding out with his umbrella and paper, not surprised at all when she smiled and bade him 'good morning' on only their second head-nodding.

'Do you think I'll need this?' he asked now, brandishing his umbrella.

'No, the forecast's good.' Daphne smiled, hauling the spaniel in from its foray in the gutter. 'Come here, Rufus,' she added, but the dog was strong.

'Please, allow me,' Thomas said, taking the lead and pulling until the dog got the message. 'Good boy. Do what your mistress tells you.'

'Thank you, he is a bit naughty. Well, I suppose I must be going. See you tomorrow morning, perhaps?'

She had said it in such a way that Thomas would pick up the hesitation in her tone: she was hoping he would give her a better offer.

'I tell you what,' he said, as if he had just thought of it. 'Why don't I buy you coffee in town this afternoon?'

'Oh,' Daphne said, feigning surprise. 'That would be very nice. Thank you.'

'There's a lovely little café in the High Street, at the river end. Do you know it?'

'Yes, doesn't it have a baker's as well?'

'The very one,' Thomas beamed, his every gesture and nuance of expression designed to reassure her he would not turn out to be a serial rapist. 'Shall we say half past two?'

'Yes, that would be lovely,' Daphne said, cheeks pink. 'I look forward to it.'

'Oh, and by the way,' Thomas said, touching her arm lightly. 'I'm a very old-fashioned kind of chap. I would be most offended if you offered to pay.'

She laughed, a trilling sound that was not unpleasant, but which Thomas decided he could only tolerate in small doses.

'That's very kind of you,' she smiled coyly. 'I'm rather old-fashioned myself and I'd not dream of offering to pay.'

He wondered if she had picked up the inference: that she never paid for anything; but Thomas gave her a salute with the umbrella and bade her farewell.

As Thomas sat by the bay window and looked down at the birds vying for the food the woman next door threw out at nine every morning, his reflections turned to his granddaughter, Beth, and what the reason could be for her silence these past few weeks.

The notes he had been receiving from her, the many questions she had posed and to which he had given honest – if a trifle biased – answers, had dried up and there had been no word from her since his unhappy meeting with her husband. Thomas was beginning to think that the boy had poisoned her against him, particularly as Grace had been so antagonistic, perhaps threatening Beth with banishment from the family if she had anything to do with Thomas Blake. He smiled at the idea of banishment – a bit extreme perhaps – but you never knew just how much influence Grace exerted on her family. If she had taken after Charlotte he would have nothing to worry about; but if she were at all like him, it could be tricky.

It was three weeks to Christmas and it would be the first one he had spent alone in fifty years. The strange thing was that it was not recent Christmases that his mind kept returning to, but the ones with Charlotte – December 1925 in particular. He was assailed by the now familiar wave of despair as the memory unfolded in the darkness behind his closed eyes, Had it been the way she told him, the callousness of her tone that had hurt him so much, or had he been truly heartbroken at the tragic turn their lives had taken? Should he have defied her and stayed, in the hope that she would mellow after the child's birth?

He had not met or even written to the woman in forty years, nor had he a recent photograph of her. Consequently, the image he retained in his mind's eye was that of a twenty-two year old girl, in the flush of youth, with a gentle nature that he had never found in anyone since; least of all their own daughter.

He laughed aloud when he recalled the evening Charlotte had lost her temper, and then only mildly.

You're cycling without lights

*

'What do you mean you're going to fine us?' she had asked Jock, half laughing, half frowning.

'You're cycling without lights,' Jock Stephens had said officiously, standing to attention in front of Thomas's bike as if he expected him to make a run for it. 'I will ask you to pay the fine now, thank you very much.'

'Hang on one minute,' Charlotte said, the first sign of anger showing. 'You're not even on duty now. Besides, there are street lights everywhere.'

'It makes no difference about street lights,' Jock had stated firmly, although he had avoided her eye. 'And whether I'm in the house having my supper or whether I'm in uniform isn't important either. The fine is two shillings each.'

'What?' Charlotte shrieked at the man, much to Thomas's horror, for she was not the kind of girl to cause a fracas. 'Two shillings, you silly man? That's a ridiculous amount. Where am I going to find that sort of money?'

At that point Thomas opened his wallet and began to hand over the sum in question. He had reckoned without Charlotte, however, who wrestled the money from his fingers on its way past her nose, and was now stuffing it in her pocket.

'You'll have to drag me to court, you daft gowk,' she said to the unhappy policeman. 'Put that in your pipe and smoke it.'

With that she stomped off, wheeling her bike away from them but hopping on, still without lights, in full view of Jock Stephens. Now that she was out of sight, Thomas drew another four shillings from his wallet and gave it silently to the man before walking off, bicycle at his side.

When he rounded the corner she was waiting for him, muttering and grumbling away in a state he had never witnessed before. At first he thought it funny, but when he saw how badly she was taking it, his heart went out to her.

'Are you all right, Charlotte?'

'No, I'm not, the stupid, glaikit fool that he is.'

Seeing that she was on the verge of tears, he leaned his bicycle against the fence and went to take her in his arms.

'Oh, Charlotte, never let them bother you like this, my love, they're not worth it.'

She sniffled and sobbed into his jacket for a few minutes and then looked at him with such a miserable expression that his heart lurched: that someone as sweet-natured and as gentle as Charlotte Shepherd should be reduced to tears by one of the world's most dim-witted men was unforgivable.

'Come on,' he told her, taking her hands in his. 'We'll go back and have a quiet

163

seat, put this all behind us.'

'A quiet seat?' she had smiled. 'Where? Father will hardly welcome you to our house and, rest assured, your mother won't even let me in your front garden.'

It had been on the spur of the moment, for he had not intended anything of the sort and later he would never understand his reasoning; but he took a deep breath and squeezed her hands tightly.

'Christmas is the day after next.'

'Aye,' she laughed, back to her usual self. 'I think I'd remembered.'

'My mother's away tonight, won't be back until tomorrow.'

'You want me to do your washing, do you?'

'You know damned fine that I do,' he said pointedly, but he had asked her to marry him so many times that it was hopeless. 'But not tonight. Why don't we take advantage of her being away and go back to my house?'

If she had suspected what was in his mind, she gave no sign of it, simply shrugged and nodded her head.

'If you think you can smuggle me in the back door without Mrs Dunbar seeing me, then fine. Let's go to your house, have that quiet seat, and put all this behind us.'

*

Thomas sighed and shifted his position in the chair. Mrs Dunbar had not been the problem that night; rather it had been his ungentlemanly behaviour towards Charlotte. Again he smiled at the old-fashioned word his mind had come up with –*ungentlemanly* – and the deceiving leniency of the judgment it pronounced upon such a scandalous event.

The clock chimed a metallic two. As he passed it, he frowned at its cheaply-painted face, the fake gold leaf of the numbers and the brown base that was supposed to look like mahogany; just the kind of thing Maria would have loved. How the hell had he survived forty four years of marriage with a woman who would even admire a monstrosity like this, far less buy the damned thing and give it pride of place?

Thankful that he was too busy to think of her now, Thomas hurried into the bedroom to change into something more suited to wooing a lady.

*

Beth was filing recent leaflets into appropriate clients' folders when there was a knock at the door and she knew it had to Charlie Webster, since Marjory was in town posting letters.

'Yes,' she called, her back to the door.

He hovered in the doorway like an errant schoolboy at the Headmaster's office.

'Am I interrupting anything?'

'Not at the moment.'

'Good. Remember that dinner we discussed, the one involving clients?'

Beth frowned, for she had forgotten. 'Er…dinner with clients?'

'We discussed it the night you were at my place,' he said hopefully. 'You said that if it was O.K. with your husband, you'd help me out.'

'Did I?'

'Definitely.'

'I think I do remember,' Beth said, locking the filing cabinet and wondering why she bothered when there was nothing of value inside. 'But I forgot to clear it with Harry, so I can't until I do.'

'Fair enough, it's not until next week anyway. D'you think he'll mind?'

164

'I have no idea, but probably not. He didn't mind at all that you kidnapped me on the street the night of the snowstorm.'

She could have advised him to close his mouth, that he looked like a goldfish, but she only smiled and sat down, waving her hand at him to do the same.

'You told him?'

'Well, of course I did,' Beth said with carefully measured surprise. 'Why wouldn't I?'

'If it were my wife, I'd hate it.'

Beth smiled sweetly. 'That's the difference then.'

'The difference?' Charlie asked, but he knew he had bungled it.

'Yes, between a man who has nothing to worry about and a man who's suspicious of her every move.'

'I didn't say I'd be suspicious,' he said patiently. 'I just said I would hate it.'

'Anyway,' she said dismissively and he found it hard to believe she was the same girl that had cried on his shoulder in front of a roaring fire. 'I'll mention it to him, see what he says, and then I'll let you know. How does that sound?'

'Sounds good,'

'Which clients are they, as a matter of interest?'

'Some guy from abroad and his new conquest apparently.'

A tiny warning flickered at the back of Beth's mind. She had allowed thoughts of her grandfather to fade these past weeks, but she had a feeling that he was not the type of man to stand back and allow others to dictate the pace.

'From abroad? Would that be America?'

Charlie stared at her. 'Wow, that's uncanny! He is from America, South actually, only just moved back here now that his wife has died.'

Now that his wife has died

'How interesting,' she said casually, fiddling with the pencils on her desk. 'And what's he after?'

'After?'

'You sell antiques,' Beth reminded her boss patiently. 'What's he looking for in particular?'

'Ah, right. A Welsh dresser for his kitchen apparently, and an old-fashioned sideboard thing.'

'So his house must be fairly big?'

'Seems like it. Well, to tell the truth,' he added sheepishly. 'I drove past it the other day, just to check it out. It's big.'

'Where is it, this big house?'

'You know Kinnoull Hill?'

'Mmm.'

'Well, it's up there, but at the bottom.'

Beth shook her head at the snobbish inference: the huge, prestigious houses were further up the hill, more in keeping with the Webster's social circle.

'I see.'

'He hasn't bought it,' Charlie divulged, and it crossed her mind that her boss was hardly the kind of confidant a client could trust. 'He just rents it, on a six-monthly lease.'

'How do you know all this?'

'He did it through Frank.'

Beth's reaction made him lean forward and she cursed herself for not being ready for anything where Thomas Blake was concerned.

'Are you all right, Beth?'

'Yes, fine. I suddenly remembered I didn't switch the cooker off.'

165

'Heavens, do you want to pop home?'

'No it's only on simmer,' she lied. 'Scrambled eggs for breakfast.'

'I wouldn't know,' Charlie said and the look in his eyes was unsettling. 'What you have for breakfast, I mean.'

'What's this guy's name, this one from abroad with the rented house in the more common area of Kinnoull Hill?'

'I'd have to look it up,' he said, slightly put out by her description. 'But I think it begins with a 'B'.

*

Grace sighed when she saw the queue in the doctor's surgery. If she had not been with Lily Morris and it had not been urgent, she might have turned tail and gone to get the next bus home. Lily was relying on her, however, and she would have to wait her turn.

'Hello, stranger,' she heard a voice say and it was Molly, at the head of the queue.

'Stranger?' Grace smiled. 'Well, I could say the same about you.'

'I've been busy.'

'Of course.' Grace said pleasantly, but the implication was that she had been lazing around. 'How are you, and what are you doing here?'

'Oh, it's nothing much,' Molly said loudly, and Grace feared her old friend was about to reveal her symptoms to a dozen pairs of flapping ears. 'Just a little cold. You expect them in winter, don't you?'

'It wouldn't be winter without them,' Grace agreed, helping Lily into the only remaining seat, right at the door.

'How's James?' Molly asked and Grace's heart sank: not only was she not in the mood for conversation, but also she abhorred idle chatter in the waiting room, especially when there were older, frail biddies present. The one thing they needed here was peace and quiet.

'We're all fine,' Grace replied, short-cutting further inquiries as to the family's health.

'Did you hear about Mary Dewar?' Molly was asking now, and Lily nudged Grace in the ribs.

'Yes, I did,' Grace lied.

'Imagine that, coming home to find your husband…'

'Next please,' said the receptionist's voice, thereby denying the queue the satisfaction of a bit of gossip.

'Oh that's us,' Grace said gratefully. 'Maybe we'll see you at the bus stop,' she called to Molly as the door closed behind them.

'What about Mary's husband?' Lily whispered. 'I never heard anything.'

'Me neither. But you know what Molly's like, it's probably nothing. Just you concentrate on remembering to tell the doctor all your symptoms.'

It was a glum-faced duo that left the doctor's office half an hour later. Had Grace not been with her, she suspected that Lily would not have borne up so well, but on the other hand, there had been someone to witness the diagnosis and that was an invasion of privacy, albeit from a friend.

'Now, you're not to worry about this,' the new young doctor had said unwisely, Grace thought, for it was a sure way of putting it into Lily's head that she should worry. 'I'll prescribe heart tablets for you and you'll be fine, as long as you remember to take them of course.'

It was yet another reminder of the erosion of the 'bedside manner' of the old-fashioned doctors: no doctor in the '30s or '40s would have phrased things in such a way, especially to an elderly lady living alone. Before they left the surgery, Grace had wrapped the warm scarf around her friend's neck and tucked it into the coat; and then helped don gloves and hat against the bitter December wind that was sweeping down the main street. At last the bus had drawn up at the stop and, teeth chattering, they climbed aboard, grateful that Molly was nowhere in sight.

Once in the house, Lily was thankful that Grace had thought to light the fire before they left, for the living room was warm. She had also made up sandwiches for their lunch, a surprise for the old lady who was too despondent about the doctor's words to bother with food.

'When did you make them up?' she asked. 'I never saw you, you rascal.'

'I found them under a bush, must have been left by the fairies. Now, is it tea you want?'

'Aye, but what's this about Mary's husband?'

Grace tutted and went to fill the kettle. 'You're worse than Molly,' she chided. 'I told you, she'll have got the wrong end of the stick.'

'Lucy Webster told me something similar.'

'About Mary Dewar?'

'Aye.'

'Well I don't want to hear it,' Grace said firmly. 'If I had a penny for every bit of gossip I heard in this village, you and I would be going to Spain for our holiday.'

'Chance would be a fine thing. So, you're not interested then?'

'Not in gossip thank you. Sit down and I'll get things organised.'

'Have you heard from your father recently?'

Grace paused and turned to look at Lily. 'No. Why, have you?'

'He sent me a note, but that was a while ago.'

'What's your idea of 'a while ago'?'

'A fortnight ago, no more than that.'

Grace sat down to wait for the kettle to come to the boil. Although it was not the subject she wanted to discuss, she saw the value of it, in that it prevented Lily from dwelling on the news from the doctor. Reluctantly, she prepared to respond.

'I haven't heard from him since last year.'

'And Beth? Has she heard from him again?'

Something cold wound its way around Grace's heart: to hear her daughter's name in the same sentence as Thomas Blake's was bad enough, but to hear that she might have been in contact with him was akin to being stabbed in the back. She kept her tone light.

'What do you mean 'again'? How many times has she contacted him?'

'I shouldn't have said,' Lily grimaced. 'I shouldn't have mentioned it.'

'Listen,' Grace smiled, leaning across and taking her old friend's hand. 'I'm only asking. I'm not even annoyed, I just want to know.'

It had taken all her acting skills to pull it off and Lily appeared convinced.

'That's a relief then. As long as you're not annoyed with the girl.'

'I'm not, so don't worry. He is her grandfather after all.'

'Aye, and she seems to be fair taken with him.'

'Oh good, there's the kettle now,' Grace said, springing up and moving quickly through to the kitchen before Lily could see the pain in her eyes. 'Tea will be with you in a moment, Madam.'

She went into the kitchen and pulled the door closed.

*

167

Lily closed her eyes. What was that song again, the one about the difference a day made? Oh, yes, that was it, and it went on '*twenty four little hours*', did it not? Last night at this time she had been thinking that her breathlessness was just a symptom of the cold weather, like it had been for the past few years; treated with handfuls of Beecham's powders and Aspirins.

Now she knew the truth, that she had heart trouble – angina or whatever he had called it – and she faced the prospect of sitting in this chair for the rest of her life.

Her eyes flew open: if she had only a short time left then there was a lot to do; a lot to say, especially to Grace, for the girl was still in the dark about her mother and father and had to know the real story before things got out of hand. Lily drew several deep breaths. She would have to put it right; and she resolved to start now. When the kitchen door opened and Grace appeared with the tray, however, she lost her nerve; would wait until tomorrow, until she felt a bit stronger.

*

Thomas was discovering that it took very little to impress Daphne McDonald, by which he deduced that the poor woman had led an extremely sheltered life. When he mentioned South America – and he had stopped pretending it was 'The States' now that his daughter knew he was here– she gazed at him with admiration bordering on awe, and he realised at that point that this was going to be a dawdle.

'Oh, my,' she breathed. 'How exotic! You're a man of the world and no mistake.'

'Hardly,' Thomas said with false modesty. 'I've never been anywhere else, you know, other than the Americas.'

'I've never been further afield than Rothesay.'

'Oh, but there's nothing wrong with that.'

'Still, it's not nearly as exciting as South America. Was it your work that took you there?'

No, it was my sweetheart turning me down

'Yes, I was an engineer for the national railways.'

'Goodness! And you've come to live in a dull place like Perth?'

'Dull? Oh, it's not dull,' Thomas smiled, pausing, allowing his gaze to linger on Daphne's face for a fraction longer than necessary. 'I've found that it's anything but dull here, believe me.'

He was surprised that she did not shy away from such a remark, being as it was related to her presence. Not only did she not shy away from it, but also she appeared delighted to be the object of someone's attention.

'I know what you mean,' she said pointedly, not lowering her eyes from his.

It crossed Thomas's mind she was going too fast; even for him.

'I love the river,' he said, selecting a cake from the tiered stand. 'Strolling over the bridge, or wandering down by the riverbanks is my idea of a pleasant hour. And the architecture, it's very imposing.' He could have told her that he had trained as an architect in an office not far from here, but it brought back memories of Charlotte and his heart was already bruised from this morning's recollections.

'Did you go to South America when you were a boy?'

'Twenty I was,' he smiled. 'Just a slip of a lad.'

'You travelled all that way by yourself at that young age?' Daphne asked, a fresh flush of admiration on her cheeks.

'I did.'

'No sweetheart to leave behind?' she asked daringly.

'Yes,' he said, not having to feign sadness. 'I loved her, but she turned me down.'

She looked at him then with an expression that clearly denounced the sweetheart as a fool and, irrationally, it irked Thomas.

'She was far too good for me, as a matter of fact.'

'I doubt that.' She had meant only to flatter him, of course, but it had the opposite effect. As soon as she had uttered the words, she knew she it was a mistake. 'I'm sorry,' she stammered. 'I didn't mean to offend you, or your sweetheart. I just meant...'

'It's all right,' Thomas forced himself to say. 'I understand. Now, more coffee?'

By the end of their tête-à-tête Daphne had revealed to him each and every one of her successes and failures, the latter being in greater abundance. She was a widow, husband already gone by 1956, no children, no Aunts, Uncles or Best Friend that cared a hoot for her. He also discovered that she lived on the outskirts of Perth, almost at Scone, in one of the big semi-detached houses on the main road. Seven rooms, she told him, and there she was on her own, rattling around in them when she should be in a flat in the centre of town.

'Why don't you move?' he asked politely.

'Rufus,' she explained and he remembered the spaniel. 'He really needs a garden to run around in. It would be cruel to keep him in all day.'

'Of course.'

'And you? You must live quite near the hotel where our paths usually cross.'

'I'm staying with my niece,' Thomas lied, ever the one to give himself a way out right at the beginning. 'Kinnoull Hill.'

'Oh, that's a very nice area.'

'It is indeed. Except,' Thomas leaned forward confidentially. 'I have to fit in with my niece and her family, you know. I don't have the run of the house, you understand?'

Daphne did; and it was with some satisfaction that Thomas stood up to pay the bill.

*

The telephone rang at his elbow and Harry glanced at his watch: twenty to five and, strictly speaking, the office was shut for business, secretaries off home on the stroke of four. He sighed and wondered if it would entail a half hour one-sided conversation by a client with verbal diarrhoea, not an uncommon occurrence when you were the junior. Gilmour and Barclay had the panache – and the experience – to fob people off in the most astonishing way, but Harry, treading warily in his first year, was more circumspect.

On impulse he picked the telephone up. It was Grace and she was crying, and he thought it the most distressing sound he had ever heard.

Chapter Eight

Beth was dressed in her red wrap-over creation when Harry opened the door. She came to meet him, wiggling her hips provocatively and teetering on ridiculous heels. Every other female on the planet was wearing shoes with thick chunky heels now, but Beth had no inclination to discard the high-heeled styles that made her look like a lady of the night. Admittedly, Harry liked when she wore them, but not tonight. It seemed that she wanted to go out for dinner and he was decidedly not in the mood.

'I thought we'd hit the town, paint it red,' she smiled, waltzing up to him and draping her arms round his neck.

'What you actually mean is that you couldn't be bothered slaving over a hot stove.'

'Right first time, memory man,' she laughed. 'Your mind-reading abilities are uncanny.'

'The trouble is I've had a terrible day,' Harry said truthfully. 'I'd need an hour to recover before we went out.'

'That's O.K. The table's booked for eight. I thought it would give us time for a starter.' She added mischievously, 'In the bedroom.'

'Not at the moment, I'm afraid.'

Beth stepped back and gave him a long look. He marvelled that it took her so long to ascertain his mood when he could pick hers up in a microsecond.

'You poor thing, you look exhausted.'

'A bit.'

'Tell you what. You go and have a lie down and I'll be as quiet as a mouse for an hour. Then we'll see how you feel.'

'Sounds good to me.' He removed his coat and she took it from him.

'I'll hang it up for you. Go and lie down, I'll bring your drink in if you like?'

'Thanks but no, I think I'll just have a snooze.'

She frowned and he foresaw an inquisition. 'Are you sure you're not sickening for something? There's a throat infection going the rounds.'

'Beth, I'm fine. I'm just tired.'

'No,' she countered, eyes narrowing. 'There's more to it. Tell me the truth.'

Harry had to revise his assessment of her mood-ascertaining skills.

'I'm not certain you're ready for it,' he told her honestly and she stood very still, holding his coat, looking at him closely.

'Perhaps we should sit down,' she suggested.

'Good idea. Mine's a gin.'

'A moment ago you were so exhausted you'd to lie down,' Beth said accusingly. 'Yet now you're sprightly enough to have a gin.'

Harry sighed. 'To be honest, Beth, I opted for a lie down as opposed to having to tell you the truth. It was a cop-out.'

'Ah, now we're getting somewhere.'

She hung the coat in the hall cupboard, kicked off the high-heeled shoes and took his arm.

'You go in there,' she said, leaving him at the entrance to the sitting room. 'And I'll bring the drinks through.'

'Thanks, sweetheart.'

She paused in the doorway. 'And don't go changing your mind either, about telling me the truth.'

'I promise, I won't.'

Harry crossed to his favourite armchair and sank down, stretching out his legs until his toes found the hearth rail. The heat of the fire – and it always amazed him that Beth could clean and stoke the thing at all – warmed his feet and took the chill from his core. He had five minutes before she came back. What the hell could he say?

*

Beth tiptoed across the room and laid the gin and tonic on the table beside him. She could hardly believe that he had fallen asleep in the space of a few minutes. She felt guilty, for she had suspected him of adding feet and legs to his tiredness; now she could see that he had not been making it up.

'Harry,' she whispered and his eyes fluttered open.

'What?'

'Your G and T. You fell asleep.'

'Bloody hell,' he muttered, stirring himself and straightening up. His feet were so close to the fire that he could smell his socks. 'Sorry, Beth, I didn't mean to doze.'

'Harry, darling,' she said with concern. 'Don't apologise for being exhausted. It's me who should apologise for...' She broke off, about to admit that she had been hard-pressed to believe him.

'I accept,' Harry said, touching her cheek with his finger. 'Now, sit down and let's get sloshed.'

For a split second, Beth toyed with the idea that he and Annie... But then she shook herself. What ridiculous nonsense!

'This truth you've got to tell me,' she began. 'Is it concerning you and me?'

'You mostly.'

Her eyes widened. 'Me? What have I been doing?'

'Contacting Thomas Blake.'

'But you knew that already.'

'Yes, I did. But Grace didn't.'

Beth was shocked: he had blabbed to her mother!

'You stinker!' she cried. 'How dare you?'

The confusion on his face was either genuine or a very good act and she could not decide which. So far in this marriage he had not been guilty of lying to her, or at least she had no evidence of it; so was he really not to blame for this?

'It wasn't me,' Harry said and she heard the resentment in his tone. 'I would never have said anything to upset Grace.'

She forced herself to calm down before she responded because it was always the same: never upset Grace, never make Grace unhappy, never take sides with anyone other than Grace. He was more concerned about his mother-in-law than he was about his wife.

'I see. So, who told her then?'

'Lily Morris.'

'That's rubbish, she would never say anything to...' Beth stopped, realising she was only confirming her mother's pride of place in everyone's affections.

'She'd just been at the doctor's,' Harry was saying. 'She found out she has heart disease, must have blurted it out unintentionally, poor old soul.'

'Poor old soul?' Beth mimicked bitterly. 'She's dropped me right in it, the poor old soul. And I suppose my mother phoned you, cried on your shoulder?'

She regretted the words as soon as they escaped her lips; more so when she saw Harry's reaction. Inwardly, she braced herself.

'Yes, she did phone me,' he said slowly, eyes on his glass of gin. 'And, yes, she was upset. In fact, I think it was the saddest sound I've ever heard; certainly one I'll never forget.'

For a few minutes, Beth remained silent. She had rarely witnessed her husband in such pensive mood, and she knew enough about him to put her own demands on hold for the moment. The fire crackled and, automatically, she glanced at the rug for sparks.

'Perhaps I should put the guard up.'

Harry continued to swill the gin around his glass and Beth felt the first shiver of apprehension ripple through her. It was not his habit, to keep her waiting like this, have her hanging on, wondering what was coming next.

All at once, she lost her temper.

'Oh, for Heaven's sake, Harry, either tell me what she bloody said or not, but don't think I'm going to beg.'

He smiled but said nothing and so she sprang to her feet and left the room.

As she passed the telephone she considered calling Timothy's restaurant and cancelling the booking, but then she paused, decided to go on her own. It was within walking distance and although it meant having to wear her boots and change the wrap-over, she thought it a better option than staying here and having to cross swords with Harry Gillespie.

*

Harry was happy to see her storm from the room; even happier when, twenty minutes later, she marched across the hall and left the flat, slamming the door behind her and almost vibrating the pictures off the wall. For the first time since he had put the phone down on Grace, he relaxed. Eyeing the depleted glass, he roused himself and padded through to the kitchen for the bottle of gin, carrying it back to the sitting room, along with a large bottle of Safeway's tonic.

After another swig he began to feel better, although he was beginning to project his mind forward to food, or rather the lack of it. In preference to remaining here and facing another spat, she had obviously gone alone to Timothy's. Moreover, she intended to walk, for he had heard the clump of boots and no sound of her car driving off. Why had he confided in her right away? What was to be achieved by his moody silence, a silence that would lead, inevitably, to a temper tantrum?

He reached into the coal bucket and placed a few more pieces onto the fire; felt the instant, though temporary, dampening down of the flames. It was only seven o'clock. He supposed he could pop to the chip shop, but that meant donning coat and boots again and facing the freezing wind. Harry sighed and decided that, for the moment, the gin was working a treat; but, before it rendered him too drunk to think straight, he laid it aside and thought through what he and Grace had discussed, organising things in his mind, planning his course of action, so that he would never again have to bear the sound of her crying.

*

When James came home from work Grace was sitting by the fire. She had washed her face, applied a smattering of make-up and was determined that she would not burden her husband with this particular problem. To that end, she awarded him a bright smile and prepared for an evening of careful responses that would not reflect her inner heartache.

'Heavens. you're all dressed up,' James said. 'Have I forgotten an anniversary?'

He was joking, but she knew that the whole tone of the evening would hinge on her first reply.

'No, unless you count the first December 10th. we spent together.'

'December 1945,' he smiled, removing his coat and shaking the drops of water from it. 'It was a wonderful time for me, being welcomed into your family.'

Grace's reserve wavered: her daughter's behaviour was hell-bent on ripping this family apart. How long could they remain a family?

'It was a lovely Christmas,' she agreed. 'Remember how we all joined in the singing round the piano? It was wonderful.'

'You were wearing the green dress, the same one that you were wearing the first day I saw you.'

James sat down opposite her and glanced at the framed photograph, taken in the back garden when Grace had been sixteen; a photograph whose pride of place often irked James. Tonight, however, he was amiable.

'You don't look a day older than you did then. You must have a special secret.'

Grace laughed and shook her head. 'You need new glasses.'

James's attention was still on the photograph; but it evoked too many memories for Grace and she glanced away.

'You know you can tell me anything, Grace,' she heard James say now.

'Sorry?'

'If there's something upsetting you, you can tell me if you like and we can face it together.'

Grace had every intention of fobbing him off; but, to her dismay, she found that she had no reserves of bravado. She fumbled for her handkerchief and did her best to stem the tears.

*

It had been inevitable that James would want to know the extent of Beth's deceit. Half an hour later Grace, dry-eyed and coherent, sat looking at him, wondering how she had imagined ever being able to keep it to herself. She felt no better for the telling of it, but at least she could dispense with the play-acting and discuss the situation with him. Expecting him to take his daughter's side, she had been astonished at his disapproval of Beth's behaviour, deeming it to be against the best interests of the family.

'I'm disappointed in her,' had been his first words. 'She should have more sense.'

'I'd no idea she was so interested in the man. When I'd met him, when we all gathered at her flat for lunch, she seemed a hundred per cent in agreement with me. I don't understand it at all.'

'And you think that Harry will tell her that you know about it now?'

'I asked him to.' Grace coloured slightly. 'I'm afraid I made a fool of myself when I was talking to him, started blubbering.'

James shrugged. 'He is family, after all. He won't think you're foolish.'

'Still, I did go on a bit. Perhaps I should call him tonight, say I'm feeling better, now that I've told you.'

'Beth will be there,' James reminded her. 'Best leave it until tomorrow.'

'Of course.'

A fresh wave of despair ran through her at the thought of her daughter's actions. 'Furtive' was the only word to describe Beth's contact with Thomas Blake, whether or not he was her grandfather. Obviously, knowing how distressing the information would be to her mother, the girl had kept quiet about her dealings with the man; and, more than likely, she had never intended Grace to find out. The fact remained, however, that Beth had been sympathetic to him and by doing so she had shown where her loyalties lay.

'Grace, you must leave this to Harry and me,' she heard James say. 'You must promise not to speak to Beth until it's sorted out.'

173

Grace nodded, for it suited her perfectly not to see her daughter at the moment. Years ago, she and Charlotte had laughed in amazement when news of a similar family disagreement had reached their ears.

'Not speaking to her mother?' Grace had asked in disbelief. 'How could such a thing happen, for Heaven's sake?'

'You'd be surprised at human nature,' her mother had responded. 'The slightest wee thing and they're at each other's throats.'

'Well, you'll never catch me not speaking to you,' Grace had told her mother firmly. 'There's not a chance that you and I would fall out...not about anything.'

'So I'm stuck with you for ever then,' her mother had joked and the two of them had laughed it off.

Now, faced with the prospect of falling out with her own daughter, Grace could hardly believe that she was embroiled in the same kind of situation.

'Not only did she contact him,' she reiterated now to James, 'but she took the letters he gave her and read them.' She looked across at him and frowned. 'How could she even begin to think that he was telling her the truth? I can't imagine why she would listen to him.'

'Don't worry, she'll find out eventually, and then she'll never want to see him again.'

'I'm not so sure. You know what Beth's like.' In spite of her misery she smiled at her husband. 'She's like you, of course, and fine you know it.'

He laughed and shook his head. 'Not this time, Grace. I would never do or say anything to hurt you. I won't let you down about Thomas Blake,' he added. 'And, I won't speak to Beth until you tell me it's all right.'

Grace was uneasy at the implication. 'There's no need for you to fall out with her as well, James. I don't want this problem to spoil things for the whole family.'

James frowned. 'If I had to choose between you and Beth, I would always choose you.'

Despite the sentiment being welcome, Grace was unhappy with the idea.

'But I don't want you to choose. I just want you to point out to her how miserable she's made me.'

'Sorry, but it's my decision,' James said forcefully, standing up and stretching his arms above his head. 'I have no sympathy for our daughter at the moment.'

'Just don't fall out with her.'

'I'll try not to,' James smiled ruefully. 'Don't worry, we'll soon sort it out.'

'Anyway,' Grace said, standing up and preparing to go into the kitchen. 'I don't know about you, James Melville, but I'm starving.'

'Why don't we have fish and chips? I can pop into Craigton for them.'

'I'd feel guilty, but it would save me cooking.'

James kissed the top of her head. 'Two fish and chips coming up. I'll be back before you know it.' He paused at the sitting room door and looked back at her. 'Promise me you won't worry about this?'

'I'll try not to.'

James smiled. 'That's a start anyway.'

As she set the kitchen table, Grace accepted that there was no possibility of her not worrying: the security of family life was at stake and she would know no peace until the problem was resolved.

*

When his telephone rang, Thomas jumped. He was walking through the hall on his

174

way to the lounge when its bell jangled and took him by surprise. He knew of only two people who had his number: Gilmour, the solicitor, and the landlord of this house. It rang for some time before he finally picked it up and when he heard her voice, he could hardly speak.

*

Beth had no qualms about calling her grandfather. The only reservation she had was when she had pestered Charlie Webster for the number.

'It's confidential, Beth,' he had said several times.

'But I think I know him,' she revealed eventually, freezing to death in the telephone box at the station. 'In fact, if his name is Blake, then I do.'

'That's different then,' Charlie had said with relief. 'His name IS Blake. Why didn't you say so sooner?'

'I'm indebted to you,' Beth had said, trying to stop her teeth from chattering. 'In fact, I owe you.'

She grimaced at the choice of words, for she knew how he would take it. No matter; she had the number now and she would deal with her glib promise some other time.

'Thomas Blake?'

'Yes. Is that you, Beth?'

For some ridiculous reason, she baulked at the first name but let it go. 'Yes, it is. Are you busy?'

He told her no, and was there something he could help her with?

'A question about the contents of the letters perhaps'.

'No, I was wondering if you were free to have dinner tonight.'

'Dinner?' he repeated, and he sounded confused.

'At a restaurant,' Beth said quickly. 'Timothy's actually.'

'I think I know it,' her grandfather said, hardly able to keep the delight from his voice. For a moment, Beth was overwhelmed by a sense of disloyalty to her mother. 'Near the city hall?'

'Yes, that's it. Can you be there fairly soon?'

'I can be there in ten minutes.'

'See you then,' Beth said and hung up, wasting most of her shilling's worth.

With frozen fingers she opened the kiosk door and was almost blown away by the ferocity of the wind.

'To hell with this,' she muttered, glancing at the taxi rank. 'I'm not walking another inch.'

When she arrived at the restaurant she ordered a glass of Muscadet, her favourite wine since the French holiday, and then sat recovering from the consequences of not being dressed for a Scottish winter. Boots and scarf were all very well but underneath she was still wearing the wrap-over, and her skin was purple.

'I'm waiting for a friend,' she told the waiter, thereby invoking another bout of disloyalty to her mother. The reserved tables in the restaurant were tucked away in an exclusive little enclave, which, tonight, Beth decided, was a good thing.

It was Frank Gilmour who had recommended the restaurant, and, despite his dislike of the man, Harry regularly booked a table. Now, Beth took frequent sips of the wine, hoping the alcohol would dispel her sense of betrayal.

*

Thomas had never been so nervous in his life, not even when he had asked Charlotte

175

to escape the restrictive influence of her father and make a new life for herself and the child. Even now, as he allowed the image to drift to the forefront of his mind, Thomas could recall every word, every gesture of their final meeting.

From the street, he looked through the restaurant window but she was not at any of the tables. For five minutes he walked up and down the street, finally defeated by the weather into opening the door and stepping into the warmth.

'Are you by any chance dining with the young lady at table seven?' The waiter asked, as he helped Thomas remove his coat. Thomas followed the man's gaze, caught sight of the girl's blonde hair.

'It's my granddaughter,' he said with suppressed pride, and the waiter's glance might have reflected envy.

Beth gave him a brief smile as he sat down and it was she who spoke first.

'I hope I didn't disrupt your plans for the evening.'

'Not at all. I had no plans.'

He was apprehensive. Previous meetings between them had been in the street, impromptu, no script, easily terminated; whereas this one was more like serious business, with no quick exit, and the girl calling the shots. Thomas had not come prepared. Her very presence was un-nerving, the habit she had of looking straight at him, assessing, judging, making no attempt to follow social etiquette. His heart sank. Was that not exactly how her mother had behaved towards him?

'You want to clear up a few things about the letters?' he asked, pulling at his tie which suddenly felt too tight.

'Why did you keep them all?'

'Because they... because I... they were from my wife.'

'Did she keep yours, do you know?

'I have no idea, but if she had I expect your mother will have thrown them out.'

'Why would she do that?' the girl frowned.

'Because she didn't know the whole story.'

'And you think the letters tell the whole story?'

'I think they tell both sides of it, don't you?'

She shrugged and waved to the waiter. 'I suppose they do. Another of the same, please and something for my companion.'

Thomas ordered a lager and wondered at her use of the word 'companion' as opposed to 'friend', or even 'grandfather' for so he was.

'Have you eaten here before?' she asked him.

'No. What do you recommend?'

'Smoked salmon salad.'

'A cold dish?'

'It's Scandinavian food. Mostly cold.'

'Ah, in that case, salmon salad it is.'

Once their order was taken, Thomas relaxed slightly. After all, he had the truth on his side, backed up by Charlotte's letters, and so he took a sip of his drink and decided that boldness would be the appropriate approach.

'You're saying that she sent you away,' the girl said accusingly with no preamble. 'That you wanted to live as man and wife but she refused.'

'That's it exactly. She knew how much I loved her,' Thomas said, with no sense of embarrassment. 'I had to blackmail her into marrying me.'

'What?"

'I said if she didn't, I would tell our child that Charlotte had wanted to make it a bastard.'

Beth appeared horrified, and Thomas was exultant.

'You mean she didn't even want to marry you when she discovered she was pregnant?' The girl was aghast and it spurred Thomas on.

'No, she didn't. That's when I had to... well, get tough, I suppose you young folk would say now.'

'So what reason did she give for not wanting to marry you?'

'My mother.'

'I beg your pardon?'

'She thought my mother would make life difficult for us.'

'And would she?'

'Oh, yes,' Thomas smiled. 'No doubt about that. But I was sure that love would conquer all.' He heard the irony in his voice, but was past caring. If it were the truth she wanted, he was just the man to dish it out; or, at least, an acceptable version of it.

*

Grace sat at the piano for the first time in years, the songbook open at her favourite piece, her eyes going over the melody before she even touched the keys. When she was young and her mother had bought her sheet music from a film, she had studied it for some time, her mind travelling the lines and dots until she was familiar with the song's pitfalls. Consequently, when her fingers ran over the keys she made fewer mistakes and earned Alexander Shepherd's praise; a major consideration in anything she did. The approval on the old man's face when she came home with first or second prize from Perth music festival was imprinted on her memory.

Under normal circumstances, Beth had scorned the habit of scanning the music first, fingers flying along the keys energetically and, to Grace's astonishment, displaying an innate ability to sight-read a piece with an enviable accuracy. Her daughter's patience with her practice, however, fell far short of Grace's but the result was so proficient that Grace imagined the two elements to be inseparable. Now, as she sat at a piano that had been so neglected these past few years, it crossed her mind suddenly that Beth might never bring these old keys to life again, that she might never even...

Grace could hardly form the words: *might never even come back to this house.*

She stared, unseeing, at the music in front of her, beginning to appreciate the extent of her father's power to disrupt this family. She stood up and moved to the hearth where James had lit the fire for her, and, as she pulled her favourite armchair closer to the heat, she was beginning to understand how jubilant Thomas Blake would be should he succeed in severing her relationship with Beth, especially after the brutal treatment he had received from his own daughter. The recollection of her harsh words to him at the hotel was a sharp reminder to Grace of how he must be plotting his revenge. What better revenge was there, than to come between her and Beth? Should she stand by and do nothing, he would surely win. To have no contact with her daughter for the rest of their lives was more terrifying than anything she could think of.

As the clock struck nine, Grace sank down into the welcoming folds of the chair and closed her eyes. Only now was she feeling the effects of the day's disturbing events. She sighed and awarded herself ten minutes' rest to replenish her energy, after which she would have a great deal of thinking to do.

She woke with a start to find James leaning over her.

'I thought it was too quiet in here,' he said with a smile. 'Thought you'd lost your voice.'

'What time is it?'

'Just past ten.'

'Oh, for Heaven's sake, I only meant to doze for ten minutes.' Grace stretched and

177

yawned and eased herself from of the comfortable depths of the chair. 'You should have wakened me sooner.' She glanced at the fire. 'But you've stoked the fire, so you must have been in here before.'

James shrugged. 'I was, but you were sleeping so soundly I tiptoed out.'

'I suppose I'm glad you did,' Grace admitted, yawning again. 'I feel so much better, and there's something I want to ask you.'

'I'm listening,' he said, taking the chair opposite her. 'Or, as your mother used to say, 'I'm all ears',' James laughed. 'I miss her sense of fun, you know, even now.'

'I'm afraid I didn't inherit it.'

'What nonsense, of course you did. You're just tired, that's all. This business with *him*...'

Grace sat up and wiggled her feet in front of the fire.

'That's what I want to ask you about.'

'You don't think it's too late tonight, my love? Shouldn't you be heading for bed?'

'What, after sleeping half the evening? No, I want to do it now.'

She took a deep breath and voiced the sentence that was in her mind.

'Do you honestly think I should give him the satisfaction of breaking up this family?'

She did not have to wait for James to speak: the answer was contained in his smile.

*

Harry closed the folder of old photographs, mostly of his mother, and replaced it on the shelf in his study. He never tired of looking at her, and of matching each snap to events of the time, grateful for his father's habit of printing the date on the back of every photograph. Harry still had the camera that his father had used back then and often took it from the case to turn it over in his hands, trying to become part of the emotions that had been captured by its lens, wondering if the truth had adhered to the frame and could somehow be released at his touch.

The night was clear, the visibility breath-taking. Harry stood at the small balcony window watching the strolling couples on the Inch and the children throwing snowballs at one another when they ought to have been in bed.

As he made up his mind to have an early night, a taxi drew up beneath him and he knew instinctively that it would be Beth. She paid the driver, gave the man a cheerful wave, along with a few words that drifted away before they reached Harry; and then, unexpectedly, she glanced up, presumably to check if the lights were on in the flat.

If she saw him she did not acknowledge him, and as she disappeared round the corner towards the front door, Harry knew he had no strength for another row, yet the alternative – of appeasing her in some way – was equally daunting. He sat down by the fire that he had long since neglected and waited for her.

He knew she had been drinking by the length of time it took her to get the key in the lock and he took heart from it, for she would not be at her most lucid, a more favourable circumstance for him. The door closed quietly, yet another sign that she was merry, and then she removed her boots and crept along the hallway, pausing at the sitting room door, perhaps wondering if she should open it.

'I'm in here,' he called and the door opened.

'Sorry I'm late,' she said, even before he saw her. 'I went out for a meal and met some nice people.'

When she closed the door and made her way across the room, Harry saw that her eyes were bright, her cheeks flushed. He knew he could avoid a row by chatting inanely to her, as if they had parted the best of friends, but now that she was home he was not entirely certain if he wanted to placate her.

'I hope you went to Timothy's and didn't waste the reservation.'

'I did, and it was nice.' She sat down on the rug, hugging her knees, close to the fire, although the flames were all but out. 'D'you want me to breathe life into this fire?' she offered.

'What time is it?'

'Ten past eleven.'

'Not for my benefit. I'm going to bed.'

'Did you have a nice night?' she asked, and the use of the word 'nice' three times in a minute furnished him with a significant clue: she had an abhorrence of the word unless she were too tired or too drunk to find a more elaborate alternative.

'Yes, I popped out for fish and chips, bumped into Annie's boyfriend.'

A flicker of suspicion crossed her eyes for a brief moment and then was gone.

'Was Annie there too?'

'No, he was on his own, out walking the dog on the Inch.'

'They're not getting on at the moment.'

'Who, him and the dog?'

'Very droll,' she smiled. 'No, her and the intended.'

'Are they intending?'

'Well, they're almost engaged, aren't they?'

'He didn't seem so keen.'

'Didn't he?'

'She would drive me mad.'

'She can be a bit intense,' Beth admitted, usually loyal to a fault. 'She even gets on my nerves sometimes.' She smiled, and then began rubbing her feet as if they were freezing.

'You look cold,' Harry remarked.

'Just my toes, as usual.'

There was so much pathos in her voice that, irrationally, he wanted to take her in his arms and pretend everything was normal. Because of Grace, however, and the sound of her crying, he resisted the temptation.

'I might get a hot drink,' she said now, regarding him hopefully. 'Do you want one?'

'No thanks, I'm heading for bed,' Harry smiled, standing up. 'See you when you come through.'

'O.K.'

Just before he opened the door he turned and glanced back at her, found that she was looking right at him.

'Harry?'

'What?'

'I know you care more about my mother than about me, but ....'

'But what?' he asked unkindly, when he knew he should refute it.

'But aren't you at all interested in the truth?'

'Not if it's destructive, Beth. I can't see any advantage in truth if it's not used to make things better.'

He left her there, sitting in front of a cold fire, and went straight to bed.

*

Grace lay in the darkness of the bedroom, mulling over her decision, testing it for flaws, to the extent of carrying on silent conversations between the parties. Despite being satisfied that she had reached the right conclusion on how to deal with her father, she had

179

several reservations, the main one being her ability to act with humility when all the time she would hate him as much as ever.

Had James not shown himself to be more sympathetic to her than to Beth, she might have continued along the path of breaking the bonds of her family and having no one to blame but herself. His vociferous disapproval of his daughter's behaviour had been instrumental in Grace's final decision.

'You really did intend not to speak to Beth until she'd seen sense?' Grace had asked him an hour earlier.

'Of course,' he had frowned, as if insulted by the question. 'You're always first in my mind, Grace, I thought you knew that.'

'But you and Beth…'

'Her loyalty to you is the same as her loyalty to me.'

'Anyway, you won't have to side against her now. I've made up my mind. I'll write to Helen first thing in the morning.' She gasped suddenly. 'Oh, my goodness, I hope she still has it after all this time.'

'Helen?' James had asked, curious. 'What can she do?'

'I…' Grace had hesitated, glanced at him briefly. 'I'll wait and see if she still has it, then I'll tell you.'

He had shrugged and transferred his attention to the book he was reading.

Grace sighed now and rolled over towards James, laying her hand across his chest and snuggling into him. Her last thought concerned her determination to rid her family of the man forever: would she have the strength to see it through?

Chapter Nine

When her mother called and suggested they meet in Perth for coffee, Beth feared the worst, although it was Christmas Eve and she doubted that her mother would cause trouble at such a significant time of year.

'Yes, that would be great,' Beth agreed. 'But I thought you didn't like coming into Perth?'

'Oh, I can't go on like that forever,' her mother laughed and to Beth's ears it was convincing. 'Wait until you're my age, young lady, and you'll find out that old age doesn't come by itself.'

'I wish you'd stop saying you're old, Mum. You've hardly changed since you were a teenager.'

'So your father tells me. How about this afternoon, or is that too soon?'

'Believe it or not, I'm up and dressed,' Beth said, hardly able to believe it herself. 'I got up at seven in fact.'

'I'll have to lie down in a darkened room now,' her mother laughed, and Beth was beginning to wonder if Harry had been completely honest about her mother's reaction to the letters. 'So, if today's suitable, I'll park in the free car park along the road and I'll be at the flat about two. Would that be fine?'

'Perfect. Pity Harry will be at work, but you'll see him sometime soon hopefully.'

Beth hung up and wandered back to her cup of tea. She sat down and tried to work out the probable outcome to all of this, optimistic one moment, despondent the next. When she thought about the letters and how they told the full story, her spirits soared; when she put herself in her mother's shoes, however, she was certain it would end badly.

Many things had surprised her over the past few months but none more than her willingness to side with a man who was a virtual stranger, side with him against her father, a man she loved and revered, notwithstanding his stubborn ways. As a girl she would have rather thrown herself off the railway bridge rather than invoke James Melville's disapproval, and now here she was prepared, if necessary, to thwart his wishes and to Hell with the consequences. It was quite bizarre; and rather frightening.

She finished the lukewarm tea and turned her mind to struggling through crowds of last-minute shoppers to find two empty seats in a café. Perhaps when her mother arrived, she would suggest they have coffee in the flat.

*

Grace manoeuvred through the traffic lights at Bridgend, her mind on Helen's letter, which she had all but committed to memory. Read in the light of modern permissiveness, the whole concept was out-of-date.

Helen has a letter that some woman wrote to Thomas.
How could you possibly know that?
Because I took it from his jacket pocket.
You're saying you stole it, Lily Morris?
I suppose I did.
But, why did you give it to Helen?
Because he might have found it here.
Wouldn't she be curious and read it?
No, I put it into an envelope marked 'Copy of Grace's birth certificate'.
Why are you telling me this now?
Just to let you know it's there, in case you ever need it.

What does it say?

God willing, you'll never have to know.

For months thereafter, though ignorant of the letter's contents, Grace had been filled with doubt regarding her mother's consequent defence of Thomas Blake's abandonment of wife and child. Moreover, the horror she suffered upon hearing Lily's blithe confession of wrong-doing haunted Grace for years; prevented her from reconciling herself to such abhorrent action; until a few days ago, when she, herself, had been seeking devious ways to thwart the very same man.

As her eyes had skimmed over the letter, Grace was overwhelmed with delight. It was all she needed to sully his reputation; hopefully turn Beth against him. Even in this modern era, the girl would not be able to wave away such a cruel betrayal of trust.

Mindful of James, she had tucked the letter away from his prying eyes: sometimes, Grace considered her husband's intransigent opinions on morality to be as restrictive as Alexander Shepherd's. He would certainly take a dim view of theft. As usual, Grace could appreciate both sides of the argument; in fact, because of the 'Swinging Sixties' and their lack of values, she found herself inwardly favouring the old-fashioned principles.

'The trouble is,' Molly had complained days before, as they trudged up the village through the slush. 'I look at Donald's fiancée and I wish I was young again.'

'Would we really like to be young in this day and age?'

'I would,' Molly had said quickly. 'I'd give anything to be part of the modern era. It must be great to do what you want, compared to how we were brought up.'

'It didn't stop you from doing what you wanted.' Grace pointed out, perhaps uncharitably. 'I mean, you had lots of boyfriends, didn't you?'

'Here, steady on, not that many.' Molly thought for a moment, apparently counting them in her head. 'Only four, which is not bad considering I was a bit of a lass.'

'Did you sleep with them all?' Grace had asked daringly, and Molly had given her a triumphant look.

'What if I did? I wouldn't expect you to understand, little Miss Purity.'

Now, as she walked along Beth's street, Grace was ashamed to admit even to herself that the old-fashioned idea of a girl keeping herself pure until her wedding night had probably led to many an ill-matched pair standing at the altar.

Grace sighed. What good did it do to ramble on in this way? Perhaps she was the only one to hold such a view. Besides, her daughter – a product of the liberal sixties – had retained her virginity for Harry. Again, she suffered a pang of jealousy and had to dismiss it from her mind before it took priority over all other thoughts.

By the time Grace had reached the door of the flat, she had rid her mind of contentious thoughts. Checking that she had enough money to take Beth out for afternoon coffee, she rang the doorbell.

*

'No, that's fine,' her mother smiled after Beth suggested staying in for coffee. 'I can keep my pound to spend on something else.'

'You really don't mind?'

'No, in fact when I think of the crowds that will be milling in the city centre, I think it's the best decision.'

Beth led the way into the kitchen and fussed around with cups and spoons.

'I don't always make good decisions,' she said, carrying on from where they had left off. 'At least Harry says I don't.' She glanced at her mother, weighing up her reaction.

'You mean about the letters you've been reading?'

182

Even to Beth, normally the quickest off the starting block, her mother's forthright question was quite shocking.

'Er...possibly.'

'You have a perfect right to read them, Beth,' her mother said, no trace of disapproval in her tone. 'And you were quite justified in reminding me that he's your grandfather.'

'Harry said you...' Beth hesitated, for she realised he had said nothing at all.

'I admit I was surprised,' her mother smiled, taking the cup of coffee she was offered. 'Disappointed even. At first anyway.' She gave Beth what appeared to be a genuine smile of affection. 'It was a natural reaction considering that he's been away for so long.'

'So you're not angry now?'

'Oh, I was never angry, my dear. As I say, surprised...disappointed, but no, never angry. You're my daughter, Beth, and I don't intend to fall out with you about something like this.'

Beth was not altogether sure what '*something like this*' signified; whether her mother thought it trivial, or whether the mother-daughter bond took precedence over everything. She recalled the censure in her mother's voice when she had related the tale of some woman in the village who had fallen out with her daughter about the name of the first grandchild, and how nothing should get in the way of family.

'I feel so bad about wanting to read the damned letters,' Beth said now, and part of it was true. 'You know what I'm like about ferreting out the truth.'

'There's nothing wrong with that,' her mother smiled, selecting a scone from the plate. 'Did you make these?' she asked with a sly lift of her eyebrows.

'Very funny, but they're good, aren't they?'

'I should have taught you how to bake, you know,' her mother said sadly. 'My own mother made the same mistake with me, never bothered to pass on what she knew, and I had to learn the hard way.'

'Well, I learned the easy way. I drive to Safeways, park the car, go into the shop, buy the scones and come home and eat them.' Beth leaned back in her chair and decided that she had been too hasty in worrying about today's visit; and when Harry got home, she would tell him that his instinct had been misguided; and that everything was fine.

*

Grace spread a second scone with butter and jam and topped up her cup from the percolator. Despite her relaxed attitude and the fluidity of her conversation, she was thankful that the room was too warm, for she had blamed her damp brow and hands on the temperature and not on the strain of keeping up this charade.

'D'you want me to turn the heating down?' Beth had asked twenty minutes previously, to which Grace had replied not to bother, that she preferred to be too warm in winter than too cold.

'I love the heat,' Beth was saying now. 'Even the South of France in late summer wasn't too uncomfortable for me.'

'Your father was thinking of going to France next year,' Grace said. It could have been true, as James talked of it every year, but so far this winter he had failed to mention it. 'Would you and Harry be interested in coming with us?'

Beth shrugged. 'That's a bit out of the blue, isn't it, Mum? Just coming out with it all of a sudden? When did Dad mention it?'

'He's always mentioning it,' Grace smiled. 'And I'm always pouring cold water on it, the poor man. So this time I decided we should go,' She pulled a face. 'It would be great for me if you wanted to come, company for me. We could go places on our own since you speak the language. Will you at least think about it?'

'Well, of course, I'll think about it.' Beth sighed. 'I wonder if it would be Harry's cup of tea, to go with the family, I mean.'

'He told me once he wouldn't mind going.'

'Did he?' Beth asked, and Grace heard the edge in the girl's tone.

'Yes, he did.'

'I see,' Beth nodded, forcing a smile. 'Of course, I keep forgetting that you have these cosy little chats together.'

'I thought you'd be glad that we get on so well together.'

'I am,' Beth said hastily. 'Of course I am.'

'But?'

'But nothing,' her daughter said firmly. 'Except he hardly ever tells me what you talk about.'

'Ordinary every-day things, the past sometimes. His upbringing with his uncle George.'

'Did he tell you that his mother scarpered?'

'Yes, he did.'

'Apparently, she was ravishing.'

Grace made no comment. Suddenly, Beth's eyes widened.

'Of course!'

'Of course what, dear?'

'Nothing, nothing. Not important anyway.

'You seem shocked by something.'

'No, I'm fine. I just realised something.' Beth's spirits had lifted within seconds. 'Anyway, you're sure you're not annoyed that I'm seeing my grandfather?'

'Absolutely not,' Grace lied with a smile. 'Besides, Beth, you're an adult now, entitled to lead your own life.'

'I'm glad we had this talk. I was a bit worried.'

'Oh, darling, I'm sorry, I'd no idea.'

'Its fine now though,' Beth said happily. 'And you'll see, Mum, everything will turn out great in the end.'

'Of course it will,' Grace agreed, but she had to make a huge effort.

*

Harry finished early, although much later than the other two partners, and locked up his desk. He checked his wallet to see if he had enough money to buy Beth's Christmas present and then he slipped his overcoat across his shoulders and left the office. Sandra, the practice secretary, was preparing to lock up as soon as he left and he apologised to the elderly dear for keeping her waiting.

'I don't mind,' she told him brightly. 'I've not got much to go home to, other than the cat, and she sleeps most of the time.'

'Can I give you a lift somewhere?' he asked, out of sympathy for the woman.

'I'm only going into town to wander around and pass the time,' she said with remarkable honesty. 'But thank you anyway, Mr Harry.' He wondered if he would ever get used to the archaic term of address in the practice.

'I've got nothing to go home for at the moment, myself,' he heard himself say. 'How about I treat you to afternoon tea at the George?'

Sandra – a staid name for a staid lady, he reckoned – stared at him as if she had misheard him.

'I beg your pardon, Mr Harry?'

'A Christmas treat,' he assured her quickly. 'My wife's probably out somewhere with her mother, the flat will be freezing and if I go home now I'll have to clean and light the fire.' He paused, for she was beginning to smile. 'So if I treat you to afternoon tea, by the time I do get home, my wife will have done everything.'

Sandra laughed and he had a fleeting image of the younger woman.

'Well, if you put it like that, I wouldn't dream of spoiling your plans.'

He helped her on with her coat and they left the office together to walk the short distance to the hotel.

The hotel was busy but, after Harry's charm and persuasion, the waitress showed them to a table normally reserved for the staff.

'Nice to see you again, Mr Gillespie,' the woman said, and Harry was surprised she recognised him after only a few visits. With a start, he wondered if Beth would ever discover that he had met Thomas Blake in this very lounge bar.

He ordered a tray of sandwiches and biscuits and tea for two, after which the full realisation of his good Samaritan deed struck him forcibly: what the hell had come over him, deciding to spend an hour with an elderly stranger with whom he had exchanged hardly two words since joining the practice? Freezing flat aside, he decided he had been a bit too hasty.

'Mr Andrew was telling me you'd settled in extremely well,' Sandra said, apparently at ease in his company. 'They're thinking of giving you some hefty cases in the spring.'

She sat opposite him, legs neatly together, hands in her lap, looking like everyone's maiden aunt, and Harry found it difficult to reconcile her prim attitude with the confidential information she was spouting forth.

'I suppose I have settled in well,' he said. 'I was apprehensive at first, of course, but now I feel quite at home.'

'Don't worry about my letting slip their intentions,' Sandra said with an unexpected wink. 'I know you'll keep it quiet, Mr Harry, but I just wanted to tell you how much you're appreciated.'

'Thank you, and of course I'll keep it quiet. But I never expected advancement until next year at this time.'

'May I be totally honest with you?' she asked, lowering her voice.

'Please.'

'It's Mr Andrew who's keen to give you more responsibility. Actually, Mr Frank seems not so keen.'

Sandra raised her eyebrows at him and pursed her lips together. Harry had been grateful to her for letting him know that Frank Gilmour was a friend of Charlie Webster's but now she seemed more than willing to divulge a lot more.

'Gilmour's not the kind of person I can take to,' he felt he could tell her. 'As you said before, he's friendly with Charlie Webster.'

'I wondered about that,' Sandra said, enjoying the subterfuge, he thought. 'Was there a specific reason for you wanting to know about them?'

The waitress interrupted them, setting down the tray on the table between them and fussing around for a few minutes, after which Sandra prompted Harry with a nod.

'My wife works for Webster.'

'Does she? He's in antiques, isn't he?'

'Beth speaks French and German, translates descriptions for foreign clients.'

Sandra sighed. 'I so wanted to take languages, you know, but my father was dead against it, made me take a secretarial course instead.'

'For which, may I say, I am forever grateful,' Harry laughed. 'You turn my pathetic letters into masterpieces, to the extent that I'm being considered for an Honorary Degree in literature from St. Andrews.'

Sandra was delighted, and Harry wondered at his apprehension at spending an hour in such good company. Whilst his companion was sipping her tea, he went on:

'I have a feeling that Webster fancies my wife, if you'll excuse a coarse expression.'

'That wouldn't surprise me,' she shrugged. 'The two of them have fairly bad reputations in the city.'

'Really?'

'Oh, yes.' She leaned forward and whispered. 'Mr Frank got more than one girl into trouble, you know.'

Harry could hardly see the significance of such an event as it was almost a daily occurrence in modern times, but, in deference to his companion's age and lack of experience, he nodded slowly, feigning disapproval.

'I see.'

'And I know that people have changed and that things are very different from my day, but,' Sandra looked at him with unwavering eyes. 'I've heard it said that just because everyone's doing it doesn't make it right.'

Harry was rarely embarrassed but he felt it now, as if Sandra could see right through him, that she suspected he might be similarly inclined.

'I tried to persuade Beth to sleep with me before we were married,' he said before he could stop himself, saved from total embarrassment only by his companion's nonchalant shrug. 'But, we were engaged by then, due to marry within the month. Anyway, she said 'no'.'

'I can't see anything wrong with it,' Sandra said, adopting a maiden aunt tone to match her demeanour. 'Not if you're intention is to marry the girl. But with men like Gilmour and Webster, sowing their seed all around the county, I'd say that's a different story.'

If Harry had placed a bet on the topics of conversation he would conduct with staid, elderly Sandra, sex and promiscuity would never have been in the running. For a moment he had to pause; take stock. When he glanced across at her she was grinning broadly.

'You young people always think us oldies go around with our eyes shut.'

'I must say you've surprised me.'

'There's another thing that might surprise you,' Sandra said, cutting a sandwich neatly with the small side knife. 'You'll never guess who Gilmour was caught with when he was only fifteen. Quite disgusting it was considering she was two years younger.'

Harry could hardly believe his ears: Frank Gilmour, supercilious, arrogant creep with a criminal record?

'Did it ever go to court?'

Sandra gave a derisive snort. 'You must be joking. With his family's connections? No, she – not he, mind you, the perpetrator of the crime – she was sent off to relatives in Australia, poor child, only came back last year.'

'Well, I thought I'd heard everything, but that beats it all.'

'As you can imagine, it's a well-kept secret.'

'In that case, how do you know?' Harry asked, suddenly aware of the 'well-kept secret' passing between them at this very minute.

'Because I'm on the same committees as her mother and she regards me as a safe confidante.' Sandra's eyes sparkled at the implication. 'Shows how wrong you can be, doesn't it?'

'But you know I won't tell anyone. Your secret is safe with me,' Harry added humorously.

'Yes, I do know that. In fact,' she went on seriously. 'I can tell that you've got lots of other peoples' secrets tucked away too, Mr Harry.'

For the second time in a few minutes, Harry was astonished at the woman's perception; or was he an open book, yet thinking himself so blasé?

'Was it a local girl, the one he…?'

Sandra hesitated, but only for a moment, and then she leaned forward again, this time whispering, more dramatically, behind her hand.

'I did mention how disgusting he is, didn't I? Well, it was his sister.'

*

Thomas dodged around the hundredth pushchair he had encountered on his way down the High Street and pushed his way through the crowds to the jeweller's shop he had spotted opposite McEwens. He liked this time of day, when the light was fading and the Christmas lights were lit, and the city took on a fairy tale appearance. As a child, he would often bully his mother into taking him into Perth on Christmas Eve so that he could wander around, gazing at the city decorations, at the colours and shapes dangling above him, firing his young imagination, filling his life with magic, albeit for a day.

Even approaching seventy years of age, he was enthralled by Christmas Eve, possibly because the South American version was religious, as opposed to this gaudy but utterly captivating display: the taped carols in the shops, the dazzling shop windows trying to outdo each other, the dozens of Santas ho-ho-ing in their plastic caves; but most of all the promise of something more exciting than the dull, drab normality of the other days of the year.

He halted abruptly in front of the jeweller's window and a couple behind him crashed into his back.

'I do beg your pardon,' he smiled courteously, whilst thinking them a pair of nincompoops.

'Watch where you're going next time,' the surly youth told Thomas before marching on, his hapless girlfriend in tow.

'I will,' Thomas said effusively. 'Apologies once more.'

He smiled and shook his head as he opened the shop door and went inside. So much for the Christmas spirit! Had he been thirty years younger, he might have given the young twerp a verbal bashing.

'I just want to browse,' he told the over-enthusiastic sales girl before she could finish the sentence. 'If I require any assistance, you'll be the first one I ask.'

She melted into the background and he examined the nearest cabinet, although what Daphne would like, he had no idea. A brooch was neither too expensive nor too intimate and he had doled out quite a few in his time; or he could choose a bracelet; one of those boring things that sported little charms that she could add to until the weight was so great it would require a wheel-barrow to carry it.

A small trinket box caught his eye: neither expensive, nor intimate, nor the least bit revealing as to how he felt about her. In fact, it was perfect.

He beckoned to the sales girl and pointed it out.

'A lovely choice, Sir,' she told him predictably. 'Would it be for your wife?'

'No, it would be for my mistress,' he lied irritably. 'Could you gift wrap it for me please while I have another look?'

The girl shot him a scathing glance but dashed into the back quarter to do his bidding. Thomas ambled to the next cabinet, crammed to the sides with pearl necklaces and earrings. Pearl earrings… His heart lurched at the memory of her wearing them for the first time.

I never wear earrings

*

'I never wear earrings, you know,' she said bluntly, turning them over in her hands. 'My hair covers my ears, or haven't you noticed?'

'You can sweep it back, surely?'

'Too severe.'

'Or you could just tuck it behind your ears when you're wearing them.'

'Like a tinker,' Charlotte said scornfully. 'Next you'll be asking me to sell white heather round the doors.'

He had become accustomed to her bad moods, her taciturn attitude, but he had never reconciled himself to it; not ever. He put up with it, but that was all. Since she had told him of the pregnancy, and since he had bullied her into marrying him, their times together had deteriorated into the most hurtful, most heart-breaking relationship he had ever imagined possible. Sometimes he wished he had acceded to her wish not to marry him, and then she might have preserved some of the gentleness and humour that had first attracted him to her.

As he looked at her ungrateful expression, Thomas made a decision.

'There's a job coming up and I'm going to apply for it.'

Charlotte glanced at him and, for the first time in months, he saw a flicker of fear in her eyes.

'A job? What, here, in Perth?'

'No, in South America.'

She stared at him with disbelieving eyes, but he returned her stare, for he knew this was the turning point: either she would realise how much she loved him and beg him to stay, or she would shrug and wish him good luck.

'What kind of a job?' she asked eventually, her eyes dropping to the earrings she was holding.

'An engineer with the national railways.'

'My, but that sounds grand.'

'I'll not take it if you want me to stay, Charlotte.'

The blue eyes fluttered to his face and he could read her answer before she put it into words.

'I'll not stand in your way, Thomas.'

'You're my wife, you'd come with me.'

She laughed then, attracting the attention of fellow shoppers.

'We're married in name only, remember? You're free to go where you choose.'

'Don't you love me, Charlotte?' he whispered urgently, drawing her into a corner of the shop. 'I thought you did, I know you did.'

He had blamed himself then: how stupid of him to use the past tense, for it gave her the chance to pick up on it.

'Aye, I did.'

'You still do,' he insisted, but knew he was fighting a losing battle. 'You're not the kind of girl to fall in and out of love like that.'

'Maybe I never really loved you in the first place.'

As soon as she had uttered the words, he saw the hurt in her eyes before she turned away, and he took courage from it. She did love him!

'Will you come with me?'

'No, Thomas, Charles,' she smiled wearily. 'I will not.'

'When the child's born then?'

'Not then either.'

188

'Well, when it's older, able to travel?'

She must have taken pity on him at that moment, because she had smiled and patted his hand.

'We'll see. But there's a lot of water to flow under the bridge before then.' Her face brightened but he knew it was an act. 'I think I will let you buy me these,' she told him, proffering the pearl earrings. 'And thank you, Thomas. Every time I wear them, I promise I'll think of you.'

*

Suddenly, Thomas realised he was staring into space and that the sales girl was hovering beside him.

'Here's your gift, Sir, that'll be nine pounds nine shillings please.'

He opened his wallet and handed her a ten pound note, eyeing the remaining two notes with alarm: half past three on Christmas Eve, with the banks closed and only twenty pounds left in his wallet!

'Thank you,' he smiled graciously to the girl, cursing himself for snipping her nose off earlier. 'You've been very helpful and I must apologise for my rudeness when I came in. I do hope you'll forgive me.'

She blushed and simpered, as he suspected she would: it was the accent and the expensive cut of his clothes; it worked a treat every time.

'I'm sure I don't know what you mean, Sir,' she said, ringing up the amount on the till and handing him the change. 'We're all a little harassed at this time of year.'

'I wasn't serious about a mistress, by the way. My wife just died,' he lied solemnly.

'Oh my goodness,' the girl said, horrified on behalf of a complete stranger, and a rude one at that. 'I'm so sorry, Sir, how dreadful for you at Christmas too.'

Thomas sighed and feigned heartache. 'It is, as you say, much worse at this time, and it's my first without her,' he added plaintively.

When he raised his eyes to hers, he knew he would have no difficulty in boosting his funds for the festive period.

Five minutes later, his wallet healthier and his chequebook depleted by one cheque, Thomas stepped out of the shop, gave the girl a grateful wave and merged into the crowds.

*

Grace hauled the vacuum cleaner from the cupboard and prepared to run it over the living room carpet for tomorrow's gathering. As she fixed the hoses together, Frank came downstairs and offered to help.

'For Heaven's sake, Frank, that's women's work,' she laughed. 'If you want to help you can get the Christmas tree lights working. You know what your father's like with electrical things.'

'Yes, the same as he is with painting the house.'

They shared an amused glance before he went into the parlour to check the ancient set of bulbs, dragged from the attic to adorn the freshly cut tree that Mr Dickson gifted to his employees every year.

As her mother before her, Grace abhorred housework and, had she the financial resources, she would have preferred to employ a cleaner. Cleaning and tidying were such thankless tasks. Mrs Collins next door had her niece come in once a week; had mentioned that the girl was in need of extra cash.

'She's very good, Grace, and very reliable,' Janet had said. 'Plus you'd never have

189

to worry about her stealing things, not with her being in the family.'

Grace had said she would think about it, but that she quite enjoyed housework now and, at least, it was a way of keeping fit. When her next-door neighbour had gone, she had looked at herself in the mirror and pulled a face.

'You'll never go to Heaven, Grace Melville,' she told her reflection, wishing now that she had completed her studies after the War and found a well-paid job.

'It was a broken bulb,' Frank said ten minutes later, holding it up for her inspection. 'Do we have any spares?'

'Attic cupboard, inside the electrical box.'

Once the living room was presentable, Grace filled the kettle and made tea for herself, coffee for her son. She enjoyed the Christmas holiday, for Frank had several days off and filled the house with pop records and lively chatter, both of which were sorely lacking since Beth's departure. Grace was heartened by the change in the boy since he had professed to finding the 'right girl', a colleague at the bank; a lovely girl he said, although Grace had never met her. Tomorrow would be their first encounter and she was apprehensive.

'Her name is Emily,' Frank had said, with that particular coyness common to nineteen-year old boys and first loves. 'She's great fun, Mum, you'll like her.'

Grace poured milk into her tea and wished, rather unkindly, that she had had the courage to restrict Christmas lunch to family, not strangers who might or might not turn out to be the 'right girl' eventually.

Of course, when Frank had asked her she felt obliged to say 'yes'.

'D'you think I've got fatter?' he asked her now, regarding the plate of chocolate biscuits on the table.

'Fatter? You're like a skinned rat, Frank. What on earth makes you think you've got fatter?'

'It's just that Emily is a keep-fit fanatic and she's really slim.'

'Good for her, but how does that affect you?'

'I want to be the same.'

'Wouldn't you have to give up smoking then?' Grace asked innocently.

'I'm trying to.'

She could hardly believe it: if what Beth said were true, the boy had smoked since he was twelve, and now he was talking of giving up. Grace had to assume it was true love.

She nodded encouragement. 'Giving up's a good thing, of course, but only if you're doing it for yourself.'

Frank shrugged. 'Mostly, it's for her. She hates the smell of smoke.'

'She and your father will get on famously then.'

'Did he know I smoked when I was younger?'

'Yes, dear, he did.'

'But he never said anything to me.'

'That's because I stuck up for you.'

'Yeah, that's what Beth told me, and it always annoyed her. The cheek of her, when she was Dad's favourite.'

'Oh, that's hardly fair, Frank. Your father and I had no favourites.'

He grimaced and took a chocolate biscuit. 'If you say so.'

'Do you think Emily will want a drink if she's a keep-fit person?'

'White wine's O.K.'

'Good, I bought some in Perth today.'

'And she eats almost anything.'

'Thank you, dear,' Grace said sarcastically. 'I feel much more confident now about the guinea pig stew.'

'Sorry, I just meant...'

'It's a joke, Frank,' she had to tell him, remembering what a serious and dour baby he had been. 'Now, I must tidy the parlour in case Beth wants to play the piano tomorrow.'

'You know she will. It's obligatory, isn't it, to sing carols round the tree?'

Grace's heart lurched at the image of past Christmas eves with her mother and Lily.

'Not if you and Emily want to do something else,' she managed to say.

'She'll join in, don't worry.'

'How old did you say she was?'

'Seventeen last June.'

'Goodness me, I'll feel like a kindergarten teacher in this house tomorrow!'

*

Harry could tell that Beth had spent the best part of an hour lighting candles around the flat, including the bathroom and kitchen. He stood for a moment in a hall bereft of electric lights and peered into the gloom.

'Oh, there you are,' Beth said cheerfully from the sitting room door. 'How d'you like the aura?'

'For a minute there, I thought I'd taken a wrong turning, stumbled into the Vatican.'

'It's romantic, don't you think?'

'Not if you want to read the newspaper.'

'And when do I ever give you enough time to do that?'

It was true: every time he sat down and raised a newspaper to his eyes, she seemed to resent it; chattered incessantly until he gave up and threw it aside.

'You're in luck tonight,' he smiled. 'I didn't have time to buy one.'

'Did you have lunch in the town with your colleagues?'

'You must be joking. But I did have afternoon tea at the George, with Sandra.'

Beth paused in her inspection of her fingernails and looked up sharply.

'Who's she?'

'My secretary, the most gorgeous thing on two legs and utterly available. And, lucky for you, fifty eight years old.'

She gave him a cheeky salute and turned back into the living room.

'And you, sweetheart,' Harry said, following her without taking his coat off. 'Did you have lunch with your colleagues?'

'Mum was here, so we had something light.'

'A milky bar?'

'No,' Beth said pointedly. 'I made a toasted cheese thing, with pickle.'

'Wow, you must be exhausted. Sit down and I'll bring a drink through.'

She laughed and rushed towards him, throwing her arms around his neck and hauling his head down.

'I want a Christmas Eve kiss, Gillespie.'

'What's in it for me?'

'I've made your favourite dinner.'

Harry pushed her gently to arms' length. 'You don't know my favourite.'

'Yes I do, I asked my mother,' she said with mild reproach.

'Did I tell Grace?' he asked, knowing that he had.

'So, prepare yourself for veal marinated in Marsala, followed by home-made bread and butter pudding.'

'You're joking. You must be.'

'Well, thank you VERY much, Mr Diplomat of the year. Cheek!' She drew him towards her and her mouth was close. 'Now, where was I?"

'You're not going to let me take my coat off first?'

'Absolutely not.'

As he kissed her, the telephone rang in the hall and Beth sighed.

'Who the blazes can that be?'

'We can leave it if you like.'

'It might be Mum, wanting me to bring something tomorrow.'

Harry took off his coat and hung it in the cupboard. After a moment he became aware that the conversation was one-sided, for Beth had not spoken a word; not a clue as to who it was. He turned to look at her, but she waved away his silent query, mouthing '*Annie*'.

Eventually, he passed her and went into the kitchen, assuming it was the usual girl trouble: Annie Kerr again, with her romantic problems, seesawing between hysterical joy and suicidal tendencies.

He poured a gin and tonic and wandered to the balcony window. The Inch was still dusted with snow at the edges, but the paths had been cleared and he was amazed at the number of people going to and fro. It was half past four, a time on Christmas Eve when they should all be at home, doing what they were supposed to on such a night – being with family; mending bridges; doing the Christian thing.

Harry thought back to the few Christmas Eves he had been able to spend with his father; a man pulled this way and that by the wild eccentricities of his wife, to the extent that his only solace was to disappear for weeks on end – to God knows where. The three Christmases he had spent with Ralph Gillespie were so emblazoned on his memory that it took only the sight of a decorated tree in a stranger's window, or the sound of distant carols, or even simply the scent of the first snowflakes to invoke the sheer joy of their time together.

As a child, Harry had resented his father's frequent absences; but now, he could understand the man's dilemma; apportion a share of the blame to his mother.

Idly, Harry reflected on Beth's high spirits when he arrived home: it was obvious that the subject of Thomas Blake's letters had never arisen, for if it had, mother and daughter would surely have quarrelled.

'Hey, you said you'd pour me a drink,' he heard Beth complain.

'Sorry, I was just enjoying the view.'

'There's half an hour before the starter, time for at least three. Get pouring.'

They sat in the glow of a dozen candles, Beth in her usual position on the floor, her blonde head resting on his knee. Occasionally she would offer further snippets from her chat with Annie Kerr but he had no sympathy for the girl. She was the type who continually dumped her problems on best friends and relied on them – particularly Beth – for sympathy and solutions, and Harry had never seen anything in the girl that would change his opinion of her.

'You never asked me how I got on with Mum.'

'It's your business.'

Beth lifted her head and frowned at him. 'What do you mean?'

'What goes on between you and Grace is your business, not mine.'

'You have a strange view of the world.'

'So, how did the two of you get on then?'

'It's a secret,' Beth giggled, her words slurring from too much wine.

'The fact she came into Perth tells me a lot.'

'She says she doesn't mind that I've read his letters.'

It was fortuitous that she could not see his face, for his expression would have provoked an argument.

'That's good,' Harry said only. 'I'm glad.'

'So, we were quibbling about nothing,' she said happily. 'Mum was O.K. about it all the time.'

'Does she want to meet him?' he felt obliged to ask, although he knew the answer.

'Not just yet, but she will. Once she reads the letters and finds out what really happened, she'll forgive him.' Beth glanced up at him joyfully. 'I'm so relieved about it all, I can hardly wait to tell him.'

Harry pondered the relevance of the old saying: silence is the virtue of fools. On this occasion he considered it relevant.

While Beth prepared for bed, Harry lay drowsing in the chair, trying to imagine the conversation between mother and daughter, making futile attempts to establish a reason for Grace's deceiving the girl so blatantly. What could she hope to achieve by it? Knowing Beth, she would forge ahead now, believing the way to be clear, befriending the man, perhaps inviting him here, pressing Grace to meet him.

Harry opened his eyes and watched as the candles burned low and flickered in the movement of air from the fire. An unreasonable despondency was settling upon him, although he was reluctant to give it space in his mind. He knew it was not Grace's lying to her daughter that disconcerted him, nor her pretence of being unaffected by Beth's affiliation to Thomas Blake. No, what rankled was the fact she had chosen not to confide in him. He knew it would keep him awake.

Chapter Ten

Lily Morris rose early and had the front step swept by eight o'clock. December the twenty fifth was one and the same to her, despite happy memories of Christmases in the '30's and '40's. People were so different now and every-day life so contrary to her own times that she made no effort to keep up with modern times.

As she propped the brush up in the kitchen cupboard, she had a sudden depressing thought: was this to be her last Christmas? Despite the pills she had been swallowing by the handful recently, despite the lessening of her symptoms over the past weeks, she had been thinking about her death as often as she had done when she was in pain. To be truthful, she thought about it almost every hour, on the hour, each time the clock struck and she found she was still alive.

She wondered if it were better just to fall to the ground suddenly, feeling only a slight surprise that it had come without warning; or was it better to lie in a hospital bed for months, gradually becoming used to the idea, until even the element of surprise was removed? But what would she feel, she asked herself now, as she moved around the kitchen with nothing to do; and what would her last word be, assuming that she had time to gasp it?

Lily had always prayed that Charlotte Shepherd had not suffered great pain the morning she had died. She preferred to imagine that her friend had simply been overcome by a giddy spell and had fainted; no time to be shocked, or afraid; no moment of regret for a life coming to a sudden end.

It was the strangest thing, Lily was pondering now: despite the idea being regarded as heresy, Lily firmly believed that Charlotte had no idea that she was dead.

'Och, stop this, for Heaven's sake!' she shouted at herself impatiently. 'It's Christmas day and you're going to Grace's and you'll just behave yourself, Lily Morris, or should I call you Lily Morbid?'

Slightly cheered by her amusing pun, she took a cardboard box from the pantry shelf and began to fill it with bits and pieces to supplement Grace's table. She felt somewhat ashamed at her outburst, not because people would think she was daft speaking to herself, but because, as a Christian, her faith was supposed to assure her that Charlotte was in Heaven now and was perfectly aware she was dead.

*

James did his best to help Grace as much as she would allow but, when it came to Christmas lunch and satisfying the needs of her family, she was like her mother in many respects: standing on the sidelines whilst other people ran around not knowing what they were doing was not a happy prospect. Apart from asking him to move chairs and tables and making sure the fires were stoked, Grace was willing to assume responsibility for everything else.

At eleven o'clock, following the ritual adhered to by Charlotte Blake, the four of them sat down for a sherry, although Grace knew that her son would have preferred beer; and Lily lemonade.

'You can have something else,' she told him, but he shook his head and raised his glass.

'This is fine, Mum. Here's to a successful Christmas day.'

'And here's to another twenty-four of them,' was James's toast.

Grace was aghast. 'Have there been so many?'

'Since we were married anyway, but there was one before that.'

'You lot are ancient,' Frank grinned, no longer expecting cautionary glances from his father.

'So will you be one day,' James smiled, then, looking at Grace, added: 'Did you ever imagine we'd be this age, Grace?'

'Never.'

'You know, Frank, your mother still looks the same as the day I met her.'

'Don't listen to him, Frank, he's blethering.'

'No, he's right,' Frank contradicted. 'I've seen photos of you and you've hardly changed at all.'

'Hear, hear,' Lily chipped in, face flushed from half a glass of sherry.

Grace laughed. 'If the lot of you carry on like this, I'll consider it an extra Christmas present.'

'Speaking of which,' James said, standing up and putting his glass on the mantelshelf. 'I'll have to go and raid Santa's sack.'

When James had gone upstairs, Frank refilled his own glass and offered some to his mother and Lily.

'No, thanks,' Lily said firmly. 'I'm tipsy with just one.'

'Mum?'

'Oh, it's Christmas. Might as well.'

Frank topped up his mother's glass and sat down, occupying James's chair.

'I often look through the photo albums,' he said.

'What on earth for?'

'It's interesting.'

'What, the old black and whites?'

'They're the best. They're part of history, you know, Mum, especially the ones with your cousin. What was his name, the one that was the RAF pilot?'

'Martin.'

'Imagine being a fighter pilot,' Frank said with reverence. 'Zooming around the skies, being shot at, never knowing when you'd get hit.' He shook his head in admiration. 'He must have been a tough guy.'

'I suppose he was, although he hardly spoke about it.'

Frank looked at her in surprise. 'He didn't?'

'No, when he came up here he was on holiday, wanted to forget all about it. Your father was the same. In fact,' Grace frowned, the resentment still with her to this day. 'He didn't even tell me he'd been awarded a medal for bravery. It was Tony Kerr who told me.'

'Wow, my Dad's a hero,' Frank grinned. 'Why haven't you told me before?'

Grace shrugged. Talk of times past, particularly times that reminded her of her mother, were best avoided.

'He said it was in the past, and he's right.'

'It may be only be the past to you, Mum, but it's history to me. I had to answer a question on it in my last exam at school.'

'What, on your father's medal for bravery?'

'You should have had another drink, you're great fun when you're merry.'

Grace looked at her son, trying to decide if that meant she was not great fun at any other time. Perhaps anticipating her remark, Frank spoke first.

'Not that you're a wet week the rest of the time,' he smiled, using a quaint expression picked up from Lily Morris. 'But sometimes you're sad.'

His gaze met hers and Grace was disconcerted to discover an unusual compassion in her son's eyes. With something of a shock, she realised that Frank was no longer a little boy and that, at least for the moment, their roles were reversed.

195

'Sad? Is that what you think?'

'Are you happy, Mum, honestly?'

'For Heaven's sake!' Lily exclaimed. 'What a cheek you youngsters have now!'

'Well, of course I'm happy,' Grace smiled. 'And I'd no idea I gave you the impression I was sad, Frank. If I have, I'm sorry.'

'You looked really happy in the old photos.'

'That's because we're all happy when we're young, dear,' Lily remarked sleepily. 'Now, do you want me to go and check the turkey?'

'You'll do no such thing,' Grace insisted, standing up. 'That's my domain.'

She patted Frank's shoulder as she moved away, but the essence of the smile he gave her was doubt.

*

Beth was as effusive as Harry was withdrawn. As soon as they arrived, Grace sensed that her daughter had lost no time in telling him – boasting, perhaps – that she was free to contact her grandfather, with her mother's blessing. The accusation in the boy's eyes as he wished her season's greetings was almost too much for Grace to bear, but she intended to keep it to herself for the time being.

'Harry, Merry Christmas my dear and many of them,' she smiled, the first deceptive smile of her day. 'Beth, darling, you look stunning, quite over-dressed for this old house.'

'Rubbish, I love this house, it's part of history.'

'For Heaven's sake!' Grace exclaimed, glancing at her son. 'Have you two been colluding?'

'Why?' Beth asked.

'Because your brother's just been harping on about history and the old photographs.'

'Have you, little brother?'

'Yeah. I was telling Mum I often look through the old albums.'

'Love must be turning you into a sap,' his sister said unkindly. 'When's she due to arrive then, this vision of loveliness?'

'Beth, dear, not today, please,' Grace frowned. 'We'll have to be on our best behaviour for Emily's sake.'

'I'll be so well behaved you won't recognise me. Now, where's the wine?'

'In a moment, dear,' Grace said, wondering if it would be possible to carry on. 'There's something I want to tell you all before Emily arrives.'

Four pairs of eyes swivelled in her direction and she told them quickly, before she had time to change her mind.

*

Harry thought Emily Mackay far too flighty for his brother-in-law, or was she simply trying too hard? That was the trouble when the couple were both young: girls were streaks ahead in matters of romance and pinning you down screaming until you said 'yes', which was why his own marriage had a fair chance of success. It suited him that Beth was immature and that the age difference gave her the impression he was worldly-wise, for it kept her in check. The half hour he had been observing Emily Mackay, however, conveyed to Harry she would be quite a handful for a boy like Frank. He would have his work cut out keeping this one in check.

'She's making a play for you,' Beth had whispered in his ear as he handed her a glass of wine. 'Just watch it, Gillespie.'

196

'Not my type. Too gorgeous,' he whispered back mischievously.

Harry barely listened to the conversation during lunch, so preoccupied was he with Grace's announcement regarding her sudden tolerance towards her father. She had convinced him completely that her new approach was genuine, yet, until he could reason it out in his own mind and come up with a logical explanation, it would jostle among his thoughts, as it was doing now.

'I've come to see how destructive it would be,' she had said an hour ago, not looking at anyone in particular. 'Beth's my daughter and I don't want to fall out with her over this.'

After a few more minutes of platitudes and diplomacy, she had come to the end of her soliloquy, only then glancing at each of them in turn. Had it been his imagination, or had she awarded him the briefest eye contact? Perhaps it was the effects of the huge meal and too many drinks, but Harry was finding it impossible to join in the revelry or to shake off the feeling that he had been betrayed.

'I don't think I could see him...not yet,' Grace had remarked apologetically to the group. 'But it doesn't mean that Beth can't see him, or any of you, come to that.'

Now, as Beth took up her position at the piano and the carol book was set in front of her, Harry had already decided that he would skip the singsong, regardless of how anti-social he appeared.

When he wandered out of the parlour, with several disapproving glances trailing in his wake, he found Lily Morris clearing away the glasses and tidying the room.

'Aren't you joining in?' he asked her and she pulled an amusing face.

'I've done my share of screechling, thank you.' She frowned at him. 'I see you're not joining in either.'

'Can't stand it actually.'

'What, singing?' she asked, as shocked as if it were a serious crime.

'No, the campfire bit, everyone pretending they like everybody else.'

Lily gave a wry smile, 'You're wrong,' she told him. 'They're not pretending.'

'No, that was rotten of me,' he admitted. 'I'm just in a bad mood.'

'About Thomas Blake?' she asked shrewdly.

'What makes you say that?'

'I saw your face when she said she'd changed her mind about him.'

'I was surprised, that was all. She'd always hated him, or at least that's the impression I got.'

Lily picked up some crumpled napkins and put them in the cardboard box she was using as a wastepaper bin, and then she looked closely at Harry.

'Aye, she does hate him.'

'That's what I thought.'

'There's nothing that would change that lassie's mind about Thomas Blake, I can assure you. She can spout forth all she likes, but she's not fooling me.'

Harry felt more light-hearted than he had felt all day. A woman who had known Grace for almost fifty years had just confirmed his suspicion that she was playing a part; he was right, but what was she up to?

'Why are you telling me this? You don't like me much.'

'True,' Lily said with dispassionate honesty. 'But I love Grace more than anything and I think she's making a mistake.'

'If you want, I'll look out for her.'

'Aye, you could do that,' she said casually and then turned away to continue clearing the room, her back presented to him in a sign of dismissal; but Harry was too happy to let it bother him.

At half past three the Kerrs arrived to spend the evening with the family. Whether Annie had decided to come because of a lover's tiff, Beth had no idea, but there she was, pale and interesting, dressed like a high-class whore and probably about to monopolise Harry for the next hour.

'I didn't know you were to be here,' Beth said, as courteously as she could.

'I'd nowhere else to go,' Annie said meaningfully, but Beth refused to pick up on it.

'Come and have a drink, it'll cheer you up. Harry is here, you can chat to him,' she added with a cheeky smile.

'What's Frank's girlfriend like?' Annie asked, treading carefully, Beth judged.

'Oh, she's gorgeous. In fact, I don't think I've ever seen Harry quite so love-struck before.' Beth did not wait to witness the girl's reaction. She was content to have put the proverbial cat where she enjoyed it most. Her only regret was that she had not had time to warn her husband.

*

Whereas once it might have been Sarah Kerr who evoked Grace's sympathy, it was now Tony who was the frailer. Grace thought it quite heart breaking to see such a change in a man in the space of five years. Her mother had always maintained that the creaking gate hung the longest and the adage certainly was applicable to Sarah Kerr, who at one time, because of the cancer scare, had not expected to see in another year; yet she had survived into her fifth Christmas.

Tony, on the other hand, walked with two sticks and had suffered a second mild stroke in the summer, which had left him with slurred speech and restricted movement. For a man who had once led such an active life and who had never relied on anyone for anything, it was distressing for Grace to watch him now. The odd thing was that his wife appeared the stronger for having to take care of him, quite the reverse of what Grace might have expected.

'He's lucky to have you,' she told Sarah as they prepared sandwiches for a light teatime snack. 'And you seem to be thriving on it.'

'It's funny, isn't it?' Sarah smiled. 'But I feel better now that Tony needs me. In fact, I don't have time to be ill myself, I'm so busy looking after him.'

'But the children will help, surely?'

Sarah pressed her lips together and gave Grace a look that said it all.

'Annie's in Perth now, with fiancé trouble. I wouldn't expect her to rush through to Dundee every five minutes, and, well, you know what sons are like.'

Grace said she did, but it was not from experience: Frank seemed more sympathetic and considerate than his sister.

'You know they're living together,' Sarah said now.

'Who?'

'Annie and Alan.'

Grace shrugged. 'It's not so important nowadays, Sarah, not like it was for us.'

'But it worries me. I mean, if she breaks up with this one and she's slept with him, the next time she'll probably do the same, and before you know it she'll be branded as...'

'And how do you know she's going to break up with this one? We mothers worry over nothing, don't we? Come on,' Grace urged. 'Let's go and have another drink, make ourselves blotto.'

Sarah laughed. 'Blotto? Where did you hear that one?'

'From Frank,' Grace smiled. 'And that's not the only thing he's taught me.' She paused at the door and took her friend's arm. 'Promise me you'll not lose any sleep over Annie?'

Her friend's expression told Grace that any promise would be too late in coming, but all she said was: 'I promise.'

*

It was late into the evening by the time Harry sought her out. He found her standing by the kitchen window, gazing into the darkness of the garden, so engrossed with her own thoughts that she failed to hear him come into the room.

'Hey, a penny for them?'

She whirled round, 'Goodness, you gave me a fright! I was miles away. Have you had enough to eat and drink?'

'You know perfectly well we have, since you always cook for an army, not half a dozen of your family.'

'Have you both had a good day?'

'Yes and no,' Harry said bluntly and he saw the studied composure she had relied on all day begin to desert her.

'Harry, I meant to... I was going to...'

'No need,' he said more kindly. 'I knew anyway.'

'Knew what?' she asked him, testing him to the last.

'That you were lying about feeling more disposed towards your father.'

'I meant what I said about not falling out with Beth,' she said defiantly.

'I expect you did.'

'And I wasn't lying when I said I didn't want to see him yet.'

'We can play this game all night if you like, Grace,' Harry smiled wearily. 'But, eventually, you'll have to face it.'

She lowered her eyes and frowned. In the parlour, the piano stopped and with it, the singing of carols. In a moment Beth would be through and he would have missed his opportunity.

'You're not fooling me, Grace, I know you still hate him as much as ever, and I know that you'll never accept him into this family. So, what the hell do you think you're doing?'

He had never spoken to her so roughly before and what surprised him more than anything was her calm acceptance of his harsh tone. Did James Melville treat her with similar disrespect so that she was accustomed to it?

'I don't know, to be honest,' she said quietly. 'But I do know this, that I will never fall out with my daughter over him.' She raised her head and met his gaze. 'If that happened, he'd have won, can't you see that?'

The door crashed open before Harry could reply and Beth rushed in, grabbing him by the arm and attempting to drag him from the room.

'Come on, party pooper,' she chided. 'Time to let your hair down.'

He shrugged and allowed himself to be cajoled, but at the last minute, as he stepped across the threshold, he turned back and looked at Grace.

'Thank you for a lovely day,' he said. 'It was really lovely.'

She smiled and nodded. 'You're welcome,' she said, but her eyes were wary.

*

The clock chimed midnight and Lily Morris was still wide-awake: the boy had not

199

been the only one to wonder what Grace Blake was up to. She knew the deep-rooted hatred the girl harboured for her father and there was not a snowball's chance in Hell that she had mellowed towards the man. No, the day he had fled from her on a Dundee street was the day that had sealed Thomas Blake's fate as far as his daughter was concerned. Perhaps she could have forgiven him for accepting a good job at the other side of the world; and perhaps she might have overlooked his reluctance to return to the stringencies of the Shepherd clan; but to have rejected her so publicly when she had probably dreamt of a reconciliation one day? No, that was wholly unforgivable, and Grace would hate him for that single, revealing act until her dying day.

Resigning herself to a sleepless night, Lily rose and put on her thick dressing gown. The house, being stone-built, was so cold in winter that, more often than not, it felt chillier inside than out, and during the night, when the fires had died down, she could not imagine a colder place on Earth. Brushing aside the added cost to her heating bill, she switched on the electric fire in the living room and sat huddled in front of it, casting her mind back to the many nights she and Charlotte had sat in this very spot, confessing and inviting each other's secrets, setting the world to rights.

Lily knew that it was only a matter of time until her mind crept back to the theme of dying; and how many years she had left was anybody's guess. Her life had been of little value to her after Charlotte had passed on, for they had been constant companions every day from '25 until '44. At first, Lily had not known how to cope without her friend, especially since the two friends had planned long and active lives. Charlotte's death at such a young age had shocked Lily and had overwhelmed her with guilt. Had she known her friend's fate, would words have been kinder between them?

You're too young to be yammering on about dying

*

'You're too young to be yammering on about dying,' she scolded Charlotte angrily one day in the summer of '26. 'Any more of this and the bairn will turn out to be a right idiot.'

'It's half of one already if it's anything like me.'

'Och, stop feeling sorry for yourself now. I can't bear it.'

'Do you want the truth?' Charlotte asked suddenly, fixing her friend with a frown.

'That would be a change,' Lily had said brusquely, at which they both burst out laughing.

'The trouble with you, Lily Morris, is that you're such a know-all.'

'Takes one to know one.'

'Do you want the truth or not?'

'Try me.'

Charlotte tutted, adjusted her position on the wrought-iron bench and rubbed her stomach.

'This bairn's destined to be a footballer.'

'I told you, it's a girl.'

'Suddenly you and half the bloody villagers are expert midwives.'

'Is there any chance of this truth surfacing before the damp weather comes and we turn green with mould?'

'I'm scared.'

Lily had stared at her friend, wondering how it could have taken so long for Charlotte to grasp the full implications of her circumstances.

'Well, of course, and so you should be.'

'What?'

'You'll have to bring that wee lassie up on your own, without a father in the house, without the money an extra wage would bring in, with all the hurtful things they'll say to her at school, making fun of her because the only man at home is old enough to be Methuselah.' She had paused for breath, expecting Charlotte to interrupt. *'Are you not going to say anything?'*

'No,' Charlotte had replied quietly. *'It's all true, except you've missed out the bit about...'*

They had sat in silence for a few minutes, both of them aware of what she had been about to say.

'I suppose you did a good job of convincing him you couldn't care less?'

'Oh, it was better that 'good', Charlotte said bitterly. 'It was magnificent,'

'It didn't have to be that way, you know. If you'd only given it a chance, your father might have...'

'Stop it, Lily, that's enough! What's done is done, and that's all there is to it.'

After another silence, Lily turned to her friend and took her hand.

'But you're heart broken, Charlotte Blake, are you not?'

'Aye,' Charlotte smiled brazenly. *'I am indeed, and if you ever breathe a word of it to anyone, Lily Morris, I'll never speak to you again.'*

*

Lily jumped at the sound of an owl screeching in the garden, as it always did when it pounced on prey and wanted to let the whole world know. It was past one o'clock now and she would have to go back to bed, but only because of the cost of the electricity. When the bill landed on the mat in the front porch, Lily would look back on this Christmas night and wish she had stayed in bed.

*

Thomas Blake woke abruptly at the sound of fireworks. Fireworks on Kinnoull Hill? It could only happen on Christmas night if what the solicitor had told him about this area was to be believed. Mind you, there had been something shifty about Frank Gilmour, who had a way of looking at Thomas with suspicion, as if he, Thomas Charles Blake, were a con man. He had wiped the cynical smile off the youth's face when he signed the lease and handed over three months' rent.

'But you only have to pay a month in advance,' the twerp had said.

'I prefer to pay three,' Thomas had smiled. 'It makes me feel more secure.'

The remark had changed the state of the parties: after that, it had been Gilmour who appeared the con man and they had parted the most wary of business partners.

Now, as the popping and whirring of fireworks seemed likely to keep him awake for the foreseeable future, Thomas threw off the blankets and peered at the clock. Half past two in the small hours and someone was still celebrating...

He went downstairs to see if he had any whisky left over from his romantic dinner with the lovely Daphne, switching the heating back on as he passed the hall cupboard, to take the chill off the rooms. Finding only half a bottle of red wine, he decided it would do and poured most of it into a coffee mug. He smiled to think what Daphne would have said to such a gross flouting of etiquette.

'This is the loveliest house I've ever seen,' she had breathed as he had opened the front door and ushered her in. 'I used to admire this house when I took Benny for a walk.'

'Benny?' he had asked politely, his spirits depleting suddenly at the thought of

201

having to keep up a charade of gentlemanly behaviour for the next few hours.

'My second spaniel,' she had smiled. 'A little gem, he was, used to love when we walked up here. It isn't too quiet here for you, Thomas, is it?' she had asked shyly, using his name for only the third time.

'No, it's just the way I like it, away from the noise of traffic.'

'That's the worst thing about living in Scone,' she had said apologetically, as if she found it necessary to justify her choice to him. 'There's a slight rise in the terrain just outside my bedroom window, and the buses and tractors make so much noise, trundling up in low gears.'

He had been astonished, not only at her use of the word 'terrain' but also that she was familiar with gears, for she gave the impression of dizzy blonde joining forces with doddering old woman.

When he began to reappraise her intelligence, he wondered if she had believed his story about his niece and family being away for the festive period or whether she could see from bits and pieces around the house that he lived alone.

'Does your niece have children?' she had asked, alerting him to her suspicions.

'No, she couldn't have any,' he lied with a sad face. 'There's just the two of them, she and her husband.'

'How odd that she doesn't have photographs scattered around.'

'If you don't believe me, Daphne.' Thomas had smiled, cutting her off before truth emerged, 'I could ask her to phone you and verify my story.'

She had blushed a fiery red and the subject was never broached again.

He stirred cinnamon into the mug of wine and poured it into a pot to heat up. Mulled wine was one of the few pleasures he had discovered in this country, and it was just the ticket for a cold wintry Christmas night. He sipped, thinking of his plan to kiss Daphne under the mistletoe dangling in the front porch, but a little voice at the back of his mind had cautioned him to go steady. If he were to gain access to her hard-earned savings, he would not be so stupid as to fall at the first hurdle.

The soothing sip of mulled wine hit the back of his throat and fired him with enthusiasm. Tomorrow he was to meet his granddaughter, to hear the good news she had promised him. He knew it could be only one thing: that Grace, his daughter, was coming round to the idea of having a father again.

Thomas sighed and put his feet up on the radiator. He was extremely grateful to his granddaughter for whatever persuasion she had used to change her mother's mind. He did not even mind if it had been some kind of blackmail, for he was hardly averse to resorting to it himself.

*

Early in the morning, after a surprisingly restful night's sleep, Grace woke to find that James was already up. Anticipating that he would want to bring her breakfast in bed, she lay drowsing, listening for his footsteps on the stairs.

When she woke again to discover that it was half past nine, Grace rose and threw her dressing gown over her nightdress. She began to worry when she went downstairs and saw that the fires were still unlit, felt the unwelcome chill in the rooms.

She hurried into the kitchen, only to discover that the back door was open and it was then that her worst fears took hold, until she heard his voice. Setting aside the puzzle of why her husband had made no attempt to light the fires, Grace went outside to look for him, drawing the dressing gown tightly around her neck to ward off the freezing air. As she glanced up the path, her heart lurched.

It was Harry who reached the telephone first, although Beth was hovering at the bedroom door, trying to catch his attention. When he turned his back on her, he hoped she would assume it was business, although it was Boxing Day and who the hell was working today?

As he listened to Grace's tearful plea, Harry's only thought was how he could break it to Beth.

They trudged the hospital corridor together and his instinct was to hold her hand. Several times he contemplated doing just that but she altered her step, changed the proximity of her arm to his, and so he kept his hands deep in the pockets of his overcoat.

A nurse met them at the ward door, eyes sympathetic but not morose and it seemed to give Grace hope. The nurse stepped forward and introduced herself as Staff Nurse Gibson, held Grace's hand only briefly – another good sign, Harry decided – and then led them into the ward.

'He's asleep at the moment,' the nurse whispered and Harry wondered why she bothered, for the noise in the place was deafening. 'But he'll probably waken within the next half hour, if you're to be here that long?'

Grace glanced at Harry and he nodded.

'Of course we'll be here that long. As long as it takes for him to waken and see that his wife's here.' He avoided Grace's eye, for her distress was unbearable, and moved towards the chairs at the side of the bed. 'Come on,' he smiled to her, his hand at her elbow. 'Have a seat and I'll go and get something for you to drink.'

'I'm afraid the choice is fairly limited,' the nurse said. 'But the morning tea trolley will be round soon, if you don't mind tea and a plain biscuit?'

Grace nodded but Harry knew that she was only being polite, that the cup would sit until it was cold and that the plain biscuit would remain untouched. He was concerned at her lethargy, not to mention the dark circles beneath her eyes. During the short car journey, he had made no attempt at meaningless conversation but he was now fearful that she had taken his silence as a bad omen for James's condition.

'He's going to be fine,' Harry said now, not caring if it turned out to be a lie.

'Do you think so?'

'The Staff Nurse was too normal,' he smiled. 'If it had been bad news, she'd have wept and wailed a bit.'

A grateful but brief glance was his reward. 'You're so kind, Harry.'

'I'm just observant, and she's definitely not worried about him.'

'If anything happens to him I'll just...'

'Grace, nothing's going to happen to him, you'll see. I'm never wrong. You should have learnt that by now.'

She smiled and turned her attention to James, taking his hand in hers and looking at him with such overpowering love that Harry had to avert his gaze.

'I think I'll go and have a wander,' he said, standing up and touching her shoulder lightly.

'No, please stay, Harry. I'd feel better if you did.'

'Of course I'll stay. I just thought you might like some privacy, that's all.'

'Privacy?' she asked in astonishment.

'Yes, privacy. I don't want to...' He had been about to say 'intrude' but she frowned and interrupted him.

'I have no idea what I'd do without you, Harry,' she said fiercely, her eyes more lively now. 'If it weren't for you I'd be lost.'

If he could have chosen the words he wanted her to say at that precise moment, her admission that she would be lost without him would have been too much to hope for. Even faced with the catastrophe of James's heart attack, Harry was buoyed up by her faith in him, the knowledge that she needed him.

'If you're sure?'

'Sit down, please. I want you to be here when he wakes up.'

'Beth and Frank are due any minute. She's a darling for picking him up.'

'That doesn't change anything,' Grace frowned. 'I still want you here when James wakes up.'

Harry shrugged and sat down, trying not to appear as delighted as he felt, and making a huge effort not to rejoice at the turn of events. All he wanted to do was protect her, take care of her; and despite what she had implied about life without James – God forbid – if she were left on her own it would be Harry that she turned to. This time he would not let her down. He would rather die.

Chapter Eleven

One night in early February the snow descended on Eastern Scotland and in the space of a few hours it had deposited three feet of it on pavements and roads, bringing rural Perthshire to a halt. Buses stood in the gloom of hushed depots, trains ran reluctantly and even then only between major cities, and the most regular vehicle on the trunk road between Aberdeen and Perth was the snow plough, which passed through the village several times a morning, spraying snow onto the footpaths that villagers had been endeavouring to keep clear.

Beth was in the middle of preparing her father's lunch when the telephone rang and it was Harry, calling for the third time that day.

'Nothing to report,' she said brightly, giving her father a wink.

'Is there anything you want me to get on the way home?'

'No, I went to Safeway's before I came out here. All you have to do is have my drink poured out for six o'clock.'

She flashed an apologetic grin at her father, still obliged to justify her actions to him, even at her advanced age. He smiled and shook his head, and she realised that such trivia would hardly matter to a man confined to a chair for eighteen hours a day.

'Don't rush,' Harry was saying. 'I can heat something up and we'll have it when you get home.'

'There's only one thing I'd like you to heat up,' she whispered into the mouthpiece.

'Get off this line, you shameless hussy,' he laughed. 'And watch the roads, for Heaven's sake. It's pandemonium out there.'

'Fuss fuss fuss,' Beth said before hanging up. 'He's such a fusspot,' she told her father. 'You'd think I was a child.'

'I still think of you as one,' James admitted. 'I often think of the day I first saw you... spiky hair, cheeky face... and dirty nappies, of course.'

'Dad, please, you're putting me off this soup!'

'I washed your nappies myself when you first came home. Your mother was so unwell.'

'Was she? I didn't know that.'

'Just for a week. After that she was fine, but I did most of the nappy washing.'

'That's what puts me off having kids,' Beth said without thinking, completely forgetting her father's doctor's advice to keep the subject light.

'You'd let a little thing like that put you off?' her father asked with a frown.

'No, I was just joking. In fact, once I get started you'll be sick of the sight of them.'

'I'd never get tired of seeing your children, Beth.'

Beth paused in her stirring of the soup and glanced through the open doorway to the living room. Her father was looking at her, head on one side.

'You wouldn't?' she asked him.

'No, they'd be smart, little things. Just like you.'

'Maybe.'

'Are you ever sorry you married someone so much older than you?' James asked, catching her unawares.

'What?'

'Surely, Harry must want children by now?'

'No, he doesn't.'

Her father appeared doubtful. 'He's thirty, isn't he?'

'Yes.'

'I was a father twice over by the time I was thirty.'

'I know,' Beth said lightly. 'And I'm very grateful.'

She lapsed into silence and pretended to be engrossed in setting the table.

The fine line between not upsetting her father and telling ridiculous untruths was becoming more and more of a challenge. All of them, even the next-door neighbours, had placated James for fear of exacerbating his condition, but Beth had not thought it such a good idea.

'But when he's well again, he'll discover we've all been lying to him,' she had complained to her mother the day before James was sent home. 'I can't tell him a load of rubbish, Mum, it's not fair on him.'

Her mother had sighed and shaken her head. 'Just for once, Beth, can you not put aside your fanatical search for the truth and help your father to get better?'

Beth had said she would, but that was a lie in itself; not the most promising start. Since then she had carefully avoided tetchy subjects, sticking to the banal: the meal she was preparing, or the football results, or how well his pigeons were faring under the watchful eye of his pal up the road. Topics such as politics, village tittle-tattle, her mother's constant exhaustion, or the name Thomas Blake, were off the agenda for the moment; and for the foreseeable future.

The doctor predicted six months before James Melville would be back to his old self again, and even then he had been cautioned about strenuous exercise and needless anxiety. It was only five weeks into his recovery time and Beth was jittery already: she knew that one day, as had almost happened today, she might put her foot right in it, give her father a relapse and see him back in the hospital.

'I don't suppose I was much of an example when you were looking for a husband.'

Beth's attention flew to her father. His expression was non-committal, despite the poignancy of the statement.

'That's a stupid thing to say,' she countered firmly. 'You're a great husband.'

James shrugged. 'Is Harry exactly what you were looking for?'

Beth was irritated. Everyone was supposed to pussy-foot around the man, and here he was broaching a subject that might result in an argument.

'Yes, he is,' she said patiently. 'In fact, he's too much of a gentleman at times, far too good for me.'

James smiled and appeared satisfied, and it crossed Beth's mind that it was the answer he expected.

'Harry was a great help to your mother the week I took ill.'

'I know, I was proud of him,' Beth fibbed, recalling the tiny stab of jealousy she had suffered upon hearing her father's first words upon opening his eyes that first day.

'Thank you, Harry,' he had murmured before falling asleep again, and Beth had forced herself to smile.

'You and I haven't spoken for a while,' her father remarked now. 'You're in Perth of course, making a life of your own, but this has been nice, Beth, just the two of us for a change. I've enjoyed your lunchtime visits.'

'If you ever want me to be here, 'she offered rashly. 'I'll drop whatever I'm doing and come out. It's only half an hour, you know.'

James nodded. 'And it won't be long before I'm driving in to see you myself.'

Beth placed two bowls of soup on the table. 'I can hardly wait,' she told him, but the wave of optimism that had carried her through the morning began to wane at the prospect of a long haul. 'We'll have a celebration, just the five of us.'

'Don't forget Frank's girlfriend.'

Beth paused on her way back to the kitchen and turned to look at her father.

'You think he'll marry Emily?'

James shrugged. 'He mopes around the whole night and listens to the same record all the time.'

Beth laughed. 'It's serious! I was like that myself, as you well remember.'

'Your mother was the same, you know,' James said unexpectedly. 'Her favourite was 'My Heart and I' by Joseph Locke.' She played it hundreds of times, drove me mad.'

'Who the hell was Joseph whoever?''

'We had our pop stars too,' her father smiled. 'Now wheel me to that soup or I won't have enough energy to sit in this chair a moment longer.'

'Mum should be home in half an hour. I suppose you'll be glad my shift's over?'

She had been teasing him but he frowned and shook his head.

'They say that every cloud has a silver lining, don't they?'

'I suppose they do.'

'In that case, my heart attack has brought you and I closer together again.'

It had been her very thought, but her father was such a secretive man, never showing his emotions, that she had never imagined to hear the sentiment fall from his lips. She blew him a kiss and made no attempt to hide her feelings.

'Have you seen Thomas Blake recently?' he asked suddenly.

Beth stared, hardly able to believe her ears. 'Sorry?'

'Your mother mentioned that you were meeting him occasionally.'

'Well, yes, but only now and then.' Beth was flummoxed, treading lightly; although her father was showing no sign that the topic was distressing him. 'I thought it was only fair.'

'Fair?' James repeated with a smile. 'What a pity he didn't have the same instinct for your mother.'

'Look, Dad, I'm not on his side or anything,' Beth said desperately, more interested at the moment in keeping her father calm than waving the flag of truth. 'I've only spoken to him a couple of times, nothing more than that. Mum knows and she's fine about it.'

'I see.'

It was an expression he used so many times to voice his disapproval, an expression that was so much a part of her growing up that she had only to hear the words to be plunged into the depths of despair. From her position across the table, she regarded him with trepidation and prepared to lie.

'I won't see him again if you don't want me to.'

Her father smiled and shook his head. 'Goodness me, Beth, you're a grown woman, you don't need to ask my approval for anything now.'

'But I would never knowingly do something to upset you.'

'I'm sure you wouldn't.'

It was not the reply she had expected; nor was it accompanied by a re-assuring smile or nod and Beth was shocked to discover that she still sought her father's approval; even now.

'Do you think I should stop seeing him?' she asked.

'It has nothing to do with me,' James shrugged. 'It's between you and your mother.'

'But, I...'

'Beth, dear,' her father interrupted with a wave of his hand. 'We're all adults now. You must do what your conscience tells you to do.'

'All the same, I...'

'Dear girl,' James smiled. 'I'm starving. Let's eat.'

As Beth's spoon hovered above the bowl, her spirits were sinking at the sudden turn the conversation had taken. To an outsider, James Melville's assurances would have sounded genuine; but, to Beth, his mood was one of disapproval.

207

Molly and Grace loaded the shopping bags into the boot of Molly's car just as the first spots of rain were falling.

'At least it's only rain,' Molly said with relief, for there had been several days of sporadic snow showers. 'We should get back before it's too bad. I made a huge batch of muffins yesterday, so we can stuff ourselves until we burst.'

'D' you know, I've put on half a stone since before Christmas?'

'Where?' Molly asked sarcastically, giving her friend a quick glance. 'On your knee caps?'

'No, on my spare tyre. Why do you think I wear such loose jumpers?'

They both laughed and jumped into the car a split second before the Heavens opened and a deluge hurled itself on the roof.

'I hate this kind of weather,' Molly grumbled as she started the car and switched on the wipers. 'The windscreen will steam up in a minute and I won't be able to see a damned thing.'

Grace's heart sank, for it always seemed to be the same story each time it was Molly's turn to drive into Perth. If it was not too cold or too icy, it was a complaint about windows that misted up; or the sun was too low in the sky blinding her on the way home. Had it not been for James's illness and less money coming in, Grace would have suggested that she drive every time. At least she would not have to listen to her friend's complaints.

'Here, take my gloves,' she said now. 'They're leather, good for clearing the windscreen.'

Predictably, Molly shunned the offer, much preferring, Grace guessed, to have something to grumble about on the way home; something that would remind Grace how fortunate she was not to be driving today.

Ashamed of her uncharitable thoughts, she did her best to put on a cheerful face, but the journey seemed long, the minutes dragging; and when they drew up at the cottage, Grace was overjoyed to be home.

Once the bags had been divided and Grace's dropped at the back door, Molly made a fuss of James and then asked Beth if she would cope for another half hour. Behind her daughter's back, Grace was shaking her head.

'Oh, Molly, I'm so sorry,' Beth said obligingly. 'But I've to be back in twenty minutes. Some clients I've to see,' she finished lamely, and despite having encouraged her daughter to lie, Grace was happy to see Molly out.

'Save the muffins for tomorrow,' she smiled.

'You're more cheery now that you've been all morning,' Molly said accusingly. 'Maybe you're glad to be rid of me.'

'That's a horrible thing to say,' Beth called out from the living room and Molly blushed.

'Tell the girl I was only joking. See you tomorrow then.'

'Thanks for the lift, it was good of you.'

The door closed and Grace gave Beth a bemused smile.

'Thanks for fibbing. I shouldn't have asked you, but thanks anyway.'

'Molly's an odd kind of friend for you, isn't she?' Beth asked, the first time she had ever voiced reservations about her mother's best friend.

'She means well,' Grace said, but each time she uttered the words about someone she suspected she was actually highlighting their shortcomings.

'You're too nice to people.' Beth frowned. 'And all they seem to do is hurt you.'

Grace stared at her daughter. 'Hurt me? What a strange thing to say.'

'They do,' Beth insisted, head forward in a sign of aggression. 'You know they do.' Suddenly, she remembered her father sitting next door and the doctor's advice about anxiety. 'Anyway, I made delicious soup for Dad and it was so good he wants the same tomorrow.'

Grateful for her daughter's change of tack, Grace accompanied her through to the living room, where James was dozing. Mother and daughter exchanged glances.

'I'll be off then,' Beth whispered. 'See you tomorrow at twelve.'

'Darling, you don't have to come out every day,' Grace frowned. 'You're supposed to be working, you know, and I can manage perfectly well.'

'After this week, we'll see,' Beth smiled, putting an arm around her mother. 'He's much better now. I can see quite an improvement.'

'The doctor says he'll make a full recovery.'

'And he will. He didn't get a bravery medal for nothing, remember.'

'You're so sweet, Beth,' Grace said, adding cheekily: 'Most of the time.'

'And you wouldn't have me any other way.'

'Are you all right, darling?' Grace asked, aware of a slight change in her daughter's behaviour.

'Of course I'm all right,' Beth laughed brightly. 'Why wouldn't I be?'

'You seem a bit down in the dumps.'

Beth appeared startled, but shrugged and held her mother in a tight hug.

'You're imagining things, mother dear, now I must be off.'

'Do drive carefully and give my love to Harry.'

'He'll be out here on Saturday to chop logs and gruesome things like that. Aren't you glad you're a woman sometimes?'

Grace stood at the door until Beth's Mini had disappeared up the main road, and then she went inside to give James his medicine.

'Did you think I'd got lost?' she asked him as soon as she entered.

'You must be freezing,' he replied, his eyes on her wet clothes. 'Did you stand at the door until Beth reached Perth?' he added with a smile.

'I'm a bit daft sometimes.'

'Only sometimes?'

Grace laughed and moved closer to the fire. She took James's hand, which was gaining strength daily; squeezed it lightly.

'You've got your sense of humour back I hear.'

'That's because I have a wonderful family.'

'No,' Grace contradicted firmly. 'That's because you have an iron will and you're determined to get better in record time.'

James shrugged. 'But I'm lucky to have all of you.'

'If you say so, now I'll just stoke this fire to last all afternoon.'

'Oh, by the way, are you going to the dramatic society tonight?'

'I don't know,' Grace said, glancing at the window and the gathering snow clouds. 'It depends on the weather.'

'You should go. All you do is look after me now, it's time you went somewhere.'

'I've just come back from Perth,' Grace reminded him. 'Two hours trudging round the shops with Molly will keep me going for a few days, not to mention this damned new money that I can't understand. When the salesgirl gave me my change, she could have been cheating me, for all I knew.' Grace sighed.

'Why couldn't they just leave the pounds and shillings as they were?'

'Yes, it's lucky for me I'm stuck in this chair,' James said jocularly. 'By the time I get out and about again, you'll all be able to teach me. Anyway, I think you should go out tonight. I got Beth to ask Bill if he can come down and keep me company, so you'll just be in the way.'

'Are you trying to get rid of me, James Melville?'

'Have you only just realised?'

Grace laughed and knelt down at the flickering fire. 'I told you I was daft.'

'So you'll go then?'

'If you and Bill intend to blether about football all night, then yes, I'll go.'

'Good, but you can make my tea first,' James grinned, and Grace was overcome with joy at the gradual resurgence of her husband's sense of fun.

Moments later, as she pottered around the kitchen gathering ingredients to make a fish pie, Grace was so happy that she was tempted to sing.

*

Harry threw his keys on the hall table and went into the kitchen, where he deposited his wet coat at the sink and kicked off his shoes. He had waited in vain for the snow to stop falling and eventually had to grin and bear it, although he hated this kind of weather, hated swishing and sliding along pavements, trying to avoid being poked in the eye by wayward umbrellas or bashed in the shins by aggressive mothers and their push-chairs.

He poured himself a red wine and went back into the hall to switch on the central heating, adjusting it from the ridiculous temperature that Beth invariably selected, before going back to the kitchen, by which time the wine glass was empty. Half past three and he was already on his second drink; half past three and finished work at the office! He would be forever grateful to Sandra, his ally, for the good words she had been slipping Andrew's way these past few months. The man was now convinced that Harry was the shrewdest, cleverest addition to the practice since he himself had joined, and it was all due to Sandra's efforts.

'I'll finish these off,' she had said at quarter past three, removing the stack of letters from his hands and spiriting them into her office.

'But I've still got time to do it,' Harry had protested, knowing that she would dismiss his attempts.

'And I have even more time than you,' she had smiled. 'Besides, they've both gone for the day, why shouldn't you?'

'But they're seeing clients.'

Sandra raised her eyebrows at him. 'Really?'

They had both laughed then, each of them for different reasons, after which Sandra had ushered him from the building.

'Mind yourself,' she warned him as he surveyed the stone staircase. 'I should have cleared these steps, in case clients fall in a heap and sue us.'

Now, Harry picked up the letters lying on the mat behind the door and flicked through them. His hand paused as he thought he recognised the writing on the third one. She had not written to him in years, not since he had gone to Aberdeen and she complained about its being too far away; but it was definitely his mother's handwriting.

Harry left it on the hall table and laid the others out for Beth: they were all bills and she was the one who dealt with them.

When the telephone rang he wondered if he should answer it, being out of the office an hour early. Unlike Beth, he could leave a telephone ringing and never worry about who it might be; unless it was Grace of course.

Reluctantly he picked up the receiver. The caller was not Grace; it was Thomas Blake.

*

Thomas threw the receiver down with a crash. He had been expecting the girl to answer, as she usually did at this time of an afternoon, but it seemed that the husband was home early.

He cursed himself for having spoken first, for giving his name so readily. Had he waited, for a split-second only, the boy would have spoken, Thomas would have hung up and no harm done. Now he had divulged two things: that he had her number and that he sometimes called her in the afternoon. Furious with himself, he paced the hallway for a few minutes.

Eventually he gave up trying to calm down and reached for the bottle of whisky. He would telephone her at the office from now on; never give her husband another opportunity to take advantage. He flicked through his telephone numbers until he found Daphne's. It was not too late to invite her out for dinner and she would be so thrilled that she would suggest they go Dutch. She always did; in fact, she even paid for the wine – 'my little treat' – and so he was rarely out of pocket.

'Why, Thomas, how lovely to hear from you!'

'Daphne, my dear, I've been thinking about you all afternoon.'

He marvelled at how they were all taken in by such flattery; could never work out why they never suspected duplicity and flounce off.

'That's quite a coincidence,' Daphne was saying now, and it crossed his mind, albeit briefly, that she might be doing the same to him.

'How would you like to go out to dinner tonight, my dear lady?'

'Oh, Thomas, that's a wonderful idea! But I insist that it's my treat this time.'

'Daphne, I can't...'

'Yes, you can,' she pronounced firmly and he had to suppress a smile. 'I'm paying for everything tonight, and I won't take 'no' for an answer.'

'You sound very cheerful, my dear.'

'Oh, I am,' she chortled happily. 'I came into some money yesterday, and thank goodness they wrote it down for me in old money, not this stupid new rubbish.'

'You came into some money, did you?' he asked lightly, hardly able to believe his luck.

'Yes, and I intend to treat you, providing you can work out what the bill is in decimal currency.'

'No trouble for me,' Thomas laughed. 'I just hand over a note and they soon tell me if they want more.'

'I felt so foolish, not knowing how much ten pence was worth,' Daphne said irritably. 'I'll never think of it as anything other than a two shillings, so there!'

After they had made arrangements to meet, he hung up and sauntered over to the window. Half past four and the last of the school children were loitering with intent on the corner, the girls so forward nowadays, with their skirts so short they might have been long cardigans, and their black-tighted legs squirming along in chunky shoes; hardly the image of school uniform his generation had in mind.

He went to pour himself a quick aperitif, although it was hours to go before his dinner date, and mused to himself at his ability to charm Daphne with his personality. Suddenly, despairingly, he thought of Charlotte, the one woman he had never succeeded in charming, and the very one he had wanted most.

You could never persuade me, Thomas, never in a million years.

*

'But, you'd love it over there,' he told her, at the train station, at the last minute,

211

when it was only words, when it could never mean anything other than symbols drifting across the space between them.

'Thomas, please, not now,' Charlotte had smiled, the tragic little smile she had which made him want to crush her in his arms and hold her forever. She was looking at him, begging him with her eyes to show restraint; but it was breaking his heart.

'I'll write as soon as I arrive, let you know how things are.'

'I'd like that,' she said, glancing around as if she were keen to leave.

'Please wait until the train goes.'

She appeared astonished at that. 'Well, of course I'll wait.'

'And you promise to write?' he asked, not caring a hoot about the pleading tone of his voice.

'Yes,' she had smiled. 'I promise.'

'And you'll send photographs of...' he started to say, and then his reserve failed and she stroked his cheek.

'Yes, Thomas, I'll send photographs, and I'll tell the child how much you loved us both.'

He had never anticipated her admitting such a thing. For a moment he stared at her, filled with hope that she could yet be persuaded to join him when the child was old enough to travel.

'That's the nicest thing you've ever said to me, Charlotte.'

She grimaced. 'I haven't said very many nice things to you, have I?'

'It doesn't matter,' he lied. 'What you just said made up for all the rest.'

There was a silence then, as each of them pondered the significance of her words; but then the guard's whistle had shrilled in the background, heralding not only the departure of the train but also the undisguised anguish in her eyes.

'Charlotte, I love you, I've always...'

'Sshh,' she said quietly, her finger on his lips. 'I know.'

'I always will,' he said before she could stop him, wishing that she would say the same, even if she did not mean it.

She waited until the very last moment, the minx, just as the train began to draw away from her, and then she smiled, gave him a little wave and said:

'And I'll always love you, Thomas Charles Blake.'

For a split second, he contemplated jumping from the train, forgetting all about South America and the fancy job, starting all over again with Charlotte. It was almost as if she could read his mind, for she turned swiftly and walked away; although he stood at the open window until he saw nothing but the billowing smoke from the engine.

*

Thomas brushed a tear from his eye. What good did it do now, all this nostalgic nonsense? He would never see her again, never speak to her, never be able to convey to her the misery of a life without her. He was beginning to doubt that she would have believed him anyway. His daughter certainly did not.

He swallowed the whisky rapidly and reached for another. He could drink three before his dinner date, as long as he drank a couple of black coffees before he left. It would not be appropriate for Daphne to see him drunk; not if he were to win the lady's – Thomas laughed to himself: he had been about to say 'heart', had he not?

Chapter Twelve

Charlie Webster watched her as she leafed through the dictionary, her finger tapping the side of her mouth occasionally, the blonde hair flicking back and forth across her face as she worked. He still considered her the loveliest creature he had ever seen; and he had seen quite a few. The difference with Beth Gillespie was that she was not seeing him.

Months had passed and he had no idea whether she liked him more than she had at the beginning, or even whether she liked him at all. The girl was so inscrutable that she must have Japanese ancestors.

Just as he was about to speak, she glanced up, caught him unawares.

'You want something?' she asked, politely, as ever.

'Yes, actually,' he said, clearing his throat and swallowing nervously like a teenager. 'I was wondering if you'd remembered about this month's client dinner thing.'

'Yes, I had.'

'Do you think you'll be able to come along?'

'When?'

'Thursday evening,' he said, hearing the lack of confidence in his own voice.

'Thursday,' she repeated, a little furrow on her brow. 'Not sure, have to check. Who are the clients anyway?'

'A German chap and his daughter, looking for an unusual ring for the wife.'

'There's a few in the storeroom. I fancied one myself.'

'Take one if you like,' Charlie said rashly and braced himself.

Beth smiled. 'You mean that?'

'Of course,' he said, astonished that she had not criticised his business sense.

'Thanks, but Harry gave me this one,' she told him, waggling her left hand at him. 'It was his grandmother's, apparently.'

'It's lovely,' he said, spirits crushed once more by the shining white knight that was her husband. 'So, about the dinner?'

'I'll let you know tomorrow, when I've checked my diary. Oh, and I'm sorry about the South American client.'

'It was boring anyway.' Charlie hovered at her elbow. 'He was with a local woman who seemed to be dripping with cash.'

Beth hardly glanced up. 'Really?'

'You thought you knew him, didn't you?'

'No, I think I was mistaken.'

'But you...'

She silenced him with a stern expression. 'So, as I said, I'll check my diary.'

'You're probably out all the time,' Charlie laughed, fishing of course, for he knew absolutely nothing about her private life. It was exactly that – private.

'I hardly ever go out,' she said, her eyes on the paper in front of her.

'I don't believe that,' he decided to say, meriting a suspicious glance.

'Believe it or not, it doesn't matter to me.'

She had smiled as she said it, but he felt a bit of a fool. Why was it that he could impress half the female population of Perth, have them falling at his feet and refusing to be shaken off, and yet here he was, tongue-tied and stupid with a girl he wanted so badly that it kept him awake at nights?

'I only meant that you must have dozens of friends, a social whirl.'

'It's not my thing,' she smiled, laying down the pencil and closing the dictionary: 'I prefer quiet nights at home with my husband.'

The image cut through Charlie at the speed of light and left him breathless.

'Of course. How is he, your husband?'

She looked surprised. 'Fine, why?'

'Just making conversation,' he said stupidly.

'Is it all right if I go home now?' she asked, thankfully cutting off the conversation before he ended up looking a complete idiot.

'Of course. You don't have to ask.'

'I'll let you know about Thursday first thing in the morning,' she said as she brushed past him on her way to the door.

'You know, that perfume you wear,' he began, and she paused in the doorway.

'What about it?'

'It could drive a man crazy,' he told her in a rare outburst of bravado.

'I'm sure my husband would agree,' she smiled sweetly. 'See you tomorrow.'

As her footsteps clicked down the paved vestibule, Charlie breathed out, a long, slow sigh wherein were contained all his lost opportunities. He stood at the window and watched as she crossed the street, picking her way carefully through the ice and snow, heading home to a lucky bastard who probably had no idea how lucky he was.

*

In the street, Beth breathed out, a long, slow sigh of relief, wherein was contained her continual struggle to conceal her feelings for Charlie Webster. As she sloshed through the melting snow, mentally assessing the damage to her new suede boots, she wondered how on earth she ever managed not to tear his clothes off and ravish him on the office floor. If she had to remind herself of her love for Harry twenty times a day it was not enough: each time she saw Charlie Webster her knees went weak. Despite being rather proud of herself for resisting him for so long, a tiny red flag fluttered constantly at the back of her mind and caused her many a sleepless night.

A passing car sprayed her with filthy gutter water but she was too involved with thoughts of Charlie Webster to give the driver a rude salute; besides which, she was pretty wet already from the drizzle that was falling now. Cold and wet – her pet hates, similar to Mickey the pony that had stood in the field opposite the cottage in winter, bottom to the wind, head down, lips sulky. Wherever did people get the idea that animals loved the outdoors?

She crossed the road, trying to avoid the salty slush that lay in wait for her, and dragged her thoughts away from Charlie Webster.

*

'In here,' Harry called out. 'I've a surprise for you.'

He heard the boots hitting the floor, followed by the slam of the cupboard door as she hung up her coat, and then there was the silence as she padded along the hall in her red socks, the pair she always wore with the boots.

'Harry!' she shrieked, diving into the sitting room and throwing herself at him. 'You've lit the fire, you darling!'

'Hey, steady on, you'll get black off my hands. You never told me that coal was so filthy.'

'Poor, poor darling,' she murmured, snuggling into him but avoiding his hands. 'Did you need a map and a book of instructions to light the thing?'

'No, I phoned Arthur Scargill and he was very helpful.'

Beth sighed and hugged him tighter and he wondered if her day had been unsatisfactory.

214

'Oh Harry, I'm so lucky.'

'You've won the pools and I'll never have to work again?'

'I don't even do them.' She tore herself away from him and looked at him with raised eyebrows. 'D'you think we should?'

'No, now let me get washed and you can take up where you left off.'

She followed him into the bathroom, lounging against the doorjamb as he washed. Several times he glanced at her reflection in the mirror but when she only smiled and winked, Harry was sure she had had a bad day and could hardly wait to tell him.

'Right, let's sit by the fire with a large drink,' he said as he towelled his hands dry. 'And you can tell me all about it.'

'All about what?' Beth asked. Her expression was so innocent that for a moment he thought he had guessed wrongly.

'There's something bothering you,' he said, undeterred. 'Come on, what is it?'

'You know, that's the really, really annoying thing about you, Gillespie,' she growled at him as she turned back into the hallway. 'One day I'll fool you, wait and see.'

'White wine?'

'And don't ignore me either,' her voice floated through to him. 'Yes, it is,' she added grumpily.

Harry preferred her in one of these moods, for it indicated that she was vulnerable and he could deal with her. It was the chilling, secretive Beth Melville that defeated him most times. These moods ended, inevitably, in a blazing row, something he abhorred, reminding him as it did of his mother and father, who always seemed to be shouting at each other.

'Sit here,' he said, patting the space beside him on the sofa. 'Tell me who I should go out and beat up.'

Beth laughed on her way across the room. 'Would you really do that?'

'Try me.'

'It's rather sweet, having a knight in shining armour waiting at home.' She sat down and drank half the wine in one gulp and then she turned to look at him. 'I had a chat with Dad today.'

'If you think I'm going to bop him, you can forget it.'

She laughed again, before draining the glass.

'That's funny, that is, you bopping my Dad.'

'How is he?'

'Improving every day. I won't have to go out next week, Mum will manage now.'

'I'll go at weekends, see if there's anything she needs doing. What did you and he talk about, since it seems to be praying on your mind?'

'I think he wants me to stop seeing my grandfather.'

It took him by surprise: James more than anyone knew how Beth reacted to an ultimatum, yet here she was, calm, composed, albeit swallowing half a bottle of wine at one sitting.

'He actually said that?'

'Not in so many words, but that's the impression I got.'

'What did he say?'

Beth sighed and stood up. While she wandered into the kitchen to replenish her glass, Harry waited, trying to work out what reason James would have for being so heavy-handed in the midst of his own troubles when everyone else was pussyfooting around the man, doing their utmost not to cause trouble.

'He said he knew I wouldn't do anything to upset him,' Beth started to say even before she entered the room.

'But that doesn't mean…'

'Yes, it does,' she said sharply, sitting down with a thud and almost spilling his drink. 'That's exactly what it means. I know him and that's what he meant.'

'You're a grown woman now, Beth,' Harry smiled as they chinked glasses. 'You can do what you like.'

'It's not that easy, not with my Dad anyway.'

He bit back a quick reply, maintaining a neutral expression as she studied his face. He had never imagined she would still defer to her father, especially over Thomas Blake, an issue that was absorbing her night and day.

'What will you do then?'

'You realise it's Mum's fault,' Beth said unexpectedly. 'She has the power to make things right.'

For the second time in minutes, Harry restrained his tongue. To provoke Beth now would be to invite disaster; yet, his loyalty to Grace made him recoil from siding against her. He chose the route most likely to appease.

'But didn't she tell us all that she'd had a change of heart about her father?'

'Lip service,' Beth said bitterly. 'Do you know what she's up to?'

'No, I don't,' he replied truthfully. 'I was as surprised as anyone when she said it.'

Beth's features broke into a wary smile. 'You were?'

'It didn't ring true somehow.' He resolved to stop there, halfway between betraying Grace and invoking his wife's wrath.

'Dad said that my grandfather wasn't fair with Charlotte, or at least that's what he implied. Yet, I've read the letters and I can't see what more he could have done to keep her.' She threw him a discreet look. 'Do you want to read them?'

Harry wanted to blurt out an outright 'no', but he had chosen the path of appeasement for tonight and stick to it he would.

'Not yet.'

She leaned into him, apparently satisfied with his response, and wrapped her arms around him, nuzzling his neck, the faint aroma of her Chanel No 5 inter-mingling with the heady effects of his wine.

'He telephoned here today,' he said quickly, before she had time to alter his course.

'Who did?'

'Your grandfather.'

He felt her stiffen, move away from him slightly, and although his eyes were closed he sensed she was watching him.

'What did he say?'

'Nothing, just hung up.'

'Without saying a thing?'

'Yes, except his name, of course.'

'Why would he hang up?' Beth asked, confused, and it was a timely reminder to Harry that she knew nothing of his acrimonious meeting with the man at the hotel. Occasions like these highlighted the smudged area between lies and not telling the truth, the first being easy to bear in mind, the latter not quite so.

'I have no idea,' Harry said casually. 'He obviously expected you to answer, probably put the phone down before he knew what he was doing.'

'He's only called here twice before,' she said defensively, which was a good omen for Harry. Beth in defensive mood was easy to handle.

'Beth, for Heaven's sake, I'm not your keeper.'

'But you did forbid me not to see him, remember?' she prompted him with a wicked smile. 'I love it when you play rough.'

'Women say that, but they have no idea what it means.'

'Oooh,' Beth breathed in his ear. 'Why don't you show me then?'

216

'First things first,' Harry said, disentangling himself from her grasp and standing up. 'I've another surprise for you, bought it on the way home.'

'You've hired a cook,' Beth grinned from the sofa. 'And, let me guess, she's seventeen, blonde and voluptuous?'

'Not even close. It's a couple.'

'Ah, you've brought a dashing young man for me as well?'

'No, a couple of gigot chops and I'm about to fry them with onions.'

'What have I done to deserve this?'

'You haven't done it yet,' Harry told her and she rewarded him with a lascivious smile.

*

Lucy Webster flew across the village hall to greet Grace the moment she opened the door. Her eyes struggling to accommodate the bright lights in the room, Grace blinked at Lucy apologetically.

'Such a dark night,' she said, and it sounded ridiculous, but she knew what she meant.

'I was the same,' Lucy grinned, taking Grace's arm and drawing her from the cold area at the door. 'I was goggling like a bush baby when I came in. You look great,' she enthused. 'But how's James?'

'He's improving. I see it every day.'

'I popped down to see him yesterday, but I saw he was asleep, so I didn't hang around long.'

'You should have gone in, Beth was probably in the kitchen making his lunch.'

Lucy slapped her forehead humorously. 'Silly me, of course she was. Now I come to think of it, there was a car round the back. As if he'd be there on his own. Honestly, talk about getting old!'

As they joined the crowd sitting around the stage, Grace braced herself for the usual round of sympathy for James's condition, followed, no doubt, by solicitous furrowed brows on her own account. The guilt that accompanied her uncharitable thoughts was an old friend but did nothing to prevent future, similar bouts. Occasionally, she wondered if she were wreaking revenge on the villagers for their unkind and well-voiced opinions on hers and James's marriage in the early days.

You're marrying an Englishman? Well, I never. Fancy that.

'Grace, how great to see you,' Graham Seaton said as she took the chair next to him. 'We've all missed you.'

Grace laughed, heartened by his sentiment, which she acknowledged as genuine. 'Thank you, kind Sir, it's nice to be back.'

'Molly's been standing in for you the past few weeks,' he whispered behind his hand. 'But, to be honest, we could hardly wait for you to come back.'

'You're the kindest man I know, Graham,' Grace smiled and she was amazed to see him blush. Perhaps he, too, recalled the excitement of first love.

'They've decided to stage the play in June,' he said, clearly wrestling with his embarrassment at her remark. 'That is, if you feel you're ready.'

'The whole thing doesn't depend on me. Molly's perfectly able to play the part. Besides, the audience is probably eager for a change.'

He looked at her with astonishment. 'You must be joking,' he protested. 'They only come to see you.'

She laughed at him, not believing for one minute that he was making fun of her, but also sceptical that he was speaking for the whole village.

'You're such a kind man, Graham,' was the only thing she could think of. 'Oh, how's Deirdre, by the way? I heard she'd had an accident.'

'A stupid one,' Graham shook his head. 'Daft child slipped on the top step at the back, went all her length to the bottom.' He pulled a face. 'My fault, of course. I was supposed to salt the stairs. Never heard the end of it.'

'So there you are,' said an accusing voice and it was Molly. 'You might have told me you were coming and we could have walked up together.'

'I didn't know I was coming,' Grace assured her friend. 'It was James who said I should.'

'Well, that's a change,' Molly said snidely, at which Graham, not Grace, took umbrage.

'That's a real friendly thing to say,' he said with uncharacteristic sarcasm.

'Oh, Grace knows I don't mean anything by it,' Molly said airily.

'Well, why say it in the first place?' Graham persisted, much to Grace's discomfiture.

'How's Donald these days?' she asked Molly pointedly. 'Any word of a wedding?'

Molly's face said it all. 'Not yet, but I live in hope.' Just as she was about to continue, Marjory Robertson thumped the table and called out.

'Right, I think we've all had our little gossip, have we? Good, then I suggest we begin at the first page again, for Grace's benefit.' She awarded Grace a radiant smile, reminiscent of her brother David's. For an instance, Grace was back in her school uniform, striding down the road with a lovesick David at her heels.

The rehearsal – for '*A Woman of no Importance*' – began with Grace resuming her role as Lady Caroline Pontefract, a role that Molly had coveted and which Grace would have gladly given over to her; not because she felt Molly would do the character any more justice, but because she would have preferred the role of Hester, the American lady, as her accent was more consistent than Molly's. As ever, Grace, like her mother before her, was conscious of the old adage: *if you want something done, do it yourself.*

At the end of the first hour's rehearsal, they adjourned, in the old-fashioned way, for tea and sandwiches and a chat, which would have pleased Graham Seaton, except Joanna Baxter – Grace's neighbour – and Molly took their seats on either side of Grace, relegating Graham to the row behind.

'I hear Alice is keen to come on holiday again,' Joanna said between mouthfuls of a salmon sandwich. 'Her mother's old friend was telling Kathleen at the Birches. Have you heard from her lately?' she added in Grace's direction.

'Yes, but she wasn't sure if her new husband could get the time off.'

'Did you know they go to Hawaii for their holidays?' Joanna asked, her tone slightly derogatory. 'Can you imagine it? All that hula hula stuff and tiny grass skirts making your husband's eyes water.'

'You've been watching Elvis in '*Blue Hawaii*',' Graham chipped in from the row behind.

'Wasn't he good?' Grace said, smiling a little smile of gratitude to Graham. 'Beth dragged me to see it three times. I knew the script off by heart eventually.'

'Oh, I much preferred Steve McQueen in '*The Thomas Crown Affair*,' Joanna said. 'He looked so sultry, didn't he?'

'Oh, doesn't he have a sexy mouth?' Molly giggled. 'Kept me awake at nights after I saw the film.'

'How's Frank doing these days?' Graham Seaton asked, his eyes on Grace.

'He's fine,' she smiled, in his debt for the second time that evening. 'Quite the young business man now, with his crisp white shirts and pressed suits. Sometimes I wonder where the years have gone.'

218

'Speaking of which,' Graham pressed on, giving the others no time to join in. 'I want to take a few snaps to put in the *Perthshire Advertiser* next week, to let people know about the play. Would it be all right to pop in to see you one day to take photographs?'

'Well, Joanna,' Molly interrupted, her voice heavy with sarcasm. 'I'd say you and I were playing gooseberry, wouldn't you? Perhaps these two would rather be alone.'

'You're just being silly,' Grace smiled, feigning indifference. 'I do apologise for my friends,' she added to Graham, whose agitation was obvious.

'It's no problem,' he said brusquely. 'You know that old saying – you may not be able to choose your relatives but you can certainly choose your friends?'

Even Grace could think of nothing to say, which made the silence even worse. Molly threw her a critical glance before scowling at Graham.

'Don't mind us, will you?' she said, picking up her plate and moving off.

Joanna shrugged but stayed where she was.

'She's a real prima donna, isn't she?'

'In that case,' Grace laughed. 'She's in the right place.'

'Trust you to see the funny side of it,' Graham told her, but this time his voice was casual. 'I've a habit of plonking my feet in it. Sorry, Joanna, if I offended you.'

'You were quite right to say what you did,' Joanna smiled, patting Grace on the arm. 'Grace and I have been pals for years. She's the best neighbour anyone could have, and it's me who should be apologising, for not sticking up for her.'

'Is it a full moon or something?' Grace asked lightly. 'Are we all going mad?'

'No,' Graham said, preparing to move off and start proceedings again. 'I'd say it was just village life at its normal best.' He paused in front of Grace's chair. 'I can pop down the day after tomorrow, if you like?'

'Thank you, Graham, that would be kind of you.'

As the group rearranged their chairs for Act Two, Grace's heart was heavy. Why was it that even a simple evening spent doing something she loved had turned out to be a small disaster? She would have to seek Molly out tomorrow and make her peace, although, to be honest, it should really be the other way round, since Grace had said nothing to upset anyone.

Half an hour later, however, she had cheered up considerably at the thought of Harry's coming out at the weekend. What she craved more than anything at this moment was to be surrounded by people who loved her.

*

Harry stood at the window, gazing down at the reflections of the street lamps in the shiny pavements. The few snowflakes that were falling clung to the pane on their way down, as if seeking the warmth and comfort of the room inside. There were several people still wandering the streets, but he had learnt recently that they were probably night-shift drivers trudging from the train and bus stations nearby, as opposed to the homeless down-and-outs that had been prevalent in London.

He yawned and stretched, beginning to feel the effects of having to placate Beth for an entire evening. His mind had trodden thin ice for hours, finally capitulating, crashing through the glassy surface and plunging him into the inhospitable freezing waters. As luck would have it, she had been almost asleep by then; had not heard his last remark.

'I could never fall out with Dad,' she had mumbled drowsily, her head on his chest. 'Never, never...'

But you could fall out with Grace.

He had no intention of saying it aloud, but in the stillness of the bedroom he had heard the words, waited for her to leap up and start an almighty row. Ten seconds passed, then twenty, then a full minute, and he knew she had been asleep; not that he was not perfectly capable of taking care of himself – he was not his mother's son for nothing – but in light of Grace's current situation, in light of the fact that she needed him to be strong, Harry had resolved to keep his relationship with Beth as serene as possible for the time being.

'So I won't be seeing Thomas Blake so often,' she had assured him over dinner, with a cautionary glance at him, as if he were about to contradict her. 'I can speak to him sometimes on the phone, write to him even, but until Dad's fully recovered, I'll back-pedal.'

'And then?'

'I think it's just because he's not a hundred per cent,' Beth sighed, moulding a spoonful of mashed carrots into a castle, irritating Harry with her disrespect for the food he had prepared. 'Once he's back to normal, we can have another chat.'

The clock in the hallway struck three. Harry switched off the table lamp and went back to bed. As he pulled the blankets over him, Beth moaned and stirred, reaching out for him

'Harry?'

'Here, sweetheart.'

'I missed you.'

Harry laughed and drew her closer. 'I was only gone for five minutes.'

'And you're freezing,' she muttered in his ear. 'If I can't heat my feet up on you, then I want a refund. I only married you for your warm feet.'

She fell asleep within moments, but Harry was still awake when the clock struck four. He was not unhappy at his sleepless night, for he was looking ahead to the weekend, when he would be with Grace. That was one of the things he craved; being with the people he loved most.

*

Lying next to him, feigning sleep, Beth marvelled at her ability to keep her temper after his remark:

'but you could fall out with Grace.'

Had it not been so late, and if she did not have a rule about not rowing with him after great sex, she would have argued with him; but instinct had sealed her lips and now she was glad.

Tomorrow, however, was another day.

220

Chapter Thirteen

Thomas Blake read the letter and then read it again, after which he stood in the middle of the kitchen for ten minutes and tried to make sense of it. Only a few weeks ago he had been convinced that things were finally going his way, that even his daughter was coming round to the idea of his presence in the area; and now, here was a letter from Beth telling him that her father was ill and she had no time for Thomas Blake.

'As you can appreciate,' she had written, in a tone so formal that it worried him more than the contents,

'My father's health is the top priority at the moment and the family is pulling all the stops out to get him fighting fit again. I'm there most nights, as well as at weekends, and so it may be a while before you hear from me.

'Be assured, however,' she had concluded, as if he were a business client, a total stranger,

'Once things are back to normal, I'll be in touch.

Kindest regards

Beth Gillespie'

Thomas's feelings hovered between being annoyed and being hurt. She had even added her married name to the signature when once she would have referred to herself as 'Beth' or 'your granddaughter'.

After sitting down and drinking a strong cup of coffee, he decided not to make an issue of it: the last thing he wanted to do at this moment was to upset the apple cart and go back to square one. He would fall in with the girl's plan for now; let her believe he was a reasonable and sympathetic man – which he had been, once upon a time – and then she could have no reason to break contact.

Thomas sighed and stirred sugar into his second cup of coffee. He had waited almost fifty years, so it was feasible that he could wait another few months. Besides, he had other matters to occupy his mind these days: the lovely Daphne and her many charms, not the least of these being her money.

The previous night, he had sat with paper and pen working out exactly what she might be worth and the result was anything but disappointing. The house she lived in was valued at over eight thousand, plus the flat she rented out in the middle of Perth could easily fetch a couple of thousand; and she had stocks and shares – admitted to him in an unguarded moment – amounting to a very tidy sum that would afford her a decent private pension when the time came. One aspect had failed him, however: he could not begin to guess her exact age, estimating it to be anything between fifty and seventy.

She took excellent care of herself, did Daphne, with her hair styled once a week, the manicures and discreetly applied makeup; and the expensive clothes, bought from Jaeger and McEwens no less.

If things went according to plan, Thomas Blake could find himself a very rich man. Having to marry Daphne was a disadvantage, of course, but he suspected that, at her age, she would not be averse to a platonic relationship, and it was certainly his experience of elderly women, that they were happy to settle for companionship rather than sex. He certainly hoped so, since it would be his own preference; at least at home. Should he fancy a bit of exciting female company, he was sure he could still find it somewhere.

Thomas glanced at Beth's letter and smiled. If he were smart, he would turn this delay into his advantage. In fact, even now he was beginning to see distinct possibilities. The clock struck half past nine and he roused himself. It was time to ring Daphne, tell her how sorry he was not to be able to keep their lunch date. If his plans were to succeed, he would have to think carefully. Playing hard to get was second nature to him.

Apart from Charlotte

As he waited for her to pick up the telephone, Thomas wondered how he could possibly fill the two hours he had allocated for their lunch date without going into Perth; which was out of the question now, as she might spot him there.

He smiled as her voice came on the line. He would think of something. He always did.

*

Grace wheeled James down the front path and out the gate, already fussing over the knee blanket she had draped over him, worrying in case it would catch in the wheels.

'Please, Grace,' he laughed, pushing her hand away for the umpteenth time. 'It's fine, honestly, just leave it where it is.'

'Your first day out and I'll probably tip you from this wheelchair and you'll end up back in hospital.'

'I'm wearing so many clothes, I would bounce off the pavement, wouldn't hurt myself at all.'

'Thank Heavens it's a lovely day at last,' Grace sighed. 'How many weeks have we been stuck in the house now? Must be months.'

'It seems like it,' James said despondently, and his gloomy tone of voice reminded Grace that she was supposed to be keeping his spirits up.

'We're on the way to summer,' she said brightly. 'Another few weeks and you'll be walking around the garden.'

'I can hardly wait,' James said, more cheerfully. 'In fact, I might even…'

'No, you won't "even" anything,' Grace said, tapping his shoulder with her hand. 'You'll just wait until the doctor gives you the all-clear, that's what you'll do.'

'Yes, Matron.'

Grace leaned over and kissed his cheek. 'Good boy.'

James burst out laughing, the most welcome sound Grace had heard in a long time.

'It's almost half a century since I was a boy,' he joked. 'Far less a good one.'

'I can't believe it's over twenty years since we were married. Where on earth has the time gone?'

Their conversation was halted temporarily by a passing tractor, but Grace turned off the main road and headed up towards the station, derelict now after the Beeching railway cuts and left in such a state of disrepair that she was glad Grandpa was no longer around to see it. The man had taken such pride in his work at the old station, even earning a prize for the best-kept rural station of the year.

As she wheeled James towards the station brae, Grace had an image of her and James, trudging along this stretch of road, their shoes covering the same ground, flicking these very stones; and then, standing, forlornly, waiting for the train that would take him away for months; albeit for the last time.

'Are you remembering too?' she suddenly heard him ask.

'Of course I am.'

'I always knew I'd see you again.'

Grace stopped pushing the wheelchair and moved round to stand in front of James.

'I know. You told me.'

'But you weren't so sure, were you?'

Grace shook her head. 'I was too scared to be sure. We all were, Alice, Joanna, Molly and I.'

'Was it worth it?' James asked unexpectedly and she stared at him.

'What kind of question is that,? Of course it was worth it, at least for me.'

He reached out and grabbed her hand, tucked it in the folds of his jacket and held it fast.

'You don't regret marrying me?'

Grace bent down and kissed the top of his head. 'No, I don't, silly man. Now will you please give me back my hand, otherwise we'll be run over by the next tractor.'

They paused on the bridge to gaze across the fields, the green hues diluted by the weak April sunshine but showing signs of coming to life again after the harsh winter. All at once, Grace remembered that, years ago now, April had been her favourite month; when she had sat in the garden making a list of things she wanted to achieve by the time October flew in,

Her father coming to find her

A cool gust of wind snatched at her scarf and almost tore it from her neck, so far had her thoughts strayed.

'I think this is far enough,' she told James. 'We can go to Lily's now, have our afternoon cup of tea.'

'You'll never manage this chair up the steps,' James reminded her. 'Unless Dave's in the next-door garden and can help you.'

'Or you could walk up,' Grace heard herself say and, for an instant, she wondered what had got into her; but then it seemed like a good idea, considering that the doctor's prediction of James's full recovery was only another couple of weeks away. Surely he could manage a few steps?

'Hey, that's a great idea!' James said, his face lighting up for the first time in weeks. 'I'll take it easy, but that's just what I'll do.'

As luck would have it, Dave Simpson was in his garden and they could have asked him to help; but it was in James's mind now to mount the steps unaided and Grace could only watch and keep her fingers crossed.

'You're doing grand,' Lily Morris said by way of encouragement. 'One more and you're first in the queue for tea and cakes.'

The delight on James's face banished Grace's few minutes of anxiety, although she insisted he sit in the wheelchair once he had reached the top step.

'Yes, yes,' he said with good humour. 'I promise I'll behave now. Not much else I can do with you two fusspots standing by.'

They sat in Lily's large kitchen, with the sun filtering through the lace curtains and laying hazy patterns on the tablecloth. Grace looked at James and suddenly realised that he rarely visited Lily. In fact, she was struggling to recall the occasions he had sat here; and yet he appeared quite at home.

Home! Poor James! This was not – had never been – his home. Home for him was six hundred miles away, in a tiny hamlet on the south coast of England.

'I think we should all go to Cranbrook this summer,' she said loudly, before she had time to rationalise things and change her mind.

James and Lily had been discussing something else but now turned their attention to Grace.

'Cranbrook?' James repeated, and Grace was at a loss to understand why he was not overjoyed. 'I thought we'd talked about France?'

'It might be too far.'

James face clouded. 'I won't be an invalid for ever.'

'I didn't mean it like that,' Grace frowned, her plans going awry. 'I just thought you might like to go and visit your relatives.'

'When did you think of it?'

'The day after you landed in hospital.'

'You're serious.'

'Of course I am. You haven't seen your mother since that business trip you managed to wangle in the fifties.'

James shrugged. 'Well, of course I'd like to go, but do we have the money?'

Patiently, Grace explained that she would write and ask Helen for some money.

It was Lily who was most shocked. 'What? You'd ask that bag for a favour?'

James laughed, not at all put out by the suggestion, Grace knew. If it meant he could go back to England, all was fair in that respect. She was heartened by the flutter of excitement in his expression and was only sorry that she had not thought of it sooner, when it might have hastened his recovery.

'Well,' he said, his eyes bright. 'That's a real surprise, Grace, but the best one I've had since you said we were coming to Lily's.'

'Och, you,' Lily smiled, slapping his wrist. 'Flattery will only get you another plate of sandwiches.'

As Lily rose to pour out fresh tea for them, Grace gave James several discreet glances. Each time, she found he was returning her gaze with a smile; he was so buoyed up at the prospect of going home, that it quite made up for the fact she had been the reason for his leaving it in the first place.

*

Beth was taking out her frustration on the piano keys when she should have been preparing the dinner for her guests. Her fingers stumbled and stuttered across the octaves until, eventually, at the peak of her fit of temper, she crashed the heel of her right hand down and bruised it extensively.

'Ow!' she yelled, stuffing the hand under her oxster and writhing around in pain. 'Bloody Hell, bloody Hell, bloody Hell!'

She sat waiting for the ache to subside, but when it showed no sign of abating after five minutes she rose from the stool and marched through to the bathroom, where she ran it under cold water and uttered several swear words.

Catching sight of her grumpy face in the mirror, she forced a smile and stuck out her tongue.

'Yes, we all know you're stupid, Beth Melville, so what are you looking at?'

Fifteen minutes later she was pouring sparkling white wine into the largest glass she could find – Harry's beer glass, although he never drank beer, only wine. Wandering through to the sitting room, Beth glowered at the sheet music on the piano and contemplated chucking it on the fire. Sense prevailed, however, but even that annoyed her, since she hated the thought of being sensible, flying as it did in the face of her very nature.

As she paced the room, large glass in hand, she mulled over her reasons for blaming her mother for their present situation, for rejecting Thomas Blake and throwing the family into disarray; anarchy even.

She had to smile at the word '*anarchy*', which implied a total lack of organisation or control. She must make sure it was on her gravestone, for she could think of no more fitting epitaph.

As she brushed past the piano stool, she paused and looked at the music, feeling a slight twinge of guilt that she had been tempted to hurl it into the flames. It was hardly Chopin's fault that she had insufficient patience to practise his masterpiece. The mantra of her Italian music teacher floated into her mind:

'*A good workman never blames his tools.*'

Setting the glass down on the mantelshelf, she positioned herself on the stool and raised her hands. This time she knew she would be careful, not only because her hand still throbbed, but also because, despite everything, she loved music, loved playing this piano; could never imagine life without it.

As her fingers touched the keys and liberated the notes into the air around her, Beth sighed and decided she would behave herself for the foreseeable future; at least until the guests arrived.

*

Harry picked up the wine from the off-licence but foresaw an argument the moment Beth saw the labels. She threw money away on most things, but not wine; especially wine to be consumed by guests, and especially guests like Annie and her Prince of Darkness.

Were it not for Beth's social quirks, Harry would not look forward to such an evening, but his wife, with all her vivacity and impulsiveness, could make or break a dull dinner party, and that morning she had been in good spirits, which augured well for the evening.

Whilst he could make fun of Beth's friends, Harry was ever conscious of the fact that he had none; not that it troubled him – quite the reverse – but he had a niggling feeling at the back of his mind that he ought to have made friends by now. He had toyed with the idea of joining a gym, or some sort of class where he would meet people; or taking up rugby again where he could be 'one of the boys'.

He strolled along past the George Hotel and thought, briefly, of large-breasted Sarah, the receptionist who had greeted him on the morning of his encounter with Thomas Blake. Annoyed with himself for the sudden twinge in his groin, Harry walked briskly until he rounded the corner that led to the Inch. Once again his mind began to rumble around the idea of having no friends. Was it something he had inherited from Ralph Gillespie? Had his father been as much of a solitary figure as his son? In the middle of the pavement, on his way home on an ordinary day in April, Harry halted on the pavement. A sudden image of his father shot through his mind like lightning, an image of the argument he thought suppressed: the sight of his father weeping, pleading with his wife not to abandon him.

Harry remained, unmoving, as if the contortions of his mind were not compatible with the workings of his muscles. He swapped the heavy box of wine into his other hand.

He was nine years old, hiding in his room, afraid to go down in case they started shouting at him. What was it his mother had said?

I don't care.

*

'I don't care, I just have to be with him.'

'It's disgusting, you're disgusting!' his father had shouted, causing Harry to shrink back into the sanctuary of his room in the hope that things would quieten down again.

He remembered his mother coming to kiss him goodnight, creeping into the room, trying not to wake him when, half an hour previously, she had been shrieking at the top of her voice, waking the whole neighbourhood.

'Are you asleep yet, Harry?' she had whispered and Harry had been torn between a desire to spend even a few minutes with a woman he adored and admitting he had overheard the argument.

'No,' he said at last, as his mother turned to leave. 'I'm not asleep.'

225

'I'm so sorry, my boy, that we grown-ups don't know how to behave.'

'It's all right,' he blurted out, anxious to please. 'I don't mind.'

'You must do everything your father asks you to do.'

Harry's young heart had been seized with panic, for it implied that his mother was deserting him.

'Don't leave me!' he had called out and she paused on his way to the door. Still with her back turned, she said quietly:

'I won't be leaving you, Harry, not really. I'll always be with you. Go to sleep now, there's a good boy.'

*

In the middle of the street Harry stood stock-still, riveted to the spot, his heart aching at the memory. It had been the last time he had seen his mother and father together. A few weeks later, the house had been filled with tearful relatives and the smell of mothballed fur coats: maiden aunts and nosey neighbours pretending to bewail the death of Ralph Gillespie, a man they had hardly known.

A car hooted at the side of him and Harry jumped. He took a tighter grip on the wine box and glanced up to the windows of the flat. The light was on in the sitting room already: Beth was playing the piano, something she always did when she felt the need to regain control of her life.

Whenever he opened the door he knew she had been playing instead of cooking: no culinary aroma assailed his nostrils, no scented candle trailed to the door to greet him. He was not in the least concerned, for it was early yet and he wanted her to be in a good mood tonight, especially after the last time, when they had rowed in front of the guests.

'In here!' Beth was calling, unnecessarily. 'I'm relaxing.'

Harry laid the wine box down in the hall and hung his coat in the cupboard, checking the heating temperature, turning it down by ten degrees. He struggled to concentrate on the here and now, for his mind was constantly darting to the past, to his father and mother, to an era whose secrets were closed to him. He was consumed by a renewed desire to pore over the old photographs again, to feel part of their lives

'Had a good day?' Beth asked as he appeared in the doorway.

'So-so, and you?'

'Same.' She stood up, closed the lid carefully and picked up the sheet of music. It was a composer he had not recognised in the few minutes it had taken him to hang up his coat and announce his arrival.

'Have you forsaken old Frédéric?' he asked her, still in the doorway, hands in his pockets. 'A new composer?'

'One of my ex-music teacher's modern guys with an axe to grind.'

'It sounded modern, I must admit, but you were doing it justice.'

'Do you think so?' she asked, wandering over to and standing in front of him.

'Absolutely. Of course, I'm biased. I think you're great.'

Beth grinned and shook her head.' I haven't even started to prepare the meal yet, so do you still think I'm great?'

'I do,' Harry smiled and she gazed at him with serious and somewhat sad eyes. 'Are you all right, Beth?'

'I've had an argument with the piano.'

It was then Harry noticed the plaster, stuck on willy-nilly, on the heel of her right hand.

'No wonder you didn't tackle the meal,' he said, stepping forward and laying his hands on her shoulders. 'You can be the wounded soldier tonight. I'll do the meal.'

226

'I feel stupid,' Beth said, lowering her eyes but allowing him to pull her towards him. 'I wish I could grow up.'

Harry laughed and wrapped his arms around her, breathing in the scent of her hair.

'Oh, for God's sake, don't ever do that.'

'You mean you like being married to a three-year-old?' she asked, her voice muffled against his jacket.

'Wouldn't have it any other way.'

'It was so bloody painful, I almost screamed.'

'I can kiss it better if you like.'

She wriggled in his arms to free herself. 'I've got other painful bits as well.'

'What time is it?'

'What's that got to do with it?'

'Let's see now, it's only quarter to five and they're not due until eight. ' He looked down at her unhappy face. 'We've lots of time yet.'

'I might not remember where all the painful bits are.'

'Don't worry, I'll find them.'

'No, honestly, I'll survive,' she said, taking Harry by surprise. He had never known her to turn down an hour in the bedroom in favour of domestic chores. 'I can cope with most of the cooking,' she added, gazing at the injured hand. 'If you do the finicky bits.'

'I think you should go and sit down with a drink, let me do everything.'

Beth smiled and shook her head. 'No, *je refuse*, so what now?'

'Get your peenie on, you're on the tatties.'

She giggled at his Scottish accent. 'You don't even know what a peenie is, you impostor.'

'I do, it's the thing women wear in the kitchen.' He stood for a moment watching her as she fiddled with the plaster on her hand; suspecting that her mood was changing. 'You never told me exactly why you had to argue with the piano.'

Beth glanced at him. 'What?'

'You must have had a reason for that,' Harry remarked, indicating the plastered hand.

'Sometimes I just get annoyed with the music,' she said, but he knew she was lying.

'O.K., as long as you're fine now.'

'I am, so let's get this gourmet meal started.'

*

Beth was fastidious about the way the table looked for guests. Although it was only for Annie and her Prince of Darkness – or Prince Schwartz she decided to call him, in case she let it slip in his presence – she wanted things to be perfect, including the angle of the cutlery and the tiny flowers on the crystal glasses facing the same way. As she placed the silver candle holder in the centre of the table, she wondered how many times her mother had done the very same thing with it; and her mother before her; and maybe even her great grandmother. It was a relic of past times, which Beth liked to think had secret memories encased in the tiny scratches that countless diamond rings had etched across the surface.

She picked it up again and turned it over in her hands, noting the fluffy green base, faded and worn now but still telling its story to anyone willing to listen.

She seemed to recall one of the old photographs, taken in the garden during the War, table bedecked with the ornate damask cloth and enough food to feed the village. Beth was seized with a desire to take out the old albums, to rummage through them, reawaken slumbering memories, perhaps even – She paused in her reflections, trying to put it into words: she wanted to discover what had made her mother so bitter about Thomas Blake and why she was resistant to hearing the truth.

'Yes,' she murmured to herself as she replaced the silver holder carefully on its spot. 'That's what I should have been doing all along. Why didn't I think of it sooner?'

'Think of what sooner?'

Beth spun round to see Harry in the doorway, 'Just talking to myself.'

'You sure?'

She pursed her lips together and gave him a cautionary stare. 'Yes.'

He shrugged and smiled but waited at the door, an expression of concern in his eyes, so much so that she was tempted to tell him.

'Beth, there is something bothering you. Come on, tell me.'

'I don't know if I want to.'

'It's to do with your grandfather, isn't it? You're angry because you're having to hang back now.'

With only half an hour to go before her guests arrived, Beth could see the pitfalls in provoking an argument now, besides which the hand had started to ache again and it was a reminder of her earlier stupidity. One bout of stupidity in an evening was shaming enough.

'Can we talk about it once they've gone?'

'Of course, sweetheart, I'm only worried about you.'

She was surprised to find herself blushing. 'Thanks.'

'How's the hand?'

'Pretty sore.'

'There's still time for me to kiss it better.'

Beth laughed and glanced at her watch: it was an enticing proposition, but she would wait until later, when they could take their time.

'We'll get rid of them early, shall we?'

'It's a deal,' Harry laughed. 'Oh, by the way, for Heaven's sake remember not to call him P of D.'

'I've another name for him anyway. Prince Schwartz.'

'He'll think it's something disgusting.'

'D'you think they will get married?'

'She'd be an idiot if she married him.'

'Maybe they said the same about you.'

Beth heard the insecurity in her own voice and suspected that Harry had heard it too, for he stepped towards her and took her hands, careful to avoid the plaster.

'How about we get rid of them even earlier than 'early'?'

*

Grace waited until James was asleep before she raked in the attic cupboard for the old photographs. Not pausing to wonder why she was suddenly interested in them after so many decades, she carried the box downstairs and tiptoed into the parlour where she had lit the fire to take the chill of the room. April it might be, but the cottage was an old sandstone building and it took more than a blink of spring sunshine to penetrate its stubborn walls.

She sat on the settee with the box beside her, put on her new spectacles and picked up the first photograph. Her heart lurched to see him, a boy of eighteen in his army uniform. She glanced at the date on the back.

'1924 Thomas in his uniform.'

'Wasted years,' Grace muttered to herself. 'Wasted because no one told me the truth. They all knew he would never make a life here.'

She sat stiffly, assaulted by a swift stab of regret that something so significant could have been so deliberately concealed by her family, her mother included, a woman whose integrity Grace had never thought to question, a woman who was regarded by everyone as being honest to a fault. Grace looked at the snap of her mother.

It was the innocence on Charlotte Shepherd's face that was causing Grace the most distress; the seemingly genuine smile of a woman who had no time for duplicity and deceit, a woman whose character would preclude anything other than the truth. It was heart-rending for Grace to look at her mother's photograph and witness her obvious adoration for Thomas Blake.

With a sigh of despair, she threw the photograph into the box and removed her spectacles, rubbing the side of her nose where they had chafed.

'For Goodness' sake!' she said loudly, too loudly, causing her to pause and listen, in case she had disturbed James dozing in the living room.

'Why has this started up again?' she asked herself more quietly. 'Can't you leave things alone, Grace Blake?'

Her hand flew to her mouth at such a revealing slip of the tongue. Dispirited, she picked up the box of photographs and went back upstairs, this time forcing her mind to the more pressing matter of her father. She raked in the top drawer of her dressing table and drew out Helen's letter, the only piece of evidence that would refute his claim to have loved his child as he did; the only piece of paper that could influence Beth's opinion about the whole affair.

Grace read the letter through, trying to find the slightest discrepancy that a stranger's eye might detect, trying to view it as her daughter would; but, of course, it was impossible. She had no idea what the man might have led Beth to believe; nor would she discuss it, not just yet. No, the only thing she could do was to wait, and hope that, for the second time in her life, she would have the courage to mould the truth to suit her own purpose.

*

Annie was drinking too much and Harry's concern was solely for Beth. He knew that the girl would involve Beth in any bout of knife-throwing at Alan and that Beth would do her best to pour oil on waters that could never be anything other than troubled. For the third time in as many minutes, he tried to attract her attention.

'In my opinion,' Annie was saying now, her eyes blinking rapidly, trying to focus. 'Men only want one thing and when they've got it – they're off.'

Harry suspected that the reason he was failing to attract Beth's attention was because she was avoiding looking at him and so he felt he had no option but to plunge in.

'I slept with Beth long before we were married,' he lied casually and, instantly, Beth's head turned in his direction. 'So, you could say that I'd got what I wanted, yet I asked her to marry me.'

'Ah, yes,' Annie sniggered, before an outraged Beth could call her husband a liar. 'But that was because she'd got her claws into you.'

Harry caught sight of Beth's expression, jumped in again before things got out of hand.

'I beg your pardon, my dear,' he smiled, trying to keep things light. 'If she did have her claws in me, it was the most enjoyable experience.'

Beth laughed and gave him a look that filled him with relief.

'Well said, young fellow,' she grinned, picking up her glass and swilling the remnants of the wine around. 'Besides, I only ever stuck them in your back when we were humping.'

It was Harry's turn to laugh, but when he glanced at Annie she scowled back.

'Just wait,' she addressed Beth, supposedly her best friend. 'One day he'll get tired of you and shag someone else. They're all the same.'

There was an ominous silence and Harry had to struggle to conceal his anger.

'Well, if I did, Annie dear,' he began quietly, with a quick wink to Beth. 'If I did, rest assured it won't be you I shag.'

'Oh, come on, stop this,' Beth urged, her tone pleasant. 'Who's for coffee?'

'As a matter of interest,' Annie persisted. 'Have you shagged anyone since you met Beth?'

'Of course not,' Harry said swiftly, and he had a horrible suspicion that his reply had been too swift. 'Unless you count the gypsy that often sleeps here.'

Beth laughed again and he counted himself lucky.

'Gypsy?' Alan asked, never one to keep up with the conversation.

'Yes, he means me,' Beth said triumphantly. ' I'm extremely naughty sometimes. In bed, you know,' she added wickedly.

'I saw you in a restaurant with someone.'

It was Annie who had spoken. Harry saw the momentary flush on Beth's cheeks, heard the inward gasp of her breath. He knew it had to be Charlie Webster the girl was referring to, but he wondered at Beth's reaction, for she had told him all about it.

'Yes, it was my boss and some clients.'

'You must have seen me,' Annie said accusingly. 'I walked right past you and you just ignored me.'

'That was ages ago,' Beth smiled good-naturedly. 'And I didn't mean to ignore you, honestly.'

'Oh, for fuck's sake!'

Harry jumped up and, with an apologetic gesture to Beth, grabbed Annie by the arm and pulled her to a standing position.

'Watch what…!'

'Get out of here right now,' he said, more calmly. 'I'm sick to death of you and your bitchiness. You're not even fit for Beth to wipe her shoes on, far less be her friend. Now fuck off and don't come back until you've sobered up.'

*

'I've never heard you swear before,' Beth said as they prepared for bed.

'I know and I'm really sorry, but she bloody drove me to it.'

'You're at it again,' she told him, but her eyes were laughing.

'You're just like your mother in that respect,' Harry said, perhaps unwisely, but he had to get it out.

'Oh?' Beth mouthed at his reflection in the bathroom mirror. 'And what respect would that be?'

'She's also surrounded by women who are supposed to be her friends and they're not worthy of her either.' Beth was silent and he knew what she was thinking. 'You know exactly what I mean, Beth. Take Molly, for instance.'

'Mmm.'

'Need I go on?'

Beth shrugged and sidled up to him. 'No, I get the message, and you're right as usual,' she added, nuzzling his neck. 'It's just that I feel so sorry for Annie'

'But she doesn't deserve your sympathy, Beth, and I hate to see you having to defend her when she's such a cow.'

He smiled at her humorous expression and twisted her round until she was facing him. He could see in her eyes that she was torn between agreeing with him because he was right and betraying someone she counted as a friend. It was the quality he most loved about her, the unfailing loyalty she displayed for people not worthy enough to be in the same room with her.

'I'll try to be more neutral about it,' she said in a small voice.

'Just pretend she's the piano.'

Beth giggled and pressed herself closer. 'She's in for a shock then.'

'How's the hand, by the way? Do you think it will impede things?'

'I'll just lie back and let you do all the work for a change.'

'In that case, sweetheart, you're in for a treat.'

'It wasn't Charlie Webster I was embarrassed about,' Beth said suddenly, moving away and looking straight at him.

'What, in the restaurant?'

'It was the other one, the guy you mentioned once, ages ago.'

'Who, Frank Gilmour?'

'He just turned up,' Beth explained unhappily. 'Even Charlie Webster was surprised.'

'Did he bother you at all?'

'No, in fact he only stayed for ten minutes. I got the impression that he was more interested in the client's daughter than in any business deal.'

Harry recalled Sandra's account of Gilmour and his sister and almost wished he had never known. To have a man like him sitting within a yard of Beth was not a welcome image.

'How old was the daughter, as a matter of interest?' he asked casually.

'Still at school, for Pete's sake,' Beth said scornfully. 'She lapped it up, of course, as school kids do, but I thought he was a creep.'

'Yet you seem to like Charlie Webster well enough.'

Beth bristled. 'As a boss he's fine.'

'That's all I meant,' Harry smiled soothingly. 'And let's face it, you and Grace attract strange friends too, don't you?'

'Is it important?'

'Show me a man's friends and I'll tell you about the man,' Harry quoted, at least he recalled it was the gist of it.

'In that case,' Beth smiled archly. 'You can't exist, because you have none.'

Harry laughed and muttered the word '*touché*', and then he asked:

'Hey, are we going to make love before I lose interest?'

'You're so sweet,' Beth grinned. 'Making love sounds better than bonking.'

'Whatever you like to call it, I'm about to show you a good time, whoever you are.'

'And don't think I'm going to tell you my name either!'

As he kissed her, Harry's mind was on nothing but pleasing Beth; but later, when she was asleep, he knew that grim thoughts of Frank Gilmour would abound and keep him awake.

*

James had walked up and down the garden umpteen times since breakfast time and Grace was on the verge of putting a stop to it. The only thing that prevented her was the happy expression on his face at being out and about after months of sitting in the chair and so she waited, frequently passing the kitchen window to monitor his progress, hearing her mother's words: like a hen on a hot girdle.

She surveyed the lunch table, counted the sandwiches and hors d'oeuvres and decided it would do; and then she switched on the kettle and gathered the teapots, arranging them in a neat row, the way her mother always did, before placing three spoons of tealeaves in each. She was nervous about having invited the Kerrs, particularly after the fracas with Beth, but loyalty to Tony and Sarah was uppermost in Grace's mind. Annie and her histrionics were a matter for someone else; Harry by the sound of things.

Grace smiled again at the image of the boy jumping up and swearing. Anyone least likely to utter foul words was Harry Gillespie.

She glanced from the window and saw that James was heading towards the house, limping slightly, but striding out briskly enough for her mind to be put at rest.

'That was wonderful!' he told her as soon as the door was open. 'I can hardly believe I'm out of that damned chair.'

'Remember what the doctor said,' Grace smiled, trying not to put too much of a dampener on things. 'A little every day, that's what you need, not ten miles between breakfast and lunch.'

James grinned at her and she was thankful that he had recovered his sense of fun, sorely lacking in recent months despite everyone's efforts to keep his spirits up.

'Don't worry, I'll be careful. Can I help in here?'

'No, there's nothing to do. Why don't you have a rest for ten minutes?'

She was rewarded by a frown, swiftly followed by a growl of dissent. Undeterred, however, Grace took his arm and accompanied him into the living room and directed him to his chair, into which he sank without further argument.

Once she had satisfied herself that he would rest for a few minutes, Grace went into the garden to check the sky: the forecast was good, but her grandfather had taught her what to look for and she was doing it now, scanning the blue expanse and making a judgement.

The bizarre thought struck her, that Alexander Shepherd had known everything about nothing and nothing about important things. Grace sighed at her uncharitable frame of mind, especially when Grandpa was not here to defend himself. Deciding that the afternoon would be fine, she began making plans to set lunch out in the garden.

*

Frank and Emily were fidgeting so much that Harry suspected they intended to make an announcement, *that* kind of announcement, the kind that put a noose around the boy's neck and guaranteed him a life of abject misery. He had a brief twinge of guilt when he remembered how happy he was with Beth; but this girl, Emily McKay, was not the soul mate for young Frank.

As he watched her flirt with Tony Kerr, Harry had to concede that she was a stunning girl, but if 'handsome is as handsome does' applied to men, then 'stunning is as stunning does' should equally apply to females.

'Harry, my dear,' he heard Grace say in his ear. 'You've hardly eaten a thing.'

'Too busy wondering if your eldest son and heir is about to say something.'

She looked at him with astonishment and he assumed that she had no idea.

'How did you know that?' she whispered, eyes wide, and then he knew she did.

'Isn't it obvious, with all that fidgeting and throat clearing?'

Grace laughed and laid her hand on his shoulder. 'It's amazing.'

'Should I take up psychic readings then, d'you think?'

'Don't you dare,' she said in fun, but Harry detected another element in her tone.

'Can I give you a hand with something?' he asked, but she shook her head.

'No, Beth's doing everything.'

'Wonders will never cease.'

'Oh, come on, she's quite domesticated now; you've worked magic on her. By the way,' she added, stooping to whisper in his ear once more. 'I heard about Annie the other week. Thanks for defending my daughter.'

'I'm afraid I lost my temper rather, even said the 'f' word.'

'In this instance, it was justified. Must go and make some more tea.'

'I thought you said Beth was doing everything?'

Grace smiled and moved away, leaving Harry with nothing better to do than suffer the juvenile antics of Emily McKay.

Frank stood up from his seat on the bench and meandered over. Harry was kindly disposed towards his brother-in-law, being as he was the most obliging and timid boy on the planet; the type of chap whose cause Harry frequently took up.

'How are things in the legal world?' Frank asked, his normal introit, but one to which Harry never took exception.

'Lots of people making money and lots of people losing it,' replied Harry, varying his reply, not for Frank's sake but for his own, since he hated being predictable.

'Hopefully you're one of the people making it,' his brother-in-law smiled.

'Of course. How's the banking world then?'

'People making, people losing,' Frank said, and Harry wondered if there were more to the boy than met the eye. 'Beth seems on top of the world,' he added. 'She wouldn't be pregnant, by any chance?'

Harry almost choked on his drink. 'God, no! What makes you think that?'

Frank shrugged. 'She was telling Mum about some baby she'd seen.'

'Ah, yes, Catriona's. She did mention it.'

'Cat had to get married,' Frank stated blandly.

'Did she?'

'I've asked Emily to marry me,' came the announcement out of the blue.

'You have?' Harry asked, trying to inject enthusiasm into his voice. 'Well, that's great, Frank, just great.'

'She said 'yes'.'

Harry studied the boy's face for a moment, trying to figure out the reason for the lack-lustre delivery of the words.

'That's good, isn't it?'

'I'm not sure,' the boy said, with characteristic timidity.

'She's a lovely girl, you should be ecstatic.'

'I suppose.'

Harry turned in his chair, giving the boy his full attention.

'Do I get the impression you're sorry you asked her?'

Frank blushed and grunted something under his breath. There were so few similarities between the boy and his sister that, occasionally, Harry mulled over the possibility that Frank had fallen from outer space; but in this respect, the one concerning his refreshing lack of guile, Frank Melville was as like his sister as two peas in a pod.

'Do you love her?' Harry asked bluntly, at which the boy blushed fiercely.

'Yes, of course I do.'

'Well, go ahead, take a chance.'

Frank frowned. 'You think it's a chance?'

'Isn't everything?'

'But you and Beth…I mean, you're happy, aren't you?'

'Yes, but there's still a chance she'll find someone else.'

'Not her,' Frank said with conviction. 'You're stuck with her forever, mate.'

They both laughed and Harry was about to reply when Grace interrupted.

'The worst thing imaginable has happened,' she whispered despairingly.

'What?' asked Harry, rising from his chair.

'Annie's turned up, wants to apologise.'

'What's terrible about that?'

'I think she's been drinking.'

Without Harry's presence, a full-scale row between father and daughter would have been inevitable. Because of his diplomatic and sympathetic approach, however, he had Annie sobered up and coherent within the space of half an hour, succeeding in keeping the two main players apart until the last moment, Tony's lack of mobility was helpful, for he could not see the girl in her pitiful state from his position at the top of the garden. Sarah Kerr was not so fortunate, but Harry steered her towards Grace and turned his attention to the girl.

'I'm such an idiot,' Annie mumbled for the twentieth time, slouched at the kitchen table, stirring sugar into a black coffee Harry had poured out for her. 'Will Beth ever forgive me?'

'Probably,' he replied, a shade unkindly. 'As long as it doesn't happen again.'

She gazed at him with huge green eyes, the wisps of blonde hair fluttering in the movement of air from the open door and Harry had a fleeting vision of her in bed with Prince Schwartz.

'Right,' he said briskly, standing up and pushing the chair back. 'I'll get back to Beth, leave you to it.'

'I'm really, really sorry, Harry,' she pleaded and he turned back to look at her, his fingers on the door handle. 'I'd never want to hurt Beth, honestly. It's just...' She paused and lowered her eyes to the cup.

'Just what?' he asked, understanding the folly of it.

'I'm jealous of her.'

He should have left it at that, nodded politely, closed the door and gone back to Beth; but he waited, somewhat curious as to her meaning.

'She's a talented girl,' he smiled. 'You should be jealous.'

'I mean about you,' she said quickly and appeared as surprised as he was at the words.

'Annie, this is silly. I must get back.'

'I think about you all the time,' she whispered desperately, her eyes fully focussed on his face, hands holding the coffee cup tightly. 'I can't help it, I...'

'Stop this, please,' Harry said abruptly. 'I don't want to hear it.'

He opened the door quickly, hurried down the steps and bumped into Grace.

'Harry, you look terrible.'

'You can deal with her,' he breathed out heavily, jerking his head towards the kitchen. 'She's a fool.'

He went into the garden to find Beth, aware of Grace's eyes following his progress as he walked up the path.

*

Grace took her daughter aside at the earliest opportunity and asked if there were something troubling Harry.

'Troubling him?' Beth asked in surprise. 'No, why?'

'I think he had some bother with Annie...in the kitchen an hour ago, at least that's the impression he gave me.'

'Oh, that. Yes, he told me she'd made a pass at him.' Beth laughed at her mother's horrified expression. 'Mum, it's all right, it's just Annie's way.'

Grace was forcibly reminded that it had been Molly's way too, with her frequent eyelash fluttering at James.

'She's supposed to be your friend,' Grace said feebly. 'It's not a very nice thing.'

'She's always fancied Harry,' Beth whispered in her mother's ear. 'But I can assure you, mother dear, that I'm such an expert in bed that she'll never succeed.' She laughed uproariously at Grace's reaction. 'And don't pretend you're an old fuddy-duddy either, because I know your generation had fun too, you know. See you later,' she added with a twirl, before dashing from the room and slamming the door.

Grace shook her head and began piling some of the dishes into the deep sink where they would lie until the guests had departed, after which she would stand for hours washing and drying. For an instant she was annoyed with herself for such gloomy thoughts; it had been her own idea to invite everyone this afternoon, for she wanted the family together when Frank made his announcement.

'I'm sorry about Annie,' she heard Sarah say behind her.

'It's not important. It's just a phase she's going through, they all do.'

'Beth didn't.'

Grace had to smile, for Beth had been the most problematic teenager in the county.

'Oh, yes,' she contradicted wryly. 'Beth was a monster when she was fifteen.'

Sarah's eyes widened. 'You're joking? I never saw that.'

'You should have lived here then,' Grace smiled. 'It drove me out of my mind, I can tell you. In fact, if it hadn't been for James, I'd have chucked her out.'

'No!' Sarah exclaimed, sitting down on the nearest chair as if the revelation were too much. 'I'd no idea, Grace. You should have told me, I could have...'

She stopped and glanced at her friend. 'Hark at me,' she said bitterly. 'Telling you I could have helped you with Beth and look at my own daughter.'

'Listen; let's forget all this for the moment. Frank wants to tell us something.'

'Tell us something? You mean, he and Emily McKay?'

There was nothing in Sarah's tone to indicate either approval or dissent, but she was avoiding Grace's eye and it was most uncharacteristic.

'She's a lovely girl,' Grace said, having had months to come to terms with her own reservations about the match. 'I'm sure she and Frank will be very happy.' She almost cringed at the banality of her words and tone, wondering if Sarah had heard.

'Oh, it's pot luck anyway,' Sarah said suddenly. 'I often wonder what keeps Tony and I together.'

'Love,' Grace told her firmly, although she could have no real idea of their relationship, other than the way they had each stuck by the other in times of ill-health. 'That's what keeps you two together, the same as with James and me.'

'I suppose so,' Sarah smiled, but there was resignation in her voice.

'Come on,' Grace urged. 'Let's go outside and pretend to be surprised at the good news.'

*

Beth was relieved when the announcement was over. They had been hanging on all afternoon, watching and waiting, trying not to appear as if they were watching and waiting; and now the deed was done and they could all get home.

To Harry and to her mother, she had laughed off Annie's pass at Harry, but, if the truth were known, she was quite miserable: she had been more than a good friend to the girl, through thick and even thicker, and this was to be her reward? Even half an hour bashing the old piano had failed to banish the blues completely.

One unexpected and surprising aspect had been Emily McKay, who had sought Beth out after the somewhat brief announcement and had sat down with – Beth imagined – the purpose of ingratiating herself with her future sister-in-law.

'So, what do you think about me and Frank?' the girl had asked once she had helped them to tea and slices of Grace's home-made cake.

Taken aback at the directness of the question, Beth had floundered to start with, at which Emily had smiled indulgently, belying her tender years, and patted Beth's arm.

'It's all right, I know what you're thinking, and you're not the only one.'

Under normal circumstances, Beth would have been outraged at the notion of her mind being an open book but, oddly enough, she took no exception to the girl's comment.

'I suppose we're all thinking,' Beth had said, plunging in at the deep end. 'That you're too sophisticated for Frank.'

'Golly, that's a new one.'

'Sorry?'

Emily smiled broadly, her tiny, perfectly white teeth causing Beth a moment's pang of envy. 'My family would die laughing if they heard you describing me as 'sophisticated'.'

'How would you describe yourself then?'

'I'm so shy that it took me months to pluck up the courage to speak to Frank.'

Recalling Emily McKay's propensity to flirt with anything in trousers, Beth had nodded politely, but reserved judgement.

'He'd said 'hello' to me countless times in the bank,' Emily had continued and Beth wondered if she had let herself in for a marathon. 'But I froze every time I tried to say anything back.' She giggled and threw Beth a guilty glance. 'I felt like a silly schoolgirl whenever he appeared.'

'So did I, with Harry,' Beth revealed, much to her own horror. 'In fact,' she whispered, compounding the situation, 'I still feel like one when he bosses me about.'

'He's so nice,' Emily had said, no trace of flirtatiousness on her face. 'He reminds me of Steve…'

'Yes,' Beth butted in patiently. 'People keep telling me.'

'Sorry. Who d'you think Frank reminds you of?' the girl asked and, considering she was his sister, Beth thought it the daftest question, as she had been tempted to say 'Godzilla.'

'I don't know,' she had shrugged tactfully. 'I suppose he looks like my great granddad, at least from photos I've seen.'

At the mention of photographs, Emily leaned forward, more enthusiastic about them than her engagement announcement Beth noticed.

'Do you have old family photos?'

'Yeah, lots.'

'Of Frank?'

Well, yes, since he's in the flipping family

'Yes, of course. On the bearskin rug and everything.'

'I love looking at old photos,' Emily had announced wistfully. 'Especially the one of my gran when she was young. There's something so sad about them I think.'

'Is she still alive?'

'Oh, yes, but she's never interested in talking about the past, and I could talk about it all day.'

'Not your own past, surely?' Beth smiled. 'You haven't got much of one yet.'

'Did you see that film with George Peppard and Elisabeth Montgomery?'

'What, *The Carpetbaggers*'?'

'Yes, it was great,' Emily sighed. 'The bit where he asked her about the most exciting thing she'd ever done, and she told him she was hoping she hadn't done it yet?'

'I liked that,' Beth had agreed. 'In fact, I wish I'd thought it up myself.'

'Me too.'

Rashly, and knowing she should discuss it with Harry first, Beth said:

'You and Frank must come to our place for dinner some time.'

'Really? That would be great!' the girl had exclaimed. 'We'd love to.'

'Remember he's my brother,' Beth said dryly. 'Ask him before you commit yourselves.'

'Oh, he'll want to come, he thinks Harry is the bees knees.'

It had been news to Beth, but not unwelcome: brother and sister had long since come to the conclusion that past intolerances were exactly that.

*

As Harry sat pondering the afternoon's events, his mind refused to let go of Annie Kerr's remark. He had known she liked him too much, but he was not unaccustomed to silly young girls trying to attract his attention. Until he met Beth he had never courted any girl for longer than a few weeks.

Sitting in his favourite chair by the window, he wondered now if Beth had inherited Grace's play-acting skills and had wanted him from the beginning.

'I meant to ask you this ages ago,' he began, whenever she came back into the room. 'Did you notice me before I spoke to you that first day in Aberdeen?'

She grinned and flopped down on the sofa, tucking her bare feet under her before taking a sip of her wine.

'That's confidential, Gillespie.'

'You had noticed me, then?'

'Not telling.'

He laughed and shook his head. 'Unless you tell me otherwise, I'll presume now that you had, and that you were so besotted with me that you'd have fallen at my feet if I hadn't spoken to you.'

'Think what you like, it's a secret and I'll take it to my grave.'

She had spoken lightly but the words made him shiver.

'What did you think of Emily?' he asked.

'Actually, she's O.K.'

'I saw the two of you having a girly chat.' Harry paused and then frowned. 'You're not intending to pick up another lame duck, are you?'

'What a horrible thing to say!' Beth protested animatedly. 'She's anything but a lame duck, she's very nice and very interesting to talk to.'

Harry sighed. 'Ah, you *are* going pick one up.'

'She and I will be good friends, and before you say anything, I've half invited them over for dinner some night.'

'I don't mind that,' Harry smiled. 'I rather like your brother.'

'That's good, because Emily says he looks up to you.'

'The idiot!'

'No, he's not, and I'm glad the two of you have hit it off.' Beth pressed her lips together and he knew it meant more to her than she was admitting. 'Frank's a poor thing sometimes.'

Harry laughed unkindly.' Oh, come off it, you were horrid to him when I first met you.'

'A sister's prerogative,' Beth said haughtily.

'Not all sisters and brothers hate each other,' he told her.

237

'Do you like your brother?'

It stopped him in his tracks. 'What?'

'Your brother,' Beth said, her eyes narrowing. 'The boy that your mother and her new...'

'I never think about him.'

'Liar.'

'I don't,' Harry insisted. 'That's why I was shocked when you mentioned him. I haven't given him a thought for years.'

'I might believe you. Anyway, where he is now?'

'Not a clue. Nor do I want to.'

'Maybe he's nice.'

'Maybe I couldn't care less.'

Beth sighed and rose from the sofa, padding across the room and sitting down in front of the open fireplace, decorated with flowers and candles in summer.

'Still, I often wonder about him. I saw your mother's letter, by the way.'

'I left it for you to read.'

'She seems sad.'

'Beth, sweetheart,' Harry said gently. 'She made her bed and all that.'

'You could write something nice to her.'

'That's enough. Hold it right there.'

'I could hold it,' Beth smiled wickedly. 'Only you've got your trousers on.'

'Your mind, Beth Melville, is the grimiest one I've ever known.'

'They say Leonardo da Vinci was the same.'

'Do they?'

'And he could write backwards as well,' Beth said proudly, referring to one of her own abilities that occasionally invoked envy in him.

'So you're in good company then.'

'I'm in good company now,' she said seriously. 'Harry, I know I'm sometimes... well... annoying, shall we say?'

'Yes, let's say that.'

'But I honestly can't imagine life without you.'

'Why would you have to?' he asked in astonishment, and then, seeing it in her eyes, he added: 'Darling girl, if I even thought that you were in the least worried about Annie Kerr, I'd take you over my knee this minute and wallop you.'

'I'm really worried then.'

'You have no idea, do you?'

'Of what?'

'Of how lovely you are and how I could never find a single trait in any other woman that would remotely interest me.'

She looked at him silently, only half believing him he knew, and he had a sudden image of Grace Blake sitting at his feet.

*

'I'm so glad everything went well.'

Grace sat with her feet on the leather stool, sipping a hot drink, and it recalled memories of nights with her mother, after walking home from the picture house in Craigton to a roaring fire and the comfort of old armchairs.

'She seems a pleasant girl,' James said, his nose in a pigeon fancier's glossy magazine.

'I was worried at first,' Grace confessed. 'But Beth told me they'd had a little chat and that she likes her, thinks they could turn out to be good friends.'

James looked up from the magazine. 'That's good, because Beth needs good friends. The same as you do,' he added unnecessarily, for it was not the first time he had broached the subject.

'You don't know Molly like I do,' she said, her usual retort. 'She and I get along just fine.'

'You know what I think about it,' James told her, eyes on the magazine.' So there's no need to go into it all over again.'

'Beth was saying that she's invited Emily and Frank for dinner sometime.'

'How things change,' James said wryly. 'A few years ago they couldn't stand the sight of each other.'

'Brothers and sisters' – Grace started to say and James glanced at her as she added: 'I would have liked a sister.'

'In theory, it's all very well.'

'But you like your sister.'

'Most times.' James peered at her over the rim of his glasses. 'You look tired, Grace. With the play on next week maybe you should have held the engagement party some other time.'

'Oh, I feel fine, and, besides, it's only a village play, James, not the West End.'

'I just don't want you to be doing too much.'

'After next week, with the play being over and everything coming to an end for summer, I'll be bored stiff.'

James gave a wry smile. 'You don't know the meaning of the word, my dear.'

Grace shook her head. 'I'd rather be busy, unless it's housework, of course.'

Her words fell on deaf ears.

*

Switching on his bedside lamp, Thomas picked up the library book he was reading: an Ian Fleming novel that he had read twice already, once in South America, once in France, where he had lingered for a few weeks before coming here. He paused and laid the book aside; pondered the word 'here'. How significant was it that he regarded this place as 'here', not 'home'?

Had it been solely because of Charlotte that he once considered Perth his home and, now that she was dead, he had reverted to 'here'?

Now that she was dead!

The words echoed round his mind and, even now, he had difficulty in reconciling himself to their meaning. Never had he imagined she would not be here when he came to look for her. How and where she had died was beginning to preoccupy him: would anyone ever tell him?

There was Lily Morris, of course, but she was refusing to answer his calls or notes, and so he had given up on her; and, as for his daughter, well, he had a feeling that he was wasting his time pinning his hopes on imminent reconciliation.

Beth was the only friendly face in a sea of animosity and even she had deserted him momentarily. Thomas baulked at the word, for he done it to Grace, despite his protestations to Beth; an admission he had finally acceded to in recent days; ever since he had received his granddaughter's cool letter. He may not have abandoned Charlotte, but he had certainly abandoned their daughter – in the middle of a Dundee street, in full view of passers-by. The memory of that day and his undignified flight was in such sharp detail that it refused to be brushed aside. Without a couple of whiskies before he went to bed, it could easily keep him awake.

'There was nothing else I could have done to keep her,' he had told Beth, even showing her the letters that apparently confirmed it.

Now, in the silence and privacy of his bedroom, Thomas was having problems with his conscience; an unusual – if not rare – occurrence. He opened the top drawer of his bedside cabinet and took out the bundle of Charlotte's letters wondering, in a heart-stopping moment, if she had kept any of his. If she had, could Grace use them against him? He racked his brains, trying to recall any rash statement he may have committed to paper.

In the middle of the night, he was thinking now, most problems seemed insurmountable, whereas, in the bright light of a June morning he would laugh off his fears and march out into the world with renewed vigour.

*

Harry poured himself a glass of juice and pulled out a chair at the kitchen table. He wanted to believe it was the heat that was keeping him awake, but he knew perfectly well that it was the aftermath of Beth's mentioning his brother; strictly speaking, his half-brother. He had thought about the boy so rarely that he had even forgotten his name.

He had told Beth that he had never given the boy a second thought over the years and it was true; yet, since the moment she had slipped it into the conversation, Harry had thought of nothing else.

He supposed he could contact the RAF base where his father had been stationed; find out from them where the widow and, presumably, Harry's stepbrother lived; but why exactly would he want to do that? In the mean light from the street lamp, he sat pondering the consequences. Within minutes, he decided it was a waste of his time. He finished off the glass of juice and went back to bed.

Things always seemed hopeless in the dead of night: come the morning, he would laugh this off.

Chapter Fourteen

They had tea at five, but Grace had shown no appetite, citing last-minute nerves.

'I couldn't eat a thing,' she said as they sat round the kitchen table. 'But tuck in the rest of you. I slaved over a hot stove for hours.'

Frank ate heartily, never being one to refuse food, despite being as thin as a rake.

'It's because you smoke,' Beth had said frequently when he boasted of his weight. 'If you ever stop, you'll blow up like a balloon,'

As she sliced the homemade quiche into reasonable pieces, Beth kept glancing at her mother, envying her poise and composure when, in a few short hours, she would be the focus of the villagers' attention.

'I could never perform in public,' she said now, taking everyone by surprise.

'Of course you could,' her mother smiled. 'It's only the village hall, Beth, not the famous Whitehall Theatre.'

'Oh, yes, Brian Rix and his farces,' Beth said and Harry gave her a curious glance. 'Did you ever see any of them on television?' she asked him.

'I've no idea what you're talking about.'

'Oh, they were hilarious,' Grace agreed. 'I don't think I ever laughed so much, before or since. His wife was the best, Elspet Gray her name is, such great timing, so important in comedy.'

'You were great in *Sailor Beware*,' Frank said, realising too late that his father would tell him off for speaking with his mouth full. 'Sorry, Dad,' he said quickly and James was satisfied.

'I enjoyed that play,' Grace said. 'We had some good reviews in the local papers afterwards.'

'Didn't Lily Morris say that the reporter, Graham Seaton, was smitten with you?'

Beth had meant it to be light-hearted, but was embarrassed by the glare she received from her father.

'Graham was not smitten with me,' her mother said firmly. 'He's a very kind and considerate young man. Honestly, this village!'

'How many plays have you put on?' Harry asked, mostly, Beth suspected, to diffuse the situation; to rescue her mother.

'Oh, I can't remember now. I joined in '53, but didn't carry on for long.'

'Why not?' he asked, and Beth could have told him it was something to do with being tethered to the back green.

'I had two young children,' Grace said reasonably. 'And they were,' she emphasised, glancing at both of them, 'extremely trying children, I can assure you.'

'Frank was anyway,' Beth quipped quickly before her brother had time to say it first. 'Always moaning and whining about something.'

'Beth, dear,' James said quietly, and his daughter shrugged apologetically.

'Sorry, Frank, my lips are sealed about your whining and moaning.'

They walked to the hall, James and Grace in front, Harry and Beth lagging behind, Frank wandering far in their wake, smoking a cigarette, keeping his eyes on his father in case he turned round unexpectedly and caught him.

'Isn't this romantic?' Beth whispered to Harry, indicating her parents, arm-in-arm a few yards in front. 'They must have walked up and down this village street hundreds of times when they were courting.'

'Did anyone ever tell you were soft in the head?' he asked her, but despite the humour in his tone, Harry was loathe to imagine Grace Blake with anyone.

'I think it's...' Beth paused.

241

'Think it's what?"

'Sad, I was going to say. Yes, more than anything, it's sad.'

'They look happy enough to me.'

'Not them… *it.*'

'Beth, whatever are you rambling on about?'

She held him closer, wrapping her arms round his waist and impeding his progress.

'The old photos, the letters and everything. I just think it's so sad, times past.'

She looked up at him suddenly, a fearful expression on her face. 'It will happen to us as well.'

'Time passing, you mean?' Harry asked, pretending to misunderstand.

'No, not just that, I mean growing old, having sad memories.'

'I'm sure we'll have just as many happy ones, sweetheart.'

'But even the happy ones end up being sad.'

'This conversation is too deep for me,' Harry laughed, disentangling her hands from around his waist. 'For a Friday night, after a hard week's work, I suggest you stick to the weather. Heavens, look at the queue. We'll never get a seat.'

'Oh, yes we will,' Beth said smugly. 'I popped up here an hour ago and put my coat across the best seats.'

Harry marvelled at the sight of so many people; suddenly realised that he had never known how many people actually lived in the place. When he remarked upon it to Beth, she shrugged.

'Oh, they'll have come from other villages to see Mum. Miles away in fact. It wasn't only Graham Seaton who fancied her.'

Harry allowed himself to be dragged to the back door, through the kitchen and down the stage steps to the front row. He had forgotten that Beth had been born and brought up here, that she was a child of rural Scotland. In the city, surrounded by city people and city life, she had fitted in so well that her childhood environment had slipped his mind.

'Here we are,' she said proudly, lifting the coat from their seats and sitting down. 'Maybe you can get me a programme before it starts? I'll just nip back stage and wish Mum good luck. Oh, keep that seat for Dad. Frank will want to sit at the back so he can sneak out for a fag.'

With that, she had gone, leaping the steps two at a time and disappearing behind the stage. Harry glanced around and saw Lily Morris waving at him and he felt obliged to move along and speak to her.

'Your first time here?' she asked, covering her knees with a tartan rug.

'Yes, I'm looking forward to it.'

'She's a star, is our Grace,' Lily said, as if she should take credit. 'They come from as far away as Perth and Dundee to see her, you know, always have done, know a real talent when they see it.' She gave him a shrewd glance. 'Any trouble from her father lately?'

'No, he hasn't shown himself at all.'

'That doesn't mean he's not still here,' Lily frowned. 'I've heard he's got a new companion already.'

'A woman, you mean?'

'Aye, a woman. Seems she's an old friend of a friend.' Jean shook her head. 'You won't know her, of course, not being from around here.'

Ignoring the jibe, Harry glanced around. 'This friend, Is she here tonight?'

'No, she's housebound mostly.' She peered at him. 'Do you want to speak to her?'

'I might.'

'Aye well, Grace goes to see her every so often. Maybe you could ask her to take you.'

242

'Thanks, I will.'

'Enjoy the show,' Lily said, her eyes lowering to the programme in her hand; and he was dismissed.

Harry sat waiting for Beth to reappear, his mind floating between past and present. Beth had been right about it being sad, of course, for he had always found it so whenever he perused the old snaps and intruded on the privacy of the people therein. Yes, it was sad; but he would never admit it to Beth. It was one of the few things he kept to himself.

Harry was transfixed. Grace was in complete control of the production: she drifted through the performance with the aplomb of a West End star, evoking laughs and tears from the audience, knowing exactly when to pause and wait, exactly when to raise her eyebrows, curve her lips into a smile, lower her head to invoke sympathy. He had never witnessed a role so perfectly portrayed; nor so greatly appreciated by the audience.

She had always given him the impression that she and James had continually struggled against the prejudices and intransigence of the villagers, and yet, the villagers were thoroughly engrossed in her character, applauding even before she came to the end of a particularly amusing line, not waiting for the more appropriate moment. Despite everything she had inferred, he could see that Grace Blake was held fast in the affections of her audience. Harry wondered how on earth she had ever imagined her contribution to village life as being a waste of time, her very words to him only a few months previously.

'I don't know why I'm bothering,' she had confided, as she weighed out flour to bake trays of oven scones. 'They'll not appreciate it anyway.'

'Of course they will. I'm sure you have no idea of how much you're liked in this village.'

'They only like you if you're useful,' she had retorted unkindly, although later he had cajoled her into a more forgiving mood.

Now, as he watched her take a third bow, Harry began to wonder what had happened to the young Grace Blake that had clouded her judgement of her worth.

'Wasn't that fantastic?' he heard Beth whisper beside him. 'Isn't she the best?'

'Yes,' he said truthfully. 'She is.'

'Come on, let's go back stage and tell her she was great.'

'She must know she was great,' he laughed as Beth pulled him from his chair.

'No, she doesn't,' Beth frowned. 'She has no idea how good she is.'

Grace was cleaning the makeup from her face when they opened the door to the tiny dressing room. Molly and Joanna were also squeezed into the cramped space, but it was her mother whom Beth rushed to hug.

'You were wonderful, Mum,' Beth cried out, completely ignoring the other two.

'Thank you, dear,' Grace smiled, returning her daughter's hug. 'We all did remarkably well I thought, didn't you, Molly?'

'Oh, don't be so modest, Grace,' Joanna tutted. 'You were the star and we don't mind admitting it, do we Molly?'

'Certainly not,' Molly smiled with ill grace, her smile lop-sided because only half her makeup was removed. 'The audience lapped it up. What did you think of your mother-in-law, Harry?'

'I thought she was excellent,' he felt obliged to say, but it hardly did her justice.

'Now, there's a posh word,' Molly winked to him. 'You don't hear that word much in this village, unless it's from Lucy Webster, of course.'

'Can you two stay for supper?' Grace asked, the frown already appearing on her forehead.

'Yes, we can,' Harry smiled, and he sensed Beth's surprise, for he had wanted to go straight home afterwards. 'Just for half an hour anyway.'

'Good, I'll be dying for something to eat now, not to mention a little tipple to celebrate.'

She gave him the warmest of smiles and, suddenly, stupidly, Harry knew that he would do anything she asked of him.

*

They sat in the kitchen and drank the last of the sherry. James looked tired, but when Grace suggested he retire to bed, he shrugged it off.

'I'm enjoying this, just the two of us.'

'James, dear, it's always just the two of us.'

'Not tonight, it wasn't.'

Grace was wary: his expression was almost petulant. She formed the sentence in her head before she uttered the words.

'You don't mean you're sorry you bullied me into going back to the Dramatic Society?'

He was immediately contrite. 'No, of course not.'

'What then?'

'Graham Seaton still seems keen on you.'

'Oh, for Heaven's sake!' Grace exclaimed. 'Not you as well?'

James examined the dregs in his glass. 'He's a very handsome chap.'

Grace took a deep breath. 'I was thinking we should go to England at the end of August.'

Taken aback at her change of topic, James remained silent, and Grace carried on as if he had shown willing.

'Is the end of August too late, do you think?'

'What for?' James asked, his attention on his plate.

'The weather. What will it be like in the South of England so late in the year?'

Grace touched his arm and forced him to look at her. 'Will it be warm?'

'It should be, but I can't guarantee it.' He added with a faint smile, 'You'll have to take your chance.'

'We'll have to take our chance, you mean.'

'Are you sure you want to go, Grace?'

'Are you sure *you* want to go?'

'Why wouldn't I?'

'To be honest, James, you don't sound very keen.'

He shrugged and her suspicions were confirmed. Her heart sank, for the only reason he would hesitate from going home was anxiety regarding his health.

'I'm not altogether sure it's a good idea.'

'But it's your home,' Grace reminded him, aghast at the notion he would turn down the opportunity to visit his mother. 'Of course it's a good idea. You've only been once and that was over ten years ago. Your mother will be so upset if you don't go soon.'

'She'll understand.'

'Well, good for her,' Grace said, anger rising. 'But I certainly won't.'

James stopped eating and laid aside his knife and fork. She waited, heartbeat picking up at the expression on his face.

'The last time I saw her, we had an argument.'

Grace was astonished. 'You never said.'

'Well, I'm saying now.'

'What was it about?'

244

James averted his eyes. 'I'm sure you can guess.'

'You mean me?'

'Not exactly.'

'Your staying here after the war?'

He nodded. 'She expected us to go down there to live.'

'I would have, if you'd asked me.'

James gave a sigh of frustration. 'I don't want to carry on with this.'

Grace had lost her patience. 'Well, I do!' she cried, jumping up from the chair. 'If you don't have a good reason for not going, then the rest of us will go.'

James showed no surprise at his wife's outburst, sitting calmly, turning the sherry glass over in his hand. He was so calm that Grace sat down again, determined to get to the core of his reasoning.

'Ah,' he smiled. 'You've stopped giving an impression of our daughter.'

Ignoring the remark, Grace began again.

'I'm sorry, James, but I've gone through so much suffering with my own father that I refuse to stand by and watch you lose touch with your mother. The least we can do is go and visit her, try to make up for things.'

'Her idea of making up for things would entail moving down there,' James said bitterly. 'And I have no intention of doing that.'

'At least go and visit her.'

'Did you ever fancy Graham Seaton after we were married?'

Disconsolately, Grace slumped in the chair. 'No, I bloody didn't.'

'He can hardly take his eyes off you.'

'I was never interested in anyone but you.' She raised her eyes to his. 'You're not being fair, James. I've given you no cause.'

She glanced over at him, saw the remorse on his face, the desperation in his eyes; and, fleetingly, Grace suffered a shiver of shame.

'I'm sorry,' James said. 'Can we forget all this nonsense?'

'Of course we can,' she smiled, reaching for his hand.

*

Harry lay awake listening to Beth's regular breathing. The street lamp shone across the bed, lighting the blonde of her hair until it appeared white.

He had a brief image of their old age together: two elderly people with...

He paused in his reverie. Would they have kids? If he left it to Beth he suspected not; but he was beginning to imagine life with a son; the opportunity to make amends for his own parents.

It was a disturbing idea: in his immediate circle of family and friends there were numerous instances of broken or fragile homes. As a boy, he had imagined he was the only child to suffer the trauma of being cared for by aunts and uncles; and yet, Grace Blake had also been forced to defend her fatherless state; as had Harry's half-brother; the nameless boy who, through no fault of his own, had been the result of an irresponsible woman's whim.

The clock in the hall struck three. Harry rolled over and squeezed his eyes tightly shut.

As he prepared to drift off, he was thinking of Grace; and how one glance from her could take his mind off everything else.

Chapter Fifteen

Beth was ten minutes late. She flew into the outer office and apologised to Marjory, who waved it away with a flutter of her hand.

'Don't you dare apologise, my dear, May I remind you how many nights you stay on after I've slunk off?'

'You don't 'slink off',' Beth laughed, trying to get her breath back after the dash across busy streets. 'Besides, he couldn't manage without us, so just remember that.'

'Have you noticed he's in a bad mood these days?'

Beth stopped on her way to her office. 'No, I can't say I have.'

Marjory pursed her lips together before lowering her voice. 'I know why.'

'Should you be telling me?'

'Girl trouble,' Marjory pronounced with a nod. 'I've seen it before, many times before.'

'How can you tell?'

'Oh, he signs letters without reading them, mopes around staring into space, and even made me a coffee the other day.'

Beth laughed. 'Is that so unusual?'

'Has he ever made one for you?'

'Well, no.'

'He will, dear, mark my words. Then you'll know I'm right.'

'Does he have a girlfriend?' Beth asked, a tiny sliver of jealousy lurking at the back of her mind.

'Sofia, her name is. With an 'f', after the film star perhaps.'

'Goodness, is she exotic then?'

'As exotic as you *can* be coming from Bridge of Earn,' Marjory said with amusement. 'Her mother's a nurse at the hospital, father's the manager of a shop in Perth somewhere. Most exotic,' she added with wide eyes.

'Has he known her long?'

'Over a year now, but presumably she's giving him what he wants so there's no need to marry her.'

Despite her relaxed friendship with Marjory Wilson, Beth was surprised at the woman's sentiment. It reminded her of what her mother always said about this generation assuming it had been the first at everything.

'You sound just like my mother,' Beth said with a smile. 'You and she would get on like a house on fire.'

'She's a lucky lady to have you as a daughter.'

'Try telling her that,' Beth retorted, opening her office door. 'You didn't know me when I was a grotty teenager.'

'Grotty? That's a new one on me, I must write it down and...' Marjory stopped, for the front door had slammed, announcing the arrival of their boss.

Quickly, Beth slipped into her office and closed the door, grateful that the conversation about Sofia had been curtailed: the idea of Charlie Webster in a clinch with someone was almost as painful as the ones she had about Harry and Annie Kerr.

No sooner had she sat behind her desk than there was a knock at the door and she knew it was Charlie. With some amusement, she waited for him to bring the coffee in.

'Beth, can I interrupt you?'

'Yeah, sure, come in.'

Each time she saw the man she felt the same tremor of something she should resist, the mental goose pimples that triggered off the racing pulse, that triggered off the other bits that were supposed to be reserved for her husband. Beth often wondered just how long she could endure seeing him every day.

'I've a favour to ask,' Charlie said immediately, even before he sat down. 'You can say 'no', of course, but I hope you won't.'

'Another client dinner that I have to cop out of?'

'Not exactly, and you didn't cop out. You told me in plenty time and I didn't even have to change the reservation.'

'Something cropped up,' Beth said. 'I was…'

Charlie held up his hand and stopped her. 'You don't have to tell me, Beth, it was fine.'

She wondered if he thought that her decision had had anything to do with Harry dissenting on his wife going out with her boss, and for a moment she contemplated putting him right; but he had moved on now and the chance was gone.

'It is a dinner, and, yes, there are clients,' he was saying, avoiding her eye. 'But it's not in Perth.'

Beth shrugged. 'Well, as long as you're paying for the petrol, why should I mind where it is?'

'It's in Paris.'

Beth stared at him. 'What?'

'You know. Paris, France?'

'Vaguely,' Beth replied sarcastically. 'Why do you have to go over there?"

'Because it's an important client, someone who's too busy to come over here, and I said I'd go.'

'But you can't speak French.'

'That's why I'm asking you,' Charlie said patiently, but Beth could sense his nervousness. 'I'll be up the creek without a paddle if you say 'no', but I realise how awkward it might be, your husband and everything.'

Had she been in a contrary mood, and had Harry not been such a wonderful husband recently, she might have said 'yes' just to spite him; but she was not in one of her moods; nor did Harry deserve her gallivanting off with a tall dark handsome stranger. The only exciting element would be Paris, but she could always take Harry there for their fifth wedding anniversary.

'If I refused it wouldn't have anything to do with Harry, but I don't think I…'

Again, Charlie held up his hand. 'Stop right there. Just promise me you'll think about it, give it some serious thought?'

'I can't promise any…'

'Please, just think about it for a few weeks?' he asked her and she was glad she was married to a man who never grovelled.

'All right,' she said to appease him. 'I'll think about it.'

'That's all I ask,' he said, satisfied. 'It's not for another month yet, so there's plenty time.'

After he had gone, Beth sat looking out of the window, wishing he had accepted her refusal right at the start; for she knew she could never go to Paris – the city for lovers, no less – with Charlie Webster.

'That, my dear,' she told herself, 'is a trap for beginners, so just banish it from your mind.'

*

Grace pulled into Molly's driveway and switched off the ignition. She sat for a moment, wondering how she could possibly get through the next half hour, knowing as she did the full story. She had poured scorn on it at first, hearing it put so bluntly by Lily Morris, who, Grace had to bear in mind, was not enamoured of Molly anyway; but when she also heard it from Sally herself, not to mention Lucy Webster of all people – never a woman to carry idle gossip – Grace had bowed to the inevitable. Her best friend had been – She stopped short of forming the words, even in her head.

'Come in,' sang out her friend's voice and Grace went through the vestibule into the kitchen. 'You must have smelt the coffee, it's just ready.'

Now that Grace was here, about to face Molly, the notion of providing a shoulder to cry on was losing its appeal. She knew her friend's frailties, her predisposition for flirting and even for two-timing her steady boyfriend, and she also knew that views as old-fashioned as her grandfather's were out-dated. Grace felt she should be more broad-minded; yet could think of no defence for hurting Sally in such a manner. Not only might it break up her marriage, but also it took away the woman's dignity, emblazoning her private life on every billboard from here to the borders of Perthshire.

'I've left the packet of biscuits at home,' Grace said now, hovering on the threshold, her first sign of nerves and something Molly would notice.

'Oh, it doesn't matter,' Molly laughed happily, too happily for Grace's liking. 'I have dozens in the cupboard.' She glanced at her friend. 'Will I bring your coffee over there, or do you intend to sit down?'

'Of course I'll sit down. I was just getting my breath back.'

'Did you walk up then?'

'No, but I've been busy in the house.'

'Now I know you're kidding,' Molly said, without a trace of fun. 'You hate housework, almost as much as Charlotte did.'

'Beth's the same unfortunately. I seem to have passed it on to her.'

'Oh, she and Harry have enough money to hire a cleaner. No need for her to get her hands dirty.'

Bearing in mind the sensitivity of her visit, Grace tried not to take exception to Molly's tone. She went over to the coffee machine and helped herself to a cup of coffee that she knew would be too strong and would result in indigestion for hours.

'There's milk in the jug if you don't want cream.'

'No, I think I'll have cream for a change,' Grace said, another example of her humouring Molly in light of the gossip. 'So,' she smiled as she took the chair opposite her friend. 'What did you want to talk to me about?'

'You know damn fine,' Molly responded irritably. 'Even you must have heard the tittle-tattle.'

'I didn't believe it.'

'Which means you do now obviously,' Molly pointed out abruptly.

Grace frowned. 'Molly, for Heaven's sake, can we not have a grown-up chat about this, at our age?' She spoke with more confidence than she felt, but her companion cast her an apologetic smile and shook her head.

'Sorry, dear, force of habit over the past few weeks.' Molly sighed and slouched back in her chair. 'I don't know what on earth I was thinking of,' she confessed, much to Grace's surprise, for she had heard from Lily and Lucy that Molly had brazened it out, laying the blame solely on Sally for not being able to keep her husband happy.

'You mean you're sorry for it?' Grace asked tentatively.

'What do you think?'

'Well, I don't know, but I like to think you are.'

'Of course I am,' Molly tutted impatiently, lifting her cup but not drinking. 'But it's George I feel sorry for, not her.'

'George? Surely he knew what he doing?'

'Yes, he did, and, contrary to popular belief, it was his idea, not mine.'

Grace was obliged to smile and nod, but from previous experience, she doubted it; besides, George was the canniest of men, not likely to be looking for trouble.

'What about Derek? How did he take it?'

'Oh, he wasn't bothered,' Molly said bitterly. 'As long as the food's on the table the moment he sits down, and as long as he can clamber on top of...'

'Molly, please, I hate to see you like this.'

'Well, they're all the same, aren't they?' She leaned forward confidentially, although they were alone in the house, 'You know what he said when I told him?'

'It's none of my business, Molly, so, no, I don't.'

'Too bad, I'm about to tell you,' came the surly reply. 'He said 'For God's sake, don't leave me, I wouldn't know what to do.' Can you believe that? He couldn't have cared less about what I did. He was more concerned about having to look after himself.' She sat back in her chair once more and withdrew a handkerchief from her pocket. 'After all these years, you'd think he'd be jealous. Just goes to show you he probably never loved me at all.'

'Now you're being silly,' Grace sighed. 'He was mad about you, chased you round the whole county to get you to marry him.'

'I wanted to sow my wild oats first,' Molly smiled, her eyebrows rising. 'And I certainly did a lot of that.'

'I thought you told me you'd only had three boyfriends?'

'Oh, don't look so outraged, Grace,' her companion laughed unkindly. 'I'd have had more if I'd had the time.'

If Grace had hoped for the confession of a guilty woman, she was hugely disappointed: not only had Molly not shown much remorse for her present indiscretion, but she was now boasting of her youthful ones as well. Grace had two choices: either she could pretend that she was sympathetic to her friend, or she could tell the truth. Before she had decided which it would be, Molly spoke again.

'I suppose you think you can judge me.'

Grace thought she had misheard. 'Sorry?'

'I suppose you've never been unfaithful to James?' Molly asked, her tone the most unfriendly that Grace had ever heard.

'No, of course not, but I certainly wouldn't judge you, Molly,' she replied angrily. 'I didn't come here to give you lines and make you stand in a corner all day.'

Molly laughed then and leaned across the table to touch Grace's hand.

'Just as well. I dread to think what you'd make me write.'

They sat in silence for a few moments, during which Grace was planning her departure. She had come with the intention of lending support to a friend she had hoped would be remorseful, but Molly's attitude was anything but.

'You know that James once made a pass at me?' she heard Molly say now.

'What?'

It was ludicrous of course, but Grace still suffered from a swift tingle of jealousy, although she had seen her husband's reaction to Molly with her own eyes.

'Yes, Christmas Eve 1947.'

Grace's heart skipped a beat, for she had no knowledge of how James had spent that night, other than with a few of his regiment pals, which was what he had told her.

'He was with Beth and me that night,' she smiled now, raising her cup and tasting the acrid strength of the coffee.

'Ah, not the whole night,' Molly said with glee. 'He was in Perth, at Martha's parents' hotel. I should know, he danced with me a couple of times.'

Grace shrugged but her mind was darting ahead.

'He was a grown man,' she smiled. 'He could do as he pleased. Besides, I was too busy looking after Beth that winter to worry about where James was.'

Molly sighed and the hostility in her features seemed to dissipate with the outward breath, exchanging harshness for contrition.

'Oh, James may have danced with me, ' she said quietly. 'But it was you he spoke about the whole time.'

'I suppose I should be grateful.'

'He was crazy about you. He was the only man I couldn't prise off a woman,' Molly added boastfully.

'I came along to see how you were,' Grace told her companion briskly. 'To let you know that it doesn't matter to me how much gossip there is about you, that we're still friends.'

The effect on Molly was instant: she grabbed Grace's hand and squeezed it tightly, the smile on her face genuine.

'I know and I'm grateful, Grace, really I am. I'm not the hard bitch they make me out to be, you know. I hope you realise that.'

'Of course I do,' Grace lied, returning the smile. 'And so do a lot of other people in the village,' she added magnanimously, much to her friend's amusement.

'Now I know you're joking. No, I'll be branded as a hussy until Kingdom come and Hell mend me, as Sandy Shepherd would have said, the old fool.'

'He wasn't a...'

'Aye, he was, and you know he was.' Molly stood up and pushed her chair in.

As they walked out into the balminess of a summer's day, Grace's heart was heavy: her intention to help Molly come to terms with her infidelity had somehow culminated in failure.

'Thanks for popping in,' Molly said, linking arms with Grace on the driveway. 'I don't know what I'd do without you, you're a real friend.'

'I didn't do anything,'

'Yes you did, and I'm grateful. Now,' she said more briskly. 'Mind that gatepost on the way out, it's in the wrong place altogether.'

*

Harry was walking home for lunch when he saw her: he had known it was Grace, even from this distance, and, spirits soaring, he ran to catch up with her. When she turned to look at him, however, he was shocked to see the misery in her eyes.

'Harry! What on earth are you doing here?'

'I thought you'd be more pleased to see me,' he joked, and she forced a smile.

'I'm delighted to see you, silly boy. Are you off home?'

'For lunch, yes, and now you'll join me.'

'I'm not sure,' she started to say.

'Well I am. Take my arm, I'll escort you.'

Without a murmur, she walked alongside, her hand resting on his arm, her gaze straight ahead. He glanced down at her, for the first time ever struggling to think of something to say.

'You're wondering why I'm in Perth,' she said as they walked by the river.

'No, I wasn't actually, I was thinking how unhappy you look.'

He felt her hand stiffen, heard the involuntary intake of her breath, and for a moment he imagined that Thomas Blake had been pestering her again.

'I went to see Molly this morning.'

'And that's why you're unhappy?'

'Yes.' She turned her face to him and he sensed she was telling the truth. 'She's been in a spot of bother.'

'Don't tell me,' Harry smiled, aware that he was treading dangerous ground. 'She's been caught in flagrante with the postman.'

Grace stopped walking and stared at him. 'How could you know that?'

Harry shook his head. 'I didn't, of course, just a lucky guess where that woman's concerned.'

She withdrew her arm from his and stood with her back to the river, leaning on the rail and looking at him closely.

'It's the first time she's ever done that sort of thing,' she said defensively and he was reminded of Beth's fruitless support for Annie Kerr.

'No, I suspect it's the first time she's been found out,' Harry said quietly, anticipating her anger but no longer willing to keep his opinion to himself as to the suitability of such a friend.

'That's a horrible thing to say,' Grace frowned. 'And probably unfounded.' He smiled to himself, for she had said 'probably'. 'Besides, she's been a good friend to me over the years, despite what you all think.'

'Come on,' he said diplomatically, avoiding an outright lie for the time being. 'Let's go to McEwens and have lunch, save me from spreading sandwiches.'

'Is Beth at home?'

'No, she stays in the office most days, with Marjory, her new pal. I call it the witches' coven and I'm going to suggest to my own secretary that she join.'

They sat by a window, Harry giving Grace the choice of seat. For the first few minutes she gazed at the street below, saying nothing, and he found it perturbing, not characteristic of a woman who spent her entire life pandering to everyone else; but he perused the menu and waited for her to speak.

'It came as a shock to me,' she said eventually, still studying the street below. 'I'd no idea that she could even contemplate such a thing.' She turned at the last moment and frowned at him. 'I got the impression that it didn't surprise you.'

'It didn't.'

'Why not?'

'Because she's made several passes at me, all harmless no doubt, but not very elegant for a woman her age.'

There was not the surprise on her face that he envisaged and it seemed to him that Molly's discreet overtures towards him had not passed unnoticed.

'I've seen her chatting to you,' Grace said pensively. 'But are you sure she was making a pass at you?'

'Trust me,' Harry laughed. 'She was.'

'Then I apologise for her, she doesn't mean anything by it.'

'It's not that I mind being appreciated by the opposite sex,' he quipped, noting her flinch at the word. 'But in Molly's case, I'm afraid she's not the most decorous of ladies.'

'Most people like her,' Grace lied, mostly in defence of a friend she knew was not worthy of defending in this instance.

The waitress interrupted them and wrote down the order, all the time glancing at Harry as she hovered at their table. When she had gone, Grace spoke again and what she said took him completely by surprise.

'I'd like to confide in you, Harry, but I don't know how to do that anymore, not since my mother died. I could tell her anything, you know,' she smiled. 'There was nothing we didn't discuss.'

'Except your father,' he reminded her cruelly and silence presided for what felt like an hour.

'You're right,' she said eventually. 'It was the only thing.'

'They weren't fair to you, Grace, none of them, not even your mother.'

Her eyes flashed anger for a brief second and then she sighed, shook her head. 'Don't you think I know that?'

'If they'd told you the truth at the beginning, you'd never have been hurt the way you were.'

'I don't even know the truth yet, at least, not the whole truth.'

'I wish you'd confide in me,' Harry said suddenly. 'I would never take advantage of anything you told me, you must know that.'

'To be honest, is there anything left to tell?' she asked, but he knew by her expression that she thought there might be.

'There's the letter from Helen,' she told him, and he saw the green eyes flinch.

'Is that what it is you want to confide in me?'

Grace nodded. 'But it's such a big step. I'm not sure I can do that to Beth. I know I'm justified in doing it, but ....'

Harry changed the subject. 'By the way, Beth's been invited to Paris.'

'Paris? By whom?'

'By her boss, Charlie Webster. She phoned me this morning.'

'Do you think that's a good idea?'

'She won't go. Unless...' A suggestion was forming in Harry's head, and it was either brilliant or ridiculous, depending on how she reacted.

'Unless what?'

'Unless you go with her.'

She burst out laughing and was obliged to glance apologetically at fellow diners. 'Good Heavens, Harry, I could never go to Paris.'

'Why not? Beth would love it, I know she would.'

'But she'd be working.'

'Only in the evenings when they took clients to dinner. You and she could wander around the city all day, buying expensive things and drinking Pernod.'

She laughed again and shook her head, but he could see that she was not dismissing the idea out of hand. There was a flicker of interest when she spoke.

'But what would James say? I've been on at him to go to England at the end of August. We can't afford two holidays.'

'Beth says he's not keen to go.'

Grace stared at him. 'What? She said that?'

'Yes, she told me that James doesn't feel he's back to normal yet.'

She relaxed at that and he suspected there were more significant reasons.

'Ah, yes, it's true,' she said cautiously. 'He's not a hundred per cent yet.'

'So, in all probability you won't be going this year, so why not go with Beth to Paris, have the time of your lives?'

'Alice said she might...'

'Might's not strong enough,' he joked, not surprised when she picked up the pun immediately.

The waitress arrived with their order and conversation was postponed; but Harry was satisfied on two accounts: firstly, Grace had not been averse to going to Paris, but, more importantly, she had shown signs of wanting to confide in him. He smiled across at her and prepared to pour out the coffee.

'When I saw you in the street,' he began, glancing at her as he handed her the cup. 'I thought you were unhappy because your father had been in contact again.'

She suffered an immediate shiver of fear, so obvious and instantaneous that Harry

252

imagined his assumption to be correct. Her words, however, contradicted the reaction.

'No, he hasn't. Besides, he wouldn't dare to contact me. It would probably be Beth.'

He heard the disappointment in her voice and was about to reassure her on that account when she added quickly:

'You didn't tell her, did you, that it upset me?'

'No, of course not. I told you, Grace, that I would never take advantage of anything you should confide in me.'

'I wonder why she's holding back now, from seeing him, I mean.'

'She said it was because of James, that she thought he didn't approve.'

'He never mentioned it to me, but I knew that something had passed between them.' She gave a wry smile. 'Two of a kind, father and daughter.'

'Like my mother and me,' Harry said, looking at her over the rim of his cup.

'I don't know her, of course.'

'I doubt if you'd want to.' He smiled across at her. 'She's even more of a hussy than Molly.'

'I'm sure you're wrong,' Grace said half-heartedly.

'I could always hear them shouting at each other from my bedroom door.'

'Oh, Harry, I'm so sorry. It must have...'

'Sshh,' he smiled, laying a finger to his lips. 'You really must stop taking the blame for absolutely everything, Grace. There was no love lost between the two of them, nothing much to spoil.'

'It's horrible, that you should have suffered so much.'

She sighed and reached over to cover his hand with hers. Harry felt a frisson of something he was powerless to resist.

*

Thomas Blake strode along the main street of Bridgend towards the Isle of Skye Hotel. He was in jaunty mood, hailing passers-by with a hearty greeting, albeit receiving several strange glances in return.

The Hotel loomed. For a moment, Thomas slowed his step and listed his thoughts in order of importance. Whatever he achieved in the next hour, it would be attributable to his charm alone. He studied his reflection in a shop window, pretending to examine the goods; decided that no woman in her right mind could resist him, and walked briskly on.

Chapter Sixteen

During the following weeks, events moved so quickly for Grace that she hardly knew whether she was coming or going. One thing was clear, however: not only were she and Beth planning their trip to Paris, but also Alice was to join them before flying to Scotland to spend a fortnight there.

The first inkling of what was to come had been contained in Alice's reply when she had learnt of her friend's imminent holiday in France. Alice had latched on to the Paris idea with an enthusiasm that demonstrated to Grace that her old friend had lost nothing of her joie de vivre, an appropriate term, as Beth had pointed out.

'Grace, my dearest friend, isn't this just fate lending a hand? I'm so excited to be seeing you again, and Beth, of course, who was only six the last time I saw her. I can hardly wait, we're going to have so much fun!!!' And in Paris too? Can it get any better???'

Thereafter, in a whirlwind of days, Beth and Alice had assumed control of all arrangements, leaving Grace with nothing to do except pack.

At James's insistence, she and Beth had been dispatched to Edinburgh to buy a new set of clothes for the trip, because, as he had been quick to point out:

'I want you to have the best time you've ever had, Grace.'

'But that won't depend on what I'm wearing,' she protested, ever mindful of the cost.

'In Paris?' he had laughed. 'Of course it does. Here,' he smiled, pressing a wad of bills into her hand. 'Take this and don't come back with change.'

Now, as she folded crisp new blouses and summer skirts into the new case, Grace could hardly believe what was happening. How could she have allowed herself to be carried along so readily?

'Oh, Mum!' Beth had cried, throwing her arms around her mother in a fearsome hug. 'Thank you, thank you! It means I won't have to worry now.'

Grace had given her daughter a critical stare, at which Beth had shrugged sheepishly: 'Well, you know what I mean.'

'Charlie Webster?'

'I suppose.'

'Beth, dear,' Grace had said sadly. 'Perhaps you should reconsider…'

'Don't worry, Mum,' Beth laughed, patting her mother's arm in the manner of an elderly relative. 'I can handle it.'

'But you should be enjoying your job, darling, not 'handling' it.'

'I'll think about it,' Beth had said, but it was obvious she was only placating her mother.

Grace wandered to the bedroom window and watched the antics of the birds on the feeders. In three days' time, she would be miles away, in a strange country, meeting strange people, not understanding the language. She turned back into the room and regarded her reflection: was she doomed to be such a pessimist all her days?

'Honestly, pet,' she could almost hear her mother say. 'You'll really have to stop all this doom and gloom nonsense.'

Grace peered at her expression. It was perfectly true: she could never recall a time when her face was wreathed in a smile. She pursed her lips and shook her head. Perhaps gay Par-ee would banish her blues…

She turned to go downstairs and was beset by a troubling thought: what a pity that

Harry was not going with them.

*

Charlie Webster finished off the work on his desk and rang through to Beth's office. She took an age to pick up and he was just wondering if she had left early when, suddenly, her voice came on the line and he stuttered the first few words, cursing himself for being such an idiot.

'Sorry?' she asked politely. 'I missed that.'

Of course she had missed it because he was gibbering like a damned monkey.

'Beg pardon, I was eating a Mars Bar, couldn't get the words out. I was asking if you're all fixed for the trip.'

'Yeah, all fixed,' she said, followed by a silence.

'Good, that's good, and your mother?' he added, regretting his hurried agreement to allow the woman to join them, although without her it would have been curtains to the trip at all; so he should be grateful.

'Oh, Mum's the organised type, had her case packed last week.'

Charlie was none the wiser if she were serious or not. He had known her for over three years – albeit, not intimately – and he was no further forward in discerning her nature. Sometimes she looked at him as if he had just landed from outer space.

'You're joking, right?' he asked.

'No, honestly, she's all packed, can hardly wait. She's dying to see Alice, of course,' she added and he was puzzled.

'Alice?'

'Yes, her pal from America.'

'America?' he heard himself echo like the proverbial Swiss mountain.

'Didn't I tell you?'

'Er...don't think so.'

'She's coming back to Scotland with us for a holiday. You'll like her, she sounds great fun.'

'I look forward to it,' Charlie forced himself to say, although he was mystified.

'Is there anything you need, anything I can do?'

'Nope, it's all in the bag,' she laughed and he could visualise the smile, the generous mouth, the slim fingers sweeping back the blonde hair. How would he survive five days – and six nights – in the same city as this female; Paris especially?

'So,' he said, a fleeting vision of her in his bed. 'I'll see you on Sunday, D-Day, as it were, for Departure.'

She bade him goodbye and hung up. Charlie replaced the receiver with a long sigh and sat with his head in his hands for a few minutes, waiting until she left the office so that he could avoid her on the stairs and omit his bumbling nincompoop act.

Never before had he wanted to impress a girl so badly; and, perversely, never before had he bungled it quite so adeptly. She must think him an utter fool.

*

After ten minutes, Beth locked her desk and went into the outer office. She tiptoed across the tiled vestibule, trying not to make a sound, trying not to let him know she was on her way out and have to meet him on the stairs. She had never been so guileless in front of a man before, not even Harry, and it seemed to get worse instead of better. By now, he must be thinking her a complete idiot.

As she walked briskly down the street she caught sight of a familiar figure and her

255

heart stopped: it was her grandfather and he was waiting for her.

*

Thomas had been standing at the corner since three, never knowing from one day to the next when she would leave the office. From experience he gathered that it was never before three but could be any time from then until five thirty. His luck was in today, for he had only had to hang around for half an hour.

When she saw him she stopped walking and he contemplated moving to meet her, but thought it might appear threatening, so he stood where he was.

At last, she resumed her step and headed towards him, the blonde hair bobbing on her shoulders, the mini-skirted legs striding out, looking for all the world like a model on the cover of Vogue and not like one of the Shepherd clan.

As a man he might have admired the effect, but as her grandfather he condemned the skirt as too short.

'Are you following me?' was the greeting she awarded him.

'Hardly, but I've been waiting for you, yes.'

'Why?'

'I don't know really,' he said, injecting a careful measure of wistfulness into his tone. 'I just feel you're my only hope to get at the truth.'

He may not know everything about her but he did know her fixation with the truth, for every second word to him during their initial encounter had been 'truth'; and he had taken advantage of it. It was either that or kiss goodbye to Charlotte's daughter forever; not to mention the memories and photographs that he would never share. It still pained him to accept his ignorance of the time and place of Charlotte's death.

'Make it quick,' the girl said brusquely, glancing around as if she expected to be spotted by someone she knew.

'Here,' Thomas said, proffering a letter. 'I'd like you to read this one, forgot all about it, but it's important.'

The girl turned the letter over in her hand. 'It can't be all that important,' she said sardonically, 'if you forgot all about it.' She looked at him, the green eyes hostile and Thomas was startled by the change in her.

'I know, and I'm sorry,' he grovelled. 'But I'd still like you to read it. Please.'

She shrugged. 'O.K., I'll read it when I'm away.'

He saw her flinch, knew that she had let it slip and was annoyed at herself.

'You're going on holiday?'

'No, it's with my job actually. I'll be working.'

'Ah, not so exciting then,' Thomas smiled, thinking this encounter such an uphill struggle.

'I have to go now,' the girl told him, already walking off.

'See you when you get back,' he called after her, but she made no sign of having heard him.

He stood for a moment watching her hair flouncing around her shoulders and then he turned and strode off in the opposite direction. It was only four; he might call Daphne, take her out for tea, spend time with someone he could impress.

*

Lucy Webster walked past the Melville's cottage but paused to admire the flowers James had planted recently. She found him the kindest, gentlest man she had met in the area, far too kind and gentle for this village, she often thought, with its inference that unless you lived in the place for a hundred years you were still an incomer; and even then, unless you were Scottish through and through, they continued to view you with suspicion.

Being English herself, Lucy had endured her fair share of bigotry, which was why she felt so drawn to James Melville: a fellow outcast.

She was about to move on when there was a tap on the window, and it was Grace beckoning her in.

'I hope you weren't intending to walk past,' Grace smiled, wagging a finger at Lucy.

'I wasn't sure if you'd be in.'

'That's a lame one, if ever I heard one, now come on in and help me demolish a cream cake or two.'

'You'll be excited about the holiday,' Lucy said as she sat down in the kitchen and Grace dashed around preparing the afternoon tea.

'I don't know if I did the right thing,' she was astonished to hear Grace say.

'What on earth do you mean? Of course you've done the right thing. You'll have a wonderful time with your American friend.'

'I expect I will,' Grace said with a brief, nervous smile. 'But I'll be worried about James, him not being quite back to normal and just back to work again.'

'But your son-in-law will keep an eye on him, surely?'

Grace turned to look at her and Lucy wondered if she had said something wrong.

'Yes, of course he will. Did James tell you that?'

'Yes, he did, as a matter of fact,' she said lightly. 'I stopped to speak to him the day he was planting out the front garden.'

'Ah, yes, I thought it would be too much for him, but he insisted.'

'He told me about Beth's husband, that he would pop out most days when you were away.'

'Dear Harry,' Grace smiled, setting down the tray between them. 'I have no idea what I'd do without him.'

'Charlie's rather jealous of him.' Lucy said before she could stop herself.

Grace's eyebrows rose. 'Is he?'

'He's an ardent admirer of your daughter,' Lucy smiled. 'Strictly above board, you understand, but he's quite bowled over by her.'

'Thank Heavens we're old and sensible,' Grace laughed, and yet, to Lucy, her tone was doubtful. 'I couldn't go through all of that again.'

'Were you young and foolish?'

It was simply something she would have said to make conversation, but it had an extraordinary effect on her companion. Grace blushed.

'Yes, weren't we all?' she asked, her attention on the cake in front of her.

'I certainly was. In fact, when I look back, how silly I must have been.'

'Beth's very happy working for Charlie,' Grace said, perhaps to change the subject. 'She loves it there. In fact,' she raised her eyes to Lucy's. 'I'll always be grateful that you mentioned it to me.'

'I was delighted to help. Besides, don't forget it was to Charlie's advantage too. His French is lamentable, you know. I wonder why I spent so much money on his education.'

Inwardly, Lucy cringed, for it was an oblique reminder of the difference in their situations: Charlie Webster educated at private school, Beth at the local secondary school. Oddly enough, Lucy pondered, it was the girl's education that was the more significant with regard to Charlie's work. It was the girl who was pulling in clients because of her language skills and business acumen.

'I'm so proud of Beth,' Grace was saying now, as if reading her friend's mind. 'She was such a wayward teenager that I despaired of her ever amounting to anything, and here she is now, quite a woman of the world, holding her own in situations that would terrify me.'

'And Frank?' Lucy felt obliged to ask, for, as usual, the boy was being left out. 'I heard he'd become engaged a few months ago.'

'Yes, to Emily, a lovely girl. She and Beth are firm friends already.'

'Emily McKay, isn't it?'

'Yes, do you know her?'

'I know her cousin,' Lucy said, wondering at the sudden frown on Grace's brow. 'He lives next to us in Perth. Not that I know him, but we often nod over the hedge.'

'Isn't it a small world?' Grace smiled, fiddling with her napkin, leading Lucy to believe she might be over-staying her welcome.

'Well, I should be going.'

'Oh, not so soon, surely?' Grace asked with genuine disappointment. 'I was hoping we could sit in the garden for a time. James is out there, pruning and planting. He'd not be pleased if I let you go without saying 'hello' to him.'

'Of course I'll go and see him,' she smiled. 'I want to ask him what these flowers are in the front garden.'

'They're from seeds he collected years ago,' Grace told her as they stood up. 'I'm sure he'd be delighted to share them with you. He probably smuggled them over the Scottish border,' she added with a mischievous grin.

Outside, James was leaning on his spade but had obviously been hard at work, evidence of freshly dug flowerbeds in almost every section of the garden. At sight of Lucy he waved and straightened up, his hands on the small of his back as if to ease aching muscles.

'You've arrived just in time,' he told the two women, but his glance was directed more at Grace. 'I was trying to find an excuse to stop.'

'You don't need an excuse,' Grace told him predictably, taking the spade and holding it fast. 'That's enough for one day, James Melville, unless you want to end up in PRI again?'

'No thanks,' he smiled, this time at Lucy. 'The Matron in that place would make a fine prisoner warder.'

Grace laughed. 'She certainly made sure you did what you were told. I think she deserved a medal.'

'You look fit as a fiddle,' Lucy said. 'And Grace was telling me you're back to work.'

'I could have been back weeks ago,' James scoffed. 'But the doctor seemed to think I was a weakling.'

'You know that's nonsense,' Grace said pleasantly, with a cursory glance at Lucy. 'If he'd left it up to you, you'd have gone straight to work from the hospital, not even stopping to change out of your pyjamas.'

James laughed to Lucy, inclining his head towards his wife.

'You see what I've to put up with? Grace is just the one to keep me right.'

'You've got some English flower seeds, Grace was telling me?'

'Yes, do you want some?' James volunteered eagerly. 'To remind you of an English meadow?'

'I'd love them, if the flowers in your front garden are the result.'

'I'll look them out for you.'

'Thank you, I could pick them up next time I was passing.'

'Why don't you come down when I'm away?' came the unexpected suggestion from Grace.

Lucy and James both turned and looked at her, but it was Lucy who responded first.

'No, I don't think that would be quite the done thing,' she laughed. 'Can you imagine what the villagers would say?'

'Oh, they'll say it anyway,' Grace retorted, somewhat bitterly. 'What haven't they said about James and me for the past twenty-five years?'

'Grace, dearest,' James began, but she waved off his attempt to placate her.

'So, you'll come down when I'm away,' she insisted to Lucy. 'Keep an eye on him, make sure he's not doing too much?'

'Well, if...?' Lucy looked at James who appeared to be in agreement.

'In fact,' he said, winking at her. 'I can walk you home afterwards and really set the tongues wagging.'

*

Harry heard the telephone ring in the hall but left it for Beth to answer. It was invariably Annie Kerr, whining and whingeing about the state of her love life, or lack of it, since the Prince of Darkness had run off to seek out pastures new; pastures that presumably were free of whining, whingeing females. Harry wondered how on earth the man had stood it for as long as he had.

'That was Annie,' Beth told him on her way back to the kitchen. 'She's coming round later.'

'Bloody hell!'

'Harry,' she said, her tone heavy with censure. 'Please be nice to her, she's going through a miserable time.'

'No, I'm not going to be nice to her,' he snapped, temper rising. 'She's a pain in the arse and you can see her yourself. I'm going out.'

'Out? Where out?'

'Anywhere out,' Harry frowned. 'If you want to listen to her weeping and wailing, be my guest, but my shoulder isn't water-proof, so I'm going out.'

'She and I could go out then,' Beth suggested magnanimously, he thought. 'You can stay here, I don't mind.'

'She'll only get pissed and you'll not be able to carry her home,' he said unkindly, at which Beth sighed and darted him a disapproving glance.

'She won't, and I won't have to.'

'Well, don't phone me and tell me she's flat on her face then, because I refuse to help her.'

'But you wouldn't refuse to help me, would you?' she asked sweetly.

'I might.'

'No, you wouldn't, 'cos you love me,' Beth twittered, coming over and planting a kiss on his cheek. 'How will you manage without me for a week?'

'It's only five days, I think I'll be O.K.'

Beth knelt down in front of him, her hands wandering around his waist.

'Are you sure?'

He laughed and slapped her hands away. 'Yes, I'm sure, you hussy, now go and make the tea, for Heaven's sake.'

'You'll be sorry, Gillespie, mark my words. Hey,' Beth said suddenly, pausing at the door. 'Don't' forget to check on Dad when we're gone.'

'I've already planned to go out twice, sweetheart,' Harry said patiently. 'Does that meet with your approval?'

She grinned. 'Yup, that's fine. Tea's in twenty minutes. Switch the news on, see if anything's happened.'

Harry sat thinking about Annie Kerr. For a brief moment, he decided that what the girl needed was a good slap. With a sigh of exasperation mingled with guilt, he stood up and switched on the television.

*

Thomas was in two minds: should he kiss Daphne goodnight, or should he simply carry on the tradition of squeezing her hand and promising to see her in a few days?

'I've had a lovely evening, Thomas. In fact, I've had a lovely few months, thanks to you.'

He smiled his most beneficent smile at her and decided that he would kiss her.

'Would you mind terribly if I kissed you goodnight, Daphne?'

She flushed bright pink, which often suited women, but not Daphne, with her fair skin that sprouted blotches at the slightest provocation.

'Well, of course not, Thomas,' she simpered, lowering her eyes in what she must have considered a maidenly gesture.

He leaned over and lightly touched her lips with his, and then stepped back, following his plan; knowing she would be disappointed,

'I'm so glad we bumped into one another that day outside the Isle of Skye,' he told her as she opened the front door. 'I'd have been pretty lonely on my own, in a strange place.'

'You wouldn't have remained lonely for long,' Daphne said, her hand lingering on his arm. 'Some lucky lady would have snapped you up.'

Thomas gave her another of his winning smiles. 'But one did, dear lady, one did, and I'm very glad it was you.'

He stepped into the front garden before he had to endure another bout of simpering, for there was only so much he could take. The main road was still busy, even at this time of night, and he doubted if he could ever live here after the tranquillity of the Hill. As they walked towards the gate and his waiting taxi, Thomas turned to appraise the house, whose value he had estimated to be nigh-on ten thousand; a tidy sum for them to share ultimately, enough for a round-the-world cruise and a rented villa in the South of France; a promising start.

'I love this house,' he lied. 'Such architectural flair, most impressive.'

'Don't you think it's a bit large for a woman on her own?"

He saw the trepidation on her face, wondering if she was exceeding the expectations of such a brief kiss, and he congratulated himself on the perfect execution of his perfect plan.

'Well, I expect it is,' he agreed. 'But if you've lived here for years, it won't be so easy to leave, will it? So many memories for you, my dear, not simply bricks and mortar.'

'Trust you to think of that,' Daphne said with admiration. 'You're the kind of man who's so busy thinking about others, Thomas Blake, that you never have time to think of yourself.'

He shrugged and affected modesty. 'Oh, I wouldn't say that.'

'No, but I would,' she persisted daringly. 'And one day...' She paused, changed her mind, but he knew what she wanted to say and it was too soon; even for him.

'The taxi driver's getting restless,' he smiled. 'Best be on my way.'

'Thank you again, Thomas, it was lovely.'

He slammed the car door shut, gave her a wave and mouthed 'goodnight and thank you' before the driver pulled away and Daphne faded into the distance.

*

260

Beth was sitting up in bed reading *Rebecca* for the fourth time. It was a close-run thing, whether it could be called her favourite book or not, the other ones jostling for top position being *Flight from the Enchantress*, *Madame Bovary* and sometimes, if she wanted a laugh, '*1066 and All That*'.

She heard Harry moving around in the kitchen, opening and closing cupboard doors, making a list of where things were for when she was in Paris, she thought unkindly. So much for her women's lib notions, the child of the sixties, the new-age female who ought to have been running the world but was stuck with shepherd's pie and cleaning out log fires; married to a man who would die rather than wash a dish.

Her mind distracted from the poor heroine's clumsy antics at knocking over a priceless figurine, Beth sighed and closed the book, taking note of the page number, which annoyed Harry who always had to mark his place with a sliver of paper.

'Why can't you remember where you've got to?' she had asked him a long time ago, when she was still getting used to her new husband's foibles.

'If I mark it with a piece of paper I don't have to remember.'

'But remembering is good for your brain cells.'

'Maybe I've got more than you then and don't have to mollycoddle them.'

In the face of his Law degree and the way he was whizzing through the course work, she had desisted from further argument; but it had not changed her mind on the benefit of mental exercises. To that end, she had memorised all her friends' telephone numbers, the doctor's, dentist's, garage, not to mention the library and building society. If she had hoped to impress Harry with it all she was doomed to be disappointed, for he never seemed to notice.

'Oh, good, you're awake,' he said from the doorway. 'Where do you keep the wooden spoons?'

'Won't that be too much sugar in your nightcap?' she smiled sarcastically.

'That's the thing I'll miss most about you next week.'

'Not my talents in the bedroom?'

'Not at all. I can always take cold showers. So, where are they, the spoons?'

'Hanging up above the cooker.'

He gave her a cheeky salute and went back to the kitchen, from whence came the sounds of further door-openings. She slid beneath the covers and wondered if going to Paris was the best idea: leaving Harry Gillespie in the same city as Annie Kerr seemed innocuous enough, given that he disliked the girl; but she did not trust Annie as far as she could throw her, and therein lay the problem.

'How long will you be gone?' Annie had asked casually the day before.

'A couple of days.'

'Oh, I thought it was six.'

'So why ask then?' Beth had retorted sharply and she knew it had been a blunder. Unless she had pleaded with the girl not to sleep with Harry while she was in Paris she could not have made it any clearer.

'You'll have a great time, with your Mum being there,' Annie had smirked, and Beth had read too much into the remark.

'Mum being there is the best bit actually.'

'Not Charlie Webster?'

'Are you mad? He's just my boss, for Heaven's sake, nothing to write home about.'

'He's lovely, wouldn't mind a piece myself.'

'He's available,' Beth said, too quickly. 'If you're at a loose end, that is.'

'I am, but he'll be in Paris with you, won't he?' Annie had smiled, at which Beth had jumped to all the wrong conclusions and they had parted soon after, hardly the best of friends.

'I've brought you a chocolate biscuit,' she heard Harry say beside the bed.

'What?'

'Here, I've gone through Hell and High Water to get it.'

'It was on the table, in the tin. If that's your idea of Hell and High Water...'

'Will you miss me?' he asked as he climbed into bed.

'That's a stupid question, of course I will.'

With difficulty, Beth refrained from asking him the same, for she was still grappling with the Annie problem. She munched the chocolate biscuit, trying to keep the crumbs on the plate.

'I hope Grace has a great time,' Harry said.

Beth looked at him. 'I'll make sure she does.'

'She's not happy these days, have you noticed?'

Even if it were true, it irked her that he should be so concerned with her mother's welfare. At times, he seemed obsessed with Grace Melville.

'Mum's perfectly happy if you must know. She's tired just now, what with the play and the engagement party and the excitement of Paris. She's fine.'

'It's just as well Alice will be there. At least Grace won't be on her own at any time.'

She bristled at that, for it implied she had never given a thought to her mother.

'Don't you think I'd taken that into consideration? If Alice hadn't been going, I'd have turned it down.'

'And regretted it forever.'

Beth glanced at him, discovered he was serious. 'You and I can go to Paris.'

'I know,' Harry shrugged. 'But Grace won't have another chance to go and you're making it possible for her now.'

She bit back a hasty reply, opting for a lie instead. 'Yes, that's the best bit about it.'

'Were you thinking of going for our fifth?'

'Yes, how romantic would that be?'

'Speaking of romance,' Harry smiled. 'Fancy some just now?'

'What, as well as a chocolate biscuit? Is it my birthday already?'

'Play your cards right and you could even get breakfast in bed.'

'Oh, too much! '

As she wrapped her arms around him, Beth found it impossible to dismiss the image of Annie Kerr in this huge bed.

*

Grace lay worrying about the trip. She regretted now having agreed to go, for the whole idea was so out of the ordinary, so complicated, such an unknown situation, that over the previous few days, she had come to dread every aspect of it; even the thought of seeing Alice after all these years. The only compensation was that Alice's husband was not to be there, having broken his ankle in a baseball game, and so Grace would be spared the dilemma of liking him or not liking him, being sympathetic to him or not.

She wanted to come up with a valid reason not to go, but could think of nothing that would avoid her looking like an idiot. Besides, Beth was so looking forward to the excitement of Paris that she could hardly let the girl down at the last minute.

At the back of her mind, in a place she had tried to ignore, was the dreadful, but recurring aspect of leaving Harry and how she would miss him more than James. Before Grace drifted off to sleep, it was her final, guilty, thought.

262

*

Waking in the small hours, Harry rose and wandered into the sitting room. Despite the hour, he poured himself a half measure of gin, splashed some tonic into the glass and sat staring into space. The whole idea of the Paris trip was now upsetting him, being as it was so out of kilter with their normal routine, which he liked, contrary to the assumption that only old fuddy-duddies refused to accept change.

He worried now that Grace would find it all too strange, for she hinted to him on the telephone the previous day about the uncertainty of it all.

'I think it's the language problem,' she had told him. 'I've never been in a place where I won't know what anyone's saying.'

'But most of them speak English,' Harry had countered. 'They'll be only too glad to help you out.'

She had laughed, relaxed a little. 'Anyway, I know I'll feel like a fish out of water, but at least Alice will be the same.'

Harry had had a flash of inspiration then, recalling suddenly her continual efforts to put other's needs before her own.

'Yes, and surely you'll want to help her have a great time?'

'Well, of course.'

'Let's face it, she'll be feeling more of a stranger than you, won't she? I mean, with her recent divorce, not seeing you for years, worrying how you'll react.'

Grace had sighed. 'I hadn't thought of it that way. Of course she'll be the same, worse maybe.' She laughed. 'What would I do without you, Harry? I dread to think. You're such a good friend.'

Harry had spoken quickly, before disappointment at the blandness of 'friend' flooded his mind.

'So, remember, think of poor Alice and how anxious she must be.'

He sat now in the harsh light from the street lamp, reflecting on his advice to her, knowing how it would encourage her to set aside her own concerns. In the recesses of his mind, however, he acknowledged that his problem was not how Grace would cope without him, but how desperately he was going to miss her; more than he would miss Beth. As he dozed off in the chair, it was his last, guilty thought.

Chapter Seventeen

Beth felt a lump in her throat as she watched her mother and Alice greeting one another in the airport concourse. Not only was it touching to see two long-lost friends meeting after almost twenty years, but it was also a poignant reminder to Beth of bygone days; days and events that the two women had lived through; times and memories that were as remote and inaccessible to Beth as the moon.

Alice was not as she had expected: her hair was neatly coiled in a French roll, appropriately named, Beth mused, and her clothes, though sophisticated, were more suitable for a twenty-year-old, unlike Grace Melville who dressed in keeping with her age. Not that Beth would have allowed her mother to leave the house in the guise of a frump – far from it – but she admired the way her mother instinctively knew what was right for her. The sleek, dark green suit with its box pleated skirt and tapered jacket was exactly what Beth would have chosen for her, along with the crisp white blouse, ruffled at the neck and looking as fresh as the moment she had taken it from the wardrobe.

Conscious of Charlie Webster hovering at her elbow, Beth waited until the two friends had exhausted their joyful exclamations before stepping forward and introducing herself.

'But you're so grown up!' Alice cried, much to Beth's embarrassment, considering that her boss was nearby. 'The last time I saw you, you were this high.' Alice indicated the height of her knee and Beth hoped that such reminisces would end before the naked baby on the bearskin rug was mentioned.

Charlie was the epitome of charm, although Best did her best to ignore it. He appeared to be in his element with elderly women and, after only a couple of minutes, Alice was completely under his spell, monopolising him on the way to pick up their hired car, chattering away in her American accent and impressing him with her prowess in French.

'If I'd known you were to be here,' Charlie was saying. 'I wouldn't have twisted Beth's arm to come along.'

Beth felt her mother's cautionary gaze on her and she shrugged, torn between being slighted and relieved to be out of Charlie's spotlight.

'Oh, Beth, it's so good to see Alice again. What a wonderful idea this was.'

'She seems great fun,' Beth felt obliged to say. 'I hope you have the best time ever.'

'And isn't it lucky that she likes Charlie so much?' Grace whispered. 'It means you won't have to fend him off!'

'Mum!' Beth exclaimed, her cheeks belying her outrage. 'What a thing to say!'

'Well,' her mother went on, voice lowered. 'I know you were a bit worried about the situation, so don't deny it.'

'Maybe Alice can act as his interpreter and you and I can paint the town.'

'Not a bad idea, is it?'

Beth grinned. 'I'd spend too much money and Harry would throw me out.'

'I've brought plenty with me, so spend what you like and he'll never know.'

The Penta Hotel, in the heart of La Defense, was fairly luxurious, As soon as the rooms had been allocated – Beth and Grace in one, Alice next door and Charlie safely tucked away on a lower floor – Beth rummaged around until she was satisfied they had everything.

'But it's perfect,' Grace said, for the umpteenth time. 'I've never seen anything quite so grand.'

'Well, I have,' Beth said, trying not to sound smug. 'So I'm just checking.'

'It's lovely,' her mother sighed, sitting on the bed and running her fingers across the bedspread. 'I can't recall the last time I even stayed in a hotel.'

Beth turned to look at her. 'You're not sad, are you, Mum?'

'Goodness no! Whatever made you think that?'

'Something Harry said.'

'I keep forgetting,' Grace said with a frown.

'What?'

'Nothing,' Grace smiled, jumping up and moving over to the television set. 'I wonder if they have 'Z Cars' here?'

Beth burst out laughing. 'I doubt it, unless it's called 'Zee Voitures'.'

'I'm going to enjoy being here with you,' Grace said suddenly. 'It was a good idea after all.'

'You mean you weren't keen?'

Grace gave a rueful smile. 'I was a bit worried.'

'About what?'

'Everything.'

Beth grinned. 'Oh, well, if it's just everything you're worried about, we'll soon have that fixed.'

*

Charlie Webster unpacked his case and tried not to be irritated that he was on a different floor; not that he had any plans to sneak into her room and ravish her during the night – not with her mother in the next bed – but he had a notion to pop in and share a nightcap on their way back from dinner with clients, and that was looking decidedly unlikely with his room down here and hers up there. If he did suggest a nightcap, it would have to be in the bar, hardly conducive to an intimate tête-à-tête. Why had he assumed she would have a room to herself?

He ambled to the window and looked out. How amazing it was, in a place of this size and splendour, to see so many green areas. Trees and more trees met his eye and he marvelled at the Frenchman's ability to include so much nature in the midst of such a cosmopolitan city.

He glanced at his diary and noted the number of Monsieur et Madame Blanc – so much more romantic than 'White' – along with the time of their table reservation in the hotel restaurant. He had three hours until they arrived and no idea how to fill them. Charlie's mind tried to break free of the fantasy of sharing a sunlit walk on the Pont Neuf with Beth before dinner, for if her mother and this Alice had not come along then neither would Beth. He sighed and turned his mind to business, taking out the catalogue he had printed, preparing to read up on the items Monsieur Blanc had listed. At least it would keep his mind off Beth Gillespie.

*

Grace lay in the bubble bath, unable to recall the last time she had enjoyed such luxury. Her gaze fell upon the little box beside her toilet bag, the box James had insisted she take with her; the box containing her pills, out of date by several months but no matter. Should she need them, there they were.

It was the strangest feeling having nothing to do, no one to please, and for the first hour she had revelled in it; but then, when Beth had gone to see if Alice were happy with her room, Grace had found the solitude unsettling, not to mention the slow passage of time compared to home. She glanced at her watch, propped up beside the bath, and saw that she had only spent ten minutes in the bath when it seemed like an hour.

She closed her eyes and sank deeper into the froth, a stray thought of James flitting across her mind, how he was coping without her after eight hours. Harry was on hand, of course, and Lucy Webster, who had appeared thrilled at the idea of popping in to see James.

Grace rejoiced to hear the room door open and then her daughter's voice.

'Have you gone like a prune in there?'

'No, it's lovely. I feel so decadent.'

Beth giggled outside the bathroom door. 'The last person on the planet I'd think of as decadent would be you, Mum.'

'Oh, I've had my moments,' Grace retorted in fun, but then she thought it the silliest thing she could have said, for it inferred behaviour akin to Molly's.

'Really? Well, you know what they say, don't you? 'Still waters run deep'.'

'Is Alice happy enough with the room?' Grace asked, to change the subject.

'Loves it, and so she should, it's a gorgeous hotel, and wait 'til you see the restaurant!'

'Is it expensive, do you think?'

'I thought you said you'd brought plenty money?' Beth laughed.

'I have, but I want to spend it on you, not a plate of snails.'

Beth hooted with laughter and rapped on the bathroom door.

'You'll be glad to know I ordered them 'specially for you tonight, mother.'

'In that case, I'll go and find a chip shop.'

'Not in Paris, you won't. The French are far too sophisticated for that.'

Fifteen minutes later Grace was wrapped in the huge towel, a glass of sherry in front of her, at half past four in the afternoon when, at home, she would be rushing around the kitchen taking care of James's evening meal.

'Well, if I felt decadent in the bubble bath,' she said with amusement. 'I feel a fallen woman now, perfumed to high heaven, with a glass of sherry in my hand.'

'Did you and Alice talk about things?'

'Of course we did. In fact we had quite a laugh one day about …you know.'

'What, sex?' Beth asked in disbelief.

'Yes, and I don't know why you're so surprised.'

'But things were stricter then, weren't they? I mean, didn't you tell me that Grandpa stopped you doing what you wanted?'

'He stopped us doing what was bad for us anyway, which was good. At least we always knew the rules, unlike you lot who don't seem to have any.'

'And whose fault is that?' Beth laughed, waving her glass at Grace. 'You must have allowed us to chuck away the rules then, *you* lot.'

'Not you in particular, dear, your generation.'

'Harry and I have rules.'

Grace looked at her daughter, saw the faint signs of apprehension, heard the slight doubt in Beth's voice.

'You don't have to worry about Harry, darling.'

'I'm not.'

'Yes, you are, I can sense it.'

Beth smiled and shook her head. 'If I ever have a daughter I hope I'm as shrewd with her as you are with me.'

'You will be. I can hardly wait to be a grandmother.'

As she spoke, she waited for the tiny flicker of dissention in Beth's expression; but none came.

'Steady on! Plenty time yet, you know.'

'Don't wait too long, otherwise you'll be too old to wash nappies.'

266

'A thing of the past, mother,' Beth grinned, rising to replenish their glasses. 'I'll be using disposables.'

'Your Dad did yours.'

'For Heaven's sake, don't say that in front of Charlie Webster,' Beth frowned. 'Leave me with some dignity!'

Grace looked at the sherry bottle Beth was proffering. 'Don't you think I've had enough?'

'This is Paris, Mum, of course you haven't had enough. Drink up, then I'll put some makeup on you, give Monsieur Blanc something to look at.'

'But Alice and I won't be...'

'Tonight you will be,' Beth said primly. 'This is more of a social occasion than a business meeting, so hurry up and get your gladrags on. What are you wearing, by the way?'

'I've no idea.' Grace cast a sly glance to her daughter. 'Won't this towel do?'

'The poor guy will have a heart attack! You're right, Mum,' Beth went on seriously. 'About you and me having fun here.'

'Will you speak French with Mr Blanc?'

'Oh no. Only when it turns to business. Now do get out of the toga, Queen Cleopatra and let's go!'

*

Much to Beth's amusement, Monsieur Blanc was captivated by Grace Melville. He bowed, raised her hand to his lips and endowed her with such an appreciative stare that Madame Blanc was obliged to make light of it. As they took their seats, Philippe Blanc ensured he was next to Grace. Alice caught Beth's attention.

'Well,' she whispered in Beth's ear. 'I guess your boss will make a tidy profit with Grace around.'

'She looks so lovely, doesn't she? Quite the Parisienne really.' .

'Your mother was gorgeous,' Alice said, no trace of envy in her voice. 'She could have had her pick of fellas.'

'Did she have many boyfriends?'

'She was too fussy,' Alice laughed. 'Before James came along she couldn't have cared less about that sort of thing.'

'Her grandfather was strict though, wasn't he?'

Alice shuddered. 'I always thought he was a horrible man.' She glanced at Grace who was nodding obligingly to Philippe Blanc. 'She was afraid of him, to be honest, never took a step without his approval.'

'Thank Heavens I live in modern times.'

Alice smiled. 'Ah, but you have your own problems, I suspect.'

Beth's mind flashed to Annie Kerr. 'Do we?' she asked pleasantly.

'We all do,' Alice said solemnly. 'If we say we don't, we're only fooling ourselves. Oh, hark at me,' Alice laughed. 'I'm hardly the best example of womanhood.'

'Lots of people get divorced and remarried now.'

'I daresay.' Alice brightened up. 'Hand me the menu, will you, sweetie? I'm simply famished.'

*

Charlie was content: not only was he lapping up Alice's attentions and letting Beth see how women flocked to him, but he was also onto a winner with her mother: Philippe

Blanc's money was as good as in Charlie's pocket. As he watched Grace chatting and smiling at anything the man said, Charlie was counting the pennies, working out to the last one how much he could wheedle out of the Frenchman.

At his side, Alice was professing interest in the acquisition of antiques as an investment, although Charlie suspected she was only being polite. He might ask Beth later if the lady from America had any spare cash to throw his way.

Foolishly, he kept glancing at Beth, imagining that they were a couple, that she was Mrs Webster, ensconced in his house and bed; but eventually the idea gave him goose pimples and he had to think of something else.

'Have you known Beth long?' Alice was asking now.

'Since 1969, or thereabouts.'

'She's so lively, isn't she? I wish I'd a daughter,' she said wistfully. 'I've three sons and sometimes, you know, I think it would have been nice...'

'Beth plays the piano,' Charlie said and immediately felt like an idiot.

'Just like her mother,' Alice smiled, opening a cigarette packet and offering him one, to which he shook his head.

'No, thanks. I often invite her to come to the house and play our baby grand, but she never has.'

'You like her, I can see that,' Alice remarked, lighting the cigarette, blowing the smoke away from them. 'Her husband's certainly a lucky man.' He sensed it was a reprimand, although he hardly knew the woman. 'Have you met him?'

'No, I haven't. Can I pour you a glass of wine?'

'Why, thank you, young man, you may.'

Again, the correction of his choice of word made Charlie wonder if he had been scolded; yet, when she smiled at him and allowed her fingers to brush his as he handed her the glass, his impression was that she was falling under his spell.

*

Harry yawned and laid the book aside, peering at the clock and being amazed to find it was only half past nine when he imagined he had been sitting here for hours. Idly, he wondered what they were doing at this moment, but his mind soon relinquished thoughts of Paris and turned to thoughts of his journey to see David Routledge; perhaps his only friend. *'Well, you don't exist then, because you don't have any friends.'*

It was true, and the reminder had sapped his confidence slightly since then, despite the fact being somewhat inconsequential. It had prompted Harry, however, to telephone David Routledge and arrange to go and see him, perhaps to counter Beth's 'no friends' claim. The man was old enough to be his father, but they had shared so many interests that the age difference hardly seemed to matter and now, faced with the week on his own, Harry was looking forward to the trip, mostly to keep alive his friendship with David, but also to pass the time. He had booked into the hotel at the bottom of Union Street, the Atheneum.

'But you must stay with Margaret and me,' David had protested. 'We have at least three spare bedrooms for you to choose from.'

Harry had declined politely, just in case Margaret Routledge turned out to be a dragon, although he had no reason for thinking such a thing. Besides, it was only for one night, preferable to remaining here and rolling around the massive bed being reminded of Beth's absence. He smiled to himself at how much he was missing her; and Grace.

He yawned again, decided to call it a night. He would have to be up early anyway to get on the road by half past eight. As he switched off the sitting room lamps he tried to imagine Grace in Paris, and was beset by a sudden onslaught of jealousy.

James sat with his book, but his mind was on Grace They had spent so few nights apart since the end of the War that he was missing everything about her: her voice around the house, the way she could bring cheer to a room by walking through the door; he even missed the small feminine touches that the house had become used to, and would glance at the space where the fresh flowers would have been, at the sparse table settings that reflected her absence.

Over the past twelve hours he had been shocked to discover how much he had taken her for granted, had tried to imagine the house without her permanently, but the image was so distressing that he had forced himself to go into the garden and work. The only consolation was that Lucy Webster was due to pop in the next day, to pick up the flower seeds he had selected for her; and that would pass some of the time.

*

'How about we have a degustif,' Alice had suggested after they had wandered from the restaurant and said their 'adieus' to the Blancs. The idea appealed to Charlie, who was reluctant to let Beth go so soon.

'Yes, let's,' he had said cheerfully and the others had agreed, albeit Beth reluctantly.

The cocktail bar was all but empty and they had their choice of seats. Despite his desire to sit with Beth, Charlie held back: there was no point in pushing his luck.

'Charlie, why don't you sit beside Beth?' Alice was saying now and he had to force himself to act casually. 'Grace and I have some catching up to do.'

'Fair enough,' he said nonchalantly, overjoyed that Beth was sitting on a two-seater settee. 'Can you catch the waiter's eye, Alice? I think he's more likely to be looking at you than at me.'

She smiled and wagged a finger at him. 'Flattery, dear Charlie, is wasted on me.' She winked. 'But do keep trying!'

'Did you have time to sell anything?' he heard Beth ask beside him.

'They're very keen on the thimbles, surprisingly enough. Can you imagine?'

'It's not my thing, but it takes all sorts.'

'What is your thing?' Charlie asked, adding hastily: 'Antiques, I mean.'

She afforded him a puzzled glance. 'I know what you meant, and it's linen, although you could hardly call it antique.'

'Linen? Do we have any?'

'No.'

'We'll rectify that,' he said at once, an idea forming. 'Why don't you have a wander round the salerooms when we get back, see what you can find. Buy anything you fancy and we'll add it to the list.'

He was nervous in her company and he had ceased laughing if she were around, for it ended up in a hiccough sound, made him look like the village idiot. He cleared his throat.

'I'd never thought of linen before. That's what the business needs, a woman's touch.'

Inwardly, he cringed at the remark, but she appeared to be agreeing with him.

'Yes, Marjory and I were thinking the same.'

'Why didn't you say?'

'It's your business,' Beth said, turning to look at him, causing his stomach to lurch. 'We didn't want to interfere.'

269

'But I want you to interfere,' he frowned, but saw she was suppressing a grin.

'What?' he asked as she clapped her hand to her mouth.

'Nothing.'

'All I said was I want you to...' He paused, then grinned himself. 'You're being risqué, o nymph of the ivories.'

She laughed then, and it occurred to Charlie that she may have been nervous too; something he had not considered until now.

'That's good. 'Nymph of the ivories'. Do you still have the baby grand you keep rabbiting on about?'

'Yes, mother will never sell it.' He hesitated, for he could not be sure how she would react.

'What?' she prompted.

'Unless you wanted to buy it, of course.'

Beth stared at him. 'But I could never afford such a piano.'

Charlie smiled, suddenly holding all the cards in his hand. 'Yes, you could.'

'No,' she frowned. 'I couldn't.'

'Mother would sell it for a reasonable price if she knew it was going to a good home.'

Beth was silent for a long moment, but he could tell she was weighing things up; not about to refuse such a tempting offer, even if it did mean a closer link between them.

'I'd have to discuss it with your mother,' she said at last, her eyes on his, taking his breath away. 'Besides, I already have a piano. My husband bought it for me.'

'That's nice.'

'Although it's not a grand.'

'Think about it anyway.'

'I might do.'

When Charlie sat back in his seat, he felt his shirt damp against his skin.

*

That night, lying on their beds, Grace and Beth exchanged snippets of conversation. The room was hot and stuffy and they were clothed only in their nightdresses, a T-shirt in Beth's case, one of Harry's. Grace looked at her daughter's long legs, tanned from the months of good summer weather, and recalled a time, during the War, when she and her friends had relied on a tan to cover the absence of stockings. When she mentioned it now to Beth, she was not surprised at her daughter's reaction.

'What, you mean you couldn't buy them anywhere?' came the horrified question.

'No, and sometimes women painted the seam down the backs of their legs, to pretend they were wearing them.'

'But that's ghastly! Why didn't they just wear trousers?'

'Women didn't at that time.'

'Oh, my flipping heck! I'd have hated living in the forties, you poor thing.'

'It had its compensations,' Grace said, but she was hard-pressed to think of one.

'Like what?'

'Oh, such as we didn't have to lock our doors. No burglars and thieves around.'

'What else?'

'Well, we had a great time, going to the pictures, to dances, a huge crowd of us.'

'Not pairing up, you mean?' Beth asked now, and Grace detected an element of guile in her daughter's tone.

'No, I didn't pair up, as you put it, until your father came along.'

'But you must have had boyfriends before Dad, surely?'

270

Grace turned and looked at Beth who returned the look with an innocent smile.

'No, I was too interested in schoolwork.'

'Where did you meet Dad?'

'Beth, dear, I'm sure I've told you a hundred times. At a dance in Perth.'

'What was he like?'

'Extremely tall, and quite impatient. He used to drag me round the floor, not waiting for me to pick myself up.'

'That doesn't sound like Dad at all.'

'I soon changed him,' Grace smiled knowingly. 'As all women do.'

'Alice was saying she didn't like your grandfather much.'

'I'm sure she's having you on.'

'She said he was a stubborn old...'

'Beth, dear,' Grace said patiently. 'My grandfather was not the man that Alice may have led you to believe. He certainly wasn't a religious fanatic, nor did he ever stop me doing what I wanted either. You must take what Alice says with pinch of salt. She was terrified of him for some reason, so she's biased.'

'But, she told me that...'

'Beth, please, I'm tired of this, especially on holiday.'

'I know, and I'm sorry,' Beth mumbled, pulling the sheet over her. 'I'll make it up to you tomorrow.'

Grace smiled at her daughter and leaned over to switch off her bedside lamp.

'I suppose I just wanted you to have a few secrets,' Beth whispered. 'The way you looked back then, you must have had boys flocking around you.'

'I didn't say I had no secrets,' Grace laughed and Beth sat up again.

'Tell me!'

'You were a twin, did you know that?'

Grace had no idea why she had mentioned it. She heard Beth's intake of breath.

'A twin? I'm a twin? You mean it's out there somewhere?'

'No, I had a bad fall one day when I was washing windows.'

Beth leaped from the bed and rushed to comfort her mother.

'Oh, Mum, how terrible!' It was so heart-rending to see such compassion that Grace felt a lump in her throat. 'Why didn't you tell me? I could have been nicer to you.'

'Beth, darling, you do say the funniest things. You *are* nice to me.'

'But not when I was a teenager,' Beth groaned, sitting on the edge of the bed and grasping Grace's hand. 'If I'd known how sad you'd been, I would never have acted so childishly. Oh, I'm so sorry, Mum, forgive me?'

'I suppose I'll have no peace until I say I do?'

'None.'

'In that case, you daft little girl, I forgive you.'

'The twin,' Beth said hesitantly. 'Was it... how old was...?'

'A few months only, hardly formed really.' She was reliving the pain, both physical and mental but it was her own fault for mentioning it at all. 'The doctor said you must have been tough to hang on.'

Beth was silent for so long that eventually Grace prepared to speak, but her daughter held up a hand to interrupt.

'I wish you'd told me,' she said plaintively, as would a small child. 'In fact, it's been like that all along, hasn't it? You not telling me anything.'

Grace's heart sank, for she envisaged now the inevitable mention of her father.

'Anyway, it's late,' Beth said unexpectedly, moving across to her own bed. 'I should get some sleep. You too.'

'Will you be busy tomorrow?'

'Charlie wants us to take the Blancs and their friends to lunch. It seems they're interested in some of the items too.' She looked at her mother, no sign of discontent in her expression. 'I'll be free about half past three. Do you and Alice fancy a stroll along the South Bank to look at the art work?'

'How exciting,' Grace smiled. 'Try and stop us.'

As they lay in the darkness of the room, Grace thought back to her conversation with Alice.

'She's been asking me questions about our past,' Alice had laughed. 'As if we had one! She was telling me about your father turning up'

It came as a shock to Grace, that Beth would have discussed it with Alice, albeit she was an old friend. Perhaps Beth had decided that the more people she told, the more support she was likely to find.

'That's another fantasy she has,' Grace frowned. 'She seems to think he's a paragon of virtue and I'm the big bad witch.'

'No, she doesn't,' Alice contradicted. 'She's young; it's a mystery, that's all. I think it's natural she'd want to find out about her grandfather.'

'She contacted him without telling me.'

'Mm, that's hard,' Alice had agreed, her eyes sympathetic. 'She'd be afraid you'd disapprove, of course.'

'He abandoned me and my mother, and yet she wants us all to kiss and make up,' Grace had said bitterly. 'I can't, Alice, it's too much to ask.'

'Have you told her this?'

'No, I've let her believe I'm thinking it over.'

'Ah,' Alice smiled and it seemed to Grace that in the ensuing silence her friend was passing judgement.

'You don't agree?'

'Grace, it's none of my business and you know your daughter better than anyone.' Alice finished off her dry martini and glanced around for the waiter.

'Fancy another, since we're being decadent tonight?'

Thankful for an end to the rigours of the conversation, Grace had been only too happy to change the subject.

'Speaking of being decadent, do you remember the bit in the F. Scott-Fitzgerald book we read years ago?'

'The bit about drinking cocktails in the back of limousines?' Alice laughed.

'Yes, and we'd no idea what a limousine was either.'

'Weren't we so young and foolish, Grace?' Alice asked quietly, her gaze on her red-painted fingernails.

'I suppose we were, but things change and now we're old and foolish.'

The two women had burst out laughing, inviting curious glances from Beth and Charlie.

'Sounds like you lot are having fun,' Beth had smiled.

'Oh, we are, dear,' Alice assured her, but discussing the past had never filled Grace with anything other than sorrow.

Now, as she lay listening to the muffled sounds throughout the hotel, her only thought was how much more of Beth's search for truth could she endure?

Chapter Eighteen

The drizzle had begun by the time he reached Forfar, an intermittent drizzle that made a fool of the windscreen wipers, scraping back and forth with a sound like a drowning cat.

Harry was astonished at how long the journey seemed and yet, just a few years ago, he had travelled this road every weekend; there and back, with scant regard for anything other than seeing Beth at the end of it. When he reached Brechin he contemplated stopping at a café somewhere in the town, but then, in view of the drizzle showing a desire to turn into steady rain, he carried on, anxious now to be at his destination.

It was incredible how much of the city he had forgotten, not even recalling how to find his way to David's house, although it was close to the Bridge of Don, an area he had come to know like the back of his hand when Beth Melville had boarded here with a friendly landlady; although the elderly dear was an expert on winding Beth around her little finger.

'She's taking advantage of your good nature,' Harry had said. 'You're even doing her shopping for her when you should be studying.'

'I do it because I want to,' she had told him indignantly as he had driven her into the city after picking her up at her digs. 'She's a lovely woman, I'll have you know.'

'What, she gives me the creeps.'

Beth had relented, but only slightly. 'Once you get to know her she's great fun.'

It was his first taste of his future wife's penchant for lame ducks and he supposed he should have been firmer at the beginning, but Beth, along with her short temper and volatility, was quite capable of digging her heels in on certain issues, and taking in lame ducks was one of them. His mind drifted to Annie Kerr, the latest of Beth's ducks. Harry had an instinct about the girl, that she had no qualms about testing Beth's friendship to the limit and, if it were up to him, Annie Kerr would never darken their door again.

The rain was showing no mercy by the time he drew up at David's house, a large detached villa – granite, as they all were – with a neat front garden and dark blue door. David had told him once that personalities could be discerned by the colour of a front door and Harry had thought it the most ridiculous idea, particularly when he heard that dark green was a sign of affluence. He doubted that Grace and James Melville would have agreed, despite their door being painted dark green.

David had been looking out for him, for as soon as Harry stepped from the car, the front door opened and David ran down the path wielding an umbrella. It was a fleeting thought, but Harry wondered if it were the sort of kindness that his own father would have shown.

'Harry, my dear boy!' David yelled from half way down the path. 'You couldn't have chosen a worse day, could you? Never mind,' he went on joyfully, not requiring an answer. 'Let's get you in before it gets any worse.'

In an effort to protect Harry from the rain, David was so generous with the position of the umbrella that he himself was dripping wet when they entered the vestibule.

'Oh, it's of no consequence,' he laughed when Harry apologised. 'For Heaven's sake, my boy, it's only water. Come on in, meet the better half.'

Margaret Routledge was a petite, grey-haired woman whose features were arranged in a permanent smile, reminding Harry of Sandra, his legal secretary, who had a similar cheerful disposition.

'I've heard so much about you from David,' she said, ushering Harry over the threshold of the sitting room. 'He said you were the brightest student he'd ever taught.'

'Margaret, dear, don't embarrass the boy so,' David frowned. 'Next, you'll be telling him I said he'd be the next Procurator Fiscal in Perth.'

'I'll bring tea in soon,' Margaret said, happily ignoring her husband. 'And then you won't see me for hours, so you can chatter away to your heart's content.'

'Lame ducks,' David said soulfully as his wife left the room.

'I beg your pardon?'

'She has a new one,' David explained ruefully. 'This time it's the young girl at the corner shop. Her mother's just died apparently and Margaret's doing a good imitation of a stand-in.'

Harry laughed at yet another similarity between him and David: wives with causes.

'Beth's exactly the same, funnily enough.'

'It's my own fault, of course,' David admitted as he sat down opposite Harry. 'I was so wrapped in my work that she was left alone for hours on end. No children, you see, which made it worse.'

'Beth's not keen,' Harry heard himself say before he could think about it.

'On having children, you mean?'

'Yes. She'll come round, obviously, but she says she's too young at the moment.'

'We couldn't have any,' David said lightly. 'But to be honest, and I wouldn't say this in front of her, you understand, I like it the way it is. If you ask me, children are nothing but trouble from the moment they pop out.'

Before Harry had time to respond, the door opened and Margaret Routledge came in bearing a large tray, her face flushed, smile hovering.

'There you are,' she announced, setting it on the table between them. 'Now, I'm off to see Muriel, won't be back for ages. Do be careful that you don't talk yourselves hoarse!'

'For her age, she's quite the whirlwind,' David smiled as they heard the front door slam. 'I loved her the moment I set eyes on her.'

Harry was neither surprised nor embarrassed by the older man's confession. They had shared many confidences during tutorials, when they ought to have been discussing Harry's course work, and now, despite it having been several years since they had last met, it seemed as if it had been only a matter of days, so easily were they resuming the habit.

'It was the same with Beth, but she was at a disadvantage because I'd come up here to find a Scottish wife.'

'Had you? Sensible lad,' David smiled. 'Shall I be mother?' He poured tea into the cups, handed one to Harry and then regarded him with shrewd eyes. 'But I suspect you didn't come all this way to talk about your wife.'

Harry was shocked, mostly because he had only just figured it out himself, during the latter stages of the journey: he wanted to confide in someone about Grace and he was aware that David Routledge was as good a friend as he would find.

'It's odd you should say that,' he began with a frown. 'I was thinking about something on my way up here, wondering if I should ask your advice.'

'I'm also presuming it's not a legal problem?' David asked with a wink.

'There is one, but it's not important at the moment,' Harry said, referring in his own mind to Grace's father. 'No, it's about a woman actually, not a par amour,' he added with a smile. 'An older woman, in her forties.'

'Ah, a wonderful age,' David sighed. 'A child of the war years. It made them tough, you know. In fact, if I could choose to live in any particular decade, it would be the war years.'

'Wasn't it grim, never knowing if you'd survive until the next day?'

'Of course it was grim,' David conceded. 'But people stuck together, against all odds. They couldn't care less now.' He paused, shrugged apologetically to Harry. 'I do ramble on sometimes. Tell me, who was the woman?'

'Grace, my...' Harry paused.

'Is it some relative you're trying to find, is that it?'

'Not exactly. It's my wife's mother.'

David's expression was polite. 'Is there a problem between the two of you, the old mother-in-law joke?'

'No, nothing like that.'

David sank deeper into his chair, a small sign to Harry that, perhaps, the man was in the process of grasping the implications.

'I feel sorry for her,' Harry said, avoiding David's eye. 'Her father ran out on her and her mother years ago and has suddenly turned up in Perth.'

'Oh, how sad,' David breathed. 'Poor girl. Have they been reconciled?'

'Quite the reverse.'

'And you want to help her,' David stated quietly.

Harry nodded, still avoiding his companion's eye.

'But there's something more, isn't there?' the elderly man queried gently.

Harry had reached a decision. 'It's pretty stupid, the way I feel about her. Not in a romantic way, if you know what I mean. I just can't explain it.'

'Did you have a good relationship with your own mother?' David asked shrewdly.

'No.'

'In that case,' David grinned, sitting forward in his chair again and beaming at his companion. 'I suggest that your fondness for your mother-in-law is simply a way of dealing with it.'

'You think that's all there is to it with Grace?'

'Yes, I do. Now do you want my advice?'

'No, if you don't mind, because I suspect you'll tell me to be sensible.'

David's smile said it all.

*

It was with a lighter heart that Harry walked into the foyer of the hotel and picked up his room key. Beth had been right about the disadvantage of having no friends, for, as soon as he had unburdened his troubles onto the unsuspecting David Routledge, Harry had felt the weight lift from his shoulders; not that it helped to lessen the intensity of his feelings for Grace, but the mere fact of confiding in someone was the most rewarding sensation, the likes of which he had never known.

'Will you be dining in this evening?' the receptionist asked, her fingers lingering on the keys a second too long for Harry's liking.

'Yes, two of us.'

'Oh,' she intoned with some disappointment. 'Your wife will be joining you?'

'No, a friend,' Harry said curtly, irrationally annoyed at the girl's interest which was probably only professional. Was he seeing Annie Kerr in every female who spoke to him?

He let himself into the room and leaned against the door. All at once he felt the full significance of his talk with David and, had it involved any other man, it might have given him cause for concern: blabbing about Grace, hinting at his feelings for her may have been an enlightening experience for him, but he was alert to the possibility – however slight – that his confidences would stray beyond this city and cause her distress.

Harry locked the door and went to check the contents of the mini bar. He had a couple of hours before David arrived to join him for dinner; time enough to relax and mull things over; or, to be accurate, to mull one thing over.

Not a par amour.

Not in a romantic way.

Harry poured the small whisky miniature into his glass, carefully avoiding his reflection in the wall mirror.

*

Alice and Grace were resting their feet in a café on the South Bank. The day was hot, sticky, tiring, and even the effort of raising the glass to her lips was proving too much for Alice.

'You'd think I'd be used to such heat,' she grumbled, fanning herself with a huge sunhat. 'Living in America all these years.'

'I remember the first letter you wrote, telling me you'd had to sit in the bathroom in your petticoat. Any time I thought of you, I imagined you there.'

'Boy, did I sweat! Oh, I mean perspire,' Alice corrected with a laugh. 'You'll hardly believe this, but I cried buckets the first time I wrote to you, missed you for ages, Grace.'

'Me too.'

'I wish I'd...'

'You wish you'd what?'

'It wasn't my idea to emigrate,' Alice bemoaned. 'I should have been more forthright, told him I wanted to stay at home.'

'But you would have been miserable in Scotland,' Grace said,, sipping the cold orange juice that had cost the earth. 'You're too exciting a person to spend your life in a backwater. And you're very happy now, aren't you?'

'Oh, yes, I've never been so happy.' Alice gave her friend a swift glance. 'Are you happy, considering you've had to live your life in a 'backwater'?'

'Yes,' Grace replied, surprised. 'You know I love James more than anything.'

'Love's young dream, my mother used to call the two of you, wandering down the village gazing into each other's eyes.'

'Did we?'

'You know you did,' Alice teased. 'How's Molly, by the way?"

'She blotted her copybook recently, but I shouldn't be telling you.'

'You mean she was finally caught?' Alice laughed, draining her glass of mineral water and giving Grace a mischievous look.

'What do you mean 'finally'?'

'She was always at it, you must have known.'

Grace was horrified, mostly at not having known. 'No, I didn't. Who with?'

'Oh, for Pete's sake,' Alice sighed. 'It would be quicker to say who she hadn't been with.'

'Come on, she's not that bad.'

'She tried it on with James, you know.'

Grace stared at her friend, believing it to be a joke; but suddenly, Alice was quite serious and, for Grace, the heat of the day seemed to dissipate rapidly.

'I can't believe that. James would have mentioned it to me.'

'He mentioned it to me.'

'Yet neither of you told me,' Grace accused her friend, and it was the old story of the truth emerging when she least expected it.

'And what good would that have done?' Alice asked, shading her eyes with her hand and gazing up the street towards Notre Dame. 'You might have said something to Molly and then she might have said something back.' She looked at her companion and shook her head slightly. 'No, dear Grace, it was best to let it go. At least, that's what James thought, and I agreed with him.'

'Was it long ago?'

'Once upon a time long ago,' Alice smiled, enjoying her observation. 'Before you were even married.'

'What?' Grace was incredulous that her best friend and fiancé had not thought to mention it to her; and now, after almost thirty years, here she was again, the last to know. 'I wish you'd told me.'

'Well,' Alice said cheerfully. 'I just did, honey. Now, who's for wandering around that old church over there?'

As they sauntered up the street to Notre Dame, Grace should have been struck by the beauty of the building, by the hushed reverence of its stones. Instead, she was struggling with the resentment of another truth having been withheld from her; of her going about daily life in blithe ignorance of the duplicity of her supposed best friend. Did no one care that she might feel more betrayed by the secrecy than with Molly's flirtatious nature?

The coolness of the interior of Notre Dame greeted them as they walked across the threshold, causing an involuntary shiver to run through Grace. Alice walked on ahead, peering at the carvings, reading the information boards, silently mouthing to herself the history of the building; and as Grace trailed along behind, her over-riding thought was relief, for, believing Alice to be a trusted confidante, she had planned to unburden her soul to her friend that very evening, Now, of course, she considered that she had had a lucky escape.

*

Beth was making friends with Madame Blanc and it had two advantages: the woman was eager to buy antiques because she felt she was helping the business, and it kept Beth away from Charlie Webster.

'Your French is excellent,' Yvette Blanc remarked again. 'I can even place your accent as similar to the Parisians.'

'That's because my tutor was from Paris,' Beth explained. 'She came from Rue des Trois Freres, eighteenth or eighth section, can't recall which. She was so lovely that the boys fell under her spell.' Beth laughed at the memory. 'The class results had never been so good.'

'We girls have the same fascination for your British boys,' Yvette winked.

'Sorry?'

'We love your men, so discreet, so cool, but underneath,' Yvette paused and pretended to fan herself with the menu. 'Ah, the torment, yes?' she asked in English.

'You think our men are passionate?'

'Of course. You do not know this?'

Beth was glad of the heat in the café, for it could explain her flushed cheeks.

'I suppose they can be passionate, but not like Frenchmen I suspect.'

'We have the 'arrangement',' Yvette whispered, although no one was listening to their conversation. 'You know? The husband has a mistress and the wife is very happy, oui?'

'We have something similar,' Beth smiled. 'But the wife isn't very happy, non.'

'This boss you have,' Yvette said unexpectedly. 'He is your arrangement?'

Beth's horrified expression was enough to change Yvette Blanc's opinion.

'Oh, I am sorry,' she frowned, biting her lip in consternation. 'I have upset you, my dear Bet, have I not?'

'Bet' took a few deep breaths and calmed down, but was riven with guilt at how remorseful her companion was, for the idea of Charlie Webster being Beth's 'arrangement' was ever uppermost in her mind.

'No, I'm not upset, just surprised. Charlie and I... well, it's business between us, that's all.'

'For you maybe,' Yvette suggested, eyebrows raised mischievously. 'But not for Monsieur Webster.'

'He... I...'

'Of course, I understand. You are married then?'

'Yes, his name is Harry and he's wonderful and I'm missing him.' She had said it without stopping for breath and, because of that, the words rang false.

'But you are tempted sometimes?' Yvette asked without guile, and Beth was reminded of the cultural differences.

'Tempted?' Beth repeated, to gain time.

'Yes, with your boss?'

'I like him, but I would never... no, never.'

'I have had the grand passion once,' Yvette sighed. 'With an English man too.'

It was not Beth's idea of a cosy chat, discussing the woman's love life, and she was racking her brain for a way out when she heard Alice's voice.

'Co-ee, Beth! Over here!'

Without turning to look at Alice, Yvette shrugged and gave Beth a disappointed smile.

'Ah, well, we continue our interesting conversation this evening, yes?'

Beth returned the smile, but she intended to move Heaven and Earth to avoid a repetition of this cosy chat, even if it meant taking to her bed for the next two days.

*

Grace listened to her daughter's tale as they lay on their respective beds, feet throbbing, legs aching after a few hours' meandering in Alice's wake. She had typified Grace's idea of an American in Paris, by seizing hold of every conceivable French souvenir as if her life depended on it, finally forcing Grace to call a halt before she and Beth dropped from exhaustion.

'You may be used to this kind of heat, Alice, but we're not. If I don't get back to the hotel soon, I'll drop where I stand.'

Alice had capitulated gracefully, loading some of her purchases onto Beth who had shown willing.

'Thank you, my dear, you're the sweetest thing. Just one more perhaps? Oh, good, that leaves these three and I can manage them. I can tuck the Eiffel Tower into my pocket.'

Grace had counted every step to the hotel, envisaging arriving in the foyer in bare feet, having kicked her tight shoes off somewhere between one Bank and the other.

'I'll never wear these shoes again,' she vowed now, eyes closed, hands folded across her bosom. 'I was an idiot to buy them in the first place. I should have known they'd pinch my toes.'

'I'll take the blame,' Beth laughed, wriggling to a sitting position and squinting over at her mother. 'It was my idea, remember?'

'You weren't to know how hot it would be here and that my feet would grow to size twelve. Oh, by the way, did you persuade Madame Blanc to part with her francs today?'

'Easy peasy. She's buying two pestle and mortars and an old-fashioned iron that heats up on the stove.'

Grace opened her eyes in disbelief. 'What use can she have for that?'

'Oh, they don't buy them to be useful, Mum,' Beth informed her mother. 'They want to show them off.'

'Goodness, what strange people.'

'It takes all sorts, so you told me once.'

'Did I? How astute of me.'

'And she says her friend wants to see Charlie about some jewellery he has.'

'Well done you,' Grace smiled. 'I could see that Yvette Blanc was under your spell.'

'Maybe I should go into business on my own then?'

'Why not?'

'Because I'm lazy, that's why not.' Beth rolled onto her side and lowered her voice. 'By the way, Yvette was telling me about the 'arrangement' the French have.'

'What kind of arrangement?'

'The kind where the husband has a mistress and the wife is happy, oui?'

Grace turned to look at Beth. 'You mean the *ménage a trois*?'

'And how would you possibly know about that, mother dear, living in the wilds of Scotland and leading a sheltered life?'

'It's common knowledge, isn't it? I read it once in a magazine. They all do it here apparently.'

'She was wondering if Charlie Webster and I had that kind of arrangement.'

'Well, of course you don't,' Grace said indignantly. 'What a cheek!'

'Steady on, she was only asking.'

Grace sat up and wiggled her aching toes. 'I still think it was a cheek, trying to tar us all with the same brush. That's always the way with different cultures.'

She had said in such a way that Beth gave her a scrutinising look, head on one side, eyes full of interest.

'Was it like that with you and Dad?'

'Beth, dear, he is only English. You'd think he was from the subcontinent.'

'What were the biggest differences between the two of you?'

'I was a female, your father was a man.'

Beth burst out laughing and Grace hoped that the flippant reply might distract the girl from embroiling them in the sort of conversation she had come hundreds of miles to escape; one that would, inevitably, lead to Thomas Blake.

'Apart from the obvious, smarty-pants.'

'Beth, do we have to do this now?' Grace asked wearily, at which her daughter shook her head vigorously.

'No, of course not, I was just curious. D'you think they'll be missing us?'

'Who, our husbands?'

'Yes.'

'More than you think,' Grace smiled, knowing it was what Beth wanted to hear. She had picked up the insecurity in her daughter's voice as she had related the story of Madame Blanc's 'arrangement' and suspected that Beth's imagination was hard at work. She was not unaware of the effect Annie Kerr had on her daughter, despite countless reassurances to the contrary.

'I wonder what he's doing at this moment.'

'Working probably, since there's nothing else for him to do.'

'I confided in Alice,' Beth frowned, avoiding her mother's eyes.

Grace knew that it could only relate to Thomas Blake for, had it been any other matter, her daughter would surely have confided in her. Inwardly she resented Beth for raising the subject under the guise of chitchat with Alice.

'We all need someone to talk to,' she said pleasantly. 'And Alice is a lovely person, very understanding.'

'When I told her...' Beth threw her mother a swift glance, gauging her reaction, Grace suspected. 'When I told her what I told her, she was really sympathetic. You were lucky to have her as a friend when you were young, especially when your mum died.'

'No, Alice had gone to America by then.'

'Did Molly comfort you?'

'Yes,' Grace said with exaggerated patience. 'She did indeed. Now, unless you're deliberately trying to provoke me, dear girl, I suggest we discontinue this conversation and get ready for dinner.'

'I was only interested,' Beth said in a peevish voice. 'Anyway,' she added resentfully. 'At least I had someone to confide in.'

As she watched her daughter flounce into the bathroom and slam the door, Grace refrained from a hasty retort. It was not Beth's desire to unburden herself upon Alice that was irking Grace at that moment, for she had almost given way to the very same impulse earlier in the day; rather, it was Beth's continual quest for information, an obsession that could only wreak havoc in the family. Her father had succeeded in filling the girl's head with his version of the truth and was most probably revelling in the disruptive effect it was having on Grace's family.

Furthermore, he would not be fooled into believing she was coming round to the idea of accepting him back into her life: if she had inherited anything from him it was the propensity to turn the truth into a form that might best suit her own purpose. Time would tell which of them was the more devious, but Grace was certain that, should she have the strength to survive this temporary impasse with Beth, she could outmanoeuvre Thomas Blake and be rid of him once and for all. Besides, she could rely on Harry, if no one else.

*

Lucy Webster sat in the sunroom with her book, waiting until dinner was ready. She had read the same page at least five times and, yet again, the meaning of it had flown over her head, so little attention was she paying to the story. Somewhere in the garden a blackbird was singing its heart out and, foolishly, she envied the creature its burst of happiness.

With a sigh she laid the book aside and removed her spectacles, tucking them into the velvet case and setting them carefully on the book, covering the title lest the maid see it on her way past. *The Virgin and the Gypsy* was not the kind of novel her staff would imagine she read; and, to be honest, not the kind of book she herself would have imagined she might read; but during her perusal of the books in the library upstairs, she had come across several D.H. Lawrence novels and selected one at random. Who had bought it in the first place, she had no idea, but it seemed like the sort of thing Matthew would choose.

The silent sound of his name inside her head filled her with pain. The boy had been away for years now – almost three – with no letter or telephone call, no word if he were alive or…

Her thoughts were interrupted by the clock striking seven, its warbling tones threading their way through the house, into each room and out again, finally coming to rest with a whisper in the sunroom. Lucy gazed at the newly dug flower bed, where James had worked only hours earlier, digging and planting, choosing the best position for her seedlings, taking over from the gardener for a short time, encouraging her mind to project forward to spring, when she would witness the result of his labours.

'These delphiniums will be lovely against the wall,' he had assured her, as if she were about to contradict him. 'Their height, you see, gives the other flowers a strong background.'

He had insisted on dividing his own plants so that she would have instant results, promising to return in late summer to work in the glasshouses on next year's batch. Lucy had been overjoyed at the suggestion, at the thought of James taking an interest in her garden, such a sprawling, haphazard arrangement of beds and shrubs; not neglected, but not *cherished*, as he had pointed out. To hear the word falling from the man's lips had unsettled Lucy. It was not the kind of word she had ever heard from her husband, or sons, or even the gardener; but coming from James Melville it had not jarred in the least and the effect it had on her was disturbing.

'Yes, I suppose you're right,' she had agreed, stepping back, standing alongside him, casting a critical eye over the untidy borders, trying to suppress the notion that he and she were more than just neighbours.

'We can do so much with this,' James had announced happily. 'I have so many ideas.' He had frowned then, had turned to her apologetically. 'But, perhaps you wish it to remain like this?'

She had rushed to assure him that his opinion reflected hers and that she would be delighted at the changes, wondering as she spoke if this were the wisest thing she had ever done.

'I think we should have a cup of tea now, don't you?' she asked, as casually as she could. 'That's the least I can do after all your hard work.'

He had smiled and nodded and, as they sat together in the shade of the huge cherry tree, Lucy could hardly believe the difference in the man: where once she had thought him aloof and unsociable, now he was as comfortable in her presence as she was in his. For several hours she had enjoyed his company, perhaps even silently congratulating herself on the effect she was having on him. He had seemed completely at ease in her company; and when he had promised to visit within the next week, Lucy had been hard-pressed to keep the delight from her face.

*

Harry awoke with a start, unsure if he had been dreaming or if there had been a knock at the door. He waited and it came again, louder this time. He rose and glanced at the clock: half past nine. Before he had even reached the door he knew it would be Annie Kerr.

'Who is it?' he demanded rudely, with no intention of opening the door.

'It's me,' she said and Harry let his breath out in a long sigh.

'Piss off,' he told her, more roughly than before. 'Go home.'

'I've no money, I lost my purse somewhere.'

'Wait then, I'll give you some,' he called to her. He ran to the bedroom, took out a five-pound note and went back through the hall, where he slipped the note to her underneath the door.

'There you are, that's enough to get you home.'

'Don't leave me here,' she wailed, perhaps expecting him to let her in out of sheer embarrassment in front of the neighbours.

'I've given you money, now go home,' he said, before turning away, switching out the light and retracing his steps to the living room. Once inside, he closed the door and turned on the television, so that he would not hear her if she called out. After ten minutes, his curiosity got the better of him. He stood up and tiptoed to the front door.

*

Charlie Webster lay on his bed and estimated how much he was likely to make from his trip, summing it up, approximately, in his head. Without Beth, the takings would be a quarter of what they were and he acknowledged her part in the proceedings, charming both Philippe and – more surprisingly – his wife, not the most friendly of women, at least not to Charlie. With Beth, however, Yvette Blanc had appeared to enjoy the girl's company, had come out of her shell and had plunged her husband's hands deeper into his wallet. The result would be roughly one fifty, a tidy number, not bad for a few days' work.

As for his plan to seduce Beth in the most romantic city in the world, well he had not been so lucky. Oddly enough, it had not been her mother's presence, or the long-lost pal from the States that had blighted his chances; it was the girl's attitude. She had been polite, friendly, amusing and a social delight, but his advances towards her, however subtle, had been repulsed at the start with a tiny frown, a weary sigh, a bored glance, a tolerant smile.

He suddenly realised it was half past six and leaped from the bed to get ready for their last night out; and the surprise he had in mind for Beth.

'Tonight we're going to Montmartre,' he had informed them when they met in the lobby of the hotel in late afternoon. 'A lovely little Italian restaurant halfway up. You'll love it.'

'An Italian restaurant?' Alice had laughed. 'In Paris? We were hoping for a real taste of French cuisine, weren't we, fellas?'

'I love Italian food,' Beth had said, and he had thrown her a grateful glance.

'Bring on the pasta, I can hardly wait!'

*

Without the slightest engineering on his part, he found himself sitting opposite her, the frequent recipient of her smiles and winks. By now, of course, he knew they were meaningless, that she was only being polite; nevertheless, he savoured her witty, colourful conversation, appreciated her ability to wind Yvette Blanc round her little finger.

'Does anyone have a wine preference?' he asked before the waiter came round.

'Oh, how formal you are,' Yvette Blanc smiled, winking at Beth, which made him think they had discussed him earlier. 'You Englishmen are so stuffy.'

'What?' he joked. 'Like a teddy bear?'

As predicted, she failed to see the humour in it and he was aware of Beth's disapproving sigh across the table.

'I'd like dry white,' she said only, without glancing at the wine list.

'And I'd like a full-bodied red,' Alice smirked, perhaps at yet another remark going above Madame Blanc's head. 'Have you ever had one, Philippe?' she added with an air of flirtation and Charlie feared she was going too far.

'Ah, no,' Philippe Blanc said sadly. 'I prefer blondes.' He looked straight at Grace as he spoke, stark admiration in his eyes. 'There is nothing quite so appealing as a blonde.'

'And you should know, *mon cher,*' his wife commented sarcastically. 'You must have had quite a few in your time.'

Everyone, including Grace, laughed, but Charlie suspected that Beth had taken umbrage at the admiration Philippe was bestowing on her mother. He had an inkling of a previous argument between them, a disagreement that was manifesting itself in the coolness of Beth's manner towards her mother, although Grace appeared as gracious as ever.

He lowered his eyes to the menu and as he caught sight of the prices he almost had a heart attack.

*

Yvette Blanc was regaling Grace and Alice as to the advantages of marrying a Frenchman, She had openly discussed the 'arrangement' she and her husband had, a topic that Alice considered quite shocking.

'It is so good,' Yvette told them in English. 'He goes out every Friday night and I never have to ask, never have to be the sad wife. We are both very happy.'

'You'd hardly believe there could be such a difference in behaviour between the two nations,' Alice remarked, a tiny furrow creasing her brow. 'I'd hate my husband to go out every Friday night, I'd just hate it.' Turning to Grace she added: 'I imagine so would you, Grace, if it were James?'

Grace, torn as ever between offending one or the other, saw no middle ground on this occasion and had to confess that her friend was right.

'Can you imagine?' Alice went on and Grace foresaw dissent ahead. 'The very thought of your husband touching another woman… in that way…' she emphasised with a shudder. 'Well, I'd chuck him out at the first whisper.'

'But we all have different values,' Grace pitched in. 'Take James, for example. He has a few strange ones, believe me.'

The look she received from Alice signalled that her friend considered this to be untrue, but Grace was more concerned with Charlie and Beth's business profit than with supporting Alice's opinions.

'Did Beth tell you that my friend Simone le Fevre is very rich?' Yvette Blanc interrupted, before Grace was obliged to appease Alice, although she knew she would have to do it later.

'No,' Grace said, trying not to catch Beth's eye.

'She is very, very rich, and she wants to buy many things from Beth.'

'It's Charlie's antique business,' Grace started to explain, but Yvette waved her words away.

'Ah, but it is your daughter who is the best at persuading,' Yvette smiled, glancing down the table to where Beth was in conversation with her boss.

'She should do this for herself, such a delightful girl. Perhaps she thinks this already?'

'I'm not sure,' Grace said, although the very thought had occurred to her as she had seen Beth's skills in action that week. 'She's only twenty-four, time enough yet.'

'I expect she's still finding her feet at the moment,' Alice said, without thinking, until she saw the puzzled look on Yvette Blanc's face.

Even Alice laughed at the colloquialism that had Yvette stumped and the happy atmosphere was restored, much to Grace's relief. Falling out with her daughter was bad enough, but falling out with Alice only an hour or so later was a dismal prospect.

As she half listened to the ensuing discussion on the merits of French perfume, Grace was planning the best way to console Beth before the night was out. The trouble was that appeasement in this case could only lead to a resumption of the girl's incessant questions about the past. Would there ever come a time when Grace would be granted the luxury of leaving it behind?

*

Charlie was listening to Beth, but the only thing he could think of was that, if he were to succeed in wooing and winning her, it was taking so long that the two of them would be leaning heavily on Zimmer frames the day of their joining.

283

'But have you had a good time?' he asked her now.

'Of course I have, especially with Mum being here.'

'Oh? I thought for one moment that you and she had fallen out.'

Beth's eyes narrowed; he had said the wrong thing again.

'No, we haven't fallen out,' she smiled coolly. 'Besides, what business is it of yours anyway?'

'None, except I hate when you're not happy.'

Her face softened; at last he had said the right thing.

'D'you know how much we'd made this week?' he whispered, leaning across the table.

'Yes, I worked it out before we came out tonight, and it's a very tidy sum.'

'You were the one who wowed the clients, not me. Credit where it's due.'

'Oh, well, whatever helps,' she shrugged casually, but she was pleased.

He raised his glass, took a deep breath and dived in.

'Here's to our new partnership,' he smiled and the expression on her face was the sweetest moment of his life so far. When it was clear to him that she was completely flummoxed, he added: 'I'm offering you a full partnership, Beth and if you turn me down I'll jump off the Pont Neuf.'

The girl blinked several times, recovered her voice, fiddled with cutlery.

'Are you serious?'

'Couldn't be more,' Charlie affirmed nonchalantly, feeling like a character out of a Raymond Chandler novel. 'But, obviously you'd like to think it over.'

'No, I accept.'

'Just like that?' he laughed, hoping that she would pick up his deliberate scepticism, the doubt that she was her own woman, that she could bypass the husband on such a major decision.

'Yes,' she said quickly. 'But you realise I know nothing about antiques.'

'And everything about people,' Charlie responded, trying to appear a man of the world and gazing at her over the rim of his glass.

'Why don't *you* think it over?' she suggested pleasantly. 'Perhaps you've been carried away with the success of the trip.'

He would have liked to tell her that the only 'carrying away' that appealed to him involved Beth Gillespie, away from the husband, into Charlie Webster's lonely bed.

'I've been thinking it over for weeks,' he lied now. 'My mind's made up.'

'In that case, so is mine.' She offered him her hand across the table. 'Here's to the partnership.'

'We'll have to come up with a new name for the business,' Charlie said, almost distracted by the electric touch of her fingers.

'Wow! ' she breathed. 'You really are serious.'

'We'll put our heads together when we get home,' he smiled, cursing himself for such a stupid remark, one that propelled him right back into his lonely bed.

*

Grace listened to the rhythmic breathing of her daughter and wondered at the ease with which the two of them had shed the effects of their argument. The news about the business partnership had been the key, of course, for it was not something that Beth could ever have kept to herself. With Harry being hundreds of miles away, there was only one person to tell – her mother; but Grace would have seized on any excuse to be on amicable terms again and how fortuitous that it had come from Beth.

Grace sighed and closed her eyes. She was so looking forward to going home, although she had thoroughly enjoyed most of the holiday, particularly her time with Alice, for, despite the tiny hiccough relating to cultural differences, they had resumed their friendship and had benefited from the long chats. She wished now that she had confided in her old friend, that she had given in to the strong impulse to talk about the past, about her hatred of her father, about her obsession with never allowing him in her life again. If she could only unburden herself to Alice, perhaps it would bring an end to the constant anxiety, her irrational fears.

Fear of what? Grace's head was beginning to ache. She had no idea why she should be entertaining such fears, for all she had to do was to read out Helen's letter and the whole situation would go away. With a sigh, she made a last attempt to stop the turmoil in her head.

As she prepared to drift off, yet another distracting idea popped into her mind: that Beth's decision to accept Charlie's partnership offer had been reached without talking it over with Harry; but, very quickly, she decided it was quite ridiculous to think he would be anything other than delighted for his wife.

*

Charlie sat up, suddenly wide-awake. He had dreamt vividly and could recall each small detail of the dream. He laughed out loud and jumped out of bed. Grabbing his dressing gown, he shoved his feet into soft shoes, opened the bedroom door and hurried off in the direction of the lobby; and the telephones.

Chapter Nineteen

Thomas Blake yawned and stretched, eyeing the brooding sky from the warmth of his bed, deciding to stay where he was for another half hour. Despite the advent of summer, the house was cool, only warmed by the sun from mid-day onwards. First thing in the morning he was loathe to dispense with his thick dressing gown and usually kept it on until well after ten; unless he had somewhere to go, of course. Today, however, he had nowhere to go.

He closed his eyes and ruminated on the girl's return from Paris. Marjory had been so helpful, a tender-hearted woman who had been convinced she was doing her best for Beth when he made inquiries about his granddaughter.

'Oh, they'll be back to work on Monday,' she had said, endowing Thomas with a dazzling smile. 'Shall I tell her that you called?'

'Of course,' he had smiled, for to say otherwise would not have been to invite the woman's curiosity, give rise to doubt. 'Do tell her I'll be in touch whenever she's back.'

He sighed and switched on Radio Four, idly following the brief weather forecast and most of the news. His complete lack of interest in the local press was compensated for by the snippets he picked up on the radio, and his command of what was going on in the world seemed to work wonders with Daphne, who thought him the most knowledgeable of men.

'Is there anything you don't know?' she had chirped the previous evening as he had expounded forth on the evils of the communist system, gleaned from an article he had once read in Reader's Digest. 'You make me feel like a ninny,' she added, obviously expecting him to disagree, which he did, naturally.

'Daphne, dear lady, you are anything but a ninny. In fact,' he had confided, leaning closer to her on the settee. 'I can't think of anyone with whom I'd rather spend an evening.'

He sighed now at the banality of his rhetoric and changed his mind about staying in bed. If his granddaughter were coming back soon, he had to lay his plans, take on the spirit of the Boy Scouts – be prepared.

As he washed and dressed, he pondered on the route his 'romance' was taking. Apart from the confession about his imaginary 'niece' and her husband and the house not being his, he had given very little away to Daphne. He had revealed nothing of his past life, other than having lived in South America; nothing of his Brazilian wife and family, nothing of Charlotte and his daughter here; in fact, now that he came to think of it, Daphne knew absolutely nothing about him and that was very satisfactory. He was sufficiently confident in her being under his spell that he had confessed to the house being his.

'But why didn't you tell me the house was yours?' she had asked, both mystified and hurt. 'Why was it important?'

'Because I'm an old-fashioned man,' Thomas had said, having rehearsed the sentence for days previously. 'And I like to take things slowly.'

'I can't see how...'

'If you'd known this was my house and that I lived here alone, you might have thought my reticence to entertain you here had something to do with not being attracted to you.'

She had blushed then, and her hand had squirmed beneath his. 'I see.'

'I hope you do, Daphne, because I know that most men would have...'

He had left the sentence hanging, for he could see that she was following his train of thought and that she was accepting it as a compliment.

'Oh, Thomas,' she said, lowering her eyes. 'You are the most gentlemanly of men.'

Now, as he selected casual trousers and shirt from the wardrobe, Thomas mused over his play-acting abilities, congratulated himself on the way he could so easily manipulate women.

Except Charlotte

A momentary shiver enveloped him at the silent sound of her name, a shiver that encompassed the full horror of her death, the irrevocable end to their love, the crushing loneliness of his existence without her.

When the hall clock struck nine, Thomas roused himself, tried to concentrate on the here and now; but shrugging off his memories was even more impossible than he had imagined, and – worse – they were accosting him on a daily basis, standing firmly in his way, impeding his attempts to carve out a new life.

*

As soon as Harry saw the smile on Frank Gilmour's face and heard the hearty morning greeting, he knew it had to do with Beth. The man had been invisible for months, going out of his way to avoid Harry, even to the extent of working at their smaller office in an insalubrious street in the town, an office the size of a box room and with no access to Sandra's secretarial skills.

This Monday morning, however, he stood in the doorway of Harry's office with a smirk adorning his features and an imminently devastating remark on his lips. Harry steeled himself.

'May I be the first to congratulate you on your wife's promotion?'

'Thank you,' Harry smiled, his voice steady. 'I'm only surprised it took Charlie Webster so long to discover her worth.'

It was a bluff, of course, but the idea that this man would ever get the better of him spurred him on, vetted his words, controlled his expression; and even when Gilmour's face fell, Harry let nothing show.

'So you know then?'

'Why wouldn't I?' Harry asked with a puzzled frown. 'I'm her husband, I'd be the first one she telegrammed.'

'What, in the middle of the night?' Gilmour asked rudely, thereby letting slip that Charlie Webster had been on the telephone in the middle of the night.

'No, this morning actually,' Harry lied, looking at the papers on his desk.

'Well, anyway,' Gilmour said grudgingly. 'Good for her.' With that, he turned on his heels and left the office, allowing the door to stand open.

Before Harry had time to stand up, Sandra appeared, cup of coffee in hand. She closed the door quietly and looked at Harry with inquisitive eyes.

'What did he want?' she asked, with no preamble.

'Wanted to tell me that Beth's been promoted.'

'How could he know?'

'I expect Webster wired him right away.'

'But you knew anyway,' Sandra said, although she seemed doubtful.

'No, I didn't,' admitted Harry. 'But I pretended I did.'

'Thank Heavens,' Sandra sighed, setting down the coffee cup at his elbow and taking the chair opposite him. 'I'd never let that little rat get the better of me.'

Harry laughed. Despite their age difference, he had discovered that he and Sandra had several traits in common; mostly relating to pride.

'I can assure you, he didn't. You should have seen his face.'

'What kind of promotion is it?'

'Haven't a clue,' Harry shrugged. 'She'll be home late tonight. I'll find out then.'

'I have a better idea,' Sandra smiled, head on one side, eyes bright. 'What if I called her now, at the hotel, through the practice switchboard?'

'She might be out.'

'Mr Harry, thy middle name is negativity!' Sandra exclaimed, slapping him on the wrist as she stood up. 'I'm going to try anyway, so don't go away, young man, I'll be back in a jiffy.'

Harry sipped the coffee and rummaged through the papers on his desk. Now that he had ruined Gilmour's coup de grace, his mind was roaming around the implications of whatever promotion she had been offered. It could be a pay rise, or her own client list, or even a share in the business; in other words, something he would have expected her to mention to him first, something you would talk over with your husband.

Within minutes Sandra was back, face radiant.

'She's on the line, pick up quickly!'

'You're a magician,' he told her but she was shaking her head.

'No, dear boy,' Sandra grinned as she left the room. 'A witch.'

*

Beth had been in the middle of packing her case when the hotel reception had rung up with a call for her and she could hardly believe her ears when it was the woman from Harry's legal practice.

'Beth?'

'Harry! Oh, I've missed you!'

'Me too. I thought I'd just call and wish you bon voyage, sweetheart.'

'I can hardly wait to get home, I've been so miserable without you.'

She waited for him to say something similar, but when he remained silent, she had the first tiny inkling that there was trouble; and her mind immediately darted to Annie Kerr. With bated breath and an over-active imagination, Beth waited for him to speak.

'Did you have a good trip?' he was asking, skipping over the bit she most wanted to hear.

'Yes, we made lots of money and I met so many nice people and Charlie Webster was so impressed with me that he's offered me a partnership.'

She had blurted it out, taken no time to phrase it properly or to break it to him gently. As usual, Beth Melville had put her foot right in it.

'A partnership?' Harry repeated and she thought he sounded pleased.

'Yes, a full partner in the business. We're even going to change the name.'

'Beth, sweetheart, I'm happy for you, you've worked hard for it.'

'I'm so glad you called, because I've been dying to tell you.'

'Oh, but I knew already,' Harry said and she thought she had misheard.

'What?'

'Frank Gilmour told me first thing this morning.'

Beth's heart froze. 'How could he know?'

'I expect Webster wakened him up in the middle of the night.'

She could think of nothing to say. It was the most horrible thing that could happen to her in the midst of such joy; that it could be spoilt in this way, for she knew it was spoilt, sensed that Harry, for all his false good wishes and cheerful voice, would resent her for not wiring him right away.

'Why would he do that?' she was inspired to ask.

'Because he wanted to have a smirk at my expense I suppose.'

'But why?'

'Listen, sweetheart, we'll talk about this when you come home, this call is costing the practice a small fortune.'

'I'm miserable now, you realise that?'

He laughed and sounded like the old Harry. 'Beth, don't be silly, I'll be at the airport to meet you all, see you then.'

'I don't understand why he should do that,' were her final words to thin air before the line went dead and she was left, feeling like an idiot, holding the unresponsive receiver.

Her enthusiasm for the day had vanished within the space of five minutes. Even the packing that she had tackled with eagerness was suspended while she sat on the edge of the bed and waited for her mother to return from the kiosk in the lobby. She glanced at her reflection and saw a pathetic creature stare back. She wanted someone to suffer for this; preferably Charlie Webster.

*

Grace listened to her daughter's tale of woe, her over-riding thought being that she should have paid more attention to her niggling doubt about Harry being consulted first. Her heart sank as Beth, in her usual dramatic manner, exaggerated greatly the effect it might have on her marriage.

'I know he'll hate me now,' she mumbled, biting her lower lip. 'I should have waited, asked him what he thought.'

'Oh, Beth, I don't imagine for one second that Harry will hate you. Don't you think you're over-dramatising the situation?'

'You don't know him like I do,' Beth frowned and Grace had to suppress a tiny stab of jealousy. 'He may sound fine but inwardly he'll be seething that Frank Gilmour got one over on him.'

'But why should he dislike this Frank Gilmour?'

'Because he's Charlie's best friend.'

Grace pondered the information, let it sink in and rearrange itself into order.

'You mean Harry doesn't like Charlie?'

'What do you think?' Beth asked impatiently, jumping up and pacing the room. 'He's jealous of everyone, even the eighty-year-old geriatric next door.'

Grace kept her face impassive, for any hint of a smile would not help the atmosphere.

'Perhaps you should be flattered that he's jealous.'

'Well, I'm not, it's bloody stifling!'

'Thank goodness you're not the same with him,' Grace smiled, but her daughter was hardly amused.

'I knew you'd be on his side. I wish I'd never told you now.'

Grace wished she had the courage to tell her daughter how sad it was that she had never quite grown up. The girl was twenty-four, past the age of all this melodrama. Grace cast her mind back to when she had been twenty-four: struggling to come to terms with her mother's death; unable to cope with the villagers' intolerance of James; bringing up two children on pennies.

'I'm not on anyone's side,' she said wearily. 'Once you get home and speak to him, you'll realise he's just as happy as you are about the partnership.'

'Oh, of course, I forgot,' Beth started to say caustically. 'You and he...'

'Beth, that's enough!'

For the first time in Beth's adult life, Grace had spoken harshly and the effect on the girl was immediate. She stopped pacing and threw herself down on the bed, giving her mother a remorseful glance.

'I'm sorry, I can be such a fool.'

'You're anxious, that's all, and I'm the only person within firing range.'

Beth laughed and grimaced. 'And I give you permission to take me over your knee and wallop me.'

'I haven't done that up to now, so don't expect me to start today.'

'Mum, what will I do?' Beth asked pleadingly, taking her mother's arm and holding it fast. 'What will I say?'

'The truth always works,' Grace said, and the irony of the remark made a mockery of its sentiment.

'I suppose.'

'Just tell him it was too late to call him, that you only heard about it at midnight and that you didn't want to disturb him at that hour.'

'I could say that.'

'There is one other thing.'

Beth's arm stiffened. 'What's that?'

'This Frank Gilmour.'

'What about him?'

'It might be best to let him and Charlie think you'd called Harry last night, otherwise it implies that he didn't know, which he didn't, of course, but you don't want them to know that, do you?'

Beth's eyes widened. 'Yes, you're right, that's a great idea. Thanks, Mum, you're a wizard.'

'Now, why not finish packing?' Grace suggested gently, steering Beth towards the suitcases. 'And once we've done that we can enjoy the day. Alice and I thought that we three could go to the Louvre.'

'I'd love that,' Beth sighed gratefully. 'I feel so much better now, thanks to you.' She turned to her suitcase and placed several items inside. 'I'm so looking forward to going home.'

Grace wandered to the window and gazed down at the tiny dots below, the hundreds of people floating around the district, anonymous little dots in a huge landscape, tiny specks that had wives, husbands, children, people who lived a life not unlike her own. Somewhere out there, another woman – a Parisienne –was dealing with her daughter, straightening out the misunderstandings, doing her best to push the girl off in the right direction again.

Selfishly, irrationally, she felt an animosity towards Charlotte Blake for reneging on her role as confidante and guide to her own daughter, leaving it to poor Lily Morris, not even a relation, only a friend, a person ill-equipped to carry the burden.

Suddenly, Grace was tired of this place; weary of the pretence of liking everyone, chatting to everyone, placating everyone. She sighed and moved away from the window. She could hardly wait to be home; to see James again; and Harry.

*

Alice was finding it impossible to make space in her cases for the gifts she had bought in Paris. Her solution had been the suggestion to buy another suitcase, but after a hurried reshuffling of items, Beth and Grace had offered her the smaller one of theirs.

'But your clothes will be crammed into one case!' Alice had cried, unwilling to take advantage of them in such a way, when buying another case was the obvious solution.

'Nonsense, it's fine,' Grace said, her mind refusing to hold onto the notion that she was, as usual, putting herself out for someone else. 'I've hardly got anything and Beth had lots of space in hers. Not another word, it's settled.'

They left the suitcases in the hotel lobby, under the watchful eye of the porter, before catching the hotel taxi into the centre of Paris. No one mentioned Charlie Webster and what his plans might be, nor did Alice hear about the offer of a partnership, for Grace had advised Beth to tell as few people as possible until Harry knew the full story.

*

The sight of the queue was enough to put Beth off, for she had no patience with queues, preferring to miss an event or a show if it entailed standing for hours in a straggling line of humanity.

'I don't fancy queuing,' she said to her mother who showed no sign of surprise.

'No, I didn't imagine you would, darling. What do you want to do then?'

'You and Alice can go in if you like, but I'm going to wander around, maybe have a boat trip on the Seine.' She suppressed a smile at the matching looks of horror on the older women's faces. 'I'll be fine, honestly. For Heaven's sake, it's broad daylight!'

'Why don't we arrange to meet somewhere at one o'clock?' suggested Alice. 'That way, we can do something together in the afternoon.'

'Ah, Charlie and I have to make last minute farewells to the Blancs and Le Fevres. I'll be tied up until at least five.'

'I'm not happy at the idea of you wandering on your own,' Grace frowned, supported by Alice's nod.

'Mother, dearest, I'll be fine.' Beth checked her watch. 'What do you say I come back here in a couple of hours, meet you at this exact spot, have lunch together? Presuming, that is,' she added mischievously, 'that you've managed to get in there at all.'

'Beth,' beamed Alice. 'That's a great idea. Give us both a hug and off you go!'

Beth waved gaily as she sauntered off to explore Paris.

*

Charlie watched her take her leave of Grace and Alice and then followed her, at a safe distance, as far as the first café, where, without much difficulty, he manoeuvred himself into her line of vision.

'Charlie!' he heard her call and he glanced up, pretending to be surprised.

'Beth, what the heck are you doing here? I thought you were going to the Louvre with your two chaperones?'

'Have you seen the queue?'

'No,' he lied convincingly. 'You've no patience, I assume?'

'You couldn't be more right,' she laughed. 'Fancy a coffee?'

'Thought you'd never ask.'

They sat on the pavement in the sunshine and, knowing it would soon come to an end, Beth seemed to be savouring the sensations of Paris. His heart lurched at the sight of her, such a beautiful female, even here in the land of the sophisticated woman. With a struggle, he tore his eyes away from her and glanced at the menu.

'Shall we be really decadent and have a patisserie?'

'Mmm, yes, let's.'

'Have you enjoyed Paris?'

'Absolutely. I just love it. In fact,' she said, eyebrows raised. 'I think I could even live here.'

'Really? Oh, of course,' Charlie smiled, slapping his forehead. 'You speak the lingo,

291

I keep forgetting. You'd have no trouble with the way of life.'

'There are lots of things I like here.'

'Such as?'

'The 'arrangement',' she replied, face straight, eyes serious.

'You mean the...?' Charlie stopped. He could hardly bring himself to put it into words.

'Yes, the husband and the mistress thing,' she said solemnly and he was convinced she was serious. 'It seems like a great idea to me.'

'But you'd hate your husband to have...'

'Oh, not him,' Beth contradicted happily. 'Me! I'd fancy being the mistress.'

Charlie gaped at her and was about to say something outrageous when she burst out laughing and waggled a finger at him.

'I got you there, Charlie Webster, good and proper.'

'My God, I thought you meant it.'

'I must have inherited my acting skills from Mum then. She's the best.'

'Not after that display. I was completely taken in.'

After a quick nod to the waiter, Charlie sat back and brought the conversation around to the business.

'Have you given much thought to the partnership idea?'

'Yes, but I'll discuss it further with Harry, see what he thinks.'

'Further? You've spoken to him already?'

'Yes, of course,' she frowned. 'I'd never commit myself to anything without talking it over with him first.'

'Oh, I see.' His spirits plummeted. He and Frank had got it wrong.

'Now, can I please have the sugary, squashy thing that makes you fat just to look at it?'

The waiter was suddenly at the table, poised, so handsome and suave that Charlie wondered at Beth's disinterest in the man.

'Two coffee and that thing,' Charlie pointed to the menu. 'For the lady.'

'I'll have to go on a diet when I get back,' Beth grimaced. 'I've eaten like a pig in this place.'

'Oh, come off it, you're the skinniest thing I've ever seen.'

'Not underneath this voluminous shirt, I assure you.'

'Well, I wouldn't know, would I?' he asked unwisely, but beyond caring now.

'I think Marjory will be pleased about the partnership,' Beth said, ignoring the remark. 'She and I are the best of buddies.'

Charlie forced a smile and nodded, but his plan to capture her before old age set in was beginning to fade again.

*

Grace slept on the short flight home, while Alice and Beth carried on a hushed conversation. Beth was eager to tell Alice all about the partnership, for Alice kept asking Beth how the business side of the trip had worked out.

'You were so professional, honey,' Alice said with admiration. 'Your boss doesn't know how lucky he is, I can tell you.'

'He's very generous with my salary,' Beth felt obliged to say in his defence.

'He'd have sold diddly squat without you in Paris,' Alice told her young companion scornfully. 'You did it all, sweetie, the whole shebang, kit and caboodle. He should make you a partner, that's what he should do.'

'I'll discuss it with him.' Beth said diplomatically, avoiding Alice's gaze.

'Do you fancy him at all?'

'Alice!'

'You're blushing, so I presume you do,' Alice chuckled.

'No, I don't fancy him, although I admit he's handsome.'

'You know what they say about 'handsome', don't you?'

Beth let out an exasperated sigh. 'Don't I just? Mum never stops, and, apparently, neither did my Gran.'

'Ah, yes, Charlotte was quite a woman, poor soul.'

Instantly, and without any prompting from her, Beth saw possibilities in this line of chat.

'Did you know her really well?'

'Oh, yes, I was Grace's friend at the time, until the month Charlotte died.' Alice shuddered. 'That was such a tragedy for Grace. So sudden. Her mother had been ill during the winter, of course; never seemed able to kick the flu that year.'

'Did they ever speak about Grace's Dad, Thomas Blake?' Beth asked in as casual a manner as she could muster.

'No,' Alice said and it seemed as if she had been briefed on how to stop Beth in her tracks. 'I never heard anyone mention his name. Now, d'you think I could borrow your Marie Clair magazine for ten minutes?'

'Yeah, sure,' Beth smiled, handing it over and doing her best to conceal her disappointment. 'There's a great article in there about how to be more exciting in bed.'

'Now it's my turn to blush. Quick, tell me which page!'

*

Lucy Webster walked round to the back door of the cottage and bent down to lay the parcel where James would see it. Just as she was retracing her steps to the main street, the door opened and James's voice reached her ears.

'Good afternoon, Lucy.'

'Oh, James, I thought you might be at work.'

'I finished early,' he explained, coming down the path to meet her halfway. 'I'll be retired soon, you know, in a few years' time.' He halted a few feet away from her, stood with his hands in his pockets, looking at her with nothing more than neighbourly interest. 'I'm only working mornings now, doctor's orders.'

Lucy was plagued with worries about the man. Surely he had the all clear a few months ago?

'Aren't you well, James?'

'Oh, I'm fine,' he said firmly. 'But the doctor seems to think I should take it easy until I retire, and I don't mind.' He grinned suddenly. 'I enjoy the garden now a lot more than I did.'

'Well, my garden certainly enjoys your efforts,' Lucy told him.

'Thank you for the parcel of home-baking,' James said. 'At least, I'm supposing that's what it is?'

'Just a small token of thanks for all the tremendous work you've put into The Birches garden over the past few days.'

'Perhaps you would like a cup of tea in the garden?'

'A cup of tea would be lovely. Thank you.'

'We'll sit at the top of the garden,' he suggested. 'Just go up now, I'll bring the things in a minute.'

'Thank you,' she said again, turning to make her way up the path. She paused to examine the Meadowsweet, several of its fading flowers still clinging to the stems, petrified, determined to linger on until the very last moment. At the top of the garden, the path turned and suddenly she found herself in the most delightful oasis of colour and perfumes; 'a sight for sore eyes'. It was the loveliest little garden Lucy had ever seen. Transfixed, she moved towards the old wrought-iron bench and sat down, her eyes wandering around the flowers and shrubs, counting the hours and effort it must take to keep such a perfect haven.

Lucy was still admiring the display when James appeared with the tea tray, pride of place occupied by her homemade gingerbread.

'This is the loveliest garden I've ever seen,' she told him. 'Honestly, James, it's beautiful. You and Grace must sit up here all the time.'

'It's my favourite spot,' he smiled, placing the tray on a small wooden table he had fashioned himself, she suspected. 'Grace prefers to sit nearer the house.'

Lucy had to fight hard to keep the surprise from her expression, but she noted that James had not missed her reaction, although he swiftly changed the subject.

'How are all your new plants looking?'

'You'd hardly believe they could grow so much in a few days. I think they're extremely happy where they are.'

'And you, Lucy, are you happy where you are?'

'Yes, I love this village.'

She thought he grimaced briefly, but then he began to pour the tea.

'Beth seems to enjoy working with your son.'

'She's an angel,' Lucy enthused, glad to be back on neutral ground. 'In fact, she's saved the whole business, so Charlie told me.'

'She works hard,' James smiled, handing Lucy a cup. 'But I was disappointed she didn't go into teaching, perhaps get a good job in England.'

'And would you and Grace have gone to live there too?'

'Oh, no,' James laughed. 'Grace would never leave here.'

But she expected you to live here

'I see. So Beth wasn't keen then?'

'She met her future husband at that time.'

'He's a very nice man,' Lucy heard herself say stupidly, the kind of description you gave to a stranger in a railway carriage.

'Beth and Grace seem to think so,' James said, and she knew then that he had not approved his daughter's choice. 'This gingerbread is very good,' he smiled. 'My mother made it years ago, before the War.'

'You must miss your family.'

He looked at her with surprise. 'My family is here.'

Flustered, Lucy was at a loss. 'I mean, your family in England.'

'It's true,' James admitted, but with no sadness in his tone. 'I sometimes think of them, the way it used to be. But I have no regrets. And you,' he addressed her suddenly. 'Do you have any?'

'No, at least I don't think so.'

'Your husband died when he was very young?'

'Yes. I've been a widow for over twenty years now.'

'You must be a strong woman, to carry on yourself.'

'Strong? No, not strong. I had no choice.'

'Sometimes it's best,' James smiled. 'When you have no choice. It saves you from having to decide between one thing and another, don't you think?'

She laughed, for it was frequently her very thought. From somewhere in the flowerbed, she heard the buzzing of many bumblebees, a sound that transported her back to her childhood, to her parents' garden in Oxfordshire, to a time of misery and doubt.

294

'You look sad now,' James frowned.

'No, just thinking of the past,' she lied.

'Ah, the past,' he repeated, as if it left an unpleasant taste in his mouth. 'The past is best left alone, I think.'

They nodded to each other and Lucy could not recall a moment when she had been so content. She was roused from her reverie by a voice calling to them.

A young man appeared and, immediately, Lucy knew it was Beth's husband. Despite there being nothing immoral in her presence in the garden, that it was only a case of two neighbours chatting, she was aware of a growing feeling of discomfort, mostly on James's behalf.

'Harry,' James said now, rising to his feet and extending his hand. 'Please join us, if you have the time.'

'I was just passing,' the boy said. 'Just to see if there's something I can do for you.'

James shook his head. 'No, I'm fine. I've been home early these past days, so I've managed to do everything myself.' He turned to Lucy. 'This is Lucy Webster. Lucy, this is Harry Gillespie.'

Lucy sensed the boy's hostility, but could find no reason for it. With a gracious smile, she held out her hand.

*

Harry parked the car as close as he could to the air terminal and made his way to the concourse, still suffering the effects of driving Beth's car, an old Mini that had seen better days but which she refused to update because she insisted it was reliable.

He stifled a yawn. To compensate for the lateness of the hour, he had snatched forty winks after his meagre dinner of baked beans and cold quiche, waking to the sound of the alarm clock at half past nine – a time he would normally consider going to bed.

Now, as he locked up the car and picked up his book to read in case the flight were delayed, he tried to imagine how much worse he would feel next morning after having been up half the night.

To his surprise, the place was quite busy, although he suspected that most of the people wandering the concourse could be airport workers or individuals with nowhere else to go. He had read once that bus stations were not the only refuge for vagrants and the homeless, that airports were becoming a respite for the great unwashed, as one American wit had described them.

He discovered that the flight was on time and that he had less than half an hour to wait, and so he sat down in a seat nearest to the arrival point and drew out the book. He opened the page, but knew that his mind would be focussed on Annie Kerr.

Harry had known as soon as he laid eyes on the girl that she might bring nothing but trouble to his relationship with Beth: she had looked at him that first day and he had read quite clearly the message she was sending out. If Beth knew even of the explicit conversation he had had with Annie that day, she would have blown her top.

'You know,' she had said, regarding him with undisguised lust. 'I could show you a thing or two.'

'I've no doubt you could,' he had replied casually, but the girl's attributes were not easily ignored. 'But I'm in love with Beth.'

'So what?' she had asked dismissively. 'Doesn't mean we can't have a bit of fun before you tie the knot.'

'Beth gives me all the fun I need.'

'You haven't sampled mine,' Annie had smiled, reaching out to touch his shoulder. 'I could make you forget all about her for half an hour.'

'Half an hour?' he had laughed, too late to ponder the wisdom of even carrying on this conversation. 'Beth can do a lot better than that.'

'Ah, so it's quantity you want, not quality?'

'Look, I suggest we stop this nonsense,' Harry had said impatiently. 'Some friend you're turning out to be.'

With that, he had left her standing in the kitchen and gone to seek Beth out, cursing himself for having given even the slightest encouragement to a girl who he knew could become a nuisance; if not a threat.

He opened his book and tried to rid his mind of Annie Kerr's breasts.

*

Grace had slept for most of the flight, but was now wide-awake, peering from the window into the gloom of the night, the blinking wing light the only thing she could see. It hardly seemed possible that they had been gone only six days, for it felt more like a month; perhaps because of the itinerary that Alice had insisted on; the cramming in of sights and experiences regardless of aching feet and minds.

'Oh, look!' she heard Alice say now. 'I can see the airfield over there! See the lights?'

'Thank Heavens,' sighed Beth in her mother's ear. 'I'm so tired I could sleep for a week.'

'You should have had a snooze on the plane. I feel fine.'

'I wanted to chat to Alice, about the past.'

Grace's heart sank. 'Goodness me, child, you do seem to have an obsession with it. At your age I never gave it a moment's thought.'

It was blatantly untrue, for she had thought of nothing else, especially where her father was concerned, a man she had doted on for years, until that fateful day when she had witnessed his flight on a Dundee street.

'I bet you did,' Beth disagreed guardedly. 'I bet you thought about my grandfather a lot.'

'Did you manage to put the thumbscrews on Alice, find out what you wanted?'

Beth back-pedalled and Grace surmised she had picked up the cautionary tone.

'It was a general chat about the past,' she insisted. 'Not just about our family.'

'Hey, you two,' Alice said from the seat behind. 'I hope Harry hasn't forgotten he's meeting us.'

'No,' Grace assured her. 'He'll be there. He's the most reliable person.'

She caught sight of the comical face that Beth pulled at Alice but was too happy to be home to make an issue of it.

As the plane rushed towards the runway, Grace's heart skipped a beat, for in a few short hours, she would be at home, surrounded by familiar things and people, a stranger no longer, completely at ease. All at once, she was beset by guilt: it was a feeling that James had known only once, almost twenty years ago; a visit to his childhood home. Was he resentful at having been forced to give it up for her? If it were Grace being asked to relinquish her home, she knew what the answer would be.

*

The first Harry saw of Beth was the blonde hair flying around her shoulders, and then came her shriek of joy. He might have minded the attention she attracted were it not for the fact it was always glances of admiration, this time from the men waiting for their own relatives. For as long as he had known her, she had exercised that effect on the male

296

population, although, like Grace, she appeared oblivious of it.

'Harry!' she yelled, throwing herself at him, not stopping to wonder if she was embarrassing him. 'I missed you so much, I'll never go away again!'

'Suits me,' he murmured into her hair. 'I missed you too.'

She stepped back and grinned at him.

'You mean you haven't eaten anything this week?'

'Apart from the rotten apple you threw out to the birds last week, no.'

She hugged him again and, over her head, he caught sight of Grace. He disentangled himself from Beth and went to carry the cases.

'How wonderful to see you,' Grace smiled, allowing him to take her case. 'This is Alice, my best friend from years back,' she added, gently pushing Alice forward. 'Alice, this is Harry.'

'Well, I'll be damned,' Alice laughed.

'Why, what have you done?' Harry joked. He smiled, shook her hand, but turned to look at Grace.

'I hope you told her good things about me.'

'Well, of course,' she responded lightly. 'Now lead me to Beth's jalopy, let me sink into the back seat or I'll expire on the spot.'

'Golly,' he heard Alice whisper to Grace. 'Ain't the boy handsome?'

He missed Grace's reply, for Beth was dragging him by the arm and forcing him to speed up.

'Come on, do,' she tutted, her heels clicking across the floor. 'I can hardly wait to get home, show you what I've learnt from the Parisiennes.'

He laughed and realised how much he had missed her sense of fun, not to mention her considerable bedroom skills. An unbidden image of Annie Kerr flooded his mind for a moment and he almost stumbled.

'Have you been drinking, Gillespie?'

'No, it was just the thought of you teaching me what Parisiennes do.'

'I love you,' Beth whispered, her lips close to his ear. 'By the time we get home, you won't care how late it is.'

'By the way, where's Charlie Webster?' Harry asked, glancing behind them.

'Coming back tomorrow,' Beth said airily. 'Last-minute stuff, you know?'

As the old Mini came into view, Beth let out a yelp of joy. 'Oh, it's Milly! How I've missed you, you old darling!'

*

On the way home, Grace and Alice sat in the back seat, too tired to chat, although Grace had the impression that Alice was transfixed by Harry's looks. She had to stifle the unkind idea of Alice flirting with the boy for the next fortnight.

'How's Dad?' Beth was asking.

'Fine, I popped out to see him, to make sure.'

Harry knew that, for obvious reasons, James would make no comment on the brief ten minutes his son-in-law had afforded him the day before, and so he had no qualms about accepting Beth's lingering kiss on his cheek.

'Thanks, you're wonderful. Any signs he's been working too hard in the garden?'

'No,' Harry replied cautiously, not about to mention Lucy Webster. 'He's perfectly fine, I assure you.'

Beth yawned. 'I can hardly wait to see him, give him his present.'

'You bought presents?'

'Of course, we all did, didn't we girls?'

297

'I bought so many I had to borrow Grace's case,' Alice laughed from the back seat. 'Lord knows how I'll ever manage to carry it all the way to the States.'

'It sounds so exciting,' sighed Beth. 'Living over there, I mean.'

'You should come and visit me, see for yourself.'

Harry braced himself for Beth's outburst of glee but, surprisingly, she only nodded and said how kind Alice was. He was amazed, for he could have sworn it was the sort of trip that would most appeal to her.

'I hope James has put fresh flowers in Alice's room,' he heard Grace say quietly. 'Men don't usually think of these things, do they?'

'Don't worry, I'm so grateful to be staying with you that a few flowers won't change that.' Alice tapped Beth on the shoulder and added: 'Remember not to mention divorce and remarriage, otherwise your father will throw me out!'

The rest of the journey passed in silence: Beth fell asleep as soon as they left Edinburgh, and Harry was glad of the absence of chatter; although it made room for Annie Kerr.

*

Grace's first thoughts when they arrived at the house revolved around Alice and making sure of her guest's comfort. As she carried out last-minute improvements to Alice's bedroom – Beth's old room, which had lain empty since Frank had professed a preference for the small downstairs bedroom.

Grace's mind refused to settle, alternating between joy at her friend's visit after so long an absence and trepidation at the thought of Beth's insatiable interest in her grandfather.

Despite having briefed Alice on the possibility of awkward questions and despite her assurances that she would remain tight-lipped about Thomas Blake, Grace was not convinced that the visit would pass without some attempt on her daughter's part to discover the truth – an expedient truth, the kind that could be all things to all people. Hastily, she pushed aside her own desire to manipulate the facts to suit herself.

'Grace, for Pete's sake!' she heard Alice exclaim from the doorway. 'Will you stop rushing around this minute and come down for supper?'

'I'm finished anyway, just this window to close if you'd prefer?'

'Please,' Alice laughed. 'You wouldn't believe the heat in the States. This is much more comfortable.' She gave her friend a critical look before continuing. 'You know, when I said that Beth should come over to the States, I was meaning you too, Grace. I saw how much you enjoyed Paris, how you came out of your shell a little…'

'My shell?' Grace asked incredulously. 'Do I have one?'

'Oh, you most certainly do, sweetie, and I worry about you.'

'Goodness me, I forbid you to do that, Alice Cameron – oh, I'm sorry, Alice, I keep forgetting.'

'I'll always be Alice Cameron,' Alice smiled, going over and laying red-painted fingers upon her friend's arm. 'The same as you'll always be Grace Blake to me. Now, let's go down and eat ourselves silly.'

*

After supper, Beth and Harry took their leave. With a last, tearful hug, Beth professed herself miserable at the thought of the holiday coming to an end, and Grace had to feign a similar sentiment, for now that she was home she was the happiest person on earth.

'And I'll miss you too, darling, but perhaps we can all meet up next week, for a coffee?'

'I'll phone you,' were Beth's final, sorrowful words before she ran off to catch up with Harry.

'Gosh, she's a darling,' said Alice, mostly to James. 'You should be so proud of her.'

'I am,' he smiled, glancing at Grace. 'I knew I would be the first time I saw her.'

Grace's mind flew immediately to the day that James had first set eyes on his daughter, during one of the coldest, harshest winters they had ever known.

'She looked exactly like you,' she said now. 'Except for the tantrums.'

James nodded. 'Not so many now, though.'

Alice tutted loudly. 'Only the very best people have tantrums, you know. It means they're geniuses.'

'I can believe that,' James said seriously. 'I see that the two of you had a good time in Paris.'

'Oh, we did,' Alice confirmed, grabbing Grace's hand. 'In fact, I wish we could see each other all the time.'

'How's your husband?'

'He's fine,' Alice smiled, hardly missing a breath, although Grace's heart skipped. 'Sends his regards. Now, is it time for bed yet, 'cause I'm exhausted!'

*

Grace lay at James's side, drowsily going over the past few days, sifting out the best moments, recalling them in order so that she could tell James the next day. He had been as delighted to have her home as she was to be home, fussing over her in the way she had become used to, taking care of the small things he knew were important to her.

'I missed you so much,' she told him as they prepared for bed. 'I thought about you all the time.'

He had smiled and nodded, but if she anticipated a similar compliment she was disappointed, for he had said only that he hoped it would be a long time before she went away again and she had been obliged to find satisfaction in words that fell far short of her expectations.

The familiar, comforting outdoor sounds kept her company as she drifted in and out of sleep and she rejoiced to be home again. Her last thought, however, before she succumbed to fatigue was that, after declaring his delight at seeing her home again and having kissed her as tenderly as she could wish, her husband had not wanted to make love.

*

Beth twisted and turned, eventually giving up on sleep and climbing from the bed. She donned a loose dressing gown and padded through to the kitchen, where she switched on the kettle and set about making herself a hot drink.

After a few minutes, just as she was pouring water into the mug, she heard Harry moving around, the sound of his bare feet in the hallway.

'Are you a vampire, by any chance?' he asked from the doorway.

'Batwoman, actually, straight from the comic book.'

'It's Bat *man*, you woman's libber, and make one for me before I 'pow' you.'

They sat in the dimly lit kitchen, the first signs of dawn creeping into the sky.

'Shouldn't that be 'kapow!'?' she asked, making a reasonable job of fooling her

299

husband into believing she was totally happy.

It had been the partnership thing that had kept her awake and she guessed that he knew. Harry Gillespie was a mind reader when it came to his wife's stash of secrets and it still annoyed her that he was so good at it when she rarely had any idea of what he was thinking, even in things as mundane as what he liked on his damned sandwich.

'So, what's the reason for the night-prowling?' he asked suddenly, almost causing her to drop her mug of cocoa.

'Jet lag.'

He laughed at that, for a flight to Paris could hardly qualify. 'Really?'

'No, not really,' Beth frowned. 'As if you didn't already know, Gillespie.'

She saw the flicker of a smile at the corner of his mouth, the mouth that had wreaked havoc with her self-control just an hour ago.

'I like it when you call me Gillespie.'

'I know, that's why I do it.'

He looked astonished and Beth chalked one up for her.

'How did you know I liked it?'

'Because you never asked me not to.'

'Ah, that's too deep for me at this time of the morning.'

'I could kick myself for not telling you first about the partnership,' Beth said with more remorse than a liberated woman should show. 'I should have wired you or something.'

'Beth, sweetheart, what difference would it have made? I would have thought it a great idea, whether or not you told me first.'

She stared at him, disbelieving. 'You're having me on.'

He smiled wickedly. 'If you're not too tired, it's a deal.'

'You're impossible.'

'Annie Kerr was here when you were away.'

The hand that was holding her drink froze on the way to her lips. Beth's heart sank in an instant: she had been right all along! The cow had succeeded at last.

'What d'you want me to say?' she asked, her stomach churning so much that she feared she would throw up any minute.

'I didn't let her in,' Harry said irritably. 'She came whining to the door, asked for money and so I slipped a fiver under the door and told her to piss off.'

Beth tried to hide a smile, for it was completely within the scope of Harry's character to do exactly that. 'What time of night did she turn up?'

Harry shrugged, glanced at the clock as if it would jog his memory.

'After ten, I think.'

'And you left her out there, in the dead of night, at the mercy of...?'

'Beth, stop it,' Harry said abruptly. 'Stop the play-acting. I know you wouldn't care if I left her on the doorstep, so stop pretending.'

For Beth, it was the last straw: was nothing sacred anymore? Was there not one tiny little insignificant thought that she could claim as her own?

'Yes I would care,' she denied hotly. 'I know you can't stand her but she's my friend and I'll stick with her through thick and thin.' She sat back in her chair, cheeks flushed, heart pounding. The one thing she absolutely hated was to be predictable.

'Even if she tries to screw your husband?' Harry asked rudely.

'She wouldn't.'

'Oh, yes,' he laughed, fuelling Beth's anger. 'She certainly would. God knows how you managed to pick up such a slag for a friend.'

'That's a horrible thing to say and you know it!'

'Tell you what,' Harry said pleasantly, leaning across the table in a confidential manner, signalling that she had asked for it and he was about to oblige.

'I'll invite her in next time you're not here, see who's right, shall I?'

He leaned back again, eyes on her face, smile intact, and Beth knew the argument was lost.

'I suppose you think you're smart.'

'No, I suppose *you* think *I'm* stupid.'

'Did you really send her away?' she asked after a long pause, wherein she had decided that her only course of action was appeasement.

'Of course I did, Beth. The girl's a menace.'

'And you really do think she'd try it on with you?'

'Yes, in the same way as she'd try it on with anything that wears trousers. I can't help comparing the two of you,' he went on with a frown. 'You were both brought up by strict fathers and she's a bloody trollop. What does that tell you?'

'Her Mum's ill,' Beth reminded him. 'Annie's had a terrible life, not knowing if her Mum would survive until the next day. If it was my Mum, maybe I'd be a trollop as well.' She gazed into the dregs of her mug, spirits sinking suddenly at the idea of her mother ever taking ill. 'My God, I don't know what I'd do without her.'

'Hey, come on,' she heard Harry say gently, and then she felt his arms around her. 'Grace is as hale and hearty as they make them, so don't even think about it. Come back to bed,' he whispered into her hair. 'I've a remedy for the blues.'

*

Alice woke with a start and listened for a moment. As a girl, she had lived and worked in the countryside around here, accustomed to the sights and sounds of the wildlife, some sights not so pleasant, some sounds decidedly frightening; yet for years now she had lived in a small American suburb, host to only the occasional songbird and her neighbour's two cats, with no more frightening sound than the rare feline squabble between them. Tonight, back in unfamiliar territory, she was on edge, torn between closing the window and enduring the stuffy attic room, and throwing it wide to be assailed by noises of the night.

Even in the privacy of the room, she was immediately ashamed of her castigating the room as 'stuffy' when Grace had worked so hard to please her, but the truth was that Alice was used to large rooms, air conditioning, swimming pools, vast kitchens that the whole family gathered in and still could not fill. Compared to this, her town house was huge and she had space to call her own.

She sighed at the words – 'space to call her own' – for it was, indeed, all hers now, now that Brad had found a ripe little twenty-year-old to tickle his fancy. She had no idea whether to tell Grace the whole truth or not, no idea what impression her friend might gain from such an admission; her second marriage failure and she was still only forty-eight.

The old clock in the hall began striking the hour and she pulled the sheet over her head so that she was not tempted to count.

Oh, Lordy, but how she'd messed things up!

Chapter Twenty

James finished off the previous night's supper dishes and set about making his wife's breakfast, intending to carry it up to her on a tray, to surprise her on her first morning back. A few moments before the toast was ready, however, the kitchen door opened and she appeared, still in her dressing gown but looking refreshed and as happy as he had seen her for months.

'Oh, how disappointing, I was hoping to surprise you with breakfast.'

'I couldn't lie in bed a moment longer,' she said, stifling a yawn and sitting down at the table. 'I just had to get up and see everything again.'

James was puzzled. 'See everything. What everything?'

'The house, the view from the windows, the flowers in the garden. All the things I've missed.'

He smiled and shook his head. 'But you were only away for a few days.'

'I know,' she admitted, blushing slightly. 'And it's stupid. But I could hardly wait to get home.'

'And see everything again,' James teased.

'I missed you most of all.'

He laid the crockery and cutlery at her place and then touched her shoulder fleetingly before moving to pour the coffee. He knew she was expecting him to say something similar and there was no excuse for the delay, but by the time he sat down opposite her and gave her his full attention, it was already too late and she was speaking again.

'Did you keep busy while I was gone?'

'Yes, I helped Lucy with her garden.'

'Good,' Grace said, her eyes on the toast she was spreading. 'She's a poor soul, being a widow for so long. I'm glad you're helping her.' She looked up at him. 'She's so different from Molly, don't you think?'

'Like chalk and cheese'.

'She couldn't be more different, and I enjoy her friendship.'

'I think it is a good idea if you see her more often,' James said casually. 'I like the woman and she's the best kind of friend for you, Grace.'

He wondered if he had sounded too eager but Grace appeared to be in total agreement.

'Why did you never tell me about Molly making a pass at you?'

James was astonished. 'When did she do that?'

Grace shrugged. 'Maybe my information was wrong.'

'Alice?'

Grace raised her eyebrows. 'How did you know?'

'Because she's the only one you've kept company with recently.'

'Anyway, it's not important. And you're right about Lucy being a good friend. Especially now with Beth and her son.'

James was shocked, but, before he could speak, Grace laughed and waved her hand at him.

'No, no, not that, James! I'm sorry, I should have explained right away. Charlie has asked her to become a partner in the business.'

Had she made such an announcement only a month ago, James knew that his reaction would have been disappointment, disappointment that Beth was squandering her language degree on a fly-by-night scheme with no prospects. Now that he had come to know Lucy Webster better, however, he was pleased that it would draw her closer to

Grace.

'I'm delighted,' he told Grace.

'You are?'

'Of course,' he affirmed, his attention on his plate. 'If Beth's happy, then I'm happy.'

'She'll be relieved to hear it,' Grace smiled. 'I think she was dreading telling you. That's why she asked me to do it.'

James was horrified. 'Dreading telling me? Am I such a horrible father then?'

Grace sighed. 'Don't be silly, James, you know what I mean. A year ago, you'd have told her she was wasting her degree on a job like this.'

'I've changed a lot since the heart attack,' James said truthfully. 'Some things aren't so important for me now.'

'Am I important to you now?' she asked warily.

'Of course you are. You are always important to me. I only meant that my attitude to some things has changed. I can see now that I was too set in my ways.'

'But I liked you set in your ways,' she said with a touch of desperation. 'That was what made me love you in the first place.'

Try as he might, James could not conceal a smile. 'Grace, that's not true and you know it. You and I were always arguing about it.'

'No, we weren't,' she contradicted strongly. 'Not about your values, never about them. I admired you – I still admire you – for your old-fashioned values. I would hate it if you let them go.'

James shook his head. 'Anyway, I'm glad you're home.'

*

As she climbed the stairs with Alice's tray, Grace's mind kept returning to her conversation with James. He had seemed distant, uninterested, not even asking about Paris, or about the implications of Beth's promotion; and yet when she had mentioned Lucy Webster, he had talked at length about how grateful she had been for his help with her flowerbeds and how he had invited her to tea in the garden.

An inappropriate sense of jealousy filled Grace's mind and she acknowledged it to be irrational. She was glad of Alice's presence in the house. At least, for a week or two, there would be someone to distract her, perhaps even someone to confide in, if she could bring herself to do so. How many times in Paris had she been on the verge of telling Alice everything there was to tell about her intended revenge on Thomas Blake?

She knocked on the bedroom door and was greeted by her friend's welcome voice. With rising spirits, Grace pushed open the door and went in.

'Oh, my, you're spoiling me already,' Alice tutted, lifting herself into a seating position in bed. 'Look at this! You are naughty, Grace, I should be doing this for you.'

'James did it for me,' Grace lied, a small white lie that satisfied them both. 'I wanted to do the same for you. Here you are, I hope you like a boiled egg and toast.'

'You know, I haven't tasted a decent egg for years. I suppose this one's from next door's hens?'

'No, from Lucy Webster's hens. She brought them down the day before yesterday, James said.'

'Lucy Webster,' Alice repeated, as if she were trying to fit a face to the name. 'Does she live in the village?'

'At The Birches.'

Alice flashed Grace a look of mischief. 'Ah, the Kinmont's old place.'

'Don't you start,' Grace smiled. 'That's all in the past, and it was nothing anyway.'

'He was nuts about you, that Kinmont boy. I never saw such a lovesick expression.'

'It was a crush, that was all.'

'Come and sit by me,' Alice said, patting the bed. 'Talk to me while I scoff this lot.'

'Well, don't think I'm going to talk about Roderick Kinmont,' Grace laughed. 'Any other subject is fine.'

'Harry's a fine boy.'

'Yes, he is.'

'He's English, isn't he? I mean, from the accent?'

'Yes, from Newbury.'

'I'm none the wiser,' Alice laughed. 'Does he have family there?'

'I don't think so.'

'What, no mother and father?'

'His mother ran off with someone, and his father is dead.'

Alice stopped chewing. 'Oh, my, the poor boy! He must have been pretty miserable.'

'He rarely talks about it.'

'Is his mother still alive then?'

'I suppose she could be.'

'Does he ever contact her?'

'I don't think so. How's the egg?'

Alice grinned. 'Absolutely perfect. Do convey my gratitude to Lucy and her hens.'

'You can do that yourself,' Grace told her, rising from the bed. 'She left a note inviting us up for tea this afternoon.'

'Isn't it funny for you, being in that house, with all its memories?'

'Memories? You mean, of Roderick?'

'No, I mean of Charlotte.'

Grace was besieged by images of her mother – in Celia Kinmont's kitchen, peeling dozens of potatoes, washing countless dishes, earning just enough money to make ends meet. Her heart ached suddenly for things lost.

'I miss my mother more than ever. Isn't that strange?'

'No, I think it's normal,' Alice said firmly. 'I still miss mine, and she and I were never really close.' She glanced at Grace, whose fingers were already on the door handle. 'You and Charlotte were the closest pair I've ever seen.' Not trusting herself to speak, Grace nodded and opened the door. 'I'll be out of bed in ten minutes,' Alice called after her.

'No rush,' Grace said before she closed the door.

*

Thomas saw the girl at the window, watched her as she stood gazing out onto the Inch. Because of the distance between them, not to mention the fog that was drifting around that morning, she was unaware of his presence.

He had breathed a sigh of relief to know that she was back; from Paris, no less, the obliging Marjory had informed him. A business trip it had been; Paris without her husband too. Was that not the oddest thing, regardless of whether it was business or not? He had envisaged her and her boss together, flirting over a romantic dinner perhaps, or dancing to the heady melodies of the street musicians, or even side by side in the cocktail bar, exchanging confidences. It was a risk he would not have taken with his own wife, not even with Charlotte: a lovely young girl thrown into the company of a handsome rogue like Charlie Webster; at least, that's what he had heard from Sarah at the George; and she should know.

Thomas crossed the street and made his way towards the café where his habit was to take breakfast. It not only saved him from cooking in his lonely kitchen with only the infernal ticking of the clock to keep him company; but also, it had given rise to meeting a few interesting people, particularly John, a solicitor in a past life, but retired now through ill-health.

Thomas saw his new friend sitting at the window of the café as soon as he turned into the street. He sighed and walked out briskly: life was improving by the day.

'Morning!' he called as he strode towards John. 'Isn't it a wonderful day?'

'Man, it's bucketing down and you can't see your hand in front of you. Have you won the pools?'

'Not exactly, but I've had good news this morning, and, before you ask, it's a secret.' He removed his coat, hung it on the peg nearest their table and sat down. 'Family business,' he added, tapping the side of his nose.

'Ah, yes,' John smiled. 'I had my fair share of that, believe me.'

He said it with such acrimony that Thomas was intrigued: the man had given the impression of having been one of the most successful investment advisers in Perthshire, a man expected to have been in complete control of his own family. Thomas filed the remark away for future use and changed the subject.

'Did you read about the rise of the SNP?'

'Waste of time,' John said dismissively. 'A load of rubbish.'

Thomas laughed and perused the menu. 'You're one up on me, for I've no idea what they stand for.'

'An independent Scotland,' John scoffed. 'Have you ever heard anything quite so ridiculous?'

'What's ridiculous about it?'

'The best of Scotland left years ago.'

'Oh? Where did they go?'

'America, Australia, Canada, you name it, they went there.'

'I lived in South America for decades,' Thomas said nonchalantly, knowing the effect it would have, the effect it always had on people hereabouts.

John's eyebrows rose. 'You did? Banking, was it?'

'Engineering.'

'Engineering, eh? A man of mystery.'

'Hardly,' Thomas laughed, beckoning the waitress over. 'I worked for the national railway.'

'Why did you come back here? I'd imagine it's a dull life after South America.'

'I was hoping to meet up with someone I'd known years ago.'

John smiled knowingly, man to man. 'A woman, I'll bet.'

'And you'd be right.'

'And have you? Met up with her again?'

'Alas, no,' Thomas said and the rawness of his hurt took him by surprise, so much so that he hesitated, shifted his gaze from his companion's face to the view of the street. 'Sadly, she'd passed away.'

'Oh, I see. Must have been a shock for you.'

'Indeed.'

The waitress, who had been standing by respectfully, stepped forward at Thomas's bidding and raised pencil to pad. Once they had ordered bacon, eggs and tomatoes, the conversation continued, this time steered back to the SNP.

'They've no idea what an independent Scotland would mean,' John muttered. 'The damned country would be bankrupt before you knew it. One thing I can't stand and that's stupid people, especially when they don't even know how stupid they are.'

'But isn't there North Sea oil?'

'Oh, there's hardly any, I'll wager. A lot of fuss about nothing. By the way, and I hope you don't mind my asking, but are you retired now?'

'Thankfully, yes, retired over five years ago.'

'Did you...?' John paused, glanced apologetically at Thomas before going on: 'I mean, did you have family out there?'

'No,' Thomas lied. 'Never had the time, to be honest. No, I worked twenty four hours a day and before I knew it, my life was over.'

'You're still a young man,' John smiled. 'And there's many a fair maid in Perth.' He looked at Thomas, as if he had cracked some sort of joke, but when Thomas failed to respond, John shrugged and moved his attention to the street.

'I have met a very nice lady in Perth,' Thomas volunteered, wondering if the admission were a mistake: Daphne could be this man's sister; or ex-wife...

'Good for you. What's the lady's name? Do I know her, perhaps?'

'Her name's Margaret,' Thomas lied, the second time in as many sentences. 'She's new in Perth, used to live in Edinburgh.'

'Ah, well I won't know her then,' John said, almost disappointedly.

'Oh, good,' Thomas said, rubbing his hands. 'Here comes our breakfast and I'm starving.'

*

Harry was having difficulty keeping his eyes open. It had seemed a good idea the night before to cavort around the bedroom until dawn, but now he was paying the price. Sandra, who had known about the lateness of his trip to the airport, was holding the fort in the outer office, way-laying any calls that she could deal with herself, but it was only a matter of time before a client would walk in and expect Harry to exhibit a razor-sharp mind.

Razor-sharp

He was shocked by the intensity of the image.

*

'*You need a razor-sharp mind to stay one step ahead of me,' his mother said, as they sat having a picnic on the beach. 'Fortunately, your father's mind is as blunt as that plastic spade you're using.'*

'*He bought it for me,' Harry admitted.*

'*I'll buy you a better one for next time.'*

'*Didn't he want to come with us?'*

'*Of course he did,' his mother laughed. 'But it would have spoilt our day.'*

'*Will he ever come with us?' He almost gasped at the scowl his question evoked and quickly backtracked. 'I don't want him to anyway.'*

'*Suits me,' his mother smiled, taking a cigarette from its packet and doing her best to light it in the gusty wind off the sea. 'Oh, how I wish he could be here.'*

'*But you just said you didn't want him to come,' Harry dared to say.*

'*Not your father, you ninny, I mean* him.*'*

'*Who?'*

'*Never mind,' his mother had said, in the gentlest tone Harry had ever heard, one that had never been used with him. 'You would love him as I do.'*

'*Why don't you want me to know his name?'*

'*Because it's none of your business.'*

306

His mother had held the cigarette in mid-air a moment, her eyes on the horizon, no trace of annoyance on her face. Harry knew he was being cheeky, but he took courage from the silence and asked:

'Are you going to marry him?'

*

Harry breathed deeply, swamped even now by the memory of his mother's anger, the endless threats never to mention their conversation to his father. Even as a child, he had felt the anger in her tone and had assumed that the nameless man, whoever he was, was not a friend of the family.

Harry turned on the cooling fan on the desk and loosened his tie; he had plenty time to smarten up if Sandra buzzed through. He looked at his diary and ticked off three morning appointments for which the paperwork was prepared, and then he made a note of the papers he needed for the afternoon, for a Mrs Daphne something-or-other, who had sounded like a right old eccentric on the phone, but was a vague acquaintance of Sandra's and would he do her a favour?

As he leafed through the relevant sections of his law book, the telephone rang, an outside line. He looked at it for a few seconds and then picked up.

'Charlie Webster here. Is that Harry?'

'This is Harry Gillespie,' Harry opted to say, showing his disdain for any familiarity right at the start. The man may be Beth's business partner now, but he was nothing to Harry.

'Beth told you about her promotion, I take it?'

'She did, yes.'

'I was wondering if you and she would like to have dinner one night, to celebrate, maybe have a chat?'

'Sorry, I can't see what it has to do with me,' Harry said politely and was satisfied at the silence it provoked. He waited, not in the least inclined to make it any easier for the man.

'Ah, I was hoping that we could discuss things, get to know each other maybe.'

'Were you?'

'Beth thought it was a good idea,' Charlie Webster said pointedly.

'Did she?'

'I can tell you're busy,' came the short response. 'Sorry to have troubled you.'

As the line went dead, Harry sighed heavily. Although he doubted that she had thought it a 'good idea', he knew it would be an uphill struggle to fend off a tantrum.

He stood up, straightened his tie and went to speak to Sandra. At least there would be no tantrums from that quarter, and he might glean some extra information about Daphne the eccentric.

*

Alice and Grace sat in the shade of Lily Morris' sun umbrella sipping tea and pondering the passage of time, fearful of its disregard for human beings.

'Imagine,' Lily shook her head. 'The last day you two sat here, you were both gay young things.'

'We were young anyway,' Grace chipped in swiftly, before the other two could pass comment. 'I'm not so sure if we were gay.'

'Yes, we were,' Alice laughed. 'At the peak of our womanhood we were, full of vitality and enthusiasm.'

'I can't remember that far back. Are you sure it's us you're thinking about?'

'You were the lifeblood of our society,' Lily reminded Grace. 'No one had ever witnessed such a perfect Lady Bracknell, especially Graham,' she added slyly, at which Alice turned inquisitive eyes to Grace.

'Graham? Loves young dream?'

'I haven't heard that expression for years,' Grace said, deflecting her answer. 'Mum used to say it all the time.'

'He,' Lily told Alice firmly. 'He was Grace's most ardent admirer, still is as a matter of fact. He was inconsolable when we broke up for the summer.'

'Oh, for Heaven's sake!' Grace frowned. 'Are you never going to stop teasing the man over it?'

'Was he the reporter who did that piece about you in the '50s?' Alice had to know.

'Yes,' Lily replied. 'He fair got carried away too, called her the Marilyn Monroe of Perthshire.'

'He did not!' Grace renounced angrily. 'I'll not let you treat him like this, Lily.'

Lily's smile faded. 'It was just a joke, pet, that's all. You know I like him.'

'Did you make these, Lily?' Alice asked, lifting her third treacle bun.

'Aye, I did, but try one of the oven scones, they're Grace's recipe.'

'It's a pity your husband couldn't come over,' Grace said once the atmosphere had lightened and after they had all helped themselves to more tea. 'I'd have liked to meet him.'

Alice grimaced. 'I wasn't sure whether to tell you or not, Grace.'

'Tell me what?'

Alice hesitated briefly, giving rise to Lily's covert glance towards Grace.

'Well, it's over.'

'Oh, no! Alice, I'm so sorry, I'd no idea.'

Alice shrugged. 'He found someone else, that's all, a younger model.'

'But you're not even fifty yet,' Grace protested in her friend's defence.

'Maybe not,' Alice smiled ruefully. 'But she's only twenty-six.'

'That's horrible,' Lily remarked. 'But just like a man.'

'James hasn't traded me in yet,' Grace said. 'At least, not yet.'

'He'll not do that,' Alice reassured her friend. 'It's real love with you two.'

'But I thought it was real love with you and...'

'Real lust,' corrected Alice playfully. 'Once he'd sampled all my delights, it was only a matter of time.'

They sat in silence for a while, with only the droning of the bumblebees and the whirr of birds' wings as accompaniment. It was Grace who spoke first.

'You should come home to Scotland and stay here now.'

If she had expected Alice to display astonishment or disapproval, Grace was surprised to see the flicker of agreement in her friend's eyes.

'I've thought about it.'

'Well, why don't you?' Grace asked eagerly, envisaging the two of them together again, confidantes, best friends, as they had been over twenty years ago.

'I'm not sure,' Alice said slowly. 'I wonder if I've changed so much that I...'

'You haven't changed at all,' said Lily brightly. 'You'd fit in here the way you did years ago, Alice Cameron, and I, for one, would be happy if you came home.'

Alice was taken aback at the old woman's sentiment, but Grace could tell that it would need more than one person's blessing to persuade her friend to come home.

'Let's change the subject,' she said diplomatically. 'Alice will make her own decision in her own time.'

'Was it the early '50's you were here last time? Lily asked.

'1953, Coronation year.'

'I remember it as if it were yesterday, ' Lily laughed. 'I was in Edinburgh at the time and what a crowd gathered. But you know, I didn't see a blessed thing!'

'Oh, we saw everything,' Grace smiled. 'At Molly's. The whole village descended on the poor woman that day, ate her out of house and home.'

'She had the first T.V. set in the village, didn't she?' asked Alice. 'You were all so thrilled here, but, of course,' she smiled slyly. 'I had one already. We Americans always do things first.'

'You may as well blow your own trumpet,' Grace told her cheerfully. 'No one else will.'

'You know, you're a different person when Alice is here,' Lily said suddenly, causing Grace to look at her sharply.

'Am I?'

'Yes,' Alice butted in. 'You're much more fun.'

'And how would you know what I'm like when you're not here?' Grace asked patiently.

'Because you write letters to me all the time and you never seem to have any fun at all, always doing things for people, never for yourself.'

'Perhaps it's just the way I write. Believe me, I don't always do things for other people and I do have fun.'

'The last time I was here,' Alice told Lily, much to the embarrassment of her friend. 'I dragged her into Perth and made her have a good time.'

Lily shrugged. 'That's what friends are for, surely? Oh, by the way, to change the subject, I was so pleased that Beth's to be a full partner in the business.'

'She's thrilled,' Grace smiled. 'It was the only thing she spoke about that night before she fell asleep.'

'Wasn't it lucky that Lucy Webster mentioned it to you? You see how well it's all turned out?' Lily paused momentarily, as if uncertain about continuing, but then she straightened her shoulders. 'There's one thing I was wondering.'

'What's that?' Grace asked warily.

'Will she be too much of a business woman to give you any grandchildren?'

Grace laughed. 'One minute you're castigating me for doing things for other people, and the next you're putting my name down for babysitting!'

'Anyway, let's have another treacle scone,' Alice suggested.

'Heaven's, we can't,' Grace cautioned. 'We've to pop into Lucy Webster's this afternoon and she'll have baked as well.'

'What does she want?' Lily asked, her tone uncharacteristically hostile.

'Just to meet Alice, I think.'

Lily shrugged and remained silent, but her attitude had not gone unnoticed.

*

Beth was the first person Charlie told about Harry's reluctance to celebrate her success and he was rather satisfied to witness her fleeting irritation.

'He doesn't have many friends,' she said after a few moments, during which he saw her assume control of her feelings. 'He prefers it to be just the two of us.'

'Well, that's only natural, so would I,' he told her, heart pounding as it always did when he was pushing his luck. 'Do you think he'll reconsider?'

'I doubt it,' she smiled. 'And I hate to admit it, but that's one of the things I love about him, his continual refusal to conform.'

Charlie smiled and nodded and took the chair opposite her, although she had made no sign that she wanted him to stay. If she were surprised, she hid it well, only rustling papers on her desk, arranging them neatly.

'It's a pity, because I was hoping to get to know him better.'

Beth looked across at him. She could do it so easily, make him feel so uncomfortable. It took all his control not to fidget under her scrutiny.

'Better? But you don't know him at all.'

'Exactly, and that's why I thought we should all meet, especially now that you're my business partner.'

'If you put it that way,' she said reluctantly. 'I suppose I could work on him.'

The image that flashed across Charlie's mind was enough to bring him out in a sweat. Would the day ever dawn when he woke up and no longer coveted this girl?

*

When Charlie had gone, Beth sat staring into space, fiddling with her hair, twisting it round her finger, the way she always did when she was thinking things over. She was hurt by Harry's point-blank refusal to have a celebratory dinner: if she were to take this job seriously now, it could be her career for the rest of her life; and she had been certain that her husband would be keen to join in.

The trouble with Harry was that, now that he had made up his mind about this, there was nothing – short of whacking him on the head, kidnapping him and tying him to a chair in the restaurant – that she could do or say to change his opinion. She had told Charlie it was one of the qualities she loved about her husband but, to be honest, that only applied when he was agreeing with her. Beth sighed and picked up the latest additions to their stock. She took out her French dictionary, just in case, and lowered her eyes to the paper. Work was fine: she could do it standing on her head; but persuading Harry to agree to the dinner was probably impossible.

*

Harry let himself into the flat and heard the strains of a Chopin Waltz. He crept in quietly and stood inside the door, reluctant to announce his presence, for Beth would stop playing and close the manuscript and he would feel that it was his fault; as usual. He stood where he was for at least five minutes, after which the piece came to an end and he heard Beth's discontented voice.

'Will there ever be a bloody day when I can play this bloody thing properly?'

Harry slammed the door, threw his keys on the hall table and walked to the sitting room, his first sight of her being her dejected figure slumped over the keys.

'Hey, Padarewski,' he called from the threshold. 'I'm home.'

She looked up quickly, her eyes full of admiration and he congratulated himself on swotting up on all famous pianists,

'How do you know about Padarewski?' she asked, still leaning heavily on the keyboard.

'Because I know everything,' he smiled, swaggering towards her, arms outstretched. 'Now, come over here and plant one on me, I've had a busy day.'

'And I've had a rotten one, so you'll have to come over here.'

She laughed as she said it but he was shrewd enough to put two and two together: she had been hurt at his refusal to get cosy with Webster.

'In that case,' he said, stopping halfway across the room. 'I'll go and get changed and get down to some serious cheering up.' He turned and made his way to the bedroom.

She began to play again, this time more slowly, occasionally repeating a phrase that fell short of her expectations, working her way methodically through the piece; only as an exercise, however, bringing no emotion to what was, even to Harry, a highly emotional Waltz.

As he opened the wardrobe to swap city clothes for casual trousers and shirt, he rehearsed how he would tell her, projecting things forward, trying to figure out what she might say, if she would be more annoyed at his reason for changing his mind than if he stuck to a refusal. She would know immediately that Grace was the reason and, quite frankly, he was apprehensive about Beth's reaction: she could be quite vociferous regarding his soft spot for her mother; but when Grace had asked him to change his mind, he had not even hesitated. Beth was, and always would be, his second consideration.

*

Beth lowered the lid onto the keys and sat back, satisfied that she had conquered the practicalities of the Waltz and that, next time, she would concentrate on the 'with feeling' bit. Before she had begun to play this piano, she had swept aside the boring technical fiddly bits and charged on regardless; and, for a long time, it had been enough. Now, however, sitting at such a work of art, she had to do it justice, which meant paying attention to the boring technical fiddly bits.

She examined her fingers, deciding that the nails were too long and making a note to file them next day.

'Have you lost any?' she heard Harry ask from the doorway.

'No, don't think so, but they're squealing in pain.'

'I listened at the front door for ages, it was so good.'

'You creep!' Beth frowned. 'You know I hate that.'

'I needed something soothing after the client I saw this afternoon.'

'Who was that?' she asked grudgingly, still irritated by his furtive hanging around at the front door.

'An elderly woman, who'd sounded like a nutcase on the phone but who turned out to be a gem, quite sweet, in fact.'

'So why did you need something soothing?'

'Because she's met someone and she wants to change her Will.'

Beth shrugged and wandered across the room towards him.

'A boyfriend?' she asked incredulously. 'At her age?'

'I advised her not to be hasty. Anyway, I've poured you a drink.'

'Thanks,' she said, stretching her arms above her head. 'Ow, I ache all over.'

'I have a cure for it,' Harry smiled, making his way towards her. 'Here, it's real bubbly for a change.'

'What?' Beth stared at the glass, then at Harry. 'What for?'

'As a celebration of your promotion.'

She eyed him with suspicion but his expression was genuine enough.

'Oh, right.'

'Here's to your partnership with Charlie Webster,' Harry said solemnly, raising his glass. 'I'm happy for you, sweetheart, I really am.'

'Are you feeling all right?' she asked sarcastically, not reconciling the happy fellow in front of her with the morose moron that had refused Charlie's invite.

'I couldn't be happier, and I'm looking forward to the celebration dinner.' Her eyes narrowed and he knew she was wondering if it was his idea of a joke. 'You know?' he went on, a smile touching his lips. 'The dinner Charlie invited me to?'

'But you said you weren't going,' Beth said.

311

'I said nothing of the kind,' Harry retorted, convincing her she had got it wrong. 'I was taken by surprise for a moment and he hung up before I could say anything.'

'That's...' She stopped, perhaps unsure now if Charlie had misinterpreted Harry's reaction.

'So Charlie's mother, Lucy, is arranging things and it's to be at The Birches.'

In a split second, Beth had it figured out; and she was decidedly unhappy with the result.

'Lucy Webster? You must have been speaking to my mother then, because that's where she and Alice were going this afternoon. I suppose she phoned, cried on your shoulder, made your heart bleed.'

She must have seen his mouth tighten, the flash of animosity in his eyes; but it passed and he was in control again.

'Something like that,' he smiled, and it was the cruellest thing he could have said, when what she wanted him to say was that he had changed his mind for her, not her mother. Beth lowered her eyes from his and sipped the bubbly.

'I expect you'll want me to be grateful you're going at all.'

Harry shrugged. 'I expect you to be a big girl about it, yes.'

Normally, she would have flown into a rage after such a remark and, normally, she would have stomped out of the room, locked herself in the bedroom all night, eventually ending up in the spare room. This time, however, his wife's reaction was unforeseen. Shrewdly, he suspected she had an idea, and that it might have something to do with revenge.

'In that case, I am grateful,' she told him, but the smile was forced. 'You'll like Charlie, I know you will. He's the nicest person, and the best boss. He and I get on really well.'

Harry nodded and sat down on the sofa, legs stretched out, arms lying across the back, like a crucified figure, he imagined suddenly. Perhaps the same thought had crossed Beth's mind, for she shivered suddenly.

'Aren't you coming to join me?' he asked cheerfully, although he had been waiting for a tantrum and was still trying to figure out why she was behaving like an angel. He knew she would want to pay him back for having acceded to her mother's wishes and how rewarding it would be for her to make him suffer for such disloyalty to her. It was a small price to pay, however, for taking care of Grace.

*

'Lucy's very nice,' Alice said, as they sat in the garden after tea. 'Just the sort of friend you should have, Grace.'

'That's exactly what James said, so it must be true.'

'Now you're making fun of me, but I'm serious.' Alice repositioned herself on the bench so that she could look directly at her friend. 'Molly's a strange one. I never got the hang of how the two of you ever got together.'

'We've been friends since Primary Two,'

'So what?' Alice laughed. 'When I was five I was friendly with a piglet named Wally, but he and I have long since gone our separate ways, honey.'

'She means well.'

'People always say that when they can't think of a good reason.'

'Oh, come on,' Grace urged. 'Let's not talk about Molly. Why don't you tell me about the boys?'

'Boys?' repeated Alice with a shake of her head. 'They're men now, oldest one's the same age as Beth.'

'Do they ever ask about Scotland?'

'Never,' Alice replied sadly. 'And it's not for the want of trying on my part, believe me. I gave them books about Scotland as soon as they could read.'

'Yet they're still not interested in coming over?'

'I have myself to blame in a way,' Alice said quietly. 'If I'd paid more attention to my home life, instead of gallivanting around with a lover...' She stopped, threw her friend an apologetic glance 'I think you get the idea.'

'Perhaps they'll come over eventually.'

'I doubt it. Girlfriends came along and every one of them is an all-American gal.'

'But you get on all right with them?'

'Oh, I guess. Harry's a lovely boy, isn't he?'

'He is.'

'Funny that he didn't want to go to the dinner at first, don't you think?'

'Are you snooping, Alice Cameron?'

'Of course,' Alice said, pulling a comical face. 'Is he jealous of Charlie Webster, d'you think?'

'Probably, but he's no need to be. Beth's not the type to...' She let the sentence hang, suddenly beset by the familiar flicker of jealousy as she imagined Beth and Harry together. It was ridiculous, of course, but she had no idea how to stop it.

'It was nice of Harry to change his mind when you asked him.'

Grace heard nothing in Alice's tone that would suggest even the slightest curiosity; but, in her own mind, she was aware of the significance of Harry's change of heart, aware of how it would look to Beth.

'He was probably thinking of Beth, how hurt she would be,' was her explanation.

'Yes, that's it probably,' Alice smiled, her gaze returning to the flowerbed.

'You know, this is a gorgeous part of the garden. How come I never really noticed it before?'

'James has been working up here recently, since he had to give up full-time work.'

'He was telling me that Lucy dropped by when you were away.'

This time, Grace did hear something untoward in her friend's tone and she forced herself to make light of it.

'She's hopeless at gardening, Lucy is, and James's been helping out. She brought some eggs down – you ate one for your breakfast, remember? – and he invited her for a cup of tea. I think they sat up here.'

'They certainly did,' Alice said pointedly, causing Grace to look at her closely. 'I almost died of shock when he told me he'd entertained a lady here when he was alone, in a part of the garden that's so secluded.' She burst out laughing suddenly. 'When he was younger he wouldn't even invite Lily Morris in if you weren't home, remember, and she was sixty?'

'Things change,' Grace said pleasantly. 'Although I must say, I admire his old-fashioned values.'

Perhaps accepting the remark as a reminder of her own behaviour, Alice rose to her feet. 'I think we should go down and have a nightcap. What do you say?'

*

Harry sat up reading long after Beth had gone to bed. It was irrational, but he could not get Daphne out of his mind, such a gentle, considerate woman, not unlike Grace in character, a woman swept off her feet by some old gigolo most likely and a woman who needed good advice.

'I don't want him to know,' she had told Harry in hushed tones. 'But he's been so good to me this past year and I had no one, you know,' she added plaintively, tugging at his heart strings in the way that only Grace could. 'And, let's face it, I could drop dead tomorrow and never be able to thank him.'

Harry had advised her to wait, prevailed upon her to let him at least examine her finances and put things in order; and then, acting on an extraordinary impulse, he had cautioned her to keep her plans to herself for the time being, including her appointment with him.

Now, as he sat mulling over the situation, he resolved to ask her the name of her mysterious new man, after which he could do some snooping in case the old dear was about to be fleeced by some con man.

Chapter Twenty-One

Beth was in the middle of cleaning out the kitchen cupboards when the phone rang and it was her future sister-in-law, wanting to know if she would like to have lunch or did she have other plans?

'Apart from housework, which I loathe, no,' Beth laughed, removing her yellow Marigolds and chucking them in a corner. 'You could say I've been saved by the bell.'

'Is it all right if I go and meet Emily?' she asked Harry, his nose in a legal tome as was his habit on Saturday mornings.

'Yes, fine,' he said, without raising his head.

'Isn't this the weekend?' Beth reminded him caustically. 'Shouldn't you be doing something recreational?'

He looked up at her then, a tiny frown wriggling its way across his brow.

'Yes to both counts.'

She sighed and turned on her heel; nothing she could say would alter his plans for the day. As she raked through the wardrobe for a summery outfit, her mind refused to let go of the ease with which her mother was able to get Harry Gillespie to change his mind. The familiar stab of something like jealousy tried to take hold of her, but she slammed the wardrobe door on it and instantly felt better.

Emily was waiting on the corner at McEwens, her dainty little figure swathed in purple – her favourite colour – and her hair twisted on top of her head, but loosely, as if it had been done professionally. Beth walked towards her, wondering for the hundredth time how her puny, witless brother could have snared this jewel.

'Hi,' Emily smiled, taking Beth completely by surprise with a hug. 'It's great to see you.' Still recovering from her space being invaded, Beth was slow to respond and Emily added anxiously: 'Is this O.K. for you, coming out on a Saturday?'

'Yes, sure, I was just surprised at the hug.'

'You don't like that sort of thing?'

'Not much,' Beth said with a grimace, reflecting that in Paris she had hugged and kissed complete strangers, but here in Scotland it felt weird. 'But I think I'll survive. Come on, I'll treat you to something.'

'No,' Emily insisted. 'It was my idea, so I'm paying.'

'My turn next then.'

The girl was so delighted at the thought there would be a next time, that Beth had an overwhelming feeling of guilt about not being a fan of hugging people she hardly knew.

'I just have to ask you,' Beth began unapologetically, as soon as they sat down. 'What the hell d'you see in him?'

Emily giggled, reminding Beth the girl was only eighteen.

'Frank's lovely,' she said, cheeks red. 'He's the nicest person I've ever been out with.'

'You can't have had much experience at your age, surely?'

'I've had a few boyfriends,' Emily admitted brightly. 'Didn't you at my age?'

'I never had the time. Too busy studying and murdering Chopin.'

'What?'

'Chopin, the composer. I love playing his stuff.'

'Ah, right. Frank did say you drove him mad with it.'

'It wouldn't take much to…' Beth stopped mid-sentence. It was not very nice, what she had been about to say, especially since the girl was trying so hard. 'I had one or two casual boyfriends, I suppose, but they were short-lived.'

'Your Dad was strict, wasn't he?'

'Not that I noticed,' Beth said sharply. 'I mean,' she amended more kindly. 'I was used to it, so I never thought anything of it.'

'Frank said his Dad always picked on him.'

Beth's patience and Good Samaritan act had fizzled out. She was perfectly willing to ease up when the situation demanded but the conversation was turning out to be unwelcome.

'Yes, he did always pick on Frank,' Beth smiled pleasantly. 'But then my Mum would spoil him rotten, so it kind of made up for it, but I expect he forgot to mention that.'

Emily blushed. 'No, he did say she was extra nice to him.'

'Swings and roundabouts,' Beth said cheerfully, her eye on the menu. 'I think I'd like a sandwich, that'll do me.'

'I've done it again.'

'What?' Beth asked, glancing across at the girl.

'Put my foot in my gob.'

The sound of such an uncouth word falling from the lips of an immaculate mannequin had Beth stifling a laugh. She took one look at the poor girl's face and felt instant remorse.

'I'm sorry, Emily, I'm a bit tetchy today. Nothing to do with you. Apology?'

'Don't be silly, it was my fault. I get a bit nervous in your company.'

Beth stared at her. 'Nervous? In my company?'

'You can do absolutely everything,' Emily sighed. 'Speak languages, play the piano, talk about anything under the sun.' She paused for a moment before adding: 'And your mother likes Harry, that's another plus.'

'But she likes you as well,' Beth frowned. 'She told me she thought you were a lovely girl.'

'She said that?'

'Don't you know you're a lovely girl?' Beth smiled wryly. 'No mirrors in your house then?'

'It's all very well looking presentable,' Emily agreed. 'But I'd rather be good at something and I'm not.'

'You'll be good at having kids probably,' Beth grinned, causing the girl's cheeks to redden again. 'In fact, I can hardly wait for you to start, because it'll take the heat off me.'

'You're not keen to have them?' Emily asked, as if it were the most abominable sentiment known to humankind.

'I wouldn't go so far as to say I wasn't keen, but, put it this way, I won't shed a tear if I never have one.' Emily's expression of horror had the opposite effect on Beth: she burst out laughing.

'You should see your face,' she managed to say eventually. 'You'd think I'd just admitted to being Jack the Ripper.'

'Sorry, I just meant that, well, you know, we get married to have kids, don't we?'

'You might,' Beth said, still laughing. 'But I certainly didn't.'

'Gosh, how odd.'

'No, I married because I couldn't keep my hands off Harry.'

Once more, she was conscious of the girl's tender years, not being able to fend off a fiery blush.

'Oh, good,' she said with relief. 'Here's the waitress at last, let's order.'

As Emily dealt with the waitress, Beth watched her out of the corner of her eye, wondering why she always felt like an alien in the company of the rest of the female sex.

'Oh, by the way,' Emily said as they were left alone again. 'Frank and I have been invited to your celebration dinner.'

'That's nice,' said Beth inanely. 'You'll meet my boss... er... sorry, my business partner, Charlie. He's dishy, you'll like him.'

'As long as Frank doesn't get jealous.'

'Does he?' Beth asked, trying to imagine her brother having any emotion whatsoever.

'I'll say, and it makes me feel he really cares about me. Is Harry ever jealous of other men?'

'I shouldn't think so,' Beth told her truthfully. 'Of course, I never look at any other men.'

She caught the look, inwardly grimaced at the implication: was there the slightest chance that, in the next half hour, Beth Melville could keep her mouth in check?

*

When he heard the door close behind Beth, Harry closed the book and stood up. He crossed to the window and caught sight of Beth's blonde hair disappearing round the corner, and then he went through to the small room where he kept his files and opened the one marked 'Legal differences Scot/Eng'.

Minutes later, easily distracted from his task, he was poring over the old photographs again, something he was doing more frequently these days, ever since the onslaught of vivid dreams and flash-backs about his father.

He had had another during the night, had woken up with a blinding headache and a sense of utter despair, for the dream had involved his father's car accident, about which Harry knew very little. His imagination, however, had not held back and even now he could still see the blood and gore and the mangled wreck with its spinning wheels. He shuddered as his hands flicked over the pages. The only time that he overcame his feeling of loneliness, the isolation he had suffered after his father died, was when he looked at these photographs. Somehow, they drew him in, into the circumstances of the picture, allowed him to take part in Ralph Gillespie's life, albeit as an observer.

He picked up a snapshot of his parents, in a group of people that had gathered for her birthday in 1939, a few months before war had broken out. His mother and father were standing together, their attention drawn to the antics of a scruffy, wiry little dog that was sitting dutifully at his mother's feet.

Harry had lost count of how many times he had perused this shot, how many times he had tried to imagine what she was saying to his father at that precise moment. From the date on the back, he knew she was only nineteen. By the time she was twenty-three, she would have begun to destroy his father's life.

He threw the photograph into the folder and closed it quickly. Normally he had the patience to look at several, but today the sight of the two of them together only heightened his isolation.

At least he had Grace; and she would never ruin *his* life.

*

Thomas Blake was glad that the day was hot and sunny, for it gave him an excuse to don dark glasses and a boater, an ideal disguise for his afternoon jaunt. He picked up the keys of the hire car – small and not likely to attract undue attention – and left the house.

The warmth accosted him as soon as he opened the car door, not the type of heat he had been used to in Buenos Aires, but stifling nevertheless, especially at his age. He wound down all the windows and left the door ajar while he checked he had brought his wallet, then threw his jacket onto the back seat, by which time the inside of the car was bearable. He examined the controls again, having only driven it half a mile from the hire company, and familiarised himself with the basics, the most notable being that they drove on the left here and so sitting in the driver's seat felt quite wrong. He turned the key, took a deep breath and wished himself luck.

The traffic was light, despite its being Saturday, and he assumed that the local holiday had something to do with it, most of the inhabitants having fled to the Costa Brava or some such dreary place. He sighed again at the advent of cheap flights for the masses and longed for the old days, when only those and such as those could travel.

As he drove through Scone, past Daphne's house, he lowered himself in the seat and pulled his boater down over his face, although the chances of her being at a window and recognising him were less than slim; yet he breathed easier once he was on the open road, on his way to look at the Shepherd house for the first time in almost fifty years.

*

Grace and Alice stood at Molly's gate, making futile attempts to take their leave. They avoided each other's eye in case they should be overcome by a fit of the giggles, for their lunch with Molly had been plagued by unintended ambiguities and innuendos and Grace knew that she would burst out laughing at the slightest encouragement. It was such good fun having her friend around, but it only highlighted Lily's accusation: that Grace was dour and unhappy the rest of the time.

'Next time,' Molly was saying to Alice. 'You'll have to stay for longer, maybe meet Jonathan and Donald.'

'I'd like that,' Alice said sincerely, but Grace saw the telling flicker of amusement at the corner of her friend's mouth. 'The trouble is, I only have another week, and I've made so many plans.'

'Surely you can fit me in?' Molly asked brusquely and, once more, the connotation, considering her indiscretion with poor Sally's husband, was not lost on the two friends.

'Of course we can,' Grace said firmly, almost rudely, in an attempt to stifle her laughter. 'We'll pop up in a day or two, but I'll phone you, let you know.'

Molly appeared satisfied. 'That's a promise,' she nodded. 'And I'll hold you to it.'

They walked away, their gaze ahead, until Alice turned briefly to check if Molly had gone inside. By her sudden burst of laughter, Grace assumed she had.

'Oh, my!' Alice exclaimed, stuffing her handkerchief to her mouth. 'I thought I'd collapse in a heap! How on earth did you manage to keep your cool?'

'I must be a good actress,' Grace grinned, linking arms with Alice. 'I just pretended that the dog had died and I was heart-broken.'

'Hey, that's a grand idea! I'll try it next time, only it would have to be Wally, the piglet.'

'You were worse than me,' Grace whispered, although the street was deserted. 'When she told us she'd have to get a man in, I could have strangled you, rolling your eyes at me like that. Honestly, Alice Cameron, you're wicked! You knew she meant the painter.'

'Come on, you were just as bad,' Alice scolded. 'I never thought anything of it when she said she'd lost her oomph. One look at you and I thought I'd make a right fool of myself.' Alice squeezed her friend's arm. 'Anyway, didn't we have fun?'

'I feel a bit guilty that it was Molly. She is supposed to be...'

'Yes, yes,' Alice interrupted briskly. 'Your best friend, we know. Your record's stuck, honey.'

'Oh look, there's a pony,' Grace pointed out and they both turned towards the fields

318

opposite the cottage. 'It must be the new girl from the Post Office. Her mother said she'd taken up horse riding to get fit.'

'Come on,' Alice said eagerly, grabbing Grace arm tightly and beginning to drag her across the road. 'Let's go and say 'hello' to the poor little thing. It looks so lonely.'

'Watch out,' Grace warned, stepping back. 'Car coming.'

Alice ran over without waiting but Grace stood by the kerb, her attention drawn to the driver and the way he was draped over the steering wheel, hardly able to see the road in front of him. She was just about to say something amusing to Alice when she noticed the jacket lying in the back seat.

'O.K.!' she heard Alice call. 'All clear now, over you come!'

Grace stood stock-still, her heart pounding, for she had recognised him: it was Thomas Blake.

*

Thomas cursed himself for driving too slowly. She must have had a good look at him, with him dawdling along at fifteen miles an hour. What the hell had he been thinking about? He glanced in the rear-view mirror and saw that she was looking in his direction and, for a split-second, momentarily confused, he turned left at the crossroads before he had time to think.

What the hell was wrong with him? To turn off here meant that he knew where he was going – it led only to the deserted station and to a back road to nowhere – so he had awarded her another clue to his identity, for a stranger would never have left the main road.

He drove past the station, another mile to the farm on the corner, and then he slowed down, looked for a place to park, to gather his thoughts. As he drew to a halt, a tractor lumbered down the road and he pulled his straw hat down over his ears and pretended he was adjusting the height of his seat, sweating so profusely that his dark glasses were slipping off his nose.

The tractor disappeared into the distance and Thomas lay back in the seat, completely drained of energy, furious at himself for such a ridiculous idea. If she had seen him – and he knew that she must – he had just made a huge blunder. No matter how much he pretended she meant nothing to him, no matter how blasé he acted in front of the rest of her family, if she refused to acknowledge him as her father, forced him to abandon her again, he would never forgive himself for letting Charlotte down.

He sighed and idly tried to work out the odds of her being on the main street when he had been driving past: it had to be thousands to one; just his luck.

*

Harry was sitting at the window watching the people strolling on the Inch. He had long since dispensed with the folder of photographs, although he knew it would only be a matter of time before he searched through it again. He was doing his best to improve his mood before Beth came home expecting him to be enthralled by her lunch date. The slightest sign that he was out of sorts and she would embody all the worst elements of the Inquisition in her quest for the truth.

Reluctantly, he smiled. If Beth embodied one trait it was commitment to the truth, like it or lump it; and he had to admit he rather liked it. He liked it because he had known so many gormless women in his time, women who slaved over a hot stove and had no opinion on anything other than the best way to clean it after use. Beth Melville was lively and provocative and, despite the tantrums – or could it be because of them? – there were

319

more advantages than disadvantages in being married to her.

The telephone rang and he glanced at his watch: half past two. His heart gave a stupid lurch at the thought that something might have happened to her, but then he steadied himself: she was only having lunch in the middle of Perth.

He picked up the receiver and it was Grace.

'Is anything wrong?' was his first question. It was unheard of for her to call at the weekend, as she had a quaint idea that he and Beth should spend it in splendid romantic isolation.

'He was here,' she said, and he heard the panic in her voice.

'Thomas Blake?'

'He was driving past and we were crossing the road and I saw his jacket, the one he was wearing at the hotel that day and I...'

'Did he stop?'

'No, he... he drove past and then I thought I... the jacket, I knew it was his, and then he turned left at the crossroads, so it was definitely him.'

'Because he turned left at the crossroads?'

'It goes nowhere, just to the station and the farms.'

'You're sure it was him?'

'Yes, I'm sure. Harry, I don't know what...'

'Hey, come on,' he said gently. 'I told you not to worry the first time and I'm telling you again. Don't worry, Grace, I'll handle it. Where's Alice?'

'I'm in the phone box, she's at the house. I didn't want to worry her.'

It was typical of her, but he found nothing in it to condemn. The only thing he could do was to protect her.

'I'll be at Lily's in half an hour,' he told her, not expecting to be contradicted. 'Can you let her know?'

'I suppose I could phone her from here.'

'Do you intend to tell James?'

'No,' she replied swiftly. 'I don't want him to worry.'

'Right. Phone Lily,' he repeated slowly. 'And I'll be there soon.'

'Are you sure, Harry, because I know that you and Beth like to spend...?'

'She's out with Emily. Now, if you stop arguing, I can leave now.'

'Thank you, Harry. I'll call Lily right now.'

After she had hung up, Harry caught sight of his smug reflection in the hall mirror. As he grabbed the car keys he thought of leaving a note for Beth, but decided there was no time. Uppermost in his mind was the thought that he had failed to get rid of Thomas Blake after promising Grace she need never worry about the man again. Harry had been given another opportunity to take care of her and this time he would not fail.

*

Alice knew that there was something wrong and so she pitched in gamely and helped Grace to deal with James, who was put out by his wife's last-minute visit to Lily Morris.

'It was my fault,' Alice said dolefully. 'I forgot to pick up the berries she gave me for making jam tomorrow.' She ignored Grace's confusion and ploughed on. 'I should be the one going for them, but I've got some sewing to do. Is there anything you'd like me to sew for you, Grace, while I'm at it?'

Briefly, Grace struggled to come to terms with the ease her friend could lie, but then her own response implicated her in the very same lie; with equal ease.

'No, but thanks for reminding me about the berries, I'll be as quick as I can.'

Now, as she sat in Lily's kitchen waiting for Harry, she was grateful for her friend's innovative mind. Two pounds of blackcurrants had been weighed and poured into kilner jars, only to persuade James she had been telling the truth, as there were still berries hanging on their own bushes.

Lily paced around the kitchen, glancing at her unexpected guest from time to time. Eventually, she spoke.

'I knew you were lying when you told everyone you'd mellowed.'

'My acting skills must be fading.'

'And the boy wasn't fooled either,' Lily volunteered, halting in her pacing.

'No, I didn't expect he would be.'

Lily resumed her restless meandering of the kitchen and Grace was tempted to tell her to sit down, that she was making her nervous. Suddenly, the old woman stopped in front of Grace and asked:

'Would it not be easier if you just met him and pretended to be friendly?'

Grace could hardly believe her ears. She looked closely at her friend, wondering how to respond without losing her temper. Meeting him had been bad enough, but feigning friendship was absolutely impossible.

'No, Lily it wouldn't. I'll never change my mind about that.'

'Ah, well,' Lily sighed, coming to sit at the table. 'It was worth a try. He'll cause you and your family nothing but trouble, mark my words. He's the type of man you can't reason with.'

'I could tell the police,' Grace said feebly, but they both knew that a father wanting to see daughter was hardly a crime.

'It's Beth you have to worry about,' Lily reminded her. 'She's the one he'll work on again, try to get her on his side. She only stopped seeing him because James was ill.'

'She hasn't mentioned him since,' Grace said hopefully. 'Maybe she's too wrapped up with her new job.'

'Hope springs eternal, so they say.' Lily raised her head and listened. 'That's the boy now, I'll make myself scarce.'

'No, I'd prefer you to stay.'

Lily shook her head. 'Best if I know nothing. Then if he ever asks me, I won't be lying.'

'If no one had lied in the first place,' Grace complained bitterly. 'This wouldn't be happening now.'

Lily frowned as she moved towards the door. 'Maybe not. Give me a shout if you need anything.'

*

Harry let himself into the house and went straight to the kitchen. He caught sight of Lily disappearing upstairs but she made no attempt to greet him, although she knew he had paused in the hallway.

'I feel so awful,' were Grace's first words as he entered the room. 'Honestly, I shouldn't have let you come out here.'

'And how would you have stopped me?' he asked cheerfully, sitting opposite her.

'Was Beth annoyed?'

'I told you, she's out. With Emily, actually.'

'Frank's Emily?'

'It seems they're the best of buddies now, she and Beth.'

'Oh, I'm so glad,' Grace smiled and he thought how little time she devoted to herself: even in the midst of this fracas about her father, she was still thinking of others.

'Emily's a lovely girl, but quite shy. Beth will be good for her.'

'I doubt that,' Harry laughed. 'The poor girl will spend half the time blushing.'

'Beth is a bit naughty sometimes,' Grace admitted with a rueful smile. 'But she has a heart of gold.'

'You would say that,' Harry teased, doing what he could to ease the tension in her face. 'You're biased.'

'I don't know what I'd do if she took his side against me.'

Harry was silent. There was no point in handing out platitudes to her now, platitudes that would lead to false conclusions. He had no option but to tell her the truth.

'She hasn't spoken about him since James took ill, but that doesn't mean she won't in the future.'

'Has she asked you to read the letters again?'

'No.'

'What do you think I should do?'

'The letters seem to indicate that his version of the story is true,' Harry said slowly, his eyes meeting hers. 'Why do you think that is? Why would your mother's letters to him paint him in such a good light?'

'Because she was quite adept at telling lies,' Grace stated unexpectedly. 'At least she told me quite a few. So I presume she told him lies as well.'

'There is the possibility that she was like you,' Harry smiled, fiddling with the edge of the tablecloth, feeling suddenly ill at ease. 'You do everything in your power not to hurt people. Couldn't she just have been the same?'

Grace shook her head, 'You have the wrong idea about me, Harry. I can be just as vindictive as the next person.'

'Vindictive is an ugly word. I prefer to say 'resourceful'.' A spontaneous smile touched her lips but she remained silent. 'So,' he continued. 'If you're asking me what you should do, I'd advise you to hunt through every document, every letter, every note, any tiny scrap of paper you have that can back up your side of the story.' He made a gesture of irritation. 'I mean, that can back up the truth of the story.'

When she avoided his gaze and began to trace the pattern on the tablecloth with agitated fingers, Harry suspected that there was, indeed, such a piece of paper, a letter that she had, something that confirmed Thomas Blake as an unscrupulous man who had abandoned his child to further his own ambitions.

He waited, watching her face, seeing the transitory expressions that reflected her innermost thoughts, until at last she looked at him with resignation.

'I might have such a letter.'

'You have?'

She nodded.

'Would you mind if I read it?'

'No, in fact I'd like you to read it.'

'Can it be used to refute his story?'

She appeared uncomfortable at that and it confused him, for if she had in her possession anything at all that would rid her of the man, why would she not be overjoyed?

'It's a letter written to him by some woman.' She paused, seemed to struggle for breath. 'Whilst he was courting my mother.'

Harry's mind absorbed the implication of old-fashioned etiquette, but he passed over it swiftly.

'Shall I pick it up, or do you want to send it to me at the office?'

Again, she was uneasy, her eyes flicking from his face to the table and then back again, making no attempt to act, to adopt a role that would hide her true feelings. He wondered how many people had been witness to Grace Blake's deepest feelings.

'I brought it with me.'

He was struck by her trust in him, that she should be prepared to hand it over, to allow him access to so significant a letter, especially one that was causing her such anxiety.

'I could read it now, if you like?'

'I have to explain first,' she said, lowering her eyes in what he took to be an admission of guilt. 'It's not what it seems. It's a letter about a child, but the child mentioned wasn't me. He had...' She glanced across at him, the hatred in her eyes catching him unawares.

Harry took a few moments to grasp the significance.

'He had a child with someone else?'

She nodded.

'Whilst he was leading your mother on?'

Again, she nodded. 'She never knew, of course. Lily stole the letter in case my mother should find it.'

'And the child?' He was incredulous.

She sighed and sank into the chair. 'It's all in the letter.'

'I can hardly believe it.'

'Neither could I.'

'How did you come to know about it?'

'Lily hated him for what he did, put it an envelope marked as my birth certificate.' Grace pursed her lips together. 'Then she gave it to Helen for safekeeping.'

Harry had to smile. 'The minx.'

'I suppose she thought it would be safer in Holland.'

'When did he write this letter?'

'In 1923, after the war.'

'Did Helen just hand it over to you?'

'I wrote and told her I needed my birth certificate.'

She sighed and withdrew a crumpled, faded envelope from her pocket, proffering it across the table, averting her eyes as he took it, as if she had renounced responsibility for it. Harry turned the envelope over in his hands.

'I'd prefer to take it away with me, read it when I'm alone.'

'Of course,' she frowned. 'I wouldn't expect you to read it here. Of course you must take it with you.'

Harry placed the envelope in his inside pocket and stood up.

'You'd better go home,' he told her gently. 'I don't want you to get into any trouble.'

'Alice would save me,' she said humorously, the tension fading from her features. 'She's the best friend anyone could have.'

He felt the familiar, irrational pang of jealousy at the idea of someone else being entrusted with her friendship; but he nodded his agreement.

'We all need friends.'

'I can't bear the idea that he's snooping around the village,' Grace said dejectedly. 'Knowing he was in Perth was bad enough, but...'

'I doubt if you'll see him here again, now that he's been spotted.'

'I'll be scared to go out now.'

'Come on, where's that fighting spirit? I know you have one.'

'I'll look for it when I go home,' she said with a reluctant smile.

Harry could have asked her to find some for him as well, but it was encouragement she needed now.

'You don't have far to look,' he said, standing up to take his leave. 'I won't see you until the dinner at Lucy Webster's, but if you want to call me, don't hesitate. I'll be in the office all week.' He turned at the door and looked back at her. 'Oh, and I know it's easier said than done, but please don't worry. I'll not let him hurt you again.'

Without waiting for her response, he hurried out of the house and walked quickly down the path.

*

Grace had been gone less than half an hour, an acceptable absence to James, considering Lily Morris' propensity towards chattering. From his vantage point at the top of the garden, he saw her at the back door, the jars of berries in her hands and, involuntarily, he glanced at their own blackcurrant bushes – hanging with fruit ripe for the picking – and wondered at the necessity for more.

A few moments later, he saw Grace and Alice in the garden, pulling up deck chairs and settling down for yet another chat. For the life of him, he could not imagine what women talked about; endlessly, from one day to the next. A sudden, unwelcome thought entered his mind: they might be discussing the past, reminiscing fondly perhaps about the old days; days before James had met her; her love affair with Graham Seaton.

Never a day went by without his dwelling on Seaton's obsession with Grace, the man's blatant attempts to woo her, even after she had been married for a few years.

Married for a few years

He had to struggle to dismiss the unbidden memory of Sabine, the French girl, with her willing eyes, the softness of her skin. He had been engaged to Grace at the time.

James sat down on the bench and turned his face to the sun. At least he had something to look forward to: he was going to see Lucy Webster at the end of the week. He looked at his watch – four o'clock – and wondered what Lucy was doing at that very moment.

*

Beth wandered from room to room, eager to tell Harry about her conversation with Emily. Frustrated at the absence of a note from Harry, she paced the hallway for ten minutes, after which she went to pour herself a drink. It was only four o'clock but she had spent an entertaining afternoon.

She kicked off her shoes and raked in the magazine rack for something to read. A copy of House and Garden came to hand, although it was months old. She leafed through the pages until a house caught her eye. She supposed it was every girl's dream house: small-paned windows, tall chimneys, red-brick façade, huge French doors; plus the most enormous sunroom stuck on the side, large enough for an army to billet in.

Beth took the magazine and her whisky into the sitting room and sat by the window, where she could see the antics of children on the Inch and the lovebirds canoodling on the grass, oblivious to passers-by. She was always amazed at the kind of things couples would do in full view of the general public: as far as her father was concerned, until she was a married woman, even holding hands had been frowned on, yet she had accepted it easily, had no qualms about setting Harry straight over it.

'But that's silly,' had been his first comment, when she let go of his hand forcibly in the middle of Perth. 'We're only holding hands, not fornicating.'

'If you don't like it,' she had told him archly, walking on briskly. 'You can go and find someone else.'

'Is this the way it'll be when we're married?' he had asked incredulously, at which she had turned back, retraced her steps and grinned at him.

'You must be joking! You'll be begging me to keep my hands off you then.'

She laughed at the memory and began to leaf through the magazine again.

No sooner had she become engrossed in the photographs of the 'dream house' than she heard the front door open. Harry was home.

'It's me,' he called. 'I went for a walk, lost all sense of time.' He appeared at the sitting room door and gave her a cheeky salute. 'Miss me, sweetheart?'

'Not a bit,' Beth said, her nose in the magazine. 'Now, go away, I'm busy.'

'Don't you want to tell me all?'

'All what?'

'Emily's all, that's what. Is she as shy as you thought?'

Beth raised her eyes from the magazine, closed it with a snap and jumped up. 'Oh, much worse. She spent the whole time blushing.'

'That's what...'

'That's what?

'That's what I thought she'd be like,' he said, coming towards her. 'I don't deserve a hug?'

'No, you didn't leave me a note.'

'If only someone had taught me to write, what an exciting world would have opened up for me.'

'Honestly,' Beth muttered, resisting his attempts to put his arms around her. 'You might have been in an accident or something. I was worried.'

'You little fibber,' Harry laughed, drawing her close. 'You never gave me a second thought.'

It was mostly true, but how annoying it was to be read like an open book. She laid her cheek on his shirt and sighed, supposing there were worse things than having a husband who understood you completely.

'Where did you walk then on this mammoth trek?'

'Over the bridge, then down the Norrie Miller walk. It was lovely.'

'You'll be running for Scotland soon.'

'England, you mean.'

Beth stepped back. 'What?'

'I'm English, you twit. How could I run for Scotland?'

'You could change your nationality,' she suggested warily.

'No thanks.'

Beth frowned and disentangled herself from his arms. His loyalty to England had not occurred to her before.

'What difference could it make?'

'My accent tell everyone I'm English. Why should I pretend to be Scottish?'

'I hardly notice your accent,' Beth mumbled, keeping her distance.

'And since when have you been interested in anything Scottish, I'd like to know,' Harry laughed. 'You couldn't care less about Scottish things, Beth Melville. You're as European as they come.'

Reluctantly, she smiled, because it was not only true but also something of a compliment. She invariably aligned herself more with volcanic, bad-tempered, impatient and bluntly spoken people like the Gauls, than with reserved, unfriendly people who were ensnared in eighteenth century values.

'Come on,' Harry prompted when he must have known she was in a better mood. 'Tell me about Emily and what you could possibly have said to make the poor girl blush.'

325

Thomas poured out a cream sherry for Daphne and clinked glasses. She had stopped gazing at him with wondrous eyes now, but her expression was much more satisfying, bordering as it did on the romantic. There was no mistaking it: there was a distinct element of love in the woman's eyes and he was beginning to congratulate himself on a task well in hand.

'Here's to a most exciting life,' he smiled, allowing his fingers to touch hers as their glasses met. 'Thank you, Daphne dear, for bringing so much joy to this old man.'

'Thomas Blake, if you're an old man, then I'm Methuselah.'

'I certainly don't feel old,' he said meaningfully. 'Since meeting you, I've had a new lease of life. Quite remarkable.'

They moved apart, taking their usual seats in the bay window of Daphne's living room. Thomas never failed to be impressed by the house. Each time he visited, he was discovering further delights. Today it had been the wine cellar.

'A wine cellar?' he had asked, wide eyed, to encourage her.

'Oh, yes, my husband's, you understand. He was...' she had paused, not wishing, Thomas assumed, to brand dear old William as a drunkard. 'He wasn't very strong, the dear man, but I did my best to help him.'

'I'm sure you did,' Thomas had purred, glancing around the cellar, clocking the rows of expensive-looking bottles – dozens of them, if not hundreds. 'Goodness me!' he had almost exclaimed, before he remembered he was feigning indifference. 'It can't be.' He examined the bottle closely. 'It is, it's a twenty-year-old malt, laid down just after the War. Well, well, fancy that.' Now, as he surveyed her from his side of the bay window, Thomas was undecided: should he move to the next stage with Daphne or leave things as they were for now? He was convinced she would be susceptible to his suggestion that they go on holiday together – separate rooms and at her expense, naturally – but was there any great rush? Was he not perfectly happy with things as they were? Thomas's only niggling doubt stemmed from his next thought: but was *she* happy with how thing were? Until he voiced the holiday idea, he could never be sure.

'I was just thinking, Daphne, dear,' he began, suddenly gripped by an uncharacteristic nervousness when she turned and looked at him, her face alight with interest. 'I was wondering...' He paused for effect, head on one side, smile hovering.

'Yes, Thomas?' Daphne asked, leaning forward slightly.

'Perhaps you'll consider me too forward,' he said, giving her an apologetic smile. 'But I was wondering if you'd like to accompany me on a short trip.'

Put in such a way, he hoped it sounded a lot less risqué than going on holiday together and as soon as he had uttered the words, she blushed and lowered her eyes. Inwardly, Thomas rejoiced: he was on the second rung.

*

Harry had been on the verge of pleading a headache by the time Beth exhausted her account of lunch with the blushing Emily. The only thing he had wanted to do was to disappear into his study, take out the letter from Helen and read it thoroughly, find out if it held anything that could be used to rid Grace of her father, once and for all. He had a moment of despair when Beth had suggested going out for dinner, but he succeeded in persuading her to stay in and sample the delights of his cooking. At least, alone in the kitchen, he would have a modicum of peace.

'Why don't you go and play something soothing?' he asked her as he stood up to prepare the meal.

'Like what?'

'Like Beethoven's Moonlight thing, it's lovely.'

Beth shrugged. 'I'm a bit rusty.'

'Don't tempt me.'

She giggled and slapped him playfully on the shoulder before rushing off to rake through her music sheets for the Sonata. A grateful Harry went into the kitchen and half closed the door.

He swung the fridge door open and peered in: fresh vegetables, tins of soup and boxes of pasta stood on one shelf, while another boasted eggs, various types of cheeses and yoghurt, one of Beth's latest fads. For a moment he wondered what he could prepare, eventually settling for a cheese and mushroom omelette. As he chopped and peeled, his mind drifting between images, he suddenly recalled the last time he had broken eggs into a bowl.

You can't make an omelette without breaking eggs

*

'*I'm sorry, Harry, but if you want an omelette, there's no other way.*'

His mother sat on the arm of the chair, cigarette in hand, a distant expression in her eyes, monitoring her son's progress.

'*But there's a chicken inside, someone told me once, and if I break it and cook it, I'll kill the chicken.*'

Instead of being angry, his mother's face had softened and Harry thought he would never understand her. When he expected to be punished or praised, the reverse usually happened. His mother drew on the cigarette before replying.

'*There's a chicken in certain eggs,*' *she said gently.* '*But not in ones you buy in a shop.*'

'*Honestly?*'

'*Cross my heart, hope to die.*'

*

Hope to die. Harry waited for the pain to subside, a pain he had only known these past few months; never before; not until Grace's father turned up and reminded Harry of his own miserable past. He took several deep breaths to steady himself and then picked up another egg to crack into the bowl.

'Are you all right?'

He jumped at the sound of Beth's voice. He had been so pre-occupied with thoughts of his father that he had failed to notice the lack of music or her presence in the doorway.

'Yes, I'm fine. Concentrating so much on this that I didn't hear you come in.'

She remained at the door, her eyes fixed on him, her stance obstinate, in a way that only Beth could convey. Harry dropped his gaze to the chopping board and waited, rehearsing in his mind what he might say, for in this mood – and he recognised it – Beth would pry until she was satisfied he had no secrets left.

'You seemed edgy when you came back,' she said innocently.

'I was edgy. I had a meeting with an old dear yesterday and I think she's being conned by some trickster.'

He could tell that she was both disappointed and intrigued: disappointed because there was no secret for her to prise from him; intrigued because it was the kind of tale that caught her imagination. A lame duck was involved...

'Ah, a victim-to-be. Is that what you suspect, Perry Mason?'

'She's a nice old thing,' Harry said, drying his hands and taking the frying pan from the highest shelf. 'I'd hate to see her being fleeced.'

'Did you give her any advice?'

'Yes, I told her to wait, not to do anything hasty.'

'Good advice, Perry, said the lovely Della.'

Harry smiled, paused in his egg whisking and looked at her.

'Sometimes I forget how funny you are.'

'A laugh a minute, that's me.'

He studied her face, thought he might have detected a degree of animosity in her tone, but then she laughed and walked towards him, an exaggerated wiggle to her hips and a seductive raising of her eyebrows. Harry was not detracted, however: there was something bothering her and he wondered if she had spotted him parking the car after his 'walk.'

He poured the egg mixture into the pan, placed a lid on it and turned the cooker to simmer; then he ran his hands under the cold tap, dried them on a kitchen towel and gave her his full attention.

'What's up, sweetheart?'

'Annie,' she said without preamble. 'She told me she'd screwed you that night.'

Despite his pounding heart, Harry spoke quietly.' She's lying,' he said, well prepared. 'I told you what happened.'

'Don't you think I know that?' Beth frowned. 'What worries me is why she would say such a thing to her best friend.'

'You may be *her* best friend, Beth, but she is definitely not *yours*. How much longer will it take before you dump the bitch?'

'I was disappointed, hurt, to be honest.' She meandered over to him and flicked an imaginary speck of fluff from his shoulder. 'I've done everything for her...and more...and yet she'd do this awful thing to me.' She gave him a doleful look. 'You were right, Mr Know-all. I should dump her, but don't call her a bitch because it's not nice.'

Harry sighed and took her in his arms. 'What did you say to her anyway?'

'I asked her what part of your bum had a birthmark on it.'

'I don't have any birthmarks.'

'I know, but she said where she thought it was, so I told her you didn't have one and it had been a trick question.'

'That's clever,' Harry smiled. 'I approve.'

'How long 'til the culinary masterpiece is ready?'

'Long enough, if you mean what I think you mean.'

'I do mean.'

'Then I'll switch the cooker off, just in case you drag your heels.'

'It's not my heels I want you to look at.'

Something woke him in the middle of the night. He lay for a few moments, listening, but the sound, whatever it had been, never came again. Beside him, Beth was fast asleep, her hand across her face, the pose of a young child.

Harry rose and crept from the room, tiptoeing across the hallway to his study, where he closed and locked the door. The letter, still in his top pocket, felt so light in his hand that he could hardly believe it could present such a threat to Thomas Blake.

He switched on the desk lamp and unfolded the sheet of paper. Whenever he read the first sentence, he knew it would work. It was exactly the kind of deceit that would make Beth change sides.

Furthermore, it would take her mind off Annie Kerr; at least for the moment; until Harry had the opportunity to frighten the girl into keeping her mouth shut.

328

Chapter Twenty-Two

'Did your grandfather get in touch when you got back?'

They were sitting on the North Inch during their lunch break, only a hundred yards from Harry's office, enjoying a balmy summer's day and relishing the fresh air, for the atmosphere in the office was unbearable. When Marjory asked the question, Beth almost choked on her sandwich.

'My grandfather? When did you see him?' Her heart sank, for although she was aware that her father's illness and the trip to Paris had only postponed meeting the man again, Beth was not yet prepared to pick up where they had left off.

'Oh, he popped into the office one morning,' Marjory said happily. 'I told him you were in Paris and he said he'd be in touch when you came home.' She turned and gave Beth an anxious smile. 'I didn't do anything wrong, did I?'

'Gosh, no,' Beth said convincingly, at which the older woman puffed out an exaggerated sigh of relief. 'No, I haven't got round to it yet,' Beth assured her. 'But I will this week.'

'Such a nice man. So gentlemanly. Old-fashioned, if you like.' Marjory gave a mischievous grin. 'Is he taken, by the way?'

'What?' Beth could hardly conceal her shock, but not for the reason Marjory had in mind.

'I was only joking, dear, but he is rather handsome and distinguished.' She laughed and patted Beth's arm. 'But of course you're his granddaughter, you probably don't even notice these things.'

'No, I don't.'

'Is your grandmother still alive?'

Marjory was simply making conversation but Beth had a resistance to this particular line of chat: the fewer people who were privy to the Shepherd skeletons the better, especially in a small place like Perth where everyone seemed to know everyone else's business.

'No, she died years ago. Do you fancy one of my sandwiches? I've had too much already.' Marjory tutted in a maiden-aunt manner, usually a prelude to a remark about Beth's skinny frame. 'And before you tell me how emaciated I am, I had porridge this morning, half a ton of it.'

'Oh, that was hours ago, dear. How about this Mars Bar to give you energy for the afternoon?'

'Later maybe. Is Charlie to be in this afternoon?'

'Yes, he wants to finalise the partnership document, then you'll be a fully-fledged business woman.'

Marjory spoke with as much pride as if she had been Beth's mother, and the thought of her own mother gave Beth something of a jolt: the time was fast approaching when she would have to fly the flag for Thomas Blake's cause, do it all over again; the cajoling and the wheedling, pleading and persuading, being the only one in the family who was on his side.

'I'll have to start wearing something sophisticated to work now, will I?'

'What you need, young lady,' she heard Marjory pronounce primly. 'Is a shopping trip to Princes Street, to buy a whole new wardrobe, something stunning for your celebration dinner for a start.'

Beth laughed. 'One of the few opportunities for us to don our cocktail frocks and drink Pimms, whatever that is. By the way, I saw a fabulous dress in Jaeger's window, but, if I do buy it, I'll have to cut the price tag off before Harry spots it.'

'Men only pretend to be annoyed about that sort of thing,' Marjory said confidently, a woman who had often boasted of remaining single. 'But I'm sure they'd rather pay the price than have a wife who looks like the rear end of a cow.'

'Now, there's an interesting philosophy, but excuse me if I don't test it on Harry. What are you wearing by the way? New frock?'

'Goodness me, no. I have an old faithful, so it will do just fine. I'm so looking forward to seeing Lucy again,' Marjory went on, tidying away the remnants of her sandwiches and brushing crumbs off her skirt. 'She and I knew each other years ago, when her first husband was alive.'

'Really?' asked Beth, her senses alerted. 'He died in a crash, didn't he?'

'Very sad,' whispered Marjory, which Beth thought odd when there was no one around to hear. 'He was such a pleasant man too, quite devoted to her.'

'She must only be fifty, same as Mum. Why didn't she marry again?'

'Never met the right one, I suppose,' Marjory sighed. 'I know the feeling only too well, I'm afraid.'

'Have you... I mean, were you ever...?'

'You mean, did I ever do it?' Marjory asked humorously.

'Yes,' Beth opted to say, despite her blush, for her companion seemed as keen to tell all as Beth was to hear it.

'Well, yes, I did do it, as they say nowadays, but to be honest I think I prefer making jam.'

They burst into unrestrained laughter, attracting the attention of an elderly couple walking nearby, but the sight of their disapproving glances only added to the hilarity.

'Goodness me,' Marjory said eventually, her cheeks flushed. 'You must think I'm a dreadful influence on you, my dear.'

'Not at all. In fact, my family would say it was the other way round.'

As they walked the few hundred yards to the office, Beth's joie de vivre began to desert her. The more she thought about Thomas Blake and the renewed demands he would make on her, the more she wanted to find a way out. The strange thing was that nothing had changed: she was exactly the same person as she had been before her father's heart attack, and the circumstances had not altered in any way; yet the fervour that had gripped her months ago to read his letters, to hear him out and take his side, had long since muted to a feeling of slight resentment. Not only did she regard the whole affair as encroaching on her time, but also truth seeking was all very well; but it was also a hell of a lonely path.

*

Sandra waylaid Harry on his route to the photocopier, drawing him aside in her quaint, staid manner and glancing around to make sure they were alone, which they both knew was the case, Gilmour and Barclay having both left ten minutes before.

'I know it's supposed to be confidential, Harry,' she said in hushed tones. 'But I was wondering how you got on with Daphne the other day?'

Harry opened the machine and checked for paper, noting that he seemed to be the only one who restocked things, be it the copier or the coffee maker.

'Is she a good friend?'

'I've known her for years,' Sandra said evasively, not usually one of her traits. 'But I don't think you'd call us great friends, to be honest. I do see her at the City Women's Guild, things like that.'

'It is, as you say, confidential,' Harry agreed. 'But has she mentioned meeting anyone lately, a man, I mean?'

'Funny you should say that,' Sandra told him pensively. 'I think she did say something to me a few months ago, just in the passing, you understand. We were both helping at the church fete.' She paused, appearing to be searching for the exact words. 'Yes, she said she had an escort now, which she thought was rather nice at her age. Yes,' Sandra's nod confirmed. 'That's the way she put it.'

'Is there any chance you could find out anything about the man?'

Sandra's face lit up. 'I love any kind of intrigue,' she smiled broadly and it took all of Harry's strength not to laugh. 'Yes, I could do that, although I can't say for sure when I'll bump into her next, but if you think it will help her?'

'Oh, it will. I have a suspicion that she's on the brink of doing something really foolish.'

Sandra's hand flew to her mouth. 'Oh, no! You don't mean…?'

Harry, for all his experience of women, not to mention the sang froid he had inherited from his mother, felt his cheeks warming up.

'Sandra, honestly, you have a one-track mind,' he told her, much to her enjoyment. 'No, I didn't mean that kind of thing, I meant something else.'

'Of course, and she's probably a bit old for it anyway.'

'Will you stop distracting me with all this innuendo and let me get my work done?'

Sandra laughed and squeezed his arm. 'Certainly, Mr Harry,' she parodied with a curtsey. 'And I'll do my best at the Mata Hari thing.'

She darted into her office and left Harry to the photocopying. As he stood waiting for the machine to kick in, he thanked his lucky stars for a woman like Sandra. In fact, she was wasted on her cat.

Back in his office, he was about to lock the copy of Helen's letter in his top drawer when he had a sudden impulse to read it through again, although he suspected he knew it off by heart. Grace had been correct in assuming that the letter would read in her favour, especially the bit about Thomas Blake 'hating the child' and wanting 'nothing to do with it'. Harry was filled with a ridiculous sense of pity for the writer; an unmarried mother struggling to be accepted in the rigid atmosphere of the religious fervour of the time was a dismal prospect and Harry could sympathise with the unknown woman.

Valuable though it was, this letter paled into insignificance alongside the bigamy issue, one that Harry had never discussed with Grace, but one that could prove far more destructive to Thomas Blake, in that it would sully his reputation – even in these modern times – and make him think twice about setting up permanent home here. In legal terms, it was a much more valid route than the letter.

Harry tucked the letter in the drawer, locked it and popped the key into his wallet and then, seeing that the time was past four o'clock, decided to call it a day.

*

Alice and Grace were raking through the upstairs cupboard for suitable dresses to wear at the dinner. The first sight of her haute couture legacy from Celia Kinmont had caused Grace a brief, though intense, heartache, for it recalled to mind her silly dalliance with Roderick, a silly, though painful, infatuation that had stood in the way of any other romantic notions. She had never given other boys the slightest opportunity to get to know her, keeping them at a distance, clinging to the vain hope that one day Roderick would look at her and discover how much he loved her. When she had opened the cupboard door and caught her first glimpse of the clothes Celia had left her, Grace's heart had ached for times lost.

Alice must have noticed, for she laughed and joked about the amusing moments in their past, recollecting the risqué, secretive chatter that had always cheered them up when James and Martin were out together; the naughty references to sex – a taboo subject in 1940's Scotland.

'Didn't we have such fun?' Alice said now as they selected several dresses to try on. 'If it hadn't been for you, Grace, I dread to think what I'd have done.'

'I think it was the other way round,' Grace smiled. 'Remember how your letters helped me when Mum died? I'd been sitting in my room for weeks when you wrote something really hard-hitting about self-pity, and forced me to go to Lily's.' She stopped searching for dresses and looked at Alice, serious for a moment. 'You were so right, you know. I suddenly felt so selfish, thinking only of myself for so long, never giving a thought to poor Lily. I never really thanked you properly, Alice, but I'm thanking you now.'

She stepped forward and hugged her friend.

'Hey,' she heard Alice say softly. 'No more of this doom and gloom, Grace Blake. Come on, let's have a mannequin parade!'

They took the dresses into Alice's bedroom and tried on each of them amid gales of laughter at the fashions of the time and gasps of disgust at their spreading waistlines.

'Look at this,' Grace bemoaned, only just able to fasten the green silk dress that had once been her favourite. 'Did I ever get into this?'

'Yes, you did, and how lovely you were, just like an angel, sang like one too.' She paused and raised her eyebrows at her friend. 'When was the last time you sang?'

'I can't remember,' Grace said casually, anticipating what was coming next.

'You must sing and play while I'm still here,' Alice demanded. 'Tomorrow night, I insist.'

'Have you heard the old piano? I'd be more successful playing the spoons.'

'No, that's my instrument, you're on the piano, like it or not. What d'you say we have a good old sing-song, get out all the old music?'

Grace shrugged, for she knew perfectly well that Alice would not take 'no' for an answer. 'Very well, but I expect I'll sound like a drowning cat now, so don't say I didn't warn you.'

The remainder of the afternoon was taken up with trying on the dresses, Alice settling for a shade of blue that suited her complexion and dark hair, whilst Grace was drawn to the green silk dress she had worn as a girl, despite the tight fit around the waist.

'I can always starve until tomorrow night,' she said despondently. 'If I ask for anything at all to eat between now and then, you have my permission to slap my wrist!'

'Why do you think I chose this loose thing?' Alice grinned, twirling and whirling in front of the mirror. 'It covers a multitude of sins.'

'And will you look at the length of the hems compared with the ones Beth wears nowadays? We'll look like old biddies, the two of us.'

'They'll be back in fashion in no time,' Alice predicted, stepping out of the blue dress and eyeing her figure with a sigh. 'Whatever happened to us, Grace, turning from princesses into frogs?'

'Ugh! Speak for yourself, Alice Cameron, I'll keep pretending I'm a princess.'

'What will James wear?' Alice asked suddenly.

'James? Oh, he'll not go to something like that,' Grace said dismissively.

'Won't he?'

'No, he never goes anywhere, you know that. It almost caused us not to marry in the first place, remember?'

'It's just that I heard him tell Frank.'

Grace paused in her changing from the green dress back into her ordinary clothes and looked inquisitively at her friend.

'Tell him what?'

'That he couldn't decide whether to wear a suit or a jacket and trousers.'

'James said that?'

'Yes, I definitely heard him.' Alice shrugged. 'Seems like he's going after all. For Beth's sake, I would think,' she added with a reassuring smile.

'He wouldn't, not even for Beth.' Grace sat on the bed and looked at Alice. 'You know, when she had peritonitis… remember I wrote to you in '62?'

'Yes, the poor dear. It was touch and go, wasn't it?'

Grace nodded. 'She was rushed into hospital on the Friday night and James didn't go to see her until the Sunday, and d'you know why? Because he had a football match on the Saturday.'

Alice grimaced. 'Grace dear, men are quite different from us. He's just the same as any other man, taking care of his own needs.'

Grace stood up, doing her best to conceal her anger from Alice, not wishing to inflict her own grievances on her guest, but she felt it rising in her, the sense that he had neglected his daughter on the point of death and yet he could pander to Lucy Webster because she had fluttered her eyelashes at him.

'You're angry now,' she heard Alice remark. 'Come on, cheer up chicken.'

Grace forced a smile. 'I'm fine, just surprised, that's all. Now, if we want to get into those dresses tomorrow night, we'll have to eat a lettuce leaf for our tea.'

'Don't be mean, honey, I'm sure we can have two or three.'

'Oh, Gluttony, thy name is Alice!'

*

As was his wont at the end of the week, Charlie Webster called an informal meeting with Beth and Marjory to ponder the highs and lows of the previous seven days' sales. Since they had returned from Paris, Beth's efforts to woo Madame and Monsieur Blanc and their friends had paid off handsomely and Charlie was delighted with his new partner's social skills. When he mentioned it at the meeting, Beth burst out laughing.

'Only when money's involved,' she told him. 'Aside from that, I have all the social niceties of a flapping goose on the warpath.'

'Not that I've noticed,' he smiled, earning two glances of disapproval.

'Our German clients have rather fallen by the wayside,' Marjory said flatly, her gaze on Charlie's embarrassed face. 'What do you think the reason could be?'

'Beth hasn't been to Cologne yet,' he said with an attempt at a joke. He was considering taking on a male P.I. to redress the balance of the sexes in this place… 'Do you fancy that?'

'No, I don't as a matter of fact, but you could go.'

'I don't speak a bloody word of the lingo.'

'They all speak English,' Beth said helpfully. 'And you could always ring me if you got into difficulties. For instance, if you said something embarrassing.'

'Like what?'

'I remember someone at school asking the German student if she was hot, one day in the summer when we were all boiling in the classroom.'

Charlie shrugged. 'What's wrong with that? Just being polite, I'd have thought.'

'Except it actually meant are you a hot bit stuff?'

'Ah.'

Marjory suppressed a laugh. 'Thank goodness I only speak English. Did she biff him one?'

'No, he was rather dishy, I think she might have fancied him.'

'Did *you* think he was dishy?' Charlie had to know.

Beth frowned. 'I thought this was a business meeting.'

'Quite so,' Marjory agreed, effectively dismissing Charlie. 'Now, about the German clients. Any suggestions as to how we can woo them back?'

'I suppose I could write to them,' Beth suggested, the easy option.

'A good idea,' Charlie picked up on, casting her a grateful glance. 'Send them catalogues, see if they're tempted. I wonder why they've lost interest recently?'

'Could be the effects of the Berlin Wall,' Marjory said and the other two turned to look at her.

'What about it?' asked Charlie.

'Well, perhaps there's trouble at the borders or something. I've read of people being shot.'

Beth shivered and turned back to business. Twenty minutes later, after a brief mention of the dinner the following evening, Charlie offered to lock up. As he did so, he was torn between looking forward to the dinner, seeing her at The Birches again, pretending she was a permanent fixture. He suppressed the notion that he would see her with her husband and be forcefully reminded that she belonged to someone else.

*

Beth and Marjory left the office, going their separate ways at the Queens Bridge. On impulse, Beth decided to go into town to look for an evening bag to match her old faithful red wrap-over – the Jaeger dress was too risky – and took a detour up the High Street towards McEwens. As she walked past the jewellers on the opposite side of the street, she paused to admire a gaudy ring in the window, as gaudy and bulky a ring as she had seen and one that would not go amiss alongside the other six on her fingers.

'How do you manage to play the piano with that lot clunking at the ends of your wrists?' Annie had once asked.

'I take them off first,' Beth had replied.

She opened the door to the shop and came face to face with Thomas Blake.

'Beth, isn't this an unexpected pleasure?' he beamed, not the least put out by her sudden appearance. 'I do hope you enjoyed your trip to Paris?'

'I'd rather you didn't snoop around the office asking questions,' Beth found the strength to say bluntly. 'There's no need to involve Mrs Wilson.'

'Well I wouldn't have needed to,' her grandfather said smoothly. 'Had I known of your absence.' He must have regretted the arrogance in his tone, for he quickly amended it. 'I was only wanting to see you again, my dear, and I certainly wouldn't have gone to your office had I known you were away. I apologise profusely, especially to Mrs Wilson.'

'Apology accepted,' Beth said with a brief nod, seeing no point in rushing off into the street with some feeble excuse of washing her hair. No, she would act normally and fend him off gradually.

'Are you buying something?" she asked.

'A trinket for a friend,' he said, and she thought he grimaced, as if he wished he could retract it, that it was the last thing he wanted her to know.

'Lucky lady,' she smiled and he shrugged, changed the subject.

'Have you had any success with Grace?' he asked now, guiding her out of the shop doorway to allow a couple to enter.

'We've been so busy with my father that we really haven't had the time.'

It was plausible, she thought, and from his expression he thought so too.

'Of course, a dreadful, dreadful time for you all. How is he?'

'He's had to give up work,' Beth said, supposing it was half-true. 'And also they have visitors from abroad staying just now. Life goes on,' she added, possibly cruelly, as it inferred a life that excluded him.

'Just so,' he smiled, but showed no sign of moving away. 'I think I saw Grace and her overseas guest a few days ago actually.'

Despite her inbuilt defence mechanisms against being ambushed, Beth had to admit to surprise. 'Did you? She never mentioned it.'

'No, perhaps she didn't recognise me. In fact, I only realised it was her after I'd driven past.' He paused, looked at her with innocent eyes. 'On the spur of the moment, once I'd realised it was Grace, I turned off at the crossroads with the crazy idea of going back to speak to her.'

'But you didn't, obviously.'

'No, I have no desire to cause friction in the family,' he told her, with just a touch of sadness that Beth might have applauded had she been in an audience. Still, there was no law against good acting: she and her mother were star performers...

'Have you finished with Charlotte's letters to me?' her grandfather asked.

'Yes, I have. You'll want them back.'

'No hurry, but they mean a lot to me, the only part of her that I have left.'

This time there was no mistaking the pain in his expression. Beth knew that he had not taken Charlotte's death lightly and, involuntarily, she felt a tiny surge of pity for the man.

'I'll give them to you at the beginning of the week.'

'Have you made up your mind about the truth of the matter?'

There was no getting away from it; she would have to be brutally honest.

*

Thomas waited, for the girl appeared to be searching for the right words, and when people had to do that it meant the result would be unpleasant.

'The thing is,' she began slowly, not meeting his gaze. 'Even if I believe that you cared for my mother and grandmother, it won't matter much.' She raised her eyes to his. 'If she doesn't want to see you, that's her decision.'

'But you led me to believe that she was coming round to the idea,' Thomas reminded the girl, recalling the days thereafter when he had walked on air.

'Yes, she was... is, probably, but it's not going to happen overnight. She did tell me that she had no objection to my having contact with you, and I took that as a promising beginning.'

His spirits clambered upwards again, trying to find daylight.

'As you say, perhaps it's too soon. She needs more time, that's all.' He smiled broadly, forcing himself not to be too disappointed. Besides, he was taking Daphne on a trip next week and they would be gone for several days, which would pass some of the time.

'I'm sure that's all it is,' the girl said, apparently genuine in her concern for him. 'Meantime, I'll do my best. She and I have already talked about you.'

'Have you? Did she seem...? I mean, had she mellowed at all?'

'I think so,' the girl smiled. 'I'm sure that she'll get used to the idea. She's not an ogre, you know.'

Thomas thought back to their meeting at the George, when his daughter had looked right at him, relishing the moment she told him Charlotte was dead. Wisely, he had kept it to himself.

'No, I'm sure she's not. After all, her mother was the kindest, sweetest person you could ever hope to meet.'

For an instant, he felt foolish when his eyes filled with tears, but then the girl leaned forward and touched his arm, her eyes showing the first tenderness he had witnessed in her.

'I'll do my best,' she said quietly and, before he could respond, she had turned and walked away.

*

Harry saw her striding down the pavement ahead of him, blonde hair flying as always, short skirt and shapely legs attracting admiring male glances. He had no idea why she would be in town, unless it was to buy something for Lucy; a gift for the hostess.

Even at this distance he could tell she was in a bad mood and if, as it seemed, she was going home, the kindest he could do for her was to give her time to let it out of her system, whatever it was. As the Salutation Hotel came into view, he veered off and went in for a drink, confident that, by the time he arrived home, she would have exhausted her temper and they could share a cosy conversation.

Half an hour later, he let himself into the flat and was greeted by an ominous silence. He stood for a moment trying to ascertain where she was, but all he heard was the ticking of the hall clock. With more noise than usual, he opened the cupboard, hung up his jacket and slammed the door closed, to herald his approach.

'Beth, it's me. Are you home yet?' To let slip that he had seen her flouncing down the street in a foul mood was not advisable: second on Beth's list of pet hates was being spied on, even accidentally.

Harry walked towards the kitchen. As he passed the sitting room doorway, he glanced in and saw the result of her bad mood: every sheet of music was strewn around the room, Chopin's labours being the most obvious, lying, as they were, at his feet, right on the threshold. Rather than stoop to pick them up, he stepped into the room, suspecting her be huddled on the floor somewhere in the throes of remorse.

'I'm over here,' came her voice and he turned to see her at the piano.

He could say something funny, or he could shut up, never an easy decision when she was sulking; but from her expression, he deduced that she might tolerate a comic remark.

'Play it again, Beth.'

She sighed and shook her head. 'No chance, Gillespie.'

'Had a good day?' he persisted with the humour.

'Did you?'

'Fair's fair. I asked first.' He began making his way across the paper trail.

'I did have a good day,' she replied slowly. 'Until half an hour ago.'

'And then?'

'Oh, Harry,' she said despairingly, jumping up and clutching his arm. 'I don't know if I do the right thing sometimes.'

Involuntarily, Harry's gaze lowered to the manuscripts on the floor.

'Maybe I should plead the fifth amendment here.'

She laughed then, hanging onto him as if her life depended on it. He loved her more when she was vulnerable, rather than when she was assertive and in control. He wondered if Grace Blake had held a similar appeal for her suitors. He never included James Melville in their number.

'Come on,' he said gently, prising her from his arm and leading her to the sofa. 'Sit down, I'll make us a drink and then you can tell me all about it.'

'I'm not sure I want to.'

'Confession's good for the soul, so sit down there at once, Madam, and prepare to start talking.'

'Oh, I rather like it when you're Clint Eastwood.'

She sat obediently on the sofa, tucking her bare feet beneath her.

'What's yours?' he called, halfway to the kitchen.

'Whisky, please.'

He paused in the hall: whisky was something Beth drank only when she was utterly dejected and, as he searched for glasses, Harry was trying to figure out what on earth could have happened at work to make her so miserable.

He opted to sit opposite her and, as he looked across at her, his heart skipped a beat: she was the loveliest creature.

'So, tell me,' he prompted. 'Why are you fed up?'

'I was going into the jewellers opposite McEwens and I bumped into him.'

He waited for a moment but when she said nothing more, Harry smiled.

'I'm not a mind reader, sweetheart.'

'Him, Thomas Blake, who d'you think?'

He caught his breath at the unexpectedness of it, and yet the man had been snooping around the village; why should he not way-lay Beth? Had he been following her from work?

'What did he want?'

'Nothing really,' she said, but her tone was nervous. 'He was just passing in the street.'

'I see.'

Immediately, Beth took umbrage. ' 'I see'. What does that mean?'

Without responding, Harry rose, picking up their empty glasses and went back to the kitchen, where he poured another two of the same. By the time he returned and sat down, she was repentant, as he suspected she would be. Her continual struggle not to be a child was familiar territory for them both.

'I'm a bit tetchy, that's all.'

'I know and I accept your apology,' he said with amusement.

'Don't push it,' she cautioned, but her eyes were laughing and he envisaged the whole story pouring out in the next few minutes.

'He wanted to know if Mum was mellowing, if there was any chance of her coming round, wanting to see him.'

'And is there?'

She threw him a look of the utmost contempt. 'If anyone knows, it's you.'

'Well, I don't, as it happens, so I'm asking you.'

She shrugged and picked up her glass, drinking half of it in one gulp.

'I haven't spoken to her about it for ages, not since Dad's heart attack.'

'What do you think she'd say?'

'I have no idea, but if you're so interested why don't you ask her yourself?'

'I think I will, tomorrow night at Lucy Webster's, perhaps.'

He knew she would take exception to her mother being troubled on a night that was supposed to be a joyful occasion, and so he was hardly surprised when she shook her head vigorously.

'No, don't do that. I'll ask her when the time's right.' She gave him yet another conciliatory glance. 'Don't you ever get cheesed off being such a goody-two-shoes?'

'No, I rather like it, and I fervently hope that you never get cheesed off being the most volatile, stubborn, argumentative, wild creature I've ever met.'

It was exactly the right thing to say to Beth – the coup de grace – but he meant every word. She uncurled from the sofa, padded across the space between them and sat at his feet.

337

'You're safe enough there,' she smiled, gazing up at him. 'In fact, I might even get worse.'

'Don't make promises you can't keep.'

She laughed and averted her eyes. 'Now I suppose I'd better clean up in here.'

'I'll help.'

'No, it's O.K.,' Beth disagreed brightly. 'I made the mess, it's only right that I should clear it up. Why don't you just sit and watch me, cheer me on?'

'I've a better idea. Why don't I just sit and watch you, cheer you on?'

*

Lucy Webster threw the dress onto the bed with a sigh of disgust. How could she ever have worn such a monstrosity and considered herself the belle of the ball? She surveyed the array of dresses, skirts and blouses that she had already tried on, and saw that there were so few possibilities left that she would be forced to drive into Perth and buy something new, only three hours before the guests were due.

It was ridiculous, of course, and she quickly dismissed it as such. The combined cash value of the bits of material discarded onto her bed must be in the region of a thousand pounds, enough to put down as a deposit for a small house; and here she was, casting them aside with the scantest of respect. Lucy shook her head and began looking through them once more.

The most shameful aspect was, had James Melville not been coming for dinner, she would have selected the first dress off the hanger. At her age, with her plain looks, and with a propensity to be dumbstruck in mixed company – especially when Grace Blake was a social delight – Lucy was aggrieved.

The telephone rang for the umpteenth time that day and for the umpteenth time she feared that he might not be well enough to join them. With trepidation, she picked it up; but it was only Kathleen with a query about the table settings.

'I'll come down in five minutes,' she told the hapless girl. 'Just leave things until I'm there.'

With a brief but despairing backward glance at the outfits on her bed, Lucy left the room and made her way to the top of the stairs.

*

Lily Morris was in no hurry to get ready. She would change into her old faithful at the last minute and walk twenty yards up the lane. The sad thing was that she would need to wear stout shoes, for the potholes in the lane were lying in wait for a pair of wobbly ankles like hers and she was fearful of ending up in PRI with a broken hip and no hope of escape until the hearse arrived.

As she passed the living room mantelshelf, she chanced to look at the photograph that took pride of place, right in the middle: she and Charlotte Shepherd; arms linked, long dresses sweeping the ground, laughing out at her, catching her by surprise and obliging her to pause on her way to the kitchen.

She picked up the photograph and turned it over: *summer 1923*, she read and she could hardly believe that so many years – nay, decades – had flown by and, so quickly that she had not even noticed half of them.

She examined Charlotte's happy face, which had scarcely altered over the years. Of course, you were lucky if you died young, because you were spared the ignominy and ravages of old age. Not for Charlotte the sallow, sagging skin, or the nagging pains in joints and muscles, or – the very worst thing – the necessity for a pot under the bed because her bladder had given up its fight to stay in shape.

Lily thought of her other childhood friend, Nan, still content but confined to her flat these days unless some Good Samaritan took the bus to Perth, walked half a mile to Nan's house and pushed her wheelchair around the park for a while. If Lily had been able to drive, she might have gone more regularly; and she supposed that she could have taken up Grace's offer to give her a lift now and then; but the trouble was her bladder again, for she had to go every half hour now and the prospect of disgracing herself on a Perth street was enough to bring on her angina.

She shook her head at such pathetic whingeing and hurried through to the kitchen. The cake she had baked for Lucy Webster had cooled now, and so she wrapped it in greaseproof paper, slid in into the old Coronation tin and left it in a prominent place for her to pick up on the way out.

*

At the last moment, both Grace and Alice changed their minds about which dresses they would wear. With great hilarity, and only an hour before they were due to leave, they attacked the contents of the upstairs cupboard anew and could hardly try anything on for laughing.

'This is daft,' Grace said. 'There's nothing wrong with the green silk dress. I should just go and put it on now.'

'No!' shrieked Alice, grabbing her friend's arm. 'That'll make me look like the only idiot in this house!'

'Honestly, what on earth's come over us? You'd think it was a ball at Buckingham Palace.'

'I suppose it's almost the same thing,' Alice grinned, holding up a red flowery dress and examining her reflection in the mirror. 'The Birches is surely your equivalent of Buckingham Palace, don't you think? The landed gentry, lots of money, important people in the community.' Alice paused for breath. 'Not to mention the way the villagers bow down to the likes of the Kinmonts and the Websters; something I never see in the States.'

'I suppose they do,' Grace had to admit reluctantly, for she had grown up in this village and had experience of the kind of subservience Alice was alluding to. 'The only one who didn't do it was my Mum,' she added with a smile.

'That's true, but she was unique, was Charlotte Blake.'

Grace stood for a moment, weighing up the advantages of saying nothing or revealing just how un-unique her mother had been when it came to matters of honour.

'You know,' she heard Alice say. 'When we were in Paris, I had the feeling you wanted to talk to me about something.'

Grace looked at her friend sitting demurely on the edge of the bed, her eyes filled with compassion. When they were young, no subject had been out of bounds, no tears, no pain, no heartache too much to confide or to hear, but now, approaching fifty, it was not so easy, nor so wise perhaps, to reveal all, especially where Thomas Blake was concerned. In this village, only Lily Morris knew the truth, and when she was gone, Grace's secret was as safe as she wanted it to be. Harry knew, of course, but that was tantamount to her knowing. She had a sudden shiver: she was relying on the boy to such an extent that she dreaded the day he might leave.

'Hey, did you hear me, Grace Blake?' Alice was complaining.

'Yes, I did, and no, I didn't.' She laughed. 'Didn't have anything to talk about, I mean.'

'I'd never tell a soul.'

'But there's nothing to tell,' Grace smiled, looking at Alice with what she hoped was sincerity. 'Honestly, if there were, you know I'd tell you.'

'Whatever it is,' Alice insisted pleasantly. 'For Heaven's sake, don't tell Molly. She'd blab it all over the county.'

'I think I'll wear this one,' Grace said, deliberately steering the conversation away from dangerous ground. 'What d'you think?'

'Listen, you,' Alice frowned. 'You'd look good in a tatty sack, you horrible woman.'

'Oh, no,' Grace said, feigning disappointment. 'How terrible!'

'What is it?'

'I don't think I've got a single one left.'

'A single what?'

'Tatty sack.'

'Get into that damned frock, woman. It's time we were away!'

*

James sat downstairs, uncomfortable in his dark blue suit, which he wore only to funerals and weddings and they were few and far between. He recalled that the last time had been at Beth's wedding, almost five years before. The fact that he could still get into the same suit when some of his peers were developing hefty stomachs hardly consoled him, although he knew he should be grateful that he was here at all, considering the severity of his heart attack.

Thankful for his stubborn resilience, which he had passed onto his daughter, his mind floated back to the War, to days of conflict, to moments he had believed to be his last; and yet, when the noise and chaos had died down, he had not been surprised to find he was still alive. Going home to see Grace again had been his strength. Grace! With a start, he remembered how loving she had been, how gentle and patient, particularly when the sights and sounds of warfare had haunted him in dreams. She had been there during the long nights, sitting up with him, encouraging him to talk, to unburden himself of the terrors he had survived.

He heard now faint sounds of the two women moving upstairs and he stood up, moved off to give his shoes a final polish. It was the sign of a tidy mind, or so he had read somewhere – a pair of clean and polished shoes. It had been the first thing he had noticed about Harry Gillespie, but, instead of accrediting it to the boy's advantage, James preferred to believe it was a result of his daughter's insistence on good grooming. He had a swift and unwelcome thought that the short skirts young girls wore nowadays were most unseemly, especially for Beth, who had been brought up to act modestly. Perhaps it would not go amiss if he were to mention it.

*

Harry called to Beth, still in the bedroom, fiddling with her dress.

'One more minute!' she replied, and he had lost count of how many. However, as he wandered down the hall towards the bedroom, she emerged, rushing as usual, hair flying, cheeks flushed.

'I'm speechless,' he told her truthfully. 'You look utterly gorgeous.'

'I should think so too,' she said with a smirk. 'I wasn't going to buy it, but Marjory persuaded me. It cost you the earth.'

'A small price to pay if this is the result.'

'Funnily enough, that's what Marjory said, and it seems she was right.' Beth suddenly looked him up and down. 'Hey, you're not so bad yourself. I could eat you right now.'

'And when you look at me like that, I wouldn't put up much of a fight.'

'You really like the dress?'

'You have good taste, considering you're such a Scottish peasant.'

'And I love you too, now let's go and try to behave.'

Harry gave her an appraising glance as he locked the door.

'I hope you won't behave too well once we get home.'

'Depends how nice you are at The Birches.'

She spoke lightly but he sensed her eagerness for him to make an effort with Charlie Webster. He supposed that even that were possible.

Descending the staircase, Beth took his arm to lean on, her heels so high and spiky that he expected her to tumble at every step. Moments later, they walked to the car beneath gathering skies, the sun making a final, desperate attempt to flaunt itself before the clouds drifted closer and snuffed it out.

Chapter Twenty-Three

When Lucy's first guests arrived, the air was sultry, the clouds threatening rain, precluding any prospect of sitting outdoors with the cocktails. As a result, Kathleen had been setting out glasses and wine decanters in the sunroom.

'If the weather improves,' Lucy said hopefully, 'we can go outside later, after dinner.'

She wondered if the girl could see how nervous she was. After all the dinner parties and soirees Lucy had hosted in this house, she was having the greatest difficulty in maintaining her composure, and the last thing she needed was the maid's tittle-tattling to all and sundry. There was little that these sort of girls missed.

When the doorbell clanged, Lucy jumped, fortunately out of sight of Kathleen.

'Shall I get it?' the girl called from somewhere and Lucy was amazed at the girl's use of '*shall*' as opposed to '*will*'. She had learnt a lot more than laying tables and cleaning out fires in the few years she had worked there.

'Yes please, Kathleen, I'll be in the sunroom.'

Lucy walked up and down the room, trying to cool her flushed cheeks in case it should be James and Grace arriving first; but it was Lily Morris and Lucy's heart had fluttered needlessly.

'Lily, how nice to see you. Did you survive the potholes?'

'I think I travelled twice the distance, avoiding them all.' She leaned her walking stick against the window ledge. 'It's high time someone did something about the state of it.'

'I suppose it's up to all the householders who back onto it,' Lucy said without thinking, for Lily was one of them and could ill afford the expense, albeit shared. 'Actually,' she added quickly. 'I feel it's more my responsibility, what with this house extending half way down the lane. I think I'll speak to Charlie about it, get him to organise something.'

'That would seem to be the solution,' Lily said bluntly, scarcely a trace of gratitude in her tone. 'It will make quite a difference, to my spindly ankles anyway.'

'Speaking of which, take the weight off them and have a seat,' Lucy said, waving her hand in the direction of the most comfortable settee. 'Would you care for a drink now or would you rather wait for the rest?'

'Oh, they could be long enough. I'll have a wee sherry, thank you.'

Automatically, Lucy pressed the service bell at the side of the hearth and caught her guest's disapproving glance. The deed was done, however, and within seconds, Kathleen was at the door.

'A sherry for Miss Morris, please, and a dry Martini for me. Thank you, Kathleen.'

'I always thought this was a fine room,' Lily said, looking around the sunroom, her eyes resting on each and every piece of furniture, every ornament. 'But it's a lot cleaner since you took over.'

Lucy was invariably at a loss in the older woman's company. She was unable to find the balance between being magnanimous to her elders and adjusting to Lily Morris' outspoken nature. In Lucy's society, there were few occasions when people said exactly what they were thinking.

'Is it?'

'Oh, aye,' Lily smiled. 'Celia Kinmont was a nice enough woman, but her housewifery skills were sadly lacking, even if she did have more servants than you.'

Lucy's spirits sank at the way Lily had pronounced the word 'servants'. She must see it as an outdated term in this modern age, especially when even some of the village women had a cleaner. She soldiered on.

'I didn't know her, of course, but I believe that Grace and her mother had their work cut out to clear the place after Mrs Kinmont's death.'

'They did indeed, but neither of them was one to shirk duty.'

Again, Lucy took the comment personally, believing it to be a slight on her own, privileged life. Thankfully, the door opened and Kathleen arrived with the drinks on a small silver tray, enabling Lucy to fuss around for a few moments and try to recover her composure; but she was so despondent and fearful that the evening would be a failure, that the first sip of Martini made her feel quite ill.

When the doorbell rang a second time, she jumped up, almost spilling her drink.

'I'll only be a moment, Lily,' she said, already out of breath in case it should be James. 'If you need anything, just...' She had been about to say 'just ring for Kathleen', but common sense cut her off mid-sentence.

Before she reached the door, she heard James's voice and her heart skipped a beat.

*

Grace and Alice were straggling behind, wandering up the path to the house, admiring the flowers and shrubs. James was already up the steps and ringing the doorbell when the two women were still breathing in the scent of the old-fashioned roses on the wrought-iron archway halfway up.

'James!' Lucy said, her cheeks turning pink, something that, in James's eyes, defined her as modest and old-fashioned. There was also an element of satisfaction that, at his age, he could still cause a lady to blush. 'I'm so delighted that you could come. You're looking so well.'

'Of course I would come,' he said, waiting politely for her to invite him in. 'It's a very important occasion for Beth.'

'Yes, it is,' Lucy said, inexplicably flustered, which he considered rather endearing. 'Are the ladies with you?'

'Just admiring your garden,' he smiled, glancing over his shoulder in the direction of the path.

'Ah, yes, well I'm sure they won't mind if you come in.' She stepped aside to let him pass and, briefly, their shoulders touched. Under normal circumstances it was the sort of contact that James avoided with other women but with Lucy Webster, being as she was a most genteel and well-bred woman, he thought nothing of it.

She led the way through the hall towards the sunroom, whilst, behind her, looking at the décor and furnishings, James could hardly believe his eyes: he had never seen such opulence, such extravagance; not even during the War when they had fallen heirs to the contents of abandoned houses on their trek across Europe. It took his breath away; but for all the wrong reasons. His mind flashed back to the small village in East Sussex, with its basic amenities; the outside toilet, the sporadic supply of spring water; and the homemade curtains whose creation had drawn blood from his mother's fingers. He paused to examine a portrait on the hall table, of Lucy and her husband – James presumed – set amidst such an array of wealth and splendour that the cost might have fed everyone in the village for a month.

'James?' he heard her call and he shook himself, forced himself to walk on; but, in one significant moment, James had discovered that Lucy Webster, whether or not she appreciated flowers and the joys of gardening, whether or not she found him pleasant company, was as removed from his world as she could possibly be.

*

343

Harry carried Beth up the stone staircase leading to the front door of The Birches, not because her feet were hurting, but because he had spotted Charlie Webster at the window above the entrance and had decided to start the evening with a statement of intent.

'Golly,' Beth murmured into his neck as he deposited her gently at the top. 'That was the most romantic thing you've ever done for me.'

'Was it?' he frowned. 'It doesn't say much for my romancing skills then, does it?'

'You have absolutely nothing to worry about on that score,' Beth smiled wickedly, her arm lingering around his neck. 'In fact. I could ravish you here and now.' Her mouth touched his just as the door opened and Charlie Webster's voice reached him.

'Oops, I can go away and come back later if you like?'

To Harry's surprise, Beth seemed in no hurry to disentangle herself from his grasp and it was he who drew back first, much to her irritation, although it was short-lived.

'Charlie, how lovely to see you dressed up,' she said airily, offering him her hand and stepping daintily across the threshold. 'You look extremely suave.'

'And you are a knock-out,' Charlie whistled, an action which Harry deemed to be more prevalent among building workers than the gentry. 'Stunning, that's the only word I can use to describe you.'

Harry waited patiently for them to remember he was there, examining the end of his tie and rehearsing various opening lines, none of which were pithy or clever. Perhaps he would simply opt for 'hello'.

'And you must be Harry, the lucky husband,' he heard Charlie say, and he looked up then, patting his tie back into place and fixing the man with a smile.

'I am indeed,' he said only, taking the proffered hand.

'Harry, this is Charlie,' Beth said beside him, her tone warm and friendly. 'And Charlie, this is Harry. There, I think that's the done thing, isn't it?'

'You must be very proud of Beth,' Charlie said as he led the way inside. 'She's quite a girl.'

It was said in such a way that it implied more than a working knowledge of her but Harry had no plans to appear peevish in front of Beth and so he agreed and let it go.

'I think Lily Morris and your mother and father are here,' Charlie told Beth as they walked across the tiled vestibule, the sound of her high heels echoing around the walls. 'Oh, and Alice, of course, an exceptionally nice lady, I really like her. Oh, and Marjory's just phoned to say her taxi's there at last and she won't be long.'

'Alice is lovely,' Beth agreed, throwing Charlie a comical wink. 'And she's single now, I believe,' she winked suggestively, but if he had heard her, he made no sign.

The sunroom was lit by candles, which would immediately endear Lucy Webster to Beth, Harry guessed, for to live with Beth Melville must be akin to living in the Vatican; at least where candles were concerned…

'Oh look, there's Mum,' he heard Beth mumble in his ear. 'And doesn't she look fantastic? Alice must have done her hair, thank goodness, otherwise Mum wouldn't have bothered. And the dress! Where the heck did she buy it? It's utterly gorgeous! People are spot on when they say she's like a flipping film star!'

Harry had to admit she was right. He had a sudden thought that the sight of Grace Blake must have caused many a young man untold heartache.

Despite his desire to speak to her, Harry held back, remaining at Beth's side, in case she accused him of deserting her in favour of Grace, an inevitable consequence at some point in the evening; but preferably later.

'Harry and Beth,' Lucy Webster was saying now. 'How lovely to see you. Imagine our not having met properly,' she added apologetically to Harry. 'And Beth being my husband's colleague too. I should have had this dinner ages ago. Kathleen's around here somewhere, fetching drinks for everyone. If you see her, just grab one'

She moved away to speak to Grace and Alice and as Harry looked for James, he saw him sitting alone in one of the bay windows, a full glass by his side, looking as out of place as a fish floundering on the riverbank.

'Do you mind if I pop over and speak to your father?' he asked Beth.

'You're a darling,' she whispered. 'I was just going to do that, he looks so lonely.'

'If the lovely Kathleen comes round, mine's a g and t.'

Harry tapped James on the shoulder and was surprised to be greeted with a spontaneous smile.

'Harry, good to see you. Come and sit down, keep me company.'

Harry sat with his back to the room: it would give Beth the impression that he was unconcerned about the attention her business partner might bestow on her; but in truth, he could see her in the reflections in the windows and would be quite aware of who she was with.

'Beth's a sight for sore eyes,' James said solemnly.

'She's the loveliest girl I've ever seen,' Harry agreed, thereby evoking a nod of approval from her father.

'And she seems to be very happy,' James said, his eyes on Beth as she chatted to her mother and Alice. 'You've succeeded in making her happy.'

Harry was wary: he had never seen or heard James Melville in such agreeable mood.

'I hope I have made her happy,' he said now, wondering at James's sudden sorrowful expression. 'She certainly makes me happy.'

'What is it you love most about her?' James asked unexpectedly.

Harry hesitated, for he was cautious about such an intimate conversation with James, having skimmed over inconsequential topics until now. He decided to tell the truth, come what may.

'I love the way she flies into a temper and throws things around the room.'

It must have been the right thing to say, for James laughed heartily and slapped Harry on the knee, a most extraordinary action for a man Harry considered so reticent.

'Just the thing I love too,' he said, still laughing. 'She's a fiery little thing, my daughter, and I was afraid there would be no man strong enough to deal with her.'

'I'm not sure I always deal with her,' Harry said ruefully. 'I love her so much that she usually gets her own way.'

'Ah, but that's not always so bad,' James smiled. 'I was the same with Grace. She could wind me round her little finger.'

It was uttered with such affection that Harry had to fight the inevitable flare of jealousy that resulted from any romantic reference to Grace. He gazed from the window and waited for James to speak again.

'Have you ever been in this house before?'

'No, I haven't, but I think Beth has.'

'To play that piano,' James explained, his head inclining towards the baby grand in the corner. 'She was here twice, she told me. She would do anything to play such a piano.' He looked at Harry again, eyes appreciative. 'I was very glad when you bought her a good piano.'

'I enjoy hearing her play. In fact, I could listen to her for hours.'

'But she hates playing in front of people.'

Harry smiled and nodded. 'She does indeed, but I creep into the flat and hide in the cupboard so that I can listen.'

He was astonished when James grabbed him by the shoulders and shook him heartily, if a little roughly. 'You're a good man,' he said firmly, releasing Harry eventually and sitting back in his chair. 'It's good that you love her so much. I can see that now.'

Harry could think of nothing to say. He had never had such a personal conversation with James Melville in all the years he had known him, and it would take some time to reconcile this happy, sympathetic man with the distant, taciturn man who had caused Harry so many despairing moments.

'This house,' James was saying now. 'I think that the cost involved could feed an African country.'

'Yes, it's true,' Harry said, treading warily. 'It seems to be a fact of life in this country.'

'But not in America,' James said, almost triumphantly. 'Alice says that people are more equal where she lives.' Then he added, almost as an afterthought:

'I could have taken Grace to live there, you know, after the War. But she would never have left this village.'

'Did you ask her?'

'No,' James smiled. 'I knew what she would say. Besides, she...' He stopped, glanced at Harry for a moment with an expression of suspicion and then remained silent.

'She what?' Harry dared to ask.

'It's not important,' James told him but his eyes reflected otherwise.

'I'd like you to tell me,' Harry heard himself say, inwardly preparing for a sharp retort, risking relinquishing their present camaraderie and returning to the status quo.

'She was very fond of someone before me.'

Pulse quickening, Harry decided that he had come this far and had nothing to lose by further probing.

'A serious boyfriend?'

'He was very fond of her.'

'She told you?'

'She was still going out with him when I arrived in the village.'

'Does he still live here?'

James mouth tightened. 'Yes, he does.' He looked away, towards Grace, who was laughing with Lucy Webster. 'It was Graham Seaton.'

Before he knew what he was saying, Harry had blurted out the first thing that came into his head, in an effort to spare Grace further trouble.

*

Across the room, Grace saw James and Harry deep in conversation. Had the boy's expression not been so intense, she might have convinced herself that they were discussing daily, inconsequential matters; but the way he was looking at James, the urgency of his mannerisms, was beginning to trouble her.

She only half listened to Lucy and Lily ruminating over the disadvantages of rural living but, as soon as a suitable pause came along, she excused herself and moved closer to the bay window.

As they became aware of her presence, it was the boy who appeared more embarrassed, whilst James was regarding him with what could only be described as wariness. She was at a loss as to what Harry had said to engender such a look from her husband.

'Grace, dear,' James said, standing as she approached, taking her hand and raising it to his lips. 'Sit down and keep me company while Harry goes to speak to Beth.'

Harry caught her eye, appeared to be trying to warn her, but about what? In the split-second before he moved off, however, he had conveyed to her that he and James had discussed something significant.

Suddenly, James attitude altered completely. He gave her a contrite glance. 'I think I've been a bit of an idiot,' he said remorsefully. 'Please forgive me.'

'What for?' she asked lightly. 'What terrible thing have you done?'

'I can't tell you, but I'm asking you to forgive me.'

'In that case,' she laughed. 'I forgive you, James.'

'Honestly, I don't know if I can forgive myself.'

'James, for Heaven's sake, this is supposed to be Beth's happy night,' she reminded him.

'Of course, how stupid of me.' He took her hand and rubbed it against his cheek. 'We should go and tell our daughter how proud we are of her.'

'Yes, I think we should.'

As they stood up to go and find Beth, Grace tried to attract Harry's attention but he was engrossed in a conversation with Beth and did not turn his head. Until she spoke to him, she would know no peace.

*

Beth raised her glass and began her short speech. She had planned to say several witty things, a soliloquy laced with intellectual sparks and mind-boggling puns; but as she looked at Harry she wondered at his sudden lacklustre expression and was distracted from her original speech.

'I was going to be funny, witty and highly intelligent,' she began. 'But, to tell the truth, I'm none of these things really, so I'll just be sullen, impudent and dopey, as usual.'

The strange thing was that she meant it to be serious, but everyone took it in fun and she pretended to go along with it.

'Charlie's been the nicest boss that anyone could hope for,' she continued. 'And I'm hoping he'll be the nicest partner too.'

'I'm hopeless at the twist,' he quipped before she could go on.

'Partner, as in lots of money,' she smiled. 'Not on the dance floor.' She looked straight at Harry, saw that he was paying only scant attention to what she was saying and opted to restrict her ramblings to a couple of sentences in order to speak to him as soon as possible.

'So, in short, I'm looking forward to being more involved with the business and hopefully sacking Charlie as soon as is decently possible. Thank you.'

She sat down and drank from the glass of bubbly. When she glanced across at Harry he was looking at her, applauding her speech, smiling at her; but she suspected his mind was elsewhere. She just had to get to the bottom of it; to find out if it had anything to do with the hushed conversation he had had with her father earlier. The trouble was that the pudding was only just being served and then there would be cheese and coffee and little sweetie things that you swallowed in one bite. By the time she had a chance to speak to him, she might have lost the courage to ask him.

*

Charlie was, at last, having a word with Harry Gillespie. He had been disheartened by how good-looking the man was, for there had always been the slimmest chance to prise her from an ugly husband, but now Charlie knew his quest was hopeless. His stomach was still churning at the thought of Gillespie in bed with her, sampling the delights she had to offer, crawling all over her and…

347

He halted his thoughts right there, before he ruined the evening completely; and tried to concentrate on what the man was saying.

'I know she'll put a hundred percent into the job,' he thought Gillespie had just said and so he moulded his reply accordingly.

'Are you pleased she has this kind of a job?'

'It's a job,' Harry Gillespie shrugged. 'Is there any other kind?'

'I mean, she could have used her languages to teach, something like that. I was thinking she might be wasted in the antiques business.'

Harry raised one eyebrow at him and Charlie caught a glimpse of the man who had scared the life out of Frank Gilmour.

'You sound as if you want to get rid of her already,' Harry Gillespie smiled.

'No, that's not what I meant,' Charlie said hurriedly, on the back foot, just the last place he wanted to be with his rival. 'I only meant that she could have a really successful career with a language degree, but if she's happy where she is, then, believe me, I'm happy to have her.'

Inwardly, he froze at the ambiguous expression, but Harry Gillespie appeared not to notice.

'That's good,' he smiled, preparing to move off, Charlie thought. 'And, believe me, if she's not happy, you'll be the second to know.'

He walked off, leaving Charlie with the implication ringing in his ears and a sense that he had gone two rounds with Cassius Clay. He glanced around the room, spotted Marjory chatting animatedly to his mother and decided to butt in before his boyhood antics were mentioned.

*

As the evening was coming to an end, the foreboding sky threw down its burden at last, hurling sheets of rain earthward, accosting the sunroom windows with a venom that continued for at least an hour, confining the guests to their retreat until the storm had eased.

Lucy Webster was undecided as to whether she should be grateful or miserable: the inclement weather had resulted in everyone's remaining after ten o'clock, everyone including James, to whom she had said only half a dozen words since his arrival; not that he had been avoiding her but, before dinner, when she expected to chat to him, he had been so wrapped up in a serious conversation with his son-in-law, and then with Grace, that Lucy could find no opportunity to interrupt; nor would she have had the courage to do so.

'Thank you for a lovely dinner.'

She turned round quickly, caught off-guard, to see James smiling at her, and was tongue-tied again.

'I'm – I'm so glad you enjoyed it.'

'It must have been a lot of work for you.'

She would have liked to take the credit for a successful evening but she resolved to be honest.

'I hardly did anything,' she smiled, avoiding his eye. 'It was the cook and Kathleen who worked hardest.'

'Ah, but you're a charming hostess, and that's important too.'

She felt such a fool, standing there, hands fidgeting, with nothing to say that would matter to a man like him.

'Did you see the flower bed on your way up the garden?' she asked, returning to safe territory. 'I'm so pleased with the way it's turned out.'

'Ah, but it's not finished yet,' James smiled and her heart skipped a beat.

'Isn't it?'

'No, I'll have to come back in a few weeks' time to plant the rest.'

'Will you?'

'Of course.' He frowned. 'Did you think I would only do half the job?'

'No, not at all,' she said quickly, trying to make amends for her thoughtlessness. 'I just thought it looked lovely as it is.'

'You'd rather I didn't come back?' he asked, the frown deepening.

Lucy sighed and shook her head. When he seemed about to speak again, she laid her hand on his arm, prepared to apologise.

'James, I'm so sorry. I always seem to say the wrong thing. Of course I want you to come back. It's just that I don't want you to feel you have no choice. You must come and work here only if you want to.'

He had made no attempt to remove her hand, and now she lifted it and placed it by her side.

'It's my choice,' he said, his eyes on Grace who was wandering towards them. 'I'll be back at the end of August, if you don't mind.'

Lucy was spared a reply by Grace's approach, and it had come not a moment too soon. She was utterly exhausted with the continual swinging from high to low, feeling more like a silly schoolgirl than a woman in her late forties. Now, as she welcomed Grace into the conversation, Lucy was having the greatest difficulty in dealing with the latest 'high', finding it impossible to conceal her delight: she was buoyed up once more at the prospect of James's being a regular visitor again, when, only moments ago, she had feared that her foolish, tongue-tied state would result in his never coming back.

*

As they gathered in the vestibule, waiting until the worst of the rain had passed, Harry made a point of moving closer to Grace, trying to find a way of letting her know what he had discussed with James. Just as he despaired of ever being close enough to speak to her, she moved next to him and took his arm.

'Can I phone you tomorrow?' she whispered in his ear.

He nodded, aware of Beth's eyes on him. So far that evening he had escaped the accusation of monopolising her mother and he was not about to spoil things now.

'Thank you,' she said quietly. 'Ten o'clock.'

'Yes, it was a lovely evening,' he said more loudly, in case Beth were eavesdropping. 'Do you want us to drop Lily off at her back door?'

'No, thanks, James has run down to get the car. We'll drop her off.'

She squeezed his arm as they went towards the top of the stone staircase and as she removed her hand from his sleeve, her fingers lightly touched his. He felt it again, that delicious sensation he knew he should resist.

*

Beth threw herself into a chair by the hearth and emitted a long sigh. She had had a reasonable night, but nothing to write home about, not the excitement of the Left Bank or the thrill of a restaurant in Montmartre. She eyed Harry as he sat down opposite her, a glass in his hand.

'I've changed my mind,' she said with a grimace. 'Can I have one as well?'

'I brought one,' he smiled, standing up and lifting her glass from the mantle shelf. 'Here, I thought you might have second thoughts.'

Beth sat upright, frowning at him. This habit he had, of predicting exactly what and how, where and when, could sometimes irritate her.

'I knew you'd bring one through,' she said smugly, although it was a fib. 'So, that's why I said I'd changed my mind.'

'Liar,' Harry laughed, but there was something so suave and reckless about him at this precise moment that she forgave him. She had had her eyes opened, comparing him directly with Charlie Webster, for as expensive as Charlie's suit had been, as immaculately as he had been turned out, he did not possess the panache Harry did. She sat sipping the sparkling wine and weighed things up.

'You hardly spoke to my mother all evening,' she told him. 'In fact, I only saw you say one thing to her and that was at the end.'

Harry smiled and shook his head. It seemed that there was no pleasing her but he knew she preferred it this way, castigating him for *not* paying attention to Grace.

'I had a really good conversation with your father.'

'I noticed. What did you talk about?'

'You want the truth?'

She sat upright again, insulted by the question. 'You know I do.'

'Well, he was comparing the wealth and extravagance of the Webster's life with the poverty of his own village when he was a child.'

Beth stared at him, for it was so ridiculous it had to be true. Also, it helped explain both her father's mood later, and Harry's too.

'He said that?'

Harry nodded. 'Yes. I got the impression it bothered him.'

'I've never known him to say such a thing.'

'Perhaps it was the first time he'd been in such a grand house.'

'Well, there is that,' she admitted, settling down again. 'And I suspect he's right about the primitive conditions in some villages before the War.' She frowned. 'I bet it was gruesome. He told me that the toilet was outside.'

'Just as well you've never had to sit in a loo at the top of the garden.'

Beth grinned. 'I'd probably have loved it.'

Harry laughed and wondered if he would ever truly understand this girl. As if she had read his mind, she puckered her lips and blew him a kiss.

'You see, Gillespie, I'm not always predictable.'

'Your father asked me what I most loved about you.'

He had to stifle a laugh at Beth's shocked expression. 'What?'

'And I said it was when you flew into a temper and threw things around the room.'

'You horror!' she exclaimed, hurling the cushion at him. 'How could you, when my Dad thinks I'm an angel?'

'Do you want to know what he said to that?'

'No, I don't.'

'He said it was what he loved most about you too and that he was glad I could deal with you.'

'Are you sure you weren't hallucinating? He's never said that many words to anyone in his whole life.'

'He also said,' Harry went on, enjoying her confusion. '...that he never thought there was a man alive who could tame you.'

'Cheek!' Beth said, feigning indignation. 'Taming me? That'll be the day.'

'Or night.'

She gave him a mischievous smile and slid down the chair until her feet were touching his.

'This could be your night to try it then.'

'Try what?'

'Taming me.'

'Sounds good to me. Time for bed, Kate.'

'Hey, are you insinuating I'm a bloody shrew?'

'Absolutely.'

'Well, you're spot on. Let me finish this drink first.'

He nodded and stood up. 'I'll give you five minutes and then I'll come and drag you through by the hair.'

*

Grace sat by the hearth drinking the cup of tea James had made her. She heard him moving around the kitchen, washing his own cup, drying it, replacing it on the shelf, and then she heard him fill the kettle for morning. She had no idea why he should be fussing over her like this, nor why he had asked her to forgive him, for she could think of nothing that he had done or said recently to merit such a request.

'That's everything ready for the morning,' he told her as he came back into the living room and sat opposite her. 'You looked lovely this evening,' he added, which only compounded her confusion. She could not recall the last time he had said anything similar, although she knew that he meant it.

'Thank you. I think it was Alice's hairdressing skills that made the difference.'

'I never even noticed what your hair was like.'

'Now I know you're joking.'

'Has she gone up to bed?'

'Yes. Only another few days and she'll be gone.'

'But she might come back to Scotland and live, didn't she say?'

Grace nodded. 'Oh, I hope so, James. I've had so much fun with her these past weeks. It's been wonderful having her here.'

'I think she will come back,' he said firmly. 'She told me as much.'

'Did she?'

'Yes, she's not keen to live there now, now that she and Martin are divorced.'

Grace stared at him. 'How do you know that?'

James laughed and kicked her slipper with his foot, the way she had done once upon a time with her mother, sitting with hot drinks after walking home from the cinema.

'Because she told me, of course. I never liked him much anyway. She's better off single.'

Her mind on the hapless Brad, Grace averted her eyes to her cup.' When did she tell you?'

'This morning, after breakfast, when you were sewing your dress upstairs.'

'Thank Heaven you know now,' Grace said with a mixture of relief and trepidation. 'I was trying not to say anything, worried in case you'd find out.'

James frowned. 'You're always worrying about everyone else when you should be worrying about yourself.'

'I do worry about myself.'

'If you say so.'

'You seemed to be having quite a chat with Harry this evening,' Grace said casually.

'Yes, we did have an interesting conversation,' James agreed, but when she glanced at him she saw that he would give nothing away. She would have to wait until tomorrow, when she could speak to the boy herself.

'I do love you, Grace.'

'I know you do,' she said with surprise.

'But sometimes, I get things wrong.'

'You're not the only one,' Grace smiled, hoping to encourage him to tell her more; perhaps let slip what he had discussed with Harry.

'Anyway,' James sighed, standing up. 'I think I'll go to bed now. Are you coming up?'

'Yes, as soon as I've washed this cup.'

He paused at the door and she waited, expecting him to speak again; but he only smiled before leaving the room and closing the door quietly behind him.

Chapter Twenty-Four

At ten o'clock precisely, the telephone rang at Harry's elbow and he persuaded Grace to drive into Perth and have lunch with him, despite her reservations that she might be seen.

'By Thomas Blake you mean?' he had asked.

'No,' she replied, surprising him. 'I was thinking of Beth.'

'She's out at Bridge of Allan with Charlie Webster, should be there until late afternoon.'

'I remember she mentioned it. A house clearance, isn't it?'

'I could pick you up and take you to Dundee if you'd rather?'

'Can you get away?'

'Yes, I'll stay on later, finish any work then.'

'No, I don't want you stuck in the office when Beth's expecting you home. No, I'll drive into Perth, meet you at the 'Isle of Skye' Hotel.'

'Good choice. It's far enough from the centre.'

'I'll see you in half an hour,' she said and hung up.

Harry had arrived at the office before eight thirty in order to work through a pile of papers before lunch. Despite Sandra's loyalty and her influence over the other two solicitors, he was not lulled into complacency: Charlie Webster had been unable to keep the lust from his eyes when he had looked at Beth the night before, and the man's friendship with Frank Gilmour, though innocuous on the surface, could spell trouble for Harry should he let his work slide.

When he refused his regular cup of coffee, Sandra shrugged and made no comment, as if she anticipated his taking a longer lunch break.

At half past twelve he locked his desk and handed her the key.

'For your eyes only, Miss Moneypenny,' he told her seriously, delighting her instantly.

'Certainly, Commander Bond, Your secret is safe with me.' She gave him a knowing look. 'That is, if you have one?'

Harry laughed and wagged a finger at her, moving towards the main door, anxious to be out of the building before Barclay could ask him to pop in for a meeting. He turned to Sandra as he opened the door.

'Not a secret that will be easily wrenched from me anyway,' he replied lightly. 'I'll be back before two if anyone wants me.'

'Can't think of a female who wouldn't.'

Harry was stopped in his tracks. He turned back to look at her but she grinned and waved him away.

'See you later, James,' she laughed, already turning her attention to the typewriter. 'Go and save the world from SPECTRE!'

*

Grace was there by the time he reached the hotel, although he was ten minutes early himself. He though she looked tired, and it crossed his mind that perhaps James had broken his promise not to mention what he and Harry had discussed regarding the Melville's marriage.

'Of course I'll never mention it to Grace,' he had said firmly at the end of their conversation. 'But I'm grateful for what you've told me.'

Now, as she caught sight of him, his fears seemed to be confirmed, for she was unsmiling, frowning slightly. Harry prepared himself for the worst, although, given a choice, he would not change his decision to tell James a little white lie.

'Grace, you look worried,' he said at once, giving her no time to rehearse.

'Do I?' she asked, perplexed. 'I suppose I am, but how dreadful of me to let it show.'

He took her elbow and guided her towards the foyer of the hotel.

'Do we have to go in here?' she asked him.

'No, of course not. Where would you rather go?'

'To the flat, if you don't mind.'

It was the last place he would have thought of, since it was exactly where Beth would go on her return from Bridge of Allan.

'Beth might ....' he began, and she smiled at last.

'I was being ridiculous about Beth,' she said, shaking her head. 'Imagine a mother being scared of her own daughter.'

'In that case, we'll go to the flat, and I'll make you the best sandwich you've ever tasted. Leave your car here, we'll walk.'

She did not resist his hand on her arm as they crossed the street, but her uncharacteristic silence unnerved him, to the point where he was struggling to think of anything sensible to say.

'You're very quiet,' he told her when it became obvious that she might say nothing at all until they reached the flat.

'I'm sorry. It's just about Alice leaving, that's all.'

It was feasible, but he suspected there was more than one reason, and now, as he held her arm to cross the bridge, she apologised again.

'I'm sorry, Harry,' she said haltingly and he felt her arm stiffen beneath his hand. 'I've been thinking a lot lately about, well, everything really.'

'Thomas Blake?'

'Yes.' She seemed about to continue, but then sighed and paused at the entrance to the block of flats.

'Has Beth said anything?'

'Not to me,' Grace replied. 'Has she said anything to you?'

Harry was in his least favourable position, yet he had led himself to it by his mentioning the man in the first place. He could lie, of course, but then Beth might find out.

'She has, hasn't she?' he heard Grace ask anxiously. She looked up at him. 'You can tell me.'

'She did say she'd bumped into him accidentally in the town one evening, but I'm sure it was an accident. She was in a foul mood afterwards, so I know she hadn't made plans to see him.'

'What did he want?'

'Nothing much, she said, just making conversation.'

'I've decided to meet him again.'

She had taken him completely by surprise and it was Harry's turn to stop walking. As he scrutinised her face, tried to ascertain how and what she was feeling, she smiled at him, the old sparkle back in her eyes.

'It's nice to think I can still shock people,' she said brightly, leading the way up the stone staircase. 'Are you really as shocked as you look?'

'More so. What on earth forced you into such a decision?'

'Oh, I wasn't forced,' Grace said wearily. 'It was my own choice.' She turned back to look at him, her eyes suddenly doubtful. 'What do you think? Is it a wise decision?'

'It depends what you hope to achieve by it,' Harry said, wondering as to her motive. 'The letter from Helen...?'

'I haven't forgotten it and I intend to use it, but at the right time, when it will have the greatest effect.'

'Sounds like you're indulging in subterfuge again.'

'I suppose if you've done it once, it's a lot easier the second time.'

'I wouldn't know,' he said with a laugh. 'I've never indulged in it myself.'

'Liar,' Grace smiled.

'Here we are. Time for that sandwich.'

*

She sat watching him as he worked, her offer of help having been politely turned down. She could not help but ponder on how good looking the boy was and how lucky Beth was to have...

'Penny for your thoughts?'

Grace caught her breath. 'I was miles away.'

'Penny for them anyway?'

'I wasn't thinking about anything in particular.'

'Fibber,' Harry said kindly, wiping his hands on a kitchen towel. 'You were thinking how expert I've become at making sandwiches.'

'Of course. She has you well trained, my lad.'

'James was telling me you could wind him round your little finger,' he said unexpectedly, carrying the tray of food to the table and setting it before her.

'Did he? Goodness, I'd no idea.'

'You're making a habit of this.'

'Of what?'

'Fibbing,' Harry smiled, sitting down opposite her and pouring the tea. 'That's the third one you've told in as many minutes.'

Grace lowered her gaze to the table. She had come with the sole purpose of asking him about his conversation with James, what had made James so apologetic and attentive after last night's dinner, and here she was, having divulged her innermost intent about Thomas Blake, throwing caution to the wind, blurting it out, and yet being no nearer to the peace of mind she had anticipated after speaking to the boy.

'You seemed to be deep in conversation with James last night,' she said slowly, raising her eyes to his at the last moment, witnessing the trepidation therein.

'He was bothered by the opulence of the Websters' way of life.'

Grace smiled and shook her head. 'Now who's fibbing?' she asked archly.

'Honestly, he was,' Harry confirmed strongly. 'He honestly said that the cost of all the items in that house could have fed his village down South for a month.' Grace frowned, for it was just the kind of thing James would have said. 'So, you see,' he carried on confidently. 'I wasn't fibbing after all, honestly.'

'My mother always told me that if you said 'honestly' more than once in a sentence, you were only trying to convince yourself.'

Harry burst out laughing. 'Good God, that's too deep for me.'

Once he had stopped laughing, she persisted. 'What else did you discuss?'

'Nothing, why?'

'I don't believe you,' Grace said, but with no animosity.

'Well, I'm sorry to disappoint you but that was it.' Harry cut up the last of his sandwich, placed it in his mouth and washed it down with the dregs of his tea. 'What did he say when you got home?'

'Not much, just made a fuss of me.'

'And is that something to complain about?'

'Not normally, no.'

Grace lifted her cup to her lips and drank the tea – too sweet and strong for her liking, the exact opposite of Beth's – and wondered why she had ever believed he would tell her what he had discussed with James.

'So, you're determined to meet him again?'

'My father? Yes.'

'May I ask why?'

Grace suppressed a smile at the rigorous attention to grammar.

'You can ask, but I won't tell you.'

Harry shrugged. 'As long as you don't get hurt.'

His concern was moving, poignant even, but she had resolved to deal with Thomas Blake herself this time, not to involve her family, for fear that the man would take great delight in wreaking revenge for her original, callous treatment of him. She was under no illusion as to his character, a man who had shunned his own daughter in public, never pausing to reflect on the damage it might cause her.

'That locket you were wearing last night,' Harry said suddenly, taking her breath away.

'What about it?'

'Did James give it to you?'

'I think so,' she lied, pretending to reflect.

'It was lovely, just the kind of thing that Beth would like. Perhaps I'll ask James where he bought it.'

They regarded each other for some time, but it was Harry who backed down first. He shrugged, averted his eyes.

'Perhaps not.'

'Thank you for the lunch,' Grace said now, carefully replacing her cup on the saucer, the spoon neatly at the side. As she stood up to leave, Harry reached out and touched her hand, briefly, as a gesture of family loyalty; but she felt it again, that shiver of something she knew she should resist.

*

Harry sat at his desk, catching up with the work that he had postponed for a couple of hours, having little time to mull over his conversation with Grace. When he had drafted out several letters for Sandra to type, he took care of the telephone calls, the last one to Daphne, having relegated it to the end of the queue because he wanted to give her his full attention.

As he held the receiver in his hand, rehearsing how he would deliver the advice he thought she needed, the door flew open and Sandra rushed in.

'I do beg your pardon, Mr Harry,' she gasped, adhering to the formal mode of address in case the other partners were listening. 'May I see you for a moment about one of the client's letters?'

He waved her to sit down, but she stood just inside the closed door.

'I see you have Daphne on your list of calls this afternoon,' she whispered.

'Yes, have you seen her yet, to ask her about the gigolo?'

Sandra smiled broadly. 'I certainly did. I pounced on her at the Red Cross coffee morning and she didn't stand a chance. Oh, and I'll expect a pay rise, and an allowance for my spy costume.'

'I'll consider it,' Harry smiled. 'Did she tell you who he was?'

'Oh, yes,' Sandra said, eyes widening. 'He's rich, handsome and she's besotted with him. He used to work abroad apparently, South America.' She had not missed the flicker of shock on Harry's face and, intrigued, she stepped further into the room. 'You know him?' she asked incredulously.

'What's his name?' Harry asked, but he knew already.

*

Beth was in the bath by the time he arrived home. He called to her that he was home and then went to pour himself a drink, flopping down on the nearest chair, still wearing his jacket.

He had spoken briefly to Daphne, only to make an appointment for later in the week, after which he had sat for over an hour pondering the implications of her dalliance with Thomas Blake. Notwithstanding that Perth was a relatively small city, and despite the fact that he had already experienced the phenomenon of the most unlikely links between its inhabitants, Harry could not believe that the man was preying on the likes of Daphne, for preying he most certainly was, that much Harry knew: at this very moment, she was hesitating over a decision to marry the man and, thereby, hand him her considerable fortune.

The effect of such news, however, helped to obliterate the ignominy of his fruitless meeting with Thomas Blake, his ridiculous ultimatum concerning the man's bigamous past, for, quite frankly, even if the man were brought to justice, it was unlikely that a harsh sentence would be meted out. Besides, who would care? If Beth were to be believed, her grandmother's letters seemed to paint Blake in a golden light; furthermore, it would be difficult to prove one way or the other if Charlotte had granted or refused him a divorce. An insignificant incident in the '20's, particularly in rural Scotland – the middle of nowhere – was hardly the stuff of Fleet Street, and Harry wondered now why on earth he had thought it would be.

The telephone rang and he went into the hall, glass in hand to answer it. Even before she spoke, he knew it was Annie Kerr.

'Is Beth there?' she asked, in an unusually meek voice.

'No,' Harry lied. 'She's not back yet.'

'Are you sure?' she asked, this time tearfully.

'Yes, I'm sure,' he said quietly, lest Beth should hear. 'I'll get her to call you back.'

'Please, it's urgent,' she said before he ended the call abruptly.

Harry sighed and wandered to the hall cupboard, where he hung up his jacket and turned the central heating down. It never failed to amaze or irritate him that, in the height of summer, albeit a Scottish one, Beth could never bring herself to switch the heating off, even for a few days.

Half an hour later she emerged in a flimsy wrap from the bathroom, her face flushed, cheeks aglow, hair piled up on top of her head. He wondered if there would ever come a time when she lost her looks.

'Drink, Cleopatra?'

'Thanks, Mark Anthony, I think I will forsooth.'

'Ah, I'm not sure if there's any forsooth left. You might have to settle for white wine.'

Beth laughed and clambered onto his knee, the scents of the bath oil wreaking havoc with his senses. She put her arms around his neck and laid her head on his shoulder.

'I thought you wanted me to get you a forsooth?' he asked into her hair.

'You said there might be none.'

'I'll check. Maybe I missed one.'

'You were late home,' Beth remarked, but there was only concern in her voice. 'You work too hard sometimes.'

'How was the house clearance?'

'Great,' she enthused, lifting her head and looking at him. 'We have lots of really good items, including the most elegant dining room suite you've ever seen. Oh, and some lovely canteens of cutlery I might fancy myself.'

'Silver, I presume?'

'Is there any other?' She slid from his lap and wandered to the door. 'I'll go and get decent, then I'll have that forsooth you promised me.' As she reached the door she turned and frowned.

'Did the phone ring when I was in the bath?'

'Yes, it was Annie.'

'Why didn't you tell me?' Beth asked, agitated now. 'She's going through a really bad time.'

'Beth, darling,' Harry said patiently. 'When is she not going through a bad time? She'll come out of it as usual, with or without your being lumbered.'

'I am *not* lumbered,' Beth said angrily, turning to face him, her temper rising. 'Despite what you think, she and I have been friends for years and she needs me, so did she say she'd phone back, or what?'

'She was in a call box,' Harry lied. 'Said she'd call later, from her flat.'

'I might go round there,' Beth told him sullenly, although it was an hour's journey there and back.

'That's a good idea,' he said cleverly, for it was the surest way of keeping her at home.

'She said she'd phone back?'

'That's what she said, sweetheart.'

'I suppose I could wait, see how she is when she phones.'

'It's six already,' Harry said, glancing at the clock. 'Do you fancy having a Gillespie special for dinner tonight?'

'Thanks, but I've got something in the freezer that Mum gave me last month and we'll have to use it up soon.'

'I hope it's shepherd's pie,' he smiled, instantly regretting it. Beth's rivalry with Grace seemed to know no bounds.

'What's wrong with *my* shepherd's pie?'

'You never remember to put a shepherd in it.'

Reluctantly, she stifled a laugh and left the room to get dressed.

Harry breathed a sigh of relief, congratulating himself on having inherited such a sharp mind from his mother. Without it, he would be in serious trouble.

He took their drinks through to the sitting room and went to the window, to watch the activity on the Inch. In a few weeks' time it would be the Perth Show and the place would be choc-a-bloc with vehicles and people. This evening, however, there were only promenading couples and children playing. As he followed the antics of a golden Labrador and an unwieldy stick, Harry's thoughts drifted, unwillingly, to Annie Kerr. He should have told Beth the truth about the phone call, he supposed, but he was past caring: the sooner that trollop disappeared from their life, the better for everyone; especially him.

*

Grace sat upright in bed: the telephone had rung, in the middle of the night. James was already out of bed but she rushed after him, down the stairs, not taking time to throw on her dressing gown, heart pounding, her mind on her family, for it could only be bad news at this time of the night.

When she heard James speaking in hushed tones, she was convinced the news was serious. She crept closer, put her ear to the receiver. When she heard Tony Kerr's voice, she thought it was news about Sarah and her heart sank; but then, when Sarah came on the line and asked to speak to her, Grace knew it had to be Annie.

*

In her bedroom upstairs, Alice, who had been fast asleep until the telephone woke her, was trying to come to terms with the sound of Grace Blake sobbing her heart out. Alice climbed out of bed but waited for a few minutes before going down, to give her two friends time to absorb the full significance of whatever bad news had been delivered.

As she donned her dressing gown and slippers, she was praying as hard as she had prayed in her life; so hard that she imagined that God would have to pay some attention, although it was years since she had crossed the threshold of any church. Idly, she thought of the part of the Bible that told of their names written in God's book and despaired of hers still being listed amongst them.

When she entered the living room and saw Grace Blake in such a wretched state, Alice made up her mind to stay in Scotland until her friend was happy for her to leave.

Chapter Twenty-Five

Thomas Blake was poring over the deaths in the inside page of the *Perthshire Courier and Advertiser*, as he had done since he had arrived here, fearful at the beginning of being confronted with the death of one Charlotte Blake or Shepherd. Now, as he read the line pertaining to '*best friend of Beth,*' his heart skipped a beat. It might be his granddaughter. The girl, Anne Kerr had been the same age, the child of a local couple; therefore it was not beyond the bounds of reality.

Thomas contemplated the death notice for a few minutes, wondering if he should turn up at the funeral, stand at the back somewhere, just to see if his daughter were there. Of course, if the '*Beth*' referred to happened to be some other Beth, he would feel a bit of a fool, standing grieving for a total stranger. He smiled to himself at the idea, for was that not the norm nowadays, that people flocked to funerals out of a sense of social etiquette rather than because they had known and liked the person in the box?

He roused himself, threw the newspaper aside, still open at the page, and started to make his breakfast. All at once, he remembered that he would not be here the day of the funeral; he would be in Cornwall, with Daphne.

Of all the times for the girl to die! Still, there was nothing he could do about persuading people to die on cue, otherwise half of his acquaintances would have perished years ago.

He hummed a little tune as he waited for the toaster to eject its slices, and mulled over the idea of taking Daphne to Cornwall the week after next. His plan to become a rich man was on a satisfactory course; but could he resist the opportunity to attend the funeral and catch a glimpse of Grace?

*

Grace and Alice spent three days in Dundee comforting Sarah Kerr. As they met from time to time in the privacy of their room, they marvelled at the woman's strength, a woman whose periods of respite from cancer were less numerous than her bouts of treatment.

The day before the funeral, as they sat in the Café Val d'Or, taking a rare half hour to themselves. Alice studied Grace's face, trying to see any sign that it was proving too much for her; for at the first inkling, she intended to whisk her friend back home, take care of her until she was well.

'Are you all right?' she asked now, and Grace nodded.

'Yes, I'm fine, and you, Alice, on what's supposed to be your holiday, are you fine?'

'There's nowhere on earth I'd rather be at this precise moment,' Alice said, with such fervour that she surprised herself.

'Alice, you can't mean that,' Grace smiled reproachfully. 'It's nice to hear, but it just can't be true.'

'Well, it is,' Alice confirmed, leaning forward across the table and taking her friend's hand. 'And d'you know why?'

Grace sighed. 'I'm afraid to ask,'

'Because you'd do exactly the same for me.' Grace lowered her eyes and said nothing and Alice continued in a whisper. 'It's about bloody time that someone did something for you for a change.'

'Alice, for Heaven's sake,' Grace frowned, glancing around. 'You make me out to be a blooming Saint!'

'I'm only hoping you'll put in a good word for me when we're standing at the Pearly

Gates. Maybe I'll sneak in behind you and He'll never notice.'

'I'm not so sure they'll be pearly,' Grace said grimly. 'Or even gates.'

'Come on, now, less of this…'

'I know,' Grace interrupted with a wry smile. 'No more doom and gloom. But how can we not be doomy and gloomy when this has happened?'

Alice shrugged, her eyes wandering around the restaurant, seeing normal people, doing normal things, but knowing that they too, at some time in their lives, would have suffered similar drama.

'I only know we have to have faith, Grace. Surely some of Sandy Sinclair's religious fanaticism rubbed off on you?'

She was joking of course, but there was a thread of truth running through it, and Grace appeared surprised to hear it mentioned.

'I…He wasn't really a fanatic,' she frowned. 'Was he?'

'Yes, dear, he was. He absolutely hated to see anyone hanging a washing out on the Sabbath, or even digging in the garden as he went up to church. No, if your grandfather had had his way, it would have been a life of sackcloth and sore knees for the entire Christian flock.'

Grace was too tired to argue, but she recalled how kind her grandfather had been to most people, how forgiving to his daughter Charlotte, accepting her pregnancy with little recrimination.

'Do you think we should get back to Sarah now?' she asked, banishing selfish thoughts for the moment.

'You know, it's Beth I'm more worried about,' Alice said, making no move to stand up and leave the restaurant. 'I hope Harry is patient.'

Grace's spirits sank even lower at the thought of her daughter blaming Harry for Annie's suicide. It was so irrational, so utterly unreasonable that Grace knew it was not something that could be talked away, or left to heal by the passage of time.

'At least she's still at the flat,' she heard Alice say quietly now. 'I thought…'

'Well, she's not coming to me,' Grace said harshly, with so much venom that her friend was taken aback.

'But where would she go?'

'Not to me anyway,' Grace reiterated more calmly. 'I won't be used as piggy in the middle, Alice. She made her bed, she can lie on it.'

In the light of day, in a public place, surrounded by the hubbub of people's chatter, it sounded less damning to Grace's ears as it had done the previous night, on the telephone to James.

'You're tired and worried about Sarah,' he had told her. 'I'll see to Beth until you get home.'

'I don't want her living with us,' Grace had said forcefully, to be greeted by an ominous silence. 'If I come home and find she's been there, I'll be most upset, James.'

'She won't be here, I promise,' he said, and it only served to let her know that he *had* allowed Beth to stay while Grace was away.

'I'll see you at the funeral,' was all she had said in closing before putting the receiver down.

Neither of them had mentioned that Tony's priest had refused to conduct a service for a suicide victim and that the arrangements had been made at Sarah's church, which seemed to have no similar qualms.

'I'm staying in Scotland for the foreseeable future,' Alice said now, as she had done at least half a dozen times that day, in front of so many people that it seemed she was gathering witnesses to her decision.

'But I'm worried about your sons,' Grace responded, as she had done an equal

361

number of times. 'I know they're old enough to take care of themselves, but...'

'All I want them to do is wire some more money to me,' Alice said, highlighting the practicalities of the situation. 'I've plenty.' She grinned sheepishly. 'I can recommend divorce if your coffers ever run dry.'

It was the first laughter between them and neither felt guilty.

'Come on then,' Grace said, searching for her handbag. 'My treat and don't argue!'

*

James looked across at his daughter, surrounded by papers and her French dictionaries, eyes on her work, mouth resolute. He felt so guilty at having deceived Grace, especially since he knew she was right: it was hardly the boy's fault, whatever the mix-up in communication; and it was unjust that Beth should burden her husband with what were, in truth, her own failings.

She had had the opportunity to go round to Annie's flat, to check for herself if the girl was in any trouble, and she had opted not to do so. As far as James was concerned, that was the crux of the matter and she should be facing up to it, rather than off-loading her guilty conscience onto her husband.

He averted his eyes a split second before she glanced in his direction and resumed his place in his book.

'Am I getting in the way?' she asked suddenly.

'No,' James said. 'You're over there, I'm over here. Neither of us has moved for the past hour.' He smiled and she joined in. 'How can you be in the way?'

'When the... when it's all over... when Mum comes home...I'll have to leave.'

It would not have occurred to James to lie to her, not in the present climate of grief and doubt; but he had another option for her.

'You haven't had a summer holiday yet, have you?'

Beth looked at him closely, frowning slightly. 'I suppose not.'

'You could always go away for a couple of weeks, until your mother is back to normal.'

'She won't change her mind on this,' Beth said firmly. 'Don't you know that?'

'Of course she will,' James countered. 'She's upset just now, worried about Sarah and Tony. Once it's all over, she'll settle down and see reason.'

Inwardly, he cursed himself: his resolution not to lie to her or give her false hopes, had lasted only as long as the sentences before it.

'I doubt it.' Beth smiled, going back to her work. 'But you know what they say? 'Hope springs eternal.'

In the human breast James added to himself, for it was one of the few sayings his mother had quoted almost every day; a saying that seemed suitable for any occasion. He would bear it in mind for the foreseeable future.

*

Harry was undecided as to whether he should attend the funeral or not. If he did go, Beth might cause a scene and only Grace would suffer. If, on the other hand, he chose not to go, then she would have an excuse to hurl further recriminations at him for the rest of their married life; presuming that there was to be a 'rest' at all and, again, only Grace would suffer.

He looked up the Kerr's number and dialled. It rang so long that he thought they must all be out, although, the day before the funeral, he expected one of them to stay in the house. Just as he was about to hang up, someone picked up, and it was Grace.

'How are you?' he asked, his only concern being her welfare; unconcerned if people thought him impolite by not asking for Sarah or Tony.

'We're doing our best,' she replied, scolding him marginally with the 'we'. 'Are you coping?'

'Yes, I'm coping. Could do with a resident cook maybe, but, apart from that, I'm managing.'

'When I get back again, I've some things you could stick in the freezer, if you want?'

'I most definitely want,' he said, keeping his voice serious in case she imagined he was being flippant.

'In that case, I'll come into Perth one day next week, load your fridge and freezer up for a month.'

He wanted to ask if she thought Beth would stay away so long but, if he did ask, it would only hurt Grace and she had endured more than her share lately.

'You're an angel,' he told her and he heard the smile in her voice when she spoke again.

'Alice will be pleased to hear it.'

'Sorry?'

'Nothing, just something she said this morning about the pearly gates.'

'Are you having time to rest?'

'Yes, and it's so wonderful having Alice here. I could never have faced it without her.'

Harry was seized by the familiar sense of envy that someone else was providing her with comfort and support. He acknowledged that there would never be a day when he would be immune to such a feeling.

'I was wondering if I should come to the funeral.'

'Harry!' she exclaimed, almost shouting in his ear. 'Of course you must come. What gave you such a stupid notion, not to come?'

'I don't want Beth to have any reason...'

'Stop right there,' she said tersely. 'She has nothing to do with it. It's your decision and I'd like you to be there.'

'Doesn't that sound more like your decision?' Harry teased her gently.

'But you want to come, don't you?'

'Yes, but I had to check with you first.'

'You're so considerate,' Grace said humbly and he could imagine her face as she spoke: the green eyes, dark with sorrow, the mouth slightly curved.

'I'll be on my own, of course,' Harry reminded her. 'I won't sit beside the family, in case.'

'In case what?' she asked, the acrimony returning to her tone.

'Grace, please, I'll see you there probably, but I'll be at the back somewhere and I don't want any more argument about this.'

'I'll look out for you,' was the last thing she said before hanging up.

He went into the kitchen and turned on the ceiling light. The days had been dull and dreary – dreich, he had heard Lily Morris often say – and although it was only four o'clock, it was almost dark in the flat, except for the front windows overlooking the Inch. The lure of the whisky bottle had long since dwindled, for he had spent three nights lying in a stupor and he was not a fan, especially when the hangover kicked in at three in the morning.

The telephone rang and he knew it would be Sandra, for she had learnt of the family's situation and was calling him every night, like a maiden aunt, to see if he were fine.

'Harry, are you still fine?'

'Yes, Sandra, considering you only saw me half an hour ago.'

'I've got an idea, if you're not busy, that is?'

'I'm not busy, but, knowing you, I suspect it's a daft idea.'

She giggled. 'I love it when you say 'daft'. No, it's a meal at my house, tonight, eight o'clock. Just a few friends, nothing spectacular, only a bite to eat and some company.' She stopped speaking and he heard the anxiety in her silence. What harm would it do when her heart seemed set on it?

'Sounds good,' he said and she was over the moon.

*

Beth took over the role of chef, much to the chagrin of her brother, whose nose was out of joint because of her presence. She scorned him when he suggested that she was a pain in the arse, did her best to get rid of him with a well-worn phrase and a scathing glance.

'What are you doing back here anyway?' he had asked her as soon as he realised she was staying. 'Haven't you got a home to go to?'

'None of your business.'

'Sorry to disappoint you, sis,' he began, using a term that drove her up the wall. 'But it is my business, seeing as how I live here.'

She had been about to point out to him that, at the age of nineteen, he should be married and living in his own house, but that seemed pretty childish under the circumstances.

'I'm helping Dad while Mum's away,' she opted to say.

'I can help him, you're only using it as an excuse.'

'For what, may I ask?'

Her acid tone and aggressive stance had deterred his next remark, but she was horrified to think that he knew anything about her and Harry and the row over Annie's death. Rather than ask him outright, however, she had waited patiently for him to speak, eventually having the satisfaction of seeing him slink off; to the luxury of the downstairs bedroom, while she was relegated to the bed settee in the parlour.

'Tea's ready,' she told her father and he glanced at the clock.

'It's only half past four,' he said, aggrieved.

'What difference does that make?'

'We always have it at five.'

Beth chose to count to twenty before responding but, by that time, her father had risen from his chair, aware, perhaps, of the delicacy of the situation. He sighed and placed his book on the small table at his elbow.

'You'd better tell Frank,' he said, his gaze moving to the door. 'He'll not be ready yet. He's only just got home.'

'A part-timer,' Beth said dismissively, before remembering the advent of 'flexi-time', which entailed her brother working the hours that suited him as long as it amounted to forty a week.

They sat at the table in the living room, beneath the harsh ceiling lights that James had installed, lights to read by, to thread needles by, but certainly not to promote an atmosphere, Beth thought, unless it was of a German prison camp.

'Will Harry be picking you up tomorrow?' Frank asked innocently, but he was her brother, she reminded herself, and was most probably out to cause trouble.

'No, Dad and I are going on our own,' Beth said, effectively excluding her brother from the car. 'Are you picking Emily up?'

'Emily?' he echoed with surprise, fork halfway to his mouth. 'Why would she be going?'

'She's not?'

'No, she's not.'

'But she's family,' Beth said with disbelief. 'She should go.'

'Beth, dear,' her father said quietly and she desisted.

'She said you had a good time in Perth a few weeks ago,' Frank told her, but the doubt in his tone belied his words.

'Are you surprised?'

'I didn't say that. She seemed to have a good time, that's what I said.'

'She's very sweet,' Beth smiled, avoiding her father's eye. 'We did have a good time.'

'She said you paid for it.'

'So what?'

'She wanted to pay her share.'

Beth sighed, glanced at her father, but dared not air her thoughts: if it were meaningless, empty, inconsequential drivel that you were looking for, look no further than a chat with your brother.

*

The most dismal time of the day was after tea, when Sarah realised all over again that her daughter would never be coming home. Grace and Alice did their best to ease the situation but there was only so much they could do, for the woman was so distraught that words seemed to get in the way rather than help.

'I'm going to stay with Grace for a little while,' Alice said now, as the three of them sat together in the best room, Tony already in his downstairs bedroom, too fragile to endure company.

'That's good,' Sarah smiled automatically, but she was staring into the fireplace, oblivious to their presence.

Grace and Alice exchanged glances, imperceptible shrugs of despair.

'I've stocked the fridge and freezer for you,' Grace said, touching Sarah's hand, feeling how cold it was. 'There's enough food for you...' She broke off, about to say 'for you and Tony'.

'That's good,' Sarah said again, and they knew she was not listening.

'I think you should go to bed,' Alice suggested, more loudly, and Sarah glanced up.

'Bed? You think I should?'

Alice nodded, backed up by Grace, who stopped herself in time from pointing out that they had a long day ahead of them.

'Yes,' she said. 'Alice is right, you should go up now.'

Sarah rose from her chair and offered no resistance when Grace held her arm. Together they moved across the room, whilst Alice hovered in their wake, prepared to offer another helping hand if necessary.

Once in her bedroom, Sarah thanked them and closed the door. Before Grace had even reached the halfway stair tread, she heard her friend crying.

Even with a mother's sobs ringing in her ears, however, Grace Melville was not sufficiently moved to bring her daughter in from the cold.

*

Harry was both astonished and pleased at Sandra's abode; astonished because of its display of affluence – on the salary of a humble typist too – and pleased because she had become such a good friend and ally that he had often imagined her in a dowdy setting when she should be more comfortable.

'Oh, I'm so glad you could come along,' she whispered, squeezing his arm and refusing to let go. 'The others are here already, but you're not late,' she rushed to assure him, still clutching his arm. 'They're always early when free food's up for grabs!'

Harry took in the small circle by the French windows, older couples mostly, with the exception of a dark-haired girl, a niece perhaps, standing with her back to him, gazing into the drizzle and mist that was shrouding the garden.

'Everyone, this is Harry, a very dear friend. Harry, this is the motley crew I dread to introduce to you as my friends.'

Sandra was in her element and Harry could understand now why she had been so eager to play Mata Hari: the woman was a natural on stage. He thought fleetingly of Grace and wondered if the two of them would try to out-act each other.

Sandra did the rounds of introductions, leaving the dark-haired girl until last.

'Come on, Foxy, don't be anti-social, this is Harry and it's his first time here.'

The girl she had addressed as 'Foxy' turned and looked at Harry, her head on one side, eyes polite, hand out-stretched.

'I was engrossed in the garden, sorry. I'm Kate.'

'No you're not, you naughty child,' Sandra scolded. 'It's Foxy to the family and it's Foxy to her friends.' She gave Harry a knowing look. 'Don't take any nonsense from her. She's a social delight if she's put in her place.'

With that, she left them, the girl, Foxy, following Sandra's departure with her eyes before focussing once more on Harry.

'She's my mother's aunt,' she explained. 'So that makes her my great aunt, I expect. She's an absolute scream, did you know?'

'I do. In fact, if I had to name the person I've been most happy to meet since I came to live here, it would have to be Sandra.'

'You work with her?'

'She's my – our – secretary.'

Foxy smiled and leaned against the glass doors, her eyes travelling around the room but returning, as Harry knew they would, to rest upon his face.

'You're English,' she stated bluntly. 'What made you come to live here?'

'My wife,' Harry said, his ego taking a knock when he found no disappointment in the girl's eyes.

'Is she here this evening?'

'No, she's not speaking to me at the moment.'

She smiled, a slow smile that spread from the corners of her mouth to her eyes within the space of a few seconds. Harry found it almost impossible to tear his gaze from her mouth; but he had had no sex for over a week and it was an inevitable consequence.

'She must be an idiot,' Foxy said contemptuously. 'Fancy a drink? Sandra's a bit of a flop on the hostess front.'

'Show me where they are and I'll get you one,' Harry told her, suspecting that Sandra had been up to dirty tricks inviting him to this dinner, pairing him off with this girl. He was hungry, though, and the flat was empty and lonely without Beth and so it seemed churlish not to take advantage of Sandra's hospitality.

'I hope she's got something cheap and nasty,' Foxy said under her breath as they moved towards the drinks table.

'Cheap and nasty?' Harry repeated, surveying the table and seeing nothing less expensive than Martini. 'There's no shandy, if that's your poison.'

Foxy laughed and turned to look at him closely.

366

'Shandy? Now that's what I call really cheap and nasty. No, I was thinking more of plonk. Ah, good,' she added, her hand seizing a bottle of Blue Nun. 'This will do nicely.'

Harry could not reconcile the elegant outfit, the sophisticated looks and dripping jewellery with a bottle of Blue Nun, but he did his best to conceal his surprise, picked up a glass of whisky and followed the girl back to the French windows.

'They're a load of fuddy-duddies, aren't they?' she whispered in his ear. 'I'm glad she invited you, otherwise I'd be like a spare prick at a wedding.'

As worldly as he liked to think himself, Harry was not fond of coarse remarks from women. He had no such worries with Beth, who, at best, was an utter delight in company and, at worse, was stubborn and argumentative; but never coarse. When they were in the bedroom, however, he waived the rules.

'So, you're a solicitor,' Foxy murmured, turning her glass in her hand, trailing her fingers up and down the beads of condensation. 'You must hear people's darkest secrets.'

'Nothing so interesting,' Harry smiled, having already mentally dispensed with the girl after her unfortunate decision to be uncouth. 'Just Last Wills and Testaments, marriage settlements, house purchases, boring things like that.'

'My other half's a solicitor,' she said unexpectedly.

'Really? In Perth?'

'No, in Edinburgh,' she smiled. 'The senior partner.'

'Good for him,' Harry nodded, bored out of his skull and looking for a way out.

'You don't like me, do you?' she asked him, her smile fading.

'I hardly know you,' he said tactfully, in deference to Sandra.

She bit her lower lip, an uncharacteristic action he thought for someone who had appeared so arrogant and self-assured.

'I'm sorry, I was trying to put you off me.'

He stared at her, thinking that she had done a pretty good job.

'Sorry?'

She sighed, long and loud. 'I always do that, can't seem to help myself. I say the most disgusting things, trying to put men off.'

She was regarding him with an apologetic air and Harry found himself sympathising with her, for it had been something of which he had been guilty at Aberdeen, spouting forth on a subject they all detested, so that he might be left in peace.

'I've often done the same,' he admitted ruefully and her eyes widened.

'You're joking?'

'Nope.'

'So you understand then?'

'Sadly, yes.'

They both laughed and he was surprised to see the difference it made to her features. They spoke at the same time.

'What do you...?'

'Where do you...?'

'Sorry,' Foxy said. 'You first.'

'I was just going to ask where you worked.'

'In the library.'

'Ah.'

'Bet you've never been there,' Foxy smiled, contemplating her glass.

'How did you guess?'

'It's a fallacy, you know, that libraries are only for the decrepit. You should come along, sample what's on offer.'

There had been no innuendo intended he knew, but now, in the wake of her suggestion, she blushed and he was intrigued: the girl was two for the price of one.

'I might do that,' he said, meeting her gaze. 'But you'll have to give me a map.'

'What, you don't even know where it is?' she asked in disbelief. 'Jings, now I've heard everything.'

'I take my work home. Besides, my wife gets annoyed if I read while she's in the room.' He paused for a moment. 'And what does '*jings*' mean?'

Foxy grinned. 'A Scottish version of 'oh, golly, gosh.' She peered at him more closely. 'I hate it too, you know, when my better half brings work home, or even picks up a newspaper when I'm around.'

'Ah, I'm beginning to think conspiracy here.'

Sandra's voice interrupted them. 'Dinner is served, friends and anyone else who's crawled in.'

Harry held out his arm. 'May I take you into dinner?' he joked.

'You most certainly may,' Foxy said, placing her arm on his.

As he accompanied her from the room, Harry was grateful that he given her a second chance.

*

In their cramped bedroom, Alice and Grace were whispering long into the night. Despite the sad circumstances – their reason for being at the Kerrs' house – they were rediscovering the depths of a friendship that had once sustained them in the darkest years of the War, and they were frequently struggling to suppress laughter at their recollections.

Grace was buoyed up by her friend's decision to move back to Scotland – for Alice's mind was now firmly made up – and she had the greatest difficulty in not admitting to the advantages of the situation, for, had poor Annie Kerr not taken an overdose, Alice would be on a plane heading for the States; perhaps never to return.

'You know you can stay with us as long as you like,' Grace whispered now, lying on her side in the single bed alongside Alice's and propping her head on her hand. 'You don't have to rush and get your own place, remember?'

'I heard you the first time, Mrs Parrot,' Alice whispered back. 'How many times have you told me now? A thousand maybe?'

'This has been the happiest time in ages.'

'I suspected you were fed up whenever I saw your skinny, pallid face at the airport.'

'Cheek! It was the middle of the night in Paris, don't forget. I could say the same about you.'

'Anyway, it's been the happiest time for me as well,' Alice grinned.

'Oh, come on, what about Brad?'

Alice pulled a face. 'The trouble with men is that you've to keep making such an effort. With girlfriends there's no such problem.' She slid down the bed and turned on her side to look at Grace. 'Take sex, for example.'

Grace feigned shock. 'Alice Cameron! How can you think of such a thing at this time?'

'You want the truth, honey?' Alice asked now, her eyes serious.

'Probably not.'

'In my opinion it's over-rated. When I think of the trouble I had to go to keep him interested, well, I wonder if it was worth it.' She laughed quietly. 'I mean, he buggered off in the end anyway, didn't he? All that dolling myself in the sheerest nighties... rinsing my hair in beer to make it shine... not to mention having to pretend that it was great sex all of the time.'

Grace was accustomed to such discussions with Beth, but to hear it from one of her own generation was quite different, and at first she had thought Alice too dispassionate. Yet, now, as she pondered her own lovemaking with James, she was beginning to wonder how often she felt the same.

'I suppose it's partly true,' she confessed with a twinge of guilt. 'Sometimes, to be honest, I can't be bothered.'

'Exactly!' said Alice too loudly, causing them both to pause and hold their breaths. 'It was always when Martin or Brad wanted to do it,' she added with a sigh. 'How about Beth?' she suddenly asked, taking Grace aback.

'Beth? How do you mean?'

'The younger generation. Any idea how often they do it?'

Grace felt the old, unwelcome images crowding in. 'Goodness, I've no idea. I've never asked her.'

'Pity,' Alice said disappointedly. 'I often wonder when I look at the two of them together.' She waited for Grace to speak but, when it became obvious there was no reply in the offing, she added: 'I know it's naughty, but how d'you think Harry will manage without sex?'

'Alice, really,' Grace forced herself to say. 'It's high time you got to sleep, otherwise Heaven knows what you'll be discussing next!'

'I suppose you're right,' Alice said gleefully, turning over and pulling the blanket over her. 'Well, it's going to be a horrid day tomorrow, my friend, so I hope we get some sleep. Goodnight, Grace.'

'Goodnight,' Grace answered dutifully.

A few minutes later, as she lay listening to her friend's peaceful breathing, Grace was wary of falling asleep, for she knew that her night would be plagued by images and snatches of dreams that she would not wish to recall come the morning.

*

Beth tossed and turned in the old bed settee, wondering how visitors had ever professed it to be comfortable. The night sounds were keeping her awake, sounds that she had loved and looked forward to as a girl here, sounds of the countryside that had been music to her ears before she dozed off in this very house.

The green dial of the alarm clock was at 1.18. It was the second time she had glanced at it in the past few minutes and she contemplated getting out of bed and turning it to face the wall so that she would not be tempted to keep looking.

Every time an image of Harry tried to creep into her mind, she biffed it one before it took a grip but now, in the middle of the night, when he should have been lying beside her, his arm around her, his head nestled in the curve of her neck, she was finding it impossible to stop thinking about him.

Suddenly, her heart pounded: would he find someone else, even after such a short separation? When she thought back to how often they made love, would he...?

She dived beneath the covers and groaned, setting her mind to putting the facts in the right order: Annie, her best friend, had phoned for help and he had deliberately told a pack of lies, stopped her going to see what was wrong. Beth groaned again, stuffing her fingers in her ears as if the facts she were recalling could be kept out.

Poor Annie! Beth could imagine the girl, desperately wanting to speak to her best friend, fobbed off by a man so callous that he had pushed money under the door of the flat and left her to the terrors of the night; and then, when Beth had not called back, what on earth had gone through Annie's mind?

Beth threw the covers off and sat upright in bed. She could never forgive him; not for that; nor for refusing to sympathise with her grandfather.

*

The day of the funeral dawned bright and sunny, but the afternoon's forecast was for showers, some of them heavy, especially in the East. Grace and Alice went through their tasks like robots, seldom talking to each other, even if they found themselves alone; trying to ensure that Sarah and Tony had nothing to do but to grieve for their daughter.

At lunchtime, no one mentioned food, for Alice's idea had been to have a large breakfast then nothing else until teatime, and Sarah was only too happy to go along with it, since it meant she could stay in her bedroom for hours before they had to leave the house.

As the morning progressed slowly for Grace and Alice, they found themselves glancing at clocks and watches several times a minute, eventually shaking their heads at each other and sitting out of sight of clock dials.

'I wonder if Sarah's ready yet,' Alice whispered as they sat in the garden for a few minutes, taking advantage of the temporary sunshine. 'Maybe I should go up and see?'

'Would you? I'll see to Tony then, make sure he's...' She shrugged, for she had been about to say *'make sure he's all right'* and how could he be? 'See if he's ready,' she amended.

Now that the day was upon him, Tony Kerr was less melancholy for some reason and Grace had an easier task than she had imagined when helping him to get ready. He was washed and dressed and sitting on the bed when she knocked and went into the room and, for a brief moment, she saw his eyes light up.

'Ah, Grace, my dear,' he smiled, waving her forward. 'So, you've come to make an old man happy at last.'

'I've come to put you in that wheelchair,' Grace said. 'Where's the knee-rug you always have?'

Tony pointed to the wardrobe. 'In there,' he grinned and it was more disturbing to Grace than if he had been morose. To see him grinning so happily rang alarm bells in her head.

'James will be here any moment,' she told him as she helped him into the wheel chair and tucked the knee blanket round his legs. 'He'll push you this afternoon.'

'No!' Tony cried, grabbing her wrist and holding it fast with a grip that belied his condition. 'Not him. You can push me.'

'Why not James? He's your best friend.'

'He's my Sergeant-Major,' Tony corrected her sullenly. 'I let him down.'

He released her wrist and sat dejectedly in the chair, folding and re-folding the fringes of the knee blanket.

'You didn't let anybody down,' Grace said gently, but he was shaking his head.

'I was closest to the gun,' he said and Grace was mystified. 'I should have been the one to take over.'

'Tony, please, just think of today, what you have to do for Annie.'

She held her breath for it was either the silliest thing to say or the most appropriate; for a long moment she waited. With a long sigh and a quick apologetic glance, Tony nodded to her and touched her hand.

'I'd still like you to push the wheelchair, Grace.'

'Of course I will.'

She wheeled him into the living room, where Sarah and Alice were sitting. There had been no further word from Annie's brother, Tommy, who worked in the Midlands; but his intention had been to fly up in time for the service and stay the night, thereby relieving Grace and Alice of their obligations.

'He'll be late,' Tony frowned now as they waited for the cars. 'He's always late, was even late for his own wedding.'

Sarah made no response other than to move her head and look at Grace.

'I was late for mine,' Grace smiled to her. 'Deliberately, of course, to keep him on his toes.'

There was a flicker of a smile on Sarah's face and then she averted her eyes.

In the silence of the room, Grace and Alice, having no way of knowing what the other was thinking, were, in fact, of the same mind: despite the satisfaction of having helped the family out for a few days, they were greatly looking forward to a normal life back in the Melville household.

Grace, pondering the fact, glanced at the Kerrs and was filled with an overpowering sense of futility when she remembered that life for them could never be normal again.

*

Harry drew up at a safe distant from the church and went to the passenger side to let Sandra out. She had insisted on coming with him, an idea that seemed preposterous considering she was neither family nor friend, but he had submitted, finally, to the request as the last guests had dwindled from the house.

'You can't go on your own,' she had tutted at him as he and Foxy helped to clear up. 'Tell him, Foxy, that I'm right.'

Foxy had shrugged and picked up a clean dishtowel. 'Nothing to do with me.'

'A man on his own?' Sandra asked, her eyes filled with horror. 'No, it doesn't bear thinking about, especially at a family funeral.'

Neither Harry nor Foxy could see the reasoning behind her remark, but it seemed she would have her way.

'You can say I'm your fancy bit,' she had chuckled to them both, eliciting a despairing look from her great-niece.

'Sandra, honestly! Have I taught you nothing all the years you've known me?'

Harry thought that a knowing glance passed between them, but it was late; perhaps he was tired.

'Why don't you take Foxy home?' Sandra suggested, much to Foxy's displeasure.

'What? Over my dead body,' the girl had said, giving Harry's ego its final battering of the evening. 'I'll walk home myself, thank you.'

Later, as he had stood at the front door with Sandra, watching Foxy's long legs stride off down the street, dark hair swinging, heels clicking on the pavement, he had suffered a fleeting pang of doubt as to the Gillespie magnetism: she must be the only girl in history not to fall, metaphorically-speaking, at his feet.

He sensed Sandra giving him a sly glance. 'Did you like her?'

'Of course I did, she's charming.'

'Tut, tut, a dreadful word that only characters in pantomime use.' She had regarded him with mischievous eyes. 'She liked you anyway.'

'You must be joking,' Harry laughed, his eyes still following the girl, although she was long gone. 'My ego's never taken such a pounding.'

Sandra chuckled again. 'Doesn't mean what you think it means.'

He had turned then to look at her closely. 'What's your game, Miss Moneypenny?'

'Oh, I do love it when you call me that! All I'm saying is that she's an extraordinary girl and it calls for extraordinary tactics.'

Harry was astonished. 'Tactics? I don't need tactics, as you put it. I'm a happily married man going through a rough spell that will only last a week, if that.'

'I'm just saying,' Sandra shrugged cheerfully. 'If you get lonely and change your mind, here's her number.' She had passed him a small slip of paper, crushed it into his hand and refused to take it back.

Now, as he helped her from the car, he wondered what her response would be were he to tell her that his fingers had already dialled the number.

'Thank you, kind Sir,' Sandra smiled, one of only two woman ever to emerge in a lady-like fashion from the sports car, the other being Grace. 'Now, point me in the direction of the corpse.'

Harry shook his head. 'What the heck am I to do with you, woman?'

'If you take Foxy out,' Sandra said wickedly. 'I promise to behave.'

'I'll think about it,' Harry told her, but the arrangements were already in place.

*

Beth and James sat together, whilst Grace and Alice occupied the far end of the pew. Harry saw Beth's blonde hair at least seven places distant from her mother's and his heart sank, for he had imagined that the tragedy of the circumstances might have brought the impasse to an end.

He sat beside Sandra in the last pew, nearest the door, watching proceedings with a feeling of detachment, as if the people and service had nothing to do with him; and yet, he knew that, had he been at Beth's side, his involvement would have been total.

As they stood to sing the first hymn, Sandra touched his arm.

'It's my favourite,' she told him. 'But then I suppose it's everybody's.'

He could have said he had never sung it in his life – nor, indeed any hymn – but it was irrelevant and cruel when she had been so considerate as to come with him. As the congregation stood, hymnbooks raised, Harry tried to catch sight of Grace, but his view of her was obscured by a wall of humanity.

*

Thomas Blake hovered near the door, his height being a disadvantage when his only desire was to be inconspicuous. He had sat in his hired car a fair distance from the church, watching and waiting for the family to arrive, and he could hardly believe his eyes when they all appeared separately: his daughter and various others came in one car, his granddaughter and Melville came in another, and then, the most surprising thing of all, Beth's husband arrived in his red sports car, complete with a very attractive, if elderly, lady with whom he chatted and joked all the way up the church lane.

Thomas had sat for at least twenty minutes, mulling over what he had just seen. There was no logical explanation for any of it, other than they had all fallen out about the funeral, but how ridiculous was that? No, it must be something to do with etiquette, some ancient Wee Free custom that had slipped his mind; and there had been plenty to go round in the '20's, *that* he did recall.

As the service was coming to a conclusion, he shuffled near the door, awaiting a propitious moment to make his exit. After all, he had seen his daughter, brought her facial image to life again after months of its fading until he despaired of remembering even the most obvious detail; and perhaps he had seen more than they might have wanted him to see. The thought that they had arrived, not as a family, but as separate units, was intriguing him. He would do some homework, find out what was going on; and, if his luck were in, he might even discover a tiny chink in the façade of his daughter's life, a chink just broad enough for him to step through.

Grace sat with her feet up, Alice lying on the settee, each with their eyes closed, savouring the moment. It had been half an hour since they had flopped down and not a word had passed between them. Grace opened one eye and yawned, at which her friend sighed and stretched.

'Wasn't that the most delicious half hour you've ever spent?' Grace asked.

'It comes a close second,' Alice grinned mischievously.

'You, Alice Cameron, have a mind like a dung heap.'

'Takes one to know one,' Alice quipped happily, swinging her legs to the floor and finding her slippers.

'I think we should have tea now,' Grace said, stifling another yawn. 'James is up the garden, doing Lord knows what, but I'll make it anyway.'

'See what I mean?'

Grace paused on her way into the kitchen. 'What?'

'About us serfs having to make such a huge effort for men?'

Grace laughed. 'I hardly think that making the tea will be a huge effort.'

'But the first thing you said was 'James is up the garden but I'll make it anyway'.'

Alice frowned suddenly. 'I was exactly the same with Martin and Brad. I always had to think of them first, never ate until they wanted to, never went to bed until they wanted to, never said or did anything of my own.' She stopped, grimaced at her friend. 'Hark at me, little Miss Womens Libber.'

'I've had enough social and political comment to do me for one day, thank you very much,' Grace smiled, saluting her friend and going into the kitchen.

'Did you have a chance to see Beth?' she heard Alice call.

'Yes, I saw her.'

'And did you see Harry with an older woman?'

'It was his secretary,' Grace called through, but when she recalled the cosy chat the woman had shared with Harry in the church lane, she found it difficult to even speak the words. 'Her name is Sandra, probably came with him to make him feel less isolated.'

'She was very well-dressed, did you notice?'

'No,' Grace lied, doing her best to keep her voice cheerful. 'D'you fancy chips tonight? I could make some if you like?'

'Great idea,' Alice said, right behind Grace, making her jump.

'For Pete's sake! Creeping up on me like that. Here, take the chip pan, fill it with that block of Cokeen.'

They worked together, occasionally bumping into each other as they criss-crossed the kitchen. Finally, when the chips were crisping in the pan, Grace glanced out of the window.

'I should go and tell him tea's ready.'

'It's five o'clock, isn't it?' Alice asked brusquely, hands on hips. 'And he's wearing a watch, isn't he?'

'Golly, you've changed since '53, when you were so obliging and easy-going with him.'

Alice shook her head. 'Don't remind me. Heavens!' she exclaimed suddenly. 'What a slave to men I was, I see that now.'

'What's got into you?' Grace frowned, hand poised above the back door handle. 'Have you lost your marbles?'

'*Au contraire*, as Beth would say – except her accent's better than mine – no, I think I've just found them!'

'Set the table. Do something useful,' Grace laughed. 'I'm off to play the part of a

373

serf. See you in a minute, your Highness!'

'Grace,' Alice called after her, and she put her head round the door.

'What?'

'Aren't you at all worried where Beth will be spending the night?'

Grace's heart sank, but she smiled convincingly.

'Of course I've been thinking about it, but it's her choice, Alice. She has a home to go to.'

Alice shrugged but said nothing, only turned and continued setting the table.

*

Beth lifted the lid of her suitcase and took out her nightdress. She laid it carefully on the bed and straightened it out, as she usually did, except this was someone else's bedroom, not hers. She looked from the window, at the small, neatly kept garden, the table and chairs on the even smaller patio, and castigated herself for not being more grateful to Marjory for her kind offer of help.

'I refuse to allow you to stay in a hotel,' she had told Beth angrily, the day she had mentioned the row with Harry. 'I have two spare rooms and you will occupy the larger of the two, whether you like it or not.'

'Considering I'm being evicted from my parents' house,' Beth had said woefully. 'It's a very generous offer, Marjory, and I'm most grateful.' She had paused, hesitated, and Marjory had picked up her mood.

'What is it, my dear?'

'Please don't tell Harry.'

Marjory's features arranged themselves into a combination of indignation and disappointment and Beth wanted the ground to open up and swallow her.

'I would never...'

'I know that,' Beth had tried to reassure her. 'But sometimes, even without thinking...'

Marjory had mellowed, smile returning. 'Of course, you mean accidentally.'

'What on earth did you think I meant?' Beth had bluffed and it was her turn to be indignant.

Now, as she stood watching the chaffinches feeding on the bird table, she would have given anything to be back in her own room, her own bed; anything, that was, other than having to grovel to Harry Gillespie.

*

Harry had accepted Sandra's offer to stay for dinner, although she had prepared the food for six o'clock, normally too early for him. They sat now in her dining kitchen, consuming the tastiest bowl of pasta that he had eaten for months, hardly speaking; but the silence was comfortable.

Eventually, when the plates were clean and they sat with cups of coffee in front of them, Sandra sighed and opened the conversation.

'She looked pretty lonely, I thought.'

'Who, Beth?'

'No, her mother, the blonde lady you pointed out to me. Grace, wasn't that what you said her name was?'

'Yes, Grace.'

'Pity you didn't have an opportunity to introduce me to her, Actually, I thought her face was familiar.'

374

Harry shrugged. 'Her photograph's been in the local paper a few times. Maybe you recognised her from there.'

'Yes, that's probably it. She's on lots of committees, didn't you say once?'

'Did I?' Harry could not remember having discussed Grace at all.

'And the local amateur dramatic society, you said.'

'Am I getting old or something?' he laughed, pouring more coffee into their cups. 'I haven't the slightest recollection of discussing her with you.'

'You're fond of her, aren't you?'

'Yes, I am,' Harry said, for with Sandra the truth would out.

'She's lovely, like a doll.'

'A doll? I don't see her like a doll.'

'A beautiful, porcelain doll,' Sandra smiled, her eyes twinkling. 'In fact, I could hardly take my eyes off her. She looks like a film star.'

'She has no idea,' Harry started to say, but changed his mind. Such revelations were of too intimate a nature to pass between solicitor and secretary.

'No idea of what?'

'That she's attractive.'

'She must be blind then,' Sandra said dismissively.

The topic changed and Harry was thankful that the moment was behind him, for he was often too close to blurting it all out, to anyone, even to Sandra.

'Well, I should be going,' he said, pushing his cup and saucer away.

'Why don't you give Foxy a call?'

Harry threw her a cautionary glance before standing up.

'Are you aware that you're wicked?'

'I do hope so,' Sandra grinned, still sitting at the table and watching him pick up his jacket. 'Did you have a nice chat with her last night?'

'I did, as you well know.'

'Doesn't it seem the perfect arrangement to you?

'You're incorrigible.'

Sandra's mouth curved into a smile. 'I do hope it's contagious.'

'Goodnight, Miss Moneypenny.'

'Well, are you going to?'

'No,' he said firmly. 'I am not going to call Foxy. Now behave yourself.'

'It's just...'

'Just what?'

'She hasn't been well lately,' Sandra told him evasively.

'What do you mean 'not well'?'

Sandra hesitated, and then opened her mouth to speak, hesitated again. Oddly enough, despite having only just met Foxy, Harry was intrigued.

'She had cancer a year or so ago.'

'Bloody hell.'

'Not always fatal, and not in Foxy's case, but still... So traumatic for her.'

'Poor thing.'

'No one else knows except me,' Sandra said meaningfully.' Not even her nearest and dearest, if you know what I mean?'

'Why are you telling me?'

'Because you'll go easy on her if you know.'

'Easy on her?' Harry repeated with a frown. 'What a strange turn of phrase.'

'I just wanted you to know,' Sandra sighed. 'Do be nice to her.'

'There's no need to ask. I will be.'

'And it's only for a little while, isn't it? Until your wife gets fed up of all this prima donna rubbish and slinks back home.'

'I'm sure she will,' Harry agreed, ignoring the personal nature of her reply. 'Anyway, thank you for today. It was so good of you to come with me and to ply me with food and drink.'

'I'd hardly call coffee 'drink',' Sandra smiled. 'If you stay longer, I have a very nice Bordeaux...?'

'Thank you, but no,' he said, heading for the door. 'I'll go home and drown my sorrows in a bath.'

'Oooh!' Sandra cried, her hands over her ears in a comical gesture. 'Don't say that kind of thing to an old woman, for Heaven's sake. It's very cruel!'

She saw him to the car and shook his hand in an old-fashioned manner, which he thought contradicted her modern outlook on matters of a sexual nature.

'See you tomorrow,' she said warmly. 'And please call Foxy, but,' she warned at the last moment, 'not a word of this to her. She mustn't know you feel sorry for her.'

He drove out of the street and smiled, looked at his watch. It was eight o'clock: perfect timing. When he turned into the side street off the Inch, she was striding towards him.

'Hi!' she called as he opened the driver's door. 'That was lucky, I've just arrived.'

'Good timing,' Harry said. 'Thanks to your great aunt.'

Her eyebrows rose. 'You've been there?'

'She offered me dinner.'

Foxy pretended to pout. 'What, dessert as well?'

'No dessert,' Harry smiled and she brightened up.

'In that case, I've brought one with me,' she said lasciviously, patting her bosom. 'Or should I say two?'

Harry laughed and led the way.

*

Beth sat on the edge of the bed staring into space, her over-riding thought being that the flowers on the bedspread would never have survived on such skinny stalks; they would have been flattened and broken to bits by the first gust of wind, ending up like a nursery school child's collage of scrap paper and glue.

The sound of Marjory bustling around downstairs was somewhere in the background of this puny flower collage idea, and eventually Beth was forced to tear her eyes away from the bedspread and give herself a mental shake. The prospect of sharing a meal with Marjory, having to chit chat and possibly scintillate for a couple of hours was a deterrent to leaving the bedroom. She was hopeless at scintillating when she was so depressed, and what she really wanted to do was go home, get the Chopin manuscripts out and play the piano until she had surmounted her troubles. The only fly in that particular ointment was that *he* was there, enjoying all the home comforts that she should have been enjoying at that moment, and it dawned on Beth, albeit too late, that she could have insisted that Harry be forced to seek refuge in a shelter for the homeless; not her.

It had been the fiery temper again, the whoosh! as she blew up, yelled and shouted, paced and marched, gesticulated and postured; in other words, if she had only waited for five minutes, thought through the consequences, imagined what would...what if...when could....?

'Beth, dear!' she heard Marjory call from the bottom of the stairs. 'Tea's ready when you are!'

Beth sighed and reluctantly dragged her gaze from the pathetic flowers she was sitting on and moved over to the mirror, practising the smile she would need for the next few hours to ward off the sympathy vote from her hostess. Marjory was not the kind of woman to sit idly by when one of her protégées was down on her luck and if Beth showed the slightest inclination to 'spill the beans' Marjory would launch in, all guns blazing, until her guest had no secrets left.

Beth suppressed the urge to run from the house and rush back to beg Harry's forgiveness. The only way she could maintain some vestige of dignity was to sit this out, make them all come to realise how much they missed her, force them to come and look for her, sling her on their shoulder and take her back to the fold; to join the other ninety nine.

*

Grace turned out the light and slid beneath the blankets. James was already asleep beside her and she envied him the ability to set aside the row with Beth, to appear unconcerned as to where his daughter had found a bed for the night – and many other nights, presumably. She thought, fleetingly, of Charlie Webster, but dismissed it quickly; not because it could never be one of Beth's preferred options, but because the consequences were too dangerous to entertain.

Her mind flashed back to the telephone call that had started it all, to the incredible hostility in her daughter's voice as she expounded her theory regarding Harry's heartlessness.

'He drove her to it,' she had shouted down the receiver. 'He could have insisted that I go round there and see how she was.'

'But surely that was your decision,' Grace had countered unwisely, only unleashing a torrent of words that spilled and merged into one another and which passed over Grace's head. She had no intention of placating Beth over someone like Annie Kerr, who had enjoyed every possible advantage a girl could have, growing up in a secure and loving family; not to mention the effect her disgraceful behaviour had had on her parents, already struggling with Sarah's illness.

'I won't listen to this, Beth,' Grace had said, shocking herself anew. 'When you decide to see reason, you know where I'll be.'

Grace closed her eyes, resigned to a disturbed night's sleep and when she thought back to how she had imagined her life would be, she shed a silent tear.

Chapter Twenty-Six

It was with a heavy heart that Grace ringed her birthday on the calendar. It would be her birthday on the last day of September and her daughter would not be there to celebrate. The conversation she had once had with her own mother had been flitting to and fro in her mind for days now, the words bobbing up and down, taunting her, just out of reach, evading all attempts to suppress them.

'I could never fall out with you,' she had told Charlotte Blake years ago. 'Imagine, not speaking to your own daughter!'

She put the pen in its holder on the desk and stood looking at the last day in September. What had amazed her more than anything was the stubbornness of her conviction, the refusal to give in to Beth, even knowing that she might never see her again. When it had been Thomas Blake luring Beth away, striving to divide the family, Grace's heart had broken at the thought of what might happen; yet now, because it involved a slight to Harry, she had discovered just how much a heart could harden.

She heard Frank's step on the stairway and moved swiftly away from the calendar, lest he guess she was relating the date to the impasse with Beth.

'Can I get you anything in the town?' he asked, swinging into the room, hanging onto the door handle so tightly that Grace was waiting for the door to be wrenched off its hinges.

'No, dear, but thank you. You just go and enjoy your Saturday, have a lovely day with Emily'

'You're welcome to join us,' he said hesitantly.

'What, an old fogey like me? Not at all, I've plenty to do.'

'She likes you,' Frank told his mother, embarrassed. 'She envies your complexion, she says.'

'Tell her it's held together with Polyfilla.'

He laughed at that and wandered over to her. 'The big day soon, right?'

'Yes,' Grace agreed, there being no point in trying to fool him when he might suspect she had only just marked the date.

'Where would you like to go?'

'Let me see,' Grace said slowly, pretending to mull it over. 'How about Davey Brown's cowshed? That wouldn't break the bank and your Dad could gather cow pats for manure.'

Again, Frank laughed, slapping his mother lightly on the shoulder.

'You know, since Alice came to live here, you're a hoot.'

'So previously, you're saying I was a right wet blanket?'

'Nah,' he said, with one of those words that, were she Edward Heath, Grace would punish with life imprisonment. 'But you were sad.'

He turned and walked away, towards the kitchen, leaving her baffled, baffled as to how she had failed to conceal her innermost feelings from a teenage boy; she who prided herself on her acting skills; a player whom people had described as the finest Elvira in the history of amateur dramatics.

Grace sighed, glanced again at the calendar. Perhaps her attributes were fading; perhaps she had miscounted; was it not more likely that she would be seventy at the end of the month?

*

Harry opened his eyes and stared at the ceiling. He remembered it was Saturday and that, for the first time in ages, he had not bothered to set the alarm. Normally, with Beth around, Saturdays had no significance, for she was up with the lark and clattering around before he even realised he had been asleep.

He heard the faint sound of traffic and then car doors closing, slamming mostly, as if they knew he was still in bed and envied him; wanted him up and about. He yawned and glanced at the clock: half past nine. Sighing, he sank back onto the bed and closed his eyes again, not enough to drift off, just enough to visualise Foxy writhing beneath him.

'Doesn't it seem the perfect arrangement to you?'

Harry recalled Sandra's words, so many weeks ago now that he had lost count. He smiled to himself, for it certainly was the perfect arrangement.

'Mine's through in Edinburgh,' Foxy had breathed into his ear. 'And yours is in the huff somewhere. What could be better?'

There was more to it, of course, a lot more, and when she had done with explanations he was torn between relief and disappointment, relief that a lesbian would never be cited in any divorce action that Beth might fantasise over, and disappointment that she was taken – especially by another woman – for she was a delightful creature, full of promise.

He stirred himself and threw back the covers, only to find a note pinned to her side of the bed.

'Good morning lazy git!
Thanks for another great bonk.
Any more of this and you'll be
converting me!!
Will call during the week.
Lustfully yours
Foxy.'

Harry smiled and tore the note into miniscule pieces before chucking it in the waste paper basket at the side of the dressing table; and then, suddenly, he remembered he was seeing Grace that afternoon and he sprang out of bed with renewed energy.

*

Thomas tiptoed around downstairs, creeping like an idiot, fearful of waking her. He still had to pinch himself at the thought of her lying upstairs in the West bedroom, of her sharing his house, chatting to him before she went to work, flying in the door at night with snippets of news. He could hardly believe she was here.

He thought he heard her moving now, faint steps padding to and fro, and so he switched on the kettle and popped a couple of bread slices into the toaster.

She had no preference, she said, for things to eat of a morning, but at the very start he had stacked the cupboards full of absolutely everything that you could eat at breakfast time and, by a process of elimination, had discovered that the muesli, porridge oats, and fancy energy bars had lain unmolested on the shelves, while the bread, butter, orange marmalade and coffee had melted away. These were the things he bought regularly, only for her; for his granddaughter.

He heard the bathwater running and put the cost of gas out of his mind. From experience, he knew she only popped in and out of the bath, and would be washed and dressed within fifteen minutes, and so he set the table, checked the supply of milk – she preferred hot milk in her coffee – and then stood by the toaster, waiting. Life could not get much better. He loved to remember how it had all come about.

*

'Are you following me?' she had frowned, glaring at him.

'No, for Heaven's sake, I was heading to the chemist. Why should I be following you, Beth?'

She shrugged, appeared in a bad mood. 'Dunno, it just looks like it.'

'I'd like to buy you a coffee,' he said, a lot more confidently than he felt.

He almost collapsed in a heap when she nodded and said it was okay.

Trying to keep his voice and movements as normal as he could, Thomas had steered her towards the George, still his favourite hotel, and ordered a tray of coffee and shortbread.

'Do they have any doughnuts?' she had asked, and the waitress had said they did, upon which his granddaughter cast him an enquiring look, as if he would refuse her anything at that moment!

'How's life?' he had asked nonchalantly, as if he had coffee with her every day of the week.

Her eyes were wandering. 'So-so. How's yours?'

'I feel pretty lonely,' he said, injecting just the right amount of chagrin.

'Do you? Don't you have friends?'

He was still trying to come to terms with the fact she was sitting here in front of him, in the same seat her mother had occupied so acrimoniously several years ago; his granddaughter chatting, passing the time of day. Previously, he had calculated his chances as a million to one that she would even say one word to him again.

'Oh, I have friends,' he lied, discounting Daphne in his mind. 'But it's family that matters.'

He had averted his eyes at that moment, conscious of her gaze coming to rest on him. Holding his breath, he waited, pretending to be occupied solely with stirring sugar into his coffee.

'In my opinion,' she said tersely. 'Family's over-estimated.'

It had taken only nine more minutes to span what he had believed to be a chasm of impossible proportions; for her to agree to board in his house, to pay him a monthly rent.

As casually as he could, he extended his hand at the end of negotiations. 'You're free to come and go as you please,' he told her, feigning indifference. 'Here's a key to the front door. When you want to move on, just leave it on the hall table.'

She had given no explanation for her decision, but he had fed Daphne a bundle of lies in order to attend Beth's best friend's funeral, and there were clues littered around the church and its environs. He had put two and two together; made four. The only fly in the ointment had been when she had mentioned her mother.

'Oh, by the way, although my mother won't know where I am,' she said off-handedly. 'She gave her blessing to my seeing you.'

'That's good,' Thomas had lied, for he wanted to hear it from her own lips. 'I'm very glad.'

*

Thomas jumped when the toaster burped out its slices. Quickly, because he had been wasting time daydreaming, he slotted in another two and pressed the lever. She would be down in three minutes.

*

Beth chose a dark grey, pin-stripe trouser suit, a welcome change from miniskirts that prohibited movement, unless you wanted to give a man an eyeful.

She picked out a white frilly blouse to go with it and dressed in under five minutes, taking great care, as always, not to meet her eyes in the mirror.

It was the strangest sensation, to go through the motions of working, eating, sleeping, mixing with clients, and never feeling a thing. She was so used to the absence of any emotion, neither high nor low, neither happy nor sad, that she was dreading the moment when her mind would snap open suddenly and there she would be – happy or sad, high or low, not knowing how to deal with it.

She adjusted the frills of the blouse to sit neatly outside the wide collar of the jacket and then surveyed her choice of shoes, most of her belongings still residing in the flat. The black, strapped shoes that no one had liked except her leaped out as presentable. They would do nicely. She pushed her feet into them and went downstairs.

'Good morning,' her grandfather said, his back to her. 'There's toast if you'd like, and your favourite marmalade.'

Beth stifled the familiar resentment that inevitably reared up at the idea she was predictable, and wandered to the table. He turned and smiled at her, proffering two slices of toast.

'Did you sleep well?' he asked.

'So-so. Thanks for the toast.'

He was nervous, she could tell. She knew he would be on tenterhooks in case she found somewhere else to go, and she was not beyond doing just that; but, for the moment, she had her reasons for staying here and it suited her.

'Anything exciting happening today?' he asked warily.

'Yes, as it happens,' she said more sociably. 'An auction in Montrose, Charlie and I are both going, should be interesting.' She could have added that it was the first time in her entire life that she had ever worked on a Saturday; the reason being she had nowhere else to go.

'Montrose? Doesn't it have a beach?'

'Yeah, it does. We used to drive past it on the way down from Aberdeen.' She looked at him closely. 'Did you live in a city in South America?'

'Buenos Aires,' he said. 'Huge, smelly, too busy for me, and that was in the twenties.'

'You didn't like it at first,' Beth reminded him. 'I read your letter.'

'I hated being apart from Charlotte,' he said, truthfully it appeared. 'I couldn't sleep for worrying about her.'

'Worrying about her? Why? What could have happened to her?'

Her grandfather sat down at the table, a cup of coffee in his hand.

'Her father, Sandy Shepherd, that's what could have happened to her.'

She stopped chewing. 'Was he really the religious tyrant that Lily Morris says he was?'

'Oh, yes, and more. You know, he tried to stop her from seeing me off at the station, said it was the Devil's work, that he was trying to snare her.'

'Golly, that's a bit heavy.'

'Anyway, I was sure she'd come out to join me when your mother was older.'

He lowered his eyes to his cup, compressed his lips together. 'If I'd known she'd no intentions of coming out there, I'd have come home on the next boat.'

Beth nodded, having no reason to disbelieve the man. She had read all the letters.

'Well, must fly,' she told him, picking up the remainder of her slice of toast. 'I'm not sure when I'll be back tonight. Oh, and Charlie and I will grab a bite to eat before I get back, so don't wait up. ''Bye!'

She rushed down the hallway and out of the door before giving him time to catch his breath. At the bottom of the driveway, she paused, emitted a huge sigh and carried on more sedately.

Imagine what Harry Gillespie would say if he saw her coming out of this house! Beth smirked, until the reality set in: Harry Gillespie was not the reason she was staying with Thomas Blake; it was all to do with her mother, Beth slowed to a stroll, pondered a crazy idea for half a second, but then picked up her pace again. She would think about it some other time.

*

Grace freshened up, changed into a lighter dress – the old green silk – and raked around for her make-up bag, the one that Beth had pounced on so many times in an effort to glamorise her mother. As she laid out a pink lipstick and a block of mascara – which she had worn only when Beth had applied it – she examined her skin in the mirror, trying to find what Emily had so admired about it. Grace peered at every line, some old, many recent, and decided that her complexion was not so bad after all. It was something she rarely did – gawp at herself in mirrors, although Beth did it all the time, even in shop windows, glass-fronted cabinets, and, more bizarrely, the back of her pudding spoon.

Grace applied a smear of lipstick, pressed her lips together and reached for the mascara block. It was hardly used, of course, the surface smooth and level. The unhygienic element of spitting on the brush and then rubbing it on the block had once put her off, until Beth had reminded her of mothers spitting on hankies and wiping squirming children's faces at the bus stop; after which spittle on the mascara brush seemed insignificant.

Tentatively, she brushed the black, gooey stuff onto her lashes, just one coat, whereas Beth applied at least three, and then she studied the result: similar to Coco the clown and much more obvious than Grace had imagined. The trouble was she had seen Beth trying to wipe the stuff off and having to walk around like a panda for hours. She shrugged and left it, hoping that James would not notice.

If he did, he made no mention of it, merely smiling at her, telling her she looked nice, to drive carefully and to give his regards to Harry. He gave the clock a furtive glance.

'Be sure to tell him that I'd be coming too if it wasn't for the football.'

'James, dearest, I think he knows that already, having known us for years. Oh, and if Alice phones with news of the flat, tell her I can help her move in any day she needs me.'

She threw her bag and coat into the back seat and drove into the stream of traffic, busier on Saturdays but with fewer commercial lorries and vans, which made the journey more pleasant. As she bowled along, past the fields ripened by the prolonged sunshine that summer, Grace was ashamed to find that she was quite happy. Despite Alice having moved out, temporarily to a hotel, but now with the possibility of a flat in Perth, and despite her continued rift with her daughter, she was singing more often now: in the bath, preparing the meals, doing the housework; and now, when she should have been commiserating over the split in her family, she was singing out 'How Can You Solve a Problem like Maria' with gusto.

As if in deference to her guilt, she stopped singing, concentrating on the heavier traffic as she approached Perth, but she kept the melody ringing on in her head until the tune had come to its silent conclusion.

*

Harry fiddled with his collar and tie, and it reminded him of the trouble it had caused him on his wedding day, when the thing just refused to sit correctly. He had not given a

382

thought to his wedding day, or, indeed, to Beth, for some time, being as he was preoccupied; not so much with Foxy, for she was only too happy to fit in with his plans, but with Daphne and her determination to hand her money over to Thomas Blake.

Harry had not breathed a word about knowing the man, as it would have jeopardised proceedings, but he had been as vociferous as was tactfully possible, citing the cases of various vulnerable women who had been conned. He used the word 'cheated', as it sounded less common.

'I strongly advise you,' he had told her often enough. 'To wait until you're sure of his intentions.'

'Dear Mr Gillespie,' she replied, her eyes sympathetic to his duty as her solicitor. 'His intentions are so honourable that your generation would be at a loss to understand them.' She blushed slightly and he suspected it was a prelude to a confidence. 'He could so easily have taken advantage of me months ago, you know, and he's been the perfect gentleman. No, I'm happy to sign over everything I have to him, in fact, I insist,' she had concluded with an uncharacteristic firmness.'

To give himself more time, Harry had said he would draw up the document and have it ready for her signature by the end of the month.

'That will do nicely,' Daphne had said the day before. 'I want it all out of the way before we get married.'

Even after hearing the words several times, Harry was appalled at the idea. He had no choice, however, but to go with her decision until the last minute, scurrying around for some legal loophole that he could write in without her knowledge. To that end, he proposed to call David Routledge in Aberdeen as soon as possible.

Now, however, he was standing at the mirror, still fiddling with his uncooperative tie, and Grace would be here any minute. At last, as he smoothed his collar down and decided it would do, he heard her steps on the stone staircase outside. When he opened the door, he was surprised to see the difference in her. There was a glow in her cheeks; she was even wearing makeup, but more than that, her smile was radiant. It had been a few weeks since they had met and he could only imagine that she and Beth had been reconciled.

'You look great,' he told her, moving aside to let her pass. 'Have you had good news?'

Grace appeared puzzled and, with a shock, he realised he had misjudged the situation.

'Good news? Not unless you count Alice finding a flat in Perth.'

'Ah, no, I thought perhaps you and Beth...?'

He was more astonished when she seemed unaffected by hearing Beth's name.

'No,' she smiled, pausing in the hallway to look at him. 'I doubt if Beth has the slightest intention of speaking to me again, at least not for a long time.'

'Why should you think so?'

'Because,' she said slowly. 'She wants to punish me for taking your side.'

Harry was stunned; not by her opinion, depressing though it was, but by her complete indifference. It was as if she had uttered words that applied to someone else.

'Forgive me for saying,' he said hesitantly. 'But you don't seem all that worried.'

Grace laughed and he knew it was spontaneous. 'No, why should I be?'

He let out his breath in a long sigh and took her elbow, leading her into the sitting room, where he had laid out afternoon tea.

'Come in, Madam, the café's open.'

'Oh, Harry!' Grace exclaimed joyfully. 'You're a wizard! How lovely this looks, and all by yourself too.' She turned and frowned suddenly. 'I'll never forgive her for what's she'd doing to you. She thinks she's doing it to me, but you're the one who's suffering most.'

He felt a huge pang of guilt at the word 'suffering', at the thought of Foxy embellishing his bed so soon after Beth's departure. He walked over to the large window overlooking the Inch to draw attention away from his embarrassment.

'Why don't you stand here and watch the world go by,' he invited her, his back to her for the moment. 'And I'll go and put the kettle on, get the tea made.'

He was aware of her behind him, could even hear her breath close to him, and when he turned to face her, he was not surprised to see her scrutinising him closely.

'Are you managing without her?' she asked.

'Yes. As you see, the house is clean, the meals are on time, and I even have peace and quiet to read the newspaper.'

She moved to his side and gazed from the window, saying nothing, but he suspected that she wanted to say much more. He even thought he knew what it might be.

*

Grace stood watching the people strolling on the Inch, coats draped over arms because the autumn day was so warm, and she wondered if she had the courage to broach the subject. She was, after all, only his mother-in-law, not his mother, and had no right to bring such intimacy to the conversation. The problem was that she and Beth had frequently discussed things that would have horrified Harry, things that Beth took for granted between mother and daughter and which Grace had also taken for granted with her own mother. She would never, however, have divulged any of it to James, for he would have never understood how such private, intimate details could be passed on so callously between women.

She was despairing of ever finding the right words when she felt his touch on her arm.

'You can ask me, you know,' Harry said quietly. 'You have a perfect right to ask me anything.' She blushed, bit her lower lip and shook her head. 'I mean it,' he insisted, keeping hold of her arm. 'If you want to know anything, just ask me.'

She looked up at him and, although he knew what was in her mind, to his shame, he was enjoying her confusion. It was something beyond his power, this ridiculous pleasure he derived when her acting ability faltered and she revealed more than she wanted to.

'I don't want to ask you anything.'

'Yes, you do,' he smiled patiently. 'And the answer is that I can wait for Beth, for as long as it takes.' It was the most blatant lie, since he had waited only a few days before bedding Foxy, but it was what Grace would want to hear. 'Now,' he added, as she was about to protest. 'You go and sit down, make yourself comfortable, and I'll bring the tea through.'

She nodded; let him go without further eye contact. When he reached the doorway he turned to find that she had resumed her window position and was watching the activity on the Inch.

He was gone only five minutes, as long as it took the kettle to boil, and when he returned to the sitting room she was still standing by the window.

'I was wondering,' she said, as soon as he crossed the threshold. 'I was wondering how Beth was faring without her piano.'

'I hadn't thought of it.'

'I had,' she said, turning and walking over to the hearth, where she sat in one of the chairs before continuing. 'She'll go mad without one, you know.'

'Will she? Even with all that's going on?'

'Oh, yes, she'll not be able to last very long without playing.'

'Do you know where she is?'

'I think I can guess,' she said, frowning slightly.

Harry, who had no idea where his wife might be, was astonished; mostly because it was the first time Grace had mentioned it. Had she known all along and not told him?

'When did you discover where she was?'

She seemed shocked. 'I haven't... discovered I mean. Goodness me, Harry, if I'd known for certain where she was I'd have told you. Surely you must know that?'

Suitably chastised, he made a gesture of apology. 'Sorry, I just thought...'

'It struck me just the other day,' Grace went on pensively, accepting the cup he offered. 'Where would she go to really hurt me, at least to imagine she was hurting me?'

He stared at her, for the notion was too preposterous.

'You can't mean what I think you mean?'

She nodded. 'Yes, I think she's with him.'

Harry sat back in his chair with a sharp out-take of breath. 'But, it's unthinkable.'

'No, it's exactly how Beth would think, given that I've thrown her out, so to speak.' Grace smiled, albeit sadly. 'I never forget how volatile she is and it stands me in good stead.'

'I know where he lives,' Harry told her, much to her horror. 'Wait!' he added, his hand raised to cut off her imminent remark. 'I have a client who knows him, it's confidential, and I can't say more.'

She lowered her eyes from his. 'I'm sorry, I thought...'

'I've never been to the house, nor had Beth, at least not to my knowledge. She did have his phone number though. I found it one day in the waste bin.'

Grace gave a wry smile. 'You rake in waste bins?'

'How else would I get my information,' he asked with a wink.

'Anyway, she's probably with him, crying on his shoulder about her wicked witch of a mother.'

'Why isn't it bothering you?'

She caught her breath, her eyes flicking to his face and then away again.

'Because it's unjustified, what she's doing. We all know what Annie was like. Even James and I knew. The girl was unhinged,' she ended with contempt.

'A good word,' Harry agreed. 'But I'd no idea you knew.'

'She came to me one day with a story that you'd slept with her.' The words, so bluntly stated, and with such little sign of emotion, stabbed the air around them. She shrugged, sighed. 'Perhaps I should have warned you, but, to be honest, I didn't think that Beth would ever believe such tripe.'

Harry was astounded at the venom in her tone and had no time to conceal it. She smiled a slow smile, head on one side, eyes dancing and he could hardly believe that this was the same woman who, only minutes ago, had been unable to broach the subject of two months without sex, and yet here she was looking at him, completely at ease, making references to him and Annie Kerr.

'Grace Blake, sometimes I think you must be the most unpredictable woman on the planet.'

She appeared delighted by his observation but he waited for the remonstration over the use of her maiden name. 'I'll never understand you,' he added, when she made no such remark.

'Oh, I think you understand me fairly well.'

'As you do me, I should imagine.'

A silence fell then, and he felt the underlying implications of their last words heavy in the space between them, for it was not the kind of conversation that took place between mothers-and-sons-in-law; it was the kind of conversation that he and Beth might have.

Perhaps she realised it too, for she leaned forward and examined her shoes.

'Oh, by the way,' she said, fiddling with the buckle of her left shoe. 'I've some stuff in the boot, things that you can stick in the freezer.' She glanced across at him. 'I made quiches and tarts and things, some odd bits and pieces. I hate to think of you having to cook for yourself.'

'Why don't you come in and do it for me then?' he suggested rashly, but she was already shaking her head.

'No, I don't think so. If Beth found out I was here at all, she'd...' Grace paused, frowned, looked at him for some time before she went on. 'It's silly, isn't it, that I should think of her when she's not thinking of me?'

'She will be thinking of you,' Harry assured her. 'You and she were as close as two peas in a pod. Just wait. She'll soon come to her senses.'

'That's the trouble,' Grace said bluntly. 'Beth has none.'

He saw the necessity to tread lightly, but the words he had intended to utter kept changing in the few seconds before he chose the right ones.

'One day, when this is all over and things are back to normal, we'll be glad we didn't say too much.'

She should have shown surprise, or even remorse, but she hid her feelings well and he had no clue. He reached out and poured them a third cup of tea, for he wanted her to stay.

'I shouldn't have any more.'

'Oh, come on,' Harry cajoled. 'When you leave, I'll be fed up again.'

'I'm sorry,' she said, immediately contrite. 'I forget. Of course I'll have another, and keep you company.'

'Have you thought any more about seeing your father again?'

She showed no surprise at the question, as if she had been mulling it over herself. 'Not lately. Now that Beth's flounced off in the huff.'

Harry had two choices: he could leave it hanging, say nothing further, or divulge her father's intention to remarry, without actually breaking a confidence between solicitor and client.

'Don't ask me where I got my information,' he started to say.

'Not in another waste basket?' she asked with a faint smile.

'You're on the ball today, but no. He's planning to remarry.'

This time she was surprised, her eyebrows rising dramatically, the eyes growing wide and troubled.

'Marry? But who?'

'Can't tell.'

'I see. Goodness me, that means he intends to stay here.'

'Seems so.

'I don't know what to say,' Grace frowned. 'The idea that he'll be here for ever...'

'You could put a spoke in his wheel, of course,' Harry said casually. 'I mean if anyone can, you can.'

'You know something else, don't you?' she asked shrewdly. 'Why did you bring the subject up in the first place?'

'I may not be able to tell you who she is, but I know they always have afternoon tea at the Isle of Skye.'

'That's not far from Alice's new flat.'

'Really?' Harry laughed. 'Fancy that.'

She said nothing but he could see she was absorbing the information, filing it away for later. The other thing he sensed was that she was not averse to putting a spoke in this particular wheel.

'Why don't we arrange to have lunch next week?' he asked, while she was still pondering the usefulness of what he had divulged. 'I could treat you and James to a slap-up feed at Timothy's.'

She was trying not to laugh. 'I don't think you'd be able to drag James to a posh place like that.'

'Why not?'

'Because he'd have to get dressed up and he hates it.'

'He made the effort for Lucy Webster,' Harry said on impulse, gauging her reaction. Once more she hid her true feelings and had him fooled. 'He did, yes.'

'But perhaps that was more for Beth.'

'No,' Grace said evenly. 'I think it was for Lucy.'

Had he been braver, he might have gone further, but he was not. As the clock struck four, she glanced at it and he knew she was thinking of leaving.

'I'll help you with my rations for next week,' he offered, standing up at the same time as she did.

'Next week?' Grace laughed. 'More like next month.'

'I don't know what I'd do without you.'

She flashed him a bright smile. 'You'd be fine, but I'm glad to help.'

Five minutes later, after he had stacked the last of the plastic boxes in the freezer and closed the fridge door, Harry walked her to her car. It was a mellow autumn evening, one of the final spells of settled weather before the Equinoxal gales, and they stood for a moment on the pavement appreciating the late afternoon sunshine.

'Thank you,' she said unexpectedly, offering her hand to him.

He ignored it for the moment. 'What for?' he asked.

'For filling my time, allowing me to forget Beth for a few hours.'

'Same here.' As she stood with her hand still hovering in the space between them, Harry lowered his head and, for the first time in their relationship, he kissed her cheek.

'Your dress is lovely,' he said. 'You suit that soft shade of green.'

'It's an ancient thing.'

'It's still lovely.'

Grace turned and opened the car door. 'Thank you, Harry, for being so nice to me.'

'Is he nice to you?' he heard himself ask, stupidly, and she turned.

'Sorry?'

'James. Is he nice to you?'

'Yes, in his own way,' she qualified, not meeting his eyes, and not making a fuss. He waited until she reversed into the street, made sure her way was safe, and then he waved her into the flow of traffic, watching the car until it had turned into Tay Street and disappeared from view.

His over-riding thought was not of her appearance and the effort she had made for him. No, it was the intimacy of their conversation; the acceptance of his kiss on her cheek. As Harry walked back to the flat with a light step, the scent of her hair still lingered around him.

*

The house was silent as she let herself in. It was too early for James to be back from the football match and Frank would probably treat Emily to an evening out in Perth; and so Grace revelled in the idea that she had the place to herself for a change and set about removing the silk dress and make-up.

She had to laugh when she ended up looking like a panda, just as Beth always did, but with persistent reliance on cotton wool and Ponds Cream, Grace had the mascara removed at last, mentally consigning the little box to the waste bin.

The waste bin.

How odd that Harry should resort to raking in bins to glean information about Beth's activities; and how odd that Beth should be indulging in any that she wanted to conceal.

Grace dressed in an old skirt and cardigan and went downstairs to prepare the tea. As she worked, she would glance from time to time at the garden, although there was nothing to see apart from familiar bushes and flowerbeds, flowerbeds that James had pillaged for Lucy, trudging up and down to The Birches during August, digging, planting, spending hours with the woman, hours that Grace had found herself counting up. His efforts had amounted to seventy-five hours in one month, an astounding revelation to her the day she had sat with pencil and paper to work it out.

Now, in the silence of the kitchen, she paused in her labours and stood at the window. How many times had she stood here watching James tending to the garden; keeping an eye on her children as they played; watching the light alter from morning 'til night; posing for the inevitable photograph her mother always insisted on taking.

Grace moved from the window and resumed her preparations for the tea, surprised, as always, by the ache she suffered for past times.

She sat down for a moment on one of the chairs and lowered her head onto her hands. The effort she had made for Harry, the dress she had chosen so carefully, the make-up she had worn, and the audacity of some of her remarks to him were coming back to haunt her in the calm and normality of her kitchen.

She knew why she was doing it all, of course, and it was all made worse by her age, for she fully expected that her ambiguous feelings were a result of being almost fifty; but it was wrong, quite wrong, the way she was using the boy to take revenge on her own daughter, trying to supplant her in Harry's affections.

Grace gasped and jumped to her feet, standing stock-still, her mind abruptly rejecting the words, refusing their plea for a hearing.

*

Charlie and Beth had given up looking for a restaurant on the way down from Montrose and had driven back to Perth, where they were sitting in Charlie's villa on the Glasgow Road, eating fish and chips.

'What will Harry have been doing, with you working on a Saturday?'

'Legal stuff, I would imagine,' she smiled pleasantly.

'You mean he takes his work home?' Charlie asked, so incredulous that she stared at him.

'Of course he does. So do you, remember?'

'Yes, but I don't have a wife like you waiting for me.'

Beth threw him a tolerant glance, for it was no longer much of an issue between them: she had long since accepted that his advances were as much a part of their working day as the obligatory cup of coffee at ten o'clock and now neither of them put much store on such remarks. Her knees going wobbly at the sight of him, however, or her pulse racing if he happened to touch her hand, were not relegated to normality, and she had to fight the urge to tell him.

'Do you fancy a night cap?' he asked now and, this time, she did look at the clock.

'I suppose.'

'Good,' said Charlie rising to his feet and gathering up the greasy plates. 'I'll just pop them in the kitchen.'

'Mine's a whisky, if you've got any.'

'Malt, single or double, or Safeway's plonk?'

'Anything, as long as you don't put ice in it.'

'Did you have a good day?'

'Yes, it was fun.'

'I love old warehouses stuffed full of antiques.'

Beth laughed. 'Some of it hardly qualified as antique. Did you see the bicycle wheels?'

Charlie nodded. 'But they were nineteenth century.'

Beth shook her head. 'Who the hell would want them?'

Charlie shrugged. 'A hundred-year-old farmer with an old bike?'

They laughed, and Beth caught her breath: he was so easy to talk to; so easy to spend time with; maybe so easy to...

'What?' she heard Charlie ask.

'Nothing.' She glanced at the clock. 'I'd better go. My grandfather gets worried.'

'Of course,' Charlie said, the perfect gentleman. 'I'll walk you to your car.'

Beth gathered up her handbag and coat and walked to the door. Instinct made her pause. She glanced around, saw Charlie smiling at her.

'What's so funny?'

'I'd give my right arm to kiss you.'

Beth's pulse rate speeded up, giving rise to a faint blush in her cheeks; she wondered what harm it would do.

*

Harry sat in the study until after ten, perusing his finalised document for Daphne to sign. Even after speaking to David Routledge, he had found nothing that might be slipped surreptitiously into the thousands of words that would preclude Thomas Blake from falling heir to her fortune. How her husband – a drunk, she had implied – had ever succeeded in accumulating eighty thousand pounds in the fifties and sixties, Harry had no idea; but, had he had the good fortune to be a colleague of the said 'Mr Daphne', he would have hung on the man's every word.

Harry was pinning all his hopes on the note he had sent to her, anonymously, and the intensity of Grace's desire to have tea at the Isle of Skye.

He closed the file, removed his reading spectacles and rubbed his eyes. He had been so occupied with his work that the glass of gin and tonic sat untouched, ice long melted, at his elbow. He picked it up now and swigged it down in one, grimacing at the warm liquid.

In the kitchen, he refreshed the glass, adding more than a fair share of ice cubes and, as he was replacing the ice tray in the freezer compartment, he saw the results of Grace's labours on his behalf. He looked through the various dishes and selected an onion and mushroom quiche, popped it into the oven and set the timer for twenty minutes. She had labelled, fastidiously, each bag and box, with contents, shelf life, cooking times, even the position in the oven. He was filled with pity for her when he imagined the work involved on his behalf; especially when her daughter was causing so much heartache; and worse, considering how he had deceived her about Foxy. The more he thought of it, Harry considered himself to have been more unfaithful to Grace, than to Beth.

Unfaithful!

He gasped at the implication and slopped the gin and tonic all over his shirt; swore loud and long, not at the temporary damage to the shirt, but at the idea of...

He took a deep breath and gave the front of the shirt a perfunctory wipe with a kitchen towel, and then he swore loud and long again.

He knew that everything about his relationship with Grace was unwise. Not only was he using her to get back at Beth, but also, he was slackening the rein on his fantasy; beginning to regard it as reality.

Harry stood in the middle of the kitchen, trying to arrange his thoughts in some kind of order. He simply had to stop it; before things got out of hand.

Eventually, he went into the sitting room and turned on the television, to distract himself with the prospect of miners' strikes and every other kind of strike Edward Heath would have to contend with in the – presumably – short life of his government. It served him right, Harry decided, for foisting decimalisation on people; not to mention the Common Market.

As he sat looking at the screen but seeing nothing, Harry forced himself to admit that considering Grace in a romantic light was the most foolhardy thing he could ever do; something that could only lead to folly.

He had dozed off, for he woke suddenly at the sound of the doorbell ringing. Glancing at the clock, he knew it could only be Foxy at ten to mid-night and she was the one person he wanted to avoid tonight. Despite her considerable charms and how good she made him feel, his mind was focussed on Grace. It would be sheer folly to entertain Foxy tonight.

With a prepared speech in his mind, he ambled to the front door and unlocked it. It was not Foxy, however; it was Beth.

*

Charlie Webster sat for hours, drinking far too much and feeling sorry for himself. Rather than be elated that she had finally succumbed to his charms – well, partly anyway – he was utterly miserable at knowing now what he was missing. To have to work alongside her now, to see her every day and not be able to grab her, touch her any time he wanted, was the bleakest prospect he would face; not to mention the image of the husband doing just that.

He lolled in the armchair, one leg over the side, feeling quite sick. When he tried to stand, the nausea increased and he knew, with a horrible premonition, that the maid would be disgusted at him in the morning.

*

Beth stood looking at him, wondering why he was still up and dressed at midnight. Resisting the temptation to peer over his shoulder into the flat for signs she did not want to see, she kept her gaze firmly on his face.

'Beth, are you all right?'

'No.'

'D'you want to come in?'

'Dunno.'

She knew what had flashed across his mind: she had a degree in languages and could not even speak English.

'I'd like you to come in.'

'Are you sure?'

He smiled. 'You know I do.'

She shrugged, tried not to dive into his arms, and walked calmly across the threshold. As she passed him, she felt his hand on her wrist, inexplicably a gentle reminder to her that she had been such an idiot. When he might have yelled at her, called her names, told her to get out – and rightly so – here he was laying his hand on her wrist,

390

winding her fingers around his, forgiving her even before she had begged him to.

'I can't kiss you,' she said wearily. 'I've just kissed Charlie Webster.'

*

Harry was fair; he awarded himself that much. He could never have condemned her for sleeping with Webster when he had been frolicking with Foxy for the past few months. He knew before Beth told him that she had been unfaithful only once, for that was the kind of person she was: incapable of carrying on the deceit for longer than it took her to find him and confess.

'I don't care whether you've kissed King Kong,' he told her seriously. 'I still want to kiss you.'

He saw that she was too remorseful and too tired to laugh, but her eyes told him that she was grateful and would never hurt him again.

'I might ....' She hesitated, glancing towards the bathroom. 'I might freshen up, if that's O.K.?'

He released her hand and nodded. 'Help yourself. When you come out, I'll be waiting for you.'

Perhaps it was what he said, or the way he said it, but he knew that she was going to cry and he put his arms around her before the first tears fell.

*

She lay in the crook of his arm, sleeping soundly, but having bad dreams. He had to smile at the way he had dismissed her infidelity as if it were nothing more than running out of coffee because she had forgotten to add it to her list.

A few months ago, if she had come to him and admitted to allowing Webster anywhere near her, Harry would have gone berserk, shouted and yelled, chucked her out most probably. Not now, however, and not only because he had been pretty unscrupulous himself, but also because he had been so miserable without her. No; despite the irrational behaviour, the temper tantrums, and the petulance, the prospect of a Beth-less life had turned out to be fairly miserable.

He sighed quietly so as not to disturb her, but she moved and he sensed she was awake.

'Harry?' she whispered.

'Yes?'

'I didn't go the whole way with him.'

Harry's heart sank; and for the most idiotic reason.

'What?'

She squirmed her way to a position where she could look at him and gave him a smile that was both woeful and embarrassed.

'I was a bit naughty, I'll admit, but it was heavy petting, that was all. I found I couldn't, hurt you, I mean, even if you didn't know I was hurting you.'

He hugged her tightly, in case she saw the alarm in his eyes. Where once he had imagined that her behaviour would negate his own; where only an hour ago he had thought that it hardly mattered if she ever found out about Foxy, it had all gone wrong, was not working to plan, even if Foxy's alibi were full-proof.

'I never thought you would go all the way,' he lied as she snuggled closer.

'Didn't you?'

'Not for a minute.'

'Well, you're one up on me,' she giggled into his chest. 'Because I did.'

391

'You're not the unfaithful type,' he said, the words compounding his own guilt.

'That makes two of us then,' she said happily, settling down again and closing her eyes.

'It sure does,' Harry said, closing his eyes too, but for a very different reason.

As he turned over and prepared for sleep, his last thought was of Grace, and how Beth's return would spoil everything.

Chapter Twenty-Seven

Daphne sat with the letter in her hand, numbly staring at the words, having the greatest difficulty in understanding how someone could think they applied to her Thomas. There must be dozens of Thomas Blakes in Perthshire. It had to be one of them, surely; not hers.

She took off her spectacles, placed them in the case and snapped it shut. Lying in her hand, the letter was heavier than it had been five minutes previously but she continued to hold it, seeing some of the words and phrases that she knew off by heart and could have recited at a concert.

'never granted a divorce... bigamy... lucky to escape a jail sentence....' She opened the case with silver flowers embossed on the lid, removed the spectacles once more and unfolded the letter. It was obviously a mistake and she would consult nice Mr Gillespie as soon as his office was open for business. She trusted his judgement and was convinced that he would know exactly what to do.

*

Grace and Alice were in the throes of unpacking. The floor of Alice's new flat was littered with boxes and bags, crates and suitcases and, despite the fact they had worked for hours to clear everything and put it away, progress was slow.

'Is it only my imagination or have we achieved nothing in the past two hours?'

Grace laughed at her friend's question, for it had been on the tip of her tongue to ask the very same.

'Oh, come on, we've done half of it already.'

'What?' Alice shrieked, throwing a cushion at Grace. 'You mean there's another half like this?'

Grace grinned. 'Or perhaps we've done seven eighths,' she conceded.

'Now you're talking, honey, and it's time for a cuppa, that's for sure.'

'But you haven't unpacked the kettle,' Grace pointed out quickly.

'Ah,' Alice said, scratching her head and looking at the boxes. 'D'you know, I don't even have a clue as to where the darned thing might be.'

'We could always boil up a pot of water,' Grace suggested, but there was no enthusiasm in her voice.

'Ugh! It will taste foul. No, we'll go out to a café somewhere.'

Grace pretended to mull over the location of the flat in relation to cafés. She told Alice that she could think of no eatery within half a mile, apart from the Isle of Skye and that was a brisk walk away.

'So, what are we waiting for?'

Fifteen minutes later they were sitting in the lounge of the hotel with a tray of sandwiches, a 3-tiered column of cakes, and a pot of tea for two. Alice, who rarely bowed to the Scottish tradition of dressing to go out, was still clothed in her cleaning outfit – a pair of baggy Levis, an equally baggy T-shirt borrowed from Brad and never returned, and a bandana to keep her unruly hair from her eyes. Normally, she wore it tightly curled into a neat bun at the nape of her neck but today it was loose, fluffed around her head like a dark halo.

'I can stay the night if we haven't finished,' Grace offered now, as they ate the last of the sandwiches and eyed the half dozen cakes. 'I don't even need to phone James, he'll know.'

'We'll be finished, dearest pal,' Alice said, her mouth full of salmon sandwich.

'Besides, I don't have a bed for you anyway at the moment, or hadn't you noticed?'

'Do you have somewhere for yourself?' Grace asked mid-chew, suddenly failing to recall a bed that had been assembled for Alice.

'Yes, I'll be fine on the settee for one night.'

Grace was horrified. 'I can't let you sleep on a settee, Alice. You can come home with me for one night, and I'll bring you back in the morning.'

'Okay,' Alice said quickly, as if it had been in her mind all along. 'It's a deal,'

She had been choosing a fruit slice from the selection of cakes, but now raised her eyes to Grace's, whose gaze had been drawn to a couple who had just entered the lounge bar.

Alice glanced over her shoulder and discovered that Grace's attention was fixed upon an elderly couple: a tall, distinguished-looking man and his diminutive, elegantly dressed wife. They were going to sit by the window overlooking the main road, too occupied with each other to notice Grace and Alice.

When it became obvious that Grace could not tear her eyes away from the couple, Alice whispered nervously:

'Is it someone you know, honey?'

'Yes,' Grace replied without turning her head. 'It's my father.'

Alice almost choked on her sip of tea. She had never met the man, of course, had only befriended Grace in the forties, long after her father had deserted her; and, apart from the occasional oblique reference on Charlotte's part, Thomas Blake had evaporated into the mists of history.

'Do you want to speak to him?' Alice whispered and, at last, Grace moved her position to face her friend once more, turning her back to the couple.

'I might,' Grace said evenly, picking up her cup and drinking. 'It depends.'

'On what?'

Grace smiled. 'There's no need to whisper, Alice. They're miles away.'

Alice shrugged. 'I didn't know if you wanted him to see us or not.'

'I don't really care one way or the other.'

'Have you spoken to him since he came here?'

'Yes, once. I think I told him I never wanted to see him again, or something similar.'

'Oh, dear,' Alice grimaced, whispering again. 'I suppose that didn't go down too well?'

'I think Beth's staying with him.'

Alice's hand paused on the way to her mouth. She stared at her friend, for it was the first time Beth had been mentioned since Annie Kerr's funeral.

'Staying with him? What on earth do you mean? She lives with her husband, doesn't she?'

'Not recently,' Grace said dispassionately. 'She was angry that he didn't pass on Annie's message to her, thought that if she'd gone round to the flat, Annie might still be alive.'

'Heavens, that's a tad unfair,' Alice said scathingly, recalling Grace's account of the girl's problems. 'How can she blame poor Harry?'

'I think I might go and speak to him after all,' Grace told her friend. She swept the crumbs off her knee, rose to her feet and had walked off before Alice could stop her.

*

Thomas was having the worst of days: he had never known Daphne to be in such a sullen mood in the months they had stepped out together. It was such an uncomfortable experience that he had no idea how to deal with it. He could either ask her outright and risk being fobbed off with a lie, or he could weather the storm for however it lasted and console her when it was all over. He assumed, rightly or wrongly, that it had something to do with her finances. Perhaps the eighty thousand had dwindled to seventy nine thousand nine hundred and ninety nine.

He suppressed a smile and asked her politely what she would like.

'Just tea please,' she said impersonally. 'Nothing to eat, thank you.'

Briefly, he wondered if it were the menopause, for he had read something about it in a doctor's waiting room once; but Daphne must be sixty if she were a day, and he guessed that 'women's troubles' would be over by now.

He looked for the waitress and his heart lurched: he saw his daughter advancing towards him. Such was his shock that he stared at her, flummoxed for the first time in his life into a dumb silence. As she approached, he was flabbergasted at the smile on her face. Instantly, he suspected subterfuge.

'Grace,' he said, with false bonhomie. 'How lovely to see you again.'

*

Daphne glanced from one to the other and, utterly confused as to the identity of this lovely woman, was even more surprised when the stranger addressed her, not Thomas.

'Hello,' the woman said warmly, extending her hand to Daphne. 'You must be Mrs Blake?'

'Not yet,' Daphne blurted out before she caught sight of Thomas's face.

'This is my friend, Daphne,' Thomas said, his hand on Daphne's shoulder in a protective gesture. 'Daphne, this is my daughter, Grace.'

Daphne was astonished, for he had assured her there had been no children.

'Daughter?' she repeated stupidly, her hand resting limply in the woman's – Grace's, for she had a name now. 'I'd no idea that Thomas…'

'Well, to be honest,' Grace said pleasantly. 'It was all a long time ago and there's no hard feelings.'

Daphne threw Thomas a pleading look but he was staring at his daughter and it was the first time Daphne had seen him speechless.

'Perhaps we could go somewhere more private,' Thomas said to his daughter. 'There are things we need to discuss, Grace.'

'I said there were no hard feelings,' the woman smiled, glancing at Daphne. 'What happened in the 1920's is hardly relevant today.' Before either of them could respond, she gave Daphne a beaming smile. 'Oh, and congratulations on your forth-coming marriage. If only my mother had lived to see it, poor thing.'

Suddenly, Daphne remembered the anonymous note. Could it have been this woman who had sent it? Just as the daughter was turning to leave, Daphne jumped to her feet, face flushed, heart pounding and asked loudly:

'Was it you who wrote the note?'

Even in such a heightened state of emotion, Daphne could see that the woman was perplexed.

'The note?' she repeated slowly. 'I think you must have confused me with someone else. I haven't written any note.'

'Well, someone did,' Daphne protested feebly, sitting down again.

'What note?' Thomas asked angrily, his eyes darting from one woman to the other. 'You never said anything to me about a note, Daphne.'

The daughter, Grace, turned to Thomas and looked at him.

'I do apologise for mentioning my mother. I didn't intend to cause any trouble. She bore no grudge against you for deserting us, nor do I. I hope you'll both be very happy,' she concluded with apparent sincerity before she walked away. 'Oh,' she turned back, glanced at Thomas. 'Give my love to Beth. I do hope you're making her do some housework. She can be a lazy little madam at times.'

Daphne's heart was sinking, not so much at what the woman had said, but the way that Thomas was looking at her: if ever there was an admission of guilt on a man's face, she was privy to it at this moment.

*

Alice sat dejectedly, waiting for Grace to return to the table, her eyes flitting to and fro, from Grace to the couple, but particularly to Thomas Blake, who appeared the most perturbed. When, at last, her friend turned and made her way back to their table, Alice's own shoulders lowered six inches with relief. Heaven knows what the little old lady was thinking!

She greeted her friend with an anxious, 'Grace, dear, are you all right?'

'I'm perfectly fine,' Grace smiled and, to her friend's amazement, she did appear fine. 'How lucky, to meet him here today, especially with his intended.'

'But he's a...' Alice paused and reconsidered. 'No, of course he's not, since Charlotte's dead now.' Grace's raised eyebrows prompted Alice to add: 'Of course, the idea that he once was a bigamist might not be so attractive to the new bride.'

Grace nodded imperceptibly and picked up the pot of tea. 'I think this has gone cold. Shall I ask for a fresh pot, or would you like to go back to the flat now?

Weighing up the situation was made easier for Alice when she spotted Thomas Blake and his companion leave the hotel without glancing to left or right.

'Oh, I think we can have another one,' she smiled, at ease with the departure of the couple. 'And we can guzzle the cakes now to our hearts' content!'

Grace smiled, surveyed the cakes and pointed to an angel cake.

'I wouldn't mind the angel cake, unless you desperately want it?'

'Oh no, I much prefer the almond slice. I just love almonds.'

'Don't I remember?' Grace laughed, and Alice could see nothing in her friend's demeanour that reflected an adverse reaction to meeting her father in such odd circumstances.

*

Grace sat drinking tea and eating cakes, marvelling at her ability to remain so calm when all she wanted to do was rush out of the hotel, back home, to recover her strength after such a traumatic encounter. Despite the fact that it had not actually affected Alice, she, nevertheless, felt a tiny twinge of guilt at having deceived her friend by feigning innocence and suggesting they have tea in this particular hotel.

When it became clear that Alice was content to drink tea and eat cakes without asking questions, Grace began to suspect that her friend knew now that she had deliberately chosen the hotel. She prepared to tell the truth.

Once she had come to the end of her short speech, she looked at Alice.

'I'm sorry for not telling you they'd be here.'

'For Heaven's sake!' Alice laughed, dusting the icing sugar from her mouth. 'It's your business, not mine. I'm only sorry that I haven't been able to help in some way.' She grinned. 'I could have said I was his other daughter from South America. With my accent, she'd have believed me.'

'*He* might have believed you,' Grace joined in, the relief flooding in now, making her heady. 'I had him completely baffled.'

396

'What will he do now, do you think?'

'I have no idea. Nor do I care. I said what I wanted to say, especially the bit about Beth, and now it's over as far as I'm concerned.'

'I wonder if he'll tell Beth.'

'Oh, most likely,' Grace said wearily. 'And she'll have another reason to stick pins in my little voodoo doll.'

Alice shrieked with laughter. 'I love being with you, Grace, you're such great fun.' She must have seen her companion's scepticism, for she added, 'You are, you know. The trouble is, you seem to hold back most of the time.'

'Most of the time I'm worrying about all and sundry.'

'Come on,' Alice said cheerily, clattering the crockery as she piled it onto the tray. 'Let's go back to the flat, call it a day and go back to your place.'

'That, Alice Cameron, is the best idea you've had all day!'

*

Beth rushed around the house, stuffing her meagre belongings into the holdall, opening and closing cupboards and drawers to make sure she had not forgotten anything and would be obliged to come back for it. Once she had satisfied herself that she had missed nothing, she pulled off the bed sheets and pillow cases, stuck them in the washing machine – a new Hoover that her mother would have loved – filled up the powder container and switched it on. He would have to hang them out, of course, but she had explained how sorry she was in the note that was lying on the kitchen table, a note that had been so difficult to write; just the right balance between apology for leaving and gratitude for helping her out.

With a frantic glance at the clock, she unfastened the front door key from her key ring, laid it alongside the note on the kitchen table and fairly flew out of the house. A few minutes later, as she drove towards the Isle of Skye, she was horrified to see his car going in the opposite direction. Beth's heart flipped: he never came back before four o'clock! She had had a lucky escape.

Hands shaking for no apparent reason, she drove on, stopping at the red light at Bridgend. Something caught her attention: a silver Austin 1100 was sitting just in front of her and her heart pounded. It was her mother.

*

It was Alice who spotted her first, although Grace's powers of observation kicked in only a split-second later.

'Oh, look!' Alice cried, pointing needlessly, grabbing Grace's arm. 'It's Beth!'

'So it is,' Grace said tonelessly.

'I wonder what she's doing here?'

'She's living with him, remember? He lives in Kinnoull somewhere.'

'I think she's spotted you,' Alice said, her eyes on the wing mirror. 'She has, and she's trying to attract your attention.'

'She knows where I'll be,' Grace said bluntly. 'If she wants to see me, that is.'

'Oh, Grace,' Alice groaned. 'She's only a child, for Pete's sake. You're a grown woman. You should know better.'

Grace was stung by the censure, the first from Alice in all the years of their friendship. Silly, pointless tears sprang to her eyes.

'Oh, good, the light's green,' she said in reply, and moved off.

When Beth continued on the main road without lowering her speed, she knew that her daughter was heading to the village. After the strain of dealing with her father, pretending she was happy for him, maintaining a demeanour that betrayed her entire being, Grace could not face a confrontation with Beth. When they approached the village, she turned off and drove towards Lily Morris' house, despite a shocked exclamation from Alice.

'Grace! You can't!'

'I just did,' Grace murmured, trying to muster a smile. 'I need some peace and quiet, Alice. If you want, you can walk from here, no offence meant.'

'None taken,' Alice said sympathetically. 'I'll see you later.'

'Oh, and I'd be grateful if you didn't tell her where I was.'

'My lips are sealed,' Alice grinned as she stepped from the car. 'See you later, alligator.'

Grace gave her friend a brief wave as she strode off, suspecting, in her heart of hearts, that Alice would waste no time in telling Beth where she was.

Lily was sitting outside, coat and scarf on, thick gloves that a goalkeeper would envy. She glanced up at Grace's approach.

'Hello, stranger.'

'You know where I live,' Grace said wryly, sitting beside the old lady.

'Your legs are younger than mine.'

'They sure don't feel younger some days.'

'You've got the beginnings of an American accent now,' Lily frowned, as if it were despicable. 'You'll be calling me honey-pie soon.'

Grace had to laugh. Even these harmless barbs reminded her of her youth, when she would sit listening to her mother and Lily sparring with each other, bantering back and forth, wondering if she would ever have such fun with Molly. Time had shown she would not.

'You look wabbit,' Lily said, turning to give Grace a close scrutiny.

'I've been helping Alice move into her new flat.'

'So, she's staying then?'

'Yes, and I'm so glad.'

'Aye, and how's the family?'

'They're all fine. But how's your angina?'

'Och, I could drop dead tomorrow an' I wouldn't give a damn.'

'Well, I would,' Grace said firmly. 'I want you to be around when Frank and Emily have their first baby.'

Lily gave her a suspicious stare. 'Frank and Emily aren't even married yet.'

Grace shrugged. 'They will be, soon.'

'You don't think Beth will beat them to it?'

'She doesn't want children.'

'They all say that,' Lily said dismissively. 'Until their pals all start breeding like rabbits.'

'I came here for a bit of peace and quiet, Lily Morris, not to hear your latest moans.'

'Did she really say that?' Lily asked. 'That she didn't want children?'

'Not in so many words, but I know she's not keen.'

'And him, is he keen?'

'I have no idea. It's hardly the kind of thing you discuss with your son-in-law.'

'I doubt if you think of him as that,' Lily said unexpectedly, taking her friend by surprise.

'Of course I do,' Grace protested, pulse quickening. 'How else would I think of him?'

'More of a friend, I'd say.'

Grace picked up the disapproval in Lily's tone, and she was angry: rather than go home and face Beth, she had chosen to come here, to get her breath back, sit quietly, talk about inconsequential village events, and here she was, at the sharp end of Lily Morris' dissent.

'Oh,' Lily said suddenly, glancing down the path. 'Speaking of your lovely daughter, here she is.'

*

Beth marched up the path with a vigour that belied her nervousness. When she saw her mother's head swivel in her direction, saw the anguish on her face, the sadness in her eyes, even the dejected way she was slouched on the bench, Beth's heart turned over. Before she had reached the bench, she had burst into tears.

'Beth, darling,' she heard the voice say and then her mother's arms enfolded her and she wondered how she could have stayed away so long.

*

The telephone rang as they entered the house and, because Beth was so distraught, Grace picked it up, keeping a firm hold on her daughter.

'Grace, it's Harry, I've something to tell you.'

'She's here,' was all Grace said.

'Thank God,' he said. 'I'll leave you to it then. Tell her I'll see her later.'

Grace replaced the receiver, by which time Beth had recovered sufficiently to speak coherently.

'Was that Harry?'

'It was, and he says he'll see you later. Now, come on, there's a nice fire in the parlour, we can sit in there.'

'Good. I'm freezing,' Beth grimaced.

'I could say it has something to do with the flimsy thing you're wearing,' Grace said humorously. 'But I won't say a word.'

They went into the parlour and Grace threw heaps of coal on the fire, followed by some kindling to get it going. When it flared up after a few minutes she sat opposite her daughter, who was staring into the flames.

'Oh, Mum, I've been so... stupid.'

'Yes,' Grace smiled, about to steal Charlotte Blake's phrase. 'You certainly exceeded my interpretation of the word.'

Beth glanced across and laughed. 'That's a good one, never heard it before.'

'I have,' Grace said ruefully. 'And, just like you, I deserved it.'

'You don't mince your words, do you?'

'Should I?'

Beth shook her head slowly, her eyes fixed on Grace. 'Never.'

'That's fine then, because I'm about to do it again.'

'Can we not wait a bit?' Beth pleaded. 'Maybe have a cup of tea first?'

'If I drink any more tea today, I'll float.'

'A glass of whisky then?'

'What? At half past four on a Tuesday afternoon? Good idea!'

'Oh, Mum, I've missed you so much, more than Harry.'

Grace paused at the doorway. 'That's not very nice, dear.'

'Maybe not, but it's true. I could bear it if he never spoke to me again, but I could never bear it if it was you.'

399

Grace was torn between disapproval on Harry's behalf and gratitude on her own.

'Two whiskies coming up,' she smiled, for it was better to keep her daughter in a good mood, especially when she was going home to her husband to make up. Grace felt the jealousy well up, but she opened the door and walked quickly to the kitchen before it took hold.

'Here, I've put water in it,' she told Beth a few minutes later. 'No ice.'

'Good, I hate ice in it.'

'Do you have your suitcase in the car?'

'Mm. Not that I took much to his house.' Beth sighed, her features seeming to collapse before Grace's eyes. 'I'm so sorry, Mum, for screwing it all up'

'But you didn't.'

'What? Of course I did. Running off to take up with a man you hate and...'

'Wait a moment,' Grace said, her hand up. 'I don't hate him,' she lied. 'Not now, not after mulling things over. In fact, I was speaking to him only an hour ago.'

Beth stared at her mother, fingers clasping the glass so tightly that the knuckles were white. 'You were? Is that why you were in Perth?"

'Well, I was helping Alice too, of course.' Grace suddenly looked around. 'Where is she, by the way?'

'She went for a walk, said she'd give us half an hour on our own.'

'The daft thing. She'll be frozen stiff with only her baggy t-shirt on.'

'She took your anorak, don't worry. What did you and he talk about?'

'Drink up first, we'll have another,' Grace said and her daughter raised her eyebrows.

'Golly! Are you turning into an alcoholic?'

'No, but I rather enjoyed it, so I'll have another.'

Grace took their empty glasses to the kitchen and filled them up. She knew it was Dutch courage, as people termed it, but whatever it was she needed to gather her strength for the second time that day. She was about to tell her daughter the same pack of lies she had just spouted to Thomas Blake.

*

Harry heard her heels clicking on the stairs, and it was quite strange, that he should recognise them as Beth's, not Foxy's: different heels, different women. He had sent a hurried word to Foxy, left a message with her flat mate that he was George Porter, a business colleague and would be in touch sometime; their planned euphemism for ending it.

Briefly, his heart turned over at the thought of never seeing the girl again – at least not in his bed – but then he turned his mind to Beth and Grace, tried to work out what they might have said to each other. He would ask Beth later, but expected to hear half of it.

When she opened the door and he saw her face, he breathed a sigh of relief. She was happy and vibrant, the same old Beth; except she could never be the same old Beth again; and neither could he be the same old Harry; not after surviving only three days without sex and ending up with a complete stranger in his bed. At least Beth had lasted two months and at least she had picked someone she knew; and at least she had resisted full-fledged adultery.

Harry's reverie was thankfully cut off when Beth threw herself into his arms.

'Oh, I'm so happy!' she almost yelled in his ear. 'I'm so very, very happy!'

'Was it all right, between you and Grace?'

She drew back, looked at him with shining eyes, so sparkling in fact that, with something of a shock, he realised that she had been more concerned about falling out with her mother, not with him.

'Let's sit down,' she said cheerfully, dragging him towards the sitting room. 'I've lots to tell you.'

He noticed now that her breath smelt of whisky and he wondered if she had stopped off somewhere on the way home.

'Mum and I had two whiskies,' she told him over her shoulder, as if she had read his mind. 'Can you believe it? Mum guzzling whisky?'

Harry laughed, followed her into the room; but, whereas Beth seemed to think it was a matter of humour – her mother drinking whisky – Harry knew that only the prospect of a nerve-racking conversation would lead such a woman to seek courage from a bottle.

He listened, however, not interrupting, as she told him how her mother had made up with Thomas Blake, had met him and his new lady friend at the Isle of Skye hotel that afternoon and had wished them both well for the future. He heard of Beth's slight change of heart towards her grandfather, her growing disillusionment with the glittering lure of truth and how she had allowed her obsession with truth to drag her off the path. She also told him, with some tearful interludes, that she had been stupidly jealous of her mother and it was ridiculous. At last, when she was coming to an end, she gazed across at him and bit her lower lip. He braced himself for any eventuality.

'I told her about kissing Charlie Webster.'

'Goodness me,' laughed Harry, slightly relieved that the biting of the lower lip had signified only an introspective criticism. 'What did she say?'

'She said it wasn't important,' Beth said evasively and he suspected that Grace would have said much more than that. 'Anyway, she was great. I told her how much I'd missed her and that I'd never do such a thing again.'

'What, kissing Charlie Webster?'

'No, funny man, rushing off in the huff.'

He watched her, sympathising with her for baring her soul, first to Grace and now to him, for she had the courage to do it whilst he would harbour his guilty secrets forever.

'I think you're very brave,' he told her truthfully. 'You have more courage than anyone else I know.'

Except Grace

'Do I?'

'Yes.'

'But if I hadn't been so stupid in the first place, there'd be no need for me to be brave, would there?'

Harry smiled, shook his head at her logic. 'Don't short sell yourself, Beth. Courage is courage, whatever the circumstances.'

'I think I might look for another job.'

Caught unawares, he stared at her. 'What?'

Beth averted her eyes from his. 'I don't fancy working with him now, after...' –

'But you only kissed him,' Harry reminded her. 'I mean, you didn't...'

'No, I know, but it's awkward now.'

'It's your choice, Beth, but it doesn't bother me.'

Beth sighed, slid off the chair and across the floor to drape herself over his knees. He stroked her hair, wound his fingers around the strands.

'I'll never be able to make it up to you,' she said meekly and he twisted her head back, suddenly furious with himself for allowing her to think, even for a moment, that he was the victim.

'Ow!' she squealed, rubbing her head when he let go. 'What was that for?'

'I refuse to let you think it was all your fault,' he said harshly. 'It was my fault as well, and Grace's if you must know, and I won't listen to you taking the blame for everything.' Beth sat back on her heels, intrigued. 'So' he went on, moving his legs to encompass her body. 'There's to be no more of this self-pity after today. Understood?'

She nodded. 'But it was…'

'Sssht!' he said, finger to his lips. 'Any disobeying of direct orders will result in severe punishment.'

She giggled then, slid her hands onto his knees, worked them up his thighs.

'I like the sound of that,' she said wickedly. 'But I'm starving. Is there anything to eat in this place?'

'Grace brought a whole box of things she'd made, enough to last a month.'

He detected the tiniest flicker in her eyes at the mention of her mother, but then it was gone and she was grinning at him.

'Race you to the freezer then!'

*

Thomas sat in the darkness of the room until his head ached from hours of deliberations. He switched on the lamp closest to him and looked around. Although there had been nothing of hers in this room, he still felt her loss, and when, eventually, he could rouse himself long enough to empty the washing machine, he would be reminded all over again that she had been here once upon a time, but was gone now.

He supposed that he should be glad she had lived here at all, that she had chosen him over her family when things fell apart; but the truth was that he knew his daughter was bluffing and that her little bout of play-acting was nothing more than an attempt to scupper his chances with Daphne; which, indeed, it had; at least where an imminent marriage was concerned. The minutes they had sat in the car outside her house had been the longest and most unbearable Thomas could recall; apart from the hours after he had learnt of Charlotte's death. Nothing could compare to such tragic news.

Daphne had brought up the subject of the note first, but since Charlotte had died and Daphne knew nothing of Maria, the bigamy issue was quickly dealt with.

'You never told me you had a daughter,' Daphne had said then, as they sat in the car outside her house. 'You told me you'd no family.'

'I'd only just met you, Daphne,' he began, already planning his strategy. 'I had no idea that I would fall in love with you. How could I?' He turned to look at her, found the balance between pathos and sincerity. 'I loved Grace's mother fifty years ago. She refused to come with me when I left for South America, but promised she'd join me when our daughter was older. Why would I not believe her?' He waited, observing her discomfort. 'When I finally realised she'd had no intentions of coming out there, I was settled into an excellent job, with a good living. And,' he added, suddenly recalling. 'I sent money for Grace regularly, as any father would.'

He moved his gaze to the road and tapped his fingers on the steering wheel, but still she remained silent and he had to launch in again.

'I could show you her letters, if you like,' he offered, comforted by the certainty of refusal. 'Then you can see for yourself how often I begged her to join me. After ten years,' he turned to her, frowning. 'Yes, I waited ten years for her to make up her mind, and then she stopped writing altogether, never heard from her again. She even sent the money back, the money for Grace.'

It was true, of course, but that was only a consequence of his pleading poverty in his final letters. 'I think it's extremely unfair of you, Daphne, to blame me for any of this, but if you never want to see me again, well, I won't hold it against you. In fact, I would wish you good luck and every happiness.'

He sat back in the seat, drained of energy, feeling the perspiration seeping through his shirt to his jacket. When he looked at her again, taking his time, pretending to be unconcerned, she was gazing at him with the old adoration, and he knew he had earned himself a respite.

Now, as he mulled over the postponed marriage, he could at least console himself with her final words.

'Of course I want to see you again, Thomas, but it's been a bit of a shock, all things considered. Perhaps we should postpone the wedding, just for a few months, until spring maybe?'

He had given her a patient and gracious smile, of which he had an inexhaustible supply.

'I think that's the best idea,' he had agreed, noting her anxiety when he jumped at the suggestion with alacrity. 'Let things settle a bit, see each other occasionally. Now, my dear, you'll excuse me, I really must get back.'

Thomas smiled to himself when he recalled the excellence of his modus operandi: she would fall at his feet long before spring and, if she were lucky, he might just be around to catch her.

*

Grace and Alice took turns in telling the story of Beth's return to James, who was obviously content to have his wife and daughter back on speaking terms. He nodded and smiled, without butting in, although he must have been tempted on more than one occasion, and finally, when the tale had been told, he leaned forward and patted Grace's knee.

'You've been so brave,' he told her. 'I don't know anyone as brave as you, Grace.'

Grace was consumed with guilt, for her 'bravery' had extended only as far as telling so many lies in one day that she needed extraordinary courage to recall each one. She had omitted the parts about pretending to be reconciled to her father when she had 'bumped into him' at the hotel, and the fact that he had been about to marry again and how she had well and truly scotched that particular path. Alice was a fellow conspirator, for they had discussed it at length after Beth's tearful departure.

'So, I can tell him you met your father accidentally, had a pleasant conversation?' Alice had asked, a worried frown across her forehead. 'But I can't tell him that you were only pretending to make up?'

'That's it,' Grace had said, racked with shame that she was putting her best friend through this charade. 'Nor should we let on about him getting married again, although we can say he was with someone.'

At last, Alice had been word-perfect, but now, as they sat with James, it was clear to Grace that her friend was exhausted.

'I think you should go and have a lie-down, Alice,' she told her. 'I'll give you a call when it's suppertime.'

Alice complied, her weary smile of gratitude lingering in Grace's mind long after she had gone upstairs.

'I'm so glad for you, Grace,' she heard James say. 'It's so heartbreaking, for a mother and daughter to disagree.'

'Well, it's all over now,' she heard herself say brusquely. 'Is there anything special you'd like for supper?'

'Whatever's easiest for you,' he said kindly, and she was reminded of his recent consideration to her and wondered again what had evoked it.

'I'll go and see what there is,' she smiled, rising to her feet and moving away. 'I

403

think there's some steak pie left from last night, unless you ate it at lunch time?'

'It's still there,' James said jocularly. 'Although it took a lot of will power not to eat it!'

As she worked in the tranquillity of the kitchen, a thousand images and words bustled around her mind, jostling for position, trying to attract her attention. She sat down heavily on the nearest chair and put her head in her hands. What had she achieved? Because of her intransigent, though heart-breaking, stance, she had her daughter back in the fold, displaying a more circumspect attitude about her grandfather; also, by her word-perfect acting performance, her father's bluster had been quelled, plus any idea he might have had about wreaking revenge; but, in the wake of it all, as she sat weighing things up in her mind, all Grace could think of, the most rewarding result of her dishonesty and deceit was that Beth's change of heart had resulted in the saving of her marriage, thereby allowing Grace to keep the boy within her family circle; in other words, to keep Harry Gillespie close by.

She raised her head, looked at her hands, seeing them in a different light: the lines etched by years of washing and ironing, dusting and polishing, cleaning out coal fires and gathering kindling; familiar, easy things. She lowered her hands and prepared to stand up. There were things to do and she wanted nothing more than to turn her mind to the mundane.

Chapter Twenty-Eight

Harry hesitated outside Sandra's office door. He was aware that she had known of his liaison with Foxy and that it was over now, his wife having been safely gathered in. Sandra had ceased to mention her great niece, not even in the passing, as she had occasionally done before the dinner party. Her name was often on Harry's lips, but he had the impression that it was not to be discussed. The strange thing was it could never have worked out, even if Beth had never come back; and so one morning, a few days before Grace's birthday, Harry knocked at Sandra's door and went in, making up his mind to ask, nonchalantly, how Foxy was.

'Oh, she's fine,' Sandra smiled, looking for a paperclip in her drawer. 'In fact, she was asking for you just the other day.'

'I hope you told her I was missing her,' Harry said boldly, at which Sandra shook her head.

'I wouldn't dare,' she smiled, giving up on the search for a paperclip and closing the drawer with a thud. 'But I think she misses you.'

'She's quite a girl,' Harry said, suddenly realising that he wanted to talk about it to someone who understood the situation. 'Why did you introduce us?'

She blinked at him several times, as if the question were ridiculous.

'Why? Well, because your wife had gone off and I thought you'd be lonely.'

'And I would have been,' he confirmed, regarding her with interest. 'But why Foxy? Was it just because she was committed to someone else?'

'Not just *someone else*,' Sandra responded, eyebrows raised. 'And don't pretend not to know, Harry, because she told you, I know she did.'

'Yes, she did, but I often wondered ....' He recalled Foxy's enthusiasm in bed and could never reconcile it with her being a lesbian. Somehow, he had always assumed that they hated men, and yet she had more than matched his passion in matters of lust.

'Oh, she's had a few boyfriends as well,' Sandra said casually, as if she discussed such sexual issues every day. 'And that's precisely why I thought she'd be perfect for you.' She gave him a mischievous smile. 'Let's face it, if your wife ever found out, she'd look pretty silly standing up in court accusing Foxy of adultery, for Foxy would take Mike with her and profess her undying love for another girl. Not much cause for divorce there, I should think.'

'Mike?' Harry asked, a sudden, ridiculous stab of jealousy flashing across his chest.

'Yes, Michelle to you and me,' Sandra smiled. 'A gorgeous girl too, quite wasted, although I shouldn't say that, Foxy would kill me.' She stood for a moment looking at him, seemingly weighing up her next sentence, and then she shrugged and grinned.

'But I think you'll agree, it was the perfect arrangement.'

'It was indeed,' he nodded, sensing, as she turned to her typewriter, that the chat was at an end.

However, once he was back in his own office, attempting to get some work done, Harry was unable to rid his mind of Foxy's presence in his bed, or the tenderness they had shared in the aftermath of their energetic sexual romps. It was crazy, but he missed her.

*

Beth was experiencing difficulty in persuading Charlie Webster that she should look for another job but would stay on until he found a replacement. His reaction, as she anticipated, was one of bafflement.

'But why? I thought you were happy here.'

'I am, but it's not right.'

She was sitting on the edge of her desk, her knees fairly close to his as he perched beside her, imitating her, dispensing with the formality of chairs, but stopping short of kicking his shoes off.

'But nothing happened, Beth, not really.'

'How can you say that?' she frowned. 'If you hadn't been a gentleman, I dread to think what might have happened.'

'Hey, less of the 'dread',' he joked. 'You'd think sleeping with me was a fate worse than death.'

She threw him an apologetic smile. 'You know what I mean.'

'I can't,' he said suddenly, looking at her despairingly. 'I can't let you go. I mean, from the job, not seeing you every day. It's unthinkable.'

'Seeing you every day is more unthinkable,' Beth said ruefully, glad that it was out in the open, now that they had both confessed attraction for each other and moved on to more practical matters. 'I was lucky that Harry was understanding, but he wouldn't be another time, nor would I expect him to be.'

'He just welcomed you back like that?' Charlie asked with a click of his fingers.

'Yes, just like that. Even I was…'

'Even you were…?'

'If he'd been the one that had been canoodling with someone else, I'd have murdered him and then chucked his dead body in the Tay.'

'If you don't mind my saying so, he struck me as the fiercely jealous type.'

Beth smiled, shook her head, although it had been her own opinion until the night he had opened forgiving arms to her.

'He's not, you know,' she lied convincingly. 'He's older, of course, as he keeps reminding me.'

'What does being older have to do with going berserk every time a man letches after your wife?'

'Older means wiser,' Beth quipped, sliding from the desk and locating her shoes. 'He's got more experience than I have.'

'I think he's a Saint,' Charlie said, remaining on the desk, following her progress round the room with his eyes. 'I'd have made you suffer first.'

'Oh, he made me suffer,' Beth frowned. 'Have you never read the bit in the Bible? Being nice to someone who's done the dirty on you is akin to heaping coals of fire on their head?' She shrugged, coloured slightly. 'Something along those lines anyway.'

'You mean because he was nice to you, it made you feel worse?'

'Now you're getting the hang of it. But, to get back to the job…'

'Please, Beth, don't go,' Charlie pleaded. 'I promise I'll never even touch you.'

She hesitated, but not for the reason he was imagining: she was envisioning a lifetime of never being touched by Charlie Webster and it was not a happy prospect.

*

Alice's hair was streaked with white emulsion paint when Grace knocked and went into the flat.

'You have more paint on your hair than on the walls,' she laughed. 'For goodness' sake, woman, can you not wear a head square?'

'Couldn't find one,' Alice grinned. 'Besides, it's almost finished now, only the hall to do. Come in, the kettle's on and it'll be the first break for me today.'

Grace was amazed to see the transformation in the place: the furniture was set out to best advantage, whereas she often looked around her own living room and thought it was more like a storeroom; and the curtains, made by Gillies in Broughty Ferry, hung so beautifully that the room could have been worthy of a scene in a Hollywood film.

Grace gazed around and wondered if it would galvanise her into improving her own house. Inwardly she suspected not.

'By the way,' Alice called from the kitchen. 'Have you decided what you're wearing to your birthday bash?'

'Yes, the red thing I wore to Beth's celebration.'

Alice popped her head round the living room door. 'Let's buy new ones.'

'Not just for one night out,' Grace said firmly. 'The red dress is fine.'

'Well, I know it's 'fine',' her friend laughed, before disappearing back into the kitchen. 'But, as I told you years ago, you'd look 'fine' in a tatty sack.'

Grace rose and meandered to the kitchen, a long narrow room with a small window facing east and black and white squared linoleum on the floor, scuffed and scratched over the years, not only from shoes but also from dog claws. She recognised the kind of marks that little Mirk had delighted in making.

'What are you wearing?' she asked Alice, who was in the throes of removing cream cakes from the baker's box and laying them on a plate.

'Oh, I'm buying something new, especially for such an auspicious occasion.'

'What's auspicious about another birthday, I'd like to know.'

'Come off it,' Alice scolded. 'You know you don't look a day over thirty, Grace Blake.'

'Neither do you.'

'Maybe not,' her friend shrugged, licking the cream from her fingers. 'But my figure's kinda lost the will to live.' She pushed her stomach. 'See that spare tyre? I could use that on a car if I had one.'

'There's hardly anything there,' Grace protested. 'You still turn heads when we go out.'

'Sure, but that's because I run down the street stark naked. Now will you stop blethering and take this tray through.'

They sat amid the smell of fresh paint, drinking the tea and covering themselves with icing sugar and cream.

'Aren't these messy?' Alice laughed as they both surveyed the white dusting on their skirts. 'But, boy, aren't they delicious? Have you noticed that life's like that?'

'What, messy?'

'Something that's bad for you feels really good,' Alice remarked, her smile fading. 'Brad was bad for me but, oh my, did he feel good.' She glanced across at Grace suddenly. 'You were lucky, you know, only loving James, never having the agony of...' She stopped, pressing her lips together. 'I'm sorry now that I ever looked twice at Brad.'

'But think of the joy you shared together,' Grace reminded her. 'You wouldn't have wanted to miss that, surely?'

'Straight up?' Alice asked in her peculiarly American style.

'Yes.'

'I wish I'd stayed with Martin and never run off with Brad.'

Grace's pity for her friend was tempered by the memory of Alice's letters, the explicit and shocking description of her sex life with Brad; words and phrases that Grace could never even have uttered, far less written.

'Did Martin marry again?'

'Not that I know of,' Alice replied, eyes twinkling. 'Maybe I'll write to him, make a proposition.'

'But then you'd go back there,' Grace bemoaned, the dreadful idea dawning that she had only just rekindled her friendship with Alice and now she was might be contemplating leaving again.

'Oh, no,' Alice frowned. 'He'd have to come over here.' She studied her cup for a moment. 'He might, you know, he just might.'

'Wasn't he happy in America?'

'Not a bit, although it had been his idea to go there. And I suppose I was only too happy to escape from this place.' She threw her friend an apologetic glance. 'I didn't mean you were a fool to stay, Grace. I only meant...'

Grace laughed. 'I know, but now you're back.'

'And I love it,' grinned Alice, leaning back in her seat and laying a hand on her abdomen. 'Apart from the cream cakes and squashy stuff, that is.'

'You bought them, may I remind you?'

'No, you may not. Now, where were we? Oh, yes, buying something new for the birthday bash.'

'I'll come with you but I won't be buying anything.'

Alice smiled a tolerant smile and Grace saw her good intentions flying out of the window.

*

The last day in September started bright and cold but by mid-day, the sun had forsaken the world, at least in east Perthshire, and the weather took a turn for the worse: hard, driving rain slanting past the windows, chipping away at the panes. Beside the front door, where James had planted a clump of delphiniums, an hour's relentless rain was sufficient to flatten them, rendering them to an embarrassed, bedraggled state when once they had stood tall and regal.

'Look at that,' he complained to Grace as he looked out for the hundredth time. 'After such a good summer, you'd think we might have a decent autumn.'

'It's only one day,' Grace told him from the bottom of the stairs. 'By this time tomorrow things will be back to normal.' She knew from experience that the poor delphiniums would never again be normal; not from their supine position. It was her birthday, however, and Grace intended to keep cheerful all day.

'You feel on top of the world,' her horoscope had informed her. 'Today's the day for forging ahead with those special projects that are dear to your heart.'

She had shaken her head at such nonsense, but acknowledged her stupidity at reading it in the first place. Any horoscope, however paltry, drew her like a magnet to its meaningless forecast, and she blamed Beth for having read them out every day, Aquarius, Libra and Taurus – Beth, Grace and James. Frank, the Capricorn, had been left out, of course, as his sister rarely had time for him.

'I'll have to go up to The Birches and stake up the lupines,' she heard James say.

Grace paused on her way into the parlour and retraced her steps.

'What, just now?'

'Yes, just now,' James repeated briskly, taking his raincoat off the peg in the hall and throwing it round his shoulders. 'I won't be long, back in twenty minutes.'

With that, he opened the front door, gave her a cursory backward glance and dashed out.

She stood for a few minutes where she was – halfway between the living room and the parlour – mulling over his reason for thinking of Lucy Webster's lupines and dashing out so readily in such atrocious weather.

The telephone rang and she jumped.

'Good afternoon, my dear,' said Molly gaily. 'Happy birthday and many of them.'

'Thanks for the card, it was very funny,' Grace said, although she had thought it somewhat juvenile. 'It's on the mantelshelf with the others, right in the middle.'

'I should co-co,' Molly laughed. 'Actually, I was just wondering about the time of the birthday party of the year. Did you say half past seven at the hotel?'

'Yes, half eight, as Grandpa would have said.'

'Oh, and wasn't it a bloody nuisance? The number of times I was left standing at a bus stop because I'd mistaken the time. Honestly, I'm glad the old folks have gone and we can talk sense.'

Grace was never glad that her mother had gone, or her grandfather for that matter, but now was not the time to make a point; not on her birthday.

'Are you bringing Lily Morris?' she asked Molly.

'Yes, and Maureen, Lily's pal and Catriona as well. Catriona's pregnant again, did you know?'

It was said with some degree of smugness, perhaps to remind Grace that Beth, who had married long before Sally's daughter, was still childless. It occurred to her that Molly should have been more concerned about her own offspring who were neither married nor showing any sign of settling down; not that it seemed to matter these days, whether you had children within holy matrimony or not.

'Will I wear something long?' Molly was asking now.

'Wear what you like,' Grace responded, for it was always the inevitable question with Molly.

'Are you wearing something long?'

'Not long, but not short either.'

'Thanks,' Molly said sarcastically. 'That's a lot of help. Did Alice buy a new frock then? She said she was going to.'

'You know Alice. Of course she did, and it's gorgeous. She'll easily be the belle of the ball.'

She could not resist it, the brief dig at her supposedly best friend, and she was filled with the usual horror after the words were out. The trouble was that some folk seemed to ask for it, and Molly was one of them.

'Oh, well, in that case, should I bother coming at all?'

'Come on, be nice to me on my birthday,' Grace cajoled. 'It doesn't happen every day, you know, hitting forty something.'

'I hit it a year ago, but thanks for not reminding me, dear. Well, must get on. See you at the hotel at seven thirty. Be good, and if you can't be good, be careful!'

Grace hung the receiver back on the hook and stood for a while trying to imagine how on earth she and Molly had ever remained friends. How often had James and Beth and Lily Morris – and Alice come to think of it – declared their opposition to the friendship on the grounds that Molly's personality was utterly incompatible with Grace's; and how often had she disagreed?

Now, however, celebrating yet another birthday, she was just beginning to suspect that her family and friends had been right all along and that the similarities that had held two teenagers together had diverged over the years, Grace being the last to notice.

'Have you seen my blue shirt?' she heard her son ask from the top of the stairs.

'It's in the basket, needing ironed,' she told him, remembering that she had put it off until later, so that she could soak for an extra half hour in her morning bath. 'I'll just go and do it now, Frank.'

'I can do it,' he called to her, thudding down the stairs in his jeans and old sweater, the one she had knitted for him on the machine.

'Emily says she wants me domesticated when we get hitched,' he laughed as he flew past her.

'Hitching is what Clydesdales do, dear,' Grace said automatically, following her son into the kitchen. 'But you're too young to remember that. Give me the shirt, I'll do it.'

Frank kept it close to him. 'No, I'll do it. It's your birthday, Mum, and I want you to be happy all day.'

Grace never failed to be amazed at the unexpected affection that her son would often reveal. Somehow, she had assumed that boys of his age, growing up in the sixties – a liberal, free-for-all – would die of shame if they were caught being considerate to their mothers; yet Frank had none of these inhibitions. Occasionally, she wondered if she had done anything to deserve such affection.

'Frank, dearest, the only thing that will make me unhappy today is if you don't let me iron that shirt.'

She stood looking at him, hands held out in front of her, with a determination he would be hard pressed to match. He smiled, proffered the shirt and gave her a very brief hug before walking away.

'You're the best,' he said over his shoulder.

'And you,' she returned, but he had disappeared upstairs.

*

Harry walked along by the Inch, round the corner under the bridge, past the Station Hotel, his umbrella hoisted, shoes squelching, spirits flagging. He had used the pretext of black shoe polish to leave the flat and get some fresh air. He had no idea why he was so despondent: it was Grace's birthday party later on and he was looking forward to seeing her again, perhaps even dancing with her, something he had never done before. Each time he thought of it, he made no attempt to dismiss the image.

He splashed through puddles outside the Queen's Hotel, paused for a moment whilst he glanced around and then, closing the umbrella, he walked into the foyer.

She was there already, stretched out on a leather settee, reading a drip mat. When she saw him, she jumped up, wiggled her fingers at him, face filled with delight; the same old Foxy, not setting his heart aflame as Beth did, but instantly stirring his loins.

'Hi!' she said before he reached her. 'You look great.'

'Ah, it must be true what they say about appearances then.'

Foxy turned her mouth down at the corners. 'Tut, tut, who's Mr Grumpy today?'

Harry sat down beside her, laid his arm across the back of the settee and looked at her closely. Her eyes shifted momentarily from his, but then she grinned and gave him a peck on the cheek.

'Can I do that in public?'

'With your alibi? I should think so.'

Her smile faded and she took his hand, looked at it for a few moments and then laid it gently on his knee.

'You're not Mr Grumpy,' she said, her gaze wandering over his face. 'You're Mr Sad. Are you missing me?'

'You know I am.'

'D'you want me to say I'm missing you?' she asked, with more honesty than he might have wished.

'I suppose so.'

'I do miss you,' Foxy admitted but he suspected it was lip service. 'But only in bed. You sure can show a girl a good time, as your wife will testify.'

'Not enough to keep her,' Harry reminded her. 'She wandered off, remember?'

'Was she unfaithful?'

'Partly,' Harry told her, for he knew she was completely trustworthy.

'Partly?' she laughed. 'I dread to think…'

'She kissed and canoodled, that was all.'

'She told you that?' Foxy asked, astounded. 'Bloody Hell! She must really love you.'

'How does that follow?'

'I'd never tell Mike about you and me. She'd go nuts.'

'But that's because she hasn't been unfaithful to you, I presume.'

Foxy pouted. 'You're right, of course, she hasn't. You must have felt guilty then, forgave your wife straight away?'

'Something like that.'

'And are you happy now that she's back?'

'Yes, I truly am.'

'So how come you look like a wet week?'

Harry laughed. 'Haven't heard that one before. I don't know really, why I look like a wet week. Maybe it's my age.'

Foxy grinned. 'The menopause?'

'Probably.'

'Did you want to see me to cheer yourself up?'

'No,' Harry smiled wryly. 'Seeing you will do just the opposite.'

'Do you think you love me?' she suddenly asked, her eyes on him.

'I might.'

She was taken by surprise, sat speechless for a long while; and then, with her hand coming to rest on his shoulder, she sighed and lowered her eyes.

'I'm so fond of you, Harry,' she whispered, her mouth close to his ear. 'In fact, if I'd met you before Mike I'd want you for myself at this moment.'

To be the recipient of such frankness, despite being married to someone who shared similar principles, was refreshing, not to mention a boost to his ego, for he rarely found himself ousted in matters of romance; Mike was a first, and she was a bloody girl.

'I was wondering if you and I could still be friends,' he said now, trying to keep any sign of pleading from his tone.

'Well, of course,' Foxy frowned, touching his shoulder with a long finger, tracing the seam of his jacket, then along the collar. 'I never thought for one minute that we wouldn't remain friends. In fact,' she winked at him, smile spreading, and he knew she was about to say something to shock him, hoped he had guessed right. 'I was just wondering if we could meet occasionally, have a chat, maybe carry on where we left off?'

His heart skipped a beat, for it had been on his mind for days now; but he had not been confident of her agreeing; and now here she was, suggesting the very thing he most wanted. He had hesitated too long, however, and she took his silence for refusal.

'I didn't think you would,' she said quickly, averting her eyes.

'But I do,' Harry assured her, grabbing the hand that was traversing his collar and making him forget where he was. 'Not for a chat, though.'

Foxy hunched her shoulders with glee. 'Oh, great!' An instant later, however, and she was frowning again. 'But I forgot. Your wife doesn't live in Edinburgh.'

'What's that got to with it?'

'Mike's only here at weekends, makes it easy for me, but…' She stopped, gazed at him, her eyes asking questions.

'I'll think of something,' Harry smiled. 'I could always join a macramé class at the College.'

Foxy burst into a peal of laughter, drawing the bartender's attention.

'I'm sorry,' she whispered, glancing furtively at the man and then back to Harry.

411

'That's the trouble with having a big mouth.'

'There's nothing wrong with your mouth, in fact I can't keep my eyes off it.'

'You know,' she said in lowered tones. 'I could give you one right now.'

'And I wouldn't say 'no'.'

She grimaced, looked at her watch. 'Mike arrives at half past two; I'd only have an hour. Besides, where would we go?'

Harry knew exactly where they would go.

'I'll be back in a jiffy,' he told her, and then he went to find the public telephone to make two calls: one to Sandra; the second to his wife.

*

Thomas had ringed the date on the calendar, the date of his daughter's birthday. He sat now sipping coffee in the lounge, his eyes on the calendar, trying to figure out what kind of celebration she would have. He had already phoned three local hotels pretending he was a guest and had forgotten which hotel was hosting the party; but without success, The number of the only other hotel – and it was less salubrious – was at his elbow, in case he wanted to make sure before scoring it off his list without calling.

What would he do anyway if he found where she was going? He would make a fool of himself, barging in, complaining he was her father and should be on the guest list; then, most probably, he would be arrested for breach of the peace and that was hardly the image he wanted to present when he was trying to salvage his marriage plans with Daphne.

It had been over a week since they had met; over a week since she had promised to contact him in a few days. Thomas was determined not to pick up the telephone and let her think he was desperate. That would be the last thing he would do. The trouble was, a woman like Daphne was easy meat – had he not scooped her up after a ten-minute chat in the street? – and he knew that she was in countless organisations and on dozens of committees, meeting more men in a week than he took hot dinners. One thought consoled him, however: not all of them would be eligible; but the longer the silence from her, the more he worried. He was, after all, relying on her little fortune to keep him comfortable in his old age.

When the telephone in the hall rang, he leaped to his feet, almost spilling the coffee, charging from the room like an idiot. With trepidation, he raised the receiver to his ear.

It was Daphne and she was quite miserable.

*

Beth was in the middle of Chopin's Prelude in C when the telephone rang, and she had no intention of cutting the piece short. However, when the ringing persisted and she found it impossible to concentrate, she slammed her hands down on the keys in a gesture of frustration and marched into the hallway.

'Yes?' she snapped.

'It's me,' Harry said, sounding far off. 'Look, I bumped into Sandra on the way back and her heating boiler's gone wonky. Would you hate me if I went and helped her out, sweetheart?'

'No, of course not, O Knight in Shining Armour. I'm busy with Chopin anyhow, so don't rush back.'

'I won't be longer than an hour,' he said, even more distant, as if he were an extra in 'Quatermass and the Pit'. 'Can I bring anything home?'

'Only the usual bits,' Beth laughed. 'The ones I sometimes like to play with.'

412

She thought it was funny, that he might laugh at it, but when he remained silent she assumed he had not heard.

'So I'll see you about half three then,' he told her, before hanging up.

'Suit yourself,' she muttered into the purring mouthpiece. 'Don't mind me.'

As she sauntered back towards the sitting room, she glanced at the closed door of his study, regarding it for a few minutes, even trying the door, finding it was off the catch. It was ridiculous that she should consider herself a spy in her own house!

Beth pushed the door open, surveyed the room from the threshold: desk, grand Captain's chair, small filing cabinet, waste basket and a few screwed-up balls of paper on the floor when his aim misfired. She tiptoed across the room, leaving the door wide open, and picked up one of the balls of paper.

Feeling like the worst snooping wife who ever snooped, she gently untangled it, spreading it out flat on the desk and peering at the words. It was a café receipt, for two coffees and two bacon rolls, but it was the grimiest café in Perth and she had never set foot in the place; and, as far as she was aware, neither had Harry.

'Oh, for Heaven's sake!' she expostulated, furious at herself in the wake of her lustful encounter with Charlie Webster. 'Go and do something useful, you nosey parker!'

Twenty minutes later, however, as the last note of the Prelude faded away to merge with the air in the room, Beth sat on the piano stool looking into space, pondering the grimy café bill and finding it impossible to clear it from her mind.

'Bloody hell,' she grumbled as she stood up and closed the piano lid. 'You'll be looking for lipstick on his collar next.'

She glanced at the clock: almost half past three and he would be back soon. She knew she could hardly ask him outright about the bill, but she could ferret away discreetly; just to keep him on his toes.

*

Alice and Grace were in hysterics. Sitting with his book downstairs, James, heard the two of them giggling and squealing, suffered an ambivalent reaction, for he knew he should be glad to hear his wife so joyful on her birthday, but there was something unseemly about an elderly woman squealing like a teenager and he could not dismiss it from his mind.

He was dreading having to dress up like a penguin within the hour; having to sit listening to idle gossip all evening, not to mention being the object of censure when he refused to dance. For as long as he could remember, Grace had been fond of dancing, and her determination to go to Saturday dances in Perth had almost ended their relationship. Before they were married she had gone without him, surrounded by friends that were equally engrossed in silly activities, coming home at all hours, people had told him, with no regard for etiquette and decorum. Once they were married, of course, she had stayed at home, as he expected; a wife and mother; no longer a girl.

He loved her though, and regardless of what she did, that would never change. He liked to remember the first night he saw her: standing on the stage in the village hall, singing like an angel, dressed like one too, and it was this image that he carried in his heart for years to follow; the image that he conjured up when he was tempted to criticise her. Thanks to Harry Gillespie, James had been thinking more of the advantages of his marriage than the drawbacks. He had been heartened to hear the boy's opinion – and him an outsider too, not swayed by local gossip – that Grace was so obviously in love with her husband. It had been a turning point in James's deliberations.

Now, as he listened to a further outburst of hysterical laughter from upstairs, James buried his nose deeper in his book and counted the minutes he had left before he would be obliged to pretend he was someone else.

*

Alice lay on the bed, holding her sides, breathless, her face contorted with mirth.

'Stop it!' she gasped, tears streaming from her eyes. 'Stop it before I die!'

'Stop what?' Grace asked, her jaw aching from so much laughter.

'Oh, help me sit up, I can't move! I'm like a beetle on its back!'

Grace dragged her friend to a sitting position and they sat side by side on Grace's bed, too weak to speak, handkerchiefs dabbing at their eyes.

A few minutes later, Alice was the first to recover her breath.

'It's so cruel, not to tell him,' she said, trying to keep her face straight. 'He'll never forgive you, you know.'

'Yes, he will, as soon as she sweeps him into her arms, he'll be transported.'

'To a loony bin?' Alice shrieked, starting all over again.

'Control yourself, woman. We've to be dressed and on our way in less than an hour.'

Alice shook her head and stuffed the damp handkerchief up her sleeve.

'Ugh! My hanky's soaking, thanks to you and your nonsense.' She darted her friend a sidelong glance. 'Seriously, Grace, do you not think it fairer to tell him Lucy will be there?'

'Why should I? It's my birthday, my party, my decision who comes or gets left out.' Grace rose from the bed and took the new dress from its hanger. 'No, I want to see him forced to change his mind about dancing, that's what I want for my birthday present.'

Despite the hilarity they had shared at James's expense, Alice was not convinced.

'But he'll suspect you were trying to trap him all along,' she cautioned. 'Let's face it, honey, he might turn her down as well.'

'Do you want to put some money on it?'

'What, that new-fangled decimal stuff I can't understand?'

'How about a pound? A pound says he'll get up and dance with her when she asks him.'

'I've never known you to be so devious, Grace Blake,' Alice said accusingly. 'I thought the two of you were love-birds again.'

Grace laughed. 'James will always be a love-bird in bed, but it's the rest of the time...'

'He loves you like crazy and you know it.'

'True,' Grace confessed reluctantly, holding the new dress against her, trying to imagine it on, flowing and floating like a purple stream. 'But love is more than bed, isn't it?'

'Is it?' Alice asked mischievously. 'I never found it to be so.'

'But you're a nymphomaniac.'

'What's that?' Alice asked in horror. 'Sounds like a creepy-crawly!'

'Yes, creepy crawling all over a man in bed.'

'You must have been a fly on my wall,' Alice chortled. 'Oh, boy, do I miss all that creepy crawling lark.' She paused suddenly, her head on one side, eyes misty. 'I wonder what young people do?'

As always, Grace felt a sudden blow in the solar plexus at the idea of her daughter and Harry Gillespie in bed together, an image that she constantly had to force to the back of her mind, an image that often taunted her in the middle of the night when she lay awake, sleep eluding her.

'You should ask your sons,' she said casually. 'Or, I could ask Frank.'

414

Alice was aghast. 'What? You don't mean to tell me that Frank's doing it?'

'Aren't they all nowadays?'

'Hark at us,' Alice remonstrated, slapping her friend on the back. 'Wash your mouth out with soap and get ready to hit the town!'

After Alice had gone downstairs to have a quick bath, Grace wandered around the bedroom, wasting time, thinking things over, wondering if she had been reckless in keeping it from James. What would he say and do when he discovered that Lucy Webster had been invited without his knowledge? She shook her head at her reflection in the mirror. What had got into her, doing such a silly thing?

*

Beth knocked on the bathroom door, convinced that Harry had fallen asleep in the bath, as usual. He had hardly said a word to her as he hurtled through the front door and rushed past her; other than a comment on the boiler.

'Boiler was filthy, I'm filthy, must get washed.'

'Be my gue...' she had started to say but he had already disappeared into the bathroom, coat, shoes and all and closed the door. Beth had shrugged and gone into the bedroom to lay out her outfit for the evening.

Now, as she pounded on the door for a third time, she was becoming irritated by the silence from within.

'Have you disappeared down the plug-hole, Gillespie?'

'No,' he replied finally, and she could tell that he had been asleep in there. 'I'm out, getting dried. Pour out a gin and tonic, there's a good girl.'

Beth grumbled and groaned as she raked in the kitchen for glasses and tonic, glancing every so often at the clock, counting down the minutes to their departure for Dundee and suspecting that they would be late again. She dropped ice cubes into his gin and tonic and went back to the bathroom, glass in hand.

'Here's your...'

The door opened and Harry smiled, his eyes on the glass.

'Thanks, sweetheart, you're an angel.' With that, the door closed again and Beth was left standing in the hallway like an idiot.

'What did your last slave die of?' she shouted at him before stomping to the bedroom and slamming the door shut.

*

Harry was grateful that he had run the bath so hot that the mirrors were steamed up. It meant he could avoid looking at his reflection and seeing what a rat he was. In fact, 'rat' was far too kind a term for what he was doing.

He drank down the gin and tonic in one, placed the glass on the shelf on the cabinet and cleaned out the bath, attempting to swish away his guilt with the bath water, to purge himself of the sense of betrayal. Had it been worth it, the subterfuge, the conniving with Sandra – an innocent if willing participant – the feverish and futile attempt to satisfy something that would never be satisfied because he doubted he knew what he wanted?

He sat naked on the edge of the bathtub and wondered how he could have been so stupid. He had a good job; he had a beautiful and talented wife who may be impulsive and unstable but whom he loved nevertheless; he had been accepted into Grace Blake's family, even by James; he was respected by his colleagues, peers, clients, all and sundry... What the hell was happening to him; why the fervent compulsion to throw it all away?

Had it been Beth's flouncing off in the huff to live with her grandfather that had disturbed the equilibrium, muddied the waters, thrown a cat among the pigeons; whatever the figure of speech? Or was it his self-centred quest to put Grace's welfare above his wife's – to let Beth know in no uncertain terms that she was second best – that had sent the girl fleeing to someone who put her at the top of his list?

Harry heard her crashing around the bedroom, throwing things around, being the spoilt child, expecting him to give her a tolerant smile, pat her on the head and tell her it was all better now. He sighed, began to dry himself, and as he stood up, he caught sight of his reflection in the slowly-clearing mirror. He was shocked by the expression in his eyes, terrified at the thought of having to go out and pretend things were normal, to act as if he were the happiest, jolliest man on earth; to be someone else.

Amidst his mental contortions, though, he found something to smile about: if Grace Blake could do it – and he knew she did it most of the time – then he would join her on the stage, play any part that he could think of; except the one that was true to life.

Harry brushed the shoulders of his suit jacket with the valet brush and looked at himself in the hall mirror. The sexes apart, it could have been his mother standing there, He had inherited her looks, her posture, her arrogant assumption that the world owed her a living. Harry smiled. For a few hours he might abandon the pretence of being the kind, considerate, tolerant, unselfish man they thought he was – particularly Beth – and be himself, a chip off the old block, as they said.

'Golly, you look fabulous,' he heard Beth say from the bedroom door. 'Wow! I'll have to keep my eye on you tonight.'

He turned and looked at her, resolved to begin the metamorphosis right away. 'You think that would be enough, keeping your eye on me?'

Her face fell, the smile vanishing, the eyes reproachful; but he had chosen his role and he would not back out now.

'I was just meaning you look so good that women will fancy you,' she said sullenly, her head dropping. Any other time he would have laughed, pretended it was a joke, gone to her, given her a hug. This time, however, it was impossible: his mother would never have grovelled to anyone.

'We're late already,' he said on his way to the door. 'Time to go.'

'You go to the car,' Beth said sullenly. 'I've forgotten something.'

*

Beth sat in the car, utterly dejected. It was her mother's birthday celebration and, had she envisaged a more dismal start to an evening, she would never have come up with this. She glanced at Harry, gauging his mood, but he was staring straight ahead at the road, still saying nothing. The last words he had uttered had been 'Time to go' and that was half an hour ago.

Her heart was aching, spirits flagging, at the thought of the evening being spoilt, for it would take a miracle for him to cheer up now, whatever had upset him. Was it her fault? Was this his reaction, albeit delayed, to her choosing to go and stay with her grandfather, turning her back on him and his precious Grace? Was he paying her back for the slight to her mother?

She tried to think of something to say; but then she remembered who and what she was and her fiery nature and pride rose up to meet the challenge. If it was a fight Harry Gillespie wanted, then she would give him a run for his money.

Surreptitiously, she opened her handbag, found Charlie Webster's number tucked in the front pocket. Her pulse quickened as she imagined him turning up unexpectedly.

Suddenly, she had a bout of panic: had she made a mistake phoning him at the last minute?

*

Harry's mind was on Grace. Even whilst he had been with Foxy, his thoughts had clung to an image of Grace. He had no idea why he was taking it all so calmly: perhaps he was too shocked, too outraged at his own desires for the full implications to have sunk in; perhaps his brain would snap into action any moment and drag him into safer, less shameful territory.

He became aware of Beth beside him; sensed her anger. Usually, he would have patched things up by now, to banish her sulky mood and ensure a pleasant evening. Tonight, however, it was the least of his concerns. Blaming him for Annie Kerr's suicide; her consequent flight to her grandfather – a man she knew her mother hated; and then her assumption that she could just walk back into the house and let bygones be bygones.

Harry's mind was made up: until now, he had held himself in check with Grace, partly to appease Beth and avoid confrontation; but tonight he would say and do as he pleased; and to Hell with them all.

Chapter Twenty-Nine

Grace and Alice were in the ladies' room, although it was Alice who was preening herself at the mirror whilst her friend leaned against the sink and watched the proceedings. Alice seemed in no hurry to finish her make-up and Grace was beginning to fret, for time was marching on. Her own make-up was, as usual, limited to a smear of lipstick and a fluff of powder on the end of her nose to stop it shining. Alice, however, with her cream foundation, eyeliner and mascara and more than a smear of red lipstick, had an appearance that would have graced the cover of Vogue.

'You look lovely,' Grace smiled at Alice's reflection. 'Just like a model.'

'Whilst you, Miss Can't-Be-Bothered, look like something the cat dragged in?' Alice asked sarcastically.

'I sincerely hope not.'

'You don't seem to need all this stuff I plaster on my face,' Alice went on in the same vein. 'Look at your bloody complexion, Grace Blake! It's so smooth I could murder you!'

'Good old soap and water,' Grace grinned. 'You can't beat it.'

'Do you know how many bottles and potions I have in my cabinet? Dozens, that's how many. Cleansing creams, astringents, eye gels to keep the bags at bay.' She sighed and placed the last of her make-up tools in her bag. 'And all the time you tell me I should be using soap and water. Well I never!'

'That's not what you told me up in the bedroom,' Grace whispered.

'And don't think to blackmail me either, Madam,' Alice whispered back. 'Or else I'll tell James why you invited Mrs Landed Gentry along.'

Grace laughed and took a last look at herself in the mirror.

'Come on, Miss Pennsylvania 1948, let's go and trip the light fantastic.'

As they opened the ladies' room door, however, they met Beth rushing in.

'Hi!' she said, gently obstructing her mother's path and pushing her back into the ladies' room. 'Don't tell me you're going out into the ballroom looking like that?'

'Like what?' Grace asked, glancing Alice, who shrugged and winked, thereby admitting complicity. 'Is that why you were taking so long in there, waiting for Beth to turn up?'

'Would I do such a thing?'

Beth took her mother's arm, and the make-up bag Alice handed her, and stood Grace against the sinks. A few other women were coming and going, but Beth paid no notice, even ignoring one of them who muttered under her breath that some people took up the whole place.

'Right,' she said, brushes and jars at the ready. 'Now we'll get to work. Dad will never recognise you.'

'He'll be too busy anyway,' Grace said, before she could stop herself, receiving a wary glance from Alice.

'Too busy doing what?' Beth wanted to know.

'Trying to look as if he's enjoying himself.'

'Mum, don't be nasty. You know he does his best, now stand still, please!'

*

Harry stood at the bar waiting for the barmaid to complete the order. She kept smiling at him, even fluttering her lashes at him occasionally, and now she was giving him the benefit of her ample bosom as she leaned over to take the five-pound note he was offering.

'I've never seen you in here before,' she told him as she handed him the change. 'Are you staying in the hotel?'

'No, just a birthday party.'

'Your wife's?' she asked, eyes wide.

'No,' Harry smiled, lifting the tray and moving off.

He made his way to the table where Molly and Lily were sitting, but as he set the tray of drinks down, he saw Molly waving across the room to someone.

'Oh, good, it's Frank and Emily, and Catriona as well. Over here!'

Harry and Lily exchanged glances and he saw the irritation in her eyes. He knew her well enough to know that there was little love lost between her and Molly, especially since Sally – one of Grace's friends from the '30s – had been forced to accept an invitation to sit at the same table as the harlot who had seduced her man; albeit the situation had calmed down.

'Your sherry, Lily,' he said, sitting down opposite her. 'Here's to you and me.'

'You know, I can't think of a better toast,' she said without humour, but he suspected she was joking. 'To you and me, Harry,' she said, using his Christian name for the first time, albeit avoiding his gaze. 'Lovely,' she pronounced at the first sip, retaining the glass in her hand. 'Just the way I like it.'

'And how is that?'

'Free,' she said with a straight face.

'James paid for this round.'

'Aye, he would. He's not Scots either.'

'Oh, come off it, I've never found them to be mean.'

'You obviously don't know that many,' she frowned and he gave up, often the best way with Lily Morris, but she was preparing to speak again and he resigned himself to a list of Scotsmen's shortcomings. 'Grace deserved better.'

'What?'

'He treats her like a serf.'

Harry did his best to keep the satisfaction from his face. 'Are you sure?'

'Oh, aye. She never had a life, poor soul.' Lily lowered her voice. 'He might as well have tied her to the back gate, for all the freedom she got.'

'When she was young, you mean?'

'Aye, and even now.' Lily sipped her sherry. 'She needs a good friend, and I've a feeling you could fit the bill.'

Around him, Harry was aware of the others greeting and chatting loudly, as if they were insulted that he and Lily were ignoring them, but his eyes and ears were attuned to the old lady sitting across from him, for she had known Grace all her life and he was desperate to learn everything about her.

'James seems like a decent man,' he felt obliged to say, riven with doubt now that he should have blurted out a blatant lie to the man about the state of his marriage.

'Oh, he's very feasible,' Lily said, regarding her empty glass. 'But I've known him for nearly thirty years and you certainly wouldn't want to have his character.'

'Wouldn't I?'

Lily smiled and raised her glass. 'Another wee sherry and I'll tell you more.'

Harry had to laugh. As he stood up to go back to the bar, he wondered if she had ever said anything to make anyone else laugh, for she was a dour, old woman.

He caught the barmaid's attention – not difficult, since she had noted his progress to the bar – and as he ordered a sherry and another gin and tonic for himself, he saw Grace walking towards him. He knew immediately that she was the only woman that he could not live without.

Setting modesty aside for a brief moment, Grace surmised that Alice's intake of breath was the result of Beth's makeup skills. For a split second, she gave way to self-indulgence and enjoyed the admiration.

'Golly, you look stunning,' Alice whispered in her ear. 'Let's have a drink and get down to serious partying.'

'Good idea,' Grace forced herself to say, stepping forward again, closing in on Harry.

'Grace,' he said, unusually making no attempt to include Alice. 'You look lovely.' He raised her fingers to his lips, kissed them lightly, and then, with something of a begrudging sigh, turned to Alice.

'Alice, nice to see you again.'

'I spent three hours on my hair and make-up,' Alice laughed. 'And all you can say is 'nice to see you'. Honestly!' she feigned indignation, although Grace had an inkling that her friend was hardly pleased. 'Why did I bother?'

'What's your poison?' Harry asked Grace and she had the first sign that he and Beth had been arguing, for his mood was aggressive, more arrogant, much less considerate. He was not even interested in the censure his attitude might provoke.

'I think I'll have a Martini,' she told him, her eyes trying to convey disapproval. 'And Alice will have a dry Martini, please,' she added meaningfully, but he appeared not to notice.

'Right, one Martini, one dry,' he repeated. 'I'll bring them over.' His hand waved in the direction of their table. 'We're over there.'

Grace's heart sank at the way he was behaving. It took her back to a time when she had walked on thin ice with James, trodden so carefully, eyes focussed on him so earnestly, that she had often stumbled and lost her way. Her love for him had been tempered by his lack of respect for her. Grace took a deep breath: what was she thinking of, maligning her husband in such a way? She could hardly respond when Alice spoke to her.

'Shall we go and sit beside them?'

She and Alice moved over to greet the others and Grace was happy for the distraction of friends and family and their numerous good wishes, for it gave her time to compose herself, to dismiss the sudden onslaught of unworthy thoughts about her husband.

*

Beth sat beside Catriona, listening to the amusing anecdotes of a nursery school assistant, wondering if it was a profession she, herself, could have taken up; until she heard the catalogue of disgusting, off-putting traits of four-year-olds.

'You don't mean they walk around with runny noses?' she asked now as Catriona related tales of unimaginable horror.

'Oh, yes, in fact, if we didn't stop them and blow their little noses, they'd wipe them on anything that was handy.'

'Yuk!'

Catriona laughed and lit a cigarette, whilst Beth threw her father a swift apologetic smile in advance of the smoke that would, inevitably, drift his way.

'Ah, but they're lovely some of the time,' Catriona said, eyes misty, which embarrassed Beth: children were not her favourite topic to start with, far less the mushy, rosy-coloured, totally unrealistic ramblings she was about to hear. 'You know, one of them is so sweet that I could take her home with me, a little darling she is.'

'But you're going to have another of your own pretty soon, aren't you?' Beth asked, discreetly avoiding her friend's stomach.

'Not until March. Lots of time to work yet.'

'Gosh, it must be strange, having kids in tow.'

'I can hardly wait for this one,' Catriona grinned. 'The first one was so easy, popped out like a cork.'

Beth found the whole idea repulsive, but, for her friend's sake, she amended her next sentence.

'She's a little darling, although it's ages since I've seen her.'

'You know, her Dad's utterly besotted with her,' Catriona smiled, and Beth had a horrible premonition that she would be assaulted by baby babble all night.

'It's a pity he can't be here tonight,' was all she said, but her eyes were roaming the room in the hope of catching her mother's eye.

'It is a pity,' Catriona agreed. 'But we're grateful for any homers he can get. Anyway, as it's another girl, he'll be ecstatic.'

'How d'you know it's a girl?'

'Lily Morris told me.'

'How can she know?'

Catriona shrugged and drew on the cigarette. 'She says it has something to do with my weight, how much and where it goes on at the beginning.'

'Sounds like witchcraft to me,' Beth whispered behind her hand. 'Anyway, I'm happy if you're happy.'

'When are you and Harry planning to get started?'

Beth hesitated and Catriona gave her a close look. 'What?'

'What do you mean 'what'?'

'You froze when I mentioned you getting started. Aren't you keen?'

'He and I had an argument before we came out tonight, so I reckon we won't be starting any time soon.'

'Oh, we have them all the time,' Catriona said brightly. 'I love the bit where we make up though,' she added with a grin. 'It was one of those bits that gave me this,' she indicated the miniscule bump. 'So, watch out when you make up.'

'No fear of that,' Beth said angrily, but quietly, lest he should hear, although, as usual, he seemed to have eyes and ears only for her mother. 'I've never seen him as spiteful as he was today when he came home.'

'Really? Where had he been then?'

'I haven't a clue. Some woman's boiler was wonky, he said, had to go and fix it.'

As she spoke, she did not miss the flicker of interest in her friend's eyes; but what she thought she saw was so frightening that she did not have the courage to ask. Instead, she picked up her glass and tapped it on the table, to attract Harry's attention. When he looked across at her, she smiled and waggled the glass at him. To her immense relief, he nodded and stood up.

'Two of these, please,' she called. 'One for me, one for Cat.'

'Should you be drinking?' Lily Morris interposed before Harry could respond. 'And, come to that, you should definitely not be smoking.'

'I'm stopping them both tomorrow,' Catriona told her, face serious.

'Aye, well make sure you do,' Lily frowned. 'Otherwise, you'll give birth to the hunchback of Notre Dame.'

Beth and Catriona did their best to keep their faces straight, Catriona perhaps because she knew that Lily was one of her mother's best friends from years back, and

Beth because she was trying to decipher the expression on her husband's face as he looked at her. She had no idea whether he was in a good mood or not, whether he would take her in his arms whenever the music struck up, or whether he would continue to ignore her all night.

It was one of the most disconcerting looks he had ever given her.

*

When Lucy Webster walked towards the table, Grace saw that everyone was surprised, not only James. He glanced at Grace briefly, before turning to welcome Lucy, and in that split second, she knew that he suspected foul play. Strangely enough, what with Harry's behaviour being so out of character and her own irrational ill-feeling towards James, Grace was too occupied with her own thoughts to worry about what her husband might be thinking.

'Grace,' Lucy said warmly, apparently unaware of the lull in conversation. 'How lovely you look, and happy birthday, my dear.' She handed Grace a small package, so small that, in Grace's experience, it had to be expensive; and then she turned to James, held out her hand and told him it was good to see him again.

'I had no idea that Grace had invited you,' he said, without looking at Grace. 'But I'm so glad you're here. Please, sit down beside me, Beth will move up.'

'No, not at all,' Lucy said swiftly, moving round to Grace's side of the table. 'Perhaps Lily can move up, let me on the end here?'

'Oh, aye, don't mind me,' Lily pretended to grumble. 'You realise that there's not enough men to go round, now that you've turned up?' She smiled at Lucy. 'Could you not have brought your handsome son with you?'

'I think he's...' Lucy stopped, looked at Beth with some trepidation.

'Think he's what?' Lily asked, also turning to Beth.

'I invited him,' Beth said, mostly to Grace. 'I hope you don't mind, Mum.'

'No, darling, why should I? As Lily says, we're short of men.' She smiled at her daughter, determined not to take sides again, even with Harry, for that route had led only to disaster, sending her daughter into the conniving arms of Thomas Blake. This time she would be more circumspect.

Just then the band assembled at the far end of the room and, with a tiny pang of guilt, Grace wondered if James would dance with Lucy Webster, if she would win her bet with Alice; and then she castigated herself for being so un-charitable. She turned to speak to Frank and Emily, broaching the subject of their wedding the following year and prepared to do social penance for half an hour.

*

On any other similar occasion, Harry would have had no reservations about maintaining the joie de vivre that had so characterised his previous demeanour. He saw it now, the way he had continually pandered to Beth, to her friends, even to Grace's friends; suppressing his innate personality that, unleashed, was so akin to his mother's. Now that the equilibrium of his life had been disturbed by one small ripple in the pond, it seemed to him that he was entitled to look on it as a turning point, an opportunity to escape the stifling constraints of politeness and etiquette, as his mother had done; even with her son, whom she adored.

Even now, standing at the bar drinking a quick gin and tonic while the girl poured out another two Martinis and two sherries, Harry could well recall the numerous barbs directed towards him from a Rachel Gillespie in the throes of inexplicable rage.

422

'Excuse me,' he heard someone say and he turned to find himself face to face with Catriona. She sidled closer, standing beside him at the bar and preparing to speak.

'About that boiler you had to fix today,' she said quietly, talking to his reflection behind the optics.

'What about it?' Harry asked, not in the least perturbed.

'A friendly word of warning,' she whispered. 'I think Beth suspects something.'

Harry looked at her, realising from the way she shrank from him that his gaze must have been formidable.

'And what makes you think I give a damn about what Beth suspects?'

He had the satisfaction of seeing her swallow several times, perturbed, unsettled by the strength of his response, and then she left him there, to scurry back to the table, back to tell tales, no doubt, with no thought for the misery they might cause; as only women could.

The barmaid took the money he handed her – again, it was from James's pocket – and raised her eyebrows at him, determined, he guessed, to test him as far as possible before he told her to push off.

'Was that your wife?'

'No.'

'Is she the one with the blonde hair?'

'They both have blonde hair,' Harry smiled, putting the change on the tray.

'You have two wives?' the girl laughed, encouraged by his smile.

'Not exactly. One's the mother-in-law.'

'Phew!' she breathed, looking in the direction of the table. 'I'd be hard-pressed to say which is which from this distance.'

'Oh, it isn't any easier up close,' Harry smiled, turning away.

'Can you tell one from the other?' she asked now, an element of mischief in her voice, but to say what was on the tip of his tongue was a step too far, even for Harry.

He set the drinks in front of each of the women and then sat down, dragging his chair halfway round the table, to the great inconvenience of others, even pushing Lily's out of the way.

'I think I'll sit here for a while,' he told Grace, stretching across the table for his gin and tonic, although he had consumed three at the bar this past hour. 'Do you mind?'

'What on earth has got into you tonight, Harry?' Grace asked him quietly.

'Nothing. Why?'

'Have you had an argument with Beth?'

'Not one that sticks in my mind,' he smiled. Catriona was nowhere in sight, nor was Beth, and he presumed that they were tittle-tattling in the ladies room. He reached over, picked up Catriona's cigarette packet and took one out.

'You don't smoke.'

'I do now.'

He could almost hear Grace holding her breath. 'Why now?' she asked.

'My mother smoked. Black Cat or something they were called.' He turned to her, seeing the joke. 'Quite appropriate, don't you think, considering they belong to a black Cat?'

Grace was regarding him with curiosity, but he saw no fear or apprehension in her eyes. It was just as he suspected: she had come to accept, without question, Harry Gillespie's ways; despite what she might say.

'Care to dance, since Beth's nowhere in sight?' he asked nonchalantly.

'Aren't you going to smoke your cigarette?'

'It can wait.'

Grace shrugged. 'In that case, considering my daughter's nowhere in sight and I don't mind playing second fiddle, I would like to dance.'

They stood up and he took her arm and led her onto the dance floor. It was a waltz and he was a good dancer, but the feel of her in his arms was not conducive to concentrating on what his feet were doing.

*

Lucy's eyes followed Grace and her son-in-law around the dance floor. She was tempted to ask James to dance but there was such a thing as decorum, even in these days, and she preferred to wait until she was asked.

'Perhaps you would like to dance?' she heard him say, and was surprised at Alice's expression, a mixture of disbelief and satisfaction.

'Yes, I'd be happy to,' Lucy smiled, her pulse racing like a schoolgirl and her mind trying to clamp down on ridiculous images.

She allowed him to lead the way, meandering between tables and chairs, and then he turned to face her, holding out his arms, waiting for her to take his hand. Lucy laid her other hand on his shoulder and, as they moved off in time to the music, she had a sudden ghastly thought that she would bore him with her conversation.

'Your dress is most elegant,' he said, although he was staring past her, perhaps at his wife. 'I always think you have such a good taste in clothes.'

'I can never decide what to wear.'

'Ah, but all women are the same,' James smiled. 'Grace must be the worst.'

'She looks absolutely lovely.'

'The night I first met her, she was wearing a green dress. She looked like an angel.'

'Have you lived here long?' Lucy asked, despairing of ever thinking of a sensible question.

'I moved up here when I was a boy.'

'Really? I'd no idea.'

'I lived with relatives.'

'I see.'

'Joined the 51st Highland Division and fought in France.'

'And you met Grace after the War?'

'Yes, she was only twenty.'

'How romantic, that you met her by chance.'

'I often wonder how it would be, if I had never come here.'

'Have you been home since the War?' she asked, an innocuous enough question she imagined and yet James stopped dancing, stared at her with an expression of disbelief, not showing the slightest sign of apology when other couples bumped into them.

'You said 'home'.'

She was flustered. 'Well, yes, I suppose I...'

'You understand that England's my home?'

'Of course it's your home,' Lucy repeated, at a loss. 'Are you annoyed that I said so?'

James shook his head and smiled at her, taking up the steps of the waltz once more, holding her tightly, moving them on.

'No, I'm surprised, that's all. People never seem to understand that this isn't my home.'

'But you like it here?'

'Grace is here,' he said simply. 'My daughter and son are here. Where else would I be?'

'And have you been back?'

'Yes, once, in the late '50's.'

'But you would love to go again?'

She noticed the flicker of a frown, assumed she was wrong, but then he nodded. 'Yes, I would like to go again.'

'Then you must,' she said firmly, looking up at him, meeting his gaze. 'Life is too short not to do the things you want to do.'

The music was coming to an end, although she knew the band would strike up immediately with another waltz.

'And you, Lucy, is there anything you want to do?'

'Yes,' she told him, throwing caution to the wind. 'I'd like to marry again, have a man around the house. I miss the companionship.'

He smiled at that and she hoped she had worded it correctly; that he would know she was lonely.

'Ah, I think we'll sit down now, continue our conversation?'

Lucy nodded. As he led her from the dance floor, she felt his hand on her wrist and imagined how good it would be to have James Melville around the house.

*

Beth lingered in the foyer until he arrived. Whenever she saw him, she rushed forward, grabbing his arm and apologising profusely for the late invite.

'It doesn't matter,' Charlie said, squeezing her hand. 'I was at a loose end, glad of somewhere to go, especially as mother was invited,' he added, raising one eyebrow.

'Well, she's Mum's friend, isn't she? Come on, let's dance, find some excitement.'

'Hey, steady on,' Charlie said, pausing in their traverse of the foyer and looking at her closely. 'What's up?

'Harry's being a pig and I'm not speaking to him,' she told him truthfully, for there was no other way. 'I asked you here to keep me company because he's ignoring me completely and I'm miserable.'

Charlie laughed and continued walking towards the function suite.

'As long as I know what's what, then I'm happy to oblige.' He stopped again, so suddenly that she almost tripped. 'Wait a minute, will he bop me one if I dance with you?'

'No, he won't even notice.'

'Are you sure about that? However,' he added, walking on once more. 'You're my best pal and what are pals for?'

'Precisely,' Beth affirmed, but the idea of Charlie Webster being a pal was slightly depressing.

As they entered the room, she automatically searched for Harry and her mother: if she located one, the other was sure to be alongside.

*

Grace had been foolish enough to close her eyes. The resulting image had been so vivid that she stumbled.

'You missed your step,' she heard Harry say.

'I'm sleepy with the food and drink.'

'You've only had two Martinis and you hardly ate a thing.'

'Are you keeping a tally?' she asked abruptly and his hand tightened around her waist.

'Absolutely. Someone should.'

425

'Someone does. James does,' she said pointedly, trying to wriggle her fingers free of his hand, for he was grasping them too tightly.

'He looks preoccupied with Lucy Webster at this moment,' he said, thinking, perhaps to annoy her.

In spite of herself, she smiled broadly, and he looked confused.

'What's so funny?'

'I won a bet with Alice.'

'I'm almost afraid to ask.'

'I bet that James would dance with Lucy.' He said nothing but she sensed that he smiled. 'I won five pounds.'

'And I suppose you'll spend it on others.'

'Not necessarily,' she frowned, but she knew he was right. 'I might treat myself to a day out.'

Harry burst out laughing, held her closer, much to her consternation.

'You won't go far on a fiver, sweetpea.'

The affection in his voice caused Grace's heart to skip a beat. She lost her footing, felt his arm supporting her.

'What's wrong?'

'I don't like being called sweetpea,' she managed to say.

'It's harmless enough.'

'I think I'd like to sit down now,' Grace told him, her feet halting.

'The tune's almost finished now anyway,' he said, looking down at her with merriment in his eyes. 'And it's one of my favourites, 'Smoke Gets in your Eyes.' What harm will it do to finish the dance?'

To Grace's horror, she blushed. 'None, I suppose.'

'The scent of your hair drives me mad.'

'For Heaven's sake!' Grace whispered, glancing across at James who was dancing only feet away with Lucy. 'Stop this nonsense, Harry. What on earth's got into you this evening?'

Harry smiled broadly and took her arm, led her from the dance floor. As they eased their way between the many couples making their way back to tables, it was Grace who spotted Charlie Webster and her daughter. She averted her eyes, lest Harry should be interested enough to look in the same direction, but it was too late: he tapped her arm.

'There's Beth, with one of her many admirers.'

'I hope you didn't mind that I invited him,' Grace lied, to save her daughter.

'Why should I? It's your party, sweetpea.'

They were at the table, empty apart from Lily Morris, who was raking in her purse, oblivious to their presence.

'I don't want you to call me that,' Grace said quietly.

'Yes, you do,' Harry smiled tolerantly. 'Now sit down and I'll keep Lily company for a while.'

Short of creating a fuss, Grace had no option but to take her seat and let the matter lie; but she was disconcerted, for she had a horrible feeling that, in his present mood, Harry would have no compunction in making 'sweetpea' sound like a term of endearment; like a secret between them.

*

Lily glowered at the boy when he sat beside her. She was quite happy with her sherry – the fourth, she thought – and not having to make conversation that would be forgotten as soon as the sentence was over. When he took up the packet of cigarettes that

426

belonged to Catriona, she glanced at the girl.

'Are you not going to say something?' she asked. 'He's pinching one of your cigarettes.'

'I thought you wanted me to give them up?' Catriona smiled, not looking at Harry. 'Anyway, that's my last. No more after this one.'

Lily sniffed and turned her head away from Harry, to let him know that she was not in the mood for chitchat; but he moved his chair to bring himself back into her line of vision and she resigned herself to whatever he had to say. She knew it would be something about his Grace and James Melville: the boy had that look in his eye, the kind that people had when they wanted to dig up all your secrets, and then examine them, before trampling over your memories and finally throwing them over their shoulder as they left, not caring where they landed.

'Here,' she heard him say to Catriona. 'Can I have a light?'

Lily watched as the girl offered the box of matches to him. He shook his head, waited until Catriona had flicked the match lit and was holding it out towards him. There was something not right, Lily decided, about the way he touched the girl's hand, held it fast, until his cigarette was alight, not to mention the look that passed between them at the same time.

'That tastes good,' he said, turning his attention to Lily, blowing the smoke away from her. 'Haven't had one for years.'

'Life was never the same when pipe's went out of fashion.'

'Ghastly, smelly things, and so unhygienic, all that spittle in the bowl.'

Lily made no reply, but sat with what she hoped was a hostile demeanour, to ward off the questions on the boy's lips.

'You said earlier that I wouldn't want James Melville's nature.'

'Did I?'

He smiled, flicked the ash into the glass tray, hesitated for a few seconds.

'Yes you did, as well you know.'

She may not approve of his impudence but she had to admit he was an interesting companion; besides which, he treated Grace with respect.

'Why don't you like him?' the boy asked suddenly.

'I suppose it was right at the beginning. His arrogance got right up my nose.'

'What did he speak about?'

'Arrogant things,' she said with no trace of humour and the boy laughed loudly, his head thrown back, attracting attention from other diners.

'Oh, that's good,' he said eventually, the cigarette poised on the way to his mouth. 'That's very funny. Does he even think you're funny?'

Lily looked around the table, at Grace and Alice, deep in conversation, at Frank and Emily kissing and canoodling, at James and Lucy, heads together discussing some world-shattering event by the looks of things; and then at Beth, sitting too close to Lucy's son, gazing into his eyes, making a fool of herself; and that hussy, Molly Menzies, not even sitting with Grace now, but boring poor Maureen with village gossip, All at once Lily felt old; wanted nothing more than to go home.

'No, he never thinks I'm funny,' she told the boy wearily. 'I was wondering if you could do me a small favour?'

He stubbed out the cigarette and blew the last breath of smoke into the centre of the room, and then he nodded.

'Yes, of course.'

'Most people would ask what the favour is first.'

'I envy you,' he told her suddenly. 'You're at liberty to say exactly what you think. You can have no idea how much I envy you.'

427

Lily was taken aback by the sadness in the boy's eyes.

'If you give me a lift home,' she said, perhaps foolishly. 'I can tell you a bit more about Grace.'

'I'll get your coat,' was his reply as he leaped to his feet.

'I'll just say goodnight to Grace and James,' she said, slightly alarmed that the boy showed no sign of doing so.

'See you in the foyer,' he told her before walking off.

Lily waited for a moment, until she had recovered her breath, and then she stood up and followed the boy from the room, without bothering to tell anyone she was leaving. When she reached the foyer, he was handing a note to the receptionist.

'Can you do something for me?' he was asking. For all her advanced years and limited experience of men, Lily could see that there was nothing the receptionist would not have done for the boy at that moment.

'Certainly, Sir,' she trilled, face lighting up.

'The table booked under the name of Melville?'

'Yes, Sir, table fourteen.'

'I'd like you to give this note to Grace, whose party this is. Blonde hair, the greenest eyes you've ever looked into, a complexion that you'd pay a fortune in beauty treatments for...' He paused and the receptionist appeared speechless. 'If you'd be so kind,' he finished, prompting her with his eyes.

'Oh, of course, Sir, the lady with the blonde hair, at table fourteen, yes, of course.'

'Not the young one who's drooling over some lout with dark hair,' the boy said as an afterthought, and Lily's assumption had been wrong: he had seen his wife make a fool of herself. 'The more mature lady, speaking to an American.'

They left the hotel and Lily was glad of her heavy fur coat, for the air had turned chilly, their breath bursting out in front of them as they walked.

'I'm afraid it's a sports car,' the boy said apologetically as he opened the door for her. 'Not much room.'

'I'll manage,' Lily said curtly, then remembered the favour he was doing her. 'And thank you for agreeing to take me home.'

'I've kept my end of the bargain,' he smiled as he swung himself into the driver's seat beside her. 'Make sure you keep yours.'

Lily gathered the folds of her coat tighter to her body and said nothing.

*

Out of the corner of her eye, Grace saw Harry and Lily leaving. She was in no doubt that Lily was going home, for she rarely stayed up after ten, and it was almost eleven now; but what worried her was her old friend's sudden and unheralded departure; without even a backward glance.

She was just about to mention it to Alice, when the receptionist rushed to the table, proffering a note.

'The young gentleman asked me to give this to you, Madam.'

'You're sure it's for me?'

'Oh, yes, Madam, he was most specific.'

'Thank you then,' Grace smiled, taking the note and opening it immediately the girl had gone.

'What's this?' Alice asked, leaning in and peering at the note over her friend's shoulder. 'A secret assignation at your age?'

'No, it's from Harry. Lily's not feeling well, he's taken her home. He says he'll probably see us at home within the hour.'

She had to admit to a certain degree of relief that he had left so unexpectedly, and the bit about Lily's not being well was no cause for concern for she suspected that the old lady was simply tired and wanted to go home. In a way, it was kind of him to take her home, given that Lily had made no secret of her hostility towards him in the early years.

'That's nice of him,' Alice said, but Grace suspected that Beth's behaviour had contributed to Harry's willingness to depart. She glanced down the table, to where her daughter was flirting outrageously with Charlie Webster and despaired of ever being permitted to lead a normal life; or was she fooling herself? Was this tortuous, disruptive, unsatisfying existence as normal a life she could expect?

'Perhaps the lady would like to dance with me?' she heard James ask, and for a fleeting, spiteful moment, Grace had an impulse to refuse him. Common sense prevailed, fortunately, and she smiled and stood up.

'I saw you dancing with Lucy,' she said, not intending to sound shrewish. 'You still dance well, Sergeant-Major.'

'And you still look like an angel, Miss Blake.'

An angel, Grace said inwardly. *How wrong could he be?*

It was comforting, somehow, to be in his arms, even after the ignominy of winning the bet with Alice, after the irritation she suffered when he chose Lucy Webster to partner him in his first foray on the dance floor in over twenty years. There had been no jealousy on Grace's part, since she had danced with Harry first.

'I was just thinking about some of the things we wrote to each other,' James was saying now. 'When we were going out together.'

'Did you keep my letters?'

James tutted and she believed he must have discarded them, that they had taken up valuable space in his desk.

'Well, of course I kept them,' he frowned, looking down at her with some impatience. 'Some of them anyway. Why would I throw them away?'

'I wondered, that was all.'

'You kept mine?'

'Of course.' Grace smiled. 'I still read them occasionally.'

'You wrote some lovely things.'

'My spelling's terrible. I would be bottom of the class for English.'

He slowed their steps to a walk. 'But top of the class for everything else. Happy birthday, Grace.'

'Thank you, James.'

As she went back to the table, Grace was not thinking about the affectionate conversation she had just shared with James. She was wondering how she could make her apologies and be with Harry.

Chapter Thirty

Lily appeared glad that the fire was still lit, although Harry had offered to set it and light it as they drove from Dundee. She nodded her head in the direction of the living room, leaving him to hang up his coat while she went upstairs, presumably to put her own coat in the wardrobe.

When she joined him in the living room, however, she was carrying a small folder.

'I said I'd tell you more about Grace,' she said, handing it to him. 'That's her as a girl, before James, the Sassenach, came along.'

He ignored the barb and took the folder from her, but left it on his knee until she sat opposite him.

'May I?' he asked.

'Aye, you can,' she said with a wry smile, enjoying her little dig at his phrase.

They were of Grace Shepherd and various family members, some familiar, others not; yet Lily herself was in none of them.

'Were you the one who took these?'

'I hate cameras,' she said disparagingly, as if they were a scourge. 'Charlotte was the same, preferred to be at the other end.'

'Why do you have these photographs anyway?"

Lily hesitated, but only briefly. 'Because James acted like a wee spoilt boy whenever Grace looked at them, said he felt left out.'

'But he didn't even know her then.'

Lily shrugged. 'Jealousy's a terrible thing.'

Harry changed the subject. 'Is this Charlotte?' he wanted to know, pointing to a cheerful woman with jet-black hair and an infectious smile.

Lily was incredulous. 'You mean you've not seen one of her before?'

'No, I haven't, only Grace's wedding photograph.'

'She doesn't love him, you know.'

Harry looked at her, saw the effort it had taken for her to relay the information.

'Who told you that?'

'Grace.'

Harry was sceptical. 'She'd never do that.'

'Well, she did,' Lily affirmed, pulling her chair closer to the fire. 'The night before her wedding too.'

'If she told you, then she must trust you.'

'I hope she does.'

'You're not as daft as you look then,' Harry quipped.

'Neither are you.'

She appraised him for a full minute, and then she smiled, briefly.

'I usually have a cup of tea in the middle of the night. Do you want one?'

'Please.'

'You don't think you should be getting back to the party?'

'No.'

'You weren't enjoying yourself?'

Harry shook his head.

She stood up and spread her hands to the flames. 'There's an old saying. Maybe you've heard it.'

'Not if it's Scots.'

'Swans take no pleasure in places where crows gather'.

Harry could hardly believe that such pearls of wisdom had fallen from Lily Morris' lips; nor that they had been quoted in his favour. Perhaps he had underestimated the woman.

He lowered his eyes to the folder and flicked over the pages, As each photograph of Grace appeared, the sight of her made his heart ache. He closed his eyes; despaired of ever living a normal, uncomplicated life. His eyes snapped open: could it be that this agonising, hazardous, unpredictable existence was as normal a life he could ever expect?

*

James had been reluctant to drop them off at Lily's house, but Grace and Alice had insisted. Grace thought it odd that her husband had not jumped at the chance to be in Lucy's company for the last few yards, as he had dropped her off at The Birches, a stone's throw from Lily's back gate.

Finally, with his anxious frown etched on her memory and Lucy's gratitude ringing in her ears, Grace walked up the path and knocked on Lily's door, Alice close behind. She had seen Harry's car parked in the lane, that he was still here at mid-night, but her daughter's deplorable behaviour would have tried the patience of a Saint and Grace was not about to become judgemental.

'Come in,' Lily said, rolling her eyes in the direction of the living room. 'You must have heard the kettle boiling.'

'Are you all right?' was Grace's first query.

'Oh, aye, I was just tired, that was all, and Harry kindly agreed to bring me home.'

Grace eyed her old friend suspiciously but said nothing, only asking for a cup of coffee to sober her up.

'You're never tipsy, lassie?'

'Not exactly, but I could do with a coffee.'

They walked into the living room to find Harry poring over old photos, and as soon as Grace caught sight of the folder, she knew it was snapshots of her youth, for she had entrusted them to Lily's safekeeping rather than be plagued by James's bad temper whenever she opened the folder.

'Grace,' Harry smiled, standing up to greet her, this time acknowledging Alice in the sweep of his gaze. 'Did you get my note?'

'I did, thank you, but I wish one of you had told me you were going.'

'I didn't think,' he said plausibly, waving his hand for them to sit down, playing the host in Lily's absence. 'I'm sorry if it caused any bother.'

'It didn't,' Alice chipped in before Grace could respond. 'She was only too glad that someone had thought to take Lily home, said it was way past the old dear's bedtime.'

Resisting the urge to refute what Alice had said, Grace moved over to the fire and stood warming her hands.

'So as you see,' Alice was saying, pushing the limits of Grace's patience to the edge. 'We're grateful for your thoughtfulness, Harry.'

'I note the use of the royal 'we',' Grace said, trying to keep her voice light. 'You'd make a fine Queen, Alice Cameron.'

'Oh, sit down and stop fussing, woman,' Alice said shortly. 'Have you ever met such a fuss pot, Harry?'

'No,' he smiled. 'I can't say I have.'

'Tea for four,' came Lily's voice from the doorway. 'Maybe you could give me a hand, Grace?'

'I'll do it,' Harry offered, rising to his feet before Grace had time to disagree. 'You sit here, make yourself comfortable.' He looked at her with something akin to pity. 'It's still your birthday, at least for another three minutes.'

When he disappeared into the kitchen, Alice turned to her friend and opened her eyes wide.

'He never even mentioned Beth, did you notice?'

'Sshh, don't say anything.'

'But he doesn't seem at all interested in what she's up to.'

'She isn't "up to" anything, as you put it. She'll be at the flat now, alone, desperate for him to come home, Take my word for it.'

As she spoke, however, she failed to convince herself, far less Alice. She had seen the look that passed between her daughter and Charlie Webster a few moments before they had all parted in the foyer of the hotel, and it was just the kind of look that could lead to trouble.

They sat drinking tea and eating Lily's homemade shortbread, as if it were the middle of an ordinary day and not the final minute of a most disturbing twenty-four hours.

Whilst he admitted to himself that his behaviour had been less than gentle-manly, Harry had no regrets. His wife was in need of a good slap, metaphorically speaking, and Grace had to be reminded that she had not always been the world's dogsbody, that she had, in fact, been the centre of her family's life, cherished and desired for what she was, worthy of their love and respect. As for himself, he knew it was time to cast off the shackles of the person he had pretended to be these past five years. It was time to be himself, the Harry Gillespie that no one could manipulate.

'Did you notice Beth was in high spirits tonight?' he heard Alice ask; caught the look of horror on Grace's face.

'Yes, I did,' he smiled. 'I hope she knows what she's doing.'

'She's not "doing" anything,' Grace pointed out firmly. 'It's high jinks with Beth, that's all. She can be a handful for all but the brave,' she added with a sly glance at him.

'Well said, and I suppose I'm brave enough.' He paused momentarily before continuing. 'But can I be bothered?'

In the ensuing silence, Harry sensed that the air was fraught with individual interpretation: probably Grace imagined that he had reneged on Beth completely, whilst Alice might be assuming he was referring to this evening only; but he suspected that Lily Morris would be perfectly aware that he was simply being contentious, saying something risqué for effect. He was beginning to think that the old woman was a kindred spirit, whether she liked it or not.

'I'm sorry that most have us have forgotten it was your birthday, Grace,' he said now. 'I honestly hope that nothing we did spoiled your evening.'

'No, it didn't,' she smiled, but he could not be sure: her play-acting was far superior to his. 'Alice and I have had a wonderful time, quite like the old days.'

'We sure did,' Alice laughed. 'You'd never think we were over forty, the way we carried on today.'

'You don't even look thirty,' Harry told Grace, aware that he was snubbing Alice.

'In that case, neither of us does,' she replied, and he smiled at the constant parry and thrust that went on between them; much like that between his mother and father, perhaps.

'Did James take Lucy home?' Lily asked of Grace.

'Yes, he did.'

'Grace was telling me she won the bet,' Harry addressed himself to Alice.

'She told you that?'

'Harry, please,' Grace protested feebly. 'Is nothing sacred?'

'What will you do with the fiver?'

'I intend to take Alice out for lunch.'

'Ah, so you're spending half of it on others. I suppose that's a start.'

'I should be going now.' Grace sighed, but he picked up her reluctance. Perhaps he was not the only one averse to going home.

'Is Alice staying the night, or shall I take her back to Perth?'

'I'm staying,' Alice smiled, linking arms with Grace. 'The night is young and we've a lot more giggling to do.'

Lily saw them to the door, hugged Grace and wished her 'happy birthday' again.

'I can hardly believe you're mid-forties,' she said, shaking her head. 'I mind when you were just a wee bairn.'

Harry walked as far as the gate with them before bidding them goodnight.

'I'll phone you during the week,' he told Grace, taking her hand, 'And don't worry about Beth. She'll fall into line.'

If he had used an unfortunate figure of speech, she gave no sign, only smiled and released his hand. He watched the two of them meander down the village, arm in arm, chattering like young girls, and then, with a final wave to Lily, Harry opened the car door.

*

Beth lay in the spare room, wretched and remorseful; not for how she had treated Harry Gillespie but for how despicably she had used Charlie; especially since Harry had been too wrapped up in his mother-in-law to take any notice of what she and Charlie were up to. In fact, if a gang of robbers had rushed the place and demanded everyone's jewellery, Beth doubted that Harry would have raised an eyebrow; not that she had any intention of trudging that particular path again. His fixation with her mother was a fact of life and she would be banging her head against a brick wall if she tried to change it now; no, it was the way she had manipulated poor Charlie Webster that was gnawing away at her at one o'clock in the morning – the morning after the night of her mother's party, a night that should have been one of the happiest of the year.

Harry had been Hell-bent on spoiling it right at the start, even before they left the house, and it could only get worse. Beth tossed and turned, wondering now if a more mature woman would have handled it differently; her mother, for instance, how would she have fared? Such speculations only served to deepen Beth's sense of gloom, for her mother would never have acted so spitefully in the face of a recalcitrant husband. No, she would have smiled and nodded, laughed and complied, weathered the storm, sailed out into calmer waters with her integrity intact; not to mention her marriage secure.

She heard the front door slam and dived beneath the covers.

*

Harry kicked his shoes off in the hall, left them where they landed, and went through to the kitchen to pour a nightcap. The street lamp shed enough light for him to find his way around and, truth to tell, he was glad of the darkness, found it restful after the glare of the hotel and the hostile, intrusive strip lights in Lily Morris' house.

He had lifted the cigarette packet off the table when Catriona had gone to the ladies' room, and he took it out now, removed one, searched for a box of matches. He sat for a while enjoying the cigarette and the whisky, mulling over the photograph album. Idly, he thought about Beth, the first time she had entered his mind since he had left the hotel.

When he stood up to take the whisky bottle to the table, he thought he heard a sound from the spare room. He listened for a moment, heard it again, and hoped that she was not in tearful mood. He could not be bothered with such nonsense tonight; besides, she had a horror of people smoking, always yammering on about the smell of stale breath.

433

He had no energy for a quarrel; at least not until morning.

He must have dozed off, for he woke suddenly to find his head on his arms, the button on his shirt collar digging into the side of his cheek.

'Are you pissed?' he heard Beth ask curtly, and he raised his head to find her standing in the doorway.

'No, just tired,' he said pleasantly, vowing that it would be the last pleasant thing he uttered if she persisted in being surly.

'I'm in the spare room, so it's safe for you to go to bed,' she told him sarcastically.

'I only came home for a drink,' Harry smiled, seized with inspiration, making it up as he went along. 'The off-licence was closed.'

She panicked then, which gave him time to think it through: where the hell would he go at this time of night? Foxy was tucked up in bed with Mike; he could hardly wake Sandra up at two thirty in the morning, and the idea of driving back to Lily's – where he might not even be welcome – was not all that appealing.

'I was miserable all night,' Beth said now, her eyes filling with tears. 'You were a pig to me. I've never seen you like that before.'

Harry shrugged, knowing he had the upper hand: whenever Beth shed tears he was on a winning streak.

'You'll have to get used to it, sweetheart. You started it, remember?'

'Me?' She was outraged. 'How do you figure that one out?'

'You blamed me for Annie Kerr's death, ran off to find solace with your grandfather, of all people.' He laughed briefly, wondering when she would notice the cigarette butt smouldering in the saucer. 'Quite honestly, I'd rather you'd scurried off into the arms of Charlie Webster. You know, Beth, it's the oddest thing.' She threw him a look of trepidation, fearing, no doubt, that he was about to raise the topic of her flirtatious behaviour that evening. 'Annie Kerr couldn't get to us when she was alive. I refused to allow her to get between you and me, should have bopped her one when she came onto me. Yet now, now that the stupid bitch is dead, she's having her biggest success.' He turned away, picked up another cigarette, lit it and drew on it, leaning his head back and blowing the smoke straight to the ceiling where it drifted around, unable to make up its mind which direction to take.

'She was ill, you knew that,' Beth protested but there was no vigour in her tone.

'So you're saying I should have shagged her?'

'I didn't say that.'

'Next time, I'll shag first, ask questions later.'

She sighed sharply and pushed herself away from the doorframe, walked towards him slowly, her features concealed by the dim lighting. He could see the shiny tracks that her tears were making down her cheeks, and yet, for the first time in their married life, he was completely unmoved.

'If I apologise,' she began hesitantly. 'Will you apologise too?'

'No, I won't. It was your fault, Beth, not mine.'

In the first seconds of the ensuing silence, he weighed up his chances: fair to middling, he guessed, no more, no less; but when, after a full minute, she was still standing in front of him, he put the odds firmly in his favour.

*

Grace lay in the aftermath of James's love-making, her mind fraught, ideas and images scattering wildly, hating herself for the most prominent one that refused to be subdued: had he wanted to make love because he was smitten with Lucy Webster?

She gasped, rolled over and stared sightlessly at the wallpaper, furious with herself, ashamed at the very idea; and yet she had read in a woman's magazine, that men could...

Grace pressed her hands to her temples. James was not *men*, James was her husband, a loving, attentive, sympathetic husband who did not deserve such criticism, albeit in the silence of her own mind. Such pointless speculation was unfair to both of them, two people who had struggled to surmount numerous obstacles at the beginning and had survived to celebrate over twenty-five anniversaries. Some of her friends and acquaintances were not so lucky: a few were divorced – an unheard of occurrence in her mother's day – and some lived separate lives in the same house; Molly, for example, whose behaviour Grace found appalling.

Drowsily, her mind drifted to Harry and his hand on her back, his fingers trapping hers so fiercely that it had frightened her. Half asleep, she recalled the shape of his mouth as he uttered the word 'sweetpea'; knew she should have protested more strongly against it Her emotion should have been one of shame, for she understood the folly of her fondness for the boy. Grace closed her eyes tightly. As she began to sink into the comforting stillness of sleep, she thought of Beth; but the image had dissipated as swiftly as it had appeared, to be replaced by the memory of Harry's hand grasping hers.

*

Harry heard the clock strike four. He was trying to recover from the dream; so bizarre that he had lain awake since the clock had chimed three.

Annie Kerr!

He had felt only relief when the girl had killed herself; relief that she would never be able to prove he had slept with her that night; relief that her death had come just in the nick of time.

Despite everything, however, he had to admit that she had aroused him as no other female had; not even Foxy and she was a proficient bed-fellow. Kerr was a slut, of course, and decent men did not sleep with sluts; but each time Harry imagined the girl's pendulous breasts swinging above him, he knew that his groin would respond. He was even prepared to admit that he was in the habit of thinking about Annie Kerr before he made love to Beth. He was not averse to the occasional fantasy.

Beth stirred and moaned and he lay quietly, regulating his breathing to make her think he was asleep. One energetic bout of sex was enough for one night, especially when there were only three hours until morning. As the word flashed across his mind, he remembered Grace's whispered entreaty to pick her up next morning, to accompany her to Kinclaven, to lay flowers on her mother's grave. The only disadvantage would be if James decided to tag along; Harry much preferred when it was just the two of them.

*

Beth heard his breathing, knew that he was asleep. Frankly, she was relieved, for their lovemaking had been brutal; not so much physically but mentally. Where once he would have allowed her the pleasure of fore-play, time for her to set the mood, he had dispensed with any of it, starting and finishing within minutes, falling away from her without even a 'goodnight.'

She supposed it was her just punishment for Charlie Webster and that she fully deserved it. Yet, she had experienced a side of Harry Gillespie that had scared her.

Sleepily, she decided that it had been an unfortunate episode and that, come tomorrow, life would be back to normal and she would take care never to be so stupid again.

435

Thomas Blake woke at seven, to the sound of a distant clock clunking away, signifying it was the Sabbath probably. The Sabbath! Good Lord, where had he dredged that word from after all these years? He supposed the Good Lord would know and left it at that.

The letter from Daphne lay on the kitchen table, her badly spelt, blandly-phrased soliloquy defining her love for him, her desire to be married sooner rather than later; no recriminations about the past, not now, not ever.

He smiled at the sheer gullibility of women, apart from Charlotte Shepherd, who had been the least gullible of females, the only one who could match his flair for strategy. Daphne, on the other hand, had been only too willing to be fooled, to believe he had another love interest. He would always be grateful to Sarah at the George for playing her little part.

'It's for you,' Daphne had said numbly, holding the receiver out. 'Someone called Sarah.'

'Ah, how unfortunate,' Thomas had mumbled, feigning embarrassment. 'I do apologise, Daphne, but I told her not to ring me at home. Please excuse me.'

Sarah had provided him with the insignificant piece of information he had asked her for earlier that day – the price of a long weekend for an imaginary friend travelling up from England – calling at precisely one o'clock, when he and Daphne were having lunch in his kitchen.

He had taken the call in the lounge, thereby leaving his companion with no option but to imagine that 'Sarah' was the replacement hovering in the wings should Daphne disdain his offer. On his shame-faced return to the kitchen, she had looked at him with eyes of trepidation mixed with subterfuge as to how she could redeem the situation.

Now, as he waited for the new coffee percolator to bubble up, Thomas had to stifle a grin. He had to hand it to himself: he was certainly a smooth operator.

He decided that, because she had been such a good girl, he would buy her something quite opulent for her birthday at the end of the month; a diamond ring perhaps, to show willing.

*

Lucy Webster poured out coffee for her son and set the cup carefully on his saucer. He was sitting with his head in his hands, worse the wear for last night's alcohol, she presumed, and she had been tiptoeing around the house all morning, trying not to disturb him. As a mother, she was sympathetic to his cause – unrequited love – particularly as it was now her own cause. If she allowed herself to think about it too much, she might have found the whole matter distasteful, her son making sheep's eyes at the daughter, whilst she was doing the same at the father. She did not, however, dwell too much on the detail, preferring to languish in the foolishness of daydreams that harmed no one except herself.

'Sorry, Mum,' Charlie muttered suddenly, glancing up remorsefully. 'I've been a bit of a jerk and it's unforgivable.'

'Don't be silly, dear,' she smiled soothingly. 'It's nothing more dramatic than a hangover. Why don't you take some Alka-Seltzer?'

'Did that. It didn't work.' Charlie picked up the black coffee, sampled it and then swilled it down as if it were foul-tasting medicine. 'Ugh! I hate it without milk.'

'It's better for you.'

'Was I sick last night?' he asked, afraid to look at her.

'Not that I noticed,' Lucy smiled. 'Of course, I haven't set foot in your room yet.'

'That's great! I haven't been sick then, because my room's...' He stopped, realising the full significance of such a conversation with a mother. 'I mean Vera won't have to clean up,' he added lamely. 'I drank far too much when I got back.'

'I'm only glad you came here rather than Glasgow Road.' She did her best to keep the censure from her voice: the last thing he needed was a whining mother. 'I was so relieved when I heard you drive up.'

'You were waiting up for me,' Charlie said gratefully. 'It was nice.'

Lucy nodded, reluctant to tell him that she had been sitting in the drawing room daydreaming about James Melville, as opposed to awaiting the return of the prodigal son.

'You love her very much, don't you?' she had to ask, putting her own day-dreams to the back of her mind.

'Is it so obvious?'

'I'm afraid so.'

'Do you think she loves me at all?'

'It's hard to say,' Lucy told him truthfully. 'She's very, very fond of you, I can see that.'

'She told me she...' He cut off the sentence and appeared horrified at what he had been about to tell her.

'That she fancied you?' Lucy finished for him, her eyes on her cup of coffee, to spare the boy further embarrassment.

'Well, yes... I mean.'

She raised her eyes to his. 'Charlie, dear boy, do you imagine that you were an immaculate conception?'

He blushed furiously, but laughed and shook his head. 'Mother, please! One outspoken woman in my life is quite enough, thank you.'

'I may be forty-nine, Charlie, but I expect I'm not totally ignorant of the facts of life, by which I mean all the facts, including fancying someone.' It was Lucy's turn to blush. 'Hark at the two of us, discussing such things, and on a Sunday too.'

'I can't imagine any other bloke discussing this with his mother.'

'Am I a bad influence on you then?' she joked.

'Absolutely, I'm delighted to say.' His smile faded and he lowered his gaze to the table. 'I've been thinking.'

'Oh dear. That sounds ominous.'

'I think I'll go to London, visit Matthew.'

Lucy was aghast. 'Visit... visit...?' She was so shocked that she could not pronounce her son's name. 'But he's a reprobate, Charlie, and how do you know he's in London anyway?'

He appeared contrite. 'He wrote to me, and I wrote back.'

'When was this?'

'Mother, I'm sorry, I... can't...' He caught sight of his mother's expression and changed course. 'A couple of months ago.'

'And is he well?' Lucy asked, her heart aching at the thought of the boy, regardless of his waywardness.

'Kind of. He lives in Brewer Street.'

'Which part is that?'

'Soho.'

'Oh, goodness me.'

'It's a bed sit. One room, tiny kitchen, outside loo.'

Involuntarily, Lucy shivered. 'How gruesome.' She had a sudden, horrible thought. 'You're not going to stay there, surely?'

'No,' he said, but she knew he was lying: his right eye twitched, as it had done ever since he was little and told her he never ate worms in the garden. 'I'll probably rent a place of my own.'

'But the cost,' Lucy said before she could stop herself.

'I have some money stashed away.'

'That's for a rainy day and I won't let you waste it,' she told him, trying to redeem her outburst of meanness.

'I'll find a job down there, support myself.'

'But the business? And Beth's partnership? You can't just leave, Charlie when we're all relying on you.' What she actually meant was that she was relying on him, that she had lost one son through a lack of understanding and would not lose another.

'Beth will be fine, better on her own I imagine.' He looked at her, perhaps re-appraising what he was giving up. 'It's not that I want to go, mother, it's not my preferred choice, you know.'

Lucy waited silently, for she would have done anything, said anything at that moment to keep the boy here, and yet the words evaded her.

'I can't see her every day, ' Charlie was saying despondently. 'It's the most unbearable thing I can think of.'

'Don't you think I know that?' Lucy asked, her heart in turmoil at the idea she was not in the fortunate position of being able to escape. 'But at the end of the day, you'll still love her. Running off won't achieve anything.'

'True,' he admitted sadly, the ghost of a smile on his lips. 'But at least I won't have to face it every day, see her with him....Harry the Great... Superman... Ben Hur... Michael Caine... the 'Alfie' of Perth...'

Despite the humour, she felt so sorry for him that, had it been in her power, she would have gone to Beth Melville and begged.

'Promise me that you'll telephone me all the time,' she said, hearing the plea in her voice, hoping he would not regard her as an over-bearing mother.

He reached across the table and took her hand. 'I promise.'

'And you will come home regularly?'

'That as well.'

'When will you tell Beth?'

'First thing tomorrow.'

'How will she take it?'

'I'm not sure.'

'If she doesn't want the business, what will happen to it?' Lucy read the disinterest in his eyes, but she pushed him. 'Will it just fold?'

'She'll want to keep it going.'

'Oh, Charlie, I don't understand what's happening to us all!'

He smiled, squeezed her hand before letting it go.

'We're like little boats,' he smiled. 'Bobbing about, just drifting where the wind takes us.'

He stood up, placed his cup and saucer by the sink, gave her a perfunctory smile and left the room.

*

Beth glanced at him, furtively, across the breakfast table, unable to make head nor tail of his mood. He had said nothing for half an hour, his nose stuck in the *Sunday Times*, his hand reaching for toast, or the butter dish, or the marmalade jar from beneath the paper; and when he had needed two hands to spread the toast, he had laid the newspaper flat on the table, not even missing a word of whatever he was reading.

Had she not been too proud, she might have begged and whined and thrown herself at his feet, regardless of whose fault it had been; and, quite frankly, it was all such a long time ago now that it hardly seemed to matter. When he rustled the newspaper and spoke to her, she almost jumped.

'Do you have any plans for today?'

'Haven't thought about it.'

'Perhaps you could then, let me know.'

'Why, do you have any?'

'Yes, I'm taking Grace to Kinclaven.'

'To Granny's grave?'

'And the rest of the Shepherd clan. So, do you have any plans?' he asked again, looking right at her.

'No, but I could come with you.'

He shrugged and she knew he was against it. Besides, he would use the sports car and there would be no room for her.

'When did you plan to leave?' she asked now, her fingers tapping out Chopin's Waltz in E flat on the tabletop.

'As soon as you've finished playing Chopin.'

Beth stared at him. 'How did you know what it was?'

'Because you always play Chopin.'

'Not always. Sometimes I play Mendelssohn and Handel and Beethoven.'

'Not on the kitchen table.'

She wondered if he was in a good mood, having fun, albeit at her expense, but even after studying his brow for a few moments – the only part of him she could see – she was none the wiser.

'I've changed my mind,' she said impulsively.

'About coming with us?'

'No, about thinking you never notice anything.'

Harry lowered the newspaper, his eyes showing interest.

'What on earth gave you the idea that I never noticed anything?'

'Because you never said.'

'Why would I be stupid enough to give you clues?'

'I give you lots.'

'That's because you're young,' he smiled, raising the paper again. 'You'll grow out of it.'

'Harry?'

'What?'

'Do you want children?'

The newspaper shot down so quickly that it was crushed.

'What?'

'Children. Do you want any?"

'What's brought this on?'

'I think I want them now,' she lied, determined to stick to her strategy.

'You hate children,' he reminded her with a frown, but the newspaper remained crushed on the table.

'No, I don't. I just hate other people's.'

He smiled then, an apparently genuine smile, and her heart lurched.

'In that case, I can't see why we shouldn't have any.'

'Now?' she asked with a frown, too much of a frown perhaps, but his response had been too quick for her.

'*Right* now,' he corrected, throwing the newspaper aside and awarding her his full

439

attention.

She blushed, for it was almost like talking to a complete stranger on a train, rather than her husband, a man she thought she had known and loved for years. She had mentioned children only to drag his eyes away from the *Sunday Times*.

'Surely, you don't mean *right now*?'

'That's what I said,' Harry smiled, his gaze wandering over her face. 'I'm picking Grace up at two and it's only eleven. Plenty time to get started.'

Beth felt usurped; similar to her emotion of the previous night when he had used her as an orifice, which was how she viewed sex without love.

'Come on,' he said impatiently, hauling her to her feet. 'I'm in the mood.'

But I'm not!

She stood up, fastened her dressing gown cord around her, whereupon he leaned over and pulled the cord loose.

'You won't be needing that, sweetheart,' he said, slowly removing the gown and letting it slip to the floor. 'Or this,' he added, unfastening her nightdress.

'Can I do it myself?' she asked, suddenly, inexplicably, feeling like a whore.

'No, it's better if I do it.'

In the middle of the kitchen, oblivious to her reluctance, he undressed her, and then began taking his own clothes off. When she thought about protesting, she realised with a shock that having children had been her suggestion. What the hell had she been thinking of?

Despite the room's warmth, Beth wrapped her arms around her breasts and shivered.

*

The day was cool and showery, the grass at the cemetery damp and treacherous. Grace had been disappointed when Beth had not turned up, as she was anxious to offer an olive branch after ignoring her daughter at the hotel. Also, James had shown no inclination to go with her, despite having complained many times that she had gone with Harry without letting him know.

On the other hand, she saw the advantages in being alone with the boy, having no witnesses to what she had to say. With James and Beth around, she would have had to choose her words more carefully and she was too tired.

Harry took her arm as they walked up the short incline to the church gate, a heavy wrought-iron contraption that clanked and crashed. As they made their way to the gravestones, he indicated the bridge across the river, in the distance far below.

'Is that the river you and Charlotte had to cycle across to get here?'

'We didn't come here often, but, yes, we did cycle.'

'Did James ever cycle with you?'

'No.'

He turned and looked down at her, still with his hand at her elbow.

'You're different today,' he accused her.

'I could say the same about you.'

'That's because *you're* different today.'

'Nonsense,' she said quietly. 'I noticed it last night, right away, whenever I saw you. I didn't approve.'

She left the censure hanging; to eke some revenge for the way he had treated Beth recently; if Beth were to be believed.

'I don't need your approval.'

'Liar,' Grace said abruptly, hoping it was true. She disengaged her arm from his and walked through the archway that led to the gravestones. 'You can be so cruel.'

440

'But I'm never cruel to you,' she heard him say behind her as he followed on. 'You can't say I am.'

She stopped and turned. 'You were cruel to Beth yesterday; otherwise she'd never have behaved the way she did at the hotel. You must have said something pretty bad to make her react like that.'

He had the grace to appear chastened, shuffled his feet, took a deep breath but refused to meet her eyes.

'We did have a row, that's true.'

'It breaks my heart when she's unhappy.'

Harry stood still, eyes on the ground in front of him, apparently mulling it over but in no hurry to respond. Eventually, Grace spoke again.

'If it's your wish to keep breaking my heart, Harry, then there's nothing I can do about it.' She moved on, throwing her words over her shoulder. 'James would never do anything deliberately to hurt me. He loves me.'

She stood at the foot of her mother's grave, pulse racing, reading the inscription that she had read so many times, her eyes tracing each letter, noting the tiny signs of erosion from the last visit, the weathering of the sandstone itself. So many things had changed since the day she had sat in the church behind her, thinking her life was over, believing that she could not bear to live without Charlotte Blake and how spiteful it was of her mother to die. Now, Grace was overcome with guilt at such a lack of compassion.

She became aware of Harry beside her, heard the long sigh before he spoke.

'I'm sorry, Grace, You know I'd rather die than do anything to make you unhappy.'

She turned to look at him and imagined contrition in his eyes.

'It's partly my fault,' Grace conceded, holding up her hand to stave off his protest. 'No, I should have prevented Beth from inviting Charlie Webster last night. The trouble is I've been too soft with her and it's too late to change.' She shrugged, pulled the collar of her coat tighter to her neck. 'I'm grateful that you married Beth and that you're helping her to grow up.' She looked straight at him. 'But in your present mood you're quite the wrong kind of man for my daughter, and not the kind of man I want around me.'

*

Harry knew he should be filled with remorse. He had two choices: he could either beg her forgiveness or adhere to his natural instincts – his new-found freedom – and resist being pushed around, Despite the fact he had invoked criticism from the only woman whose respect he craved, he refused to contemplate giving in to Grace; for it signified he must give in to Beth.

'I've seen a house,' he said now, hardly relevant, but the only thing he could think of; besides, it was true. He had viewed several recently, thinking of a move to the country, to escape the hustle and bustle of a city.

'A house?' she asked, eyes fearful, and he knew what she was thinking.

'Here,' he said quickly, kinder to her than she had been to him. 'Not far from this place, in fact.'

Her relief was heart breaking. Harry reached out and took her arm again, and she made no move to stop him.

'It's time Beth and I moved into the country,' he told her. 'She says she's happy enough in the city but I know she'd love it out here. Especially now that we intend to start a family.' He saw the momentary flash of dissent in her eyes and was at a loss to understand it.

'You're going to have children?' Grace asked, biting her lower lip.

441

Harry nodded. 'We discussed it this morning,' he said, trying to banish the image of a subjugated Beth beneath him, eyes and mind closed to him. 'But when she tells you, pretend you don't know.'

'Oh, Harry, it's such good news,' she smiled then, hugging his arm, looking up at him with such pleasure that he thought he had misread her first reaction. 'Goodness, I'll be a grandmother. What a thought!'

He was just about to reply when a car appeared in the lane and he glanced over, irritated at the intrusion. Before he could speak, however, Grace had gasped.

'It's James,' she said anxiously. 'Something must be wrong.'

'You wait here, I'll go and see.'

He left her at the graveside and walked quickly towards the small car park, where James was drawing to a halt. Harry's heart skipped a beat: sitting in the passenger seat was Beth and she was waving to him, an apprehensive smile on her face.

His first instinct was disappointment that she had curtailed his time with Grace.

Chapter Thirty-One

They sat in the parlour of the old cottage, with Frank and Emily staying only for ten minutes.

'I'll just run Emily home now,' Frank said to his mother. 'Thanks, Mum, for letting her stay last night.'

It crossed Grace's mind that being relegated to the bed-settee must have been something of a shock for the girl, although she had conveyed nothing but appreciation when it had been made down for her the previous night.

'Thank you, Grace,' she had said, using the name Grace had insisted upon. 'It's very kind of you do put me up at such short notice.'

Something in her son's eyes told Grace that he would not have been averse to taking Emily to his own bed, had James not been present; and Grace wondered if, under such circumstances, she might have acceded to her son's unspoken request.

Now, as she stood at the window, waving them off, she was somewhat glad to see the back of them. Entertaining Emily for supper and breakfast had been a strain; for them both, she acknowledged. The poor girl was still trying too hard and Grace suspected she was guilty of the same. She was quite convinced that when they both stopped worrying about pleasing the other, their relationship would have freedom to flourish.

'She's very nice,' Beth was saying when Grace returned to her seat beside James. 'but she tries too hard, don't you think?'

Her question, though directed at her mother, was answered by James.

'She'll get used to our ways,' he smiled, his eyes flickering to Harry. 'You did, didn't you?'

'I'm still learning,' Harry said with a covert glance towards Grace.

'You'll do,' James told him, possibly the most gracious compliment he could ever bestow, Grace thought.

She saw her daughter glance at Harry for approval, then take a deep breath. 'We've something to tell you, haven't you, Harry?'

They all laughed and Grace was comforted to see the boy's familiar demeanour reassemble before her eyes. She wished they had had more time at the graveside, but what she had told him seemed to have hit home.

'I've seen a house,' Harry began, his gaze on Grace. 'Not far from Kinclaven cemetery. Just along the road, near Meikleour.'

'I was born behind the Beech Hedge,' Beth smiled. 'During a really bad winter.'

'And I had to walk my bicycle most of the way,' James added. 'And it was all your fault.'

'And I looked like a scarecrow when you came to see me,' Grace laughed, joining in. 'Fortunately, you only had eyes for your daughter.'

'You think so?' asked James.

'Anyway,' Grace said hastily, moving on. 'You've seen a house?'

'It's fairly big, but we need a bigger house now,' Harry explained, smiling at Beth's blushing cheeks. 'We've decided to have kids.'

'Kids are what goats have,' James remarked.

'Children then,' Harry apologised. 'The sooner the better as far as I'm concerned.'

'And me,' Beth chipped in, sitting on the floor hugging her knees.

'What a lovely surprise,' Grace said dutifully. 'Just think,' she added, turning to James. 'You'll be a grandfather.'

'Don't think I'll be washing nappies,' he smiled at Beth. 'I did it for you, but I'll not be doing it again.'

'Oh, there's no such thing as nappies now. They're pad things, aren't they, Mum? You just chuck them away when they're full.'

Harry gave a groan. 'I think I'm off the idea already.'

'Have you actually viewed the house?' Grace asked him.

'Yes, last week.'

'You never said,' Beth said lightly, but it was the first dissent of the morning.

'I didn't want to raise your hopes.'

'That's all right then. How many rooms?'

'Three reception, four bedrooms.'

'Golly, that's big.'

'And before you ask,' Harry cautioned her. 'No, it's not too expensive for us, even with you not working.'

Grace held her breath: by the look of horror on her daughter's face, she suspected that this was news to Beth; that he had not thought to consult her.

'Not working? What do you mean?'

'Obviously when we have children, you'll stay at home.'

'You must be joking!' Beth exclaimed, regarding him with disgust. 'I'll only be at home until it's born, then I'll be back at work. Don't think *I'll* be happy to be...' She stopped abruptly, looked at her mother for some reason.

'Why are you looking at me?' Grace frowned. 'It's none of my business.'

'Sorry, I got carried away. Anyhow,' Beth continued, her gaze on Harry. 'I have no intentions of staying at home. If I'm working, we can afford someone to do the housework and to take care of the baby.'

Grace was aghast at the idea but she was of another, more circumspect, generation; not to mention one that had had no such resources at its disposal. She could tell that Harry's thoughts were running along similar lines and envisaged a full-blown row flaring up when the two of them were alone. How unfair it was, she bemoaned to herself: just when one problem had been solved, another popped up to take its place.

*

Harry was treading warily, but only in deference to Grace's presence. Having endured sufficient trauma for one day, he had no appetite for further conflict. Consequently, he patted Beth on the head and smiled at her.

'A lot of water will flow under the bridge long before then,' he said calmly. 'When the time comes, you might be so besotted with her that you'll be loath to leave her with a stranger.'

He noted Grace's brief smile, sensed her approval of his tactics.

'She?' Beth repeated, a strange expression on her face. 'A girl?'

'Last time I checked,' Harry said humorously. 'That's what a 'she' was.'

'I never thought about it being a ....well, it's just an 'it' at the moment.'

Into the ensuing silence, Grace spoke.

'How about we have some lunch? I can make sandwiches.'

'Great idea,' Beth said, jumping up, using Harry's knees for support. 'I'll help.'

'Thank you, dear, as long as you don't brew the tea.'

They left Harry and James, hearing the topic turn to football even before the door closed, although Grace knew that the boy had no interest in the game, that he joined in the conversation only to appease James.

In the kitchen, Beth rushed at Grace and hugged her tightly, hardly leaving her space to breathe.

'Oh, Mum, isn't it great?'

'Well, I hope so, darling,' Grace said sceptically. 'But are you sure about this?'

'What, the house or having kids?'

'Both really. One rather goes with the other, doesn't it?'

'We had a terrible day yesterday,' Beth confessed, sitting down, as Grace knew she would, whilst her mother did everything. 'He was really, really horrible to me all day. Hardly said a civil word to me at all.'

'I could see that at the hotel, the way you were behaving with Charlie.'

Beth screwed up her face. 'Don't remind me, please.'

'It wasn't very nice, Beth, no matter what you and Harry had fallen out about, and...' Grace raised her hand. 'I don't want to know either.'

'He acted totally out of character,' Beth frowned. 'Saying and doing things that weren't him. I know it sounds daft, but that's what he was like, as if he were trying to be someone else.'

'No, it doesn't sound daft,' Grace said, choosing her words carefully. 'I thought he was a bit strange at the hotel actually.'

'Thank Heavens for that,' Beth sighed. 'I thought it was just me.'

'He's sorry about it,' Grace said before she could stop herself.

Beth remained silent for a moment, but then smiled. 'Is he?'

'He said so at the cemetery.' Grace feared she was giving too much away, considering her daughter's resentment over Harry.

'Why do you think he did it?' Beth asked casually.

Grace busied herself with the sandwich spread, layered it on thickly to James's piece of bread. 'I think he misses his mother more than we think.'

'He does talk about her sometimes,' Beth admitted, her arms around Grace, impeding the sandwich making. 'But I don't think he knows that much about her.'

'She left them when Harry was only nine.'

'Just like you and your father,' Beth observed unexpectedly.

Grace suffered the ache that invariably accompanied the reminder. Even after all these years she was still shocked by the severity of the pain.

'Are you all right, Mum?'

'Yes, a hangover from last night most probably.'

'Did you see Dad with Lucy Webster?' Beth asked now, and Grace was reminded of her daughter's ability to move on to the next subject with no real understanding of other people's distress.

'Yes, he was a changed man.'

'Mee-ow,' Beth grinned, slapping her mother's back. 'Jealous, are we?'

'No, in fact I won a bet with Alice over it, so I'm rather pleased.'

'A bet? What kind of a bet?'

'I bet that your father would dance with Lucy.'

'What's so unusual about that?'

Grace paused in her sandwich making. 'Your father hasn't taken to a dance floor since 1948, and that was only because he didn't want me to dance with anyone else.'

'Ah.'

'Exactly. Ah.'

'They were nattering on about England, he told me.'

'Next thing, they'll be going there on holiday together.'

'Do I detect a teeny bit of petulance?'

'No. Rather a teeny bit of 'what did your last slave die of, Beth Gillespie?' Is there the slightest possibility that you could carry one of these trays through for me?'

'Sorry, I was blethering too much, wasn't I?'

'You said it, not me,' Grace smiled wanly, handing her daughter two trays of sandwiches. 'I'll bring the plates and cups, just don't drop anything. Oh, by the way, what made you change your mind about coming out to Kinclaven today?'

'You know when something's going wrong and you think you'll wait for someone else to fix it?' Grace nodded, said nothing, and Beth continued. 'Well, it was going horribly wrong, Harry and me, and so I decided that I'd stop it before it got too big.' She stood in the doorway, a tray in each hand, looking so forlorn that Grace would have done anything to ease her daughter's troubles. 'So,' Beth finished brightly. 'I did, and it worked.'

'You're a lovely girl,' was the only response Grace could think of.

As she followed on through the hall, Grace refused to dwell on the possibility that her daughter might not be able to have children. It had happened to more than one of her friends' children and was always at the back of Grace's mind. However, she would have to bear in mind her daughter's determination: the girl could have anything she set her mind to.

*

Lucy Webster sat in the glow of the fire, lit for her in the library so that she could take care of some correspondence she had postponed for days. The late afternoon sun had already disappeared behind the gables of the house, but would still be shining gloriously further down the village, on James's garden.

She was still trying to come to terms with Charlie's sudden and, in her opinion, irrational decision to flee to London, to leave everything he had up here to replace it with the uncertainty of working for some long-lost rugby pal who might turn out to be a bad influence on Charlie.

She threw the pen and paper aside, moved over to the hearth and sat down in her armchair. This might be the last week she could listen for his step in the hall; look forward to his news of the day; bake him his favourite pudding; find solace in his company. The idea of life without him loomed bleakly ahead of her. Had she not been made of sterner stuff, she might have shed a tear; but she was and she would not.

When she heard his car draw up, she had the greatest difficulty in quashing the notion that it was a sound she would rarely hear again. She rose to her feet, glanced at her reflection in the mirror above the fireplace and patted her hair into place. She would never allow her selfish motives to encroach on her son's life.

'Hi, mother,' he said, head round the door. 'I'd a devil of a job finding you, thought you'd scarpered. Be back in a mo'.'

She heard him in the kitchen, opening and closing drawers and cupboards, looking for the chocolate bars she always kept in stock. With a sudden, sickening lurch of her stomach, Lucy realised there would be no further need to buy them; at least not for a long time. She almost wished that Beth Gillespie would leave the area, but it was hardly fair on the girl and only part of the solution for Charlie.

'Boy, was the traffic heavy,' he told her a moment later, hurling himself in the chair opposite, tearing off the wrapper, discarding it into the flames. 'It took me ages to get back.'

'From?' Lucy asked archly, rarely being privy to her son's whereabouts until he returned.

'Church,' he grinned mischievously.

'Don't joke,' she frowned. 'Some people in this village think it's your duty to go.'

'Suitably chastised, mother,' he winked, his teeth crunching into the chocolate bar.

'Where were you anyway?'

'At the office, leaving a note for Marjory.'

446

'But you'll be going to work tomorrow, surely?'

'Yes, but not until the afternoon, I want to take Beth out in the morning, break it to her gently.' He looked so unhappy when he said it, that Lucy's heart went out to him.

'That's a nice thing to do, Charlie. I heartily approve.'

'Gracious of you to say so, Ma'am,' he quipped. 'By the way, do you fancy coming down to spend a few days with me in the Smoke?'

'In London, you mean?'

He leaned forward, speaking deliberately slowly. 'Yes, in London. You could spend a week with me, help me settle in.'

'You've nowhere to settle,' she pointed out.

'Ah, but I do.' Charlie sat back, looked at her smugly. 'Remember I told you about Edward whatsisname, the chap from the rugby team at university?'

'Yes, Edward Forsythe, the one who's offered you a job.'

'That's the one. He used to give you the eye.'

'Charlie!' Lucy exclaimed, giving him the severest frown she could muster.

'Well, he did. You know he did. You mentioned it to me once, said he followed you around like a lamb.'

'I think I said like something on the sole of my shoe,' Lucy corrected, much to her son's amusement.

'Anyway, I called him to confirm about the job, and it seems he's got a room to spare and he lives in Kensington.'

'How much will that cost you?'

'Is that all you can think about?' he asked patiently.

'Unfortunately, yes. This place takes all of my money, you know.'

'But I'll be working full time,' Charlie told her triumphantly, and it was the final nail in the coffin of her wretchedness.

'I thought you said just a few hours a day?'

'I did, but things have changed. Edward's in the letting business, has umpteen flats and bed sits, even a house or two. He thinks there's enough work for two of us, wants me to be his right-hand man, checking potential clients' financial credentials, suitability of property, scouting for new ones, things like that.'

'It sound permanent,' Lucy said gloomily, unable to help herself.

His face fell, as if he had suddenly remembered the effect it was having on her.

'Mother, I'm sorry, going on like this. I didn't mean to upset you, but I have. Sorry,' he reiterated, his eyes asking her forgiveness.

'It's fine,' Lucy lied, forcing a smile. 'And yes, I will come down and help you settle. That way, I can check things out for myself, drag you home by the heels if I don't approve.'

'I'll be going down in two weeks, so that takes us towards the end of October, and you'll be staying for at least a week – there's a fabulous hotel nearby – and then I'll be home for Christmas. So there you are,' he announced happily. 'We'll see each other all the time.'

Lucy nodded and smiled; but her heart was breaking.

*

Harry stood at the window, looking at the activity on the Inch, wondering if he would miss this place when they moved. One thing he would not miss was the constant traffic rolling past, the noisy buses on their route to the bus depot, or the slamming of car doors in the middle of the night when taxis deposited their cargoes and made enough noise to wake the dead.

He shuddered and tried not to imagine his father in his coffin, body mouldering, eye sockets blank, mouth gaping in its last protest. He blew his breath out in a nervous stream. When it came to things like death, he was not as tough as he wanted to be.

He wondered if Grace had been right: could he ever be tough and uncompromising, as his mother had been? What Grace had told him about his not being the sort of man she wanted around, the words were still ringing in his ears, In the cold light of day, he could sympathise with her point of view. He had suffered a similar fate at the harsh end of his mother's tongue more than once.

He had longed to know her, to speak to people who had known her, and yet, if ever the opportunity arose, the one piece of advice he encountered was that he should be wary of aspiring to be like her. At first, he had attributed their attitude to jealousy, for Rachel Gillespie had possessed more than her fair share of attributes; but now, after his brief foray into selfish arrogance, Harry was beginning to suspect that his mother might not have been a very nice woman; to coin a simple phrase.

'Hi,' he heard Beth say behind him, keeping her distance until she had his mood figured out, when once she would have thrown herself at him, regardless. 'I've made something delicious for tea.'

He wanted to tell her he was not hungry but now he hesitated, wondering if it was the kind of thing his mother might say; hurting someone in the process but not caring a hoot. Grace had told him to be himself; the trouble was, his personality had undergone such a drastic change in the past twenty-four hours that he no longer knew who that was.

'Harry?'

He turned and held out his arms, whereupon she rushed to him, sighed on his chest as his arms enclosed her.

'What is this delicious thing you're trying to tempt me with then?'

'It's macaroni cheese.'

'Wow, that's a first,' he laughed. 'Hope it hasn't turned out like the custard.'

She giggled into his shirt. 'It was the birds I felt sorry for, when I threw it out and almost brained two sparrows.'

'I could have used it to fix the leaking tap until the plumber arrived.'

'Cheek!'

'Why did you change your mind about coming to Kinclaven this morning?'

She did not reply immediately, but stood stock-still in his arms, as if debating her answer.

'I don't rightly know.'

'Liar,' he told her softly. 'Come on, tell me.'

'It's stupid.'

'I love you when you're stupid.'

She broke away, stepped back a few paces and studied his face.

'That's good.'

'Is it?'

'Yes, because I'm stupid most of the time, so you must love me most of the time.'

He reached out and drew her back to him, pondering the wisdom of what he was about to say.

'Beth, sweetheart, I love you all of the time.'

'I hope so.'

'The trouble is you take it all so seriously.'

'I thought marriage *was* serious.'

'The ups and downs I mean, the mood swings we both have. They mean nothing. Not in the grand scheme of things.'

He was lying, of course, but it was the closest he would get to apologising to her for his callousness. Furthermore, it might insure him against future temper tantrums, excuse his bouts of selfishness, let him away with murder, so to speak; even his dalliance with Foxy.

'It's just that you seemed so... so different yesterday and this morning. I hardly recognised you.'

'I might accuse you of the same thing,' Harry reminded her gently and she heaved a sigh.

'You drove me to it.'

'Snap.'

She stepped back once more, eyes fixed on his. 'You started it.'

'No, I think you'll find that you started it.'

'How? When? Running off to my grandfather, you mean?'

'It didn't help.'

'I thought we'd got over that hurdle.'

'Then, just before we were leaving for the hotel, you told me you'd have to keep your eye on me at the party.'

Beth was incredulous, 'But that was just a joke. It meant nothing.'

Harry shrugged. 'You see? You know it meant nothing, but did I? For all I knew you were suspecting me of cheating on you. '

He knew he was sailing close to the wind but it was his preferred strategy, especially with someone as astute as Beth.

'That's ridiculous.'

'To you maybe, but that's what it sounded like.'

She was immediately contrite, so contrite that he was overcome by the duplicity of his own motives, albeit for only a few seconds.

'I'm sorry then, I didn't mean it to sound that way.'

'I know that now,' Harry smiled, reaching for her hand. 'But at the time...'

'Do you think I'll ever get the hang of this?' she asked despondently.

'Come on, forget it. Lead me to that macaroni cheese thing.'

'It'll be cold now.'

'What can we possibly find to do while we're waiting for it to heat up again?'

She threw him a wicked smile. 'Stop it, unless you mean it.'

He kissed her, feeling the response, the urgency of her mouth, banishing the memory of her morning, the ignominy of having been subjected to such treatment on the kitchen floor, of all places

'Oh, by the way,' he reminded her as he led her to the bedroom. 'You never did tell me why you changed your mind about Kinclaven.'

'I love you, that's all,' she smiled, but he suspected it was only half the truth.

'That's as good a reason as any.'

*

Grace was missing Alice's company, even if she had only stayed over for a couple of nights. When she had waved Alice off in Molly's car, Grace's over-riding thought had been that she was on her own now, a thought that pulled her up sharply: on her own now? What a nonsensical thing to think!

'But you can stay another night, surely?' she had asked her friend in the hallway that morning. 'I can take you back in the morning.'

'You've done enough for me already,' Alice said, but she, too, was reluctant to part. 'Besides, Molly has no one waiting desperately for her at home,' she added in a whisper, referring to the Menzies' sterile relationship since Molly's indiscretion.

'I suppose it was nice of her to offer,' Grace conceded.

'What?' Alice grinned. 'She only wants to nosey at my flat, that's why she offered.'

'Don't invite her in then.'

'Don't tempt me,' Alice said with amusement.

'You're naughty,' Grace smiled, suppressing a certain delight should Molly's plan come to naught.

Now, she switched on a few lamps, closed the curtains and began to prepare supper. James was upstairs, trying to find spare light bulbs, but Grace knew they had used them all and that it was a fruitless search. James, however, was convinced he could find one.

In the corner of the kitchen, the twin tub was spinning, filling the air with its piercing whine. James was in the room, touching her on the shoulder before Grace was aware of his presence. She jumped, feeling like an idiot.

'It's only me,' he said, amused. 'I didn't find any, but I found this.'

He was holding a packet, a thick brown envelope, which she knew held their wedding photographs. She supposed it had been all the talk about moving house and having babies that had triggered his interest in the photos, for it had reminded her vividly of their own youth, the early days of their marriage, the excitement, the passion...

She wondered if Beth would stand in her kitchen one day, mulling over the passage of the years, trying to recall the week, or day, or minute that had decided the past was past and it was time to move on and scatter their memories like personal effects in their wake.

'I thought we could look at them together,' James was saying, probably for the second time.

'During supper?'

'Can't supper wait?'

'I suppose so.'

'You don't have to look at them,' James frowned, laying the envelope on his desk.

'I want to,' Grace lied. 'All right, we'll do it now.'

He appeared mollified, picked up the photographs and sat at the dining table, spilling them onto the cloth, spreading them out singly, even arranging them in sequence. As soon as she saw the first one, looked at her skinny frame in the satin two-piece, her tiny shoes peeping beneath the skirt, the hand-picked bouquet of wild dog roses, Grace's fingers crept, involuntarily, to her wedding ring.

'You were so thin,' James said, disapprovingly, as if it had been Grace's deliberate choice. 'I could get my thumb and pinkie round your wrist.'

'I never heard you complain.'

He glanced across at her. 'No but I worried about you.'

'Because I was thin?' Grace laughed.

'Yes, and so weak.'

'James, for Heaven's sake, you could hardly say I was weak when I had to do everything in this house myself after Mum died. Who do you think chopped the logs, set the fire, carried heavy coal bags from the shed to the back porch?'

'During the War didn't the neighbours come to help you?'

'Once or twice, that's all.'

'And Graham Seaton,' James said quietly. 'I know he came to help. I think I said some unkind things about him,' James added quickly, unexpectedly, fiddling with the photographs, choosing the next in the sequence. 'Things I shouldn't have said.'

'It's over and done with anyway,' she said, more curtly than intended.

'But I want to apologise, Grace.'

'There's nothing to...'

'Please,' James insisted. 'Just allow me.'

Grace shrugged. It was of no consequence now; all it would achieve would be a few more minutes of unwelcome memories.

'Please yourself,' she said unkindly.

'Then I apologise for thinking that you and he were... that you liked each other too much.'

'I always told you we were only friends.'

'I know, but I didn't believe you until recently.'

'Why on earth are you mentioning this now?'

James appeared embarrassed. 'With your father suddenly coming on the scene again, well, it brought it all back.'

'There was nothing to bring back,' Grace countered firmly.

She was aware of the ticking of the clock, the sparking of the fire as the moments dragged by and the significance of his remark sank in.

'There was nothing to bring back,' she repeated eventually. ''Was it only because of my father that you want to discuss it now?'

'Does it matter?'

'Yes, it does. Someone's been talking to you.'

'It was Lily Morris,' he replied, but she knew he was lying.

'I'll speak to her.'

'If you like.'

Grace lowered her eyes, focussed on her wedding photographs and saw a young girl smiling into the camera; a young girl who convinced the world that she was the happiest creature on earth that day, challenging the sceptical onlooker to lay out his case for rebuttal.

James cleared his throat, as if to speak, but when she met his gaze he glanced away quickly.

The excuse of her father apart, Grace could think of no valid reason for James's bringing up the subject now when he could so easily have let it lie. What did his opinion of Graham matter anyway? Nothing had been achieved by mentioning it, other than to remind her that, for decades, he had suspected her of being unfaithful to him.

'Did you really think that I would be unfaithful to you?' she asked him, knowing she was punishing him, warning him not to raise it again.

'No, of course not, but he...'

'I've had enough of looking at photographs, James,' Grace said wearily, pushing her chair back and rising to her feet. 'I'll leave you to put them away, shall I?'

Supper forgotten, she went through to the parlour, re-stoked the fire from the coal scuttle and sat down in her favourite chair. A few minutes later, as she anticipated, the door opened and James came to sit opposite her at the hearth. As was her way, Grace looked at him and smiled. Had he not sought her out she might have stayed in this chair for at least an hour but he was here, remorseful, asking her forgiveness, and she would not be churlish.

*

Thomas held Daphne's hand while he put the ring on her finger, trying not to look at her expression lest he burst out laughing. Whenever he compared her to Charlotte Shepherd, Daphne came out second best, only marginally ahead of Maria, but that episode was dead and buried in a cemetery in a Buenos Aires suburb.

'Oh, Thomas,' Daphne breathed. 'It's so beautiful. I don't deserve it.'

He tended to agree, but of course he smiled and refuted her suggestion.

451

'My dear lady, I cannot think of anyone more deserving of this ring. Now, wiggle your fingers around and let me see it sparkle in the light.'

She duly obeyed, at which he made all the right noises, carried out all the appropriate gestures; in other words, performed like a sea lion in the circus; but for the most worthy of causes.

'I don't think we should rush into anything,' he told her, watching her face.

'But neither do we want to postpone it indefinitely,' she countered hesitantly, according to Thomas's script. 'I mean, I'm sure we both...' She looked at him coyly and he had to avert his eyes.

'It is entirely your decision, my dear,' he smiled, lifting the small velvet box and pretending to examine it.

'In that case, I'd like to be a Christmas bride,' he heard her say.

Even for Thomas, keen to get his hands on her money, Christmas seemed a step too close.

'Are you sure?'

'Aren't you?'

'Daphne, of course I am. I was only thinking of you, the upheaval it might bring to your life.'

She blushed, shook her head. 'It's the kind of upheaval every woman dreams of Thomas.'

He sighed, mostly because keeping up this façade was tedious and time-consuming but also to give her the impression he was prepared to fall in with her wishes.

'Will we be living in Perth?' she asked unexpectedly.

'Sorry?'

'I thought it best if we bought a house together, a new start for us both.'

He saw the advantages in such a proposition, but wondered if the cash pot would be diminished in any way, not knowing what she had in mind.

'You mean buy a flat in Perth?'

'Oh, not a flat, Thomas,' Daphne frowned disapprovingly. 'I was thinking more of one of these semi-detached villas in the Glasgow Road.'

Thomas almost baulked visibly: did the woman have any idea of what such houses cost?

'But would we need something so large, my dear? There's only the two of us and we...'

'Your daughter might come and stay,' she said, no trace of acrimony. 'She seemed such a lovely girl that I wouldn't mind.'

'I don't think Grace would leave her husband, even for one night.'

'Why ever not?'

'He had a heart attack last February, poor man. She takes care of him now, round the clock,' he concluded dramatically, as if he were included in the family's affairs.

'Oh, I see. Well, perhaps not your daughter then, but some of my friends perhaps.'

Since it was the first time she had mentioned friends, Thomas was confused, but considered that the conversation had run its course.

'Of course,' he smiled. 'Now, shall we go and celebrate our happy news?'

'I feel like shouting it from the rooftops,' Daphne ventured, throwing him a girlish glance.

'Will the Queen's Bridge do?'

She laughed gaily, waggled her ring finger at him. 'Nicely, thank you. I must be the happiest woman in the world tonight, Thomas.'

'And I the happiest man,' he lied with a dazzling smile.

452

Harry sat in his study poring over his work for the next day, aware of Beth moving around the kitchen, quietly, so as not to disturb him. He had long since stopped feeling guilty at her new persona, the basis of which was her belief that things were back to normal. Harry had no such illusions. Events and incidents always influenced the present, otherwise what had we learnt from them? Life would never be the same.

He rummaged around in the bottom drawer, which he kept locked, until he found Foxy's picture, the one he had taken rashly the first night she shared his bed. She was fully clothed, however, stretched out on the sofa, hands clutching a glass of red wine, eyes lively. Twenty minutes later he had carried her into the bedroom, hardly waiting until their clothes were removed before grabbing her and pulling her down.

He heard Beth approaching, stuffed the picture in the drawer and locked it, secreting the key in the file marked 'House conveyances.'

'Are you hungry yet?' Beth called from the hallway.

'Yes, I'll be out in two seconds.'

'I'll set the table then, light some candles.'

Harry folded the papers, placed them in full view on the desk and stood up, surveying the room from the doorway, just in case he had left a clue. At the back of his mind he knew he was a rat, but if he could keep it all under control, he saw no reason for it not working.

'I thought you might want to go and see the house tomorrow night, after work,' he suggested as they sat down at the table in the kitchen.

'Great, I'd love to. Except, you've already made up your mind,' Beth added, without malice. 'But I rather like you when you're masterful.'

'Gillespie.'

'Sorry?'

' 'When you're masterful, Gillespie'. That's what you'd have normally said.'

'Don't you mind when I call you that?'

'No, I told you, I like it.'

'O.K.' Beth shrugged, dishing out some ravioli and passing the plate to him.

'I hope you'll love the house.'

'I know I will.'

'It needs some work done, at least a new kitchen, new bathroom, maybe even some repairs to the chimneys, things like that.'

'Will we have enough money?'

Harry shook his head. 'Not nearly, but I thought I might rob a bank or two.'

She grinned and took a mouthful of the ravioli. 'Yuk, this is awful.'

'I thought it was fine,' he lied.

'It was Mum's recipe but I must have missed something out.'

He could have told her it had been boiled for too long and that was why it was rubbery; but for eighty percent of the time he was behaving himself; so that he could be with Foxy for the remaining twenty.

'Are you really serious about wanting children?' he asked now.

She appeared shocked, and yet only a few months ago had scorned the idea.

'Yes, I do. I think it's time I grew up.'

'It's a big step.'

'I know, but you'll be washing the nappies.'

'Hey, I thought you said they were disposable pads now?' he protested.

'Just joking.' She stopped chewing, gazed at him for a moment. 'Harry, are you happy?'

'Very,' he told her, and it was true. In fact, it was going to be the perfect arrangement.

*

Charlie was waiting for her outside the flat, although he must have been lurking out of sight when Harry left. Beth stared at him, knowing that something had to be wrong.

'Charlie, what are you doing here?'

'Change of venue this morning,' he smiled, taking her arm and giving her the electric shock she had come to expect when he touched her. 'I'm taking you for an early coffee break.'

'Is there anything wrong?'

He stopped walking, looked at her closely. 'Well, of course there is, dumpling, I'm in love with you and you're married to someone else.'

It was so starkly put, no frills or ribbons to distract the eye, that Beth was startled. She had known it, but it was the first time the words had taken root in her mind.

'Charlie, I...'

'Come on,' he said briskly. 'Let's walk; talk later.'

He took her to McEwens restaurant and ordered two coffees and shortbread.

Beth had gone through various emotions since she had encountered him outside the flat and was now in the throes of the deepest gloom, for she knew instinctively that something was wrong and she was too scared to hear it.

'There's no gentle way of putting this,' he began, and she imagined he had decided to get married.

'If you're going to be married, I don't want to know,' she said miserably.

'Oh, Beth,' he sighed, reaching for her hand, obviously not caring now who saw them. 'I could never marry, not when there's the slightest chance you'll dump him and come looking for me.'

'Why would I need to come looking, when I know where you are?' she asked, her heart sinking.

'Because I'm going to London.'

She closed her eyes and refused to allow the words to sink in, hoping that when she re-opened them he would backtrack, start the conversation over again.

'To London? Why would you go there?'

'To stay with an old pal, help him with his business.'

'If I pleaded with you to stay, would you?'

Charlie shook his head, lowered his eyes from hers. 'I can't, Beth. Seeing you every day, being with you, thinking of you with him...'

'But what about the antiques business?'

'It's yours, if you want it.'

'Mine?' She was horrified. 'But what do I know about antiques?'

'Come off it,' he cajoled, squeezing her hand. 'If it hadn't been for you these past months, there would have been no antiques business. Besides, Marjory would be thrown on the employment scrap heap if you didn't take it on.'

It was an aspect she had not considered, although as fond as she was of Marjory, it would not have constituted a significant part of her reasoning.

'The thing is, Harry and I have decided to start a family.'

Charlie grimaced, as if she had told him he had only days to live.

'Don't,' he said. 'I don't want to know.' He opened his eyes, looked at her with utter despair. She recognised it, because it was how she was feeling. 'Will you keep the business on for a while, maybe give Marjory a chance to find another job?'

She nodded. 'Of course I will. I can even work from home as a last resort.'

'Do you want me to give you my address in London?'

'Yes.'

'Will you write to me?'

'Yes.'

'Would it be all right if I wrote back to you care of the office?'

'Yes.'

They sat in silence while the waitress laid out the contents of her tray. When the woman moved off, Charlie was the first to speak.

'I know you'll hate me for saying this, but if you ever get tired of him, you know where I'll be.'

'Charlie, I...'

'Stop,' he smiled, releasing her hand. 'I know, and I shouldn't have said it.'

'When are you leaving?'

'Two weeks on Saturday.'

'Will you come into the office before that?'

'No, I've explained to Marjory. You're on your own now, kid,' he smiled.

She returned his smile but was so unhappy that she just wanted him to go.

*

Lily Morris watched Grace walk up the path, shaking the raindrops off the umbrella before she reached the front door and glancing at the window to see if Lily were there. When she saw her, she waved the umbrella before opening the door and going in.

'What a miserable day. I think my feet are soaking.'

'Take off your shoes, heat your toes at the fire,' Lily said, omitting the part about being daft not to wear boots on a day like this. 'I've just made pancakes.'

'And I'm supposed to be on a diet.'

'You mean to put weight on?' Lily asked facetiously.

'It's sneaking on now,' Grace complained, her hands prodding her waistline. 'I suppose it's my age.'

'Oh, aye,' Lily said dryly. 'Mrs Methuselah, that's you.'

They sat in the living room because the fire was blazing, Grace's shoes drying out on the brass surround and her toes wiggling before the flames, trying to get the circulation back.

'There's nothing I hate more than wet feet.'

Again, Lily resisted the temptation to mention suitable footwear in nasty weather, for the girl looked weary; hardly in need of a lecture.

'You can leave out the jam if you're worried about the pounds,' she said, handing a plate to Grace. 'Me, I couldn't care less now. That's the advantage of being an auld wifie.'

'Seventy-five's not old nowadays,' Grace frowned. 'You'd think you were decrepit.'

'Did you enjoy your birthday party then?'

'It was great, yes, but did you?'

'What, free sherries and enough food to keep me for a week? Of course I did.' She poured out the tea, waiting for her guest to explain why she had come.

Eventually, when the silence had gone on for at least two minutes, Lily decided to give Grace a prompt.

'Are you coming to the Dramatic Society next week?'

'Is it starting up again?'

'We've another two recruits,' Lily smiled. 'I'm not supposed to tell you, so you'll pretend not to know, but one of them is Alice.'

Grace was overjoyed, and then the smile faded, as if she had remembered that she was the last to know.

'I wonder why she didn't tell me.'

'Because she didn't want to put pressure on you to come.'

'Goodness, what a nice thing to do.'

'More folks would do more nice things for you if only you'd let them.'

Grace rolled her eyes at her companion. 'Come on then, say what you have to. Everyone else does.'

'Are you having bother with James?'

'Are you guessing?'

Lily would never tell her young friend that the man had tramped up to her door just the other day with his side of the story. She nodded now, eyes giving nothing away.

'Aye, I'm guessing.'

'Someone told him that Graham and I had never had an affair after I got married, and he's being extra nice to me now.'

'Well, it wasn't me.'

'I know that,' Grace said impatiently. 'But he said it was.'

At the last moment, Lily realised that she had forgotten to show the appropriate amount of surprise at the news and, to her dismay, it was occurring to Grace at the same time.

'You don't seem surprised that James has changed his mind about Graham.'

'Grace, dear, at my age nothing surprises you,' Lily said with a shrug, but she drew her guest's attention to the teapot. 'Some fresh tea?'

'Not just now, thanks,' Grace replied, her mind definitely not on the tea. 'You knew, didn't you, that someone had told him?'

Lily had an image of the boy sitting in Lucy Webster's sunroom, talking in hushed tones to James. She was wondering how long it would take for Grace to recall the same scene, how long before the penny dropped.

'Maybe you told him and you've forgotten,' Lily suggested feebly.

'And maybe seventy-five *is* old after all,' Grace retorted irritably. 'Anyway, I'm only glad the narking has stopped at last, whoever had the ability to change James's opinion. These pancakes are good, by the way,' Grace smiled. 'Do I have the same recipe?'

As Lily nodded, she was aware that the conversation would turn to trivia until her guest departed, and she would be spared mentioning James's visit.

Fifteen minutes later, she saw her guest to the door, helped her on with her coat and told her to avoid the puddles on the way home; then she closed the door and went back to seek the comfort of her own hearth, thinking back to her conversation with James Melville, turning his phrases over in her mind.

'I've been thoughtless.'

'Someone told me that Grace and Graham Seaton had been seen together.'

'I know now it was nonsense.'

'I think it best if I never mention him again.'

Now, as she sank deeper into the chair and closed her eyes for forty winks, Lily wondered what the boy could have said to change an opinion that James Melville had held for thirty years. Furthermore, Harry Gillespie could have no knowledge of Grace's life at that time. The more she thought of it, the more curious she became.

*

456

Grace and her daughter had walked around the village for the past hour or so, wrapped up like sore thumbs against the icy wind that was blowing down from the foothills of the Sidlaws and insinuating its way into the core of Grace's being. She was afraid to suggest turning for home, however, because it was imperative that Beth be permitted to unburden herself about Charlie Webster, and equally imperative that it be Grace who listened. She knew her daughter better than anyone, knew that the slightest lack of attention now would result in her never being told anything of importance again. She was not offended; it was simply Beth's way.

'So, you think I should carry on with the business, take over?'

'Yes, I think you'll make an excellent business woman, Besides, what else would you do?'

'And when kids come along?'

'Oh, I'll think I'll be able to help out,' Grace smiled, already looking forward to her new role.

'I dread to think what kind of mother I'll be.' Beth shivered. 'It's such a big step.'

Grace looked at her daughter. Where there was doubt and indecision in Beth's eyes, there had been only joy and determination on Grace's part to have her children. Not a single moment had passed wherein she had doubted she were doing the right thing, or if she were old enough, wise enough. It had never entered her head that she was not cut out for motherhood; the very idea went hand and hand with marriage as far as her generation had been concerned. These days, however, marriage stood alone; children were not the natural consequence; young women were wielding choice like a weapon.

'You'll be fine,' Grace said now. 'And you have Harry. I think he's quite excited about being a dad.'

'Heavens, here I am,' announced Beth with a gesture of frustration. 'Talking about starting a family and yet I've agreed to write to Charlie when he's in London.'

'What's that got to do with anything? What harm will it do?'

'Do you think it's wise of me to write to him?'

'Wise? We only discover what's wise in retrospect, my dear girl, but if I were you, I'd do it.'

'Really? Write to a man who wasn't Dad?'

'Yes.'

Beth stopped walking and rested her arms on a field gate. 'Did you ever?'

'Yes, I did.'

'Who?'

'Graham Seaton.'

Beth halted on the path. 'Did you and he...?'

'No, dear,' Grace said tolerantly. 'Nice girls didn't in my day.'

'So, that's the only reason you didn't?'

'It was one of the reasons, and perhaps the most important one, but not the only one.'

'What other one could there be?'

'I loved your father, only had eyes for him.' Inwardly, she flinched.

Suddenly, Beth changed the subject, took Grace unawares.

'Are you still annoyed about me seeing my grandfather?'

'Wanting to see your grandfather? Giving him the benefit of the doubt?' Grace shook her head. 'No, I'm not annoyed, Beth, I think you've been the only one in the family to give him a chance.' It was all lip service, but, for now, there was no other route with Beth.

'And you're not totally against him now, are you?'

It took all of Grace's strength to respond. 'No, of course not.'

457

Beth sighed and swung her scarf round her neck.

'Good. Let's get back, shall we, have a nice cup of tea?'

'I've made your favourite fruit cake.'

'Oh, Mum, you're the kindest woman in the world!'

Grace burst out laughing. 'Oh, Beth, I don't know what I'd do without you.'

'You are,' her daughter insisted angrily, linking arms with Grace. 'If I could be half as nice as you are when I'm all growed up, I'll be happy. D'you know, I heard the minister say once that a woman he'd known...' She paused and thought for a moment. 'Yes, that was it. He said 'it was easy to be good when she was around.' And that's you, Mum. No, don't argue, I'm not listening.'

She hugged Grace's arm tightly and they walked on briskly, hurrying the last few yards as the snow was beginning to fall again. Before they went inside, Grace held her daughter back and whispered dramatically.

'I'd rather you never mentioned writing to other men in front of your father. He might challenge Graham to a duel on the village green.'

'My lips are sealed,' Beth giggled as she opened the door.

Whenever they entered the hallway, James appeared, ushered them quickly.

'I was looking out for the two of you,' he said to Grace, taking her coat and fussing around her. 'There's a roaring fire in the parlour. Go and get warm, and I'll bring you both a hot drink.'

'Come on, mother,' urged Beth, awarding James a cheeky salute. 'Let's do as we're told.'

They stood side by side in front of the fire, spreading their hands above the heat of the flames, each occupied with her own thoughts, Grace's mind firmly on a future that included a grandchild. It was a situation that would keep Harry close for as long as she needed him; although the thought had occurred to her that it would be yet another demand on his time; and affection.

*

Thomas Blake walked over the Queens Bridge towards the Isle of Skye Hotel. His spirits were low, although there was no reason for it. She had said only that she wanted to see him, but from past experience he was not hopeful: Grace was not the sort of woman who blew hot and cold; she had dismissed him twice and he was not optimistic enough to think she would not do it a third time.

He was intrigued, however, that she wanted to meet him at all. She could not have heard of his impending marriage, for it was a closely guarded secret, nor could she know that he and Daphne were going on a cruise for six months; not exactly around the world but pretty damned near it.

'I think it's best that we begin married life on neutral ground,' she had told him as soon as the engagement ring was on her finger. 'It's years since I've had a proper holiday and I've always fancied a cruise.'

Thomas had no objections as long as someone else was paying for it. He had insisted – to allay any fears she may have had – that she keep her money in her own accounts; a tricky strategy, but one that would work.

'But why would I want to do that?' she had asked, perplexed.

'Because some people might think I'm after your money,' he had said, affecting a slightly amused expression, as if he had no need of her money and found the whole idea highly entertaining.

'I don't care what they think,' she had announced firmly, but his point of view had prevailed: for the foreseeable future Daphne would be the only one to have access to her fortune. *Softly softly catchee monkee* was Thomas's philosophy and he had no reason to believe it would fail.

He saw his daughter as soon as he walked into the lounge bar. For a split second, he wished that they met every Friday morning and were in the habit of exchanging idle gossip over cups of coffee, but then he saw the expression in her eyes and knew it was ridiculous.

'Grace, how nice to see you.'

'I've ordered coffee,' she said, glancing at the cups and pot on the table, making no attempt to take the hand he offered. 'If you want something else, you'd better find the waitress.'

'No, coffee's fine,' Thomas said, sitting down opposite her, smoothing out the folds of his overcoat. 'How is everyone?'

'We're all fine,' she smiled, but it was a smile that never reached her eyes. 'I wanted to see you before you leave.'

He stared at her: she could not possibly know about the cruise. She was bluffing. He leaned forward and poured out a cup of coffee for himself, although she had not touched hers.

'I'm leaving?' he laughed. 'It's news to me.'

She waited patiently until he had stopped laughing and he felt chastened.

'I'm sure you'll enjoy the cruise.'

'Anyway, you wanted to see me,' he reminded her, astounded by the fact she knew of his plans.

'Yes, I wanted to give you a copy of this letter.' She drew a piece of paper from her handbag, dropped it onto to the coffee table. 'It's a copy of a letter written to you by some woman years ago, when she had your child.'

Thomas's nerve failed him. He had never known of such a letter, although, heart pounding, he recalled only too vividly the wretched woman and her threats. He looked at it, reluctant to pick it up.

'Why on earth would anyone think it was mine?' he asked faintly. 'And why would she give it to you?'

He raised his eyes, met her gaze, saw then that, whatever was contained in the letter, his daughter was playing her trump card. After all this time, after years of swallowing his pride, after the effort he had made to grovel to her, subjugating himself to a slip of an insolent girl, she had known all along that she had in her possession something – whatever it was – that could end it in an instant. Thomas lowered his eyes to the letter.

'You can keep it,' she told him. 'I have the original.'

'What is it anyway?'

'As I said, you can keep it.' She lifted her cup and drank and he was perturbed to see no tremor in her fingers, no hesitation in her movements. Truly, she was not Charlotte's daughter, but his.

'You're right,' he admitted, still looking at the letter. 'I am going away, with my new wife.' He sighed, glanced across at her. 'Around the world, for want of a better place.'

'I hope you'll be very happy,' she said, but there was no warmth in her tone.

'No, you don't,' Thomas frowned, attempting to keep his voice down. 'You hate me; you've always hated me. The truth is, you have no idea how much we loved each other, Charlotte and me. But do you know something? I couldn't care less now.' As an actress, she was proficient – he allowed her that – but there was the slightest flicker in her eyes now, the first sign of doubt. 'I begged her to come with me, even went down on my knees, something I'd never done before or since for any woman.' He stood up, taking her by surprise. 'I'll leave the copy with you, my dear. I have no desire to see it, whatever it

459

is. Suffice it to say that my memories of your mother could never be sullied by anything or anyone, not even you. She was my one, true love, and that will never change. Goodbye, Grace, and good luck.'

He turned on his heel and walked towards the foyer, never expecting her to call out. When she did, Thomas halted immediately and retraced his steps.

'I know she loved you,' she said flatly. 'I have no intention of taking that away from her. All I want is for you to leave me alone.'

'Oh, you'll get your wish, my dear,' Thomas smiled, giving her a mock salute. 'I doubt if you'll ever see me again.' He looked at the letter, still lying on the table. 'I'd like to say I'm disappointed, Grace, but how can I condemn in others what I most admire in myself?'

Thinking there was nothing more to be said, Thomas turned to leave; but she spoke again.

'Do you remember that day, in Reform Street?'

He looked back, stared at her. 'Reform Street? What about it?'

She smiled a sad smile and shook her head.

'Goodbye,' she said dismissively.

'Tell me,' he insisted, stretching deceit to its limit. 'What should I remember about Reform Street?'

Still smiling, she lowered her eyes to the coffee pot and lifted it from the table, ignoring him completely.

Like a fool, Thomas waited, but after a few moments, he turned on his heel, walked quickly away, out into street; and never looked back.

Part Three: 1976

Chapter One

Harry Gillespie swivelled on the high-backed leather chair and gazed from the office window. The windows were wide open, but the incoming air was hot, lending no respite to his perspiring brow. He could have switched on the desk fan, but the constant whirring drove him mad and made it impossible to concentrate; although he had set work aside for the day, was casting his mind forward to the evening's festivities.

'Let's have a belated house-warming,' had been his suggestion to Beth several weeks previously, and, despite the pressing needs of a four-year old who was hell-bent on achieving constant attention, Beth had jumped at the chance.

'What a great idea!' she had exclaimed, no longer throwing herself at him in gratitude now, but happy nevertheless. 'I can invite the villagers as well, get to know them.'

Thinking back, Harry suppressed a smile: to have lived in the place for four years and still know diddly squat about your neighbours – one of Alice's expressions – should have sounded alarm bells, but Beth was determined to invite all and sundry, only coming to a shuddering halt when she realised she knew only a few of their names.

'Bugger,' she said, no longer throwing him an apologetic glance if she swore. 'I'll have to ask the postman what their names and addresses are.'

'Or you could drive round and invite them in person,' Harry had suggested vainly, for she would baulk at such an idea.

'No, I'll just ask Ernest.'

'Ernest?'

'The postman.'

'You're on first name terms with the postman, yet you don't know your next-door neighbours?'

Beth had shrugged. 'The nearest one's Sheila, I think, or maybe Stella. Something like that. Besides,' she had added, picking Anna up expertly and wiping the child's nose. 'They live half a mile away, even if they are our next-door neighbours.'

Now, in the stifling heat of the office, Harry tried to imagine the kinds of conversations that might be unfurling in three hours' time. He hoped that none of the women were mothers, for Beth would not take kindly to it. Despite her considerable skills as a mother, she was not prone to indulging in hours of swapping baby stories or competing for the title of 'mother of infant prodigy'. In fact, at first, he had been appalled to witness her dispassionate treatment of their daughter, but now, having profited from the results, he was beginning to reappraise his wife's prowess as a child psychologist.

The clock in the vestibule struck four and, on cue, Sandra tapped on his office door.

'Time to go home, Mr Harry,' she smiled through the half-open door. 'And you have a party tonight, so off you go.'

'I wish you were to be there.'

She raised her eyebrows. 'But I told you, I always go...'

'Yes, I know,' Harry said impatiently. 'But I was hoping you could put it off for once.'

'And miss the latest tittle-tattle? Not on your life!'

'What do you talk about anyway, on these girly nights?'

She tapped the side of her nose. 'You'd be horrified.'

'Come and sit down for a moment, Sandra, I'm fed up'

Sandra pulled a face, but drew the door closed behind her and dragged a chair to the other side of his desk. He never failed to appreciate her kindness towards him but, since

Foxy's break-up with Mike, he had wondered if Sandra blamed him. There had never been anything he could pinpoint, no visible change in her attitude to him; but, occasionally, he had a feeling that she was holding him responsible; and yet, it had been her idea at the beginning.

The other aspect was her friend, Daphne, now Mrs Blake, although there was nothing more Harry could have done to pluck the old dear from the arms of a superlative conman.

'Someone should take you by the scruff of the neck,' she frowned at him as she took her seat now. 'If you want to know the true meaning of 'fed up' I'll take you to a housing scheme on the outskirts of Perth.'

'I'm not going to genuflex to my good fortune,' Harry said bluntly, taking a cigarette from the packet and offering one to Sandra.

'Thanks, I will, since it's lousing time.'

Harry looked at her closely. 'Lousing time? Sounds itchy.'

Sandra laughed and waited for him to light her cigarette.

'It's Scots for going home time.'

'How many bloody years have I lived here and still I don't know the bloody language.'

'That's two 'bloodys' in one sentence,' Sandra frowned. 'You owe the box two pounds.'

Harry sighed and took a couple of pound coins from his wallet.

'Here, put them in your daft box.'

'Thank you,' Sandra said primly. 'Oh, by the way, did Mr Andrew tell you the interviews are on Thursday week?'

'No, I haven't seen him.' Holding the cigarette so that the smoke would drift towards the open window, Harry contemplated coming right out and asking Sandra if she blamed him for Foxy's break-up.

'There are five candidates,' she was saying now, before he had reached a decision. 'Three fresh from University, one from Glasgow, and one who's a pal of Mr Andrew's,' she concluded pointedly.

'Need I ask who'll get the position?'

'No, it's a *fait accompli*,' Sandra sighed, in her usual forthright manner. 'I feel rather sorry for the other four, coming all this way to endure a gruelling interview and unaware they'll be wasting their time.'

Harry was hardly in a position to agree, since he had secured this job on the recommendation of David Routledge, and so he merely smiled and shrugged.

'You're too soft,' he told his companion. 'It's the way of the world.'

'I suppose.' Sandra drew on her cigarette, gave him a covert glance that did not escape his notice. 'How are you enjoying being the Laird of Cockpen?'

'What?'

'A Scottish song,' Sandra explained with a smile. 'I meant, how are you enjoying life as a country squire?'

'Is that what you think?'

'You forget I've been in your house, and if you don't think it's palatial, Mr Harry, then you should get out more.'

'It's big, I'll grant you that.'

'Beth's got good taste. I think you're very lucky.'

'I know I'm lucky,' Harry lied. 'She liked you too.'

'And your little girl, Anna, isn't it? She's absolutely delightful, a credit to you both.'

'A credit to Beth you mean,' Harry said brusquely. 'She's amazed me, I can tell you. She wasn't even keen to have any, but she's raising the most obedient and unselfish child in the whole of Perthshire.'

'Are you stopping at one?' Sandra asked, never one to hesitate over introducing personal matters.

'I'd like a boy,' Harry sighed, regarding his cigarette for a moment. 'But I'm not sure that I can persuade Beth.'

'Did she have a bad time of it?'

'No, quite the reverse. Groaning with pain one minute, whisked into PRI the next, and within the hour, there was Anna.'

'Yet she's not keen to have another?'

Harry smiled. 'No, but I have ways of persuading her.'

He was surprised to see Sandra blush. 'I don't wish to know that.'

Sensing she was on the defensive, Harry dared to ask:

'How's Foxy?'

Sandra had been stubbing her cigarette out in the saucer laid aside for such purposes, but now she paused, glanced at him with an unusually severe expression, and he thought he was in for a telling-off.

*

Beth gazed at her daughter asleep on the settee, a teddy bear clutched in her hand, her tiny eyelashes flicking as she dreamed. This had always been the best part of the day: Anna dozing for an hour, Beth sitting with a magazine and a cup of coffee; no sound to disrupt the stillness of the room. It was the perfect end to a hectic afternoon. Even the dog slumbered at this time, worn out by chasing rabbits and keeping out of Anna's way.

As the clock struck four, Beth looked up from the magazine and decided to check the hors d'oeuvres in the oven, although the aroma was putting her mind at rest: nothing was burnt this time, unlike Christmas past when she forgot to set the timer and the state of the turkey had brought a whole new meaning to the word 'roasted'.

She smiled to herself as she recalled everyone's reaction, her mother's in particular.

'What's wrong with these?' she had asked, raking through the freezer and producing a packet of Birds Eye fish fingers.

'Well, nothing, I suppose,' a beleaguered Beth had replied, and so fish fingers it had been. Harry's reaction had been the least enjoyable, but she avoided looking at him for half an hour, by which time he had mellowed.

She glanced from the kitchen window, at the red squirrel diving and plunging through the fir trees, marvelling at his acrobatic skills, her heart skipping a beat if he seemed about to falter.

The kitchen was huge, but she was used to it now and wondered how she had ever coped in the flat. At first, she had been terrified to be left alone in this house, in the middle of nowhere; vulnerable to any Tom, Dick or Harry who happened to pass by; until she discovered that no one did....pass by, that was. As the weeks became months, and the months years, she had come to realise that, if she was not content with eerie silences, creaking noises, the sudden death-defying crash of a bird on a windowpane, or the diverse intricacies of the septic tank, then she had no business to live here.

When the telephone rang she presumed it was Harry, making sure she was dutifully at home.

'Is that Beth?'

At first, she did not recognise the voice, but then he spoke again and she almost shrieked with joy: it was Charlie Webster.

'Charlie!' Beth yelled into the receiver. 'Oh, it's great to hear your voice!'

'Well I can certainly hear yours,' he laughed. 'Isn't there a law about decibels down a phone line?'

'Where are you? How are you? What have...?'

'Hey, slow down,' he said loudly. 'Let's have some hush for a moment.'

'Sorry, but I'm so thrilled to hear your voice. I've missed you so much.'

'Have you?'

Beth had not lost her habit of telling the truth, despite the adage about mellowing with age.

'To be honest, I think about you all the time.'

'Have you kept up the business?' he asked, and she was disappointed that he had not replied in kind.

'Yes, well, as much as I can with Anna around.'

'Ah, your daughter,' Charlie said, and Beth guessed he had been in constant touch with his mother. 'Anna's a lovely name.'

'Dad said it had to end in 'a' because she's a girl,' Beth explained. 'Said it was more feminine and that he'd been annoyed that Mum had chosen 'Beth' for me. Anyway, how are you and what's been happening?'

'I've been doing ordinary things,' he laughed. 'Just like everyone else.'

For some stupid reason, Beth's heart sank at the idea of him with a wife and children; yet, why should he not be married and have a family? She was.

'How many kids do you have?'

'Two,' he told her and she was so annoyed at herself for being dejected that she slapped the side of her head.

'Two? Gosh, that's nice.'

'Listen,' he went on quickly, not even giving her their gender or names. 'I've come back up here to start up a letting agency for Edward. In Perth, of all places.'

'You're back?' she repeated with a mixture of delight and trepidation. 'Well, that's wonderful.'

'I live not far from you actually.'

Again, and quite illogically, Beth's mind played a duet: part joy, part fear, in the key of doubt.

'I live in the middle of nowhere,' she said, mentally running over the area, trying to figure out which house had been sold recently.

'Yes, I know. If I stand on the chimney pot I can see your gable end.'

Years ago, she would have drawn his attention to the innuendo, and perhaps he might have laughed, but now she was so excited at the prospect of seeing Charlie again that she allowed no time for frivolities.

'Where are you, for Heaven's sake?'

'You know the old mill, the one the artist lived in?'

'What, just across the river from us?'

'That's the one.'

'You mean, you've bought it?'

'Rented it for the moment, until the guy makes up his mind.'

Beth heard Anna gurgling, knew that any second she might start wailing if she found herself alone in the room; but she remained where she was.

'Are you free tonight?' she asked casually, twirling the flex around her fingers.

'Tonight?'

'Yes, we're having a belated house warming. I'd love you to come.'

There was a moment's hesitation, during which Beth held her breath; but then, and it was music to her ears, he laughed and she knew he would accept.

*

465

Grace Melville opened her son's bedroom door and surveyed the interior from the threshold. The difference in tidiness was unbelievable: there was not a single item on the floor, nor the usual unmade bed, nor even the portrait gallery of his 'young women', as she had described them in her mind for years.

The bedroom was pristine, and she had Emily to thank for that. The idea of her son becoming a responsible and organised husband, head of a household, albeit just the two of them to start with, was a constant source of amazement to Grace. The boy had grown up so much in the past few years that any doubts she might have had over his ability to settle down and take care of a wife had melted away.

When the day dawned that the young couple would move into their own home, Grace knew she would shed tears; but, for now, she enjoyed their company in the cottage and revelled in the youngsters' chatter.

The doorbell rang and she turned swiftly to go downstairs. As she stepped into the hallway, the front door opened and Alice rushed in.

'Hi!' she breathed, hugging Grace in the passing before hurrying towards the kitchen. 'I'll have to get these in water muchos pronto,' she called over her shoulder. 'They've been in the car since breakfast time!'

Grace followed her friend, followed the trail of Estee Lauder's 'Youth Dew' and found Alice filling the deep sink in the kitchen.

'They're gorgeous,' Grace said. 'You've paid a fortune for them, I'll bet.'

'Nah,' Alice grinned, arranging the stems carefully, tweaking them out. 'It was only a couple of pounds.'

'Liar.'

'Honestly.'

'More like twenty.'

'Hey, what time are we leaving?'

'Beth said to be there at half seven, so maybe quarter past seven?'

'It's only a few miles,' Alice agreed, drying her hands on a kitchen towel. 'What the heck did we ever do without these things?' she laughed, screwing the piece of towel into a ball and pressing her foot on the pedal bin.

'I couldn't live without them either' Grace smiled. 'The washing and ironing they save.'

'Of course, you were never a fan of housework, were you?'

'Would it be too strong a word to say I loathed it?'

'Come on, you've got Isobel Patterson, to help and she's a gem.'

Grace poured hot water onto two teabags and stirred briefly.

'Can you get the milk jug for me?'

'And sugar for me,' Alice reminded her friend. 'I think men prefer the more rounded woman.' She giggled suddenly. 'I guess I'm so round I could bounce if he dropped me.'

'How's your love life anyway?'

'They're both fine,' Alice smiled mischievously. 'One for escorting me to parties and restaurants, the other as a tennis partner. Quite a suitable arrangement, don't you think?'

'As long as you always remember which is which.'

'Steven's a real gentleman,' Alice sighed as she lowered her cup to the table. 'Eyes pop when we go out together, you know, and I suppose I'd be foolish to turn him down if he asks me.'

Grace stared at her companion. 'Do you think he will?'

'If I give him the slightest encouragement, he might.'

'And will you?'

Alice shrugged, sipped her tea. 'I wish I knew. Would I like him in my bed?'

'Only you can answer that.' Grace smiled wryly. 'Have you ever been in a clinch?'

'I've kissed him several times,' Alice frowned. 'But it certainly didn't set the world on fire.'

'Does it ever, at our age?'

'I read in Cosmopolitan recently that...'

'Alice, for Pete's sake! That's a magazine for Beth's generation, not ours.'

'Still, I pick up the odd tip here and there.' Alice shook her head suddenly and grinned. 'Hark at me. Mutton dressed as lamb.'

'You look lovely, Alice,' Grace said generously, although there was an American influence upon her friend's fashion sense, the continual quest to ward off wrinkles and have her grey hairs dyed.

'I've brought the blue dress for Beth's soiree,' Alice said now. 'D'you think there'll be any unattached males?'

'Isn't two enough?'

'Safety in numbers, isn't that what they say?'

'Come on you femme fatale, help me make a few sandwiches for tea.'

*

The moment that Harry walked over the threshold, he heard Anna yelling. He knew it would be short-lived, for Beth was more intolerant than he of their daughter's bad temper, and so he strolled to the drawing room door, confident that peace would reign within minutes.

His presence in the doorway went unnoticed by his daughter, so intent was she upon tearing her colouring book into small pieces, but he caught Beth's eye and was satisfied with her wink.

'Good girl,' Beth said suddenly, and Anna stopped shredding.

'What, Mummy?' Anna stared.

'I said 'good girl'.'

'Am I good?'

'Of course you are. If you weren't, you wouldn't get to go to the beach next week to paddle and make sand castles.'

Harry shook his head with admiration: she had a new approach every time, and it never failed.

Anna looked first at the remnants of her colouring book, and then at her mother, who was smiling pleasantly, sitting on her knees, appearing in no hurry to tidy up.

'A new bucket and spade?' Anna asked apprehensively.

'Of course. The old ones need thrown out now. You've had them for two years already.'

'Thank you, Mummy,' the little girl beamed, beginning to gather up the pieces of discarded colouring book. 'In the bin now.'

'I'll put them in the bin now,' Beth insisted, rising to her feet and giving Harry another wink. 'While you're clearing up, darling,' she addressed their daughter, 'I'll just pop into the kitchen for five minutes.'

'Yes, Mummy,' was the reply, although Anna did not look up from her labours.

'When you've finished tidying up, go up to your room and get ready for tea. Wash your hands and comb your hair. Daddy will be home soon.'

In the kitchen, Harry put his arms around her and kissed her briefly on the cheek. 'Thanks for not telling her I was home yet.'

'I know you need time to unwind.'

'Do you ever have time to unwind?'

'All the time,' Beth smiled, stepping away to check the contents of the oven.

'You seem happier today.'

Beth seemed surprised. 'Don't I always look happy?'

Harry was wary of her in such a mood. She had long since dispensed with the fiery tantrums – the result of being a mother, he suspected – but she still resorted to mind games, sometimes exasperating him with the sharpness of her intellect, and usually emerging the winner.

'I can tell you've had a good day,' was all he said, watching her as she moved around the kitchen. 'Did you and Anna go for a walk?'

'Yes, in the morning, before lunch.' She turned and looked at him. 'Did you know that the artist fellow has left the old mill?'

'No, didn't even know he'd been there.'

'Yes, you did,' Beth said patiently. 'He came here once, selling his paintings.'

'Ah, right. Him.'

'You said he looked like something the cat dragged in,' she reminded him.

'Well, he did.'

'Anyway, he's moved out, rented the place to Charlie Webster.'

Harry was glad her back was to him. 'Goodness, is he back here?'

'Obviously,' she said, turned and gave him a quick smile before extracting the baking trays from the oven. Harry sauntered over to the drinks cupboard and helped himself to another whisky, deciding not to pursue the subject of Charlie Webster.

'You might want to go and check on Anna,' Beth said without looking up. 'She loves when you come home.'

'And I love coming home,' he said on the spur of the moment.

'And so you should,' Beth said with a faint smile. 'Oh, hope you don't mind, but I've invited Charlie to the bash tonight.'

'No, that's great.'

He drank down the whisky and went off to greet his daughter. On the way up the ornate staircase, he was seized with the usual panic that was invoked by another man's appearance in their social circle; not just another man, but one who had once lusted after Beth. It was ridiculous, he knew, for, if his wife were to succumb to the charms of any man, it was most likely to be a Chopin addict.

*

Beth arranged the dozens of sausage rolls neatly on the plates, and then covered them with tin foil. The vol-au-vents sat, not so neatly, on the oven tray, slightly brown at the edges, but acceptable, especially when there would be an abundance of alcohol. She counted the sandwiches and slices of bite-size pizzas and quiche and decided there would be enough, although, just in case, she had defrosted trays of cheese puffs that her mother had brought over recently for emergencies. The thought of her mother filled Beth with renewed anxiety: Grace Melville had been unusually reserved, remote even, for the past year; ever since Beth had taken time off to look after Anna herself. She felt guilty that her mother was no longer so useful, but the truth was, she wanted to see Anna growing up. The time would come soon enough when the child was heading for her first day at school.

She heard Harry and Anna coming downstairs, the child excitedly relating the events of her day, whilst Harry pretended to be utterly engrossed. Beth caught sight of herself in the mirror above the Welsh dresser and gave her reflection close scrutiny: did she look like the downtrodden mother of a four-year-old yet? Was there anything in her face to suggest that she was tethered to the back green; like her mother?

She laughed, but the idea persisted.

*

Charlie Webster polished his shoes and buffed them with a soft cloth for at least five minutes; not that he had to, but it was the amount of time he spent thinking about Beth Gillespie. He stopped suddenly, trying to recall her husband's name; decided it was Harry.

Charlie had known she would have children and settle down to happily married life; but he had never imagined that he might choose to come back and witness it. He sighed and laid the gleaming shoes on the floor, and then stood for a moment, wondering if he had been a complete idiot. Leaving a lovely house, a very biddable wife and two well-behaved children – not to mention his mistress – had not been the wisest thing to do; but he was fed up being wise. He wanted to be the old Charlie Webster.

*

Thomas Blake surveyed the menu with a wary eye. It was incredible, but he was utterly bored with gracious living. Daphne, however, was lapping it up, never tiring of the best hotels and limousines, or of the finest culinary delights of top restaurants. Had Thomas not achieved generous access to her fortune, he might have packed his suitcase years ago.

The sheer indulgence of buying anything he wanted, going anywhere he chose, was too enticing, however, and he knew he would stay; despite the hum-drum aspect that the hoi-polloi believed applicable only to their own, lowly existence.

'Oh, there you are,' he heard Daphne trill. 'I was waiting like an idiot in the suite. Why didn't you let me know you were coming down?'

'Because you were in the shower and obviously didn't hear me,' he lied. He smiled beneficently at his wife. 'You look radiant, my love.'

Daphne simpered and Thomas averted his gaze.

'Do you like my new dress?'

'Beautiful.'

'And the evening bag?'

'So elegant.'

She sat perusing the menu, but he knew she could not understand a word of it. After a moment, she raised her eyes to his. 'Thomas, dear?'

'Yes, my sweet?'

'I was wondering.'

Thomas was wary: he heard a familiar challenge in her tone, guessed that she was about to ask him, for the hundredth time, if they could go back to Scotland sometime soon.

'About going back to Perth?' he asked.

She blushed. 'How did you know?'

Thomas sighed. A hasty word may be on his lips, but it would certainly never see the light of day. There was too much at stake.

'You're not enjoying my company, Daphne?'

'Goodness me, Thomas! You know I am!'

'When we get to Gibraltar, we'll discuss it seriously, shall we?'

She nodded, but her expression was not hopeful.

'I think I'll have the trout for a change,' he smiled.

She had no idea which item it was, and so she chose the same.

As they sat in silence waiting for the waiter to attend their table, Thomas's thoughts darted, suddenly and unbidden, to his daughter, Grace.

Chapter Two

Grace was always the first to arrive. She knew that her daughter was perfectly capable – something that never failed to astonish her – but it was so rewarding to say 'goodnight' to Anna, tell her a brief bedtime story perhaps, and then to sit quietly watching the little girl sleeping soundly.

Grace had counted her blessings when Beth's pregnancy had gone well from start to finish and every night, before she fell asleep, Grace sent up a silent prayer of gratitude.

She gave her daughter a heartfelt hug.

'Mum, how did I know you'd be first?'

'I have no idea, darling, you must be a mind-reader!'

'She's in her bed waiting for you to go up.' Beth indicated the stairway. 'There's plenty time for a story, but don't let her get out of bed.'

'I won't,' Grace fibbed, already envisaging Anna sitting on her knee, fingers tightly clutching the book. 'Alice can help you in the kitchen if you want.'

'Everything's done,' Beth smiled, and her mother could only marvel. 'Now, off you go, Granny, and enjoy yourself.'

Grace climbed the stairs and crept quietly towards Anna's room. As she made her way along the hallway, she glanced into open doorways, admiring her daughter's taste, envying this generation their access to what seemed to be infinite financial resources. She was delighted, of course, that the two of them had made such a success of their life together but, at the back of her mind, she was often beset by a fleeting resentment; that she and James had worked equally hard and had little to show for it.

'Granny!'

'Anna, my pet, you look lovely.'

'Do I?'

'Like a fairy princess.'

'Do you know any?'

'Oh, yes, lots.'

Anna gave Grace a look of adoration. 'Am I the prettiest?'

'Of course. Now, which story would you like?'

'Mummy bought me a new one.' The little girl pulled the book from beneath her pillow. 'Look, it's called '*Chicken Licken*'.'

Automatically, Grace turned to the final page: if there were no happy ending, she would alter the last page.

*

Next door, Harry heard Grace reading to his daughter. He should wait until the story was finished before going to greet her, but it was twenty past seven and the first guests would arrive soon, after which he would be obliged to play the part of Laird. Silently, he remonstrated with himself, for it had been his idea, this house-warming party, although now he could not recall his reasons.

He was aware of Grace's voice in the next room, heard her injecting excitement and drama into the story, imagined Anna's enraptured gaze. His heart skipped a beat at the thought of his own mother missing out on the joy of grandchildren; but then he readjusted the idea, given that Rachel Gillespie was not the kind of woman to enjoy such pursuits.

As luck would have it, he was closing the bedroom door when Grace moved into the hallway. She gasped, perhaps at his sudden appearance.

'Harry,' she remembered to whisper. 'I'd no idea you were up here.'

'I had to hear it again,' he said solemnly.

'Hear what again?'

'*Chicken Licken*. It's my favourite. Except the ending was different.'

She stifled a laugh and took the arm he proffered. 'Oh, for Heaven's sake, it was far too miserable. Far too sad for a little girl.'

'What did Anna say?'

'She took the book and turned to the last page, as if she could read it. Then she said it was different.'

'Did she mind?'

'No,' Grace smiled. 'Children love surprises.'

'I'm sure she loved it,' he smiled down at her. 'You look well, for a change.'

'I'm not listening,' she said lightly. 'And Beth looks extremely well.'

'Extremely?' he repeated absentmindedly, perturbed at an idea that was beginning to assault his mind.

'Yes, she's really happy just now.' Grace grimaced and paused at the top of the staircase. 'I mean, she's... Oh, I don't know what I mean,' she frowned suddenly.

'I thought the same, that she was looking extra happy tonight.'

'There you are then,' Grace said triumphantly. 'So you do know what I meant.'

'I think it has something to do with her old boss.'

He saw the flicker of annoyance, knew she was angry for being led along a path that compounded his own feelings about Charlie Webster. A crease appeared on her brow. For a moment, she looked at him closely, as if she suspected he had laid some kind of trap; but then she smiled and squeezed his arm.

'I should have told her he'd come back.'

'You knew?'

'Lucy told me.'

'Yet you never told Beth?'

'To be honest, I forgot,' she said pleasantly, but Harry found it hard to believe. 'Anyway, why are we talking about him anyway?'

'Because she invited him tonight.'

He had to admit that she had lost none of her acting skills: not a glint of surprise, or confusion, or indeed any emotion, found its way to the surface. Against his better judgement, he smiled.

'You seem pleased she's invited him,' Grace suggested.

They were still at the top of the stairs, and now the doorbell rang, interrupting the conversation.

'Ah, our neighbours are arriving,' Harry said, disengaging his arm and setting off down the stairs. 'Come and help me break the ice.'

*

Alice and James were on the terrace admiring the flowerbeds, always a safe topic where her friend's husband was concerned; not that he was a difficult man to converse with, but she often wondered if she were boring him rigid or if he were really so interested in what she was saying.

'Do you do most of the gardening for Beth and Harry?' she asked now.

'Some of it. But they have a gardener,' he concluded, with a tone that reflected disapproval. 'He's very good, but sometimes he puts things in the wrong place.'

'It's a huge garden,' Alice sighed. 'More like a park really. You must be proud of her.'

472

'For having a garden like a park?' James frowned.

'Yes,' Alice said, sticking to her guns. 'And for the house too, and all that's in it.' She gave him a look of determination, and he smiled.

'You're a good friend to Grace.'

'As she is to me.'

'I sometimes wonder where the years have gone,' James said slowly, his eyes wandering across the garden. 'I can hardly believe I'm almost sixty.'

'You don't look a day over fifty.' Alice said, and it was true. 'And as for Grace.' She shook her head and tutted. 'No one should look that good at our age.'

'Do you ever hear from Martin?'

The question came out of the blue and Alice had no time to plot a clever reply.

'Martin?'

'Yes.' James turned to look at her. 'Do you ever regret divorcing him?'

This time, there was no necessity for her to plot. She had regretted the divorce for years.

'Yes, I do. I wish I'd been more like Grace.'

'You mean Grace wanted to divorce me but didn't have the courage?'

Alice was horrified, until she saw the merriment in James's eyes.

'Oh, you!' she exclaimed. 'Always the joker.'

He seemed pleased to have caused her some embarrassment, but then, before he could speak, they heard a voice behind them and it was Beth.

*

Charlie was late. By the time he was in sight of the massive doorbell, it was almost half past eight and he stood for a long moment before he heralded his arrival, rehearsing what he might say in mitigation. As the clanging resonated in the house, he heard footsteps on a tiled floor and knew it was Beth.

The door flew open and she emitted a shriek of delight.

'Charlie! How wonderful!'

He was surprised when she hurled herself into his arms and hugged him with a force akin to a grizzly bear. She had never shown any affection for him in public, despite their one foray into the joys of kissing.

'Beth, you look fabulous, you really do,' he told her as they stepped back to appraise each other. 'You haven't changed a bit.'

'What?' she cried, and he suddenly remembered her volatility. 'You mean I went to all the bother of growing up and you haven't even noticed?'

Charlie had noticed; but she was a married woman – with a child – and he was not about to make a fool of himself a second time.

'Of course you've grown up. It's a few years since I've seen you.'

'And I bet I was horrible to you.'

'You were actually,' he dared to say, but that would be as far as it went.

'I'll make it up to you,' she laughed, grabbing his arm and hauling him inside. 'Now, come and meet the neighbours, although you probably know them all already.'

He picked up the omission of 'husband', but was too afraid to think it was significant. She pulled him along a grand hall, bedecked with antiques and pictures on every inch of every wall, and then into a room that was bigger than the ground floor of the mill.

'Look, everyone!' she shouted above the din. 'The guest of honour is here!'

Charlie felt a dozen pairs of eyes swivel in his direction, and it was all he could do to stand firm and not make a bid for freedom.

From his position on the terrace, where he had gone to speak to Alice, Harry saw his wife introducing Charlie Webster to the other guests. He was still a handsome man, and one with charisma, an element about Webster he had forgotten; a word that encompassed all things sexual.

Sexual!

Harry almost dropped his glass: he had a sudden image of Foxy in his arms. He gave himself a mental shake, but Alice must have spotted his momentary shiver.

'Are you getting cold, young man?' she asked now.

'No, just hungry. Let's go and raid the kitchen.'

'You wouldn't be so cruel. Come on, I think Beth wants us to meet someone. Do you know who it is?' she asked innocently.

'Yes, it's Beth's old boss apparently.'

'Not so old,' Alice chortled, and then he heard the intake of breath, as if she was aware of the implication. 'I mean, *I'm* available, that's what I mean.'

'You're a very attractive lady,' Harry told her, mostly to pretend he had missed the inference, missed the link between Webster's looks and Beth. 'Grace was telling me you've two suitors in tow.'

'She told you that?' Alice feigned shock. 'The besom!'

'You should live in France,' Harry smiled, taking her arm to go inside. 'They have the perfect arrangement.' As he uttered the words, his step faltered, so powerful was the thought of Foxy in his bed. 'Oops,' he apologised to Alice. 'Must get these paving stones seen to.'

When they entered the room, Beth appeared immediately with the honoured guest. It was true, what Grace had said: Beth did look happier than she had done for months.

'Harry, you remember Charlie, of course, and Charlie, you remember Harry?'

'Charlie, I'm so pleased you could come along at such short notice.'

Harry was fishing for information: he had only Beth's word that she had invited him that day. For all he knew, they might have been planning this for weeks; might even have been meeting for weeks.

'When I called Beth today, I'd no idea you were having guests tonight. If I had, I'd not ...'

'Yes, you would,' Beth butted in, still hanging onto his arm. 'Because I'd not have taken 'no' for an answer.' She glanced at Harry and Alice. 'Anyone hungry?'

'Starving,' Alice grinned. 'Lead me to the grub!'

'It's laid out in the dining room,' Beth said. 'Come on, let's be first.'

As she led the way, talking animatedly to Webster, Harry had to admire her organisational skills. Single-handedly, and with a young child and a dog to contend with, his wife had cooked and baked for two days, produced hundreds of hors d'oeuvres, sandwiches, cakes and biscuits, and had still had time to clean the house and take care of him. He had to hand to her: she had turned out to be a fantastic wife and mother. Furthermore, she also kept an eye on the antiques business from the downstairs study.

He had to suppress his resentment of her, for it was both uncalled for and illogical.

Grace was in two minds about the appearance of Charlie Webster. She could still recall the months of Beth's moods; the sullen, lifelessness that had over-taken her daughter when Charlie had left. Had she not suffered the same kind of love-sickness with

Graham, she might not have recognised the symptoms; but she had, and she did. Beth had exhibited all the signs of having loved Charlie Webster, but, just like Grace, when she had been young, had not known how to deal with conflicting emotions.

Now, as she watched the two of them chattering and laughing, she knew that it could go one of two ways: either Charlie would be strong enough, gallant enough, to keep things on a friendly basis, or Beth would prove too much for him to handle and would pull him into the drama that was her life.

She had seen the looks that passed between her daughter and Harry, had held her breath on countless occasions when Beth had pushed him to the bounds of endurance; and, strangely enough, he no longer seemed to take umbrage if his wife belittled him in public or cast him a scathing glance. It was not the Harry Gillespie she thought she had known.

'Hey, you're daydreaming.'

With a start, Grace turned to see Harry beside her. She was grateful that his gaze was on Beth, for it gave her time to readjust her smile.

'I was just thinking I could do with more to eat.'

'Same here. May I escort you to the dining room, Madam?'

'I thought you'd never ask.'

They passed through groups of people whose names Grace had forgotten already, although they were fairly decent people, mostly older than Beth and Harry because of the house prices around here; but friendly enough.

'I was just wondering,' Harry was saying. 'Do you think it's a good idea that Webster's come back?'

He looked down at her, an explicit question in his eyes.

'There was nothing like that between them,' Grace lied gamely. 'They were never interested in anything other than the business.'

He nodded, appearing satisfied with her lie. 'Fine. I just wanted to know.'

'You need never worry about Beth,' Grace heard herself add rashly.

'Worry about her?' Harry repeated with a frown. 'Why would I worry about her?'

'Stop pretending,' she said quietly, not taking the trouble to conceal her irritation. 'You know exactly what I mean.'

He smiled and held her arm tighter. 'Of course you do. I keep forgetting.'

'I'm not even going to ask.'

They went their separate ways at the table, Grace to speak with Beth, who had relinquished her hold on Charlie and was wandering around the table, taking note of plates that required refilling.

'Beth, dear, what a marvellous spread. Where on earth did you find the time?'

'The Aga does it all,' Beth said modestly. 'Besides, I've all day to do it in.'

'But Anna...and Hero, not to mention your work. I take my hat off to you. Beth Gillespie, I really do.'

Beth gave her mother a dazzling smile and shook her head. 'Mum, please. You'll make my head swell.'

'I'm proud of you,' Grace blurted out. 'And so is your father.'

Beth had been about to speak, but now she nodded slightly, awarded her mother a quick squeeze of the hand, and then she was off, in the direction of the kitchen. Grace followed, her glass empty and warm between her fingers.

'Is there any more sweet Martini?'

'What? Oh, yes,' Beth said, distracted by the beeping timer on the oven. 'Over there, on the tray beside the sink.'

'Your neighbours seem pleasant enough.'

'Yes, they're fine.' Beth glanced at her mother and whispered. 'Not one under the age of seventy, mind you, but that's all right. At least Harry won't suspect me of running off with one of them.' She turned her attention to the oven glove she was wielding and, for a moment, Grace mulled over the wisdom of a response. Before she could speak, however, Frank appeared in the doorway, apologetic and very late.

'Beth, I'm sorry, I...'

'It's O.K.,' Beth smiled, hardly pausing in her food preparation to look at him. 'Help yourself to anything you fancy and – oh, take this through for me, will you, if you're going back to the dining room?'

'Sure thing. Sorry again for being late,' he added, but as his sister was paying no attention to him, he directed his words to Grace.

'It's all right,' she told him. 'Go and find Harry, he has a tray-full of booze.'

'You never asked how Emily is,' Beth whispered when he had gone. 'Has she started throwing up every morning yet?'

Grace, who hated to be reminded that her son would become a father only a few months after becoming a husband, bit back a quick reply. She knew that Beth revelled in the situation, that she enjoyed the censure Frank had received from James; and it was grossly unfair of the girl to point fingers, especially since she and Harry had probably...

'Mum, stop day-dreaming, will you?'

'Frank and Emily planned this baby, you know.'

'Did they?'

'Yes, they did.'

'I'm glad I waited until I was married,' Beth said unkindly. 'Getting used to being married was bad enough, but having a baby as well...'

'Emily's very mature for her age,' Grace said without thinking.

'*Touché*, mother,' her daughter smiled, but the remark had rankled.

'Is there something I can do to help?' Grace asked to make amends.

'Bung a few more napkins on the table, would you? And maybe clear away some dirty dishes for me?'

Grace sighed. Her lady of the manor role had come to an abrupt end.

*

Charlie Webster was standing on the terrace, alone, but not lonely. He was taking in the view, relating it to his own panorama across the river, finding common aspects, foolishly delighted that he and Beth shared several aspects of this view.

He had been over-whelmed to see her again, to witness the change in her, from young girl to woman, but he had suffered so many traumas and tragedies of his own recently, that he had a new perspective on her: rather than be miserable with her around, he knew he would be content; that there would be no need to run off this time; no need to lie awake agonising over her in someone else's bed.

It was irrational, he admitted, but now that he had seen her with her husband, after years of married bliss, Charlie was satisfied that it was not a love match for Beth; more of her desire for the lifestyle, the things that money could buy.

He had no idea how he had reached such a conclusion; but he was convinced he was right.

When he heard her voice behind him, he was not besieged by the old panic; was even able to turn and speak to her without the sense of having been kicked in the solar plexus at the sight of her.

'Charlie, you're all alone.'

'I'm enjoying the view, it's beautiful.'

She sighed and took his arm, and, just for a moment, he felt the familiar electric shock; but enjoyable.

'I absolutely love it here,' she said, her head close to his. 'I wake up some mornings and wonder what I did to deserve it all.'

When he remained silent, she moved her face in front of his and gave him cheeky scowl.

'You're supposed to say something nice to me, tell me why I deserve it all.'

'Grace tells me you've worked hard, that you're an accomplished business woman now. Antiques and baby clothes, apparently?'

'Phooey!' she said, and he remembered why he loved her. 'That's cods-wallop. Marjory runs the antique business, as you well know. She's the real business woman. As for the baby clothes,' she shrugged. 'It's hardly world-shattering.'

'Do you see Marjory often?'

'Yes, and she insists I take Anna with me.'

'She'd make a good grandmother.'

'We should have paired her off with someone.'

Charlie laughed and remembered another reason for loving the girl.

Beth smiled and pulled him round to face her. 'Come on, I've told you mine, now it's your turn to tell me yours.'

Charlie hesitated, for to tell her would provoke the makings of a confidence between them, and he knew from experience that shared, secret confidences between men and women usually led to a shared secret bed…

'Suffice it to say that I had a wandering eye, that's all.'

'Only your eye?' Beth asked wickedly.

'Yes, and only the left one.'

She burst out laughing but the laugh faded so quickly that he imagined she had seen someone behind him. Automatically, he turned round, but they were alone on the terrace.

'I missed you,' she said now.

'That's a nice thing to say.'

'You were a real stinker going off and leaving me.'

Charlie was surprised at her tone of voice. She had given no indication that she had ever wanted him to stay; otherwise…

'Leaving you? What, with the business?'

'No,' she said coolly. 'Not only that.'

'Beth, it's…'

'Sshh,' she grinned, turning immediately to her old self. ''Enough said. Let's go and get you another drink.'

She refused to let go his arm and, idly, he wondered what the husband would be thinking.

*

Beth kissed her mother goodbye and stood at the door, watching her as she made her way to the car, where her father and Alice were waiting. She saw Harry make a fuss of Grace, at Alice's expense, and then he waved them off until the car had vanished from sight. Just before he turned to walk back to the house, Beth darted into the hall and hurried to the kitchen.

'Can't you leave this until tomorrow?' she heard him ask from the doorway.

'I could, I suppose, but Catriona and I are planning to take the kids out.'

'Fine,' Harry said, but there was disapproval in the tone. 'I'll clear the dining room, bring the dirty dishes through.'

Beth waited until he had gone out and then she heaved a huge sigh. He would go to the dining room on the pretext of helping, have three or four whiskies and get drunk; and when she had finished stacking the dishwasher and cleaning up in here, she would find him snoring by the hearth in a drunken stupor.

After ten minutes she almost fainted when he reappeared with trays of dirty glasses.

'What are you looking at?' he asked with a frown.

'Nothing. I was just wondering how much more there is.'

'Dining room's clear, only the floor to vacuum and I'm certainly not doing that.'

Beth smiled at his expression. 'Do I ever ask you to vacuum?'

'No.'

'Well then.'

He placed the tray near the sink and leaned against the worktop, looking at her, making no attempt to smoke or drink, which Beth considered unusual.

He used parties as an excuse to do both to excess and her mind began to rummage for reasons. She came up with Charlie Webster.

'It was so great to see Charlie again,' she said boldly, as she stacked the glasses in the dishwasher. 'He made me a business woman and I'll always be grateful to him for that.'

'You're fond of him, I can see that,' he smiled; but Beth was not fooled.

'I am, very fond of him.' She stood up and put her hands at the small of her back, to ease the muscles. 'He's great fun.'

'You must invite him more often.'

'I will,' Beth said strongly.

'I was just thinking,' Harry said, moving over to her, taking her hands in his. 'We haven't made love for ages.'

'True,' Beth smiled. 'But you're always too tired.'

A quick flicker of anger passed over his face, but was soon controlled.

'I know, and I apologise. I should devote more time to you, Beth, I know that.'

'There's time now,' she smiled sweetly.

'If you want to.'

'You never used to ask,' she reminded him curtly.

'I never had to.'

They looked at each other for a few moments, but it was Beth who spoke first.

'I still fancy you,' she told him truthfully.

'And you still drive me crazy.'

She sighed and stepped closer, amazed at his reticence in matters of sex where once he had been capable of throwing her on the bed and taking her, whether or not she were willing.

'I'll check on Anna,' she said against the smooth linen of his shirt. 'Then I'll expect you to ravish me until dawn.'

He laughed and kissed the top of her head.

'It's a deal.'

As she tiptoed into her daughter's room and tucked her in, Beth paused to look in the mirror, wondered why she wanted to make love tonight when she had been off the notion for weeks. Quickly, she moved away.

*

Harry sat at the window, listening to the screech of an owl. The sound was the most blood curdling he had ever heard, apart from the vixen that skulked the hills behind the house. She had the kind of call that, once heard, it was never forgotten. The first time he heard it, he expected a vampire to crash through the window and bite him in the neck.

It was two o'clock, yet the sky was still light, flecked with wisps of trailing clouds that seemed to be attracted to the crescent moon. He had imagined that the countryside would be quiet, and mostly it was, but the bustle and activity of wild life during the night was enough to tire him out. He watched as the owl took off from its perch on the fir tree, a cumbersome bird spreading enormous wings and yet flying effortlessly through the air.

'Harry?'

He almost jumped at the sound of Beth's voice, and then his heart sank: if she were wandering the house at this time of night, she wanted to chat, and he was hardly in the mood.

'So, here you are.'

He sensed her behind him, lifted his hand and made contact with hers.

'I couldn't sleep,' he lied.

'I was restless too,' she said, coming into his line of vision and sitting beside him on the window seat. 'I suppose I worry about parties, in case people don't enjoy themselves.'

'It would hardly be your fault if they didn't. What more could you have done?'

She laughed and took his hand. 'We might have played 'Charades'.'

'I'm hopeless at parlour games.'

She raised his hand, placed it on her cheek, and he felt the silky warmth of her skin. Despite the sex being good, Harry feared that she was drifting away, although, the more he thought of it the more he could see no difference in her; apart from her new-found confidence, her independence, the way she could wave a magic wand and sort out any situation.

'You're sad,' she said now. 'Is it the nine-year itch?'

He had to laugh, more at her comical expression than at the idea. 'God, no.'

'You're not fed up of me yet?'

Harry turned his head, met her gaze. 'No, and I might ask you the same.'

'It's a daft question,' Beth said, but she was not looking at him. 'I remember Mum telling me once that you can never stay the same, that people have to change. Relationships change.'

'She and James?'

'Yes.' Beth sighed and lowered his hand to his knee. 'She said the grand passion couldn't last forever.'

Harry was disappointed more than surprised, for he never lost hope that Grace would confide in him, even about personal issues. 'Grace said that?'

'Yes, we talk all the time.'

'I sincerely hope you don't tell her anything about us.'

Although he spoke lightly, she must have picked up the disapproval in his voice, but she shrugged and said nothing, until Harry repeated the sentence.

'I heard you, and I'm insulted that you had to warn me!'

'Women blab,' he said uncharitably. 'I hear them in cafés every day.'

'I'm not women,' Beth frowned. 'I suppose you think you can pick a fight now, now that you've screwed me?' She held gaze, tried to stare him out.

'That's unfair.'

'Sorry.' She rose from the window seat and stood looking out on the garden, winding the dressing robe cord around her fingers. 'I don't know what makes me say these things.'

'Grace is right,' Harry smiled, knowing it would annoy her. He stood beside her, his arm on her waist and felt her stiffen. 'We can't stay the same people all our lives. The trick is knowing when to move on, be different people, yet still love each other.'

'You're so sweet,' Beth said, her tone lacking sincerity. 'I'll just have to work

479

harder at it.'

'Me too.'

'Why is life so awkward sometimes?'

'Let's hope we never turn into the Watsons,' Harry opted for humour.

'Who?'

'The couple from a mile down the road. The gruesome twosome.'

'The woman with the blue hair?'

'That's the one.'

Beth giggled. 'And he was dressed like a teenager, in a bomber jacket?'

'Right again.'

'Promise me you'll shoot me if I suggest dying my hair blue?'

'You'd look fabulous, no matter what colour your hair was.'

'Are you sleepy now?'

'Kind of.'

'Come on, I'll give you a massage to knock you out.'

*

Grace woke in the early hours with a headache. She had drunk five Martinis and a sherry that someone gave her and now her temples were throbbing. She crept from the bed and threw on her dressing gown, and then she waited to see if she had disturbed James, before going downstairs for a couple of Aspirins.

The kitchen was warm from the day's heat, although there was a draught on her feet as she sat at the table and she found the window open in the bathroom. She closed it with a thud – it had always been stiff – and went back to the kitchen, swallowed the Aspirins and sat for a while, mulling things over.

She replayed in her mind the conversation she had had with Charlie Webster, a man she had discovered who was honest to a fault and who never minced words. When she had asked for his opinion, he had not held back.

'No, I don't think she's entirely happy.'

'Why not? She has everything a girl could wish for.'

He had smiled then, a slow smile that took so long to reach his eyes that Grace had a fleeting notion that the man had not lost any of his affection for her daughter.

'I think she enjoys the trappings.'

'Not being poor, you mean?' she had asked, more sharply than intended. 'I mean, not having to worry about the next bill dropping on the mat,' she amended.

'She's changed so much,' Charlie had said. 'I know I haven't seen her for over five years, but she's quite different in some ways.' He sighed and squared his shoulders. 'Not that I knew her at all really.'

'Of course you did. You can meet someone and know all there is to know about them after a single day.'

'You and James?'

'Yes,' she had lied. 'And Beth and Harry.'

She had no idea why she had said it, and it had sounded petulant and silly; but Charlie had nodded.

'She would never have married a man she didn't love.'

Grace was not so sure of that now, but it was neither the time nor the place; nor the right person. She heard the hall clock strike four, but she sat where she was, knowing that she would suffer from lack of sleep the next day. She knew, however, that, as soon as she lay down her thoughts would turn, as always, to Harry Gillespie.

Chapter Three

Catriona was as uncompromising with her two children as Beth was with Anna, and so there was never any fear of an outing being taken up with smacks and rows. It was partly the reason that Beth had adopted the more severe approach with Anna, after she had witnessed her friend's success.

As usual, the park was empty and they strolled towards the swings with the children running ahead.

'How did the house warming go then?'

'Fine, I suppose. I wish you'd been there, I hardly knew anybody.'

Catriona laughed. 'You're joking? You knew everybody. It's just that you're anti-social.'

'Exactly. I'm like my father,' Beth admitted with amusement. 'He's a sullen old bugger, right enough, sat in a corner most of the night, except when he spoke to Alice for ten minutes.'

'Julia!' Catriona shouted to her daughter. 'Come out of that sandpit at once! Little monster. I spent all morning ironing that dress and now look at it.'

'She's so sweet.'

'So's Anna.'

'What's this, a contest?'

'No, I'm just saying. How's Harry?'

'Grumpy.'

'Keith's the same.'

Beth stopped meandering around the swings and looked at her friend.

'Really?'

'Why are you so surprised?'

'I thought it was just Harry.'

'God, no, they're all the same after a while. So my Mum said anyway.'

Both girls refrained from mentioning Catriona's father's dalliance with Molly Menzies years previously, for, to be honest, the man was a paragon of virtue compared with some.

'Do they argue?'

'My Mum and Dad? You bet they do! Don't you and Harry?'

'Not arguing really, more frosty silences and cutting looks.'

'It's normal, at least I read that in 'Marie Claire' last month.'

'Mum said that people change and so relationships had to change, but I'm not sure how to handle it.'

'Not sex again?' Catriona giggled, pushing Julia on the swing and stepping back.

'You have a one-track mind, Cat.'

'I should hope so. At least we have a great time in bed.'

'Same here, but is that everything?'

'Well, it'll do until I get everything,' Catriona laughed. 'Oh, come on,' she added, nudging her friend. 'Let go for once. You're far too serious for your own good.'

'That's what Harry told me once, that I took things too seriously.'

'We're old married women now, just have to make the best of it.'

They extricated their children from the swings and, after rigorous warnings about not getting dirty or wet, let them wander down the path to the burn.

'How's the business?'

'I'll have to ask Marjory,' Beth said wryly. 'I've hardly been in the office this past month.'

'But you work from home, don't you?'

'Yes, and I go to auction sales, house clearances, things like that. Mum's good at taking Anna.'

'I wondered if you'd call her Annie,' Catriona said suddenly.

'What?'

'Seeing as how she was your best pal, I thought you'd call your daughter after her.'

Beth paused, her feet shuffling in the dried leaves. 'I considered it.'

'What made you change your mind?'

'Harry wasn't keen.'

She thought that Catriona avoided her eye for the next few minutes, but perhaps she was becoming paranoid. Before she could continue the conversation, however, Catriona had called the children.

'Come on, you lot. We'll wander over there and have the picnic now!'

*

On the spur of the moment, as she turned into the main road, Beth had an impulse to go and see her mother. After a quick glance at her watch, she decided she had time.

'We're going to see Granny now, so behave.'

'I love Granny,' Anna said firmly, as if Beth were about to contradict her. 'Can we stay for tea?'

'No, pet, we have to get home for Daddy.'

'Granny gives me fish fingers and beans.'

'I do not wish to know that,' Beth muttered under her breath.

'I can see Granny!' Anna yelled from the back seat as the car manoeuvred into the drive at the back of the house. 'I'll get sweeties!'

'Not if I can help it,' Beth smiled to her daughter's reflection in the driving mirror, but Anna was already out of the car, bounding towards her grandmother.

*

Grace was always overjoyed at impromptu visits, and it was the idea that visitors might suddenly appear that was most satisfying. Almost every day, she would glance at the clock, wonder if Beth would drop Anna off while she went to see to some business or other, and when she did, Grace's day was as happy as it could be. She had promised herself that she would take full advantage of her granddaughter's childhood: from her own experience, they had grown up so quickly that before she knew it, they were at Secondary School.

'Hi,' Beth said, lifting her handbag from the car. 'Is this a bad time?'

'I'll pretend I didn't hear that. Anna, my darling girl! What a pretty dress!'

'I don't like it,' Anna said with a furtive glance at Beth. 'But Mummy makes me wear it.'

Beth sighed. 'Only for playing in the park where you might get dirty.'

'Come on,' Grace told her granddaughter. 'I've got just the thing for you.'

They sat outside, at the top of the garden, with Anna's orange juice and Penguin biscuits, and tea and scones for Grace and Beth. The child sat munching happily, glancing from the biscuit plate to her mother.

'You see?' Beth asked Grace quietly. 'Her eye's bigger than her belly. Any moment now and she'll be asking for another.'

'That's your business,' Grace said cleverly. 'I'm not interfering.'

'Sez you.'

'I don't!'

'We'll agree to differ. Did you enjoy the party last night?'

'The house was looking its best, Beth, and there was enough food to feed an army.'

'That doesn't mean you enjoyed it,' her daughter said casually, not even looking at her.

'But I did, of course I did. And it was so nice to meet your neighbours.'

'Even the gruesome twosome?'

'Beth, how unkind.'

'So, you know who I mean then?'

Grace hid a smile and poured out more juice for her granddaughter.

'The lady with blue hair?'

'Yup.'

'I spoke to her and she's the nicest woman…'

'You would say that,' Beth said disparagingly. 'You'd think Jack the Ripper was a nice fellow who was misunderstood.'

'Anyway, blue rinse – I mean Elma – was saying how much work you've put into that house, that she hardly recognised it.'

'Thanks to Lucy and her cast-offs.'

'I wouldn't call new things 'cast-off's', dear,' Grace reminded her. 'Some of these curtains and soft furnishings were still in their wrappers.'

'I know, and don't think I'm not grateful. Anna, don't wipe your fingers on your dress.'

'Here,' Grace said, perhaps predictably. 'Take my paper hanky, darling, keep your lovely dress clean.'

'Are you not going to mention Charlie?' Beth asked suddenly, and Grace was ill prepared.

'Sorry?' she flustered.

'Charlie,' Beth repeated patiently. 'Are you going to mention him?'

'Why should I?'

'Because I saw you talking to him, wondered what you were saying.'

'Reminiscing, that's all,' Grace smiled, but her heart pounded a little. 'He was telling me all about London.'

'All right,' Beth sighed. 'And what else did you discuss?'

'I told you, Beth; the past, and how much he's looking forward to starting the letting business.'

'Did he mention me?'

It was a casual enough question, and quite logical, but Grace sensed her daughter's discomfort.

'Only that he was pleased to see you again.'

'Is that all?'

'Yes, dear. Have you seen my postcard?' Grace asked, judging the moment to be right, taking the card from her apron pocket.

'Friends abroad?'

'It's from Daphne'.

Beth studied the card, frowned at her mother.

'Who's she when she's at home?'

'You don't know?'

'No, why should I know all your friends?'

'She's not exactly a friend.' Grace took a deep breath. 'She's my stepmother.'

Beth gaped at her mother, then back at the postcard – from Bournemouth – and she could hardly take it in: Thomas Blake's new wife was sending cards to his daughter, a daughter who had probably never changed her opinion about his character; never forgiven him for deserting her.

'Why would she do that?'

'I think she's a poor soul.'

'Stop it at once, Mum,' Beth snapped, and the tone of her voice made Anna start to whimper.

'I love you, Granny,' the little girl said tearfully, and Grace picked her up to sit on her knee.

'I know you do, sweetie, and I love you. Really, Beth,' her mother added quietly. 'Little pitchers and all that...'

'Anyway,' Beth said calmly. 'She's not a poor soul; she knew exactly what she was doing. You should have shown her that letter.'

'May I remind you that I swore you to secrecy over that letter,' her mother said sternly. 'Besides, it had nothing to do with her if he never wanted to see me again; or his illegitimate child, whoever she was.'

Her mother coughed and blushed at the end of the sentence, and Beth was reminded that the past never really went away.

'I would never mention the letter to anyone,' Beth said huffily.

'Good,' her mother smiled, but it was hardly satisfactory and Beth had to make a huge effort not to say something cutting. She lowered her eyes to the postcard.

'She says they're staying down there for the foreseeable future. Do they have a house there, or something?'

'No, apparently they're renting.'

'Gosh, that will soon take care of his pile of cash.'

'Did he have a pile of cash?'

'I presumed he did,' Beth frowned. 'He told me he'd sold up everything in South America and cashed it all in.'

'Anyway, I feel sorry for Daphne and if she wants to write to me, I don't mind.'

'You have 'sucker' written all over your forehead,' Beth smiled ruefully.

'Better that than 'stinker'', her mother said pointedly. 'Anyway, tell me how business is.'

'I was going to ask you if you could look after Anna next week, every morning maybe? I have to get out and about, buy some stuff.'

'How many times must I tell you, dearest, that you don't even have to ask? I love having her here, she's a darling.'

'You never told me that having kids was such hard blooming work.'

Her mother looked puzzled. 'I never thought it was.'

'Oh, come off it, you were hassled something rotten when we were young.'

'It's like the pain of childbirth,' her mother smiled. 'Not that you had any, of course, you jammy dodger.'

''Jammy dodger?' Where the hell did you hear that?'

'Can't remember.'

'Do you think it's possible to love two men at the same time?'

Her mother was staring at her, as shocked as Beth had been at the question. She had had no intention of raising such an issue, and now that she had, she could hardly believe her own ears.

'Two men at the same time?' her mother repeated, but she had lost the expression of shock and appeared to be deliberating. 'I... I don't know.'

Beth was astonished, for it was not the reply she was expecting.

'You have doubts?'

Her mother shrugged and turned her attention to Anna, who was fidgeting on her knee.

'Down you go, darling, have another Penguin.'

Beth was so engrossed in her mother's attitude about loving two men, that she ignored the invitation for Anna to have another biscuit.

'Did you love two men at the same time?' she dared to ask. Oddly enough, now that they were both women, it was increasingly difficult for Beth to ask personal questions; she had always imagined it would be easier.

'No, of course not,' her mother said dismissively, convincingly. 'Did you?'

'No.'

'You don't sound too sure.'

'I am sure. I love Harry, I really do. He's the only one for me.'

'You sound as if you're reciting a piece from '*Hamlet*', her mother said shrewdly.

'Cheeky.'

'Oh, Beth,' her mother said suddenly, urgently, leaning her hand on her daughter's shoulder. 'Do be careful. Promise me you'll be careful.'

'I don't know what you mean,' Beth lied with a smile, but she knew she had not fooled Grace Blake.

*

Harry strode towards the town centre, his jacket slung over his shoulder, his tie loosened, something he rarely did, but today's heat was oppressive. If anyone had told him they could have heat waves in Scotland, he would have thought they were mad.

He saw her before she saw him and it gave him time to rehearse his opening line, although he had been toying with several on his way from the office. When she spotted him, her face lit up spontaneously and he knew she still loved him.

'Harry, my dear friend,' she said, perhaps for the benefit of listening strangers. 'How are you?'

He took her hand, caressed it briefly, saw the blush in her cheeks.

'I'm fine. How are things?'

'I have it in my pocket,' she whispered as they walked along, side by side but not touching.

'What?'

'The key to Sandra's house.'

'I hate doing this.'

'You mean humping or using Sandra's house?'

He gave her a fleeting look of disapproval, but it was short-lived. She had the knack of diffusing his bad moods. They walked on, without speaking, for two blocks, and then she halted, pretended to gaze in a shop window.

'I'll go first, so no one suspects anything,' she whispered again. 'See you in five minutes.'

He watched her reflection in the shop window, tracked her progress as far as the end of the street, and then went into the shop, to pass five minutes.

'Are you sure you want to do this?' Foxy asked him anxiously the moment he opened the door. 'We can leave it, if you're not keen.'

'Do you want to leave it?' Harry asked abruptly.

485

'No, you know I don't,' she said submissively, but within minutes he knew 'submissive' would hardly be a fitting description for her. 'I was just giving you the option.'

He unbuttoned her blouse and placed his hand on her heart, feeling the strong, erratic beat, hearing the change in her breathing.

'I don't need another option,' he told her quietly, his fingers tracing the lace on her bra. 'I'm perfectly happy with this one.'

She raised her face to be kissed, and at the first touch of her lips he was already past the point of no return.

*

Foxy lay on her back, naked, making no attempt to cover up, something that Beth would have done now, in sharp contrast to the old days. He touched her breast and she opened her eyes, smiled lazily at him, laid her hand over his and pulled it down to her stomach.

'Haven't you had enough?' Harry laughed, although he did not resist her.

'No, I don't think I have. It's been weeks, remember, and I never get any now.'

'Foxy, I'm sorry,' he said impulsively. 'I never meant to...'

'Hey,' she interrupted. 'I was tired of her anyway, always checking up on me. It was only a matter of time.' She wriggled to a sitting position and put her arms around his neck. 'Come on, don't look so sad. You'd think it was the end of the world.'

Harry smiled and kissed her, but as she trailed her fingers down his back and sent shivers pulsing through him, his mind refused to relinquish the idea that she had used such an appropriate expression: he did feel it was the end of his world; but felt powerless to change it.

*

Charlie Webster sat at the old baby grand and gazed at the manuscript. He had been sitting there for half an hour and had yet to play a single note. Eventually, his mother had popped her head round the door to see if he was still in the room, at which he made some excuse about his fingers being too rusty. It was true: he could not recall the last time he had sat at the piano.

'I can get you a nice cup of tea,' she had said brightly. 'And a couple of éclairs. I know you like them.'

'Thanks, Mother, but I'll get it later, if you don't mind.'

She had left him then, had not returned, even when it was teatime. He presumed she had eaten without him. The sooner he had the Mill licked into shape, the sooner she would be redundant, and he could take charge of his life again.

The telephone rang somewhere in the house, but he forgot where the telephone points were and so he let it ring, leaving his mother to answer it if she wanted. A few moments later, to his annoyance, he heard her footsteps hurrying down the tiled hallway, her knock on the door before she threw it open.

'Quick!' she called to him. 'It's Beth, on the phone, in the kitchen! Hurry up!'

His heart skipped a beat; well, more than one admittedly. He tried to walk sedately down the hall, but his mother was standing in the kitchen doorway gesticulating at him to hasten his step.

He gave her a nod in the passing and picked up the receiver.

*

486

Beth's heart skipped beat, well, more than one actually, but who was counting?

'Beth?'

'Yes, it's me. Hope you don't mind.'

'Mind? Of course I don't mind. I'm at a loose end these days, until the office is ready.'

'Oh, right. Anyway,' she took a deep breath, wondered if he heard her gasping like a fish. 'I was wondering if you'd like to come over for coffee one morning. I have a couple of questions about the business.'

She waited, holding her breath, cursing herself for being such an idiot. He would never believe it.

'Yes, of course I would.'

'You would?' Beth brushed the perspiration from her brow. The effort this was taking reminded her of wading through treacle with flippers on.

'I'll come over on Wednesday morning. How does that sound?'

It sounded wonderful.

When she replaced the receiver she indulged in a long sigh of relief; and then she remembered what she might be letting herself in for and was filled with trepidation.

*

Grace laid the tablecloth, set two places, and checked the macaroni cheese pie in the oven. James would be another half hour yet, and so she meandered into the living room and picked up a magazine, intending to pass the time reading a short story in *The People's Friend*.

After she had read the same sentence five times, she sighed and threw the magazine aside, before leaning back in the chair and closing her eyes.

Two men two different loves

With a gesture of frustration, she opened her eyes again and wondered if Graham's words would forever take precedence in her mind. She had almost gasped when Beth had asked her about it, and she was certain the girl had noticed her nervous fidgeting, the avoidance of her daughter's eye.

Sarah Kerr – God rest her soul – had once asked who would be the mother of girls, and now Grace could only agree. How lucky Alice had been to have three sons! The trouble was, Grace knew from her own experience that no one could help Beth, that she would make her own decisions, right or wrong, and would have to live with the consequences.

The other issue, of course, was the letter. Showing it to Beth had been a cold, deliberate act but, calculating though she had been, she was not even certain that the girl's attitude to Thomas Blake had altered.

It certainly seems to paint him in a bad light

The sentence, delivered with only the minimum of censure and containing the word '*seem*', had not put Grace's mind at rest; neither had she the courage to raise the subject since.

Now, she was occupied with justifying her future plans for the letter and how much more courage she must summon up if she had any intention of showing it to Daphne.

She must have dozed, for she woke with a start to find that James was home. When he smiled at her, Grace suffered a momentary sense of betrayal over her plans for the letter; despite its having nothing directly to do with James. It was a touch of stage fright she knew; nothing more.

'Has Beth been today?'

'Yes, she and Anna came for half an hour this afternoon. It was lovely.'

'One day she might come when I'm here,' James said, going into the kitchen to wash his hands before tea. 'I'd like to see my granddaughter more often.'

'You'll get your wish,' Grace told him, preparing to serve the macaroni pie. 'She'll be here every morning next week, while Beth works.'

'We can take her to the beach.'

Grace stared at him. 'The what?'

'The beach,' James repeated, his eyes full of amusement. 'The thing with sand and water?'

'You've never suggested it before.'

'I've never thought about it before.'

'She'd love it.'

'I'm sure she would,' James said. 'Did you think our daughter was happy last night?'

'Yes,' Grace said firmly, having been caught out several times already that day and not prepared to flounder again. 'She's really happy. She told me so this afternoon.'

James dried his hands and folded the towel over the hook.

'That's fine then, if she's happy. Do I have time to change my shirt?'

'No, tea's served out. Don't you dare leave this kitchen!'

As they ate, Grace did her best to put aside the reservations she had about her daughter's marriage, but if James had noticed too, it must be fairly obvious.

She conversed without much enthusiasm and, with each passing minute, her spirits sank further; although she could not fathom the reason.

*

Anna was playing up in front of her father. He was by far the softer of the two when it came to scolding the child and she was old enough now to have figured it out. He made half-hearted attempts to persuade her to tidy up her toys, but she was paying scant attention to him, carrying on with her little game of being mummy to her teddy bear.

He heard Beth's footsteps in the hall, had a moment's panic that she would blow her top to see Anna still playing, and snatched the teddy bear from his daughter's grasp. Predictably, in the split-second before Beth entered the room, their daughter let out a wail.

'Right,' he said, pretending not to know Beth was standing in the doorway. 'That's your last chance, my lady. Time's up, so I'll count to ten. One... two...'

Anna stopped wailing the moment she spotted her mother at the door and Harry suffered a pang of envy that Beth had turned out to be such an efficient mother; especially after having been spoilt rotten by James Melville.

'Ten,' Beth called sharply from the doorway, although Harry had only reached the count of four.

'Finished, Mummy!' Anna shrieked, pointing to the toy box. 'All gone!'

'Good girl,' Beth purred on her way past Harry. 'That's what I like to see. Now, go upstairs and wash your hands before tea. Oh, and put on your blue frock, it's on the bed with a pair of clean socks.'

With that, she turned and gave Harry a brief smile before marching from the room, back to the kitchen.

His daughter dashed from the room but Harry sat where he was, on his knees on the carpet, feeling an inadequate father; yet it had been his own fault: he had been so wrapped up in thoughts of Foxy that he had dealt with Anna half-heartedly. He sighed and rose to his feet, wondering if Beth was in a good mood or whether he had have to grovel.

She was in the dining room – where they usually ate the evening meal – lighting candles, putting the finishing touches to the table. He had to hand it to her: the way she took care of everything – of her business, of the house, of him and their daughter – was a cross between Mary Poppins and Cruella de Ville.

'This looks so lovely,' he told her. 'I'm a lucky man.'

She turned to smile at him, but it was an absent-minded smile, the kind she reserved for Anna when she had not heard a word the child had said.

'D'you think so?'

Slightly astonished by the question, Harry hesitated for a moment, but then gathered his thoughts and spoke firmly.

'What kind of daft question is that? Of course I'm lucky, the luckiest man in Perthshire I suspect.'

'Where's Hero?'

Perplexed by the change of topic, Harry shrugged. 'Haven't a clue.'

'His food's been lying in the utility room for half an hour. He must have lost all sense of time. Chasing rabbits again, presumably.'

She moved back into the kitchen and he followed her, pondering her new-found authority, her eligibility for Superwoman of the County contest. She had been so much easier to handle when she was young and gullible. Was that the reason he was dissatisfied now? He had a sudden thought that perhaps he was too much of a Chauvinist to be married to a strong woman.

'I'll call the dog in,' he said now. 'He can't be far.'

'Leave him in the utility, he'll be filthy. I'll brush him up later.'

Harry stood at the back door whistling for the dog, but his mind was on Foxy.

*

Beth studied her husband across the table, noting his failure to make eye contact. She contemplated making small talk, but had run it forward in her mind, coming to the conclusion that she would be wasting her time: if he did not want to speak, so be it.

Suddenly, taking her by surprise, Harry asked her if she had seen Charlie Webster recently.

'What?'

'You're blushing,' Harry smiled, which made it worse.

'You took me by surprise.'

'Have you asked him round yet?'

'Why are you so keen to throw us together?' Beth asked, hardly expecting the reaction she got.

'What a bloody stupid thing to say!' he almost yelled, making Anna jump. When he heard his daughter's gasp, he backtracked, just as Beth had been about to remind him not to swear at the dinner table.

'I'm sorry, Anna,' he addressed the child. 'Daddy's a naughty boy.'

Anna, who was ruled by the 'no talking at the table unless you're spoken to' edict, nodded and lowered her eyes to her plate. For a moment, Beth felt sorry for the little thing, having to suffer the indignity of parents who were acting more childish than she was.

'There's ice cream and jelly when you've finished,' Beth said now, patting her daughter's hand and endowing her with a dazzling smile. 'I know it's not Saturday yet, but you've been a good girl today. Mummy was proud of you.'

'I love you Mummy,' Anna said breathlessly and Beth felt ashamed.

'I was going to invite Charlie to come over,' she told Harry. 'I could do with his opinion on a couple of things I'm thinking of buying. My mother will be here, so don't worry.'

'Beth, sweetheart, I'm not worried. I only want you to feel you can do what you like.'

'I do.'

'That's fine then,' Harry smiled, but Beth had never seen him so obliging and her mind turned to the French 'arrangement.'

Her husband had a mistress?

Surely, that had to be a most ludicrous idea.

*

Grace hung the telephone receiver on the hook and sighed. Why was it that Alice could speak for half an hour when they had seen each other only a short time before? She presumed it had something to do with her friend living alone, never hearing the sound of her own voice from one day to the next.

'You should get a job,' Grace had told her friend months ago. 'That way, you'd meet people, make friends, maybe even find the Right One.'

Alice had spluttered disagreement. 'You must be kidding, sweetie. Me, working? I've never done a hand's turn in my life, and I don't aim to start now.'

'Oh, come off it, you were a legal secretary when you first came to live here, and you enjoyed that, didn't you?'

'Yeah, sure, for all of six months. After that, it all went downhill. The boss never liked me.'

'Wasn't it because you couldn't get up in the morning and you were always late?'

'That too,' Alice admitted, a twinkle in her eye.

Now, as she prepared for bed, Grace wondered if she should help Alice find a job, even a part-time position somewhere, just to improve her social life.

When she mentioned it to James, he laughed.

'Alice? Working?'

'What's so funny about?'

'She's the laziest woman I know.'

'No she's not!' Grace refuted hotly. 'She brought up three boys, remember, and she looked after Martin.'

'For a while, yes,' James replied sceptically. 'Until she discovered it was such hard work.'

'I think you're being unfair to her.'

'Why do you think she came back here to live?'

'Because she's Scottish, that's why, and she'd been divorced.'

'She left her children, Grace,' James reminded her. 'Would you ever have left Beth and Frank?'

It was an appalling thought and Grace shook her head. 'No, I couldn't.'

'Well, then.'

'Maybe she…'

'Maybe nothing,' James said forcefully, and the subject was closed.

Later, as she went around the house switching off lights, Grace discovered she had another reason for flagging spirits: she would never understand the reasons a woman could cite for abandoning her children; and it might have taken the shine off her affection for her friend, except Grace was beginning to think it was probably her fault for persuading Alice to come back. Desperate to have her friend close by again, Grace had been quite selfish, and it filled her with guilt. She had encouraged her friend to leave home and family; the very situation for which she despised Thomas Blake.

Chapter Four

Daphne Blake opened the envelope with excitement, for she recognised the handwriting: it was from her stepdaughter, Grace. She glanced over her shoulder to check that Thomas was nowhere in sight before she unfolded the notepaper and read.

'Dear Daphne,

Thank you so much for your postcard. Ibiza looked so opulent! We never usually go further afield than the North of Scotland, although one year Beth and I went to Holland to see family, and it was so different.

We are all well, especially Beth and Harry, not to mention Anna, your little great granddaughter, although strictly speaking she's a 'step', but it's too complicated to keep remembering and so we'll just call her that. She's four and a half now, going to school in August and bright as a button. In fact, I think she knows more than me sometimes!'

Daphne smiled and raised her eyes for a moment. She loved these letters, loved the whole idea of having a daughter, and was so thrilled that Grace had dispensed with the 'step' in front of great granddaughter. She would never have believed that her life could turn out to be so satisfying. The only drawback was having to keep the letters a secret from Thomas, Grace's explicit wish for the moment, and one that Daphne was only too willing to accept. Even without accurate knowledge of the Blake clan, Daphne thought that Grace was the kindest, most considerate girl; and would never make an unreasonable demand.

She was about to resume the reading of the letter when she heard the front door open. Hurriedly, she tucked the piece of paper in the envelope and pushed it into her pocket. She would finish reading it later, when her husband was asleep in front of the television. Daphne refused to dwell on the probable cause of his falling asleep in her company. He was tired, that was all, and it had nothing to do with her being boring company.

*

Charlie Webster walked up the path and rang the bell. He had tried to stop his heart pounding since eight that morning, but eventually he had given up. He only hoped that she would not see it through his shirt.

'Charlie! Up here!'

He glanced up in the direction of her voice and saw her hanging out an upstairs window. She waved him to go in, and then the long blonde hair disappeared. He recalled the effect that long blonde hair had exerted on him years ago and resolved that it would never happen again.

As he stood in the vast hallway, she flew down the stairs, almost crashing into him at the bottom.

'Charlie, it's so lovely to see you,' she said, out of breath, and he had to suppress the idea of her being out of breath for other reasons. 'Come on and meet Anna, she's dying to see you.' Perhaps aware that he had not yet spoken, she turned on her way through the hall and laughed. 'For Pete's sake, I haven't even given you a minute to say anything.'

'So far I can't think of anything worthwhile to say,' Charlie joked.

'You always had interesting things to say.' Beth grimaced. 'What twaddle! I'm nervous at seeing you after all this time.'

'Come on; introduce me to your daughter first. That should help.'

The child was fascinated by his briefcase, particularly the buckle, and he had no qualms about handing it to the child, for it was locked. From his experience, children and precious items did not belong in the same sentence.

After ten minutes, Beth kissed the little girl and dispatched her to the playroom with strict instructions not to come out until Mummy called her.

'Yes, Mummy,' the girl said, trotting off dutifully in the direction of her toys.

'You surprise me,' Charlie had to say.

'In what way?'

'The mothering bit.'

'What about it?'

'You're helluva good at it.'

Beth opened her eyes wide. 'You think so?'

'I've had two of my own. Believe me, you're good.'

She shrugged. 'Needs must.'

'Didn't you want kids?' he asked on the spur of the moment, and she stared at him. He waited, anticipating a denial, but then she smiled and shook her head.

'No, I wasn't keen.'

'Why did you then?'

'We were going through a sticky patch and I knew he wanted them, so I did.'

They stood for a long while, looking at each other but not speaking. After an eternity, she laughed, shook her head, and the blonde hair flew around her face. 'Not the best reason, I'll grant you, but she is a gem.'

'Looks like you too.'

'It's the blonde hair. Of course, Harry and I are both blond, so you'd expect Anna to be the same. Aren't you going to tell me about yours?'

'It's dark.' Charlie said mischievously. 'My hair, I mean.'

'I can wait,' she said, leaning against the worktop, an amused smile on her face.

'There's nothing to tell,' he said, but, of course, there was. 'I got married to a nice girl, had two kids, she got tired of me not paying her enough attention, left me and took the kids.' He sighed and tapped the side of his head. 'I knew what I was doing all right, sending them all packing.'

'Charlie, that's horrible.'

'But I've got my Mum,' he smiled. 'And it's great.'

'Oh, I give up! Come on, let's get the coffee going!'.

He watched her as she cut the home-made cake, her mother's recipe, she said.

'Did you make it yourself?'

'Yes.'

'Well done,' she heard him say.

She was conscious of his eyes on her, but did her best not to slice her finger off with the knife. 'You don't have to humour me.'

'Wouldn't dream of it.'

Beth laid the slices neatly on the plate. 'Wait until you've tasted it first.'

She was perturbed by the look in his eyes; suddenly realised the ambiguity of the words:

'Do you always see the naughty side of things?'

'Not always.'

'Why are you looking at me like that?'

'Because you've lost some of your volatility.'

Beth frowned, for it might be true. 'I'm almost thirty, for Heaven's sake.'

'What difference would that make?'

'I'm a wife and mother.' Beth shook her head. 'This is supposed to be a chat over coffee, not a bloody lecture,' she muttered angrily.

Charlie smiled broadly, clapped his hands. 'Bravo, you've remembered.'

'Remembered what?' she asked rudely.

'How to be Beth Melville.'

Beth was silent for a long moment, for she had suspected as much herself: that she was a shadow of the bad-tempered, selfish, erratic girl she had once been, only five years ago. She had grown up, Was that the reason?

She voiced her opinion, but he was shaking his head as she spoke.

'No. Growing up just means growing older. It has nothing to do with your basic characteristics.'

Deciding she would probably lose this argument, Beth put the lid on the coffee pot.

'Come on, I'll show you the palatial dwelling first.'

Afterwards, they sat on the terrace, drinking coffee and eating the cake. Anna was spooning her juice into the teddy bear's mouth and his fur was sticky and wet.

'I think teddy's had enough now,' Beth called to her daughter. 'He told me he's full up.'

Anna looked at her mother, and then back to the teddy bear, her eyes sceptical.

'I didn't hear him say anything.'

'Ah, but I did,' Beth said.

When the little girl set the spoon aside and went to play in the garden, Charlie sighed and leaned back in his chair.

'Golly, you've got the knack all right.'

'Didn't your wife have it?' Beth asked boldly.

'No, she was too wrapped up in her posh clothes to notice she had kids.'

It was a harsh verdict, especially for a man as gentle and considerate as Charlie Webster, and Beth held her breath, hoping he might continue. When he remained silent, she prompted him.

'Why on earth did you marry her then?'

'Why did you marry Harry?'

'Because I loved him.'

'And I loved my wife.' He paused just long enough to arouse her interest and then he added: 'At the beginning anyway.'

'What's she like?'

'Dark hair, brown eyes, very posh, My mother's ideal daughter-in-law.'

'So what went wrong?'

Charlie smiled and glanced at her, picking up his cup and touching it to his lips. Beth had to avert her eyes, but not quickly enough, not before she had imagined how it might feel to be the cup...

'We grew apart,' he said simply. 'It happens. People start out thinking they want the same things, and then they discover they don't.' He turned and met her gaze. 'Is this what you wanted?'

'What?'

He waved his hand at the house. 'This.'

'I wanted the garden,' Beth said truthfully. 'I always wanted a huge garden, no matter what the house was like.'

'That explains it then.'

'Will you stop talking in bloody riddles!' Beth exclaimed irritably, and then realised that it had been years since her temper had been tested. Illogically, she also felt more alive than she had felt for ages, and it was an uneasy thought.

'I'm sorry, I've upset you now.'

493

'I must say you look sorry,' she told him sarcastically, and he grinned.

'*Touché*. Now, if you've finished your coffee, which, I might tell you, is absolutely the worst I have ever tasted, I think we should go and see the stuff you're thinking of buying.'

Beth sighed and stood up, her eyes scouring the garden for Anna. When her daughter appeared, dragging Hero by his collar, Beth heard Charlie's gasp of astonishment.

'Flipping heck! It's a poodle.'

'A standard poodle, yes, and his name is Hero and he's lovely.'

'But he's black.'

'So?'

'Technically he should be called 'Nero' and not 'Hero'.'

'Trust you.'

'Is he good with Anna?'

'Oh, yes, quite trustworthy.'

'You'd wallop him if he wasn't, I presume?'

Beth laughed and nodded her head. 'I would indeed, now come on, I want you to cast an eye over things.'

She threw him a cautionary glance before he passed comment.

As they went inside, Anna and Hero following on, Beth had to suppress the idea that she and Charlie were an old married couple going back into the house after a stroll in the garden.

*

The air was balmy; yet another week of the heat wave that had scorched the East of Scotland since April. No one could quite believe the tropical weather that had set in – it was the end of May now – and was forecast to linger until July at least.

'Until the school holidays,' Sally had predicted wryly to Grace the day before, as they meandered, under a blazing sun, as far as the station with their grandchildren. 'Mark my words, the minute these poor kids run out the door to start their holiday, the heavens will open.'

When Grace mentioned this now to Lily, the old woman shook her head.

'What nonsense. Didn't you see the pine cones in spring time?'

'No,' Grace replied, somewhat sheepishly, for Sandy Sinclair had thought he had been passing on his knowledge of the seasons to his granddaughter and the information had gone in one ear and out the other. 'And doesn't it have something to do with spiders' webs?' she added, hoping to salvage her self-respect.

Lily gave her a puzzled look. 'I've never heard that one, pet. Anyway, the amount of cones on these trees over there told me it would be a scorcher this summer, and they weren't wrong. Do you still take sugar?'

'Yes, not sweet enough yet.' As she spoke, Grace almost shuddered to think how decidedly *un* sweet she would soon prove to be.

'Have you any exciting news for me?' she heard Lily ask, forcibly reminded that the old dear had very little contact with the villagers now, most of her own age group having been consigned to the cemetery, the latest being poor Nan Murray, weakened by a stroke, finished off by the flu the previous winter.

'Exciting news?' she repeated slowly. 'I wrote to Daphne again, if you could call that exciting.'

'You're daft.' Lily said with a shake of her head. 'It'll only end in tears, and I'm predicting they'll be yours.'

494

'I'm not writing to *him*. In fact, I told her to keep our letters to herself.'

'She agreed?'

'Yes, she did.' Grace was glad that her jam tart crumbled to pieces at that moment, for it gave her an excuse to change the subject. 'Oh, look at that! Granny's all fingers and thumbs today, Anna.'

'Fingers and thumbs?' Anna echoed from her seat beside Lily.

'Yes,' Grace smiled. 'It just means Granny's clumsy.'

'I love you Granny,' the little girl said solemnly, and Grace's heart went out to her.

'And we all love you, poppet,' Lily said. 'You're the best little girl in the world.'

'Mummy says I'm good.'

'Well, if she says it, it must be true, now, come on, can you manage another wee cake?'

'No, thank you, Auntie Lily. I'm full up now.' Anna looked across at Grace. 'Can I go and play in the garden, Granny?'

'Yes, darling, but be careful of the wet grass down there. If you dirty that dress, your Mummy won't speak to me again.' The words were out before she realised what she was saying. 'I'm just joking, Anna,' Grace added. 'Of course your Mummy will speak to me again.'

When the child had run off to play, Grace uttered a heartfelt sigh.

'You know, I can't recall having to mind my 'p's and 'q's as much with Beth and Frank.'

'You did, but it's such a long time ago I expect you've just forgotten. So, how's the lovely Mrs Blake then?'

It was a dreadful sound, the sound of someone else being Mrs Blake when the name had belonged solely to Charlotte Shepherd. Grace would never reconcile herself to her mother being relegated to third in line, for she knew he had married in South America, and now he was married again.

'She seems happy enough,' Grace said, her tone non-committal. 'They've been to Ibiza apparently, got a card from there last month.'

'Does she ever mentioned coming back up here?'

'Yes, she has, several times.' Grace took a quick breath.

'And I suppose you'd be daft enough to meet her?'

'I might.'

Out of the corner of her eye, she saw Lily's head turn sharply towards her, suspected that there was a barb in the offing.

'You'd go and meet her, the woman who's aligned herself with him?' Before Grace could reply, her old friend had tutted. 'Oh, don't tell me,' she went on sarcastically. 'You feel sorry for the woman.'

'A bit,' Grace admitted; but not for the reason Lily had in mind.

'You were aye far too soft.'

'And you were always far too unforgiving.'

They regarded each other for a few moments, the silence broken only by Anna's exultant cry when she found a frog in the damp ground.

'Don't pick it up!' Grace warned her, but it was too late. The little girl made a grab for the creature, lost her footing on the slippery bank, and went all her length on the grass.

'Oops,' Lily sighed humorously. 'I guess I'll have to find the wee thing something to wear while you wash and iron that frock.'

*

495

Marjory ticked off the items that Beth had stored, temporarily, in Charlie's old office. It was used as a storeroom now, Beth having opted to remain in her own, smaller office, with its view of the river. She and Marjory had become accustomed to Charlie's absence now but, at the beginning, they had had their own reasons to regret his departure.

'It's not so safe without a man around,' Marjory had declared the first week, after a vagrant had wandered into the outer office and tried to urinate. 'Charlie would have socked the fool, left his mark on the idiot's bum. Two women alone...' She had shuddered, but Beth wondered if a poor man needing to pee was worth all the fuss. Short of suggesting they put up a notice requesting vagrants not to pee, however, she had not offered a suggestion.

'We'll keep the door locked.' Marjory advised, and it seemed the ideal solution. 'Strictly speaking, this isn't a shop, so no one really has to come in.'

It was true: Beth had twenty clients now whom she wrote to whenever she found something of interest to them. If they professed an eagerness to view the goods, she jumped in the car and went to see the clients. It was easier for her, for she could plan her days around Anna, and it was satisfactory for the clients, who, being mainly males, were able to take Beth to lunch and show her off. This had been Marjory's opinion and Beth was too wise to argue.

'If anyone asks, they'll say you're their fancy bit,' her colleague had announced primly. 'And, if it's good for business, why not?'

Beth knew perfectly well 'why not', but she was smart enough to meet clients in the same restaurant or hotel, where she was known as Mrs Gillespie; wife of Harry; mother of Anna; owner of a black standard poodle.

'So,' Marjory said now as they pored over the contents of the storeroom. 'Who might be interest in these buttons?'

'Francis Moncrieffe,' Beth replied. 'He's an avid collector of Ruskins and Liberties. I'll call him this afternoon, see if he wants to meet.'

'Why should a man want to buy buttons?'

'He gives them to his wife, apparently, as little gifts. She has a display cabinet full of them.'

'Takes all sorts, I suppose,' Marjory smiled wryly. 'Oh, by the way, did you get rid of the matching piecrusts? And please don't say you threw them to the birds.'

'I was tempted,' Beth laughed. 'But yes, I did sell them on, but to a new client in Dundee. Here's hoping she stays on the books.'

'Why don't you nip out for a sandwich while I catalogue these?'

'Why don't you?' Beth smiled. 'You're stuck in here every day, Marjory. Go on, get a breath of fresh air.'

'Fresh air? You must be joking! Have you ever known such weather? I'll be wearing shorts next!'

When Marjory had gone, Beth wandered around the storeroom glancing at the items she had brought back from the house clearance in Brought Ferry. If she had not been in the happy position of profiting from such clearances, her thoughts might have lingered on the sadness of the occasion: this latest booty had resulted from the death of an eighty-year old widow, who had not a single person to leave anything to. Beth was turning into a shrewd businesswoman, but even she saw the poignancy of it. Not for the first time did she thank her lucky stars for family.

The telephone rang and she frowned at the clock: half past twelve, a time when the office should be closed for lunch; except it was more like a 'bring and buy' stall. She crossed the storeroom, dashed along the short corridor and picked up the receiver. It was Lucy Webster.

*

Lucy was dressed in Jaeger from head to foot. Every time Beth saw her, her jaw dropped at the sophisticated outfits; not that she could not afford the occasional Jaeger skirt herself, but she lacked the panache to wear it. Lucy, on the other hand, looked as if she had just stepped off a Paris catwalk.

She greeted Beth effusively. 'Beth, my dear, I'm so happy to see you again! It's been absolutely ages.'

'I'm down at Mum's at least once a week, too. Next time, I'll bring Anna round, show her off.'

'Oh, I've seen her,' Lucy said, sitting down at the table, sweeping her gaze over the settings, as if she were about to rearrange things. 'She's a little angel. Grace brought her one day, in March I think it was. Goodness me, doesn't she look like you?'

Beth shrugged. 'Everyone says so, but I can't see it yet.'

'I do wish...' Lucy forced a smile and moved her cutlery around. 'They never get the hang of it, do they?' she frowned, indicating the position of the soup spoon. 'I often wonder what their own tables look like. Anyhow,' she recovered her magnanimity. 'About this piano I want to get rid of.'

'You're only saying that to knock the price down,' Beth told her companion, and was met with a shocked, if rehearsed, expression.

'How can you say that? I can't stand the thing, you know I can't. No one has played it since you did, way back in...' She paused, counted. 'Sixty nine, wasn't it?'

'Something like that. Come on, Lucy, be reasonable. Do you honestly think I could steal that piano from you and enjoy playing it?'

Lucy lowered her eyes to the menu. ' 'Stealing's rather a strong word, my dear. No, I was thinking more of fifty pounds?'

'You know perfectly well it's worth hundreds, Lucy. I suggest three hundred.'

'Oh, don't be ridiculous!' Lucy exclaimed. 'That would be daylight robbery!'

'All right then,' Beth said wickedly. 'Four hundred.'

Lucy laughed and shook her head. 'I do wish you were my daughter,' she said suddenly, her eyes making no apology for the admission. 'I really do.'

'That might have landed Charlie in jail.'

'What? Oh, yes, I see what you mean.' Lucy sighed. 'I'm so glad he's back. I missed him terribly.'

'He needn't have gone, you know. I pleaded with him to stay.'

Lucy stretched her hand across the table and patted Beth's wrist.

'I know you did, Beth, and I was so grateful. I thought you were the bravest little thing I had ever met.'

'Brave?' Beth repeated, puzzled.

'Yes, to keep him here for my sake when it meant you'd...' She paused, shamefaced.

'We would have managed,' Beth said quietly. 'People always do.'

'Are you happy?'

'Yes, very.'

'Charlie's not,' Lucy said, with some degree of triumph. 'I knew he wouldn't be, told him so several times. Still,' she sighed. 'It was his decision to marry her, not mine. Now, about the piano.'

'Two hundred and...'

497

'Fifty sounds just right to me,' Lucy said firmly. 'I refuse to accept a penny more.'

Beth knew when she was beaten and, with someone other than Lucy Webster, she might have gloated for a while; but this was one transaction she would not enjoy.

*

Harry parked the car in the garage and switched off the engine. He lowered the driver's window, pressed a button and watched in the rear view mirror as the door swung closed with a metallic clunk. The sight of an automatic garage door never failed to fill him with satisfaction, for it seemed to embody everything about gracious living, and he considered his living to be fairly gracious.

When he opened the utility door, the dog bounded towards him, tail wagging, juddering to a halt when he crashed into Harry's legs. He bent down and made a fuss of the animal, rubbed its ears, promised it a long walk before bedtime, and then made his way across the room after Hero had exhausted himself and was recovering in his basket. Puppies were like children, so Anna had told him: five minutes' exercise and they were asleep again.

She was on the telephone, to Grace perhaps, and so he paused to kiss her neck before going upstairs to change. His daughter was playing in her room, toys and books scattered around, her attention on the rocking horse she had fallen heir to from The Birches.

'Daddy!' she cried happily, hurtling towards him and squealing with delight as he swept her up, held her to the ceiling.

'Anna, my angel,' Harry said, pretending to drop her to the ground.

'Do it again!'

'Just three times then,' he told her, having learnt from Beth that promises were sacrosanct to four-year olds. 'This is the second time, so there's only one more.'

'Oh, Daddy, please?'

'No, sweetpea, that's the third time. We'll have to go down and help Mummy now.'

'Mummy and I were playing hide-and-seek and it was great and Mummy couldn't find me 'cos I was in the cupboard.'

Harry laughed and picked her up, smelling the delicious scent of her hair, feeling the softness of her fingers on his neck. She was the loveliest little creature on God's earth and he adored her more than he had ever thought possible.

'Look what the cat dragged in,' he said as they caught up with Beth in the kitchen. 'A little princess, all dressed up and nowhere to go.'

'She was a very good girl today,' Beth smiled, having previously ignored the grass stains on her daughter's socks. 'Granny said she was very polite to Auntie Lily, so she's getting a special treat.'

Harry looked at Anna, who was nodding vigorously. 'What is this treat, you lucky little girl?'

'Mummy and I are going to Capdown Park tomorrow.'

'Camperdown Park? Gosh, that's a super place.' Over Anna's head, Harry raised his eyebrows at his wife. 'Just the two of you?'

'You can come if you want,' Beth said with a shrug. 'If you can get away.'

'Of course I can get away,' Harry told his daughter, at which she squealed again.

'Anna!' Beth said sharply.

'Sorry, Mummy.'

'No squealing in the house, there's a good girl.' She turned her attention back to the Aga and stabbed a potato with the point of a knife. 'Oh, by the way, I've negotiated for Lucy's baby grand.'

498

'That was quick,' Harry said, lowering Anna to the floor. 'I hope you struck a hard bargain.'

She swivelled round and looked at him. 'I robbed her blind, if you must know.'

'She wanted rid of it, so she told Grace. You did her a favour.'

'Have you seen Mum lately?'

'No, I spoke to her on the phone last week.'

'We must invite them over for lunch someday, the weekend obviously, when you're here.'

Harry was glad that she was stirring cheese sauce: she missed the fleeting panic on his face as she uttered the word 'weekend'.

'It can't be this weekend, sweetheart,' he told her casually, wandering over and putting his hands around her waist. 'At least, not Saturday, but Sunday's fine.'

She shrugged. 'Sunday it is then. I'll phone Mum tomorrow.'

Harry let her go. He was perplexed at the ease with which she had accepted his absence on Saturday, had never even asked what, where or when. He stood at the sink, watching her work, trying to read clues in her demeanour.

'I've a client to see in Pitlochry,' he said eventually. 'She's an old biddy, housebound, can't even get in a car.'

'That's all right,' Beth said. 'I've got plans for Saturday anyway.'

Despite his own flagrant flouting of the wedding vows, Harry's heart skipped a beat at the idea of Beth seeing someone else; besides, it was ridiculous. She would never...

'I'm going to see Charlie's house while his mother's still there.' She turned and gave him a sarcastic smile. 'To stop any gossip, you know?'

'What gossip?' he asked nonchalantly. 'There would never be any gossip about you.'

'Such faith in me,' Beth laughed, but Harry did not find it at all amusing.

'How much longer will the meal be?'

'Half an hour, maybe less. Why?'

'I wondered if Anna and I would have time to take Hero for a walk.'

Beth glanced at their daughter, saw the blatant excitement in the child's eyes and nodded. 'Good idea. Put your coat on, Anna, in case the air's cool now.'

'Beth,' Harry protested lightly. 'It's twenty degrees out there. She won't need a coat.'

'Do you want a coat, sweetie?'

'No, Mummy.'

'Fair enough. The majority vote having been cast, you won't need a coat.' Beth gave Anna a radiant smile. 'Behave for Daddy, you know he's been working all day and is very tired.'

'Yes, Mummy.'

On his way to the door, Harry paused and kissed Beth on the cheek and, to his amazement, she responded by entwining her arms around him.

'I hope you're not too tired later,' she smiled coquettishly and, even now, after nine years of marriage, she could, if she wanted to, set his pulses racing.

'I won't be.'

'Promises, promises.'

'Come on, Daddy!' came Anna's plaintive voice from the door. 'Hero wants to go now.'

Beth kissed him on the mouth before releasing him. 'See you later.'

As he took the dog's lead from the hook, Harry could hardly believe that a woman's mood could alter so drastically from second to second. He thought of Foxy and how stable she was: neither too joyous nor too despondent, always the same from one month to the next, and sometimes he was grateful for her predictability. Idly, he wondered if it were just potluck.

*

As soon as Harry and Anna had disappeared across the lawn, Beth sat down at the kitchen table and mulled things over. She found it unbelievable that her mood could swing from high to low in the space of a split second, and wondered if it were normal for women of her age. She sighed and leaned back in her chair, happy to enjoy half an hour's peace and quiet before she had to suffer happy families again.

'Shit!'

She leaped to her feet, disgusted with herself. A huge wave of guilt grabbed her, threatened to drag her down to the depths of the lowest pit. Aimlessly, she wandered around the kitchen, checking drawers and cupboards, trying to still her mind. First thing next morning, she would organise a heart-to-heart with her mother and find out if wild, fluctuating moods were normal.

One subject she could not raise, however, was the sudden resurgence of Beth's sympathy for Thomas Blake.

Chapter Five

Grace and Alice were walking along Tay Street, admiring the swans by the side of the river. The day was humid and stuffy, but they were both so delighted at being able to wear light frocks and sandals that neither complained. Alice had become re-acclimatised to the Scottish weather and was no longer encumbered with jackets and coats when the natives were in shorts and T-shirts.

'This is gorgeous,' she said happily, as they paused for breath. 'One day we should go over to the other side and take the Norrie Miller walk.'

'How do you know about that?'

'I was born here, remember? I haven't always been a foreigner.'

Grace laughed. 'I keep forgetting.'

That I don't love James.

'You cold, honey?'

'No, someone must have walked over my grave.'

She had meant it in fun, but her voice wavered and Alice put an arm around her.

'Grace, sweetie, don't be sad, and stop talking about graves when we're still young things.'

'I know. It was stupid. Forgive me?'

'Only if you never do it again.'

'It's a deal.'

'Now, let's go to that quaint little tearoom that you and I used to go to when I came over in '53.'

'Goodness, it's a pub now.'

'Well, let's go to a pub then. Yes,' Alice's face lit up. 'I haven't been to a Scottish pub for years. How about it, pal?

'My treat.'

'Get lost!'

*

Harry put Foxy's drink in front of her and sat down. They were taking a chance, he acknowledged, for now she could hardly be termed a practising lesbian and would not have a valid escape route from any hassle with Beth. She was obviously thinking along similar lines, because she had been less than keen to go into the centre of Perth on a Saturday.

'We can go back to my flat, pathetic though it is,' she had suggested, but the place was a dump and neither of them liked it. That was the trouble with having to share half of nothing much. It was a constant thorn in Harry's side that, if he and Beth ever split up, he would be relegated be to a dismal two-bed apartment in the city after bringing in most of the money during their marriage.

Even now, now that Beth was earning a fair bit herself, she spent most of it on the house and their daughter, and he would often study her bank book and wonder how anyone could get through seventy pounds in one particular week in March. The trouble was, she took cash out – that much he could follow – but what she did with it thereafter was mostly a mystery.

Recently, in the middle of the night, he had found himself working out what a half share of their estate would be.

'I think we should go back to my place,' he heard Foxy say now. She was looking at him with anxious eyes, fidgeting around like a hen on a hot girdle, as he often heard

Grace say.

'Fine,' he agreed. 'Drink up and we'll go.'

They stood up and made their way to the door, struggling through crowds of St. Johnstone supporters that were boisterous, though not rowdy, and then, with a sigh of relief, Harry swung the door open and stepped right into Grace's path.

'Harry!' she exclaimed. 'How nice to see you!'

'Grace,' he began, only to see Alice move into his line of vision. 'And Alice too,' he said inanely, hoping against hope that Foxy would make herself scarce, pretend she was a total stranger and push past them. It was too late, however, for she could have no idea who the women were; assumed perhaps that they were colleagues or clients.

'Hello,' she said gaily, offering a hand to Grace. 'I'm Kate, a friend of Harry's. Nice to meet you.'

'Unfortunately, we're just leaving,' he smiled, hardly able to speak for the pounding of his heart. 'Kate's a colleague of mine and we're on our way to Pitlochry to see a client.'

He heard Foxy's intake of breath as she realised she was listening to a fairy tale, but she rallied and backed him up.

'It was naughty of us to have lunch first,' she laughed, slapping Harry playfully on the shoulder. 'Men! Honestly, they'd die of a full day's work!'

Grace laughed, but Alice stood silently on the pavement, her eyes on the ground. Harry's stomach lurched: according to Grace – a confidence accidentally revealed – the woman had been unfaithful herself; she would recognise the signs.

'Oh, that's all right,' Grace said now, her smile extending to Foxy. 'Some other time perhaps?'

'I'll see you soon,' Harry said quickly, easing past her into the street. 'Beth said she'd invited you and James tomorrow for lunch?'

'Yes, and we're so looking forward to it, especially James. He never sees enough of Anna, so he tells me.'

She moved aside to let him join Foxy, who was standing uneasily beside a silent Alice. Harry made the decision not to involve Alice Cameron, for it would look as if he were trying to placate things.

'See you tomorrow then,' he said evenly. 'Nice to see you again, Alice.'

With that, he walked off, leaving Foxy to catch up, but cursing himself for being such a bloody idiot.

*

Alice was too quiet. Grace knew perfectly well what her friend was thinking, but it was none of their business and she would not pass comment. She had her own, selfish emotions to cope with: the idea of Harry and another woman was wreaking havoc with her thoughts. For the moment, she was speaking and acting like a robot.

'I think I'll have the steak pie,' she said, glancing up from the menu. 'What will you have?'

'You know, don't you?'

'I'm not going to talk about it, Alice,' Grace said brusquely. 'It has absolutely nothing to do with either of us, so will you please choose something to eat?'

'I wasn't going to say anything,' Alice grimaced, ignoring the menu for the moment.

'Well, don't,' Grace advised candidly. 'Because I'm not listening.'

'Grace, please, don't be daft. It's your daughter's happiness we're discussing here, not her husband's infidelity.'

Had it not been for the fact they were sitting in such a public place, Grace might have lost her temper with her friend; but with so many people crowding around, she chose the path of peace.

'Beth can take care of herself, as well you know. Have you any idea where she is this morning?'

Alice frowned. 'No, of course not, but I guess I'm about to find out.'

'She's having lunch with Charlie Webster.'

'Well, don't look so pleased with yourself,' Alice said tersely. 'Otherwise I might think you're egging her on to even things up.'

Grace was angry, but it was not in her nature to make a scene. All she could do for the time being was to deflect her friend's attempts to provoke her, even to the extent of telling a fib, for Beth was only at the Mill for coffee and had made sure that Lucy would be hovering in the background.

'That's silly, Alice, and fine you know it. Now, I don't mind eating alone, but I'd much rather you joined me.'

Alice shrugged and perused the menu, but Grace suspected the issue would be resumed as soon as they were in the car.

*

Beth sat in the sunshine listening to the record Charlie had found in Lucy's collection: Franz Liszt's 'Liebestraum', a piece she could never even master in her head, far less on the keyboard. It was one of her favourite pieces ever since she had seen Dirk Bogarde play the composer in a film. Apparently, or so she had read, Bogarde had had to practice the fingering of every piece of music he 'played' in the film and, if she had idolised the actor before that, she certainly revered him afterwards.

'More coffee?'

It was Lucy, innocently interrupting Beth's enjoyment of the recital, but she was such a kindly woman that it was pointless to take umbrage.

'No, thank you,' Beth whispered, hinting broadly.

'Sorry,' Lucy whispered back, her finger to her mouth. 'I'll leave you to it then.'

Beth closed her eyes and followed the pianist's progress along the lines of the manuscript, her fingers twitching as she imagined their position on the keys, her brain leaping ahead to the next hurdle. When the last chord faded away, Beth opened her eyes and found that the sun had disappeared behind vast, towering clouds. Suddenly, she shivered, as if someone had walked over her grave. She glanced at her watch and discovered it was ten past twelve.

'So, how did you enjoy the Liszt?' Charlie asked.

'It was so-so,' Beth laughed. She sat down on the window seat, not expecting him to sit beside her. When he did, she moved over, her right leg almost in mid-air.

'I'll sit over there,' Charlie said with an amused smile.

'I told you I was Scottish, hate my space being invaded.'

'They're looking for a church organist.'

'What?'

'The village church,' he explained patiently. 'The organist died last month and they need someone.'

'Not me.'

'Yes, you.'

'Not a snowball's chance in Hell.'

'We'll see.'

'No, we bloody won't!' Beth yelled, scrambling to her feet and glaring at him. There was a short silence before he smiled broadly and shook his head at her. 'What now?' she barked.

'I'd almost given up hope.'

'Stop this, whatever it is you're doing,' Beth said sharply, although her temper was reined in. 'I've left my daughter with Catriona this morning and it's high time I went to pick her up.' She refused to look out of the window, knew that the rain was beginning to fall.

'I think you should wait,' Charlie said quietly. 'I can always go upstairs, out of your way.'

'Don't be an arse.'

'And watch your language.'

They regarded each other with mutual intransigence, neither willing to give way; and Beth knew that she would always love him.

*

Foxy sat despondently on the threadbare settee that passed for her best piece of furniture in the living area, her head low, eyes closed. To all intents and purposes, she might have been asleep, but Harry knew the torment that was going on in her mind: she had let him down, been too slow to comprehend the situation; and now he was set adrift on a sea of uncertainties. Would Grace say anything to her daughter? Would Beth fly off the handle and throw him out? Would he lose Anna, his job, his livelihood?

Harry stubbed out the cigarette – his first in months – and drew another from the packet. His heart told him to be lenient with Foxy, for it had been his suggestion to have a pub lunch; yet, had she been one step ahead, as he had been, the crisis would have been averted and they would be lying in bed now, in the throes of feverish passion, not planning his defence in the divorce court.

He had to smile at the choice of words and she must have caught the smile, for she spoke then, perhaps sensing that the worst was over.

'I could kick myself for being so stupid.'

'It was my idea to go into the city.'

'But you gave me hints and I missed them.'

Harry inhaled the smoke and held it, something his mother used to do, something that his father had hated.

That's not good for you

*

'He always tells me it's not good for me,' his mother had smiled one day as they travelled back from a trip to the beach.

'Who, Daddy?'

'Yes, Daddy,'' his mother said abruptly, eyes on the road ahead.

'Does he never smoke?'

'No'

'Why not?'

'Because he's English.'

'Is that where he came from?' Harry asked, taking advantage of his mother's good mood.

Yes, miles away, in the South of England.' His mother turned and awarded Harry a bright smile. 'Not there, in the land of the roaming haggis.'

'What's that?'

'It runs around the hills firing pellets from its bum.'

When she had laughed, Harry had joined in, for it seemed safe to do so. After a while, he took his courage in both hands and asked:

'Why do we live here and not in Scotland?'

His mother had sighed then, and Harry watched the hands that held the steering wheel tightening their grip. After an eternity, the reply came quietly.

'Because he's English.'

'Do you love Daddy?'

There was a long pause while his mother manoeuvred into the driveway and parked the car in front of the garage; and then, just as Harry despaired of ever receiving an answer, she shook her head, eyes staring at the blank garage door.

'No, I don't, and if you ever mention it to anyone, I'll never speak to you again.'

Harry had shrunk back in his seat, afraid to look at her, afraid to breathe.

'So, you promise not to mention it to anyone?' she repeated.

'I promise.'

*

'What do you promise?'

Harry stared at Foxy. 'What?'

'You said you promised and I wondered what it was.'

'I didn't realise I'd spoken aloud.'

'Anyway, you never have to make any to me.'

'I know,' he said bluntly, and she averted her eyes.

'I think it's best if we meet some other time,' Foxy murmured, perhaps hoping that he would disagree.

'Yes, I think that's best.'

She tried to put a brave face on it but she was nothing like the consummate actresses in the Melville family and so she shed a few tears, swallowed several times, and then turned her head away, refused to look at him.

'I'll phone you soon,' Harry told her, picking up his packet of cigarettes and heading for the door. 'And don't worry.'.

'I hope to God your wife doesn't find out.'

'Grace won't say a word. Besides –' he broke off, fearing he would give too much away.

'Besides what?'

'Nothing.'

Foxy turned her head away again and made no response, and so Harry opened the door and walked out.

Once in the street, he stood for a moment, undecided as to where he should go. It was far too early to go home, especially since he was supposed to be in Pitlochry; nor could he wander the streets of Perth and bump into Grace again. Suddenly, he decided to drive to Pitlochry and have afternoon tea at Fishers Hotel. That way, if anyone asked him, he would have some kind of alibi; and it would award him time to recover from the frightening prospect of being shunned by Grace Melville. His wife's anger and recrimination were not of the slightest concern to him.

*

Grace set the table an hour too early and went into the garden to find Frank. He had been moping around the house instead of playing football, had complained of a sore ankle and called off at the last minute; something that had not endeared himself to James.

505

'You can't suddenly have a sore ankle,' his father had said sternly. 'It must have been sore this morning.'

'No, it wasn't,' Frank had insisted. 'I sprained it on the way downstairs. I was rushing to speak to Emily, missed my step.'

James had been about to storm off to the match without a centre forward and he was a very unhappy man. Grace had taken her son's part, as usual, but had refrained from being too vociferous in her opinion.

'Can't you put Kenneth on the pitch?' she asked, referring to a boy who was always on the substitute bench and whose mother never failed to mention it to Grace at the Women's Guild meetings.

'I have no choice now, do I?' James had snarled, and she had been glad to see him go.

Now, as she walked up the path, the scents of the wet greenery abounding, Grace thought how relieved she would be when her son could afford a property of his own and she would have some respite from the extra work entailed in having the couple in the cottage. She had long since realised that children were your responsibility until you died, regardless of how old they were, regardless of whether they were married with their own.

Spotting her son at the top of the garden, hidden away in the suntrap that was James's pride and joy, Grace paused for a moment, eyeing the boy, wondering what might be her best approach to his problem; for he had one, that was certain, and it had nothing to do with his ankle.

'So, here you are,' she said brightly, joining him on the old wrought-iron bench. 'I was just going to make pancakes. Do you fancy some?'

'No, thanks, Mum.'

'A couple of chocolate éclairs maybe?'

'No, honestly, I'm not hungry.'

Frank's not being hungry was unheard of. Grace nodded, carefully phrasing her next sentence.

'You know you can tell me anything, Frank.'

'What is there to tell?' he asked, but politely, not like Beth. 'There's nothing, only my sore ankle.'

'I can give you something to put on it.'

He glanced at her, suppressed a smile. 'I'll survive.'

'Have you and Emily quarrelled?'

'No,' he frowned. 'We're fine.'

'What's wrong then, and don't tell me there isn't anything?'

Frank hesitated and Grace waited patiently.

'You know Emily had decided to wear a pink dress for the wedding?'

'Yes, and it's a good choice. She suits pink,' Grace said tactfully, side-stepping the issue of a white bride being linked to purity.

'Well, her mother wants her to wear white.'

'What on earth difference will it make?'

'She's pregnant.'

'What, her mother?'

He laughed, struck her arm lightly. 'Very funny, but no, not her mother. Emily.'

'Of course I know she's pregnant. How can that affect the colour of her dress?'

'Emily says she feels guilty enough at getting married in church when she's pregnant, far less having to wear white.' He turned to look at his mother. 'You know what white means, don't you?'

Grace sighed. 'Yes, dear, I do. In fact, it was my generation who told you.'

He blushed slightly. 'Yeah, sorry. Anyway, Emily's determined to wear pink and now her mother says she won't go to the wedding unless she wears white.'

Grace's anger, only just brought under control after the fracas with Alice and then James, began to bubble up again.

'What a silly woman,' she said before she could stop herself.

'That's what Emily says, but it is her mother after all, and she has to come to the wedding.' He turned to look at Grace, his eyes mournful. 'What do you think? Emily values your opinion.'

'Really?' Grace was astonished. She had hardly spoken two words to the girl in the past year. 'Well, that's nice.'

'So, what d'you think, Mum?'

'I think she should wear white, not feel at all guilty. Besides, she'll only be five months' pregnant anyway, won't she, since you brought the wedding forward?'

'But... but that's...' Frank stopped speaking, gave his mother a puzzled look.

'That's the best thing to do,' Grace finished for him, touching his arm and giving him a supportive smile. 'The very idea of her mother not going to the wedding is unthinkable. Just tell Emily she should wear whatever her mother wants her to and not to mind other people. Oh, and if she really wants some good advice, tell her to speak to Lily Morris. She's the woman to put Emily straight about Christians in rural Scotland.'

Frank smiled politely, but the remark passed him by. 'O.K., Mum, I'll do that.'

'Now, about those pancakes?'

Her son grinned. 'I think I could manage a few.' As they stood up, he suddenly took her arm and restrained her. 'I meant to tell you that we didn't... we didn't plan for her to get pregnant. It just happened. We were careless. I'm sorry, Mum.'

Grace burst out laughing and was happy to see her son placated.

'Frank, my dear boy, I couldn't be more thrilled at the idea of another grandchild. Who cares about the circumstances?'

'You're not just saying that?'

Grace sobered up. 'Oh, no. Wild horses couldn't stop me telling the truth.'

Except all the time.

As they walked down the path together, Grace mulled over Margaret MacKay's edict on white dresses and had to stop herself from further, derogatory comments about human beings in general. The redeeming aspect would be that the said Mrs MacKay would attend her daughter's wedding, sit smugly behind the white dress, and never know it had been Grace's decision.

Grace tried to see the funny side of it. Honestly! If she had time, she could write a book on how to pour oil on troubled waters. Of course, if people were not so determined to stir up the waters in the first place, there would be no need for such a book.

*

Beth dried her hair and went to Anna's room to read her a story. It was too early for a bedtime story, but her daughter would not complain. The door was ajar – a precaution against accidents – and as Beth looked in, she saw Anna sitting on the floor reading a story to her favourite doll, Ruby. She stood for a moment, enjoying the sight of the little girl in her element, and then she tapped on the door to announce her presence – another rule, this time for the adults.

'Hi, sweetie, are you busy?'

'No, Mummy, I'm just finished,' Anna said, throwing the doll aside in her haste to reach Beth. 'Can we do something else?'

'I thought we'd have a story, but maybe you're tired of them.'

'No!' Anna cried, clutching Beth's skirt. 'Can I have the one about the dog that runs away?'

'Isn't that a bit sad at the end?'

'Yes, but Granny makes it happy.'

Beth shrugged and pretended to be delighted; but the old, familiar resentment was never far away.

'Here it is,' Anna was saying, thrusting the book under her mother's nose. 'Can I hear it three times?'

'No, just once. It's too sad for me.'

Having asserted her intention to read the sad ending, Beth took the book from her daughter's fingers. As she made herself comfortable on Beth's knee, Anna asked, 'Will Mummy cry?'

'Probably,' Beth replied, much to her daughter's awe. 'Now, let's start.'

As she read and turned the pages, Beth's mind was elsewhere. She had no idea if Charlie had seen anything in her eyes as she bade him farewell, nor did she have any desire to know. All she knew was that she loved the man, had probably always loved him; but now she might have to do something about it, even if it meant never going to see him again. Her voice faltered as she read, and Anna looked up at her.

'Is this bit too sad for you, Mummy?'

'Yes, it is a bit.'

'You can stop if you want.'

Beth squeezed her daughter tightly. 'No, I don't want to stop. I want to be sad.'

Anna shrugged, for anything made perfect sense to a four-year-old.

No sooner than the last words had been uttered, but Anna jumped off her mother's knee and rushed to the bedroom door.

'It's Daddy!'

'All right, go and see him, but be careful on the stairs.'

Beth tidied away the book and a discarded Ruby doll, by which time father and daughter were on their way upstairs, Harry laughing and chatting, asking Anna about her day. At the back of her mind, Beth suspected it was a shrewd way of finding out about *her* day, but it seemed so churlish that she gave herself a mental slap.

'Hi, there,' Harry said, depositing his daughter in the doorway and urging her to go and get changed. 'How are things?'

'Fine, how are your things?'

Harry appeared surprised, perhaps that she was in a good mood, for lately she had made him work hard when he arrived home. Beth snapped her mind shut as to the reason for her good mood.

'My things are raring to go,' he smiled. 'Maybe you'd like to have a look at them later?'

With a swift glance at Anna, who was standing watching – and listening – Beth coughed twice, a sign they should postpone the conversation.

'Anna, darling, you were such a good girl today for Catriona that you can wear anything you like at teatime.'

'Can I...?'

'Yes, anything, even your new nightie.' Harry raised an eyebrow but made no comment. 'You'll be ready for bed in record time,' Beth went on. 'So Daddy will read you two stories.'

'The one about the dog who ran away?' Anna asked predictably.

'Yes, of course. Now, Mummy and Daddy are going downstairs to have a drink. Get washed and changed and come down when you're ready.'

In the kitchen, Harry wound his arms around her and nuzzled her neck. Her own guilty conscience exaggerated her response and within moments, they were kissing with as much passion as at the beginning of their relationship.

'Hey, steady on,' Beth gasped, coming up for air. 'Our daughter might walk in.'

'You started it,' Harry laughed, more at ease than she had seen him for weeks. 'But you're right. First things first. What's that advert for lager, the one that you're always laughing at?'

' 'Thirst things first',' Beth replied. 'Very clever, although I doubt I'll ever sample their product.'

'Come on, I'll pour you a glass of sparkly and we can relax for a minute.'

They sat in the small den with the door open in case Anna should come down, and as she sat opposite him, Beth noticed the dark rings round Harry's eyes, wondered if he were working too hard. Being a senior partner had pros and cons, and whilst they both enjoyed the generous salary that came with the position, Harry was not the kind of man to pass his work to an underling.

'Can't some junior do it?' she had asked him years ago, when his promotion had been settled.

'It's my signature at the bottom of the page,' he had pointed out, and she had never mentioned it again.

'So,' he was saying now. 'How did the visit to the old Mill go?'

'What a fabulous place.'

'Any time we walked along there, I always thought it looked neglected.'

'There's still a lot to be done, but it's lovely. You can see the river at the bottom of the garden.'

'It's listed, isn't it?'

'The river?'

Harry smiled more tolerantly than he had done for months, and it crossed Beth's mind that he might have some good news, for why else should he be in such a great mood?

'You're on your game tonight,' he said pleasantly, and then Beth braced herself, prepared for a direct question about Charlie Webster. 'His mother's still there, helping with the move, isn't she?'

'Yes, and he treats her like a servant sometimes.'

'That's not very upper crust.'

'No, I must admit I was surprised.'

'But, you had a good time?' Harry asked patiently, taking small sips from his glass, uncharacteristically making it last.

'Yes, I did, and I'm really glad he's come back to live here.'

Beth knew she had spoken too strongly and she expected an Inquisition. She almost fell off her chair when Harry smiled and stood up and told her she should see him regularly.

'Well, of course I will,' Beth responded, heart pounding. 'I've arranged to go next week. Once Lucy's gone, however…'

Harry paused at the door, glass in hand, surveying the crystal pattern, and she wondered what he was thinking.

'Your being happy is all I want,' he said with apparent sincerity.

With that, he turned and left the room, his footsteps clicking down the hall.

Confused, Beth sat trying to reason it out: she had been convinced he would make a big fuss about seeing Charlie Webster, and yet here he was, not only not making a fuss but also encouraging her to make a habit of it.

Beth shook her head. Would she ever understand her husband?

*

Harry heard Anna coming downstairs and calling for her mother. He waited, knowing he had a good ten minutes before having to put in an appearance, for Anna liked nothing more than sitting on her mother's knee whenever the opportunity arose; and these were few and far between. For some reason, and he had yet to fathom it out, Beth was less inclined to sit with their daughter unless she were telling stories or watching 'Picture Box.' She had labelled idle chitchat with Anna as 'time wasting' and 'meaningless', a description that had disappointed him. He loved to sit and hear the little girl's chatter, for it led him to understand her more, and his sole aim as a father was not to let her down as Rachel Gillespie had let her child down.

The sheer luxury of being able to spend half an hour with Anna reminded Harry starkly of his own, bereft childhood. Now, as he dallied in the kitchen, listening to the murmur of Beth's voice, his heart still ached for his mother. Some things would never change.

As he glanced at the clock, decided he had wasted enough time in the kitchen, he wondered if Beth had noticed the congeniality of his mood that evening. He hoped not; otherwise he might be in for an Inquisition.

When he returned to the den, however, his fears were rendered groundless: with each smile and wink, Beth conveyed not only that there would be no Inquisition, but also that he was in for a bedtime treat.

*

Sunday dawned bright and sunny. After the unexpected and untypical thunderstorm of the previous morning, the way was cleared for a more comfortable, less humid day. Grace rose earlier than usual for a Sunday and even went to Church, where she sat with Molly.

'You're looking happy,' Grace told her friend and was met by a radiant smile.

'Donald's going to have a baby. I'll be a grandmother at last.'

Setting aside the obvious humour in Donald giving birth, Grace proclaimed herself to be delighted. Despite the fact they were sitting in Church, beneath a replica of the Cross, no less, Molly launched into an unkind dissertation on her future daughter-in-law's qualifications – or lack of them – to be a mother. After five minutes, Grace greeted the arrival of the Minister with a heartfelt sigh. Was there anything or anybody that Molly approved of?

Later, as they walked down the lane, Molly mentioned having spotted Charlie Webster in Craigton the week before and was Grace aware the man had moved back to the area?

'Oh, yes,' she said, treading carefully. 'I believe someone did tell me.'

'It's typical, of course,' Molly scoffed. 'His wife got so fed up of him that she'd no choice but to leave. Stupid man lost his two children as well. Not that he seems to care, mind you. He looked happy enough when I saw him, probably glad to see the back of them.'

Grace made suitable noises but resolved not to get involved, although her loyalty to Beth would determine that she convey to her the tone of local gossip, let the girl know exactly what people were saying. Charlotte Blake had done it for her daughter and Grace would do it for hers.

As she bade her friend farewell and walked on alone, Grace felt a sudden rush of guilt at censuring Molly's unchristian conduct on a Sunday: *she* was one to speak, having deliberately left Alice out of that day's lunch plans when Beth had given strict instructions to invite her.

Harry stood in the garden smoking a cigarette to calm his nerves: when Beth had told him that Alice was to be coming with Grace and James, he knew he had paled enough for her to notice.

'I said Alice,' Beth had repeated, laughing but confused at his reaction.

'Ah, right. Sorry, I thought you said *Alan*, you know...'

'You need your ears syringed,' she had joked. 'Anyway, it'll be nice for her to see the place again. I think the last time she was here, we'd only just had the kitchen done.'

Now, in the solitude of the garden, out of sight of the house, Harry mulled over possible outcomes to Alice's presence. She would either ignore him or make discreet references to his liaison with Foxy. Either way, he would have a hard time of it; and Beth was sure to latch on.

He heard the car before he saw it, had time to stub out the cigarette and pop a Mint Imperial into his mouth to freshen his breath, and then he squared his shoulders and put his brain in gear. He would have to be extra sharp.

Grace had Alice's 'excuse' at the ready, and it slipped off her tongue like the truth.

'She's terribly sorry, darling, but her back's gone again. Sciatica, you know the kind of thing.' She was glad that James was speaking to his granddaughter, for she was able to add feet and legs to her first lie. 'She phoned this morning, when I got back from Church, says she'll pop over soon, sends you her love.'

'I'm so disappointed,' Beth frowned. 'I'll call her later. What's the number?'

Grace smiled, already prepared. The note she handed her daughter was missing a crucial zero from Alice's telephone number, causing Grace a moment's stab of self-recrimination. She was of the opinion, however, that Beth and Harry's welfare was at stake and nothing would ever interfere with that; especially since Harry's welfare was akin to Grace's own.

'I've brought some trifle,' she told her daughter, handing her the old dish that Charlotte had used for the same purpose. 'I left the sherry out so that Anna can have some.'

Beth smiled. 'You think I'm an ogre, don't you?' she asked to Grace's horror.

'What an awful thing to say! Of course I don't think you're an ogre. I'll have you know that I couldn't be prouder of you as a mother, Beth.'

Although it was known only to her, Grace's response had encompassed years of anxiety as to Beth's ability to have children and her sudden rush of tears was no surprise to her; but Beth was staring at her.

'Golly, what brought that on?' she asked in a light-hearted manner.

'I'm just putting you right,' Grace said, more calmly, dabbing her eyes before Harry and James joined them. 'I happen to think you're the best young mother I've ever seen and Anna is an absolute angel because of it.'

Beth bit her lower lip, a sure sign to Grace that the girl was moved.

'Thanks, Mum. That's the nicest thing anyone's ever said to me. I often worry that people misconstrue the way I handle Anna.'

'Well, I don't,' Grace said firmly, her emotions under control again. 'You should write a book to help other women.'

Beth laughed, 'Oh, hey, that's a step too far. Come on, let's go and let Hero out and have our tights ripped again!'

*

Harry was ecstatic. He had thanked his guardian angel several times before going to greet Grace and James, although now, half way through lunch, he was thinking now that she was avoiding his eye occasionally, and it threatened to spoil his euphoria.

'So, you still enjoy living the life of a country gent?' she was asking him across the table.

'Yes, I must admit I do, although it's nice having a gardener to come in every so often and do all the hard work.'

'You could have a swimming pool down there,' James chipped in and Anna gave him a rapturous look.

'A swimming pool?' she echoed in hushed tones.

'Yes, why not?' James persisted jovially. 'We could all have a dip on a hot day like this.'

Before Anna could entreat her parents, Harry thought it prudent to nip the idea in the bud, for Beth would never agree to any kind of pool while their daughter was still young enough to topple in.

'We'll wait until Anna's older,' he proposed, at which Beth shot him an approving smile. 'We can go to the beach until then.'

'I love the beach, Grandpa,' the little girl told James.

'We must go one day, you me and Granny.'

'Can we?' Anna asked Beth, and Harry suppressed a brief notion that he was superfluous.

'You'll have to ask Daddy,' Beth said unexpectedly, and when he met her gaze he was astonished at the affection in her eyes.

'You'll have to ask Mummy,' he laughed, and everyone joined in.

As they filed out into the terrace to take advantage of the sunshine, Harry sought the sanctuary of the orchard; breathed in the scent of fresh apple blossom, and wondered why he had devoted even a single moment of anxiety to his ability to deal with adversity.

As he turned to look back at the house, he saw Grace approaching; had little time to rearrange his thoughts.

'I would never say anything to Beth,' she said evenly, as she halted beside him.

'It's not what you think.'

She smiled, but it was a cool smile. 'Harry, dear, I wasn't born yesterday. Besides, it has nothing to do with me.'

'It has everything to do with you,' he contradicted in a loud whisper. 'You're more important to be than anyone.'

Her eyes flew to his. 'I hope you don't mean that!'

'You know I do,' he went on, acknowledging the recklessness of it.

She shivered in the shadows of the trees, and he offered her his jacket. She was horrified. 'No, of course not.'

'But, if you're cold?'

'I'm fine.'

They walked on, back into the sunshine. Harry could see the others sitting on the terrace, knew he had only another minute to talk to her alone.

'Grace, I must see you soon.'

Her pace did not slacken. 'You know you're welcome at the house any time.'

'Please,' Harry insisted, halting, forcing her to turn and look at him. 'I'll phone you tomorrow. There's something I have to tell you.'

'I doubt if there's anything I don't know.'

'Oh, for God's sake, stop this!' he told her, too loudly, it seemed, for the others glanced in his direction. 'I'll call you at half past nine, and if you don't agree to see me I'll make a fuss.'

He walked off without waiting for her; nor caring what impression the others might have.

*

The sound of a lamb's bleating forced her to rise and close the bedroom window. Where, normally, she would sleep through it, Grace was unsettled by the plaintive cry. She stood at the window, gazing out onto a moonlit garden, unable to rationalise her thoughts.

During the afternoon she had made a valiant attempt to avoid his company, to the extent that Beth had noticed and passed comment, forcing Grace to utter the first words that came into her head.

'I thought you resented any time Harry spent with me?'

Beth's expression had conveyed a mixture of guilt and shock.

'What's got into you this afternoon?'

In the wake of a careless remark, Grace knew it was too late to try and make amends. She shrugged and cited Emily as the cause of her irritation; yet another rash statement she would come to regret.

'Emily? What's she done to upset you?'

'Her mother wants her to wear white.'

Beth disapproved, which made Grace think her daughter had, indeed, been a virgin on her wedding day.

'And why are you involved?'

'Because Frank asked my opinion.'

'You're sure that's the only thing bothering you?'

'Of course, and I'm sorry if I spoiled your day.'

Now, as her eyes readjusted to the gloom of the bedroom, Grace was hard-pressed to fight down the feeling of despair. Since her father's appearance in the area, her life had been turned upside down; nothing was the same, not even her personality. He had ruined everything; yet again.

She took a deep breath. She could not reconcile herself to being the only person who should suffer because of Thomas Blake. What better reason could she have for giving the letter to his new wife?

Chapter Six

The month of July was the hottest on record and some of the older people had begun to complain. Lily Morris, however, was not one of them and as she and Grace contemplated the imminence of Donald's wedding, Lily professed a desire for the weather to remain hot and dry for the foreseeable future.

'I'm getting used to walking through the garden without my wellies on,' she said with amusement. 'Do you ever get fed up with the glaur?'

'Yes, I do get fed up with the mud,' Grace replied pointedly, never one to speak the vernacular, although she sang the old Scots songs now and then and revelled in the language when it was put to music.

'I just love this sunshine,' Lily sighed. 'It seems to warm up these old bones, make them feel better.'

'Did you know that Charlie Webster's back to stay?'

'Aye, your old pal told me,' Lily replied, avoiding Molly's maiden name. 'I wondered why she was telling me and then I remembered that he had a soft spot for Beth.'

'What difference should that make to Molly?' Grace asked lightly.

'She'll most likely use the information to make trouble for somebody.'

'For once, I'm not about to disagree.'

'What?' Lily asked, feigning shock. 'You mean you've finally seen through the woman?'

'In this instance, yes,' Grace closed her eyes, lifted her face to the sun. 'If she hears that Beth's going over to the Mill now, there's no telling what mountain Molly will make of it.'

'Is she, Beth, I mean?'

'Yes.'

'I heard they're going to ask her to be church organist in the village.'

Grace's eyes flew open. 'What, here?'

'No, where Charlie Webster lives.'

'You could hardly call that a village.'

'A group of houses then,' Lily sighed. 'Anyway, the elders are going to see Beth, to ask her.'

'She'll say 'no.'

'You hope.'

'I know her, and, believe me, she'll say 'no.''

'They should have asked Sally, but she's a Roman Catholic.'

Grace laughed. 'What difference would that make? She wouldn't be worshiping in the place, only playing the organ.'

'Ah, but folks would object,' Lily said, giving her young friend a knowing look. 'It's a wonder that you and James were allowed to marry up there.'

For a moment, Grace studied her companion's face, trying to discern what lay behind the words, uttered thirty years after they might have mattered.

'What do you mean *allowed*?'

'Some folks said it was unholy.'

'You're kidding me,' Grace said weakly, but it had the ring of truth to it.

'No, cross my heart. They said that a Catholic being allowed to marry in the village church was flouting biblical rules.'

Grace sat up in the deckchair and looked at Lily. How many of those 'folks' had she smiled to, grovelled to, acceded to, in the ensuing years? She hoped she was too old to let it bother her now; but, for James's sake, she knew that the information would rankle and that she would examine every person she spoke to now; wonder if they had been one of them.

'Have you bought a new outfit for Donald's wedding?'

'What? Oh, no. Alice wanted to – when does she not? – but I was determined not to waste money. The frock I wore to Beth's wedding will do nicely.'

'Will it not be too big now?' Lily asked sarcastically.

'No, it fits just fine. I tried it on at the weekend, just in case.'

'I can see your ribs from here.'

'Can you imagine Donald married and settled down?'

'Well, he's not as steady and reliable as your Frank.'

'She's pregnant, you know.'

'Aye. Can you imagine any of our generation turning up the church like that? It's not right, even if they're all doing it now.'

'I should disagree with you but I suspect you're right.' Grace sighed and put on her sunhat. 'To change the subject, I hope Emily has a boy first.'

'Beth's not finished yet, is she?'

'Oh, I think so.'

'Look, there's your old school pal now, striding off to meet her fancy bit.'

Grace frowned and followed Molly's progress along the lane, past Lily's gate, 'Her fancy bit?'

'She's giving Eddie Cameron the eye now, didn't you know?'

'Lily, for Heaven's sake, what nonsense.'

Lily smiled and shook her head. 'If you say so, pet. If you say so.'

The telephone rang inside the house and Grace rose to answer it.

'If it's anyone but James or Beth, tell them to get lost,' Lily called to her as Grace ran into the house.

Out of breath, Grace lifted the receiver.

'Hello?'

It was Harry.

*

Harry was relieved she had been the one to take the call. He had rung her at home, had spoken briefly to James, but, having no good enough reason for calling, had hung up with undue haste.

'Grace, I wanted to speak to you. James said you were at Lily's.'

'We're discussing our outfits for Donald's wedding.'

'Yes, of course. Look,' he went on, mouth dry. 'I was wondering if I could meet you some day. It's about your stepmother,' he lied, knowing it might draw her in.

'Daphne?'

'Yes, don't forget she's a client of mine,' he told her, holding his breath.

'I'd forgotten. Let me see now. This is Friday. How about Monday morning?'

'You can't come over to the house tomorrow, by any chance? Beth will be working with Marjory and I'll have Anna.'

He knew it would be the carrot on the stick. 'Yes, I could come over, but it would have to be morning.'

'Perfect,' Harry said. 'Beth leaves at ten, won't get back until two.'

'Shall we say half past ten?'

'Look forward to it.'

He hung up, satisfied that he would have the opportunity to explain Foxy's presence in the pub that day. Grace had refused to discuss it for weeks, and Harry suspected that the longer he delayed, she would think the worse of him.

He sighed with satisfaction: he would be word perfect.

*

The doorbell rang and Beth had to halt her coffee making at a crucial moment. The new machine was playing up again, or perhaps she was just too stupid to make it work. Whatever the reason, she was ending up with pure hot water at the end of the long wait, and it was irritating the hell out of her.

'Stay in the kitchen,' she told her daughter, 'Anna stay with Hero.' She flew down the hall to the front door, the dog's frantic barking in her wake.

There was a small deputation standing at the top of the stone stairway, and they were all dressed in sombre black. She wondered if they were here to measure her up for a coffin.

'Mrs Gillespie?' the tall one asked politely.

'Yes.'

'We're with the local church.'

And I'm with the TSB.

'Oh, yes?'

'May we have five minutes of your time?'

'Yes, I suppose so,' Beth said, starting as she meant to go on, for she knew why they were here and she had Charlie Webster to thank for it. 'Mind your feet. My daughter's toys are scattered around.'

She led them into the best room, caught their over-awed expressions and felt ashamed of herself.

'Now, I'll just go and check on my daughter and I'll be back in a moment.'

She took Anna upstairs and promised her a treat in ten minutes.

'What will it be?' the little girl asked excitedly, and Beth had to think quickly.

'We'll go and see Granny this afternoon, have lots of chocolate biscuits.'

'Oh, goody!' Anna announced and, for the second time in as many minutes, Beth endured a ripple of shame.

The three men were still standing where she had left them and when she entered the room she had a fleeting vision of a den of vampires.

'Right,' she said briskly, not offering them a seat, nor sitting herself. 'What is it you'd like to see me about?'

'I assume you've heard that Morag Drysdale died recently?' the spokesman asked in reverent tones.

'No, I can't say I have,' Beth lied, unable to drag herself into the realm of common decency.

'She was our church organist,' the man went on lugubriously, in keeping with his suit. 'And we're looking for a replacement.'

'Well, don't look at me,' Beth said pleasantly. 'I'm not interested.'

'Mr Webster said you might be.'

'He was wrong then,' she persisted, as kindly as she could muster. 'He is a very nice man, probably didn't want to come right out and say it.'

'I see.'

They exchanged glances and shuffled their feet, but Beth was not to be moved. She would never offer her services on a regular basis, not now, not ever.

*

516

Charlie Webster picked up the telephone and his heart skipped a beat. He rolled silent eyes to the ceiling: he was thirty-four, going on fifteen.

'Beth, how nice to...'

'Don't give me that rubbish!' she barked at him. 'I told you I wasn't going to play their damned organ and you still stuck your nose into my affairs.'

'I did tell them you wouldn't be interested,' he lied, trying to save his skin.

'I don't believe you.'

'No, it's true,' he insisted, glad she was not standing in front of him. 'I told them not to bother going to see you, but presumably they did.'

'Yes, they did, and I felt like a heel for saying 'no'.'

'Right.'

'I would never mind helping people out, on a temporary basis, or if someone fell into their septic tank one day and drowned, but I categorically refuse to do anything on a regular basis.'

'So you won't be coming over here every Saturday then?'

There was a long silence and then the line went dead. Mentally, he rearranged the words '*went dead*,' for it was more like an explosion at the other end as the she hurled the receiver to the cradle.

For a few minutes he stood, reflecting on his options; and then he had a bright idea. He picked up the phone again and dialled Grace Melville's number.

*

Daphne Blake rushed around the house tidying and cleaning, spending more time on domestic tasks in a day than she had devoted all year. She would have everything spotless by the time Thomas came home, and she would also have his meal on the table, relying on the old adage that a way to a man's heart was through his stomach.

At half past four she threw herself into a chair and mopped her brow. She was far too old for this work, but Thomas had frowned upon hiring someone to help, and so it was left to Daphne.

'But money's no object,' she had said over the breakfast table the first day she had broached the subject. 'I can easily afford someone.'

He had smiled at her, but she had come to recognise that particular type of smile; and it signified 'no'.

'You don't want a complete stranger wandering in and out the rooms, do you, dearest? I can't think of anything more disturbing quite frankly.' He sighed, leaned across the table and patted her hand. 'If it's too much for you, we can always rent a smaller house.'

She had baulked at the very idea, for, sad to say, she enjoyed the luxury of having her own space, of being able to avoid her husband when she chose to, and it seemed he was the same, having never uttered a word against their arrangement. After four years of marriage, they were now even in separate bedrooms and, although there had never been any intimacy between them, Daphne had found comfort in the normality of sharing wardrobes and cupboards, of exchanging little endearments before they went to sleep.

Now, as she sat recovering from her spree of housework, she tried to imagine how he would react to her suggestion that they move back to Scotland; to be closer to Grace.

*

Harry sat at his desk with a sheaf of papers in front of him: two court cases

517

involving a bitter divorce and a dispute between a builder and his client to the tune of eight thousand pounds. In front of him was Daphne Blake's letter, which he was reading for the third time. He could give her advice, of course, prevent her coming back here, tell her that house prices had soared and that she might be lucky to get a flat next to the bus station. He saw the futility of it, however, for a woman with her wealth would hardly be affected by rising house prices: the last time he had checked her portfolio she had been rolling in the stuff.

No his mission was not to stop her coming back to Scotland; rather to keep Thomas Blake's hands off her fortune.

He was relieved to see that, even after four years of wedded bliss, she had not discontinued the practice of retaining the bulk of the money in her own name. Should she die, of course, the man would inherit the lot, for she had no direct next-of-kin. Harry sat up suddenly. What the hell was he thinking about? The woman *did* have direct next-of-kin: Grace Blake, her new stepdaughter. Harry slapped the side of his head at his stupidity in over-looking such a significant fact.

With renewed energy, he dived over to the filing cabinet and withdrew his tome on Scottish Inheritance Law.

*

Beth was in the garden with Anna and Hero when Harry came home. He was early and, automatically, she glanced at her watch.

'Should I go away and come back again?' he joked, picking his happy daughter up and swinging her around.

'Stay, Daddy, stay!'

'Golly! You're getting heavier by the day, young lady,' Harry grinned, setting the little girl down gently and patting her blonde hair. 'Soon I'll not be able to lift you off the ground.'

'Is that true, Mummy?' Anna frowned at Beth.

'Yes, unfortunately we all have to grow up, and that means getting too big for Daddy to swing you round like that.'

Anna shrugged. 'Will I be too big tomorrow?'

'Goodness, no,' Beth laughed. 'It won't happen for ages yet.'

'Oh, good,' Anna smiled broadly. 'Can I go and tell teddy?'

'Yes, and bring Mummy's box of hankies out with you when you come back.'

Harry looked at Beth then, at the reddish nose, the watery eyes, and he stepped closer.

'Do you have the cold, or have you been crying?'

'A summer cold,' Beth lied, patting the swing-seat for him to sit beside her. 'I thought it was coming on last weekend. How was your day?'

'Great. I had a brainwave.'

'Gosh, I need to lie down in a darkened room for a while.'

He laughed and stretched his arm along the seat behind her. 'I keep forgetting how funny you can be.'

'I doubt if I have been all that funny lately.'

He must have picked up the mournful tone, because he lowered his arm and drew her towards him.

'We've had a bit of a dip lately,' he said quietly, taking her by surprise, not giving her time to form a controlled response.

'Do you think so?'

'Oh, come on, Beth,' Harry smiled. 'You know we have. It didn't worry me too much though. I suppose when you've been married for this long, things can't stay absolutely perfect for ever.'

Beth sighed, for it was her own interpretation; apart from Charlie Webster.

'You're probably right.' She gazed at him, saw the same affection she had years ago, wondered if she had simply stopped looking for it recently.

'At least the sex has been great,' she whispered.

'True, but I liked the other bits as well.'

'Me too.'

Harry kissed her cheek. 'Let's not promise anything, but why don't we draw a line under, start again?'

'We could.'

'But will we?'

Beth nodded. If she could get this relationship back on an even keel, she might have more ammunition to fend off her feelings for Charlie.

'There is one thing I'm going to insist on,' Harry said now.

'What's that?'

'You get someone in to do the housework.'

'But I…'

'I'm not backing down on this, Beth. I hate to see you scrubbing and scraping, and I've spoken to Grace about it. She recommended Isobel somebody, says the woman's as trustworthy as you'll find.'

Beth hesitated, for she had figured out just the other day that she was only doing domestic chores to fill her time; perhaps to make excuses to Marjory for not going into the office more regularly. Seeing the determination on her husband's face, she knew she had no choice.

'I'd have more time for the business,' she told him. 'Marjory will be grateful, poor woman. She's a brick, but I shouldn't have left everything to her.'

'Isobel starts next Thursday.'

'What?'

'Don't look at me like that.' Harry smiled tolerantly. 'It's organised, nothing more to say. Besides,' he leaned closer, brushed her cheek with his lips. 'It will free you to pay more attention to me.'

'You do all right,' Beth protested, but she had capitulated already.

'What's for dinner?'

'I haven't decided yet. You came home too early.'

'That's great. I'll make it for a change and you can lie down in a darkened room.'

As he stood up to go inside, he paused, looking down at her, his hand on the bar of the swing-seat, making it move slightly to and fro.

'I love you too much to let it go, Beth.'

Somewhat chastened, Beth lowered her gaze and nodded. 'Same here.'

'Oh, and in future,' Harry called to her as he walked away. 'Don't fib about summer colds when I know you've been crying.'

Beth had to smile. There was something so comforting about being with a man who knew you inside out.

*

Grace was astonished to see Harry's car parked at the end of the lane. As she drew level, he waved her to a stop and walked over to her car.

'Slight change of plan,' he said apologetically as she wound down the window. 'Beth's cancelled her work session, so hop in, we'll go somewhere for a coffee.'

519

Although she was disappointed not to be seeing her granddaughter, Grace accepted the situation, knowing that Harry could hardly discuss the mystery girl in Perth while his wife was listening in. She pulled up her thoughts: she must never let him know she suspected why he wanted to see her.

'That's all right,' she told him. 'But I've brought some nice things for Anna. Shall I take them home again?'

'No, I'll pop them in the car, give them to her tomorrow, if they'll keep?'

'A packet of chocolate biscuits and some crisps.'

As she spoke, she saw the faint frown lines across Harry's brow, recalled her daughter's edict that chocolate and crisps were a sign of decadence for young children.

'Fine, hand them over, and we'll use my car.'

They drove to the outskirts of Perth and found a small tearoom that Grace and Molly sometimes stopped at on their way home. It was clean and tidy with checked plastic tablecloths and little posies of artificial flowers that would have pleased Beth. Grace had lost count of the times her daughter had castigated a café or restaurant for stuffing cut flowers into narrow holders.

Harry ordered coffee and a plate of cakes, although Grace thought it too early in the morning for such treats. If he were surprised that she made no comment, he gave no sign.

'Do you mind if I smoke?' he asked her.

'No.'

'I won't then,' he smiled cheekily.

Harry tucked the cigarette packet in his pocket; and then he sighed, a long sigh, and Grace braced herself for a pack of lies.

*

'The girl I was with in Perth that day,' he began, following his script to the letter.

'You don't have to…'

'She's my secretary's niece and her name is Kate.' He paused briefly, but his hand indicated that any response was premature and so she waited, her eyes on his face. 'I know it looked like she and I were having some kind of fling,' he went on carefully. 'But nothing could be further from the truth. To be honest, it shocked even me.'

He had her interest now, and he forged ahead.

'She's a lesbian.'

Grace's eyes opened wide and she almost gasped. 'Goodness me!'

'Sandra – that's my secretary – asked me to help the girl out, see her through a messy break-up.'

'With another girl?' Grace asked, having lost none of her incredulity.

'Exactly.'

'Heavens above, what an extraordinary thing!'

'The other girl's name was Mike, short for Michelle, and they broke up a few months before. I know I shouldn't have agreed to help.' Harry raised his eyes to Grace's, saw that she was in complete sympathy with him. 'But, against my better judgement, I did agree, and I'm kind of stuck with it now.'

'It's a nice thing to do,' Grace smiled. 'Helping other people. I don't do nearly enough of it.'

'That's codswallop and you know it,' he said affectionately, buoyed up now by the success of his plan. 'Anyway, I don't suppose you'll see us together again, but, just in case you do, at least you know.'

'It didn't matter to me,' Grace shrugged and he almost believed her. 'But Alice was quite convinced you were philandering.'

'Now, there's a word you don't hear very often.'

She smiled and reached for his hand, gave it a light tap and then fiddled with her cutlery, avoided his eye for a moment, intriguing him.

'Beth wanted me to invite Alice the day after we saw you, but I deliberately didn't mention it.'

'I wondered,' Harry smiled. He was bowled over by her loyalty to him; and to her daughter, of course. 'I was dreading it, if you must know, not having had a chance to explain it to you.'

'I wouldn't have allowed Alice to interfere anyway. She's not even a relation.'

The word reminded Harry of his recent plan for Daphne Blake's estate, but he could see no way of introducing the subject without arousing Grace's suspicions. He was Daphne's solicitor and there was still such a thing as client confidentiality, even if she were a distant relative.

'Did I tell you I'd been corresponding with Daphne?'

Harry was astonished at the coincidence.

'Daphne? No, you didn't. Is that wise?'

'Probably not,' Grace smiled, and then the waitress came over with their order and she paused.

' 'Morning, Mrs M.', the woman said and Grace seemed to recognise her.

'How's the family?' she asked.

'Just fine,' the woman said, but her eyes were straying to Harry. 'And you must be Grace's son-in-law?'

Harry held out his hand and the woman took it briefly. He felt the sticky warmth of podgy fingers and it quite put him off the plate of cakes.

'Harry Gillespie,' he said, making the effort for Grace.

'You're Michael Caine's spitting image.'

'So everyone tells me.'

'I expect you're fed up hearing it.'

'No,' Harry smiled, looking directly at Grace. 'I never do.'

'Well, I'll leave you to it then,' the woman said, reluctant to leave but being called to the counter. 'See you again, Mrs M.'

'That's Alice's aunt,' Grace whispered when they were alone again.

'You're joking?'

'No, they never speak to each other now, not since Alice abandoned her children – her aunt's words, not mine.'

'Families,' Harry said with a shake of his head, although he had endured more than his fair share of acrimony with his.

They drank their first cup of coffee in silence and, before Harry could think of a way of striking up conversation with Daphne as the subject, Grace spoke, the topic being Beth.

'I'll never say anything to Beth about your strange friend. If she ever hears a whisper about you and Kate, it won't be from me.'

'Thank you, but I'm sorry to put you in this position.' He was only human, he supposed, and he suffered a pang of guilt at her sympathetic expression. 'I'll never make the mistake of taking her into Perth again, that's for sure.'

Grace laughed. 'It's always the same, isn't it? You do someone a good turn and it all ends badly.'

Harry picked up his coffee cup and vowed that never again would he make such a selfish demand on Grace. As for Foxy, she was about to be consigned to history.

*

Grace drove the short distance home, her mind preoccupied with a girl called Kate. She had read of such women – lesbians – but to her generation it was unheard of; at least, no one had ever mentioned it. That did not mean they had not existed, of course. She had no prejudices one way or the other, although the idea that her daughter might have been one taunted her high principles and tampered with any sanctimonious thoughts.

When she arrived home, James was in the garden picking a lettuce for the salad Grace was planning for their tea. She stood for a moment on the path, behind the apple trees, out of sight, watching him as he worked. He hardly looked fifty, never mind approaching sixty, yet she was astonished to recall that their next anniversary would be their thirtieth. She tried to remember the first time she had set eyes on him and why she had thought she could love him.

He glanced up, perhaps alerted to her presence by the bright blue of her dress, and his immediate reaction was to grin and wave. Grace walked towards him, along the narrow slate path James had created in the middle of the vegetable patch. As she reached him, he held out his hand to steady her.

'Your sandals,' he said, looking down. 'Don't get them dusty.'

'They're ancient. I really should buy a new pair.'

'You never buy anything for yourself,' James said accusingly. 'We can easily afford things now, with the children being away.'

'Only another week to go and Frank will be gone.'

He heard the nostalgia in her tone, took her arm and drew her to him. It was tempting, Grace thought briefly, to cry and get it over and done with; but, as was her habit, she would not give way to tears until the world was asleep.

'He's only moving ten miles down the road,' James smiled. 'You can see him every day if you want.'

'Oh, I wouldn't want to do that,' Grace fibbed. 'He has his own life now. I'll baby-sit when they need me, that will be enough.'

She had been brave mentioning the baby, for James still had fixed ideas about the sequence of events relating to marriage and children.

'How was Anna?' he asked now, releasing her to walk ahead of him down the path.

'Beth had changed her plans, so I went to Perth instead with Harry.' She prepared to tell her second lie. 'He wanted to buy something for our wedding anniversary at the end of the month, but don't say anything.'

'He's turned out to be a fine man,' James said, and it was praise indeed.

As she washed and dried the lettuces, Grace tried not to dwell on her increasing flair for deceiving people. Even telling herself it was in a good cause did little to lessen her feeling of guilt and, by the time she had set the table and was ready to call James in, she had convinced herself that there would never be a moment in her life when she told the truth twice in one day.

*

Daphne Blake hugged herself with joy, although she had left the room in a composed manner, even pausing to rearrange the stems of the fresh flowers by the door. Once in her bedroom, however, she had almost danced with glee, prevented from doing so only by the creaking floorboards that might draw Thomas's attention to her Irish jig.

'I'm so happy,' she whispered to her reflection in the mirror, doing a quiet little pirouette, taking care not to step on the creakiest board near the bed. 'I can hardly wait to see everyone again, especially Grace. Oh, I'm so happy!'

She flopped down on the bed, her eyes roaming around the room, automatically selecting personal items, mentally laying them in her suitcase. He had provided no assurances, but his reaction had given her cause for some optimism.

'How long have you been mulling this over?' he had asked, but absent-mindedly, not accusingly.

'I only just thought of it,' Daphne had lied casually, her eyes on the book on her lap.

'Do you miss the old country?'

'Yes, I have to admit, I do. Don't you?'

Thomas had laughed, but again, not disdainfully. 'Strictly speaking, my dear, I don't think of it as my old country. Been away too long probably.'

His face had saddened – at the memory of his wife, she imagined – and she had taken advantage of his melancholic mood to press her case.

'I was thinking we could buy one of those houses in the Glasgow Road.'

'What, these massive things?'

'They're not really so massive,' she had told him defensively, tempted to let him know the size of his granddaughter's house in the country, but astute enough to keep quiet for the moment. 'Besides, it's a fallacy that the older you get the less space you need. I mean, you'd be able to have your own study, or your own dark room,' she suggested, reminding him of his new hobby. 'There are lots of things we could do with the space.'

Inviting Grace and Anna to stay.

'I'll think about it,' Thomas had smiled, and Daphne had been encouraged by his attitude; had already begun to make plans for the move North.

Now, as she sat on the edge of the bed, kicking off her shoes and feeling the luxurious pile of Wilton carpet beneath her toes, Daphne Blake thought herself the happiest woman on earth.

Chapter Seven

Everyone had become so accustomed to the weather being hot and sunny that it was no longer a topic of conversation. In the coolness of the bathroom Beth was dressing Anna, fussing over the way the bow in her ribbon was refusing to lie flat. She knew it was hardly a matter of importance and that, within minutes of stepping from the car, her daughter would look like something the cat had dragged in; nevertheless, she wanted Anna to look her best.

'Do stand still, sweetie,' she said once more. 'Almost finished. There, now don't you look like an angel?'

Anna regarded her reflection. 'Is that me, Mummy?'

'Yes, dear, it is most definitely you.' Beth rose from her cramped kneeling position on the floor and smoothed down her jeans. 'Now, it's time for Mummy to get ready. Go and see Daddy, he's got something for you.'

The challenge of keeping Anna clean and tidy for half an hour lay with Harry. It had been his suggestion and Beth was not going to argue. She flew into the bathroom, stripped off and ran the shower.

*

Harry sat with his daughter on his knee, reading her the story about the dog that ran away, having lost count of how many times he had read this story. Beth assured him that their daughter would tire of it eventually, but Harry had his doubts. The trouble was, he was tiring of it himself; was desperate to find another.

'You don't like this story,' he heard Anna say bluntly.

'Of course I do, it's a wonderful story.'

'No, it's not. Mummy says it's too sad for her and she sometimes cries.'

Harry paused, his finger on his place on the page.

'Mummy cries?'

Anna nodded. 'Yes, all the time.'

Harry stared at the top of his daughter's head, his heart sinking: he had been so wrapped up with Foxy and his own immature needs, that he had paid scant attention to his wife, by far the sweetest, loveliest, funniest, cleverest girl he knew. How could he have been so utterly stupid as to jeopardise his marriage?

'We can finish the story later,' he heard Anna say plaintively.

'No, we'll finish it now, sweetheart. Right now.'

She snuggled closer, put her hand in his, and Harry was so despondent about having neglected Beth, that he could hardly inject enthusiasm into his voice.

*

When Beth emerged from the bathroom, the first thing she saw was Harry and Anna sitting in the den, heads together, voices low. Suspecting subterfuge, she crept towards the doorway, padding in her bare feet, making no sound.

'So, we won't say a word to Mummy,' Harry was whispering now.

'I'll tell teddy not to say anything,' Anna replied solemnly and, before she could help it, Beth burst out laughing. Two heads turned in her direction.

'Sorry, was just passing, couldn't help over-hearing.'

Anna glanced at her father. 'Is it all right if I go and play in my room?'

'Yes, but you know what I'm going to say?'

She grinned on her way out of the room. 'Don't get dirty!'

Harry stood up and Beth saw that he was still wearing his jeans. He looked her up and down.

'You're not going in a bath towel, are you?'

'I might.'

'I'd ravish you before you got out of this house.'

'Pity there's no time.'

'There will be later.'

'Do you have clean stuff for today?'

'Yes, thanks to Isobel.'

Beth sighed. 'She is a gem, isn't she? I know she's only been here a short time, but I've come to rely on her something rotten.'

'So, you're happy about it now?'

'Very,' Beth said, stepping up to him and raising her lips to his. 'How can I ever thank you?'

'Don't start that,' Harry laughed. 'Or I'll have to take a cold shower.'

'O.K.,' Beth responded, pretending to pout. 'I'm off to get dressed. You don't know what you've just missed!'

Harry followed on, willing himself to remember from now on how lucky he was.

*

When Grace reached the end of her sentence, Alice barely reacted.

'Ah, well, that seems to explain it then,' she said with a quick smile that lasted less than a second. 'He must have been relieved to explain it to you.'

'I must admit I was shocked. I'd never thought about women being attracted to other women.'

Alice shrugged. 'We have them in the States.' She shook her head. 'I mean, we had them...' She stopped and smiled reluctantly, Grace thought. 'You know what I mean.'

'Anyway, I won't raise an eyebrow next time I see them together.'

'I'm sure you won't.'

Grace had left it at that, albeit she harboured doubt that her friend was convinced, despite being at a loss as to what reason there could be to disbelieve Harry's explanation.

She made no attempt to hold Alice back as she stood up and indicated James, alone at the window.

'I'll just pop over and keep him company.'

'Yes, thanks,' Grace said inanely.

'That pudding was disgustingly good,' she heard Beth say at her ear.

'I didn't think you'd complain about lemon meringue pie.'

'I could never make it.'

'Of course, you could.'

Beth sat down and ran a hand across her stomach. 'I'm stuffed full.'

'Me too.' Grace lowered her voice. 'By the way, I'm your new church organist.'

She had anticipated a shocked reaction, but none so forceful as the one she witnessed now: so fervent was her daughter's anger, that Grace almost shrank back.

'You're what?' Beth whispered hoarsely, eyes wide.

'They couldn't get anyone, and Edith Burton asked me if I'd step in, help them out.'

'Who's Edith Burton?' Beth asked, in quite a rage now, holding back only because she was sitting in her mother's home.

'She's one of the elder's wives. I met her at a coffee evening recently.'

Beth swallowed several times, her lips compressed, face flushed, and Grace knew it was just a matter of time.

Charlie Webster certainly had the measure of Beth Gillespie.

*

Beth was eating Harry's almond slice, and was even eyeing her mother's, for Grace was toying with the piece on her plate.

'If you don't want that,' Beth offered. 'I can eat it.'

'Of course, dear,' her mother smiled. 'Take it.'

Across the table, Beth caught her husband's glance of exasperation, but all was fair in love and Sunday lunch feasts, and so she tucked into the contents of her mother's plate and avoided his eye.

She was still angry, still mulling over the idea of her mother having been imposed upon. The very idea of the poor woman having to practise on a pipe organ, trying to reconcile herself to the note sounding a fraction behind the touch of a finger, was filling Beth with remorse. As she looked at her mother from time to time, she projected her mind forward to the first Sunday Grace Melville would have to sit at the organ, making a fool of herself.

Inwardly, Beth was not ashamed of the word, for her mother had no experience of pipe organs, would never cope with the technical difficulty of such a piece of equipment. No, the only thing she could do was to step in and protect her mother from the slings and arrows of outrageous criticism.

Half way through her third almond slice, Beth pushed aside the empty plate and resigned herself to the inevitable: she was the new church organist.

*

After confirming that Alice was occupied keeping Lily Morris happy, Harry pulled his chair closer to Grace, Anna on his knee.

'Did you and Beth have an altercation?' he asked, choosing a word that Anna would neither recognise nor repeat.

'No, what on earth made you think that?'

'You seemed deep in conversation after lunch, and she was grumpy for a while afterwards.'

Grace smiled. 'She'll be fine. Marjory will help her.'

Harry frowned. 'Marjory? You mean her business partner?'

'No, her old music teacher.'

'Why would she need any help?'

'Beth has agreed to take on the organist's job in your village.'

Harry stared at her. 'It's impossible. She'd never do that.'

'Well, she has, and I think it'll be the best thing she's done in a while.'

'I'm amazed. How on earth did you persuade her?'

Grace smiled, but this time she did not elucidate.

'Suffice it to say, your wife will be the most popular person in the church for the foreseeable future.' She laughed, looked ashamed. 'Until she gives it up, of course, and then she'll be hated by one and all.'

'No Christians in rural Scotland?'

Grace was surprised, but only at his knowing. 'How did…?'

'Lily Morris told me once.'

'She would.'

'It's true though, isn't it?'

'My lips are sealed. Now, will you please take this delightful child home and read her at least two bedtime stories?'

'The one about the dog that…?'

'Yes. Is it still her favourite?'

Harry laughed. 'You could say that.'

As he moved off, Grace was perturbed at the glance that passed between him and Alice.

*

Grace sat with her feet up, while James made supper for them all. Alice had offered to take Lily home, but James had obviously persuaded them to keep his wife company for an hour longer. She watched her husband pottering back and forth from the kitchen, forgetting spoons, having to ask where the sugar was, and appearing so lost that Grace resolved to fill her future time taking better care of him. Although she hated housework, she saw the benefit of tasks that would occupy the long hours ahead, and she did not regret dispatching Isobel over to Beth's. Besides, it would free Beth to pursue her own interests now, rediscover the hobbies and pastimes she had so enjoyed before Anna had come along.

'You're daydreaming, honey,' she heard Alice say now.

'I'm just thinking what a wonderful day we've had.'

'You're always a gracious hostess,' Alice said, and Grace gave her an inquisitive look.

'I suppose I do my best.'

'You're much too nice.'

'Alice, what on earth are you talking about?'

Alice wriggled in her seat. 'I don't know.'

James set the teapot down on the hearth with a clunk, attracting their attention.

'Anyone for tea?'

Lily pulled up a chair as Grace stretched out to pour the tea. 'Did you know that Beth's taking over as organist in the village?'

'What, here?' a delighted Lily asked.

'No, her own village.'

'That's not much of a village.'

'So you've said before,' Grace said patiently, avoiding Alice's eye. 'She starts next Sunday.'

'That's a surprise,' Alice remarked doubtfully. 'She always told me she'd never take on a regular responsibility.'

'She's a wife and mother,' Grace laughed. 'How much more of a regular responsibility can you get?'

'I suppose you're right,' Alice conceded, although Grace could have kicked herself for highlighting a mother's duty to Alice, of all people. Unconcerned, however, Alice went on: 'She'll not have any bother, that's for certain.'

'She'll have to practise.'

'But she's played in your church before.'

'Ah, but it's a pipe organ over there.'

Alice shrugged. 'So?'

'There's a big difference, but Marjory will see her through it. And Charlie.'

'Charlie?' James asked warily. 'Webster?'

Grace coloured before taking a deep breath and then letting it out slowly.

'Yes, Marjory will be helping her on Friday evening, when they have a rehearsal,

527

but on Sunday, I've asked Charlie to bring his mother.'

'Why did you ask him?' James wanted to know, a slight frown on his forehead.

'I have my reasons,' Grace said simply.

Alice shook her head. 'Ouch, she'll not be pleased when he turns up.'

Grace tried to smile, but she knew Alice was right: the moment Charlie stepped into that church, his fate was in the hands of God.

*

As the church was only a mile down the road, Beth decided to haul her old bicycle from the bowels of the garage and cycle there. The evening was mild and sunny – as they all had been this summer – and after a wipe with a damp cloth and a serious blow up of the tyres, the bike was ready and so she hopped on and wobbled her way down the driveway. It was Friday and she wondered if she had left it a bit late to practise on the thing, but she was a quick learner and she had faith in Marjory Robertson. Not only that, but she reckoned there were not many music aficionados in the middle of nowhere, not many folks that would spot the difference between a crotchet and two quavers.

She puffed and panted up the last incline and leaned the bike against the gate. With a shock, she realised that this would be the first time she had set foot in this building since she moved here, and yet, as a teenager, she had gone to church most Sundays, with one parent or the other. As she out-manoeuvred the heavy door handle and pushed the door open, she wrapped her long cardigan tightly around her, preparing for the cold interior: churches were impervious to the vagaries of outside temperatures.

Beth paused in the doorway, taking in the relative poverty of the place. Compared to her father's church – gold statues and priceless knick-knacks strewn all over – this building was positively austere, not dissimilar to the one in her old village, but furnished sparsely, without even the luxury of an expensive carpet runner in the aisle. This floor covering looked and felt like rope.

Beth gave herself a mental whack: that was the whole point about her great-grandfather's church, the fact that it was austere, that it had reflected the way of life he and his generation had endured. That said, she pondered on her way towards the organ dais that times were supposed to have changed; yet this church had refused to change with them. She gazed around, and then upwards, at the plainness of the ceiling, the disregard for comfort, the disdain for opulence.

'Don't forget that Jesus didn't even have the luxury of a building.'

Beth whirled round to see Charlie Webster standing in the doorway, and her first instinct was to swear.

'What the... what the heck are you doing here?'

'I saw you whiz by on your bike, knew where you were headed.'

Beth thought quickly, and her first idea was that he and her mother had conspired against her. She was struck dumb with the sheer audacity of it.

'Do you know how to play this thing?' he asked.

'Of course,' Beth said, treading thin ice. This building was certainly cold enough for ice to form.

'I'm bringing mother to hear you on Sunday.'

'You're to be here?'

'Yup.'

'You never go to church.'

'True.'

'What did Lucy say when you said you were going?'

'She said I'd not to sit near the lightning conductor.'

528

Beth had to smile. She was an admirer of smart one-liners.

'I suppose you think you know everything,' she said now, eyes on her purple fingers.

'Pretty much.'

'Marjory Robertson will be here in a minute.'

'Will she?'

Beth shook her head. 'And you can stop pretending.'

Charlie grinned, and her heart skipped a beat.

'So,' he sighed. 'You'd best get started before the St. Bernard staggers in and we get drunk.'

*

Harry and Anna were playing an impromptu game of croquet when Beth flew up the driveway on her bike. Whenever her daughter caught sight of her mother, she let out a shriek, more probably at the bicycle, which she had never seen before.

'Mummy's on a bike!'

Beth extricated herself from the saddle, feeling the discomfort from just one cycle ride. She let the bike fall to the grass and picked Anna up.

'Golly, my bottom's sore,' she grimaced. 'I need a hot bath.'

'Is that your bike?' Anna asked.

'No, it belonged to Granny, but she gave it to me. Come on, tell me how you beat Daddy at croquet.'

Harry flopped down on the lawn and wiped his brow, waiting for them to join him. He studied her briefly, and it crossed Beth's mind that he might also have known about Charlie's being in cahoots with her mother.

'Charlie Webster turned up,' she frowned, undecided as to his reaction.

'I know. Grace phoned just after you'd left.'

'I have a bone to pick with her,' Beth said with irritation, and it was not entirely faked. 'I was so embarrassed when he turned up. Honestly! What is it about me that compels people to push me around?'

'Love, I expect.'

Beth's pulse raced, but her back was to him and she had time to think of a reply.

'I suppose she does love me, but it's still annoying.' She sighed and closed her eyes, leaning back on her hands and raising her face to the sun.

'Well, I'm proud of you, Beth,' Harry said, and the affection in his voice caused her to look at him.

'Quite honestly, I thought you'd be jealous of Charlie,' she dared to say. It was often better to bring it out into the open with Harry Gillespie.

He shook his head, although he was not smiling. 'Nope, just happy that you're happy.'

'Happy I'm meeting another man?' Beth asked, pushing him she knew, but aware of the significance.

'No, you wouldn't want me to admit that, would you?' Harry responded quietly. 'But I know how important friends are to you and I'd never stand in the way of that.'

'You're pretty nice, did you know that?'

Harry shrugged. 'I did, as a matter of fact, but you can tell me again.'

Beth laughed and watched Anna trying to hit the ball through the hoops.

'I got the hang of the pipe thing, by the way.'

'I didn't doubt for a second that you wouldn't.'

'Flattery will get you anything you want.'

'Music to my ears.'

*

Grace hesitated before lifting the receiver: it could only be Beth, and she might be in a bad mood.

'Mum? I could murder you!'

Grace breathed a sigh of relief. 'I wonder why?'

'Don't you dare do it again!'

'I won't need to.'

'Not even if you need to!' Beth yelled, but Grace sensed that the girl was happy. 'Are you going to ask me how I got on?'

'No, I can guess.'

'And you'll be there on Sunday?' Beth asked casually, but Grace suspected the sentiment was anything but casual.

'You think I'd miss my daughter's debut?'

'Great! Charlie and Lucy are to be there as well, so you can whisper about me behind my back.'

'He didn't tell me he'd be going,' Grace said truthfully, strangely perturbed by the idea. 'You're sure that's what he said?'

'Yes, as clear as day. Anyway, I'm so happy I got the hang of it.'

'What time's the service, by the way. I forgot to ask.'

'Half past ten, so don't be late.' There was a pause and Grace knew what was coming. 'I don't suppose Dad will come?'

'I shouldn't think so,' Grace replied, her heart heavy. 'He might be afraid he'd be flattened by a falling gargoyle.'

Beth burst out laughing.' Now who's being disrespectful?'

'I'm so proud of you, Beth, and I know you'll forgive me eventually for being a bit of a schemer.'

'I've forgiven you already, you ninny. See you on Sunday. Oh, and bring a bar of chocolate. Anna will be there with Harry and she'll need a bribe.'

Grace hung up and wandered into the living room, where James was polishing his shoes, ready to leave for the football meeting. She had a strong compulsion to provoke him into an argument about Beth's debut at the pipe organ, and she knew that when he came home later, the urge would not have lessened.

For the moment, however, she walked past him into the kitchen and began drying the tea dishes.

*

Harry sat with Anna beside him, surprised that she had been sitting so long without a murmur. She could just see the top of her mother's head and he had impressed upon her the importance of keeping quiet while Mummy was busy, but she was as still and silent as a statue and Harry was hoping it would last.

He was conscious of Charlie Webster next to him, separating him and Grace, and it occurred to him that she could have sat in the middle of them, closer to Anna and possible trouble. He glanced down at his daughter and she was completely engrossed with watching Beth. Not for the first time did he wonder at the unpredictability of four-year-olds.

When the first hymn was announced, the congregation shuffled to their feet and Harry stood up.

530

*

The spontaneous lunch that Grace produced was the best part of Beth's morning. She had wanted the feeling of euphoria to last longer than the final 'Amen' and when her mother suggested sandwiches at the cottage, Beth had persuaded Charlie and Lucy, and Alice, to join them. No one, least of all her mother, mentioned James Melville's absence, a sign to Beth that the present company were united in their opinion of his character. Beth was torn between loyalty to him and disappointment at his intransigence. She was not entirely downcast, for she had got the better of yet another musical challenge; but at the back of her mind she still had a little gloomy cloud when she thought of it.

As if to compensate for her father's non-appearance, even at lunch, the atmosphere was jovial, the chatter light-hearted. Beth glanced at her mother across the dining table and caught her eye: she was rewarded with a wink.

'So,' Harry was saying now, addressing Charlie directly. 'You're back to stay?'

'I think so.'

Harry felt Beth's tap on his arm; the lightest of touches, but he received the message loud and clear; nodded and dropped the subject.

'Wasn't Anna good?' Grace pointed out, her granddaughter's ears pricking up. 'She sat like an angel for a whole hour. Well done, poppet.'

'Thank you, Granny. I finished the chocolate bar.'

'What a surprise,' Beth smiled. 'Did you like the music?'

'Yes, Mummy, and so did Daddy.'

They all looked at Harry and, for some reason, Beth saw the flicker of irritation in his eyes.

'I was most impressed,' Harry smiled, glancing at Grace.

'And I thought I'd died and gone to Heaven,' Alice contributed. 'You were great, honey. I almost shed a tear, it was so lovely.'

Beth liked nothing more than praise, but she had had enough, wanted to move on.

'Thank you. Now, anyone fancy a piece of Mum's cake?'

*

Harry was the first to wander into the garden. He sat on the old bench and contemplated the morning's events, more so the influence Charlie Webster was having on his wife. He was hardly an authority on decorum, of course, having leapt into bed with the first attractive stranger he had encountered, but that was then, this was now, and he was hell-bent on gathering her in, tethering her to the back green if needs be.

'Hi,' a voice said, and it was Alice. There had been no obvious sign that Grace had explained about 'Kate', and as she sat beside him, Harry had a fleeting thought that Alice was shrewd enough not to believe it anyway. After all, it took a philanderer to know one.

'I'm bushed,' she told him, stretching out her legs and kicking off her shoes. 'The heat in that church was enough to fry an egg.'

'It was stuffy, that's true. I think that's what kept Anna quiet. She was half asleep.'

'Me too,' Alice smiled. 'You must be very proud of Beth.'

'I am, more than you could know.'

She was studying his face, although he kept his gaze to the garden.

'I wasn't fooled, you know, about your so-called lesbian pal.'

Because he had been expecting it, Harry found it easy to fend her off.

He turned and raised his eyebrows at her, rehearsing his sentence in his head before he opened his mouth.

'You know something, Alice? I don't honestly give a shit.'

She blushed fiercely and averted her eyes. 'Well, that's clear enough.'

'And as for trying to make something of it with Beth, or indeed with Grace, I suggest you put your own house in order first.' He stood up, looked down at her, took enormous pleasure in her discomfort. 'We've just been in church too. Perhaps you remember the parable about people in glass houses?'

He walked up the garden, away from the house, to seek the peace and quiet of the suntrap.

*

Grace watched him walk up the path, followed his progress until he disappeared from sight; and then she watched Alice, witnessed her distress. It could only have been about the girl, Kate, about Alice's obsession that Harry had been having an affair and had duped Grace with a pack of lies. She lingered by the window until her friend rose from the bench and made her way towards the house. When Alice entered, Grace spoke at once.

'Is it warm enough out there?' she asked foolishly, for she knew it was.

'Oh, yes, pretty warm,' Alice smiled, closing the door and leaning against it. 'I hoped you'd all come out to join me.'

'Isn't Harry out there?'

'Yes, at the very top of the garden, I think.'

Grace hesitated. She had two options, neither preferable. She waited, dishtowel in her hand, in case Alice should say more. They looked at each other for a long moment, and Grace suspected that she would have to settle for an impasse.

'Alice, about Kate...'

Alice waved her hand airily, moved away from the door. 'Gee, that's all in the past, sweetie. I haven't given it a thought since you put me right.'

Grace glanced around, but the living room door was firmly closed. She would say it now; else she would never say it.

'If he has been having an affair, and I'm not saying he has, it's his business, and Beth's, not ours. I won't be interfering, Alice, and I hope you won't either.'

Had she slapped her friend across the face, Grace could not have invoked a stronger reaction: Alice's face turned bright red and she seemed to gasp for breath. Before she had time to reply, however, the door opened and Anna burst in.

'Granny! Come and see what I drawed for you!'

'I'm coming, darling, in just a moment.'

'No,' Alice said brusquely. 'She's coming right now, Anna. We're finished here.'

With that, Alice swept past them both and went into the living room. When Grace pushed open the door and glanced in, however, there was no sign of her friend. She had left by the front door.

*

Harry sat up in bed with a book long after Beth had fallen asleep, slanting his reading light to avoid her side of the bed. Several times she had rolled over, but was too exhausted to wake now.

He laid the book aside, but sat pondering the events of the day, the harsh way he had spoken to Alice Cameron – Grace's best friend – wondering if the woman had blurted it out at the first opportunity. She had driven off soon after their altercation and yet Grace had given no sign that there was any tension between them. Harry smiled to himself:

why did he keep over-looking her acting ability?

He was satisfied with how he had dealt with it, however, and expected no further comment from Alice. His approach to Charlie Webster was also fairly clever, in that he had not hung around Beth and Webster as they had discussed the antique business. Instead, he had hovered around Grace, helping out in the kitchen, doing his best to appear unconcerned about his wife and a man whose good looks knocked John Cassavetes into a cocked hat.

There was one more thing he had to confront though, and he would do that first thing in the morning, when he stepped across the office threshold.

*

Grace sat by the hearth after James had gone upstairs, determined to make him pay for his wretched principles when they caused their daughter so much heartbreak. It was swings and roundabouts, this marriage: one minute she worshipped the ground he walked upon; next minute she was plotting her revenge. She sighed and shook her head, glancing across at her mother's old chair, feeling Charlotte Blake's absence just as acutely as thirty years ago. How she longed to have someone to talk to!

Pushing thoughts of her mother aside, Grace tried, but failed, to dismiss the notion that Harry had been lying after all about the girl, Kate. Alice was not the type of woman to cry 'wolf', especially when it involved infidelity, for she had seen at first hand the effects such behaviour could have on spouses and children. She would not have issued the accusation lightly.

The problem was that Grace could never – would never – take anyone's side against the boy; not just because he was good for Beth and had become a valuable part of the family, but mostly because of her reliance on him, to reward him for his loyalty to her.

When she entered the bedroom five minutes later, James barely glanced at her, and she suspected he was trying to find the right words to placate her. Tonight, however, she refused to listen to any excuses and so, before he had a chance to speak, she walked to the window and swept the curtains closed, after which she turned to look at him, knowing that her intention to sleep in Beth's old room would come as no surprise to either of them.

'I'm going to Beth's room tonight. I'm so exhausted that I just want to get into bed and sleep. I've had a very tiring day, so I'll just say goodnight, James, and I'll see you in the morning.'

She walked from the room, crossed the hall and went into Beth's old room.

Chapter Eight

As much as he prided himself on staying one step ahead of the game, Harry was astonished when Sandra greeted him the following morning with an entreaty to discuss Foxy. Foreseeing no problems from the girl's aunt, he readily agreed, having planned to the tiniest detail how he would talk it through, explain his reason for ending the relationship.

'You've no appointments until ten,' she told him as she pulled up the chair on the other side of his desk. The tremor of nervousness in her voice quickly alerted Harry to her mood: Sandra was the most easy-going of women; if she showed any sign of being nervous or ill at ease, it was not a good omen.

'I wanted to talk to you anyway about Foxy,' he began before she had fully settled in her chair. 'I made a blunder the other week, took her into the centre of Perth, bumped right into Grace.'

'Yes,' Sandra said, subdued, her eyes flitting from his face to her hands. 'She told me. I felt so sorry for her.'

With a considerable effort, Harry disregarded the disclosure of where her sympathies lay and carried on as if she had not spoken.

'It wasn't Grace I was worried about,' he explained briskly. 'It was her friend, used to live here but spent years in the States.' He looked at Sandra, paused for a moment, forced her to meet his gaze. 'She actually told me she thought I'd been unfaithful to Beth.'

Sandra was incredulous. 'She said that to you, straight out like that?'

'Yes, she did,' Harry said, leaning back in his chair, hands behind his head. 'I don't think she'll get much joy with Grace, but if she tells Beth, I've had it.'

Sandra seemed to mull it over, her mouth in a tight line, eyes conveying her continuing loyalty to her niece. Eventually, she looked at Harry and he recognised defiance in her gaze. For the first time in his dealings with the woman, he experienced a wave of panic.

'It takes two to tango, you know.' Sandra frowned. 'You didn't have to sleep with her.'

He decided not to remind her of the prominent part she played at the start of the relationship, resolved to say nothing to provoke her. He was only just beginning to suspect that Sandra could prove a formidable enemy.

'I know that, but I'm sure that Foxy and I never expected things to last. There was always the possibility that Beth would come back.' He leaned forward again, trying to keep the balance between sincerity and aggression. 'You told me yourself that it was the perfect arrangement.'

She blushed slightly, for it would have been pointless to deny it. She nodded, restlessly swung one leg over the other and looked at him. She hesitated, perhaps torn between having to accept the true version and feeling sorry for her niece.

'Under normal circumstances,' she said quietly. 'I wouldn't even consider having this conversation, Harry, but there's a complication now.'

Even before she even opened her mouth to continue; long before she had uttered the words, Harry knew what she would say and, in the space of a heartbeat, his world fell apart.

*

Grace ripped open the letter from Daphne and went into the kitchen to read it. Heart pounding, she absorbed the first sentence in a daze, knew that her plan was coming to fruition.

'...so excited to be able to tell you... agreed to come back...'

Grace lowered the letter briefly, saw the hypocrisy of saying a prayer of gratitude, but almost hugged herself with delight. Immediately, she was over-come by a sense of guilt: using the poor woman as a weapon to slam the door on her father's attempts to wheedle his way into this family was the most despicable thing she had ever contemplated.

Grace tucked the letter into her apron pocket without reading the details and then wandered into the garden. For the best part of a week, she had endured a verbal stalemate with James and so she could hardly seek him out and tell him that she had lured her father back to destroy his life once and for all; not that she would have told James anyhow, for it was something she wanted to keep to herself, but she might have let him know that Daphne had written again.

'I don't think it wise that you keep in touch with her,' James had pronounced months ago when he had learnt of the correspondence. 'In fact, I can't think why you'd want to write to the woman at all.'

'It's hardly her fault, what went on in the past. I feel rather sorry for her.'

James had stared at her for a long moment before shrugging and leaving her standing alone in the room, and the subject had never been broached since.

Now, as she watched him dig in the garden, Grace had no choice but to keep the news to herself. She toyed with the idea of telling Harry, could see no reason not to, and so she went into the hall and picked up the telephone.

*

Harry heard the phone ring. When once the sound might have energised him, filled him with enthusiasm for clients and legal contra-temps, now he hated its high-pitched warble more than any other sound. He waited, but Sandra did not pick up. Tentatively, in case it was Foxy again, he laid his fingers on the receiver and hoped for the best, but it was Grace.

'Harry? It's me. Is this a bad time?'

'No, of course not,' he lied, for there would never be a good time now. 'Is there anything wrong?'

'Not exactly, but I was wondering if we could meet, just for fifteen or twenty minutes?'

'Oh, I think I can manage that out of my hectic schedule,' he joked, his heart so heavy that he marvelled he could speak at all. 'How about tomorrow?'

'Yes, that would be fine. I'm so grateful.'

'Grace, please, you know how I feel about that.'

'I can't help it,' she laughed. 'What time shall we...?'

'How about I take you to lunch, at the Station Hotel?'

'Such extravagance!'

'There's a big car park at the back with enough space even for a woman driver.'

'You cheeky thing! I'll think of something rude to say to you, my lad.'

After she had hung up, Harry sat numbly, more depressed because of the light-hearted banter between them: it was just a matter of time before they all knew exactly what kind of creep he was, the worst part being Alice Cameron's correct assessment of his character. He could hardly take the high moral tone with her now.

He opened last Friday's *Courier and Advertiser* and scoured the columns of situations vacant: for his own sanity, he had to get out of here.

As Beth walked up the lane, she saw Harry's car in the driveway. She was confused at his being home so early, but when he stepped from the car and grinned to her, she imagined it was good news.

'How great to see you,' she said now, although she would choose her words. 'I hope you've got time for iced tea in the garden.'

'I do,' Harry grinned, lifting his briefcase from the car seat and slamming the door with his foot. 'But make it a glass of bubbly.'

'What?'

'We've something to celebrate.'

'We do?'

'Absolutely.'

'Well, tell me, for Heaven's sake!'

'I've an interview with a solicitor's practice in Craigton.'

'Bloody hell, I didn't even know there was one.'

'It was Grace who told me, and it sounds just what I'm looking for.'

'Gosh, you'll be able to pop to Mum's for your lunch,' Beth suggested, a tiny wriggle of jealousy trying to surface. 'Actually,' she went on, to make mental amends. 'Now that Frank's left home, that's the best thing that could happen to her, having you to feed at lunch time.' She slapped him on the back. 'It's going to work out just great. The perfect arrangement, in fact.'

She had no idea what she had said, but his expression altered in an instant.

'Where's Anna?' he frowned, and Beth had a taste of the old Harry, the one that had made her hold her breath for fear of upsetting him.

'She's in the conservatory, I think.'

'Make my apologies; tell her I'll see her later. I've some thinking to do.'

At that, he marched into the house, up the staircase and into his office, without a backward glance.

Beth stood at the bottom of the stairs, her mind racing, thoughts jumbled. In a daze, she went to find her daughter, to warn her not to go near Daddy until further notice.

*

In the study, Harry leaned against the closed door, his head pounding. *The perfect arrangement.*

What on earth had possessed her to say such a thing, and why had he acted like an idiot, ostensibly handing her a reason to be suspicious? He opened his eyes and pushed himself off the door, laying his briefcase on the leather chair and perching on the edge of the desk, to put his thoughts in order.

A few years ago, such a situation would hardly have mattered; but now he had a daughter; a different set of rules; and he was damned if he would treat her as casually as Rachel Gillespie had treated her son. Come Hell or High Water, he would keep his family together, even in the face of Foxy's pregnancy.

'Your aunt had to tell me,' he had told her unkindly, the moment she had admitted him into her dingy flat. 'You couldn't even tell me yourself. How embarrassing was that for me?'

'I didn't mean her to tell you,' she had protested, all the while touching her abdomen, still flat, no sign, irritating the life out of Harry. 'I tried to speak to you on the phone one day, but you were too busy, told me you'd call back.'

'I was too busy and I forgot to call back,' he added harshly. 'Satisfied?'

She gulped, hardly able to speak, her eyes suddenly moist, the worst form of blackmail, Harry had discovered.

'I've had a good idea.'

'You'll get rid of it.'

She had been horrified. 'What? You'd ask me to do that?'

'I don't think I was asking,' he said meaningfully.

'I'd never have believed you could be like this.'

'You're not going to tell me that you thought you knew me?' Harry had laughed unkindly. 'Not after a dozen shags?'

When she had burst into tears, he had been about to storm out, but she called him back, rushed over to him and clutched his sleeve.

'I told you I had a good idea.'

'All right,' he had sighed, feigning boredom, acting as despicably as he could. 'Tell me then, what this good idea is.'

Now, as he sat on the edge of his desk mulling over her suggestion, he was beginning to wonder if it would work. The clock in the hall struck three and it shook him from his daydreaming. He stood up, squared his shoulders and went to make his peace with Beth.

Anna was sleeping on the settee in the conservatory when he found her, eyelashes flickering as she dreamed, fingers curled around her favourite doll. As he looked at her, his heart skipped a beat: how could he even contemplate losing this?

'She's tired after our walk,' he heard Beth say behind him.

'I love her so much it hurts.'

'You don't have to tell me, I know that.'

He turned to face her, stepped forward and took her hands in his, almost deterred by her obvious annoyance at his earlier mood. As he pulled her towards him, however, he felt the tension leave her arms, sensed that she had forgiven him already.

'If I ever lost you and Anna, I'd kill myself.'

Since they both suspected that his father had done just that, he saw the sympathy in Beth's eyes, knew that she would want to make little of his bad mood.

'Come on, you're not going to lose either of us,' she smiled, nuzzling his neck, winding her arms around his waist. 'You were excited about the interview and I spoiled it for you.'

'You did not!' Harry pushed her away from him. He would not permit her to take the blame. 'I was in a foul mood, that's all, nothing you could have done. I was to blame.'

'O.K.,' she grinned. 'If you say so Mr Grumpy. Now, let's get back to where we were when you came home. Something like – you go and get comfy and I'll bring drinks, wasn't it?'

'I want to have some time with Anna first. Is it all right to waken her up?'

'What kind of daft question is that? She'll be desperate to annoy you for half an hour. Meanwhile, I'll disappear into the kitchen and chain myself to the sink.'

Harry sat down beside his daughter and touched her blonde hair. She stirred and opened her eyes and he braced himself for her shriek of welcome.

*

As the BMW drew up at the kerb, Grace's heart fluttered at the idea he may not have been offered the position, but then she saw his energetic wave, the broad smile followed by a thumbs-up, and she sighed with relief.

'You got it?' she asked as he marched up the path.

'I did indeed, and I sincerely hope my lunch is ready.'

'Of course it is. Come in and tell me all about it.'

When James joined them, Harry suffered a moment's disappointment that he would not have her all to himself. He smiled and sat down, however, mollified by the thought that most lunchtimes, he and Grace would be alone. It had been her suggestion that, after today, they would have lunch at two, an hour and a half after James's preferred time. She had known that her husband would not wait.

'I'll have a cup of tea with him at twelve thirty,' she had told Harry airily. 'He'll be happy enough with that. Then you and I can have something to eat at two, a much more sensible time when you're busy with clients and want to fit in several appointments during the morning.'

He would not have contradicted her, but it mattered little when he took his lunch break: appointments were few and far between, since most of the work involved keeping accounts for local estates and finding loop-holes for anyone who was averse to paying too much tax. Despite the salary being less than he had received in Perth, Harry had been thrown out several hints as to the generosity of grateful land-owners should he find sufficient 'loop-holes'.

'I suppose you'll find it dull after Perth,' James said now, his knife cutting the sandwich into miniscule pieces.

'No, I prefer the country, now that I live right in the middle of it.'

'You won't miss the city at all?'

'No, apart from not seeing Beth during the day. We often met for lunch.'

'But she can come here,' Grace said with sudden inspiration. 'And she can bring Anna too. It'll be lovely!'

It was not what Harry had in mind, but he would snuff that particular spark before it flared into anything permanent.

'Don't forget, Anna will start school in August,' he reminded her gently, avoiding her expression.

'Oh, yes, I'd forgotten. Never mind, Beth can come sometimes.'

He had already dampened her spirits and was not about to do it a second time, and so he dropped the subject, held back from mentioning that Beth had made arrangements for their daughter to go home for lunch; at least at the beginning, until she made friends.

'I won't expect to be fed for nothing,' Harry joked. 'You'll have to accept the occasional food parcel.'

'As long as it's not Beth's new fad,' Grace grimaced. 'Can't you talk her out of these cardboard strips she calls crispbread?'

'She loves them, eats them by the dozen.'

'Strange girl,' Grace smiled.

'A perfectly normal girl,' James objected.

Grace and Harry exchanged brief glances and tacitly agreed not to pass further comment.

*

As she cleared up the dishes from her light lunch with Anna, Beth glanced at the telephone again. The interview had been at ten and he had still not called. One thing she was sure of, however: due to their *entente cordiale* her mother would know by now.

'Mummy, can I pack my schoolbag now?'

'No, darling, school's not for weeks yet. There's plenty time.'

'But I want to be ready.'

Beth smiled down at her daughter. 'You will be, sweetie, you will be.'

'Will Julia be in my class?'

'Auntie Cat's little girl? Yes, she will. Do you like her?'

'Sometimes.'

Beth set aside the dishcloth and studied her daughter as she hopped from one foot to the other, teasing the dog, which darted from side to side trying to keep up.

'You'll see lots of other girls and boys too, some you don't even know yet.'

Anna frowned. 'Will I have to speak to them?'

'Like daughter like Grandpa' Beth muttered to herself as Anna gazed up at her expectantly. 'They'll be so nice that you'll want to speak to them,' she said loudly. 'You'll make so many friends that we can invite them for a tea party, have ice cream and strawberry jelly.'

Her daughter's face lit up and Beth awarded herself ten points.

*

Daphne consulted the list in her hand, ticked off the contents of each box and numbered it with a black felt pen. She was so excited that she could hardly keep the pen steady. In fact, she had taken sleeping tablets for the past few nights because her mind had refused to shut down, charging around from one idea to the next until she had almost screamed out.

The trouble was she did not waken up fully until after eleven, wandering around the place groggily, looking like an old woman probably, not doing herself any favours where Thomas was concerned. It was only for another few nights, however. They were moving north at the end of the week and she would never need to take a sleeping pill again.

As the front door opened and she heard his footsteps down the hall, Daphne pulled herself together and tried to calm down. She had no wish to give him any hint of her plans once they arrived in Scotland, for she wanted it to be a huge surprise.

She ticked off another box and its contents and prepared to endow him with her most radiant smile. This time next week, they would be home, settled into the lovely house on the Glasgow Road, and she would be meeting Grace for coffee, seeing Anna perhaps, buying the little girl presents. Life would never be so lonely again.

*

Thomas waited until she had gone to the shops for a few groceries and then he sneaked into the downstairs toilet with his bottle marked Schweppes Tonic that contained a substantial measure of gin. She was so eagle-eyed these days, an after-effect of the doctor's warning to him – a decrepit, debauched man who was so overweight that Thomas had refused to listen to a word he had said.

'He must be at least eighteen stones,' Thomas had frowned at Daphne when she ticked him off for flouting doctor's orders. 'I doubt if he has any advice to give *me* on how to stay healthy.'

She had acquiesced, as she normally did, but the prospect of countless tsks and tuts had driven him into the toilet with his mislabelled plastic bottle.

Besides, he had something to celebrate: he had chanced upon her postcard to Grace, secreted in her handbag the afternoon they had gone ashore in Lanzarote. He had pretended to snooze on the beach to give her the opportunity to dash into the town and post the card, after which he had viewed the world – even the crowded beach and scruffy English holidaymakers – with a quiet jubilation.

Suddenly he pricked up his ears: he heard her key in the front door. With an expertise borne of months of experience, Thomas hid the bottle behind the laundry basket and flushed the cistern.

*

Harry toyed with the lasagne, served too early, especially after his substantial lunch with Grace. Beth had been thrilled at his news, had thrown her arms around him with delight; but, in the dark recesses of his mind, he knew she resented being the last to know. Every so often, he would glance across at her, discover that she was looking at him, a faint pucker to her brow.

'I've annoyed you, haven't I?' he asked, throwing caution to the wind.

'Partly.'

'Thank God you're honest with me.'

'You might have phoned me first, instead of leaving it.'

Harry nodded. 'I know, and I apologise for not calling you right away.'

'Anyway, you got the job. What does it matter?'

'I'm going to like it there. By the way, the secretary knows you.'

'Oh? Who's that?'

'Her married name's Duncan, but she says Grace knew her as Izzy.'

'Never heard of her,' Beth said dismissively. 'But I'll ask Mum. Pudding?'

'Can I leave it until later?'

'Fine, if Hero doesn't sniff it out first.'

'Grace invited us for their wedding anniversary.'

'Dad mentioned it.'

'I want to buy you a new outfit, something glamorous.'

'An offer I can't refuse?'

'I'd like to take you through to Edinburgh, to buy it there.'

She feigned shock. 'Edinburgh? Strewth! And what's wrong with Craigton, may I ask?'

He heard the undertone, knew he would have to tread carefully, watch out for landmines.

'We can have lunch somewhere posh, take Anna to the zoo maybe.'

When his daughter gasped with joy, Harry met Beth's gaze and suspected he had already reached safe ground.

With an inward sigh of relief he poured himself another glass of wine; but, at the back of his mind, there was an unresolved question hanging above him like the sword of Damocles.

Chapter Nine

Grace fussed around the new coffee machine that Beth had bought as a wedding anniversary present a few days previously. She would never get the hang of the darned thing, not even with the instruction leaflet stuck in front of her. As she peered into the still-empty jug, she imagined she had missed out some essential ingredient; but, a moment later, she heard the rewarding plop as the first drop filtered through.

She used the machine in deference to her daughter, but, often, she would put a spoonful of Nescafe into the mug and be done with it.

The doorbell rang and she heard Alice calling. Taking a deep breath, Grace ran over her lines, satisfied that she was word-perfect, and then she went to greet her friend.

Even the passage of a few months had not seen an improvement in their relationship. Superficially, and to a stranger's eye, everything was normal, but Grace suspected – and Alice too, probably – that, had they scratched the shiny surface, they would uncover the hostility of divided loyalties and be forced to confront the real problem.

'Oh, I'm so happy to see you,' Grace told her friend, with as much warmth as was desirable. 'You look great. Come and tell me all your news.'

'They do say that no news is good news, don't they?' Alice smiled. 'In which case, I must be the bearer of good news.'

'How's the new job?'

'Boring,' Alice sighed, pulling up a kitchen chair, but waiting until Grace sat down first. 'Lord knows how anyone could get excited about working in a dress shop.'

'I'd hardly call Jaeger's a 'dress shop',' Grace laughed. 'You must admit, it's a class establishment.'

'Oh, they have lots of money,' Alice agreed. 'But they treat me like a serf. I often want to tell them I'm an American heiress and they'd best grovel to me.'

'Is the salary reasonable?'

'So-so, and I expect I can grin and bear it for a little while longer. Until I'm sixty anyway, and then I'll retire gracefully, buy a cat, sit in an attic all day long.'

Behind Alice's back, Grace glanced at the clock, wondered if she should have invited Lucy down. Despite the ease of conversation, it was harder than she had anticipated. For a heady, foolish moment, she thought of capitulating, admitting she had been wrong and suggest a truce. It was short-lived, of course, for she could never take sides against Harry.

'D'you think we'll ever get back to the way we were?' she heard Alice ask out of the blue, and Grace's heart gave a little scurry of hope.

'I'm desperate for that,' she told her friend truthfully. 'I've been miserable.'

'Me too,' Alice confessed, lowering her eyes and fiddling with the tablecloth. 'I should say I'm sorry, Grace, and get it over with.'

'No, don't. Can we not agree to differ and leave it behind us?'

She saw the suggestion unfolding in Alice's expression, knew that she had guessed the truth, that Grace would never be disloyal to Harry, even in the event of his infidelity.

'Put it there, pal,' Alice grinned, stretching out her hand. 'Bygones should be just that.'

'Oh, Alice!' Grace cried, almost diving across the table. 'I'm so happy!'

'Same here. I was at my wit's end, and that's a fairly short distance.'

They laughed and the ice was broken. Just then, the doorbell rang and Grace was annoyed.

*

Grace could hardly believe the difference an hour could make: she and Alice were laughing and chattering like old times, joking and giggling as if they had been young girls. Surprisingly too, Molly was proving to be better fun than Grace had remembered, although, for years, she had been biased over the woman's penchant for other women's husbands.

As the talk turned to more serious matters, the three women began to confide in one another, to the extent that Grace was tempted to spill the beans about Daphne's being back in Perth. Several times she opened her mouth to blurt it out, but, fortunately or otherwise, one of the others pitched in first.

'I suppose Harry is enjoying his stint in Hicksville?' Alice asked, her first reference to him for months.

'He says it's great,' Grace confirmed. 'The pace is slower, he told me, and the pressure's not so great.'

'I thought he worked in Perth?' Molly asked.

'No, he prefers the country now, and he pops here for his lunch most days, which is nice.'

Grace cast a furtive glance at Alice, but was satisfied that her friend meant what she had said about leaving their quarrel in the past. Just in case, however, she turned the subject to Anna's imminent change of routine.

'I'll miss the visits from Anna when she goes to school next week. Goodness knows how she'll manage.'

'How did we all manage?' Alice laughed. 'We were marched to the gates, shoved into the playground and got on with it. Is Beth planning to have any more children?' she added, not pausing for breath.

'She's not keen,' Grace revealed. 'But don't say I mentioned it.'

'Men always want a boy,' Alice sighed. 'Martin wasn't happy until we had three of them, and if I hadn't scarpered, Lord knows how many I'd have ended up with.'

Catching sight of Molly's surprise at such public disregard for motherhood, Grace was quick to reply.

'Harry seems content enough with one.'

Alice wagged a finger and shook her head. 'Take my word for it, Grace; he'll be dying for a son. They're all the same.'

An hour later, as she bade her friends farewell, Grace's mind was rushing ahead. She knew of Beth's determination not to have another child, but Alice's remark about men and sons was beginning to sink in.

She was still mulling it over while she prepared the sandwiches for Harry's lunch, but she convinced herself that it was none of her business.

*

Beth sat with the letter in front of her, going over the finer points of grammar and trying to predict Charlie's state of mind when he read it. There was no other way, however, for when he was standing there, looking at her with those penetrating eyes, the half smile on lips she visualised in her sleep, she had no chance of getting the words out without blushing furiously and botching the whole thing.

Telling him in a letter was easier and less likely to provoke an argument that Beth knew she would lose; although she doubted if he were the kind of man to read the letter, nod wisely, and then put it neatly in the waste bin. She tried not to envisage the moment he opened the envelope and unfolded her epistle.

When the telephone rang, she stood looking at it, not over-anxious to pick it up in case it was him. It persisted, however, and Beth approached it warily, her first sentence prepared.

'Beth, dear, it's me,' the voice said and Beth almost gasped with relief.

'Oh, hi, Mum. Sorry I took so long to answer.'

'Are you busy?'

'No, just ironing Anna's school things.'

'Is she still keen?'

'So keen that if they cancelled the first day, she'd throw a tantrum.'

'It's just that after Monday I won't see her so often, and I wondered if...'

'Yes, we'll come over,' Beth laughed. 'But I have to do some translating first for the French bunch. Say in about an hour?'

'Lovely, you've made my day.'

'I thought it was Harry scrounging lunch that made your day,' Beth said, immediately ashamed of her petulant tone.

'Beth, dear, you know you're being unreasonable,' her mother cautioned. 'See you some time in the afternoon.'

Beth hung up and gave her wrist a slap. 'Behave, you monster!'

The envelope beckoned, and so she slipped Charlie's letter between its folds and put it in her bag. It was fortuitous that her mother had called, for the letter would be in the post box for the evening pick-up and he would have it first thing in the morning.

*

Daphne was in her element. She was giving instructions to the carpet layer and to the delivery men from Gillies, in Brought Ferry, pretending to be oblivious to their mutterings and mumblings and the disgruntled glances they were casting her way.

She knew what she wanted, where she wanted it, and how to put it there; and she refused to compromise. This was her house for the foreseeable future and it would be laid out according to her plans.

When Thomas had disappeared after breakfast time, she had been irritated for half an hour; but then, when it became obvious that the carpet layers were going to be awkward, she was glad she was on her own. Her husband tended to be too soft and obliging with tradesmen, although he had no such qualms with hotel staff and airline stewardesses, she had noticed during their travels. Occasionally, she had averted her eyes at the injured expression on the face of a young receptionist or the purveyor of an inferior airline meal.

'The hall's finished,' she heard the surly carpet layer mutter behind her. 'I'm sure it'll do.'

'I find that when anyone tells me that,' Daphne countered pleasantly, 'What they're really saying is 'it won't do, but that's as much effort as I'm prepared to make.''

The young boy looked her up and down for a few moments. 'Go and see it for yourself,' he said grudgingly. 'That's the best anyone could do.'

Daphne surveyed the hall from the living room door: she had to admit it looked fine to her, and she wondered what all the fuss had been about.

'It's fine,' she told the boy. 'What's left?'

'The small bedroom in there,' he said, a thrust of his head indicating the spare room next to the dining room, a room that Daphne was earmarking for Grace should she ever wanted to visit.

'Well, I'm sure that won't take long,' she smiled. 'Such a small room should only take half an hour.'

He blinked at her, obviously wondering if she were bluffing or if she really did know how long it would take. He decided not to risk it.

'Yeah, about half an hour,' he agreed reluctantly. 'Then we're off.'

Daphne went back into the living room and wandered to the window, her stomach turning over. She was perfectly capable of dealing with tradesmen – willing or otherwise – but she preferred the situation where she did not have to throw her weight about. Had her first husband still been alive, of course, he would have moved her gently aside and taken over the role of agent provocateur, whereas Thomas Blake…

She shook her head at such romantic twaddle: had he still been alive, it would have been a miracle had he been sober at two in the afternoon.

Suddenly, the front door banged and she heard Thomas's steps. Automatically, Daphne checked her reflection in the mirror above the fireplace and patted her hair. Even if he did not share her bed, it was no excuse to let herself down.

*

Grace watched as he spooned sugar into his coffee, and pondered over her decision to invite the boy every day. Although she had imagined it to be a good idea that he popped in regularly, she was beginning to wonder if it was exactly what she wanted. For one thing, he was too perceptive,

'You're very quiet,' he remarked now.

'I'm sorry, I…'

'Stop,' he chided gently, lifting his finger. 'That word is forbidden.' He grew serious. 'A word Beth uses all the time to Anna,' he added, and Grace heard the disapproval.

'She is sometimes a bit strict with Anna,' she responded, but it went against the grain to cast doubt on Beth's prowess as a mother.

'Do you think so?'

'Oh, dear, I shouldn't have said anything.'

'You're her grandmother. Of course you should say something.'

It had been on the tip of Grace's tongue to broach the subject of a brother or sister for Anna – the opportunity had been perfect – but she reneged at the last moment and Harry gave her a long look.

'What?'

'What what?' she laughed, hoping to cajole him from his serious mood.

'You were about to ask me something personal.'

'I was just wondering if the salary was as good at Craigton,' she lied.

Harry laughed. 'Of course not, but there are ways and means.'

Grace was puzzled, although his manner suggested crooked dealing.

'I hope you don't mean…'

'If you didn't want to know,' he whispered behind his hand, 'You shouldn't have asked.'

'Just don't do anything awful.'

'Too late,' he frowned, and it seemed to Grace that humour deserted him.

Now, as she dried dishes and put them on the dresser, Grace was dismayed that she had never learnt from previous mistakes: the boy was so shrewd, especially where her feelings were concerned.

She sighed and looked ahead to Beth and Anna's visit. It hardly mattered that she had not had the courage to ask Harry: it would be much easier to ask her daughter.

*

544

Anna insisted on carrying her new schoolbag everywhere, and so she held it up for her grandmother's inspection as soon as the car drew up.

'Look, Granny! My new schoolbag!'

As she climbed from the driver's seat, Beth rolled her eyes at her mother.

'The flipping thing will be wrecked by the time she gets to school.'

'It's good that she's keen, though. Apparently Julia's had hysterics.'

'So I heard.' Beth locked the car and followed her mother into the house.

'Cat's wondering what to do on Monday.'

'Thank Heavens I never had any trouble with you two.'

Beth thought she heard an emphasis on the word 'two', but her mother had already spoken again and she let it go.

'Now, who wants juice and who wants tea?'

'What do they drink at school?' Anna frowned.

'Milk, I think,' Beth replied, shrugging to her mother.

'Can I have milk then?'

'Maybe Granny doesn't have enough.'

'Yes, she does. Come on, you can have as much as you want.'

They sat in the kitchen, mostly because of the flies that abounded in the garden after a night's humid rain, and Beth studied her mother as she bustled around serving Anna. It was very funny really: she was sure her mother thought she was the best actress this side of the Tweed, and yet Beth had always been able to tell when there was a difficult question in the offing. Her mother's mouth gave it away somehow, although Beth would have been hard-pressed to describe precisely how she knew.

'Go on then, ask me.'

'Ask you what?'

Although impressed by her mother's sang-froid, Beth hid a smile. There it was again, the tiny twitch of the mouth.

'You want to ask me something personal.'

'Honestly! First Harry, now you.'

Beth raised her eyebrows. 'Harry asked you something personal?'

'No, but he thought...' Her mother paused, shook her head and took out the sugar bowl, despite the fact no-one would want it.

'For Pete's sake, Mum,' Beth said crisply. 'Ask it and get it over with.'

'I'll just see to Anna first,' her mother said, handing a plate of chocolate biscuits to the little girl. 'And don't look at you mother. You're in Granny's house and she's blind.'

'Mum, please,' Beth said wearily. 'She'll have nightmares now,'

'No, she won't. I've explained the old saying to her before.'

'I can eat as much as I like,' Anna grinned, and Beth could not be bothered to tell her off.

'There is one tiny thing,' her mother said now, fidgeting with her napkin.

'Fire away, mother dear.'

'Well, what with Anna going to school next week and everyone wondering how she'll get on, I was just going to ask you if you'd...' she gave Beth an apologetic smile. 'About having any more children really, that's what I was...'

'God, no!' Beth cried irreverently, and then, always conscious of her mother's old-fashioned views, amended it to: 'I mean, golly no.'

'You don't think that Anna would benefit from a brother or sister?'

'Do you think I did?' Beth asked unkindly.

'Beth, you know that you and Frank get on famously now.'

'Yes... *now*,' Beth frowned, stirring milk into her tea and clattering the spoon off the side of the mug. 'But I'd have been quite happy on my own, thanks, and so will

Anna.'

'If you say so,' her mother said resignedly. 'More juice, sweetheart?'

'I tell you what,' Beth said, having a sudden bright idea. 'Why don't you ask Anna?'

'She'll probably say what you said about Frank.'

'Oh? What did I say?'

'You said we should send him back.'

Beth burst out laughing. 'I said that?'

'One day at the table, when Frank was just a baby.'

'I suppose I got thumped.'

'No, your father said it was a phase and that you'd grow out of it.'

'Some soothsayer he turned out to be,' Beth murmured sarcastically.

There was a long silence, but Anna's slovenly manners roused Beth.

'Dearest, don't slurp like that. People will think you're a little piggy, and please don't tell me you'd like to be a little piggy, otherwise you won't get into school on Monday because they only take little children, not piggies.'

Beth ignored her mother's frown and chose a plain biscuit from the selection, while Anna knuckled down and began to drink quietly.

'So, you're not planning to have any more?' her mother persisted.

'What is this?' Beth frowned. 'Have you taken up the cause of multiple families?'

'I'd hardly call two *multiple*,' her mother smiled. 'I'd call it company for Anna.'

'And I'd call it purgatory, or being chained to the…' She was stopped mid-sentence by a shocked gasp from the other side of the table.

'Goodness me! I never thought I'd live to see the day when a daughter of mine would think having children was akin to purgatory. How dreadful!'

'Any other personal questions to get out of the way before I start enjoying myself?'

'Really, Beth, you do have the strangest ideas.'

'How's Dad?'

'Fine.'

'D'you think he'll still want to go to England next month?'

Beth could have bitten off her tongue: he had sworn her to secrecy and now her blurting it out was as good as posting a bulletin in the Post Office window. Her mother appeared puzzled.

'I'd no idea he wanted to go to England. Did he mention it to you?'

'Vaguely,' Beth fibbed, glad of her daughter's chocolate-covered fingers to distract her. 'Here,' she told Anna. 'Hold them out and I'll clean them with this napkin.'

'I'll get a damp cloth,' her mother offered, rising to her feet. 'There you are. Use this.'

'The funny thing is,' Beth said hesitantly, and Grace looked at her closely.

'What?'

'About having another child.'

'Harry wants one?'

Beth emitted a sigh of frustration. 'He's bloody discussed it with you!'

'He has not,' Grace retorted strongly. 'And mind your language in front of Anna.'

'Sorry,' Beth mumbled. 'I might want to adopt one.'

Before Grace could respond, the door opened and James walked in, and he must have wondered why the conversation halted so abruptly.

*

Beth sat in the living room listening to '*Bohemian Rhapsody*', the longest pop record she owned, apart from Bob Dylan's LP track of '*Like a Rolling Stone*'. It was ten past

546

eleven and Harry had been upstairs since ten. She was beyond caring what he thought, whether or not he knew she was still fuming over his departing remark about children.

'So, we'll leave it just now,' he had smiled from the doorway, and Beth had failed to see the significance of what it was they were leaving.

'Leave what just now?' she had frowned at him.

'Having another baby.'

'You're not still harping on about that?'

The word had caused him to scowl at her, but she was not about to back down: she would have no more children, and that was that, and he could like it or lump it.

'I wasn't aware I was 'harping' on about it,' Harry had repeated, in a tone that would have filled her with fear ten years ago. 'I thought we were only discussing it.'

'And I thought I'd made it clear that I'm perfectly happy with one.'

He had smiled then, but, even from a distance, Beth could see it was more like a grimace. She looked at him and waited.

'Well, I'm definitely going to have another one,' he said provocatively, preparing to go upstairs.

She had called him back, explained – haltingly – about the possibility of adopting a child; a boy. His reaction was mild, and Beth had stared at him.

'You don't seem to be angry, and I've just mentioned it out of the blue.'

'Why should I be angry?'

Now, sitting through the fourth rendition of the Queen classic, Beth was mulling over his calm acceptance of her suggestion. She sighed and glanced at the clock.

As she undressed in the bathroom, she thought suddenly of the letter she had posted to Charlie. She shook her head at her reflection, for she knew she might have acted too hastily, had dispensed with a listening ear and a comforting arm; in other words, a good friend. There was a chance that he would ignore the letter, of course, and she had never wished for anything more desperately in her whole life.

Chapter Ten

Harry looked at the calendar on his desk and tried to work out when the baby was due. He had no knowledge of such things, but she had told him when her last period had been and that the doctors had given a date accordingly.

The idea of the child was in danger of superseding all other aspects of his life and he saw the pitfalls only too clearly: they would have to be sharper than sharp to make this work, to pull the proverbial wool over everyone's eyes. He smiled as he ringed the date in January, already choosing a name, casting his mind over his bank balance, calculating how much he might have to fork out.

Fork out was not the most friendly of terms; not for the baby, his son and heir, in fact, if the midwife really did know her stuff and was right about its being a boy.

Harry rearranged the phrase a propos his disposable cash and came up with *spend*; and then he had a moment's panic regarding Beth's nose for finances and how it was never easy keeping one step ahead of her when it came to money. Still, if the worst came to the worst he could endure anything for the joy of having a son.

He picked up the telephone, just to make sure Foxy was all right.

*

Daphne ripped open Grace's letter and read the first sentence without her glasses, so desperate was she to find out where they were to meet. When she saw that she had been invited to the cottage she almost jumped with glee; and then she remembered that the invitation was for her alone and it cast a tiny shadow over her delight.

She donned her glasses and read on:

'James has gone to see his family in England and won't be back until the last week in October, so please feel free to come here any morning – and I mean ANY morning! – and we can meet at last.'

There was a telephone number at the foot of the page and before Thomas came downstairs, Daphne pencilled it into her diary and tore up the letter. She kept most of them, but this one was too revealing. She was determined to get Thomas and his daughter together again, but it was a bit too soon. It had been such a shock to discover that, despite the apparently cordial meeting in the Isle of Skye Hotel years ago, the two of them were not the best of friends.

'She doesn't want to have anything to do with me,' Thomas had confessed months later, as they cruised past Cannes. 'I was so happy at the idea we'd start again, but she made it obvious I've to be no part of her family.'

His chagrin as he had related the whole, sad story, had melted Daphne's heart. Come Hell or High Water, she would be the go-between and ensure a happy ending.

'Did you enjoy your chat with John?' she asked as Thomas appeared in the doorway.

'Very much. Such an interesting chap, been everywhere.'

Thomas made straight for the drinks cabinet but Daphne was unconcerned: he drank only one whisky before dinner or one glass of white wine during, after which he partook of the occasional ruby port, but only if there were Blue Stilton on the menu; otherwise, he was content to emulate her habit of a bedtime mug of cocoa, sitting opposite her in the drawing room, her favourite time of the evening. Lately, to her delight, he had taken to drinking tonic water, a sight to gladden her heart.

'You must invite John round for dinner some night,' she suggested, slightly put out by his reaction.

'John? No, I don't think he's the ideal companion for a lady.'

Daphne was torn between pride that she was still considered a lady and some disappointment that she was not to meet her husband's bosom pal. The two men had been friends since Thomas had moved to Perth years ago, and she had envisaged that the couples might get together.

'I meant he should bring his wife,' she said now, trying to ease the frown from Thomas's brow.

'Oh, his wife's dead,' Thomas shrugged, pouring the whisky and sniffing the glass before he drank. 'He's been a widower since '64.'

'Oh, poor man! All the more reason to invite him here.'

'Daphne, dearest,' Thomas began, pausing to allow the whisky to trickle back his throat. 'John and I are quite good friends, but as for welcoming him to warm his slippers by our fire, I hardly think so.'

'Oh, well, it was just a thought.'

She might have mentioned that he never took her anywhere, not even to the shops. For all people knew, Thomas Blake was a bachelor.

'What's for dinner, my love?'

'Gigot chops and cheesy potatoes,' Daphne answered dutifully.

'Lovely!' Thomas exclaimed and she was filled with happiness.

*

Thomas lay back listening to his wife chattering on about not being able to find a knitting pattern for a tea cosy. The effect of the warm room, coupled with the drinks he had sneaked behind Daphne's back, was sending him to dreamland, a much happier place than real life, he mused. It must have something to do with old age.

As he drifted between the diminishing sound of her voice and the land of nod, Thomas's mind snapped awake, darting to her most recent suggestion that he add his name to the bank account. It had taken him a few years, but she had succumbed at last.

'But I can't see the need for it,' he had shrugged, adopting his role of indifference to her little fortune. We usually buy things together, don't we?'

'Yes, but I want you to spend something on yourself for a change,' she had countered, much to his delight. 'When was the last time you bought a suit, or an overcoat, or, for that matter, anything for yourself?'

'Daphne, I'm perfectly happy to let you buy them for me,'

'Well, I'm not,' she had pouted, and Thomas's future was secured.

Now, as his mind floated out with the reach of the real world, he had just enough time to congratulate himself on a job well done.

*

Harry drew up at the kerb, left the BMW in full view of the villagers and walked round the back. Grace was at the door to greet him.

'I'm starving!' he told her. 'I've had nothing since last night.'

'I've made salmon and cucumber sandwiches, and a few egg ones because they're your favourite. Take your pick.'

They sat in comfortable silence for a few minutes, but Harry was planning the conversation in his head, running over his opening sentences so that they would have the desired effect. When Grace sighed and glanced at the clock, he seized his opportunity.

'Remember the other day, when I thought you were going to ask me a personal question?'

She fidgeted in her chair, gave herself away. 'Yes, I think so.'

549

'You were going to ask if we intended having any more children.'

She nodded, lifting her cup and holding it between her hands, as if she were cold. 'I asked Beth instead. It's more of a womanly topic, isn't it?'

'We do play a part in it,' he said unkindly, enjoying the momentary embarrassment in the green eyes. 'Beth told me you'd asked her.'

'What did she say?'

'That she was happy with one child.'

She dropped her head, stared at the tablecloth. 'Yes, that's what she told me.'

'I want another one,' Harry stated bluntly. 'I'm determined not to leave Anna without a brother or sister.' He knew he was preaching to the converted, and that Grace – an only child – would agree with his reasoning 'You know perfectly well what I'm talking about.'

'Unfortunately, Beth wasn't all that enamoured about Frank.'

'Anna says the best bit about school is seeing all her new friends. She revels in the company.'

Grace nodded again, for she must have been witness to her granddaughter's ecstasy at making three friends on her first day at school.

'She was so thrilled, the little soul. But you understand, Harry, I can't say anything to Beth. She'll blow her top. I'll have to watch my step from now on.' She laughed as she spoke, but he was not oblivious to his wife's moods. She had long-since dispensed with temper tantrums, but could turn frosty and uncooperative in the space of a split-second.

'She mentioned adoption.'

Grace's eyes widened. 'Beth said that?'

Harry nodded. 'I was as surprised as you are. Anyway, we'd best not discuss it, otherwise we'll get lines and have to stand in the corner for a week.'

They both enjoyed the gentle dig at Beth, after which the conversation turned to mundane things. Harry sat back, satisfied and optimistic. He had broached the subject of adoption and that had been his express purpose.

*

Charlie Webster passed his desk and cast an eye over the envelope lying there. He had ignored it for weeks now, having recognised her handwriting, and he was continuing to trust his instincts: she was hopelessly impulsive, not to mention reckless with her own future, and so he had decided not to open the letter until after he had spoken to her. Now, as he paused to gaze at the wild, unruly scrawl that only the local postman could have deciphered, Charlie had an urge to lift the telephone and carry on as if nothing had happened.

As he walked down the hall, he glanced at his reflection in the ornate gilt mirror his mother had gifted him as a house warming and could hardly believe how scruffy he looked. Had it not been Saturday, he might have been shamed into shaving and dressing more in accordance with his life as one of the gentry; but it was Saturday and, apart from his work plan for next week, he would be alone for the day.

After five minutes' contemplation, however, he took the unusual decision of throwing caution to the wind. He picked up the phone and dialled her number, only to find it was engaged.

*

Beth glowered at the telephone, knowing that Harry would run to answer it, since it was always his ex-secretary, Sandra, taking him away on any pretext from a leaky toilet cistern to noisy tappets, whatever they were.

At last, the ringing ceased as he picked up and she carried on with hauling the washing from the machine. Since Anna had started school, Beth had been dismayed at the extra piles of dirty clothes and, had Isobel's weekly visits not taken care of the rest of the housework, Beth would have been tempted to drive to the nearest Laundromat. The flaw in that particular argument lay in the proximity of the 'nearest' Laundromat.

She heard Harry's murmuring in the upstairs hall, probably advising the ex-secretary from Hell how she should change a light bulb; but then his footsteps sounded in the hall and she looked up.

'Don't tell me,' she said with false cheerfulness. 'It was the little old lady.'

'She can't help it if she's thick,' Harry said curtly. 'We're not all blessed with a sparkling intellect and a fund of knowledge as deep as the Pacific.'

Beth postponed folding the washing into the linen basket and stared at him, hardly able to conceal her annoyance.

'What brought that on?'

'If you must know, her niece has cancer.'

'Oh, well I'm sorry then,' Beth said grudgingly, turning back to the washing.

'And she's pregnant.'

'What?'

Harry walked over to the window and leaned against the sink, his eyes troubled, his mood dejected, and Beth felt mean for having selfishly mis judged the situation. She shrugged and moved closer to him.

'I'm really sorry, Harry. Thinking about myself, as usual. Forgive me?'

'Don't be daft,' he said affectionately as she wound her arms around him. 'I can understand how you feel. She calls all the time, interrupting everything.'

'The poor woman,' Beth sighed, snuggling against his shirt, vowing to make amends. 'If there's anything I can do, just tell me.'

'What on earth could you do?' Harry asked with a short laugh. 'You're not even involved, Beth, though it's nice of you to offer.'

She stepped away from him, determined to make up for her flash of selfishness, and fixed him with a stubborn gaze.

'There must be something I can do. Tell me all about it and we'll see.'

Harry sighed and shook his head, but when she imagined he would dismiss her suggestion, suddenly he was nodding slowly, as if she had persuaded him.

'Come on,' Beth urged, seeing his change of heart. 'Let's at least sit down and talk about it. I want to hear everything.'

'As long as you promise not to pick up another lame duck.' Harry frowned. 'I don't want you getting bogged down in someone else's problems.'

'But you're involved, aren't you?'

'I did work with the woman for a few years, yes,'

'And you said she was a lovely person, didn't you?'

'I suppose so,' he agreed, albeit reluctantly.

'Well then,' Beth smiled, taking his arm and dragging him to the living room. 'We can sit down and discuss it, and as for the lame duck thing, I'd hardly call a pregnant girl with cancer a lame duck, would you?'

Harry shook his head and allowed her to lead the way.

*

The telephone rang and he turned to look at it. Beth, however, frowned and bade

551

him continue. It was all going so well that Harry wondered why he had lost sleep over this for weeks.

'So,' she prompted now. 'She may get better, she may not?'

'It's fifty-fifty. No one can say for sure.'

'But when she has the baby, what then? I mean, will she be strong enough to take care of it herself?'

'No, but Sandra's going to look after it. She's the girl's only relative.'

He marvelled at the ease with which so many lies could slip off his tongue within the space of twenty minutes; and not for the first time was Harry grateful for having inherited his mother's character.

'But Sandra's elderly, isn't she?'

'What difference does that make?' Harry laughed. 'Grace's the same age and I'd hardly call her decrepit.'

'Maybe not. Anyway, how will Sandra manage if she has to work as well?'

'Oh, there are places you can put babies during the day,' Harry said casually, knowing the effect such a sentiment would have on Beth. He was not disappointed: her expression was one of utter horror.

'What? You can't do that to a baby!' she exploded, rising to her feet and pacing the room. 'It's monstrous! Have you any idea of how the little thing will be affected? First it has no Dad, or not one that's interested in its welfare anyway, and then it gets stuck in a day nursery from dawn 'til dusk, with total strangers.' She turned and gave him one of her most formidable frowns. 'You must both have lost your minds.'

'What the hell can I do?' he asked, feigning irritation, delighted at the way this was heading. 'I can hardly take it to bloody Craigton, can I?' He stood up and made for the door, expecting her to call him back.

'Wait! Please wait,' she cajoled, and he turned in the doorway.

'Beth, you asked me to tell you. I've told you. Now it's up to them. This has nothing to do with you or me, and I'll hear no more about it.'

He walked away, took the stairs two at a time, marched into the bedroom and threw himself on the bed, absolutely exhausted; but over the moon. Everything was going perfectly to plan.

*

Grace parked carefully, checking in her mirror for Anna, who tended to rush willy-nilly into the driveway whenever she heard a car. As she closed the door, she heard her granddaughter's shriek of welcome.

'How's the Primary One pupil?' Grace asked, to Anna's delight.

'I can read some words now, and I get to paint things every day, and we have bottles of milk and a straw, and I have a friend called David.'

Grace stopped and glanced down. 'David? That's a boy.'

'Yes, he's very nice,' Anna said happily, hauling Grace into the house. 'He sits beside me and we're very quiet.'

'Come on and tell me all about it.'

'Do you have chocolate biscuits for me?'

'I see school doesn't change everything.'

Beth was practising the hymns for Sunday's worship and the house was filled with doleful melodies. There was usually one dreary hymn on a Sunday and this week it must be 'O Love that wilt not let me go.' Even hearing it in such happy surroundings brought a lump to Grace's throat. 'and from the ground there blossoms red life that shall endless be...'

Grace took the little girl's hand and walked into the music room. Beth had moved the piano into what had been the smaller ground-floor bedroom and now it was devoted to all things musical. Grace paused in the doorway, but her daughter was engrossed with the intricacies of the melody and did not look round.

Eventually, the hymn came to an end and Beth shook her head.

'Hi, come in. Have you ever heard such a dirge?'

'It has its place,' Grace felt obliged to say in its defence. 'Some of the older members of the congregation enjoy it.'

'That's because they're at death's door,' Beth said unkindly. 'I've got coffee ready in the kitchen and it's warmer in there.'

Anna tugged at Grace's hand. 'Mummy says to put on another jumper if you're cold,' she whispered.

'I'm not cold,' Grace whispered back. 'Besides, the Aga's nice and cosy.'

As she watched her daughter deal expertly with the new coffee machine, Grace recalled her own pathetic attempts at being the perfect hostess, at trying to emulate Charlotte Blake; and now she was wondering how she could have produced a daughter who looked a complete natural with guests, be it two or twenty two; just as adept at seeing to the needs of the multitude as Charlotte Blake.

'So, how are things?' she asked as Beth set a cup of frothy coffee in front of her.

'You'll never guess how interesting life has become lately,' Beth said mysteriously, her eyes indicating Anna. 'Once Anna's had her juice and biscuits, we'll chat.'

Anna glanced from one to the other, aware of the sudden lapse in conversation. She sipped the juice through her straw, more slowly than usual, and Grace had to suppress a smile, recalling her frequent cautionary advice as to little pitchers having big ears.

'Drink up,' Beth told her daughter patiently. 'And take another biscuit up to your room.'

'But I'm not allowed to eat in…'

'It's all right, just for today, but don't tell Daddy, or he'll want to eat his fish and chips up there.'

Anna giggled and eased herself from the chair, choosing a Macaroon Bar and darting out of the room. Beth rose and gently closed the door, which gave Grace slight cause for concern.

'Where's Harry, by the way?'

'Oh, he had to pop into Perth,' Beth replied, avoiding her mother's eye. 'He'll not be long. Now,' she sat down again and leaned across the table. 'You can't breathe a word of this to anyone.'

'Of course I won't, but you're scaring me, Beth.'

'No, don't be scared, it's not bad exactly, well not for us anyway. If you hear Anna coming downstairs, stop me. She mustn't know.'

Grace was not certain if she wanted to hear what was coming next.

*

Beth sat back, her forehead damp, scrutinising her mother's face. If there were the slightest sign of disapproval, she might have to rethink.

'Goodness me, Beth, it's a huge step.'

'I know, but isn't it lucky that I decided not to have any more of my own? It means I can help the poor girl out, at least some of the time, without having the full responsibility. I mean, I can hand it back and never have to think about it until the next time I see it.'

'It's such a generous thing to do,' her mother said slowly. 'And, quite frankly, Beth,

I'm so proud of you for offering.'

'Are you really?'

'Yes, of course. Not many young people would be so unselfish and compassionate. The only thing is, what about your business?'

'I work mostly from home anyway, certainly not out and about. No, I can go in one or two days a week, more than I do now, and Marjory will be happy to see the baby.'

'But have you talked it over with her?'

'No, but I know she will be.'

'Well, if you're sure. And is Harry fine with this?'

'Not at first,' Beth smiled ruefully. 'But I got to work on him,' she winked and her mother blushed. 'After a couple of hours, he was putty in my hands.' She laughed mischievously, took pity on her mother and sobered up. 'So, now he's fine with it, even says he'll help.'

'I hope I get to help,' her mother ventured to say. 'It's no bother for me, now that Anna's at school. Oh, goodness!'

'What?'

'How will she take it, a baby suddenly appearing?'

'She'll hardly notice probably,' Beth smiled, adding humorously, 'besides, if she's not keen, we can always send it back.' Suddenly, she frowned. 'Did I really say that about Frank?'

'Sadly, yes. Have you told Anna yet?'

'Golly, no, it's early days yet. It's not due until the middle of January.'

'That's good then,' her mother pronounced. 'It will give everyone a chance to get used to it.'

'I never thought I could be so happy about another baby.'

'Yet you were quite adamant about not wanting one, and now you'll have one.'

'It's not quite the same,' Beth pointed out. 'It was the responsibility that was scaring me.' She shrugged. 'Having kids is a daunting thing. Most people have them without thinking about it.'

Beth was surprised when her mother reached across the table and squeezed her hand. Furthermore, she thought she detected a tremor in her voice as she spoke.

'I'm really so proud of you, Beth, and I know your father will be too.'

Beth's hand flew to her mouth. 'Hell! I mean, flip... I forgot all about Dad.'

'Charming,' her mother smiled wryly. 'Out of sight and all that.'

'Will he be O.K. about this?'

'Yes, he'll be as proud as I am that our daughter is so compassionate.'

'I'm lucky in having Harry. Not many men would allow their wife to take this on, far less pitch in and help.'

Her mother smiled but remained silent.

*

Harry drew her closer; murmured into the auburn curls and breathed in the perfume she wore to please him. She was motionless, silent, recovering from the sudden onslaught of the sickness that recurred daily, even at six months. He was not as sympathetic as he should have been; was irritated occasionally, as he had never experienced the same with Beth, whose life had barely altered until the second Anna had popped out. Now he was feeling guilty at his imminent departure.

'How is it now?'

'So-so.'

'Is there something I can get you?'

'Before you go, you mean?'

'Foxy, please. You know I can't stay.'

She stirred and moved away, her hair drifting from his shoulder, tumbling down his arm. He found himself wondering if the baby would have auburn hair. With a shock, he realised he wanted it to be like her, otherwise Grace might suspect; not Beth, his instincts told him, but Grace.

'But you'll come round again soon?'

'You won't be able to get rid of me.'

She flashed him a smile – the old Foxy – and shook her head.

'I'd rather have snippets of you than nothing at all.'

'Are you sure I can't do anything for you just now?'

'No, not that sex is out,' she frowned. 'Although I told you it's safe enough.'

'I'd rather not.'

She glared at him then and stood up. 'That's the kind of thing you might say if someone offers you a piece of bloody chocolate.'

'If you're going to be awkward, Foxy, I'll leave right now.'

'You're going to anyway,' she said dismissively, and he wondered if it had been wise to blurt at such an early stage his paternal intentions for the baby. 'So you may as well go now.'

Harry sat for a moment, his temper rising. If there was one thing he had learnt from Rachel Gillespie it was never to play the part of doormat, even if it did mean losing something; although tough talking had never lost him anything yet.

'Who the hell do you think you're dealing with?' he asked her coldly, and she blinked at him. 'I can walk out of here this minute and never bother about either of you again. What makes you think anyone would care a jot whether I'd fathered a bastard or not? I'm one myself, remember?'

She bit her lip and sat down again, her hand creeping towards his.

'I'm sorry, I'm not being reasonable.'

Harry spoke tersely. 'Let's hope you're in a better mood next time.' He rose from the dingy settee and made a cruel point of brushing the debris from his trousers. Foxy averted her eyes, but not before he had seen her pained expression.

'I'm trying to find another flat,' she said feebly. 'But, in my condition, it's not easy to tramp around.'

'I'll help you find one nearer the time.'

'Will you?' she asked with a gratitude that embarrassed him.

He could have enlightened her about not wanting his son living in such squalor, but it was late and Beth was patient only to a degree.

'Yes, I will, now I really must go.'

She stood forlornly at the door, and the familiar smell of urine drifted up from the stairwell. Harry could hardly breathe for the stench, and yet she seemed unaffected.

'I'll call you,' he told her over his shoulder, already at the bottom of the first flight of steps, but she had gone in and closed the door.

*

Charlie's heart skipped a beat when the phone was picked up. He held his breath, hoped it was Beth.

'Hello?'

'Beth, it's me,' he said as casually as his nerves would permit.

'Oh.'

Ignoring her deflated tone, he ploughed on: 'I've two tickets.'

She laughed then, and he awarded himself at least one more sentence before she hung up.

'Good for you,' she said.

'It's the SNO, at the Caird Hall.'

'Why are you asking me?'

'Who else would I ask?'

'Didn't you get my letter?'

'Yes, of course I got it,' he said truthfully, although if she asked him if he had opened it, that was another matter entirely.

'And you're still asking me to go to a concert?'

'Any objections?'

There was a short silence, but he heard the sigh and knew she would go.

'What's on?'

'Mozart, Beethoven and some other bits and pieces.'

'Bob Dylan?'

'Could be.'

'I'll think about it.'

'There's plenty time. It's not until December.'

'December?'

'Better soon than never.'

'Were you in church yesterday?'

'What, ours?'

'Yes.'

'No, I had a long lie.'

As she responded, he heard the smile in her tone as she thought about bringing the conversation to an end:.

'Anyway, you can phone me nearer the time.'

'I might pop round before then,' he said bravely, crossing his fingers, counting to five.

'What for?'

'I didn't think we'd stop being pals.'

From experience, Charlie had discovered that the words *pal* and *friend* were manna from Heaven to an Aquarian, which she was, as she had reminded him often enough.

'Well, I suppose it would be O.K. to be occasional friends.'

'I might bring Sarah round to meet you,' he lied through his teeth, slapping his trump card on the table. There was a long silence that felt like a month.

'Sarah?'

'Yes, the latest female my mother has chosen as her future daughter-in-law.'

'Better if it's just you. I'm not good with strangers,' she told him, and he could have jumped with joy.

*

Harry sat in the study, re-reading the documents relating to Daphne Blake. Months ago, she had intimated her intention to move back to Perth, swearing him to secrecy, although he was certain she still had no knowledge of his being an interested party. He doubted that Thomas Blake would have highlighted his own predicament by mentioning Harry's connection to the family.

As the muffled strains of Gilbert O'Sullivan floated through to him, he pencilled in a few instructions for Daphne's benefit and closed the folder, making a mental note to call her the next day. He stood up and stretched, easing out his aching muscles, and then he locked the folder in the top drawer and went to find his daughter.

'Daddy!'

'I was just coming to find you,' he told her, picking her up, pretending she was too heavy. 'Wow! You're not a little girl any more, are you?'

'No, I'm a big girl now, and I can skip with a rope and my best friend is Eddie.'

Harry put her down and looked at her. 'Eddie?'

'Yes, he sits beside me and he's funny.'

'What's the name of your other best friends?' he asked diplomatically, having learnt a few tips from Beth.

'One's called Jennifer and she has a pigtail, and Dorothy has nice shoes.'

'We must have a party and you can invite them all for tea.'

'And I suppose Daddy will do all the cooking?' Beth interrupted with a laugh.

'Yes,' Anna said happily. 'Daddy will do the cooking.'

'In that case,' Beth smiled round the kitchen door. 'You can have that party any day you like, sweetie. Now go and find Teddy, tell him it's teatime and that we have chips tonight.'

Anna rushed upstairs and Harry raised his eyebrows at Beth.

'Eddie?'

'I know, but, let's face it, Harry, she's only four. I didn't kiss a boy until I met you.'

'Pull the other one.'

'Seriously,' she assured him, too busy with the chip pan to respond to his hug. 'Careful, I'm useless at making chips. Stand back in case of accidents.'

'Here, let me do that. You're better at everything else.'

'Flattery gets you extra chips, which means I don't have to eat them.'

He spooned the chips onto kitchen towels and set the pan back on the two-ringed cooker she used for frying. His conscience was clearer since meeting with Foxy and suffering the less attractive side of her character. Besides, the bit about the cancer had been true years ago; who was to say it had not come back?

'You're really witty, d'you know that?' he smiled at Beth. 'But, to get back to the kissing thing. You honestly don't expect me to believe I was the first one you kissed?'

Beth shrugged. 'Whether you believe it or not, it won't change a thing. I'd been given mouth-to-mouth resuscitation by a guy at school, but it put me off for years. Ugh! When I think of his rubbery lips, I could throw up.'

'Come here. We have a few minutes before Anna finds she left Teddy in the airing cupboard.' He drew her close and she put her arms around his waist. 'I still can't get it into my head that you're such a softie.'

'I'm not.'

'Yes, you are, and I love you for it. Prepare to be kissed, Mrs Softie.'

At the end of the sentence, Harry had to endure a tiny flicker of guilt, but by the time they drew apart, the feeling was long gone.

'And you're not upset that I'm not keen to meet her?'

'No, not at all,' he replied, convinced that he had a guardian angel. 'In fact, it's better. She's so unwell, Sandra tells me, doesn't want to see anyone.'

'But I can still meet Sandra?'

'It goes without saying. She can hardly wait; wants to see a living, breathing saint.'

'You horror!' Beth laughed. 'You're for it, Gillespie.'

'Yes, please.'

'Chips and steak first, then dessert.' Beth smiled wickedly, running her hands over her breasts. 'What is it?' she frowned, sensing his disapproval.

'Nothing,' he lied. 'I'm just tired, that's all.'

'Right, let's get this meal out, see if the chips are like sticks of cement, as usual.'

As he went upstairs to fetch Anna, he was still trying to banish the memory of the first day he had slept with Foxy, when she had offered him her breasts as dessert. He pulled himself together, vowed to be on his guard against losing control; even for a second. Beth was too shrewd for that.

*

Grace glanced at the clock and almost gasped: the train was due in an hour and she was still not dressed. The green suit lay on the bed, together with matching gloves and shoes; bought in Perth for the occasion, with no regard to cost. She had to admit that there were advantages in children's leaving home and making a life for themselves; and the principal one was extra cash for herself.

She picked up the postcard she had received from James– only yesterday – and scanned the lines again, unimpressed with the impersonal message and dispassionate tone.

'all well, even the weather.

Hope to see you at the station.'

Grace threw it down in disgust. He had been away for weeks and the only thing he could think of pertained to the weather; no mention of his mother or cousins; no inkling if the holiday had been good or bad; no indication that he had missed his own family.

She took a deep breath and gently removed the green suit from the bed. The material was soft and pliable. She smiled at the idea: something like herself.

As she surveyed her reflection, Grace's spirits were high, notwithstanding James's intransigent, sometimes cold nature. She had so many happy times to look forward to; not the least of these being the arrival of Harry's son.

Chapter Eleven

Lily Morris was feeling better, and she attributed her new sense of well-being to the springtime air. It was always such a relief to reach April, especially for her, for she never imagined lasting another winter. As she breathed in her first fresh air since November, she was surprised to find that she was optimistic about the future; highly unusual for her.

She looked down the garden, saw the faint sign of frost still tucked in behind the wall and knew it would not melt that day, for the sun never reached there. The blackbird she fed at the back door hopped towards her, a worm in its beak, the poor thing still squirming. She glanced away, for as much as she was used to the cruelty of the countryside, she did not have to enjoy it.

'Good morning!' sang out a voice, and she turned to see Grace and Beth at the gate. Motioning them in, Lily stared when she saw the pram. The girl had had another bairn and nobody had thought to let her know!

'Are you busy?' Grace asked as she walked up the path.

'Oh, aye, I'm right in the middle of a call to Switzerland, checking up on my latest investments.'

'Isn't that what you usually do on a Friday morning?'

Lily smiled, but her eyes were on the pram. 'That's never yours,' she told Beth bluntly.

'No, of course not,' the girl laughed. 'I'm babysitting for a friend.'

'I can't think of anybody that's had a bairn lately,' Lily mused, priding herself on being in the know.

'You wouldn't know her,' Beth said, rocking the pram as they stood. 'She's a friend of a friend of Harrys'.'

Lily resisted the temptation to glance at Grace, but it took a mighty effort.

'Let's see the wee sowel then,' she smiled, peering into the pram. 'Och, it's a bonny wee thing, lovely copper hair too. I suppose it's a boy, since it's wearing blue?'

'Not guilty,' Beth smiled. 'I don't choose the clothes at the moment. Now, is there room in your kitchen for this pram, for I'm freezing to death out here?'

*

Grace had picked up her old friend's sidelong glances when she had first set eyes on the baby, but the auburn hair had allayed Lily's suspicions and she was trying to make up for it now.

'You're an obliging lassie,' she was telling Beth. 'Just like your mother, and hers before. So, is the mother working?'

'It's a sad story,' Grace said, having no intentions of relating it. 'But suffice it to say that she's not well at the moment and her aunt is helping out.'

'And she's a friend of Harry's?'

'Yes,' Beth said between sips of coffee. 'And he didn't want me to have anything to do with it. I had to twist his arm.'

Again, Grace noticed Lily's quick glance in her direction and had to suppress her own suspicions, suspicions she had harboured since Beth had broken the news to her.

'Is Anna happy with her new brother?' Lily asked now.

'Yes,' Beth smiled. 'I told her weeks before, and her only concern was that he would want to play with her dolls.'

'The very idea!' Lily exclaimed.

'Things are changing,' Beth said feebly. 'Girls can play with toy cars now, you know.'

Lily shuddered. 'Honestly, what next?'

'Are you going to the final meeting of the WRI?' Grace asked, to detract from the onset of a lecture on gender roles.

'Do I ever?' Lily frowned. 'Having to struggle to stay awake during all that boring spouting of everybody's minutes. Och, it sends a body to sleep, so it does.' She looked directly at Grace. 'Are you babysitting every day then?'

'No, only Mondays and Fridays.'

'That'll not leave much time for visits to old friends.'

'Of course it will,' Grace contradicted impatiently. 'Kathryn's aunt will take over any time I want. Besides, I'll bring him with me.'

'Oh, well, that's hunky dory. It's bad enough being tied to the house with your own, far less…'

'I saw the doctor's car at your gate last week,' Grace butted in, provoking a puzzled look from her daughter. 'Are you keeping all right?'

'Nothing that a wee dram won't help.'

'You've never started drinking?'

'Just a snifter before bedtime, enough to make me sleep .'

The baby stirred in the pram and Beth pulled back the quilt, preparing to lift him out, something Grace recalled she had never done with Anna. It had been a constant irritation to James that the child had been left to lie unattended, crying her little heart out.

'Come on, now,' Beth told the restless baby. 'You're not hungry and you're not needing changed, so maybe you just want to see Lily's kitchen.'

'Here,' Lily offered, extending her arms. 'Let me hold him for a wee while. It's years since I had a bairn on my knee. What's your name, wee fellow?'

'Michael,' Beth replied, handing him over readily, appearing surprised at the old woman's expertise with babies.

'You're sure you've never had any?' she laughed.

'Oh, I was hopeless. Far too soft,' Lily smiled, her frail fingers intertwined with the baby's. 'I was always giving in to you, my lady, trying to sneak you a chocolate biscuit when goggle-eyes there wasn't looking.'

'Was I a pest?' Beth asked her mother.

'Only on days ending in 'd.a.y',' Grace laughed and, though the atmosphere was relaxed, she felt that a shadow had passed over the day.

*

Back at the cottage, Beth packed the carrycot into the back seat of the car and checked the sleeping baby. If she did not leave soon she might be late for picking Anna up from school, but she had to broach the subject with her mother. As the morning had progressed, it seemed that her mother's mood had dampened with each passing minute, and Beth wondered if it were such a good idea to mention Thomas Blake.

When she caught sight of her mother's weary expression, Beth decided to postpone the subject.

*

Daphne sat opposite and glanced around the office while Harry leafed through the file. He figured she was too polite to pass comment on his less salutary circumstances, might even think he had fallen on hard times. Now that his life was running so smoothly, however, he could not have cared less what anyone thought.

'So, you're settled in properly?'

'Yes, it's a beautiful old house,' Daphne smiled, her dimpled cheek turned in his direction. 'We're as happy as happy can be.'

He wondered if the lady were protesting too much, but responded only with a nod.

'I've had a look at your file, and at the estimated value of your estate. There's been a bit of a dip in the market of late.' He glanced at her, waiting for her to agree, but the information appeared to drift over her head.

'Has there?'

'Unfortunately, yes, but it's not enough to bankrupt you, Mrs Blake.' Although he smiled as he spoke, he was beset by an unreasonable bout of resentment at having to address her as 'Blake', the name, in his mind, being reserved for Grace and her mother. 'Are there any changes you wish to make at this time?'

'Changes?' she repeated, flustered.

'To your Last Will and Testament perhaps?'

Harry was aware of her correspondence with Grace and had hoped Daphne might now include her stepdaughter in her bequests. For several months now, he had been working towards such an alteration.

'Do you mean my stepdaughter perhaps?' she asked hesitantly, but her flush of pleasure did not escape him.

'It did occur to me.'

She appeared to deliberate, and Harry had the desire to hurry things on. With Grace in mind, however, he waited patiently for Daphne's decision, in the sure knowledge that she would ask his opinion.

'I'm not sure. What do you think?'

Harry shrugged, tried not to appear too interested. 'Let me think.'

She regarded him anxiously, and he suspected that she was the type of woman who would agree with the last person she consulted. Still, he would tread carefully.

'Have you been in regular contact with your stepdaughter?'

'Oh, yes,' she confirmed happily, her whole face lighting up. 'She's such a lovely person, and so friendly. We've arranged to meet.'

'Really?' Harry smiled, feigning surprise. 'It certainly sounds as if you've taken her under your wing.'

'I've always wanted a daughter.' She paused and frowned. 'I didn't have any children. My husband wasn't...' She stopped and looked away from him. 'I mean, he preferred not to have any.'

'Wise man,' Harry laughed. 'I've got two and it's crazy in our house, I can tell you.'

It was out before he had had time to think ahead: they had never discussed each other's private lives, thereby allowing Harry to remain neutral, at least on paper; as soon as she discovered he had a vested interest in her family, Thomas Blake might influence her into finding another solicitor. Harry had been meticulous, had never even remarked upon the surname 'Blake', for it was common enough in the area.

'Are they boys or girls?' Daphne was asking now, out of politeness only, but he would nip it in the bud.

'One of each. Now I don't mean to rush you, Mrs Blake, but if you'd care to make any changes to your list of bequests, perhaps you could give me a call?'

'You didn't tell me your own opinion,' she said apprehensively. 'Do you think I should?'

'It's entirely up to you, of course, but if, as you say, you and she have formed some sort of attachment...' Seeing her agreeable reaction, Harry left it there, sitting back with an air of kindly disinterest, although he was sorely tempted to come right out and say it.

'I think I will then,' Daphne decided, her cheeks pink, eyes bright. 'She writes the loveliest letters to me, and she seems such good fun too. I'm so looking forward to meeting her. I'm sure we'll be the best of friends.'

He knew she expected him to make polite inquiries as to their proposed rendezvous, but he had resumed his policy of evasion and would not blurt out even the most innocuous snippet now. He smiled, began gathering up his papers to signal closure.

'I think you should give yourself some time to reflect on the size of the bequest,' he advised her now, against his own, selfish instincts. 'I'll give you a copy of your present beneficiaries, and you can make a judgement based on that.' He stood up, effectively dismissing her, and she took the hint.

When her heels had clattered from the building, Harry sat watching her make her way down the uneven path. He wanted to feel sorry for her, as he had done years ago, before she had married the man; but now he felt she was a co-conspirator, flying with the crows, asking to be shot at, and his only aim now was to secure some of her considerable estate for Grace; as a small, but long overdue recompense for her father's conduct.

The clock struck two and he prepared to leave the office. He checked in his briefcase for the small gift he had bought for Grace and then he locked his desk and grabbed his car keys.

*

Daphne fidgeted in the taxi, checking and re-checking her appearance in the tiny compact mirror she always tucked in her handbag. She thought her face too powdery, her lipstick too brash, and the hairdo that never let her down was letting her down today. She looked more like the village idiot than an affluent woman about town.

When the car slowed down and she caught sight of the speed limit signs, her heart pounded out of control. What had possessed her to agree to meeting at Grace's house when it would have been much less stressful to meet in Perth, at some neutral hotel?

'Here we are, dear lady,' the driver said cheerfully, opening the door for her, ready with his supporting arm. 'Straight to the door.'

She smiled and would never have dreamt of passing an impolite remark, although Thomas would not have missed the opportunity to remind the fellow that *straight to the door* was the whole point of a taxi.

'Thank you. How much do I owe you?'

'Two pounds exactly,' he beamed. 'Can't say fairer than that, eh?'

Having no idea whether he was being generous or robbing her blind, Daphne handed him two Scottish pound notes and a fifty pence tip, grateful that Thomas was not there to snatch it back.

Before the taxi had drawn away, the door of the cottage opened and Grace came out, her welcoming smile instantly dissipating Daphne's fears.

*

Grace was astonished at the woman's appearance: compared to Charlotte Shepherd, this person was the epitome of sophistication; not at all what Grace had expected from the substance of the letters. She had formed an image of a homely, plump woman with a ruddy complexion and unremarkable clothes. As she went forward to greet Daphne, Grace had a fleeting sense of never having been able to sum people up.

'Daphne, how lovely to see you.'

'Grace, I've been so nervous about this, You'll think me an idiot.'

'I was a bit nervous too, to be honest,' Grace lied. 'I suppose it's normal under the circumstances. Come in, everything's ready.'

She led her guest into the parlour, where the coffee tray was prepared, and then drew up the most comfortable chair.

'Please, sit here, and I'll just pop through for the hot water.' She paused at the door. 'Is coffee all right, or would you like tea?'

'Coffee's fine, but perhaps I could help you?'

'Just you sit here,' Grace said, vainly trying to dismiss the memory of Charlotte Blake sitting in that very chair. 'I'll only be a moment.'

In the kitchen, she took a couple of deep breaths, wondered if she could ever go ahead with her plan, considering the woman was turning out to be a sweet old thing. How much less complicated the plan had seemed when Mrs Blake had been more of a shrew.

Grace waited for the kettle to boil, took her time in pouring the water into a thermos jug. She had plenty time to make up her mind, of course, but how true the saying was about the best laid plans.

When she entered the parlour, Daphne was standing at the window, perhaps admiring the roses that clambered willy-nilly and dangled over the panes, as if snooping on the people inside.

'How do you manage to have them flowering in April?' she asked Grace.

'Oh, my husband's responsible for all things green. I have no idea whatsoever about flowers and shrubs.' She set the thermos jug down at the hearth and beckoned her guest to sit down. 'In fact, there's a yellow shrub in the back garden and I've never been able to remember its name, not from as far back as the 'thirties.'

'I'm the same,' Daphne smiled and Grace saw that the woman was quite delighted to find they already had something in common. Her heart sank, for, as soon as she began to feel sorry for this person, her determination to thwart her father's wishes would begin to falter.

*

Harry pulled the garage door closed and walked to the house, his mind on Foxy and her willingness to placate him at all costs. He was not ungrateful for her acceding to his demands regarding the boy's upbringing, but he lamented the loss of her wild streak, the recklessness that had been irresistible, even the ambiguity of her sexual preference. Now that she had devoted herself solely to him, he found their relationship less satisfying and frequently made excuses for not taking her to bed.

'But this new flat is lovely,' she had complained the first time he had pleaded tiredness. 'And I've worked wonders with the bedroom. It's like something out of a magazine.'

'I know, and you've done really well,' he told her, the kind of thing you might say to a well-behaved child. 'But I'm just tired, that's all. Next time it'll be different.'

She was still waiting for the next time. As he hung up his coat in the utility room, he pondered the possibility of ending it completely, although he could hardly expect her to give the boy up legally without a fight; and a fight – a public one at that – was the last thing he wanted.

Beth was sitting with Anna when he went into the kitchen and, just for a split second, Harry was irritated that Michael was nowhere in sight.

'Hi,' Beth said, glancing up. 'We're almost finished. Be with you in a jiffy.'

Anna was so engrossed in practising her reading skills that she awarded him the briefest of smiles before lowering her eyes to the book.

'Will I see to Michael?'

'Michael's fed, washed, changed and fast asleep,' Beth frowned, as if she suspected what was in his mind. 'He won't thank you for a rude awakening.'

'Fine, I'll just look in on him, make sure he's still asleep.'

When she turned her attention to Anna without responding, Harry went upstairs to his son's room.

The child was lying on his side, fingers curled beneath his chin, his small mouth puckered, eyelashes soft on his cheeks. Harry held his breath. He could hardly believe that the boy was his. In fact, had he not pried into Foxy's love life – or lack of it – he might have had doubts. The relaxed, casual questions he had posed to Sandra, however, had allayed any fears he had that the mother of his son had been sleeping around. As he had hoped, the boy's dark brown hair had been the first thing Beth had mentioned, yet Harry had suffered an anxious few days, waiting for her to make any connection – however unreasonable – between him and the child. Once she had met Sandra, of course, the compass was set, winds fair, seas calm.

'I really like her,' Beth had declared as they had driven away from Sandra's house. 'She tells the truth and you know how I feel about that.'

'Kathryn's lucky to have her as an aunt,' Harry had added, having to endure the merest flicker of guilt at the word 'truth'. 'She's a lot like Grace.'

'Yes, I thought so too,' Beth agreed, but he knew she had fallen in love with the baby and would not argue with anything he suggested. 'I think we should invite her over, just to put her mind at rest about where Michael will be. Perhaps to stay for a few days.'

'I don't think so,' he had argued, baulking at the idea of Sandra's being a live-in conspirator. 'Besides, she has Kathryn to look after and we'd never be sure we were asking at the right time. Sandra's so polite she'd say 'yes' when it was quite the wrong moment.'

Beth had turned in her seat to give him a look of the utmost admiration.

'You think of everything,' she had told him happily, and this time the flicker of guilt took longer to fade.

Now, as he stood by the cot looking down at the sleeping boy, Harry wondered if it were too much to hope for; that his life could continue so smoothly.

He tiptoed downstairs, his mood buoyant, his optimism on full power. In fact, he could not recall a happier time in his entire life.

*

'Isn't this the most fabulous place?'

Grace nodded. 'They've done well, haven't they, the two of them?'

Alice sipped her wine, her eyes following Beth across the terrace as she chatted and mingled with the guests.

'She's the most remarkable girl, you know, your daughter.'

'Yes, I do know. Sometimes I wonder what I did to deserve her. And Frank too, of course,' Grace added hastily.

'He's looking tanned and very sexy.'

Grace tutted. 'Alice, please, that's my little boy you're talking about.'

'Speaking of little boys,' Alice began, and Grace prepared to fend off disagreeable comments about Michael, for, despite their recent truce, Grace was aware that her friend might still harbour suspicions. 'Are he and Emily having any more?'

'I should hope so,' Grace replied with relief. You know my feelings on an only child.'

'Don't I just?' Alice teased, wagging a long red fingernail at her friend. 'If you've told me once, you've told me a million times. Oh, by the way, how was your meeting with the lovely Mrs Blake?'

'She's not what I expected,' Grace said guardedly.

'What, you mean she's not fat and dumpy with a complexion like a rhino skin?'

'Anything but. To be honest, she's a bit too sophisticated for him.'

'Did she mention him?'

'Not even obliquely.' Grace grimaced, then laughed. 'I must have scared her to death.'

'How old is he now?'

Grace thought for a few moments, counted the years in her head.

'He was three years older than my mother, so he must be...' She gasped. 'Heavens above, he's almost eighty.'

'He's probably hanging on in case you suddenly welcome him with open arms,' Alice suggested, but her tone was wary. 'Will you ever do that, do you think?'

Grace shook her head. 'Never,' but her heart was heavy.

'You're not sure, are you?'

'Beth was on about it the other day.'

'I thought you'd shown her the damning letter?'

Grace sighed. 'You don't know Beth. Once she has an idea in her head, it takes a volcanic eruption to change it.'

'Yet, you've struck up a friendship with the wife?'

'I have my reasons.'

'Nothing nice, I hope?' Alice asked mischievously, and Grace had to laugh.

As the talk turned to babies and children growing up too quickly, Grace was unhappy with her state of mind. Whether it was the effect of Michael's arrival into the family, or Daphne Blake's endearing personality, she could not be sure. The result, however, was an increasing despondency over her plans to ruin her father's life.

*

Thomas Blake poured himself a drink, against the advice of his doctor, and strolled over to the window, where he sat down in the quaint old rocking chair Daphne had bought him for his birthday, swaying gently back and forth, so as not to spill the whisky.

'You've not to drink while you're taking these tablets,' the young doctor had warned, and Thomas had looked on him with disdain, for what did he know about the constitution of a man like Thomas? 'Considering your age,' the lout had said, adding insult to injury.

'I'll be very careful,' Thomas had crooned. 'I intend to live for at least another decade.'

'Not if you wash these tablets down with alcohol you won't,' the slip of a boy had reiterated stubbornly. 'Make an appointment for a month's time and heed my words.'

Heed my words indeed!

What an old-fashioned phrase for a boy to have known, far less used. Thomas had left the surgery with a jaunty step, lest the young whipper-snapper had been observing his departure.

Considering your age... The cheek of it!

He savoured the first sip of the golden malt as it trickled down his throat, banishing all ills and disappointments in its quest for his stomach. He glanced at his watch and guessed that Daphne would be another hour at least. Her hairdresser's salon was the one place that could keep his wife occupied for an entire afternoon.

His wife.

Thomas sat up quickly, besieged by an ache that was all too familiar. He had wanted only one wife, and that had been Charlotte Shepherd, a girl so delightful and loving as any man could have wished for. At his time of life he had stopped dwelling upon the whys and wherefores, the reasons for dissent, the sacrifices they had both made, she more than he, admittedly. After so many empty, harrowing years of turmoil, he felt justified now in confining his memories to the happy ones, and there were so many that he was hard-pressed to recall every one.

The sight of his daughter's letters stuffed at the back of Daphne's top drawer had filled him with utter joy; not that he would ever breathe a word to her, nor spoil her little secret. It sufficed that he knew she was visiting Grace every week and that, one day soon, he would welcome his daughter into his arms, tearfully, gratefully, with no recriminations over their past acrimony. His promise to Charlotte would be fulfilled.

Charlotte!

Her name reverberated in his head, whirring around, making him dizzy. He leaned back in the rocking chair, closing his eyes against the giddiness, wondering, fleetingly, why darkness was falling so suddenly on such a beautiful sunny day in April.

*

Daphne flew down the hall, dispensing with decorum, desperate to confess to him what she and Grace had been up to behind his back. As she passed the hall mirror, she paused to tweak her hair and plump some colour into her cheeks, and then she grinned stupidly at her reflection, not caring how juvenile she appeared.

'Thomas, I'm home!' she called before she reached the living room door. 'Sorry I'm a bit late, but I've so much to tell you, I know you'll forgive me.'

She stood in the doorway, saw his sleeping figure in the rocking chair.

'Trust you to be dead to the world when I've such exciting news.'

She tiptoed over to the window, bent to kiss his cheek and noticed he had been crying. Her heart went out to the poor man and she tapped him on the shoulder to waken him up, to let him know that his wishes were about to come true, that he would never need to shed a single tear again.

As the touch of her hand provoked no response, Daphne moved round to stand in front of him and, as soon as she saw his face, she knew that her husband was dead.

*

Thomas Charles Blake was laid to rest in a cemetery of Daphne's choosing, and, as the family made their separate ways home beneath a leaden sky, his granddaughter, Beth, was the only one who cried for him.

*

Grace sat in the parlour, in her mother's favourite chair, feeling nothing at all. Her father had just been buried and she could summon up not a single emotion; neither delight at his demise, nor sadness for his wife's loss; neither relief that she had been spared yet another act of treachery; nor disappointment at her daughter's cruel remarks.

Idly, she glanced at the old record collection, recalling James's mocking tone as she had selected '*My Heart and I*' by Joseph Locke. Her mind rummaged, like a vagrant over rough ground, over past times, distant images; but the one that was surfacing now was of James sitting opposite her, kicking her feet, teasing the life out of her, making her blush, enjoying her embarrassment.

She straightened up in the chair, trying to make sense of her inner ramblings, appreciating anew the one significant benefit from her father's death: it was no longer necessary to inflict upon Daphne the pain and heartache contained in Helen's letter, and for that Grace was grateful. She had the opportunity now to bury the acrimony alongside her father, to turn her back on the hypocrisy and shame of a truth that had altered according to the lips it touched.

Grace leaned back again in her chair and closed her eyes. She knew she would have to confront Beth's animosity at some point in the following weeks, but, tonight, all she wanted to do was to sleep and forget.

*

James Melville sat by the fire and pondered the passing of Thomas Blake. He had never quite understood Grace's loathing of her father. In his opinion, a father was a father, regardless of his mistakes. James had never known his own father and, despite his mother's disapproval of her husband's lifestyle, James could never have turned his back on the man, not even in the direst circumstances.

Now, as he closed his eyes and drifted away from the sighs and whispers of the night outside, James decided that there had been one, important benefit of Thomas Blake's death: never again could the man disrupt Grace's peace of mind and threaten to tear her family apart. For that alone, James was grateful. He foresaw a new beginning for them all, akin to a long-awaited flush of spring buds after a long, bitter winter.

*

Harry switched off the lamp and slid beneath the quilt. Beside him, Beth was sound asleep, the tracks of her tears still visible, yet provoking in him nothing more than a brief sympathy, the kind he might feel for a total stranger.

The truth was that everyone's cause was best served by Thomas Blake's being dead and buried, and, although she would never admit it, Beth was no different from the other members of the family. Harry knew that her tears had been a symptom of jealousy for Grace than of genuine distress. It would always be the same: his love and loyalty for a woman other than his wife.

The one benefit of Blake's death had been the sudden lessening of urgency to protect Daphne from being swindled out of her fortune, and for that alone, Harry was grateful. His apprehension at having to tell the woman that her husband was a con man had kept him awake some nights; but tonight he knew he would sleep soundly and that, come the morning, the long years of his quest to save a damsel in distress would be nothing more than a wisp of air in the Cosmos.

*

In the middle of the night Beth woke up, her hair damp, sweat clinging to her brow, disentangling herself from the nightmare that had dragged her to a place she thought she would never have to endure again: her grandfather was dead and she had never awarded him a real opportunity to redress the past. A few letters, half-hearted promises, some callously delivered speeches from her soap box on the pavement, had been the sum total of his granddaughter's contribution. Even sharing his house for months had not yielded the results he could have hoped for, and she recalled with horror her off-hand attitude, the despicable haste with which she had abandoned him at the end, rushing off, leaving a brusque note propped up against the cereal packet.

Beth stifled a cry and turned over, her back to Harry. Had she known of the man's failing health, the short time he had left in this world, she would surely have shown him

567

a little tenderness; yet now, as she mulled over her many failings, she made a last, desperate attempt to appease her own guilt; consoled herself with one thought.

It could be argued in her defence that she had done her utmost to see his side of things; which no-one else had done. Where she might have shunned him completely, she had, at least, shown him some compassion, provided a tiny pin-prick of light on an otherwise foreboding horizon; unlike Grace Melville; and Beth would never forgive her mother, not now, when it was too late to make amends.

She squeezed her eyes tightly shut, brushing the few remaining tears from her cheeks, knowing they would be the last she shed on her grandfather's behalf.

*

Daphne Blake took out the small suitcase that her husband had used to hold his personal papers and documents. Surprised at its lightness, she clicked open the locks and raised the lid; and then she gasped. Apart from a small brown envelope, the case was empty. She stood up and rummaged in the back of the wardrobe but found nothing, and then she raked through every single drawer that had been allocated for his possessions. Still, she found nothing.

She sat on the edge of the bed and contemplated the tattered brown envelope. It was far too small to hold anything of value and so, before she went to find the paperknife, Daphne turned it over in her hand, trying to come to terms with a man who had brought nothing with him from his previous existence, who had in his possession not even a solitary box of personal items.

Finally, her mind having exhausted every possible explanation for such a strange situation, she took a deep breath and opened the envelope.

At first, finding only a newspaper cutting and a few old snapshots, she peered into it, shook it to see if it held another item, but had to content herself with the fact that her husband, after more than seventy years, had kept only a few slips of paper, whatever they were.

Perplexed, Daphne unfolded the yellowing cutting. Immediately she recognised the young girl: Grace Blake, as a skinny, optimistic youngster, holding some kind of certificate in her hand, raising delighted eyes to the beholder. With a sigh, Daphne picked up the first photograph and found herself meeting the eyes of a lovely dark-haired girl with a child on her knee. It was Charlotte, Daphne supposed, although he had rarely mentioned her. She turned the photograph over and read the inscription.

'April 1932. To my beloved Thomas in love and gratitude. You know that I will love you for ever. I thank God every day for our daughter, Grace. Perhaps, one day, you will see her for yourself.

Your devoted and obedient wife. Charlotte.'

Part Four: 1982

When the telephone rang before eight o'clock one morning in early May, Grace heard James talking in hushed tones and expected the worst. It was, indeed, news of Lily Morris and, as James explained about the postman raising the alarm and the old lady being found dead, slumped behind her bedroom door, Grace knew he was surprised to see his wife shed no tears. He would assume that she was too grief-stricken to react immediately, but the truth was so shaming that Grace could never voice it to anyone, not even to James.

As she stood at the bedroom window reflecting on her old friend's death. Grace was overwhelmed with joy, that the only surviving link to her mother and Thomas Blake was gone, heralding the closure of an era whose passing was long overdue. Perhaps now, at last, they would all be spared the heartache of backward glances and would be set free to concentrate on the future.

*

The wind howled across the cemetery, slicing through the little group of mourners in its haste to fly out of the gates and down the lane. In the distance, rushing towards the estuary with a sense of purpose, the river flowed by, unaffected, unconcerned by the group of people on the hillside. A few sheep grazed the slopes, their haphazard forms conflicting with the neatness of the ploughed fields; and from the tops of the fir trees, came the faint song of a blackbird, oblivious to the sombre mood of the figures by the graveside.

The children stood dutifully beside their parents, although Frank had to hold his younger son's hand in case he darted off and gave Beth an excuse to accuse them of disrespect.

Beth clung to Harry's hand, but Michael and Anna, standing close together, had eyes only for each other, which Beth thought rather touching. In fact, she had encouraged the friendship, for it drew the boy into her family. As the coffin was lowered into the grave, her mind, as always, was engrossed with Harry's disapproval regarding their daughter's obsession with Michael, and, even after months of discreet prying, Beth was at a loss to think of any reason to discourage the youngsters from being soul-mates. Furthermore, to her continued irritation, she had received no support from her mother either, attributing it to the usual compliance between her and Harry Gillespie; a circumstance that still rankled with Beth to this day. She had barely spoken a civil word to her mother in years.

She smiled when Michael patted Anna's hand and gave her a comforting smile, and, when her daughter gazed at him, it brought a lump to Beth's throat.

*

Out of the corner of his eye, Harry saw Beth's handkerchief discreetly dabbing her cheek and knew her show of emotion had nothing to do with Lily Morris. A funeral on a windy hilltop was neither the suitable time nor place, but he suffered a brief twinge of conscience about the situation and resolved that, very soon, he would stop this nonsense between his two children; before it was too late.

570